Art Club

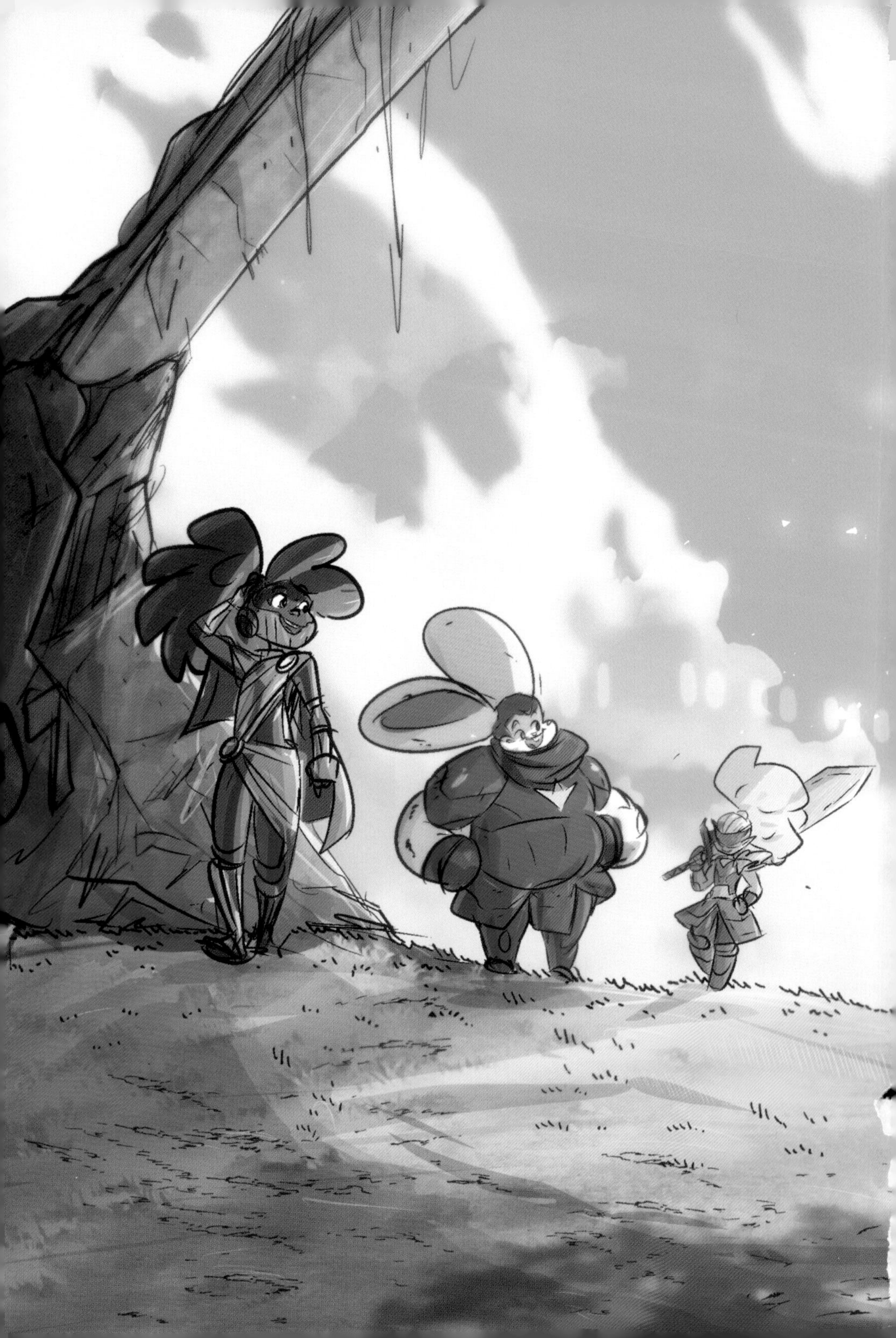

Art Club

RASHAD DOUCET

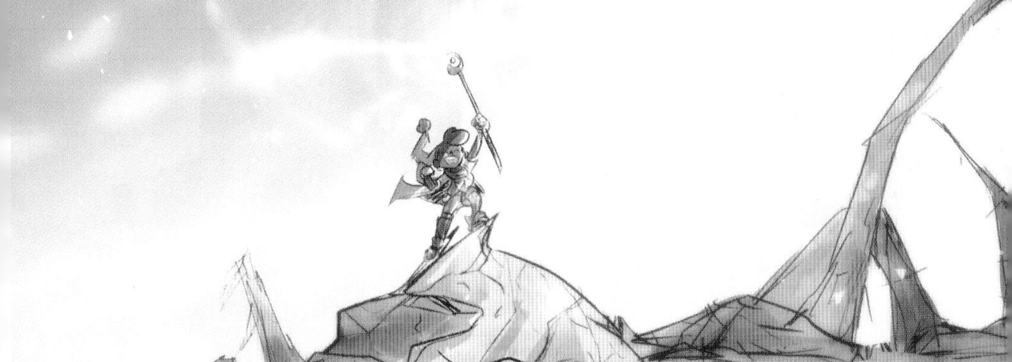

LB INK
Little, Brown and Company
New York Boston

About This Book

This book was edited by Andrea Colvin and designed by Carolyn Bull. The production was supervised by Bernadette Flinn, and the production editor was Jake Regier. The text was set in CC Victory Speech, and the display type is CC Hero Sandwich Pro.

Copyright © 2024 by Rashad Doucet
Color assistance by Andy Gordon
Lettering by Rob Steen

Cover illustration copyright © 2024 by Rashad Doucet.
Crayon texture © Agafonov Oleg/Shutterstock.com. Cover design by Ann Dwyer.
Cover copyright © 2024 by Hachette Book Group, Inc.

Little, Brown Ink
Hachette Book Group
1290 Avenue of the Americas, New York, NY 10104
Visit us at LBYR.com

First Edition: February 2024

Little, Brown Ink is an imprint of Little, Brown and Company. The Little, Brown Ink name and logo are trademarks of Hachette Book Group, Inc.

The publisher is not responsible for websites (or their content) that are not owned by the publisher.

Little, Brown and Company books may be purchased in bulk for business, educational, or promotional use. For information, please contact your local bookseller or the Hachette Book Group Special Markets Department at special.markets@hbgusa.com.

Library of Congress Cataloging-in-Publication Data
Names: Doucet, Rashad, author, illustrator.
Title: Art club / Rashad Doucet.
Description: First edition. | New York : Little, Brown and Company, 2024. | Audience: Ages 8–12. | Summary: "After the art programs are cut at his school, Dale Donavan recruits talented artists to create an after-school art club." —Provided by publisher.
Identifiers: LCCN 2021058476 | ISBN 9780759556362 (hardcover) | ISBN 9780759556393 (trade paperback) | ISBN 9780759556386 (ebook)
Subjects: CYAC: Graphic novels. | After-school programs—Fiction. | Schools—Fiction. | Art—Fiction. | LCGFT: Graphic novels.
Classification: LCC PZ7.7.D685 Ar 2023 | DDC 741.5/973—dc23/eng/20220125
LC record available at https://lccn.loc.gov/2021058476

ISBNs: 978-0-7595-5636-2 (hardcover), 978-0-7595-5639-3 (paperback), 978-0-7595-5638-6 (ebook), 978-0-316-35585-8 (ebook), 978-0-316-35598-8 (ebook)

PRINTED IN GUANGDONG, CHINA

1010

Hardcover: 10 9 8 7 6 5 4 3 2 1

Paperback: 10 9 8 7 6 5 4 3

This is dedicated to my phenomenal wife
and daughter but also to every family
member, teacher, mentor, and friend
who's supported and believed in my
dream to be a comic book artist.

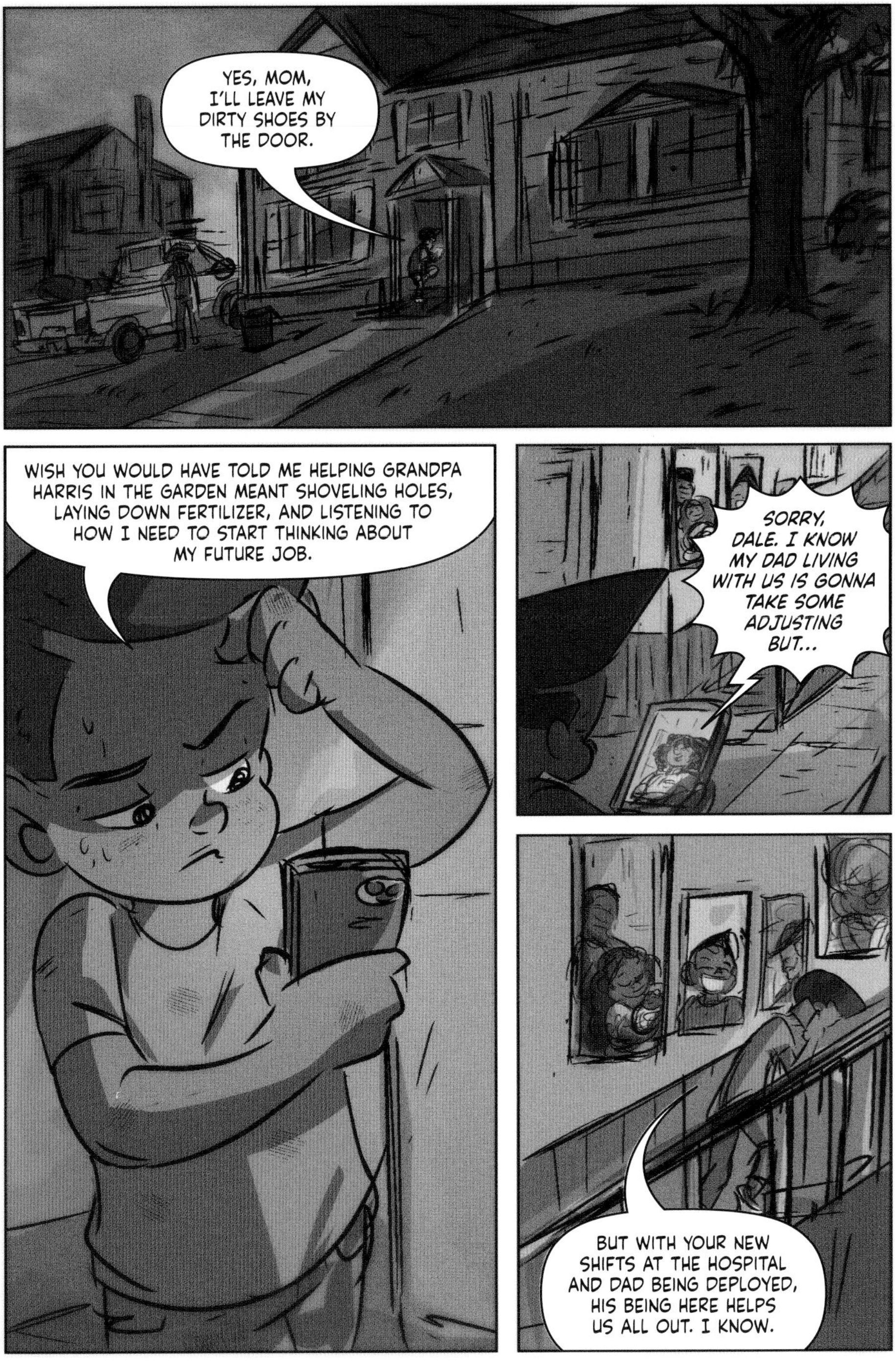
YES, MOM, I'LL LEAVE MY DIRTY SHOES BY THE DOOR.
WISH YOU WOULD HAVE TOLD ME HELPING GRANDPA HARRIS IN THE GARDEN MEANT SHOVELING HOLES, LAYING DOWN FERTILIZER, AND LISTENING TO HOW I NEED TO START THINKING ABOUT MY FUTURE JOB.
SORRY, DALE. I KNOW MY DAD LIVING WITH US IS GONNA TAKE SOME ADJUSTING BUT...
BUT WITH YOUR NEW SHIFTS AT THE HOSPITAL AND DAD BEING DEPLOYED, HIS BEING HERE HELPS US ALL OUT. I KNOW.

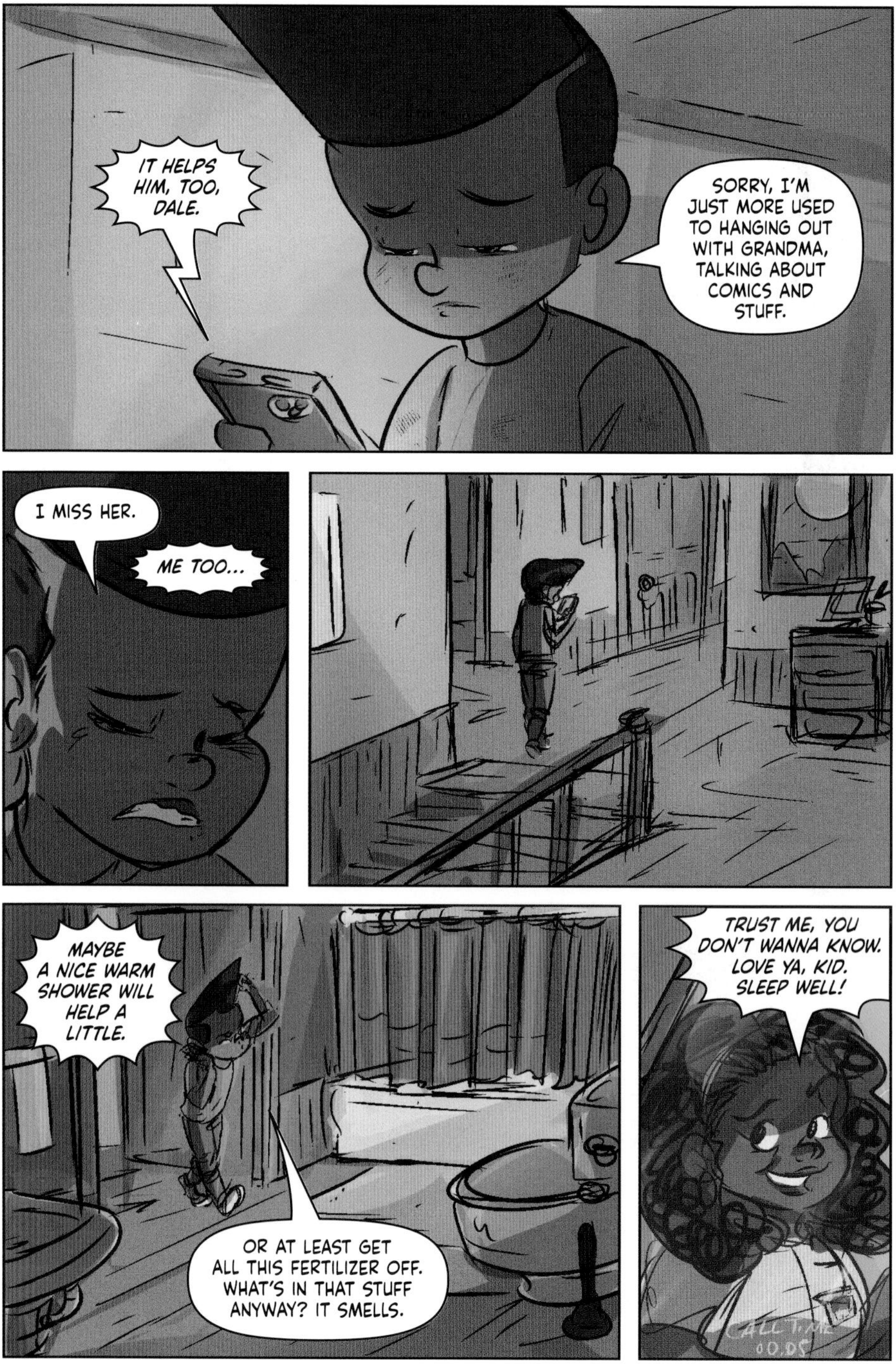
IT HELPS HIM, TOO, DALE.
SORRY, I'M JUST MORE USED TO HANGING OUT WITH GRANDMA, TALKING ABOUT COMICS AND STUFF.
I MISS HER.
ME TOO...
MAYBE A NICE WARM SHOWER WILL HELP A LITTLE.
OR AT LEAST GET ALL THIS FERTILIZER OFF. WHAT'S IN THAT STUFF ANYWAY? IT SMELLS.
TRUST ME, YOU DON'T WANNA KNOW. LOVE YA, KID. SLEEP WELL!

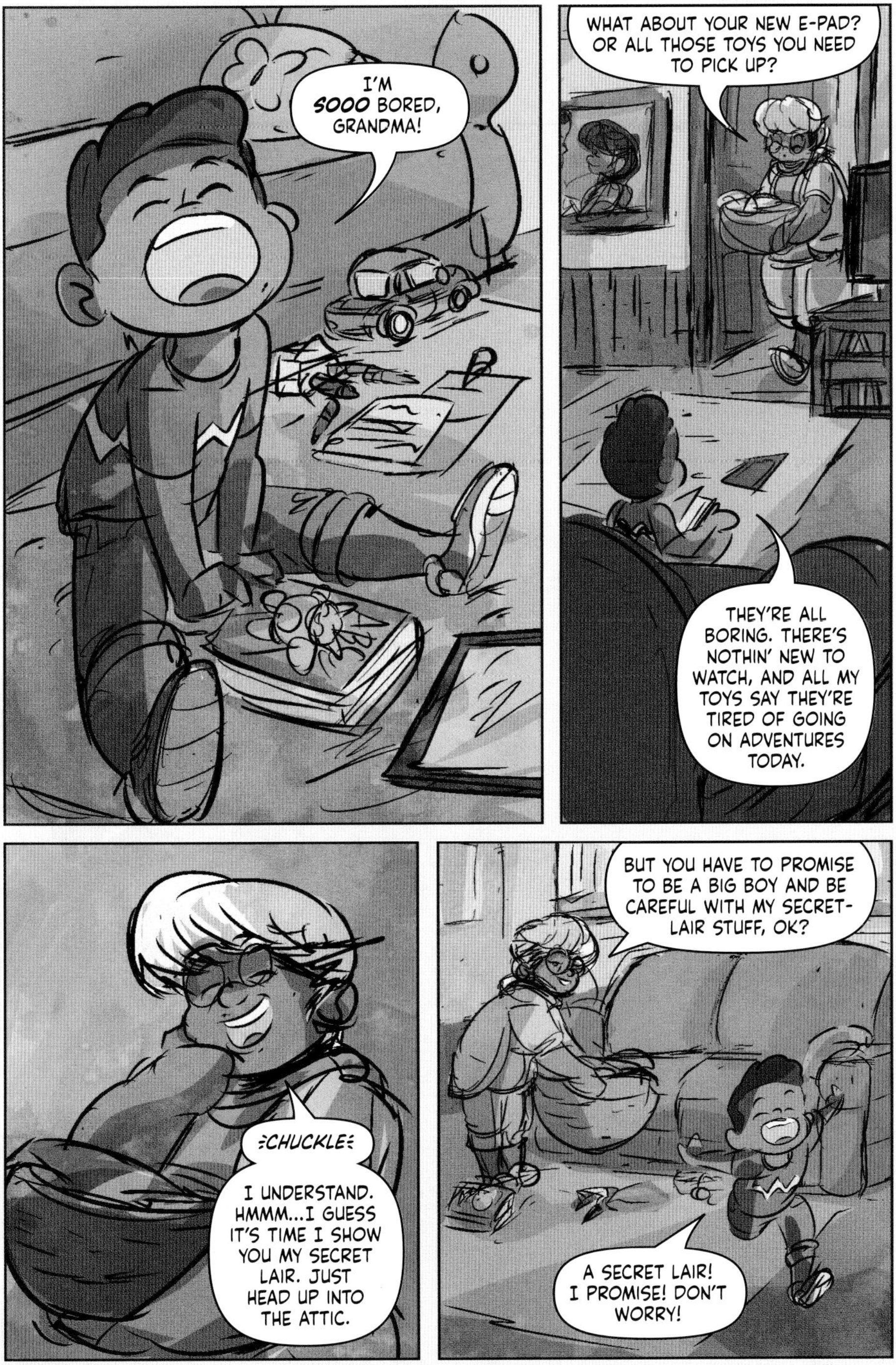
I'M SOOO BORED, GRANDMA!
WHAT ABOUT YOUR NEW E-PAD? OR ALL THOSE TOYS YOU NEED TO PICK UP?
THEY'RE ALL BORING. THERE'S NOTHIN' NEW TO WATCH, AND ALL MY TOYS SAY THEY'RE TIRED OF GOING ON ADVENTURES TODAY.
CHUCKLE
I UNDERSTAND. HMMM...I GUESS IT'S TIME I SHOW YOU MY SECRET LAIR. JUST HEAD UP INTO THE ATTIC.
BUT YOU HAVE TO PROMISE TO BE A BIG BOY AND BE CAREFUL WITH MY SECRET-LAIR STUFF, OK?
A SECRET LAIR! I PROMISE! DON'T WORRY!

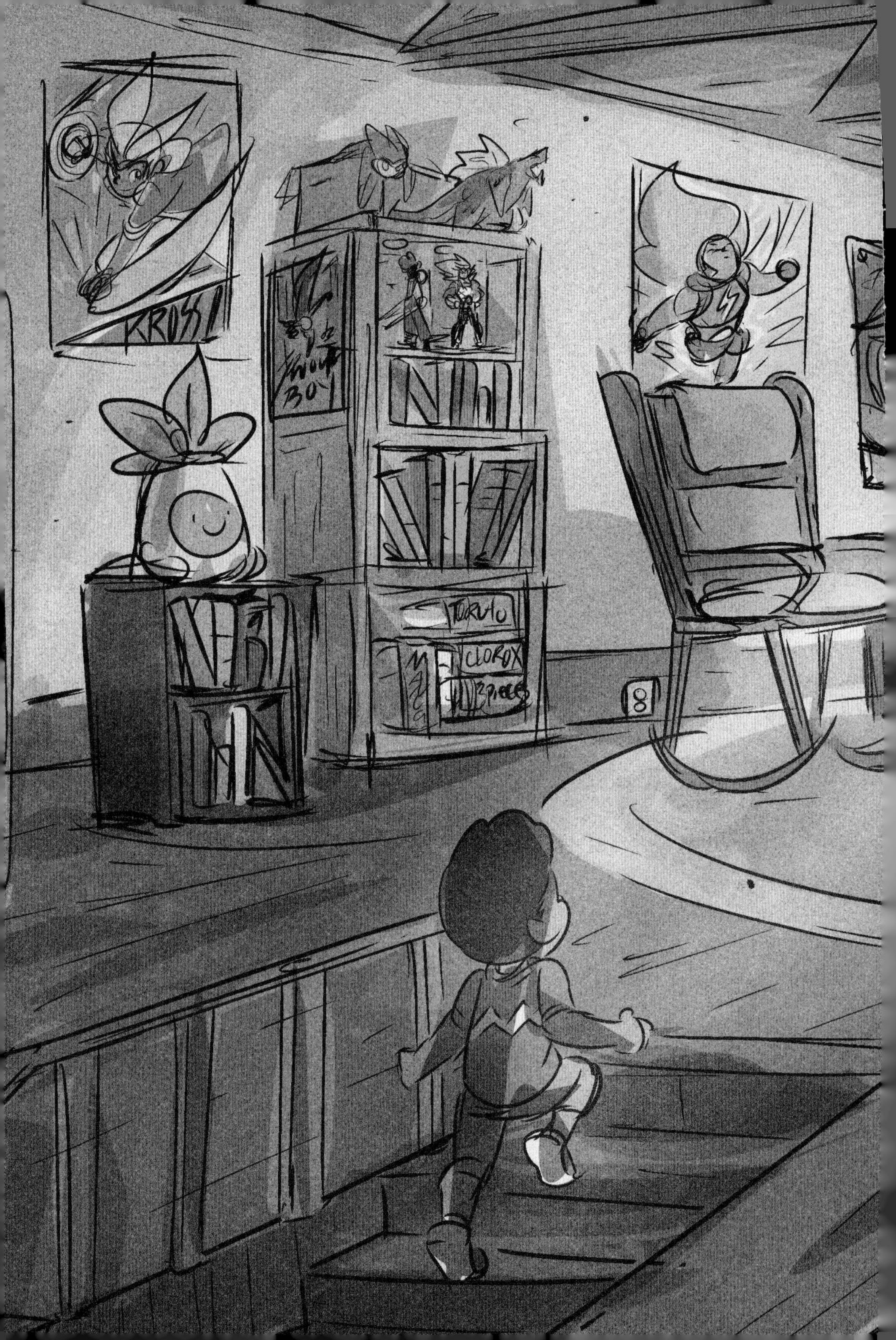
KROSS!
CLOROX

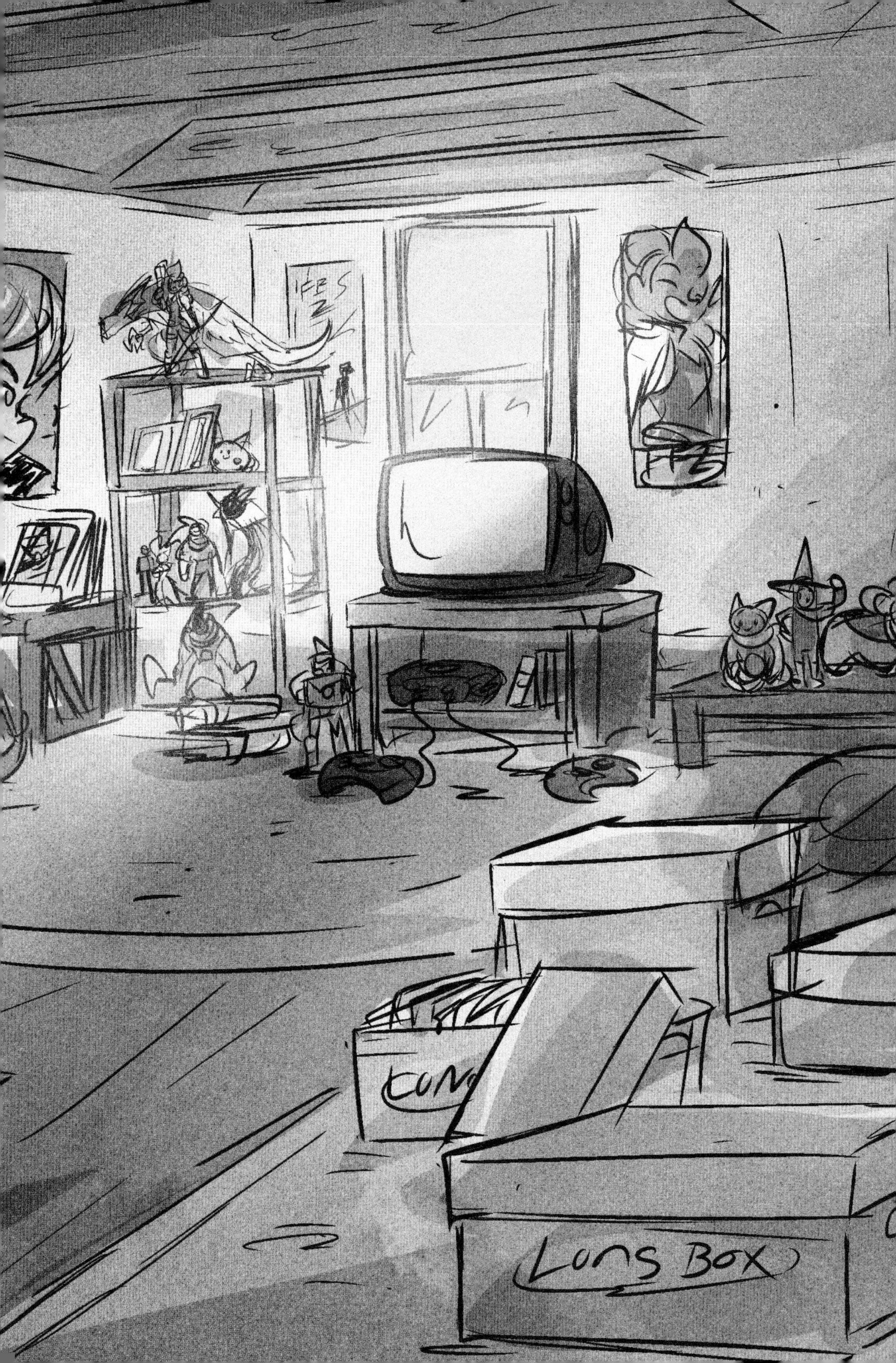
Luns Box

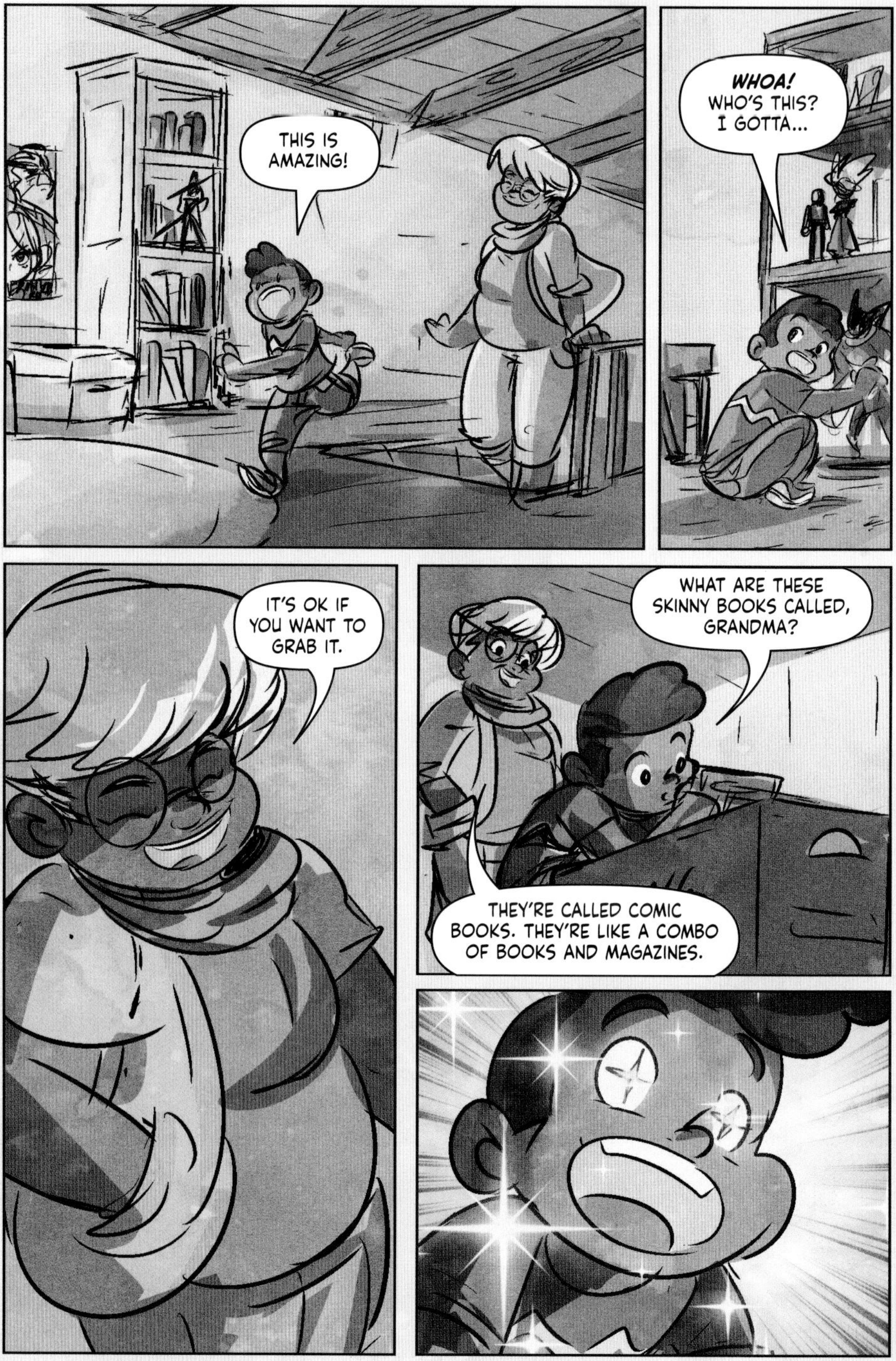
THIS IS AMAZING!
WHOA! WHO'S THIS? I GOTTA...
IT'S OK IF YOU WANT TO GRAB IT.
WHAT ARE THESE SKINNY BOOKS CALLED, GRANDMA?
THEY'RE CALLED COMIC BOOKS. THEY'RE LIKE A COMBO OF BOOKS AND MAGAZINES.

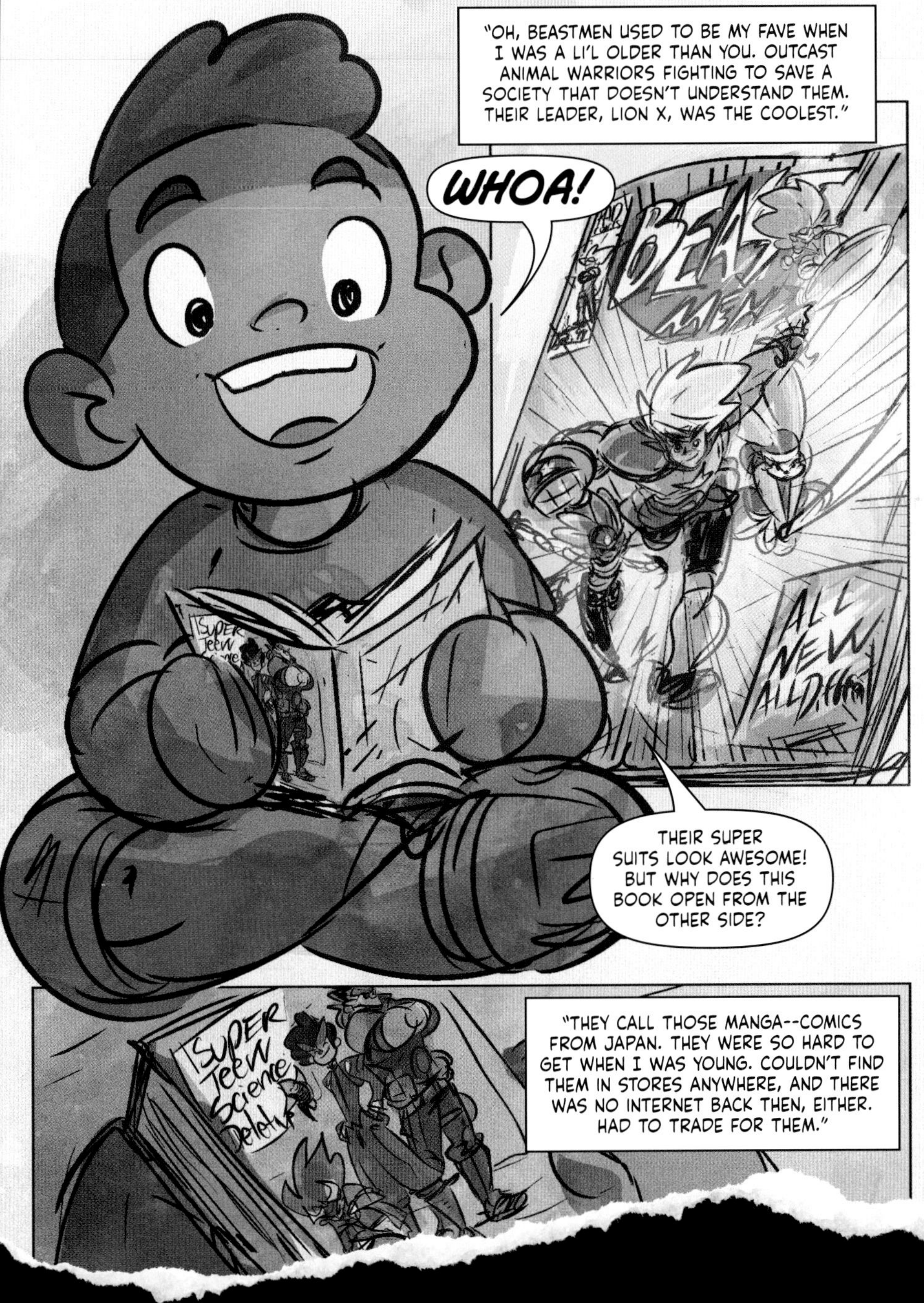
"OH, BEASTMEN USED TO BE MY FAVE WHEN I WAS A LI'L OLDER THAN YOU. OUTCAST ANIMAL WARRIORS FIGHTING TO SAVE A SOCIETY THAT DOESN'T UNDERSTAND THEM. THEIR LEADER, LION X, WAS THE COOLEST."
WHOA!
THEIR SUPER SUITS LOOK AWESOME! BUT WHY DOES THIS BOOK OPEN FROM THE OTHER SIDE?
"THEY CALL THOSE MANGA--COMICS FROM JAPAN. THEY WERE SO HARD TO GET WHEN I WAS YOUNG. COULDN'T FIND THEM IN STORES ANYWHERE, AND THERE WAS NO INTERNET BACK THEN, EITHER. HAD TO TRADE FOR THEM."

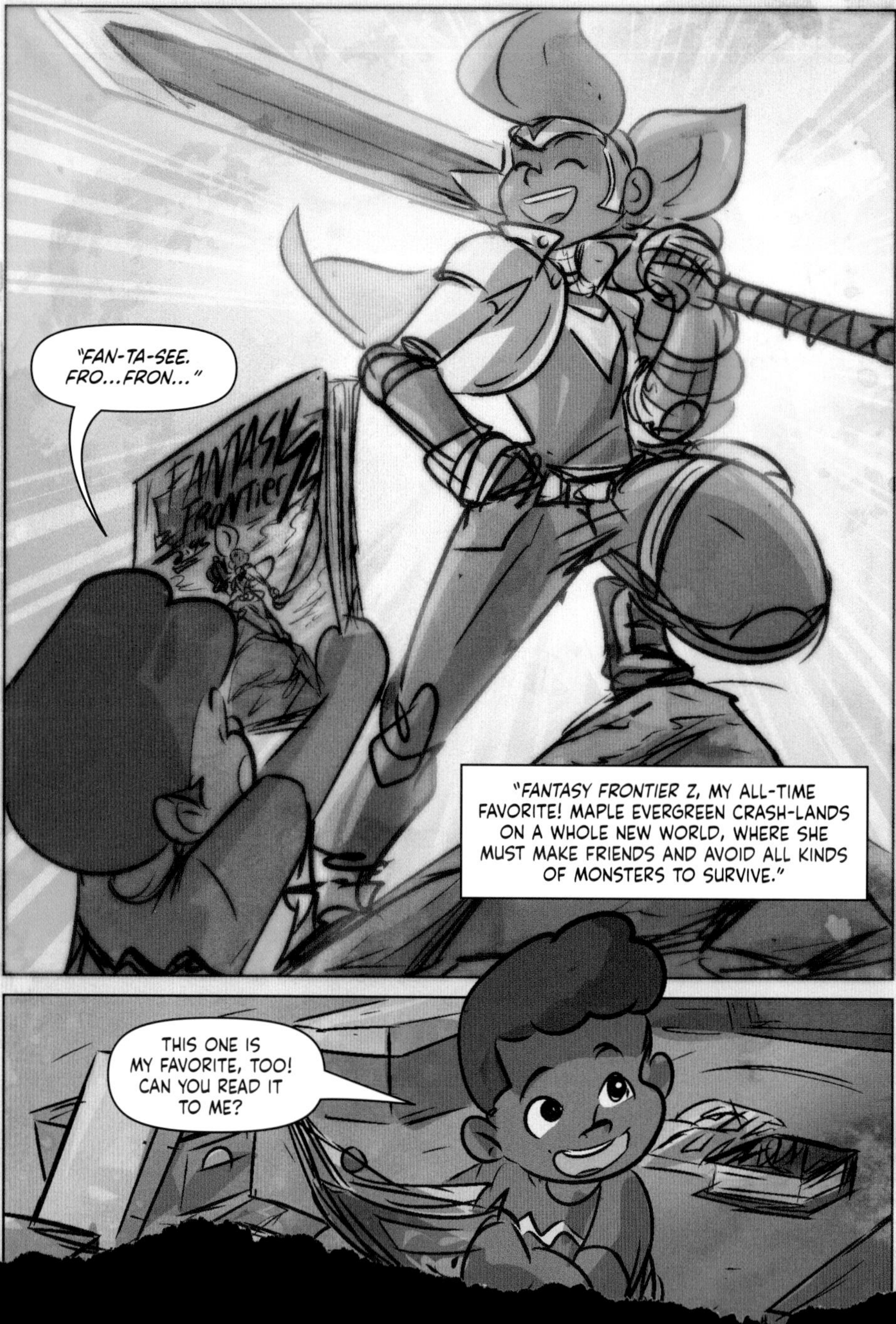
"FAN-TA-SEE. FRO...FRON..."
"FANTASY FRONTIER Z, MY ALL-TIME FAVORITE! MAPLE EVERGREEN CRASH-LANDS ON A WHOLE NEW WORLD, WHERE SHE MUST MAKE FRIENDS AND AVOID ALL KINDS OF MONSTERS TO SURVIVE."
THIS ONE IS MY FAVORITE, TOO! CAN YOU READ IT TO ME?

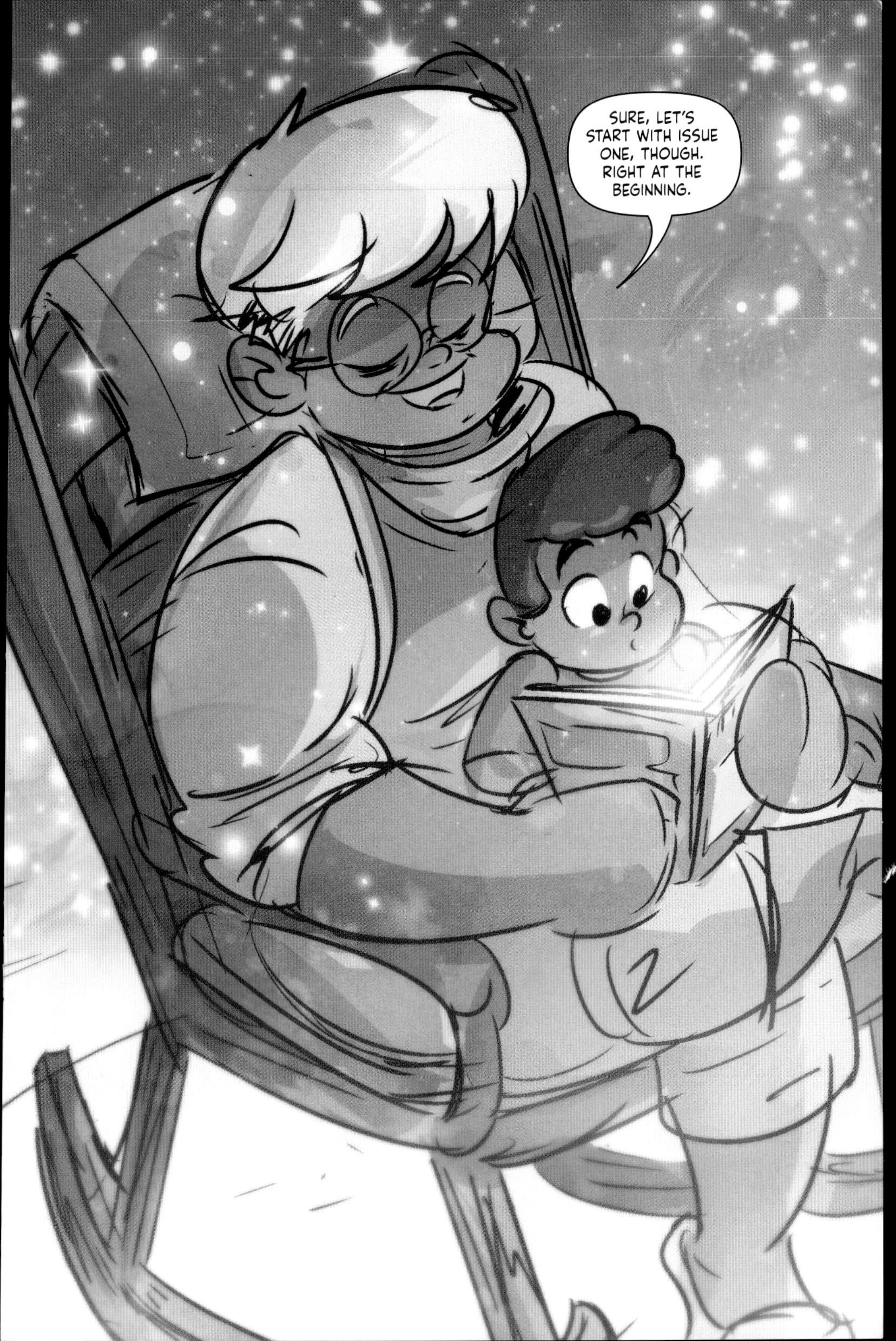
SURE, LET'S START WITH ISSUE ONE, THOUGH. RIGHT AT THE BEGINNING.

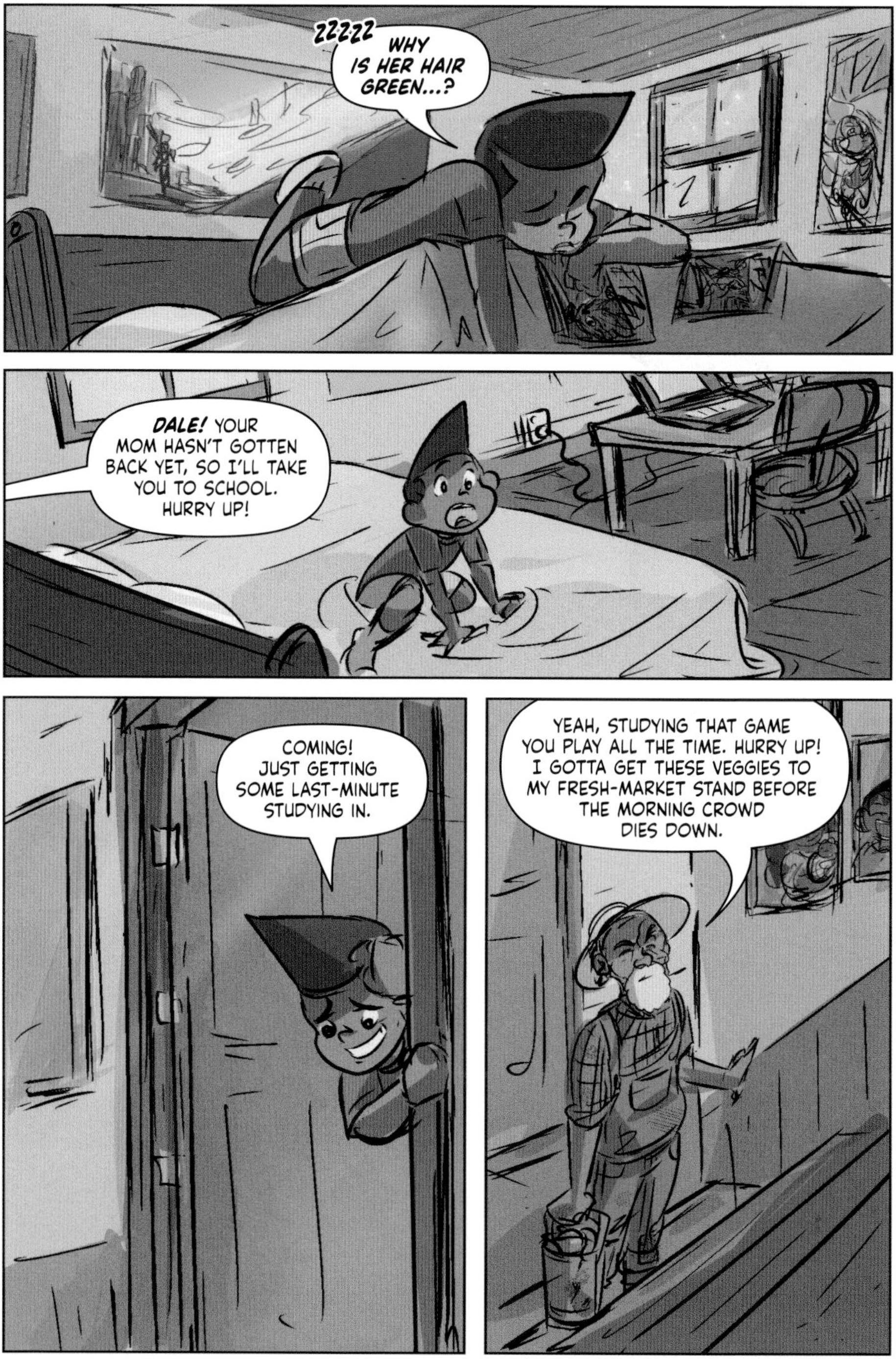
ZZZZZ
WHY IS HER HAIR GREEN...?
DALE! YOUR MOM HASN'T GOTTEN BACK YET, SO I'LL TAKE YOU TO SCHOOL. HURRY UP!
COMING! JUST GETTING SOME LAST-MINUTE STUDYING IN.
YEAH, STUDYING THAT GAME YOU PLAY ALL THE TIME. HURRY UP! I GOTTA GET THESE VEGGIES TO MY FRESH-MARKET STAND BEFORE THE MORNING CROWD DIES DOWN.

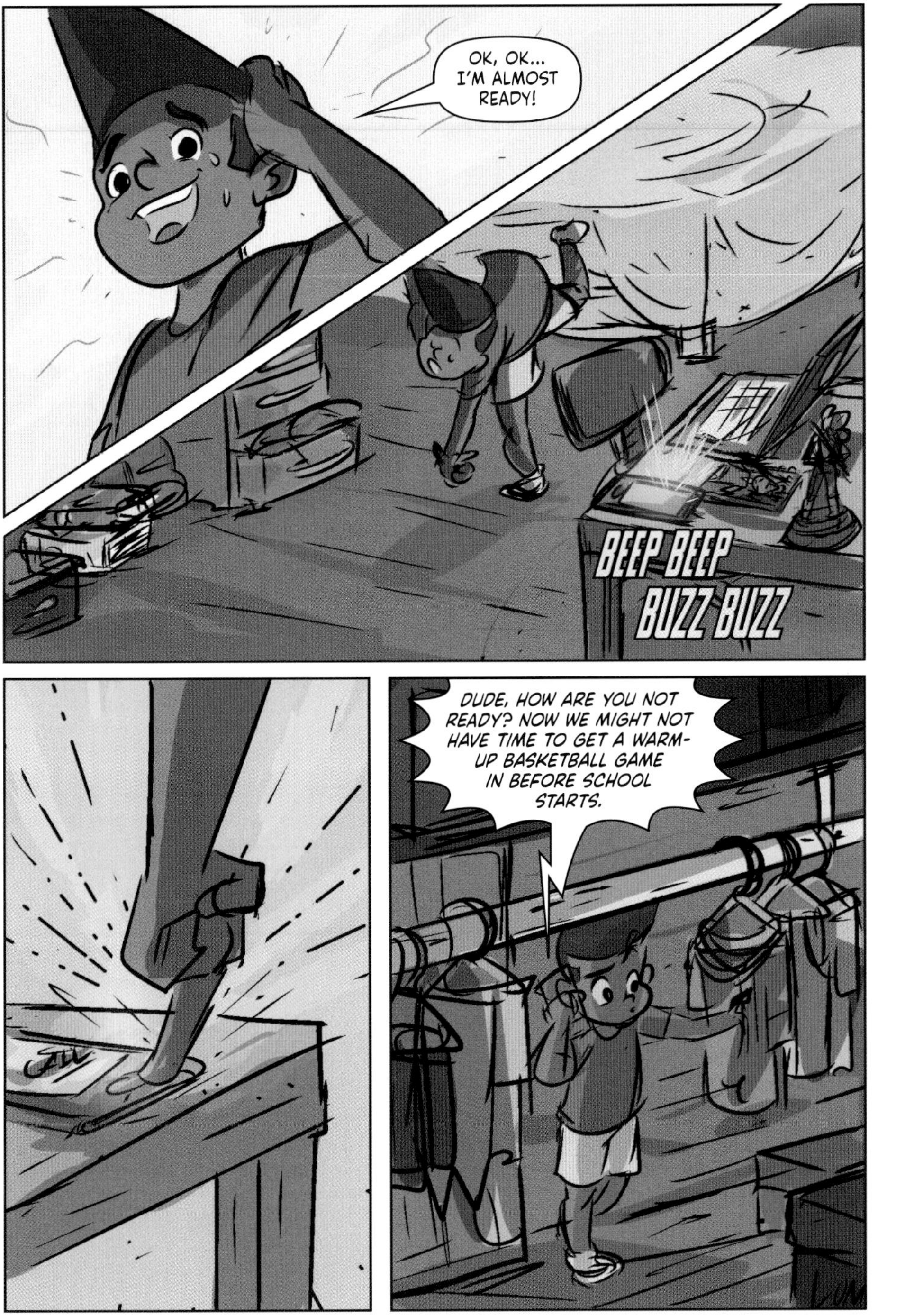
OK, OK...
I'M ALMOST
READY!
BEEP BEEP
BUZZ BUZZ
DUDE, HOW ARE YOU NOT READY? NOW WE MIGHT NOT HAVE TIME TO GET A WARM-UP BASKETBALL GAME IN BEFORE SCHOOL STARTS.

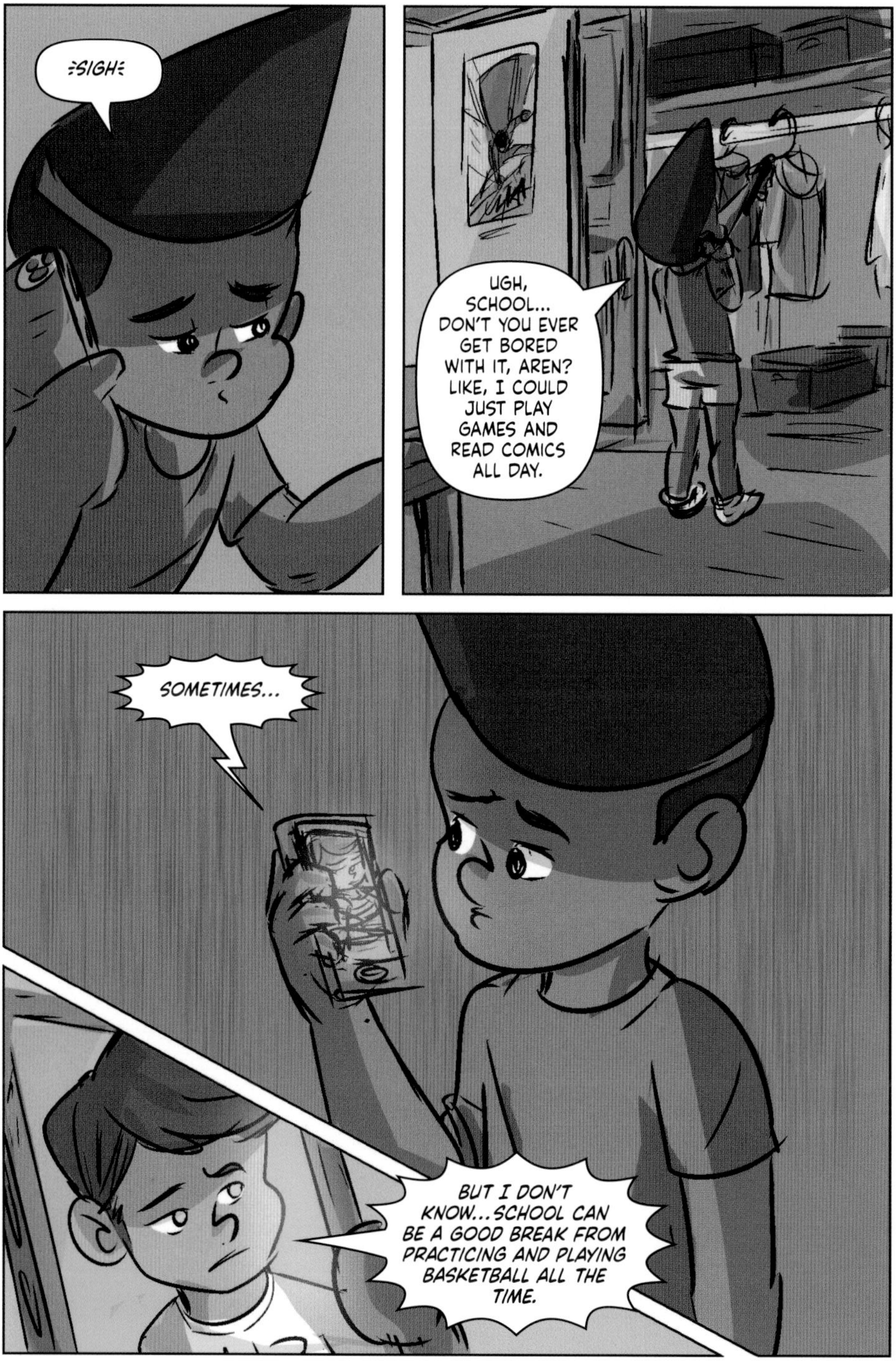
SIGH
UGH, SCHOOL... DON'T YOU EVER GET BORED WITH IT, AREN? LIKE, I COULD JUST PLAY GAMES AND READ COMICS ALL DAY.
SOMETIMES...
BUT I DON'T KNOW...SCHOOL CAN BE A GOOD BREAK FROM PRACTICING AND PLAYING BASKETBALL ALL THE TIME.

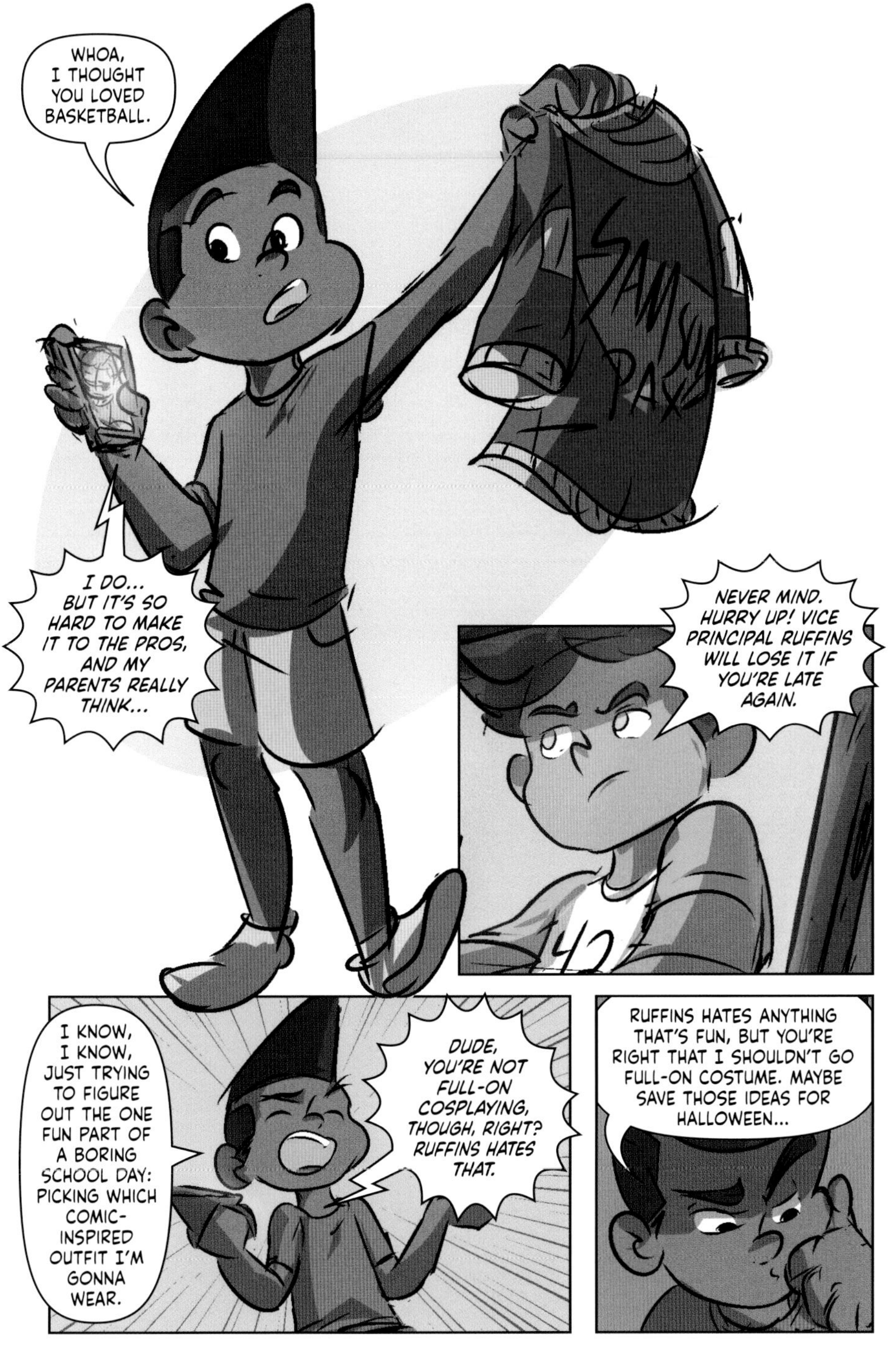
WHOA, I THOUGHT YOU LOVED BASKETBALL.
I DO... BUT IT'S SO HARD TO MAKE IT TO THE PROS, AND MY PARENTS REALLY THINK...
NEVER MIND. HURRY UP! VICE PRINCIPAL RUFFINS WILL LOSE IT IF YOU'RE LATE AGAIN.
I KNOW, I KNOW, JUST TRYING TO FIGURE OUT THE ONE FUN PART OF A BORING SCHOOL DAY: PICKING WHICH COMIC-INSPIRED OUTFIT I'M GONNA WEAR.
DUDE, YOU'RE NOT FULL-ON COSPLAYING, THOUGH, RIGHT? RUFFINS HATES THAT.
RUFFINS HATES ANYTHING THAT'S FUN, BUT YOU'RE RIGHT THAT I SHOULDN'T GO FULL-ON COSTUME. MAYBE SAVE THOSE IDEAS FOR HALLOWEEN...

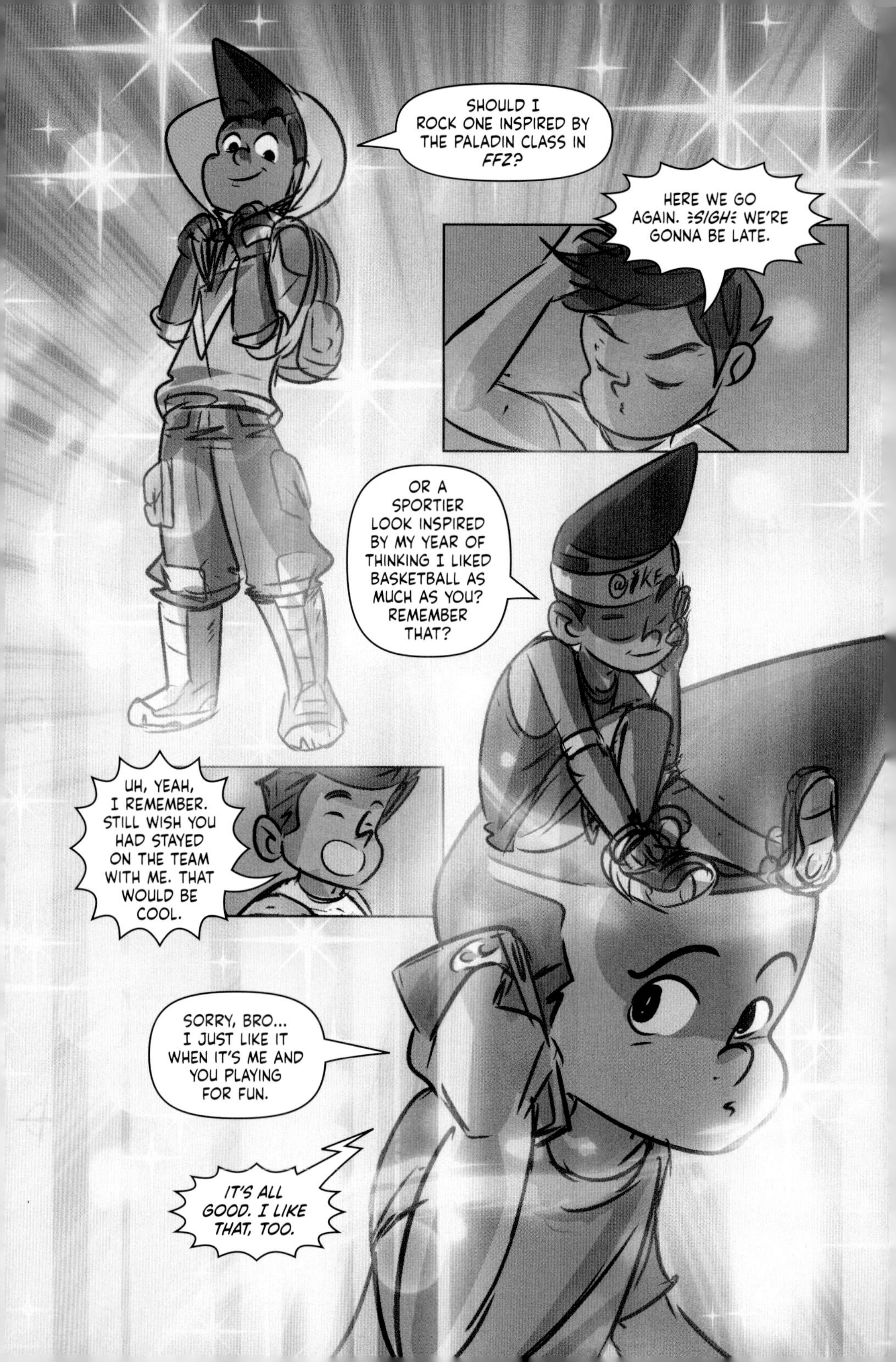
SHOULD I ROCK ONE INSPIRED BY THE PALADIN CLASS IN *FFZ*?
HERE WE GO AGAIN. *SIGH* WE'RE GONNA BE LATE.
OR A SPORTIER LOOK INSPIRED BY MY YEAR OF THINKING I LIKED BASKETBALL AS MUCH AS YOU? REMEMBER THAT?
@IKE
UH, YEAH, I REMEMBER. STILL WISH YOU HAD STAYED ON THE TEAM WITH ME. THAT WOULD BE COOL.
SORRY, BRO... I JUST LIKE IT WHEN IT'S ME AND YOU PLAYING FOR FUN.
IT'S ALL GOOD. I LIKE THAT, TOO.

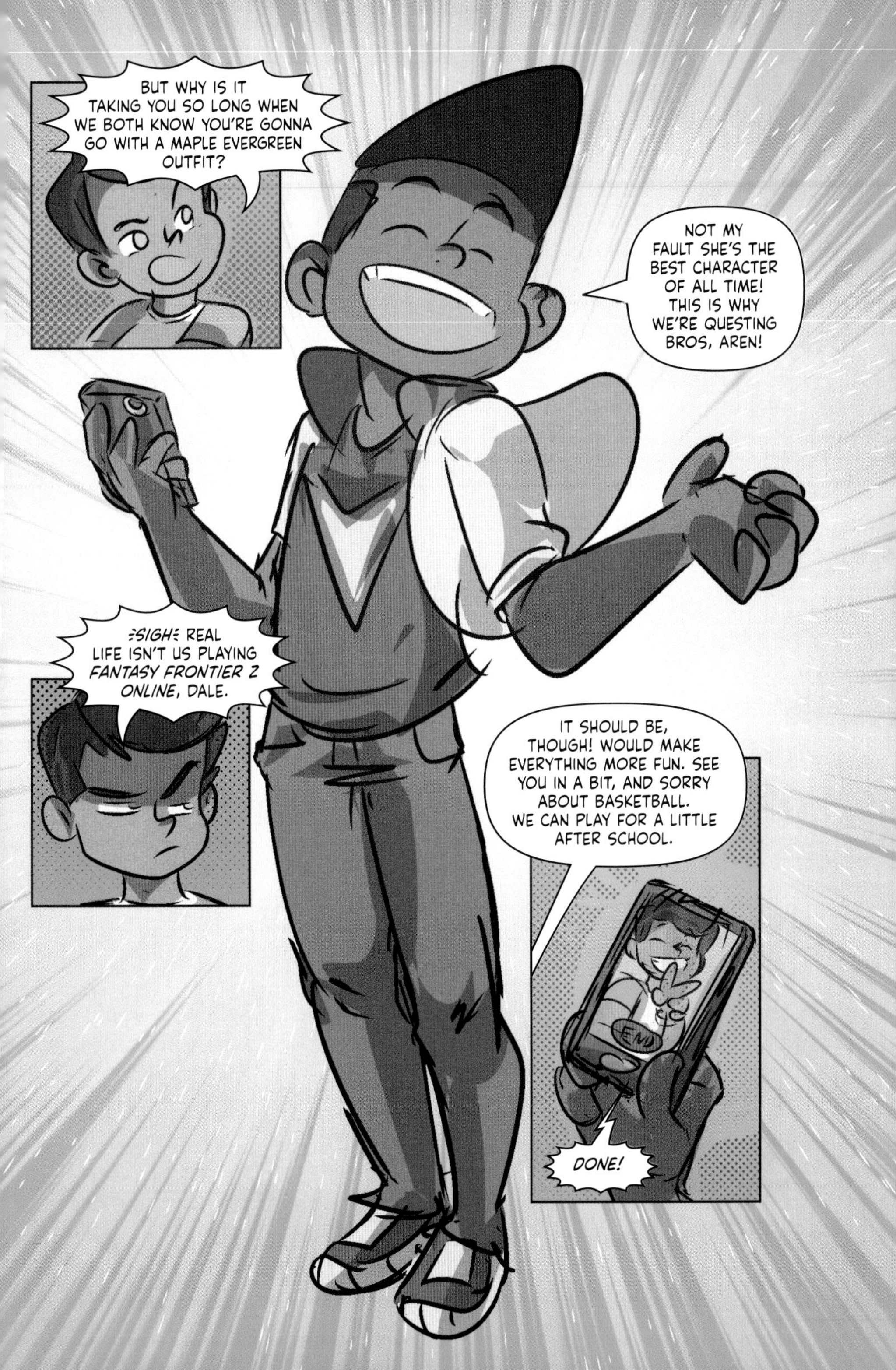
BUT WHY IS IT TAKING YOU SO LONG WHEN WE BOTH KNOW YOU'RE GONNA GO WITH A MAPLE EVERGREEN OUTFIT?
NOT MY FAULT SHE'S THE BEST CHARACTER OF ALL TIME! THIS IS WHY WE'RE QUESTING BROS, AREN!
SIGH REAL LIFE ISN'T US PLAYING *FANTASY FRONTIER 2 ONLINE*, DALE.
IT SHOULD BE, THOUGH! WOULD MAKE EVERYTHING MORE FUN. SEE YOU IN A BIT, AND SORRY ABOUT BASKETBALL. WE CAN PLAY FOR A LITTLE AFTER SCHOOL.
END
DONE!

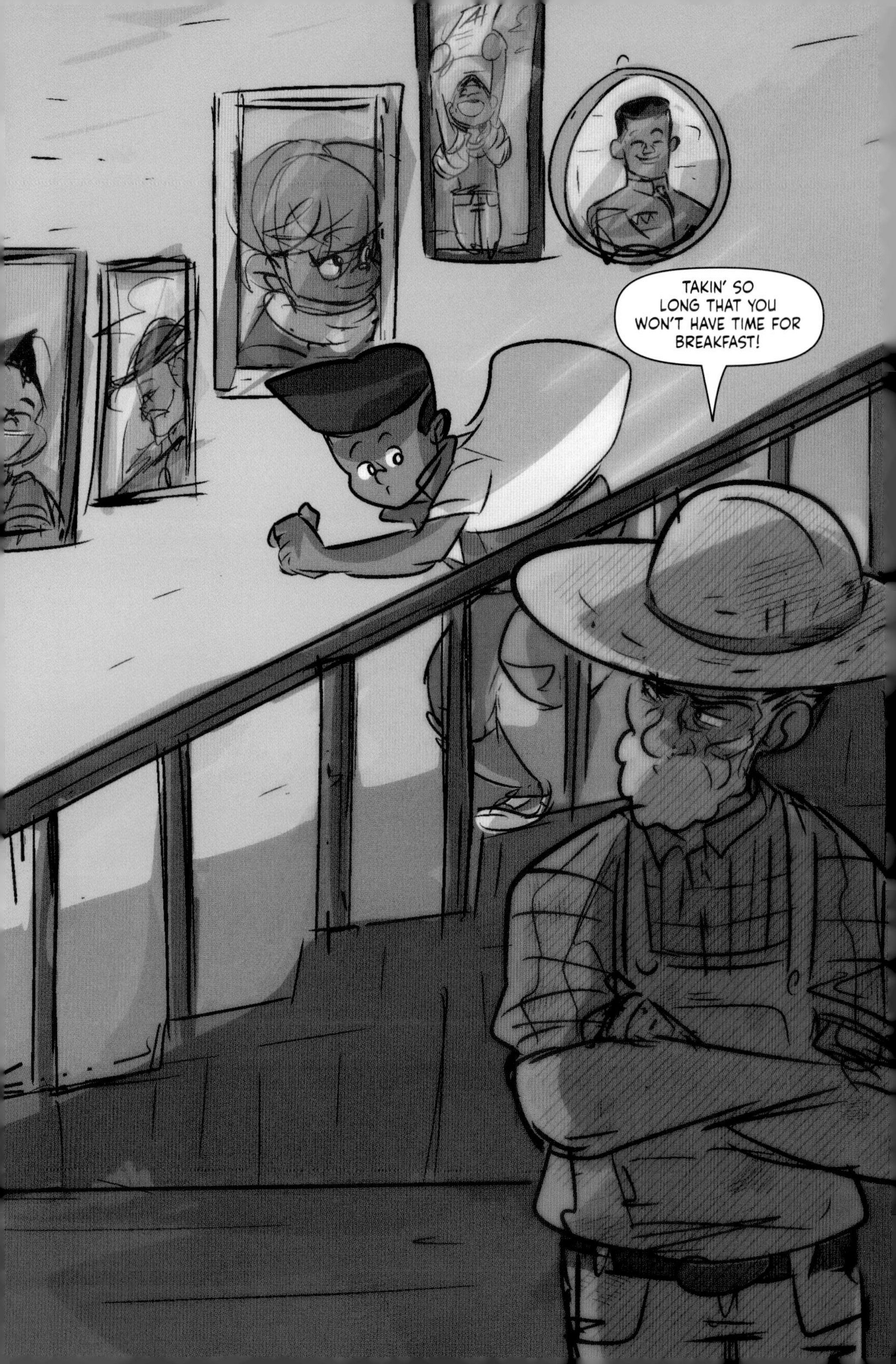
TAKIN' SO LONG THAT YOU WON'T HAVE TIME FOR BREAKFAST!

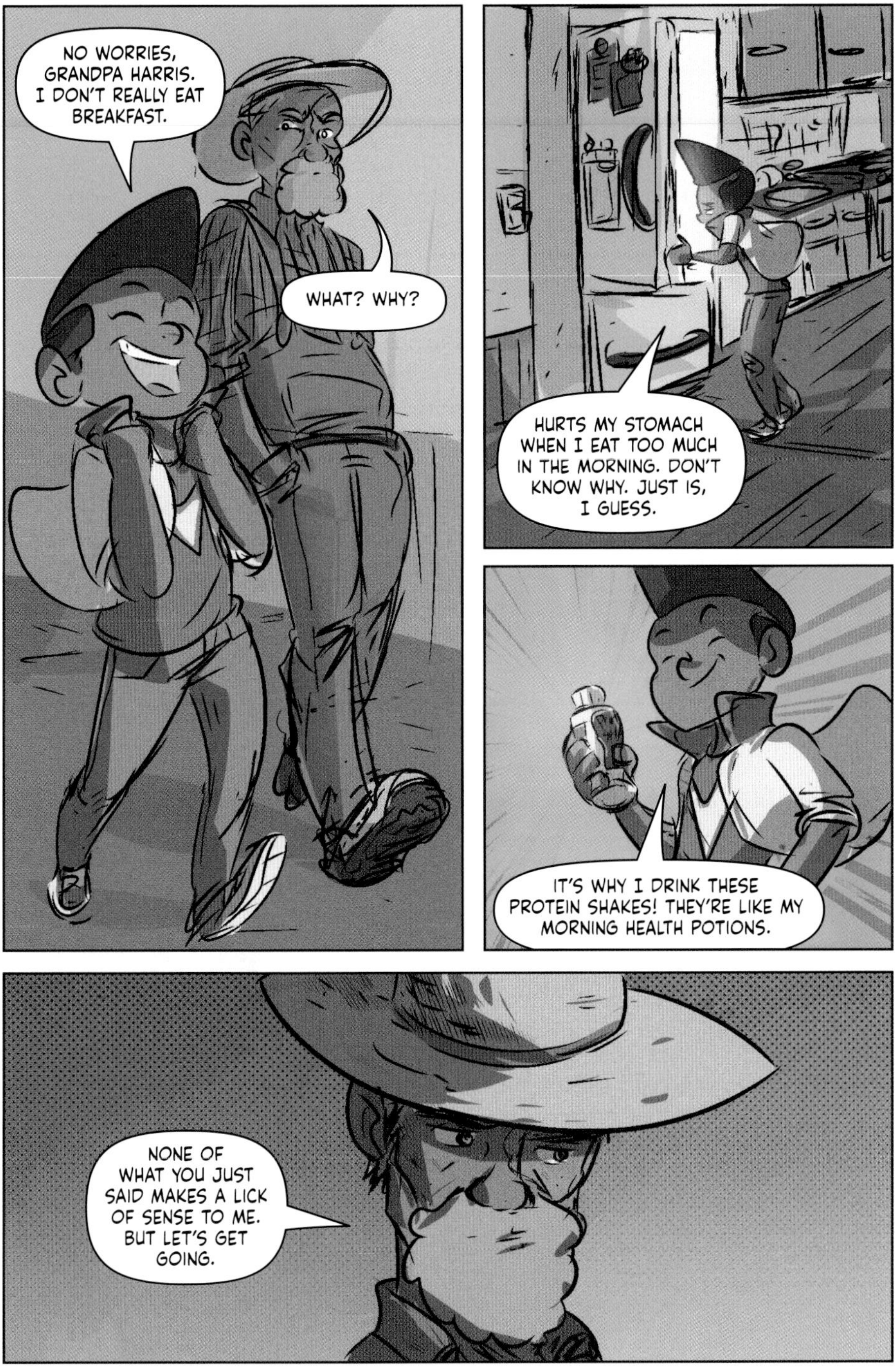
NO WORRIES, GRANDPA HARRIS. I DON'T REALLY EAT BREAKFAST.
WHAT? WHY?
HURTS MY STOMACH WHEN I EAT TOO MUCH IN THE MORNING. DON'T KNOW WHY. JUST IS, I GUESS.
IT'S WHY I DRINK THESE PROTEIN SHAKES! THEY'RE LIKE MY MORNING HEALTH POTIONS.
NONE OF WHAT YOU JUST SAID MAKES A LICK OF SENSE TO ME. BUT LET'S GET GOING.

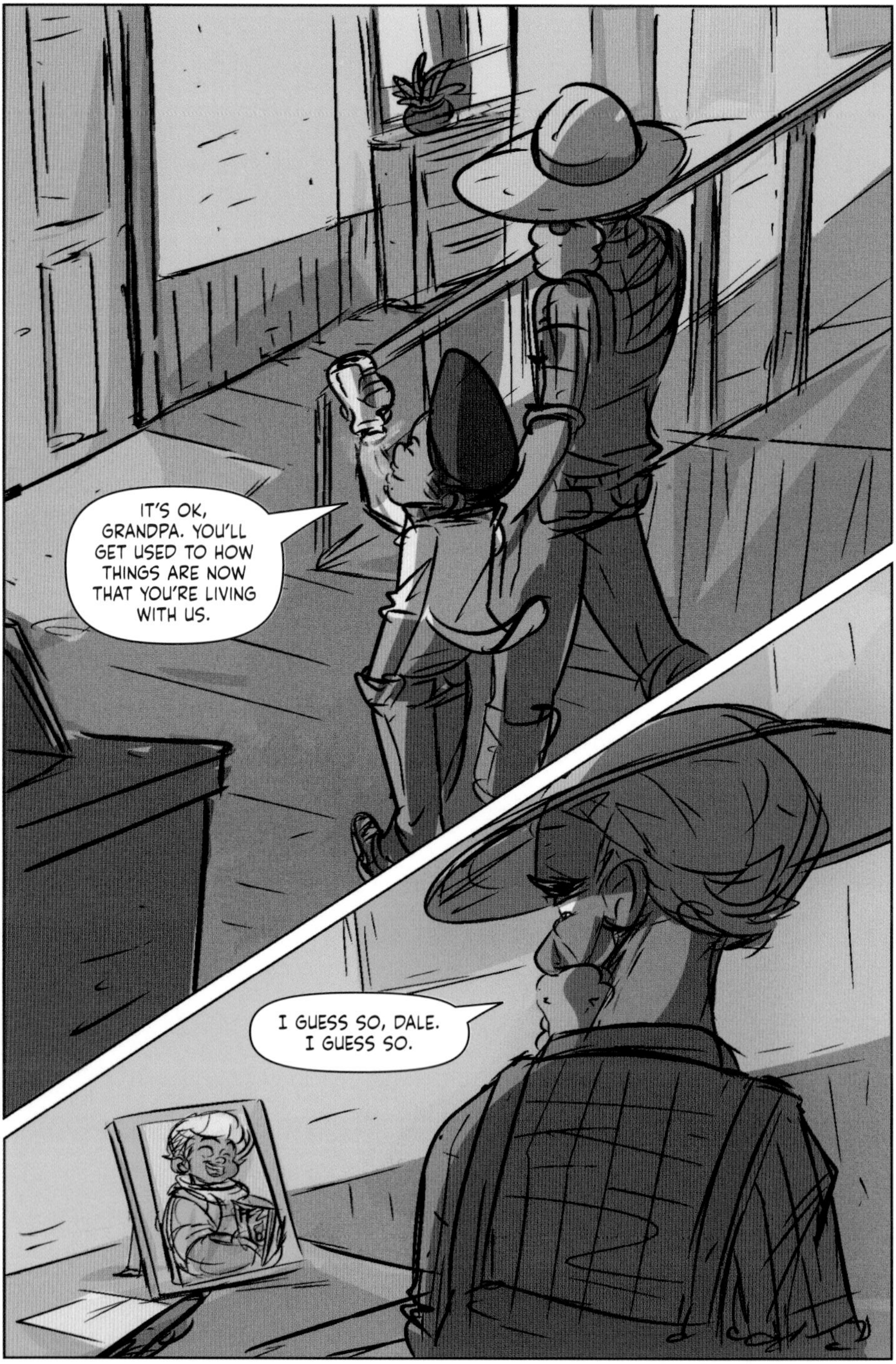
IT'S OK, GRANDPA. YOU'LL GET USED TO HOW THINGS ARE NOW THAT YOU'RE LIVING WITH US.
I GUESS SO, DALE. I GUESS SO.

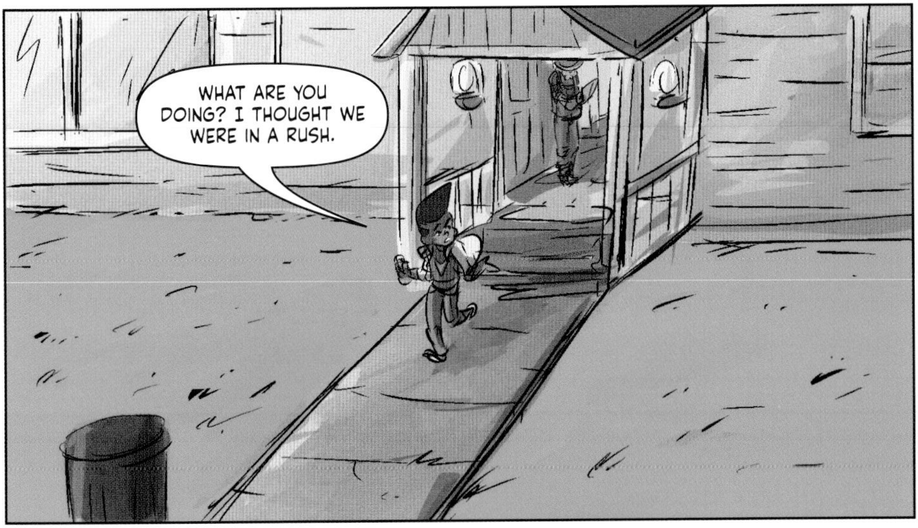
WHAT ARE YOU DOING? I THOUGHT WE WERE IN A RUSH.

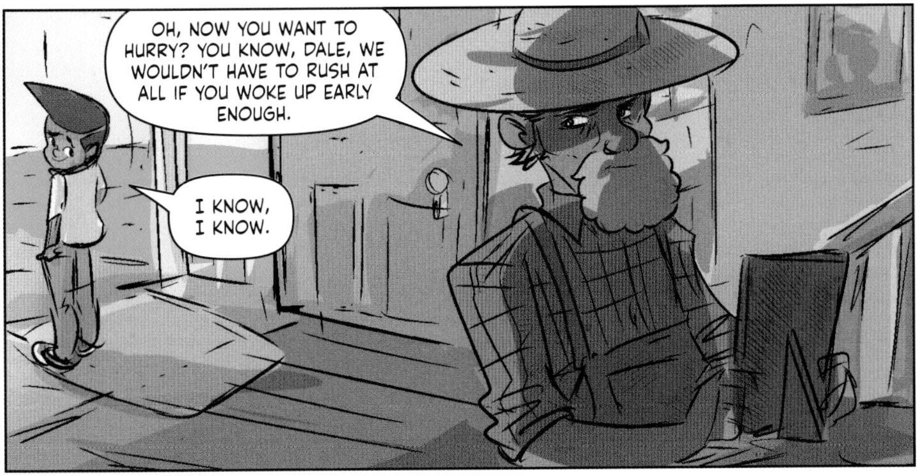
OH, NOW YOU WANT TO HURRY? YOU KNOW, DALE, WE WOULDN'T HAVE TO RUSH AT ALL IF YOU WOKE UP EARLY ENOUGH.
I KNOW, I KNOW.

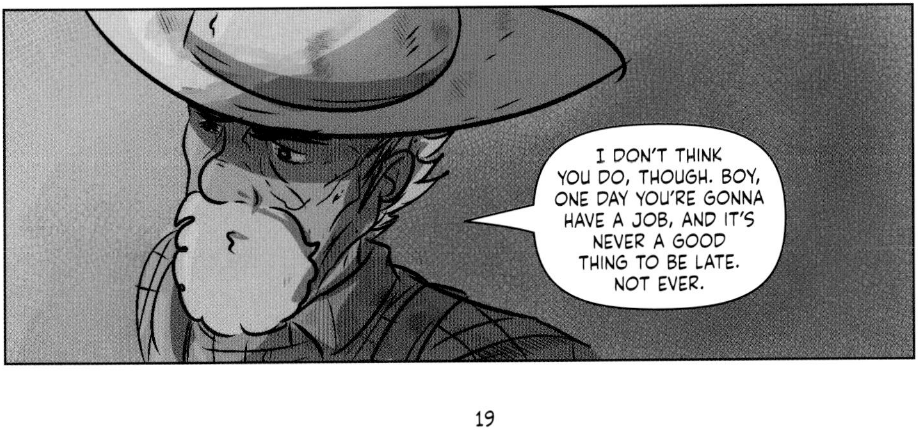
I DON'T THINK YOU DO, THOUGH. BOY, ONE DAY YOU'RE GONNA HAVE A JOB, AND IT'S NEVER A GOOD THING TO BE LATE. NOT EVER.

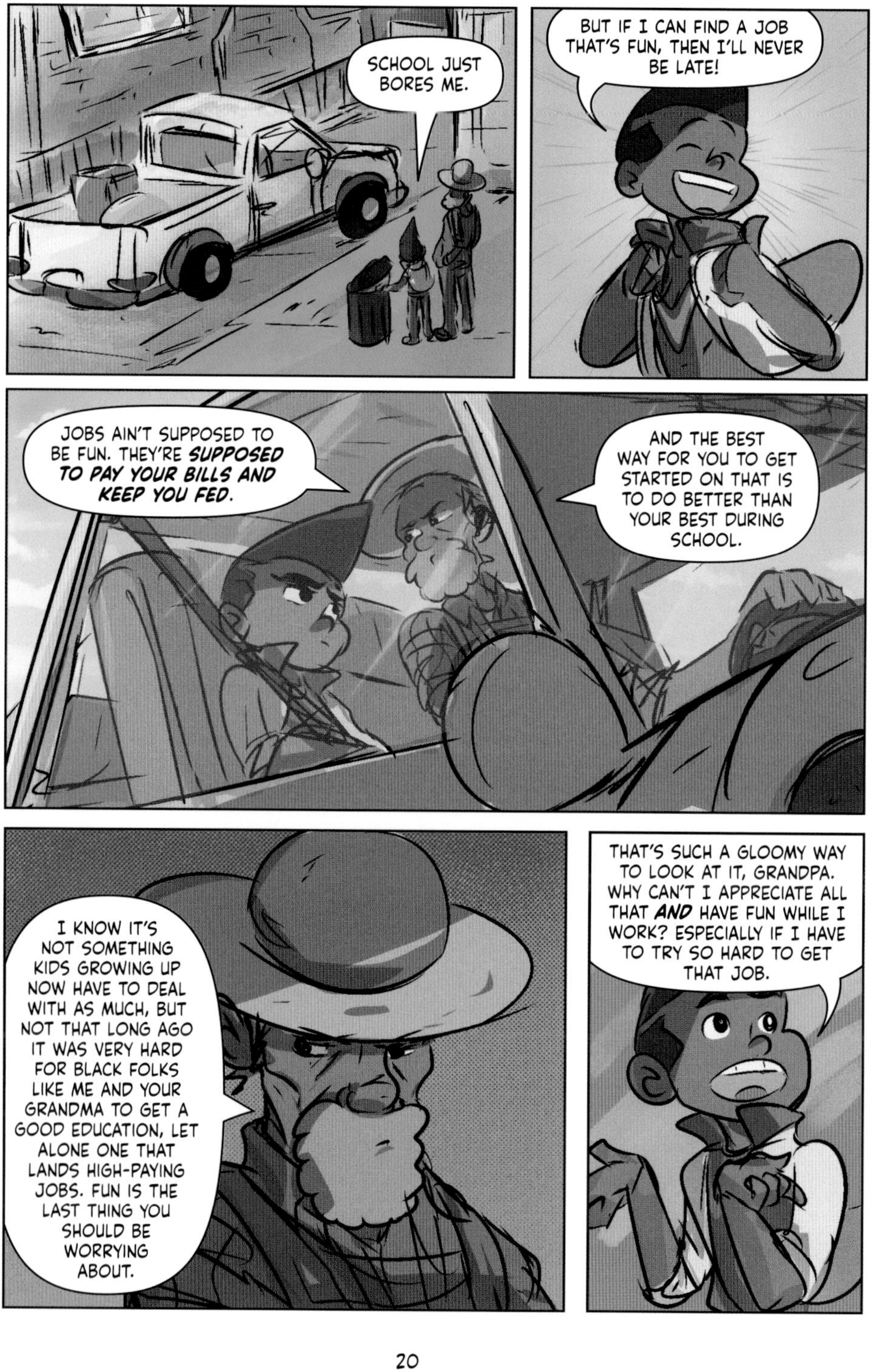
SCHOOL JUST BORES ME.
BUT IF I CAN FIND A JOB THAT'S FUN, THEN I'LL NEVER BE LATE!
JOBS AIN'T SUPPOSED TO BE FUN. THEY'RE ***SUPPOSED TO PAY YOUR BILLS AND KEEP YOU FED***.
AND THE BEST WAY FOR YOU TO GET STARTED ON THAT IS TO DO BETTER THAN YOUR BEST DURING SCHOOL.
I KNOW IT'S NOT SOMETHING KIDS GROWING UP NOW HAVE TO DEAL WITH AS MUCH, BUT NOT THAT LONG AGO IT WAS VERY HARD FOR BLACK FOLKS LIKE ME AND YOUR GRANDMA TO GET A GOOD EDUCATION, LET ALONE ONE THAT LANDS HIGH-PAYING JOBS. FUN IS THE LAST THING YOU SHOULD BE WORRYING ABOUT.
THAT'S SUCH A GLOOMY WAY TO LOOK AT IT, GRANDPA. WHY CAN'T I APPRECIATE ALL THAT ***AND*** HAVE FUN WHILE I WORK? ESPECIALLY IF I HAVE TO TRY SO HARD TO GET THAT JOB.

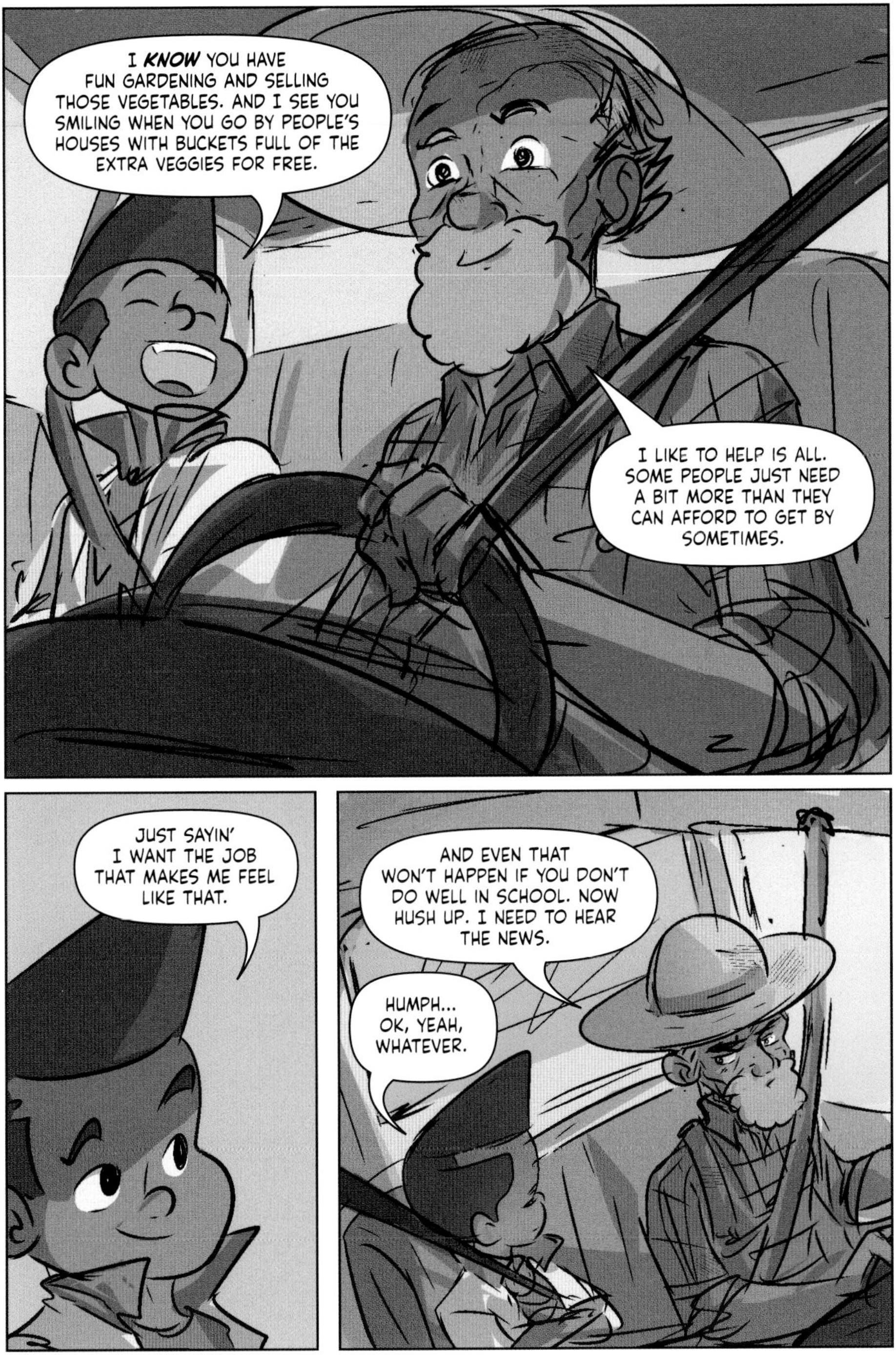
I *KNOW* YOU HAVE FUN GARDENING AND SELLING THOSE VEGETABLES. AND I SEE YOU SMILING WHEN YOU GO BY PEOPLE'S HOUSES WITH BUCKETS FULL OF THE EXTRA VEGGIES FOR FREE.
I LIKE TO HELP IS ALL. SOME PEOPLE JUST NEED A BIT MORE THAN THEY CAN AFFORD TO GET BY SOMETIMES.
JUST SAYIN' I WANT THE JOB THAT MAKES ME FEEL LIKE THAT.
AND EVEN THAT WON'T HAPPEN IF YOU DON'T DO WELL IN SCHOOL. NOW HUSH UP. I NEED TO HEAR THE NEWS.
HUMPH... OK, YEAH, WHATEVER.

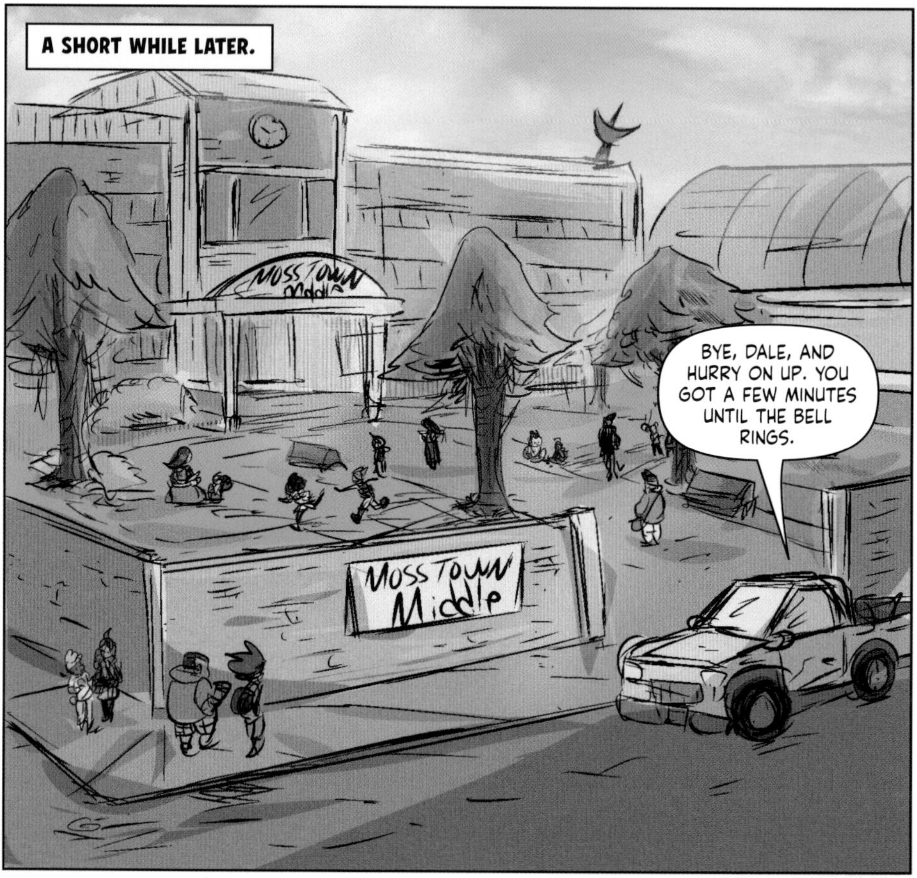
A SHORT WHILE LATER.
MOSSTOWN Middle
MOSSTOWN Middle
BYE, DALE, AND HURRY ON UP. YOU GOT A FEW MINUTES UNTIL THE BELL RINGS.

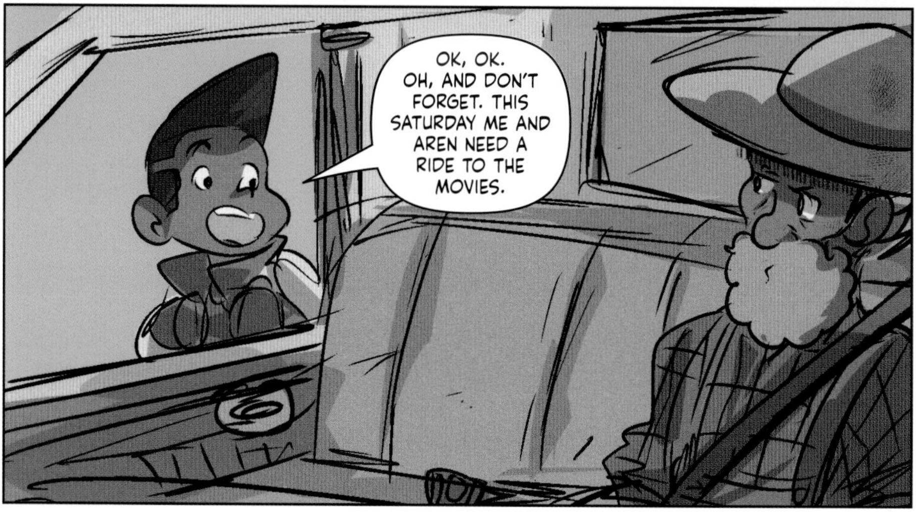
OK, OK. OH, AND DON'T FORGET. THIS SATURDAY ME AND AREN NEED A RIDE TO THE MOVIES.

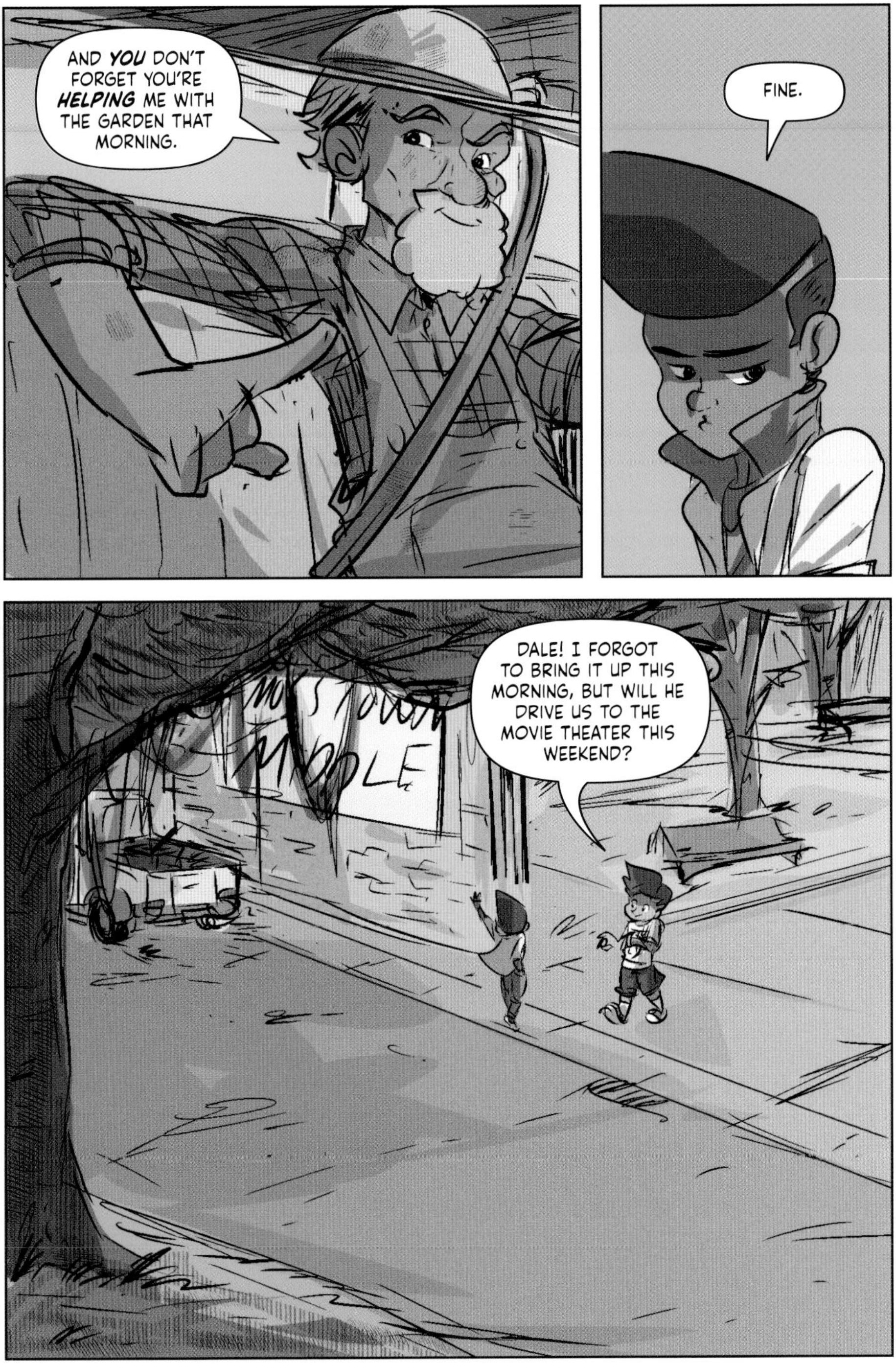
AND *YOU* DON'T FORGET YOU'RE *HELPING* ME WITH THE GARDEN THAT MORNING.
FINE.
DALE! I FORGOT TO BRING IT UP THIS MORNING, BUT WILL HE DRIVE US TO THE MOVIE THEATER THIS WEEKEND?

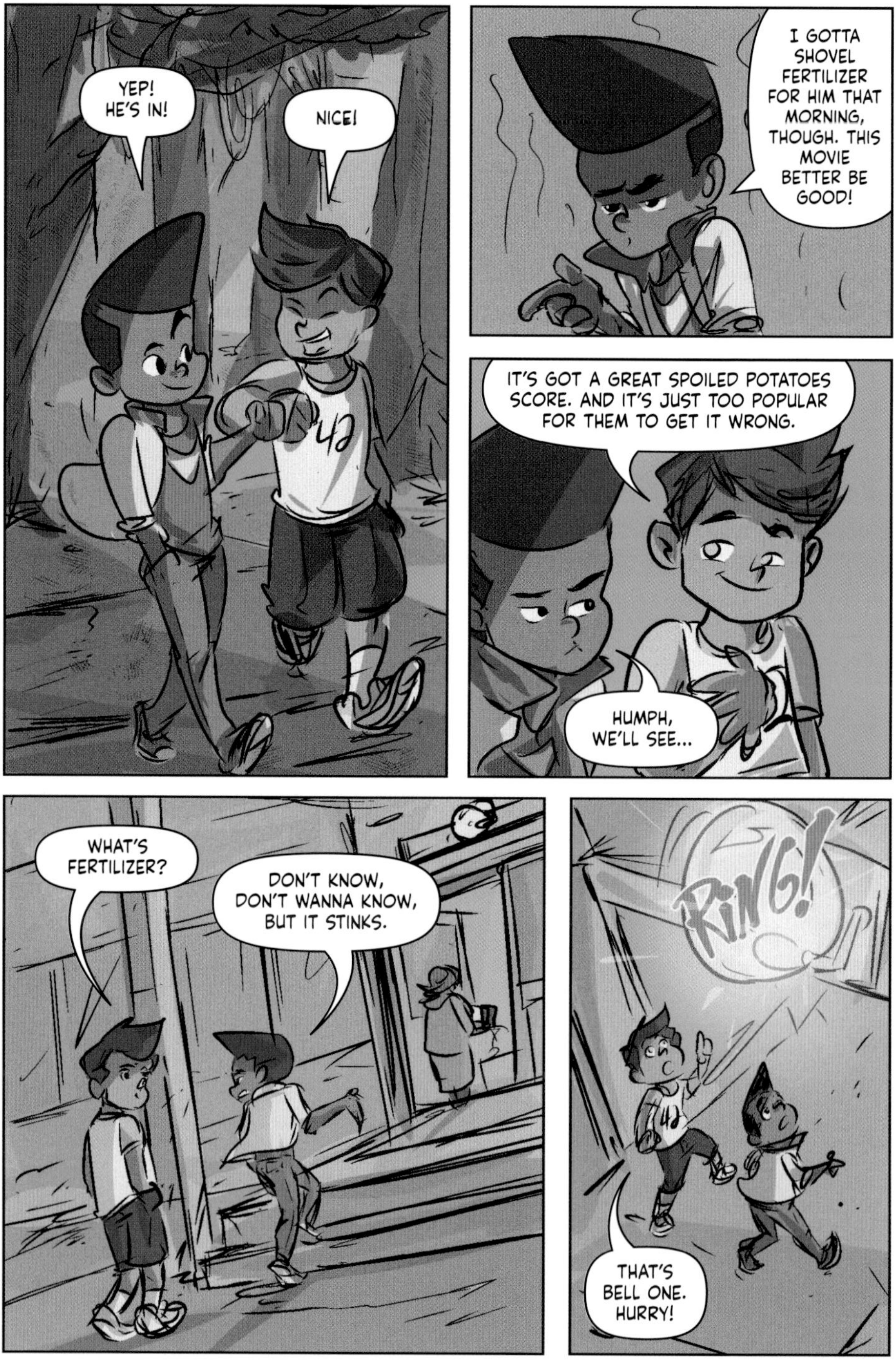
YEP! HE'S IN!
NICE!
I GOTTA SHOVEL FERTILIZER FOR HIM THAT MORNING, THOUGH. THIS MOVIE BETTER BE GOOD!
IT'S GOT A GREAT SPOILED POTATOES SCORE. AND IT'S JUST TOO POPULAR FOR THEM TO GET IT WRONG.
HUMPH, WE'LL SEE...
WHAT'S FERTILIZER?
DON'T KNOW, DON'T WANNA KNOW, BUT IT STINKS.
RING!
THAT'S BELL ONE. HURRY!

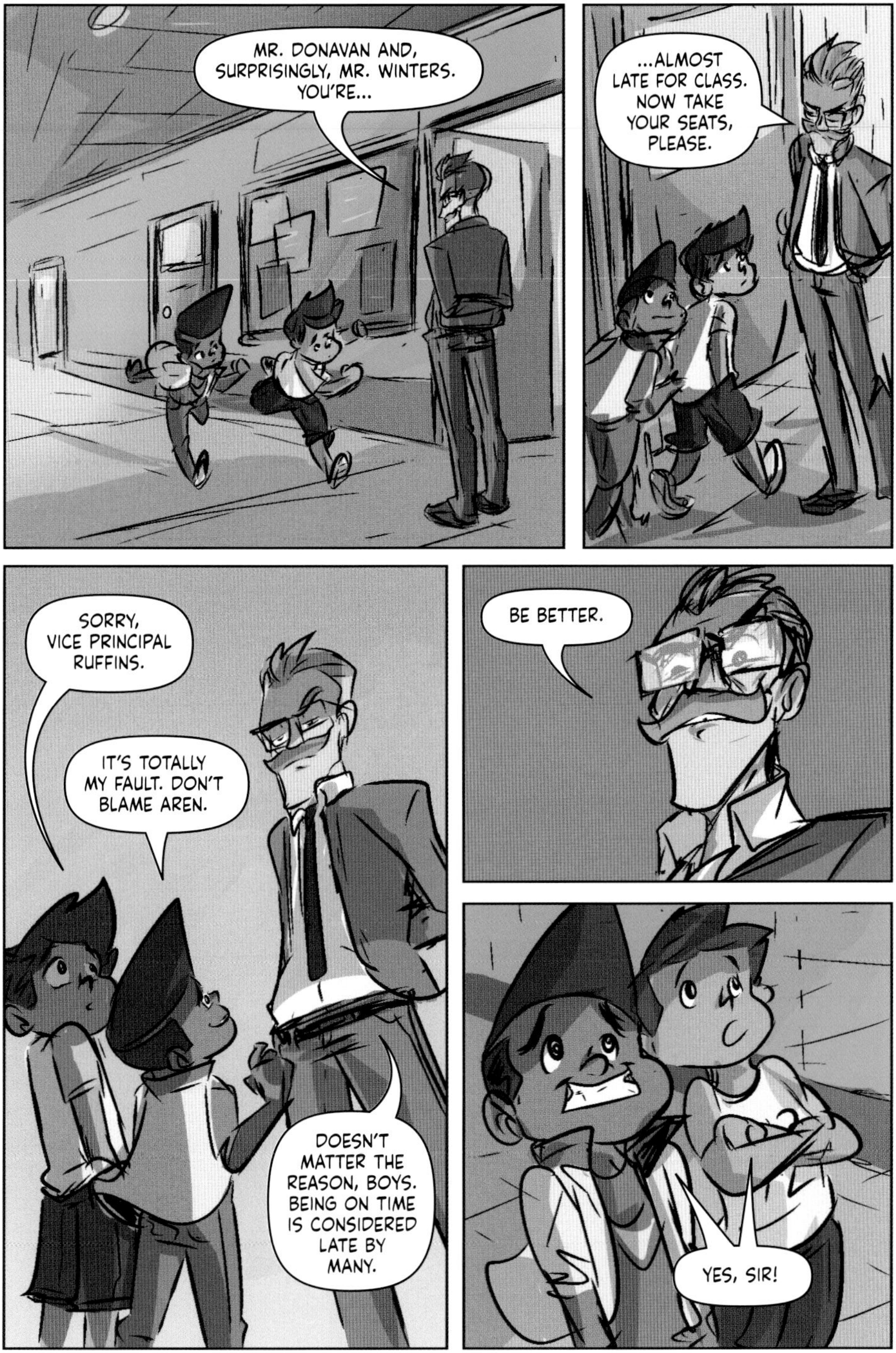
MR. DONAVAN AND, SURPRISINGLY, MR. WINTERS. YOU'RE...
...ALMOST LATE FOR CLASS. NOW TAKE YOUR SEATS, PLEASE.
SORRY, VICE PRINCIPAL RUFFINS.
IT'S TOTALLY MY FAULT. DON'T BLAME AREN.
DOESN'T MATTER THE REASON, BOYS. BEING ON TIME IS CONSIDERED LATE BY MANY.
BE BETTER.
YES, SIR!

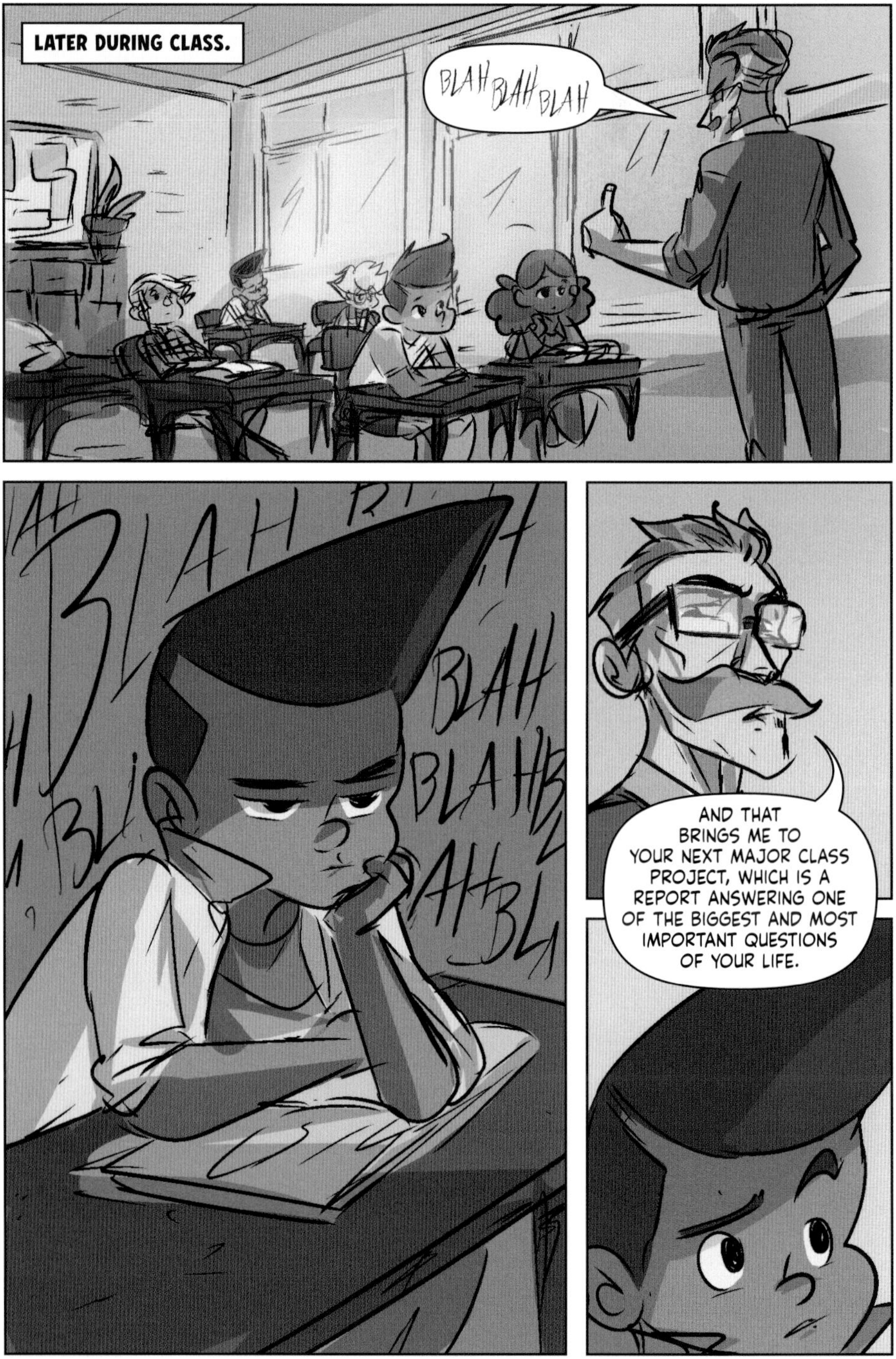
LATER DURING CLASS.
BLAH BLAH BLAH
BLAH
BLAH
AND THAT BRINGS ME TO YOUR NEXT MAJOR CLASS PROJECT, WHICH IS A REPORT ANSWERING ONE OF THE BIGGEST AND MOST IMPORTANT QUESTIONS OF YOUR LIFE.

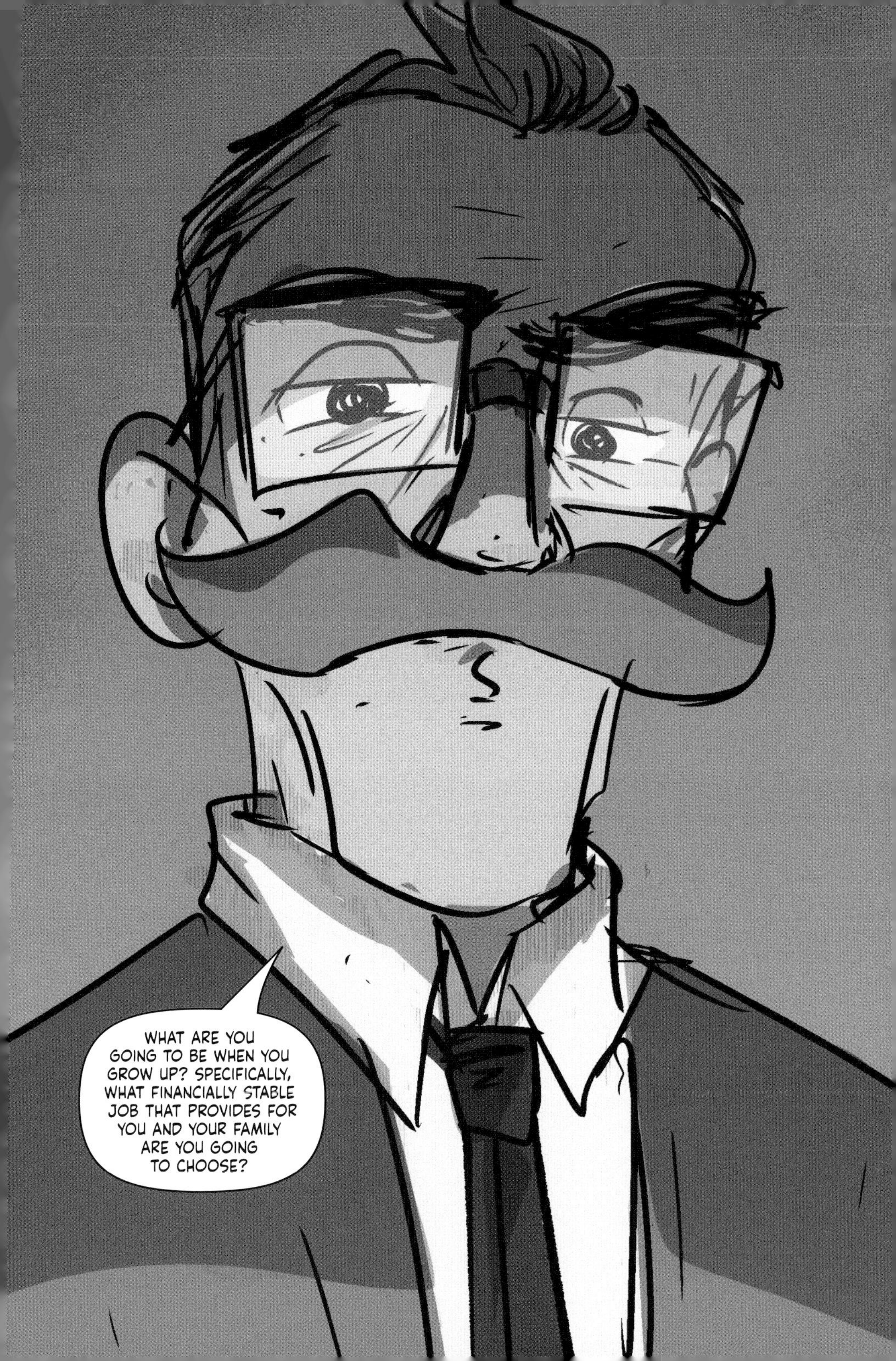
WHAT ARE YOU GOING TO BE WHEN YOU GROW UP? SPECIFICALLY, WHAT FINANCIALLY STABLE JOB THAT PROVIDES FOR YOU AND YOUR FAMILY ARE YOU GOING TO CHOOSE?

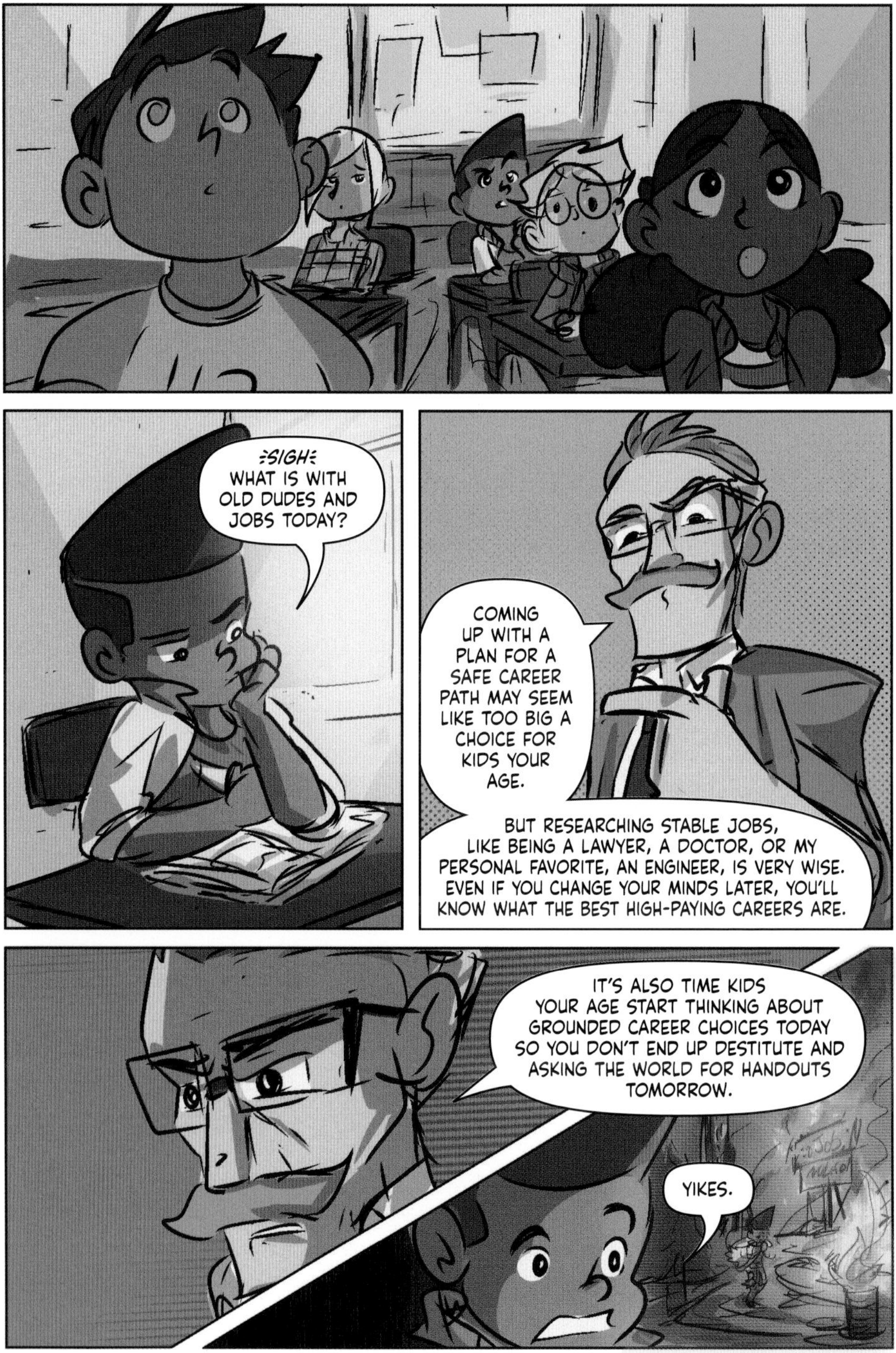

⁼SIGH⁼
WHAT IS WITH OLD DUDES AND JOBS TODAY?
COMING UP WITH A PLAN FOR A SAFE CAREER PATH MAY SEEM LIKE TOO BIG A CHOICE FOR KIDS YOUR AGE.
BUT RESEARCHING STABLE JOBS, LIKE BEING A LAWYER, A DOCTOR, OR MY PERSONAL FAVORITE, AN ENGINEER, IS VERY WISE. EVEN IF YOU CHANGE YOUR MINDS LATER, YOU'LL KNOW WHAT THE BEST HIGH-PAYING CAREERS ARE.
IT'S ALSO TIME KIDS YOUR AGE START THINKING ABOUT GROUNDED CAREER CHOICES TODAY SO YOU DON'T END UP DESTITUTE AND ASKING THE WORLD FOR HANDOUTS TOMORROW.
YIKES.

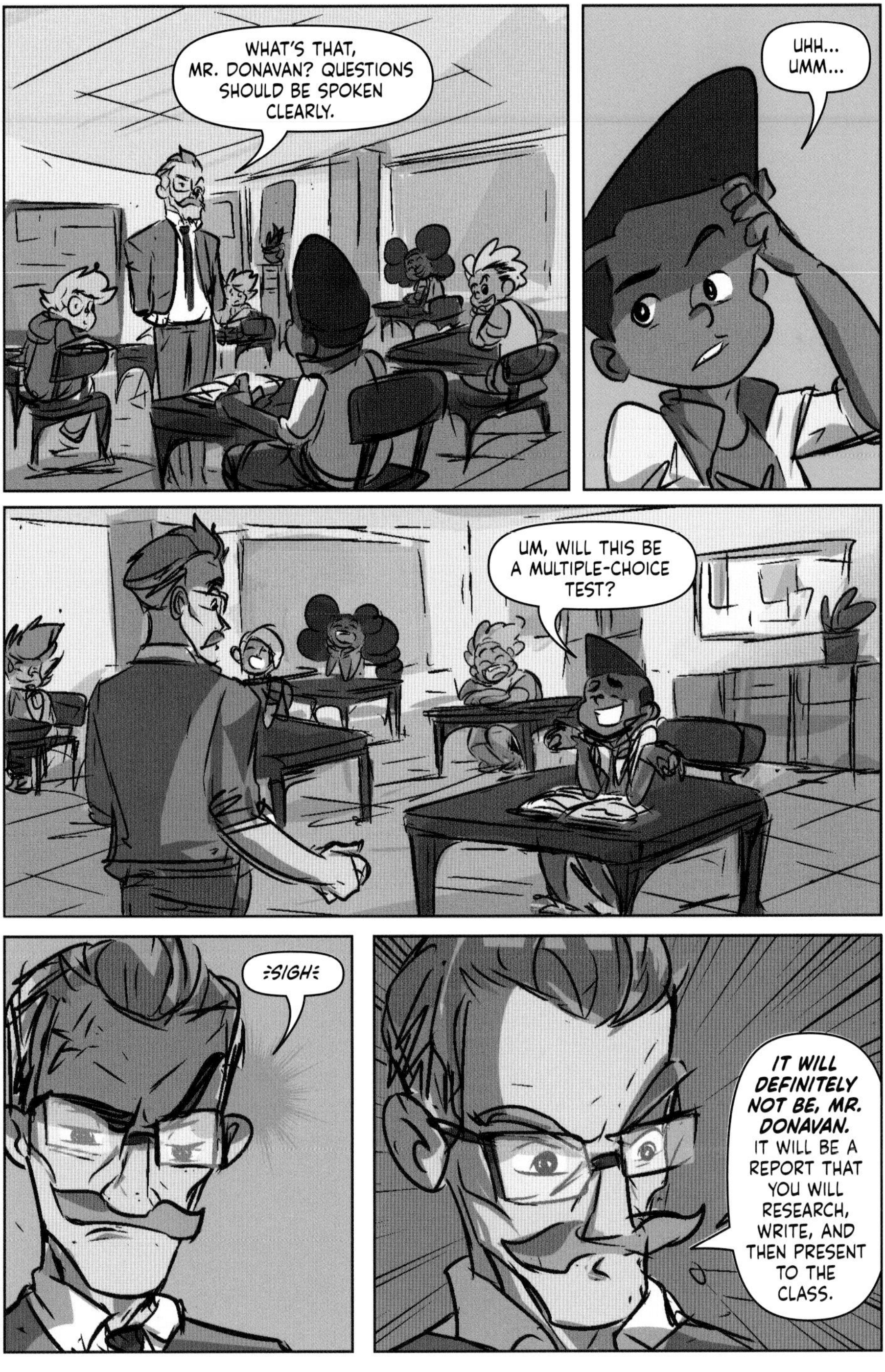
WHAT'S THAT, MR. DONAVAN? QUESTIONS SHOULD BE SPOKEN CLEARLY.
UHH... UMM...
UM, WILL THIS BE A MULTIPLE-CHOICE TEST?
SIGH
IT WILL DEFINITELY NOT BE, MR. DONAVAN. IT WILL BE A REPORT THAT YOU WILL RESEARCH, WRITE, AND THEN PRESENT TO THE CLASS.

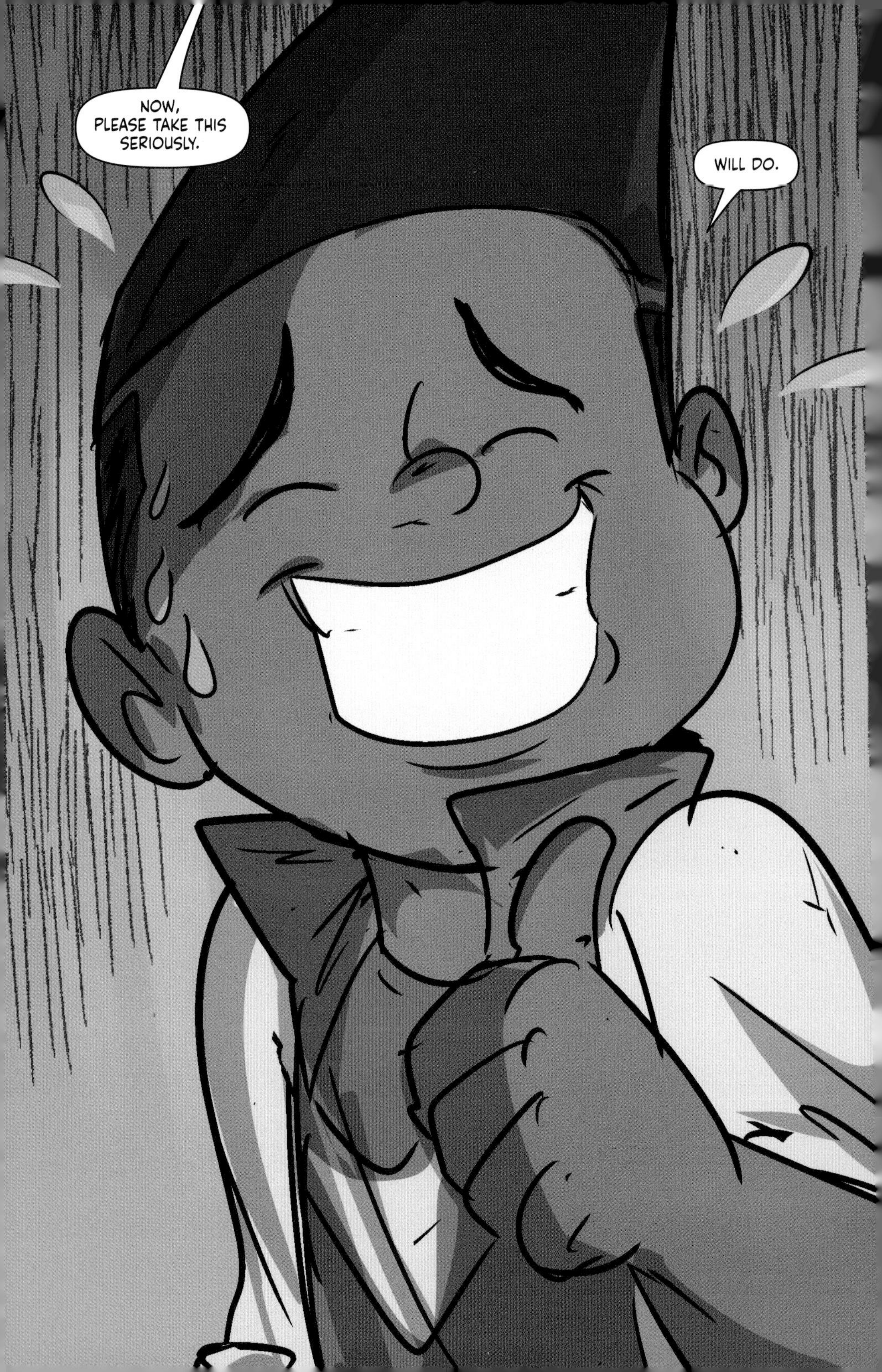
NOW, PLEASE TAKE THIS SERIOUSLY.
WILL DO.

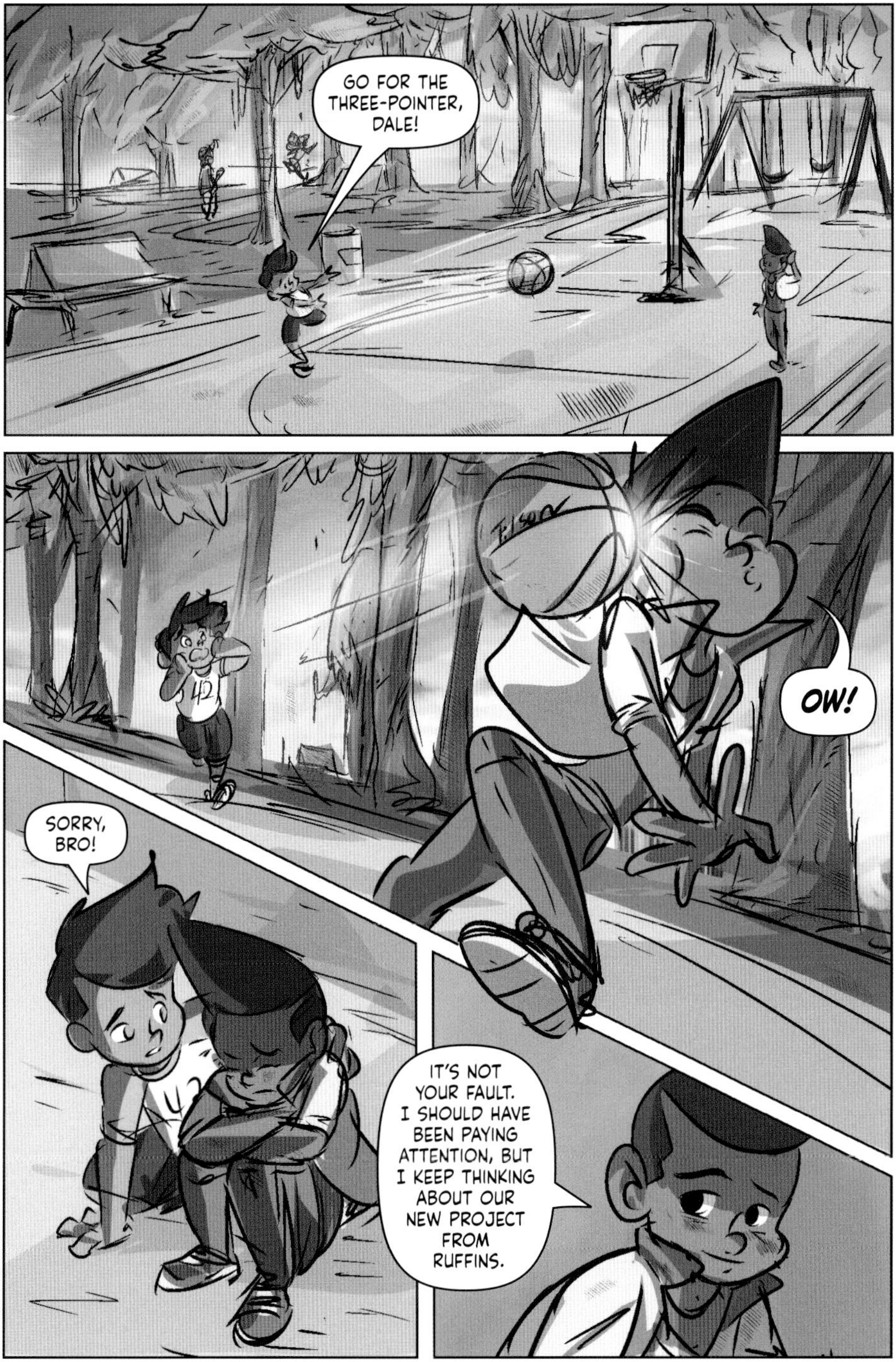
GO FOR THE THREE-POINTER, DALE!
OW!
SORRY, BRO!
IT’S NOT YOUR FAULT. I SHOULD HAVE BEEN PAYING ATTENTION, BUT I KEEP THINKING ABOUT OUR NEW PROJECT FROM RUFFINS.

YEAH? WHY?

'CAUSE I HAVE NO IDEA WHAT TO DO IT ON.

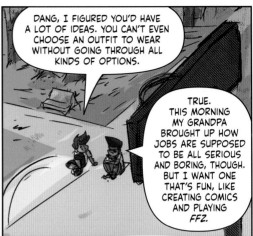

DANG, I FIGURED YOU'D HAVE A LOT OF IDEAS. YOU CAN'T EVEN CHOOSE AN OUTFIT TO WEAR WITHOUT GOING THROUGH ALL KINDS OF OPTIONS.

TRUE. THIS MORNING MY GRANDPA BROUGHT UP HOW JOBS ARE SUPPOSED TO BE ALL SERIOUS AND BORING, THOUGH. BUT I WANT ONE THAT'S FUN, LIKE CREATING COMICS AND PLAYING *FFZ*.

AND I HAVE NO IDEA IF THOSE THINGS CAN BE "SAFE AND DEPENDABLE" JOBS LIKE RUFFINS WANTS 'CAUSE WE NEVER LEARN A LOT ABOUT THAT KIND OF STUFF IN SCHOOL.

I DON'T KNOW, DUDE. I MEAN, MY ANSWER WILL PROBABLY BE BASKETBALL, AND MY DAD THINKS THAT'S PRETTY FUN. IT'S WHY WE TRAIN SO HARD. SO THAT I CAN PLAY PRO ONE DAY OR BE A COACH LIKE HIM IF THAT DOESN'T WORK OUT.

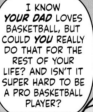

I KNOW *YOUR DAD* LOVES BASKETBALL, BUT COULD *YOU* REALLY DO THAT FOR THE REST OF YOUR LIFE? AND ISN'T IT SUPER HARD TO BE A PRO BASKETBALL PLAYER?

HMMM...

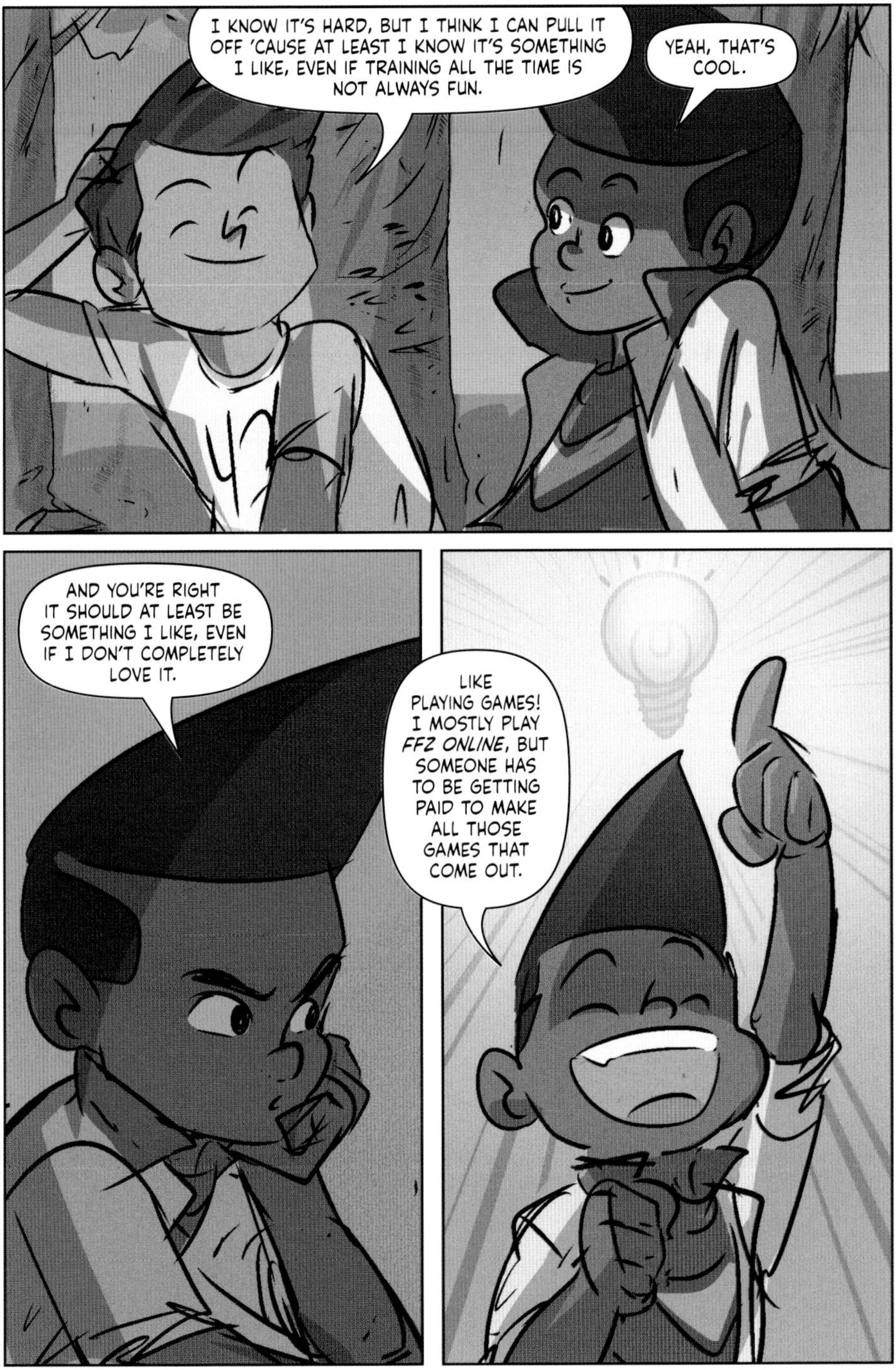
I KNOW IT'S HARD, BUT I THINK I CAN PULL IT OFF 'CAUSE AT LEAST I KNOW IT'S SOMETHING I LIKE, EVEN IF TRAINING ALL THE TIME IS NOT ALWAYS FUN.
YEAH, THAT'S COOL.
AND YOU'RE RIGHT IT SHOULD AT LEAST BE SOMETHING I LIKE, EVEN IF I DON'T COMPLETELY LOVE IT.
LIKE PLAYING GAMES! I MOSTLY PLAY *FFZ ONLINE*, BUT SOMEONE HAS TO BE GETTING PAID TO MAKE ALL THOSE GAMES THAT COME OUT.

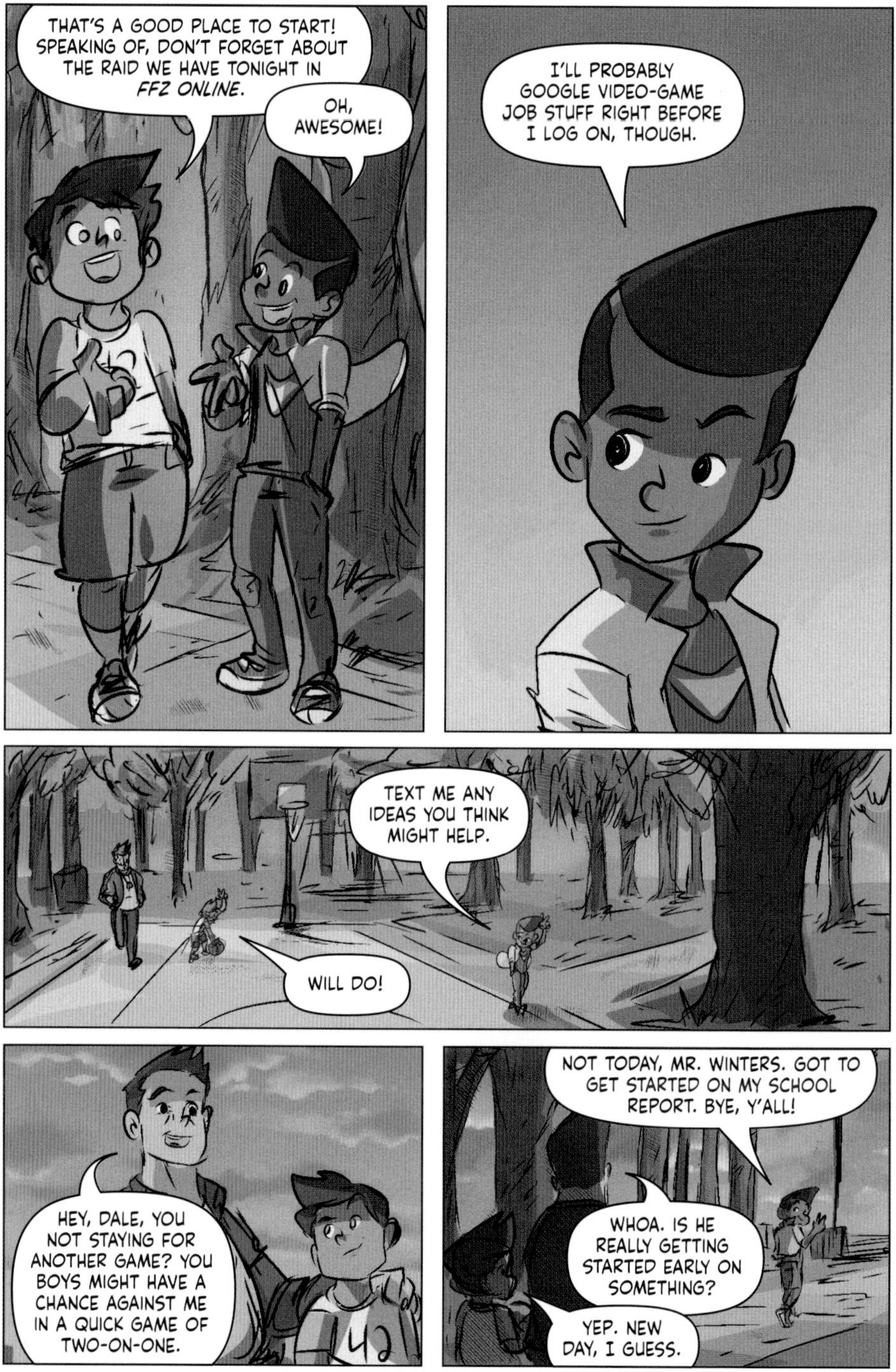
THAT'S A GOOD PLACE TO START! SPEAKING OF, DON'T FORGET ABOUT THE RAID WE HAVE TONIGHT IN *FFZ ONLINE*.
OH, AWESOME!
I'LL PROBABLY GOOGLE VIDEO-GAME JOB STUFF RIGHT BEFORE I LOG ON, THOUGH.
TEXT ME ANY IDEAS YOU THINK MIGHT HELP.
WILL DO!
HEY, DALE, YOU NOT STAYING FOR ANOTHER GAME? YOU BOYS MIGHT HAVE A CHANCE AGAINST ME IN A QUICK GAME OF TWO-ON-ONE.
NOT TODAY, MR. WINTERS. GOT TO GET STARTED ON MY SCHOOL REPORT. BYE, Y'ALL!
WHOA. IS HE REALLY GETTING STARTED EARLY ON SOMETHING?
YEP. NEW DAY, I GUESS.

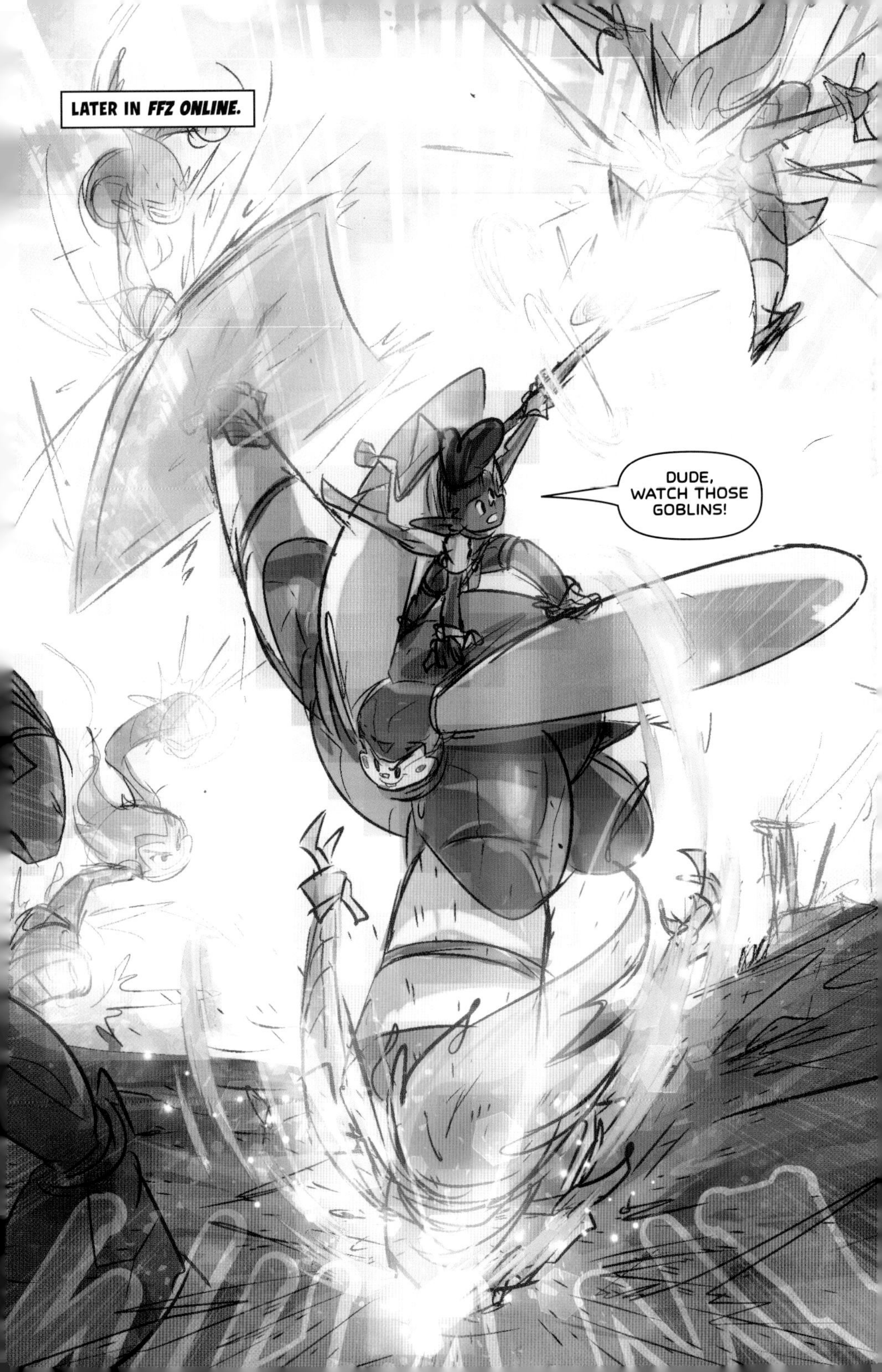
LATER IN FFZ ONLINE.
DUDE, WATCH THOSE GOBLINS!

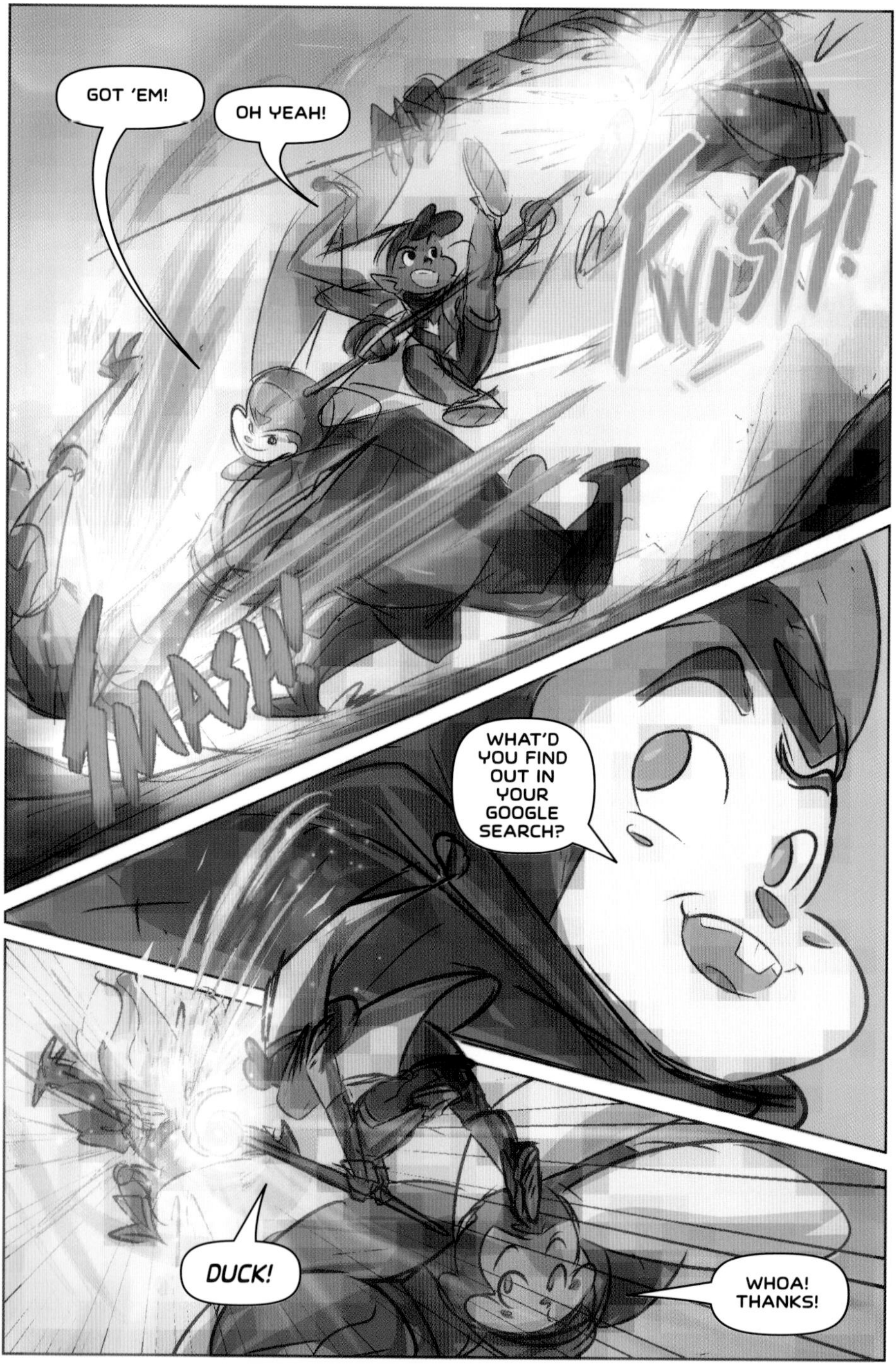
GOT 'EM!
OH YEAH!
FWISH!
WHASH!
WHAT'D YOU FIND OUT IN YOUR GOOGLE SEARCH?
DUCK!
WHOA! THANKS!

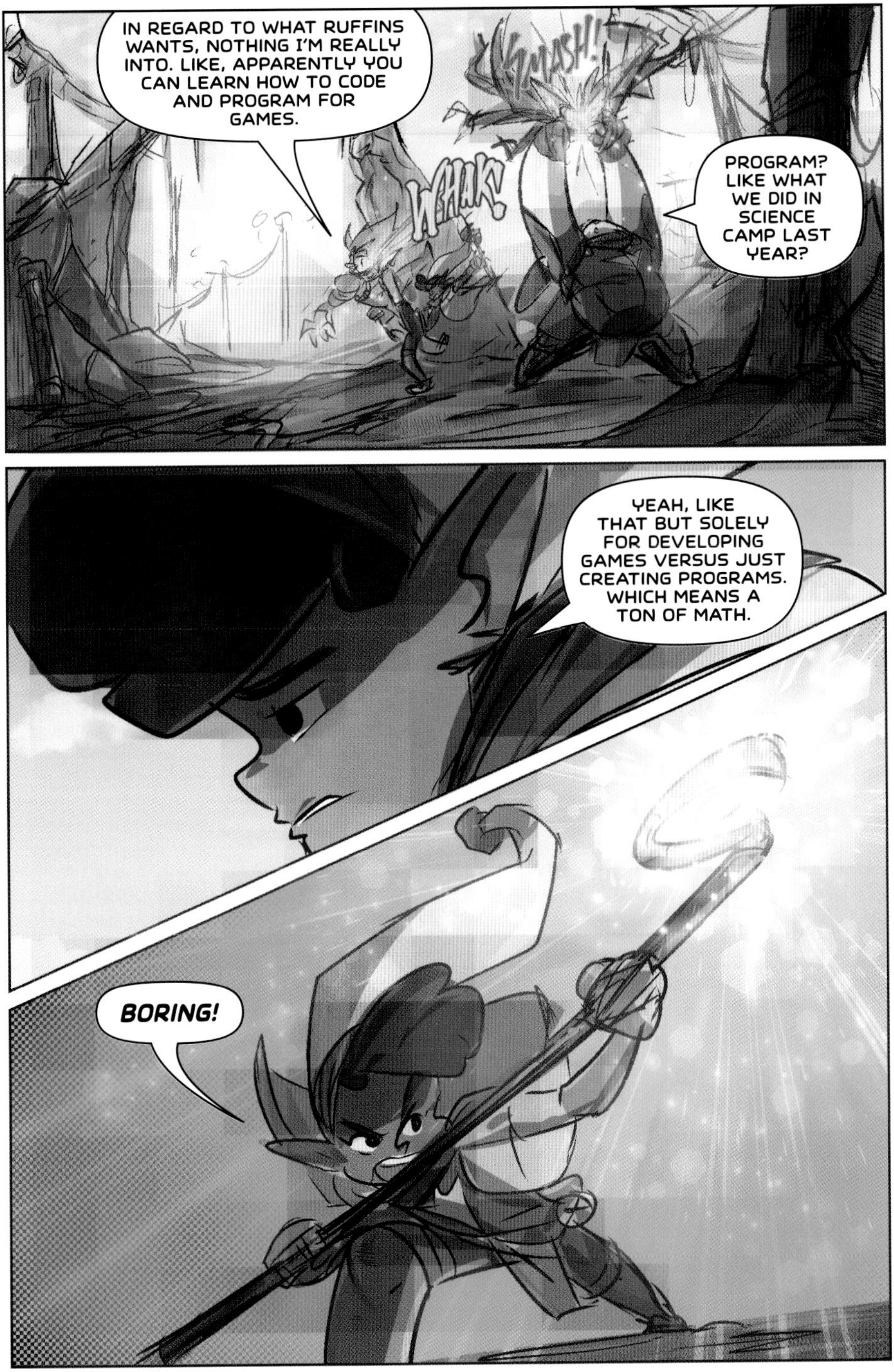
IN REGARD TO WHAT RUFFINS WANTS, NOTHING I'M REALLY INTO. LIKE, APPARENTLY YOU CAN LEARN HOW TO CODE AND PROGRAM FOR GAMES.
WHAK!
PROGRAM? LIKE WHAT WE DID IN SCIENCE CAMP LAST YEAR?
YEAH, LIKE THAT BUT SOLELY FOR DEVELOPING GAMES VERSUS JUST CREATING PROGRAMS. WHICH MEANS A TON OF MATH.
BORING!

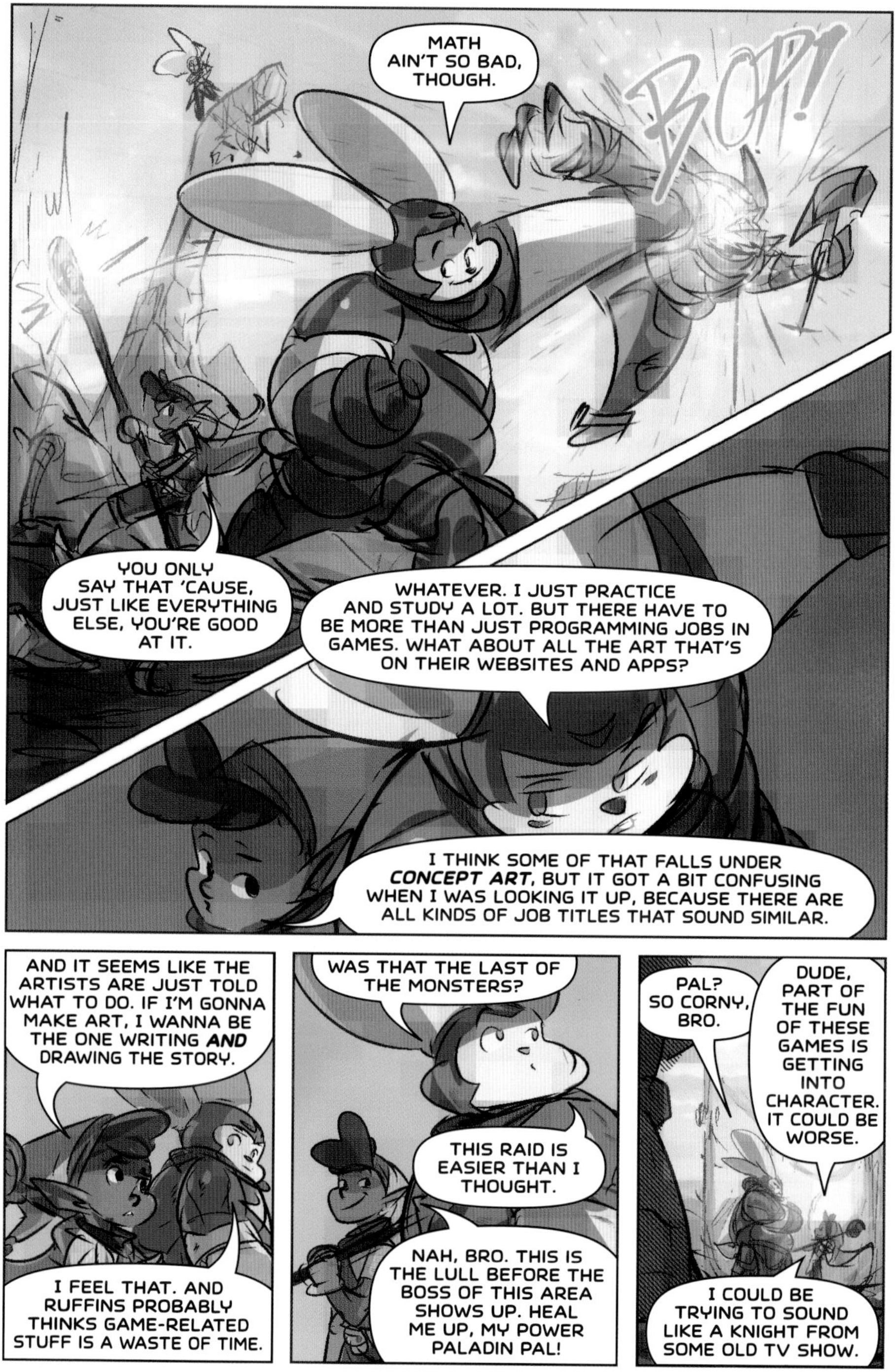
MATH AIN'T SO BAD, THOUGH.
BOP!
YOU ONLY SAY THAT 'CAUSE, JUST LIKE EVERYTHING ELSE, YOU'RE GOOD AT IT.
WHATEVER. I JUST PRACTICE AND STUDY A LOT. BUT THERE HAVE TO BE MORE THAN JUST PROGRAMMING JOBS IN GAMES. WHAT ABOUT ALL THE ART THAT'S ON THEIR WEBSITES AND APPS?
I THINK SOME OF THAT FALLS UNDER ***CONCEPT ART***, BUT IT GOT A BIT CONFUSING WHEN I WAS LOOKING IT UP, BECAUSE THERE ARE ALL KINDS OF JOB TITLES THAT SOUND SIMILAR.
AND IT SEEMS LIKE THE ARTISTS ARE JUST TOLD WHAT TO DO. IF I'M GONNA MAKE ART, I WANNA BE THE ONE WRITING ***AND*** DRAWING THE STORY.
I FEEL THAT. AND RUFFINS PROBABLY THINKS GAME-RELATED STUFF IS A WASTE OF TIME.
WAS THAT THE LAST OF THE MONSTERS?
THIS RAID IS EASIER THAN I THOUGHT.
NAH, BRO. THIS IS THE LULL BEFORE THE BOSS OF THIS AREA SHOWS UP. HEAL ME UP, MY POWER PALADIN PAL!
PAL? SO CORNY, BRO.
DUDE, PART OF THE FUN OF THESE GAMES IS GETTING INTO CHARACTER. IT COULD BE WORSE.
I COULD BE TRYING TO SOUND LIKE A KNIGHT FROM SOME OLD TV SHOW.

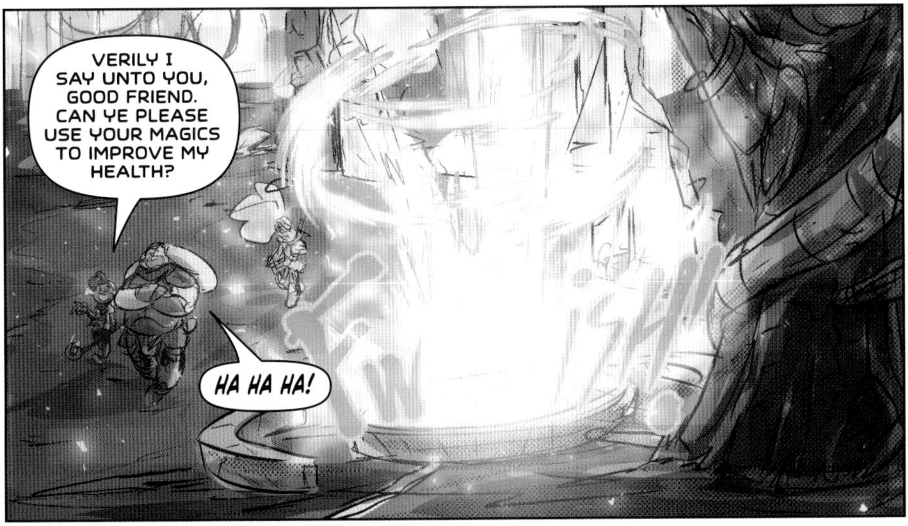
VERILY I SAY UNTO YOU, GOOD FRIEND. CAN YE PLEASE USE YOUR MAGICS TO IMPROVE MY HEALTH?
HA HA HA!

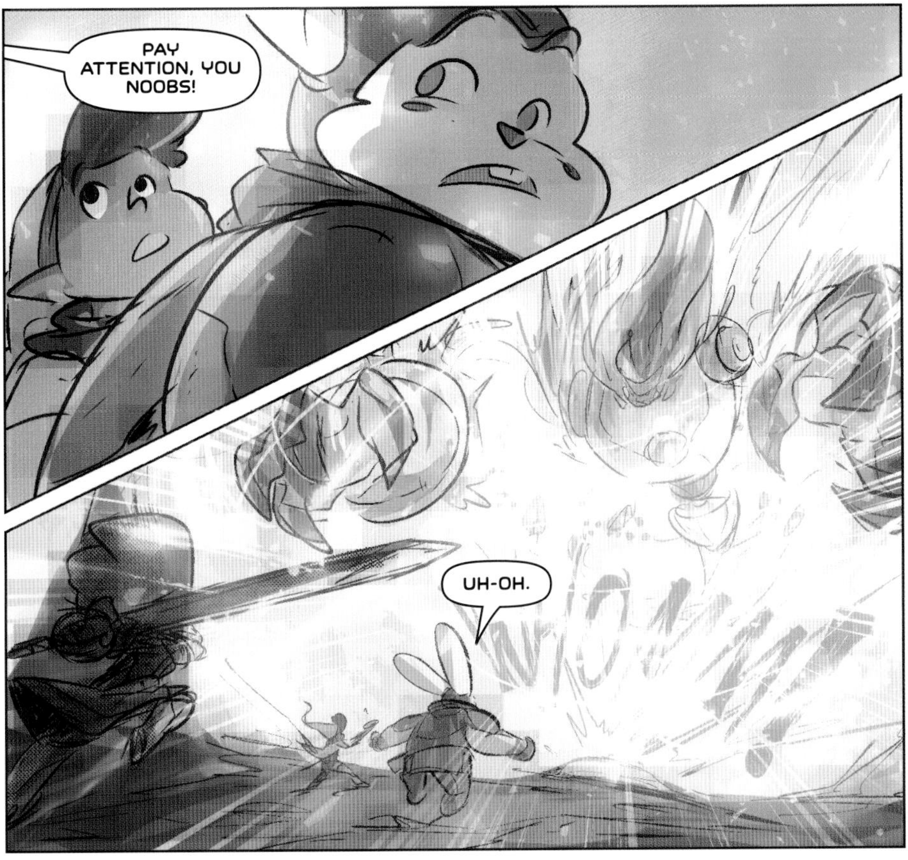
PAY ATTENTION, YOU NOOBS!
UH-OH.

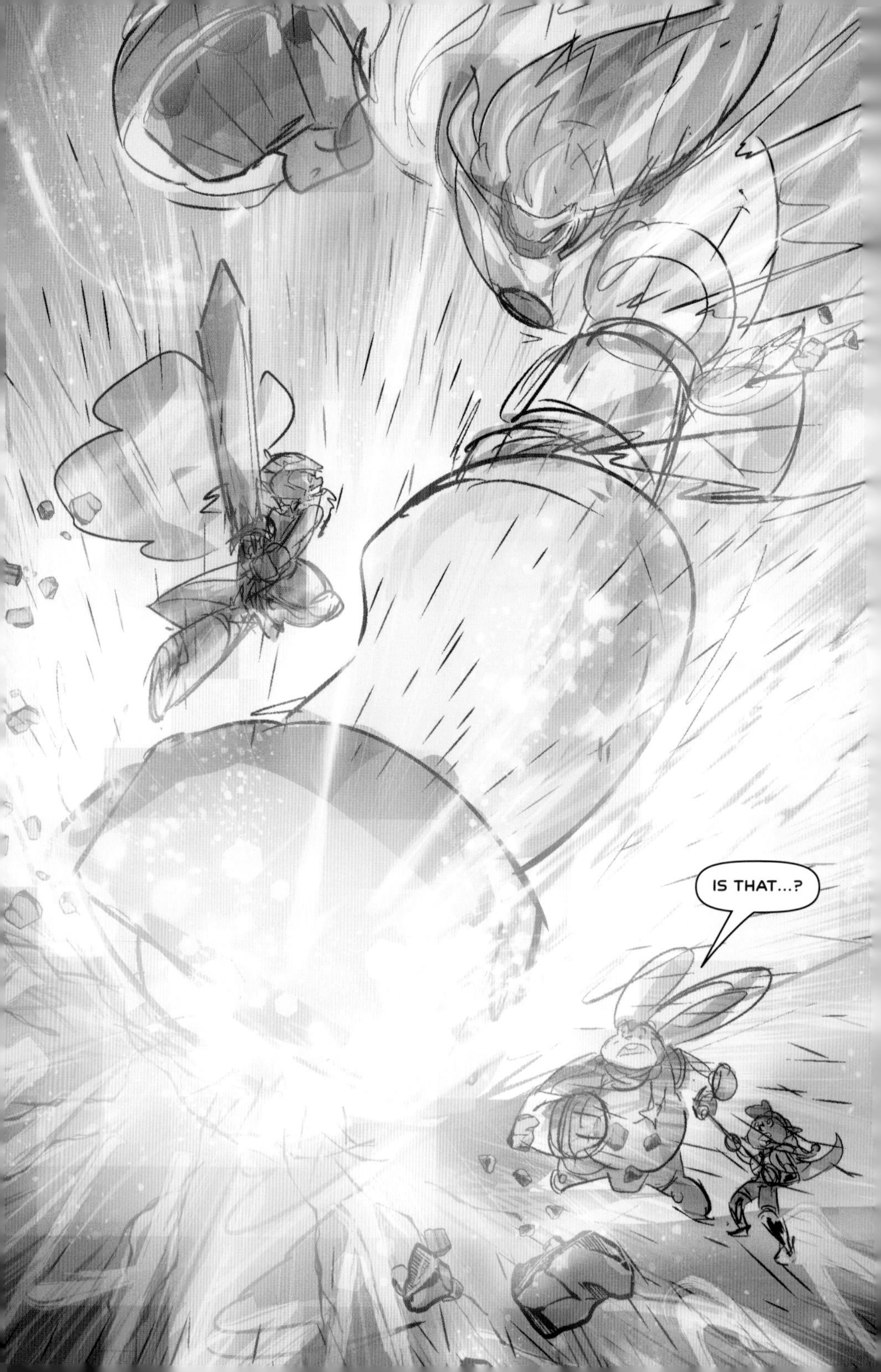
IS THAT...?

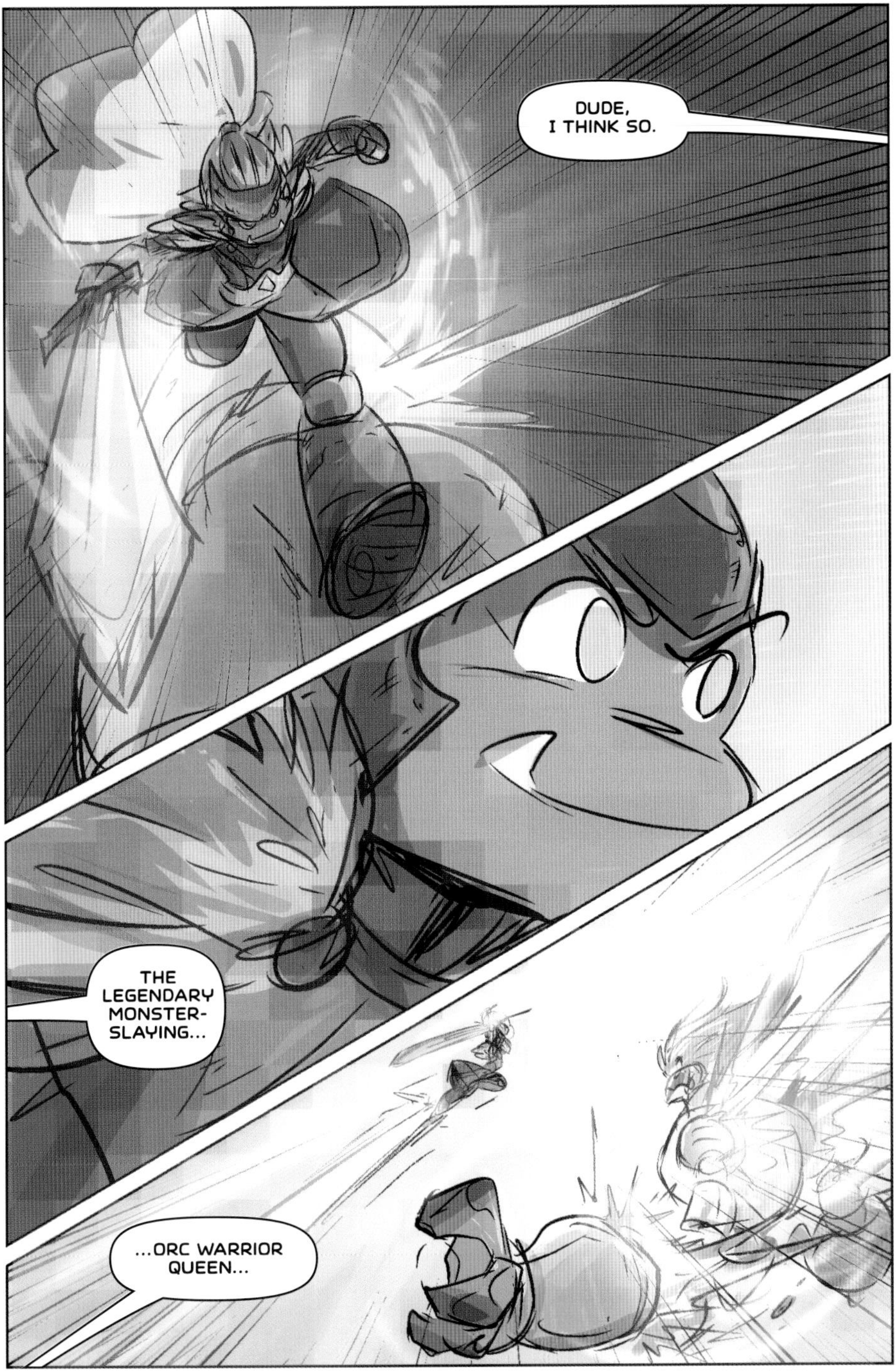
DUDE, I THINK SO.
THE LEGENDARY MONSTER-SLAYING...
...ORC WARRIOR QUEEN...

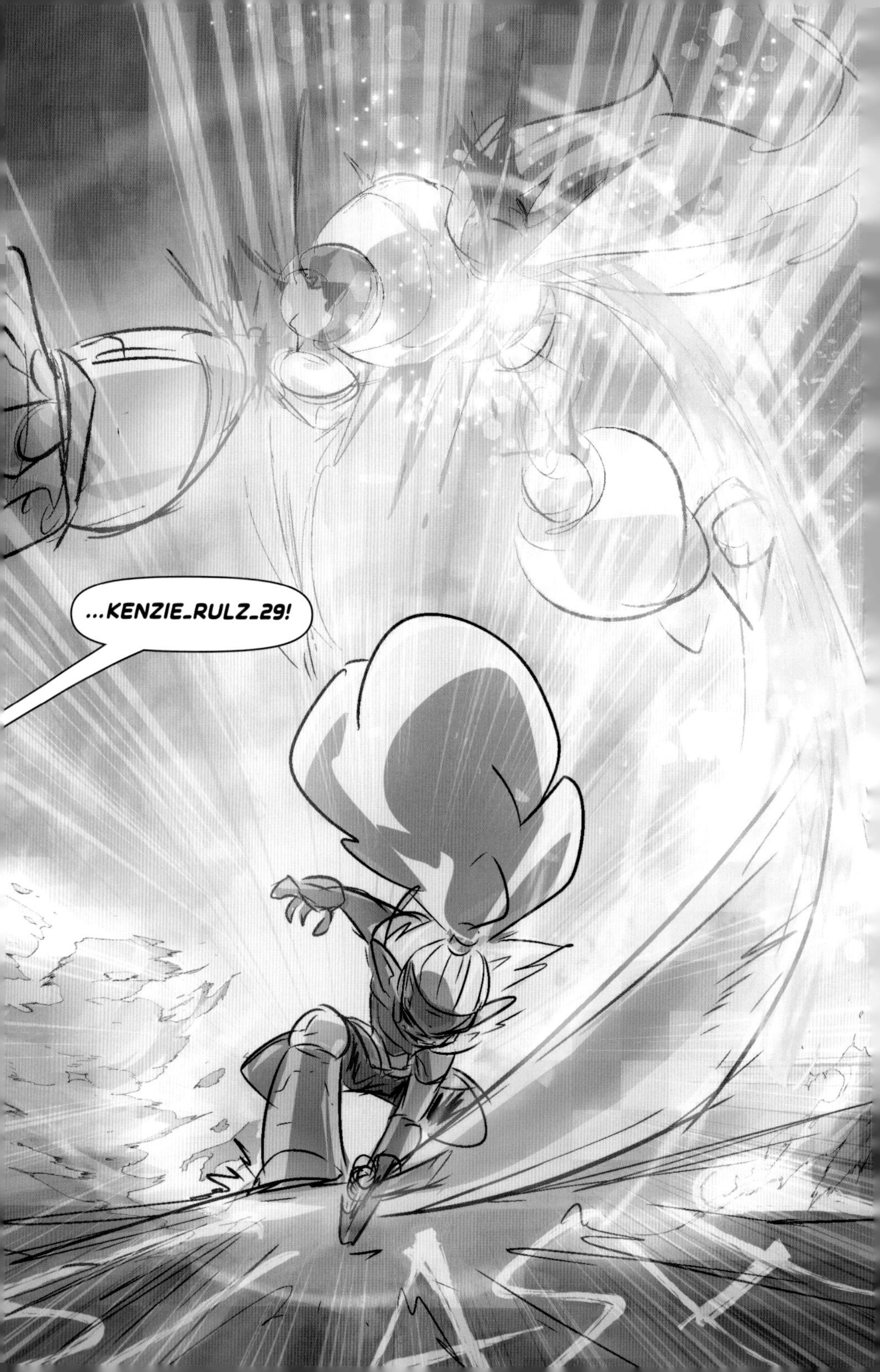
...KENZIE_RULZ_29!

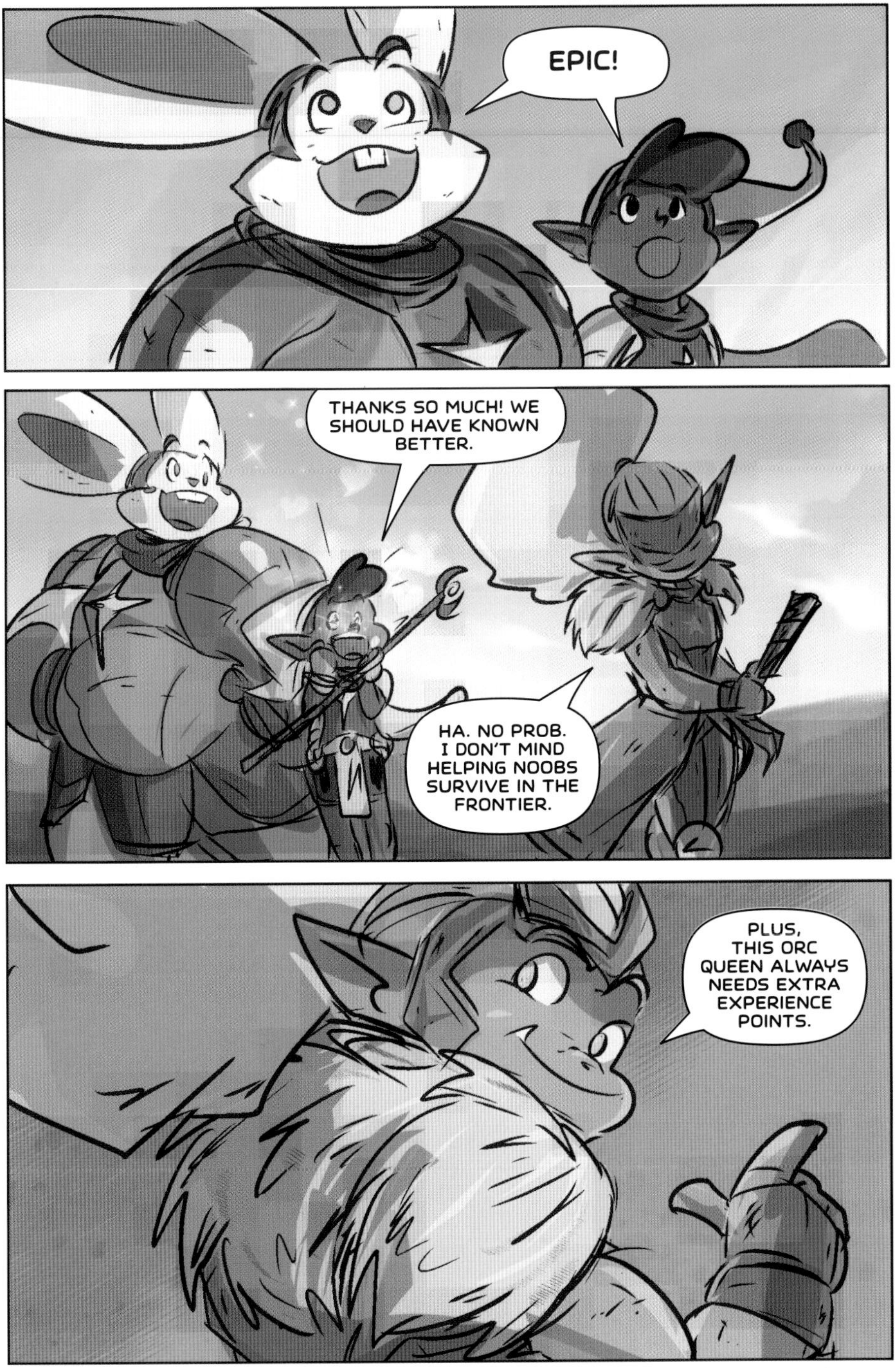
EPIC!
THANKS SO MUCH! WE SHOULD HAVE KNOWN BETTER.
HA. NO PROB. I DON'T MIND HELPING NOOBS SURVIVE IN THE FRONTIER.
PLUS, THIS ORC QUEEN ALWAYS NEEDS EXTRA EXPERIENCE POINTS.

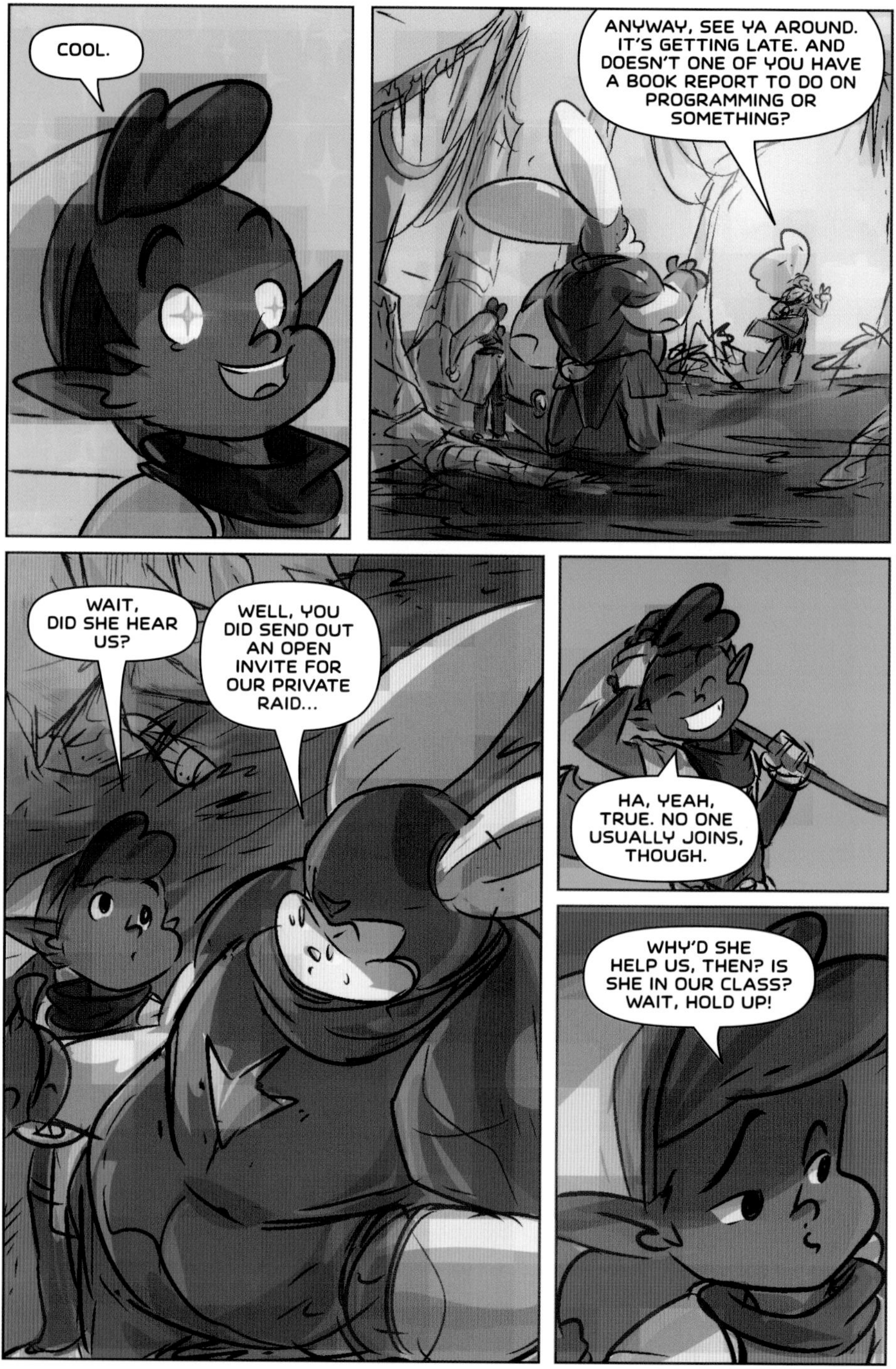
COOL.
ANYWAY, SEE YA AROUND. IT'S GETTING LATE. AND DOESN'T ONE OF YOU HAVE A BOOK REPORT TO DO ON PROGRAMMING OR SOMETHING?
WAIT, DID SHE HEAR US?
WELL, YOU DID SEND OUT AN OPEN INVITE FOR OUR PRIVATE RAID...
HA, YEAH, TRUE. NO ONE USUALLY JOINS, THOUGH.
WHY'D SHE HELP US, THEN? IS SHE IN OUR CLASS? WAIT, HOLD UP!

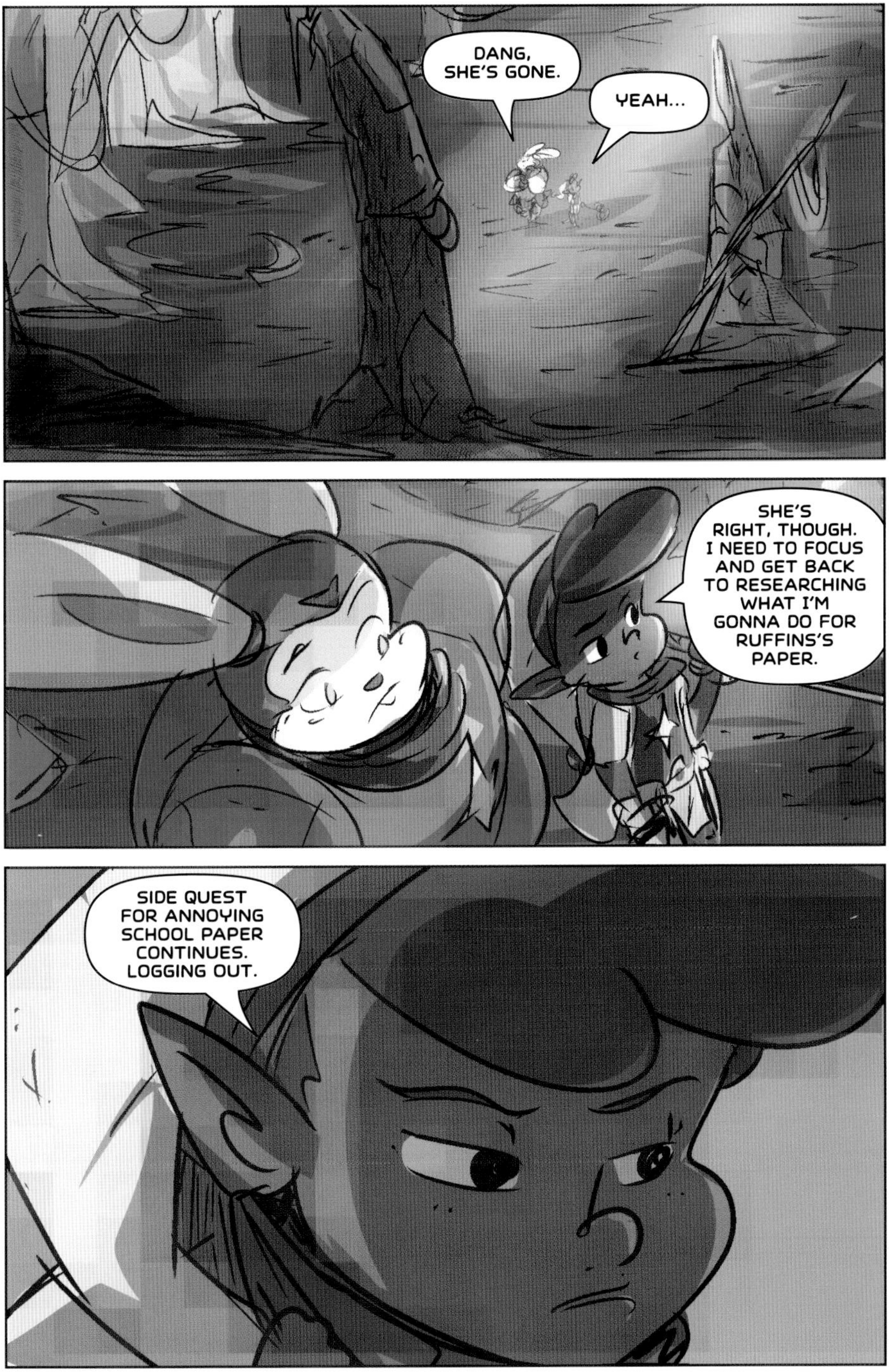
DANG, SHE'S GONE.
YEAH...
SHE'S RIGHT, THOUGH. I NEED TO FOCUS AND GET BACK TO RESEARCHING WHAT I'M GONNA DO FOR RUFFINS'S PAPER.
SIDE QUEST FOR ANNOYING SCHOOL PAPER CONTINUES. LOGGING OUT.

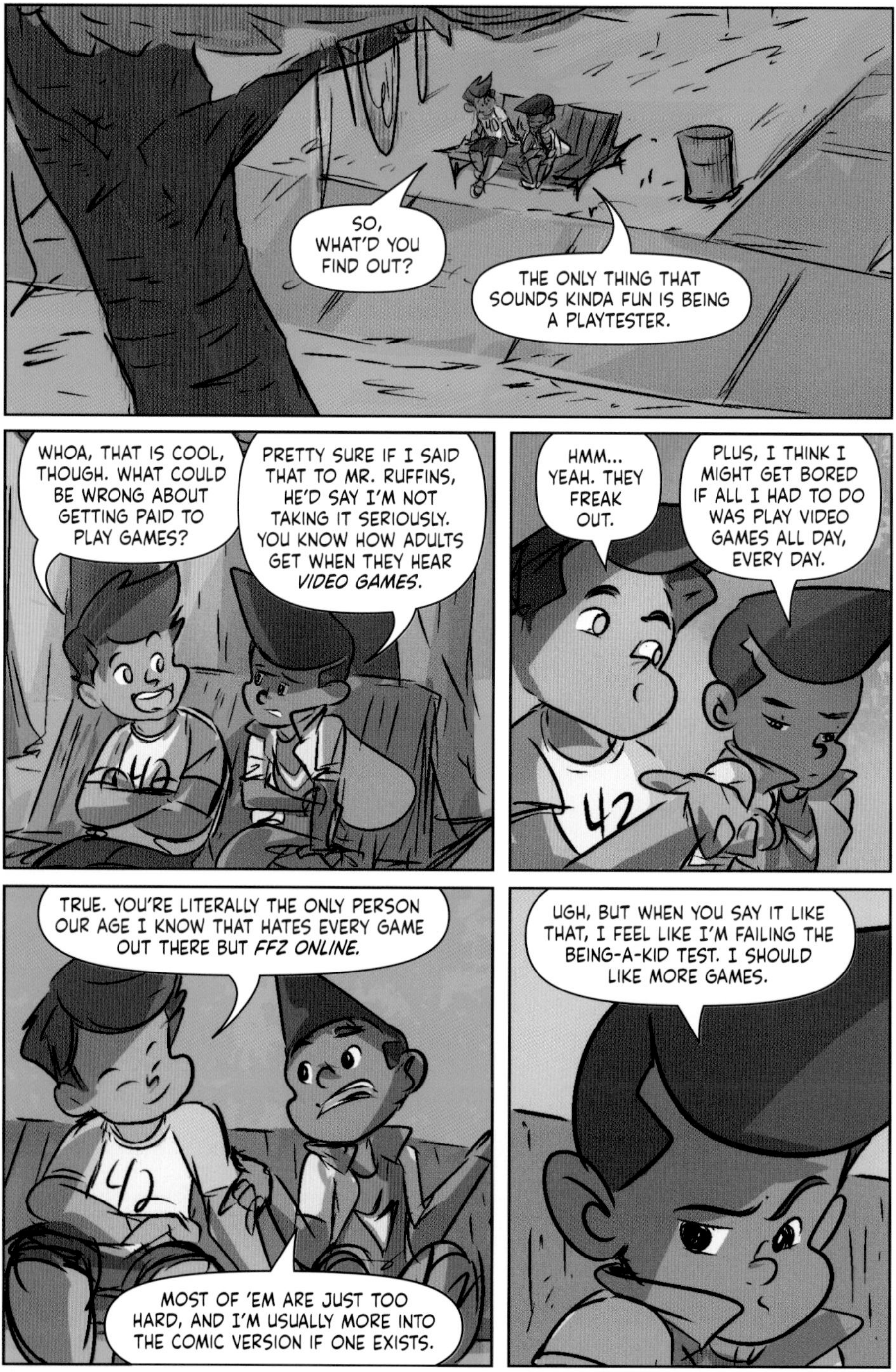
SO, WHAT'D YOU FIND OUT?
THE ONLY THING THAT SOUNDS KINDA FUN IS BEING A PLAYTESTER.
WHOA, THAT IS COOL, THOUGH. WHAT COULD BE WRONG ABOUT GETTING PAID TO PLAY GAMES?
PRETTY SURE IF I SAID THAT TO MR. RUFFINS, HE'D SAY I'M NOT TAKING IT SERIOUSLY. YOU KNOW HOW ADULTS GET WHEN THEY HEAR *VIDEO GAMES*.
HMM... YEAH. THEY FREAK OUT.
PLUS, I THINK I MIGHT GET BORED IF ALL I HAD TO DO WAS PLAY VIDEO GAMES ALL DAY, EVERY DAY.
TRUE. YOU'RE LITERALLY THE ONLY PERSON OUR AGE I KNOW THAT HATES EVERY GAME OUT THERE BUT *FFZ ONLINE.*
MOST OF 'EM ARE JUST TOO HARD, AND I'M USUALLY MORE INTO THE COMIC VERSION IF ONE EXISTS.
UGH, BUT WHEN YOU SAY IT LIKE THAT, I FEEL LIKE I'M FAILING THE BEING-A-KID TEST. I SHOULD LIKE MORE GAMES.

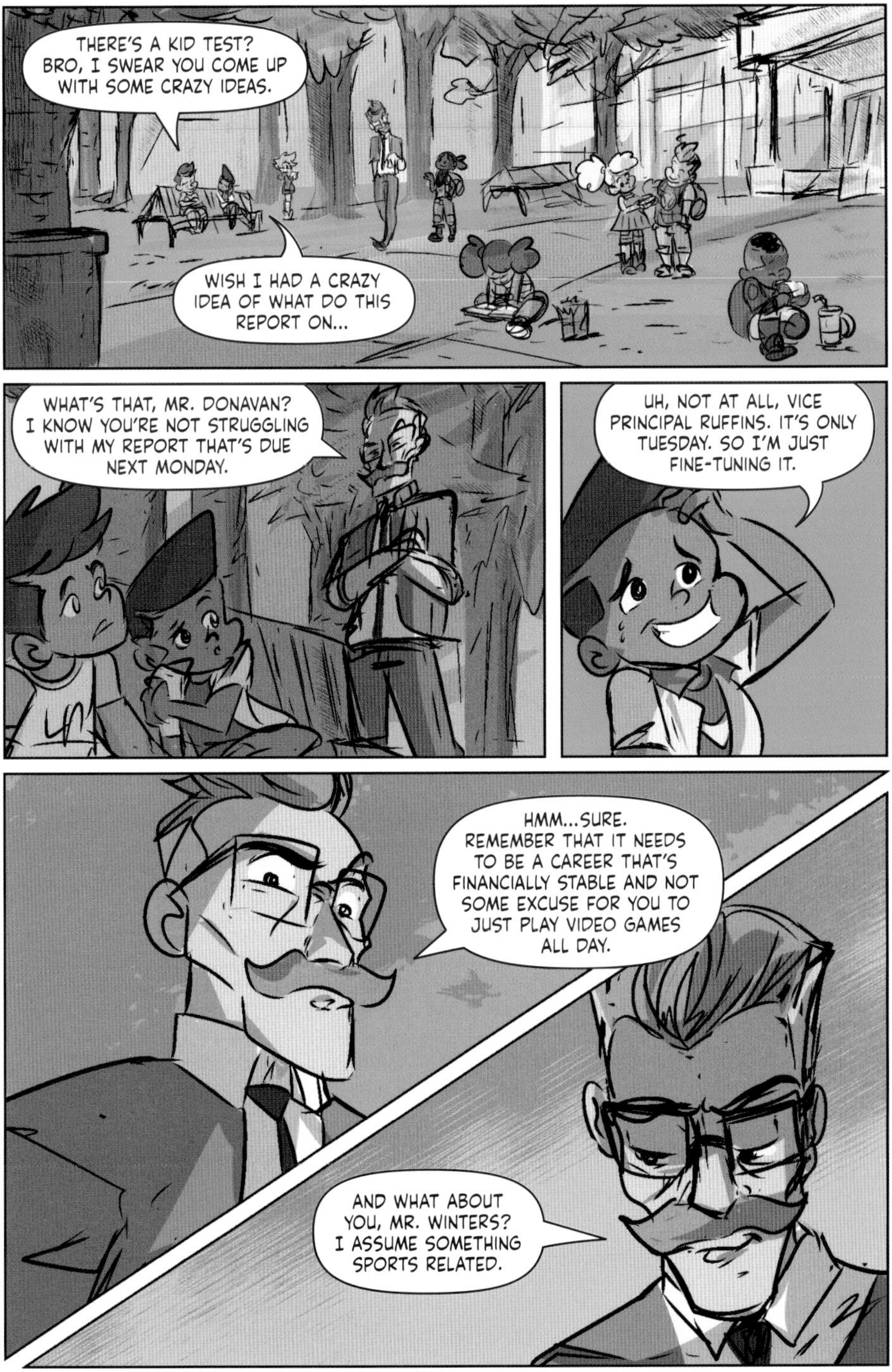
THERE'S A KID TEST? BRO, I SWEAR YOU COME UP WITH SOME CRAZY IDEAS.
WISH I HAD A CRAZY IDEA OF WHAT DO THIS REPORT ON...
WHAT'S THAT, MR. DONAVAN? I KNOW YOU'RE NOT STRUGGLING WITH MY REPORT THAT'S DUE NEXT MONDAY.
UH, NOT AT ALL, VICE PRINCIPAL RUFFINS. IT'S ONLY TUESDAY. SO I'M JUST FINE-TUNING IT.
HMM...SURE. REMEMBER THAT IT NEEDS TO BE A CAREER THAT'S FINANCIALLY STABLE AND NOT SOME EXCUSE FOR YOU TO JUST PLAY VIDEO GAMES ALL DAY.
AND WHAT ABOUT YOU, MR. WINTERS? I ASSUME SOMETHING SPORTS RELATED.

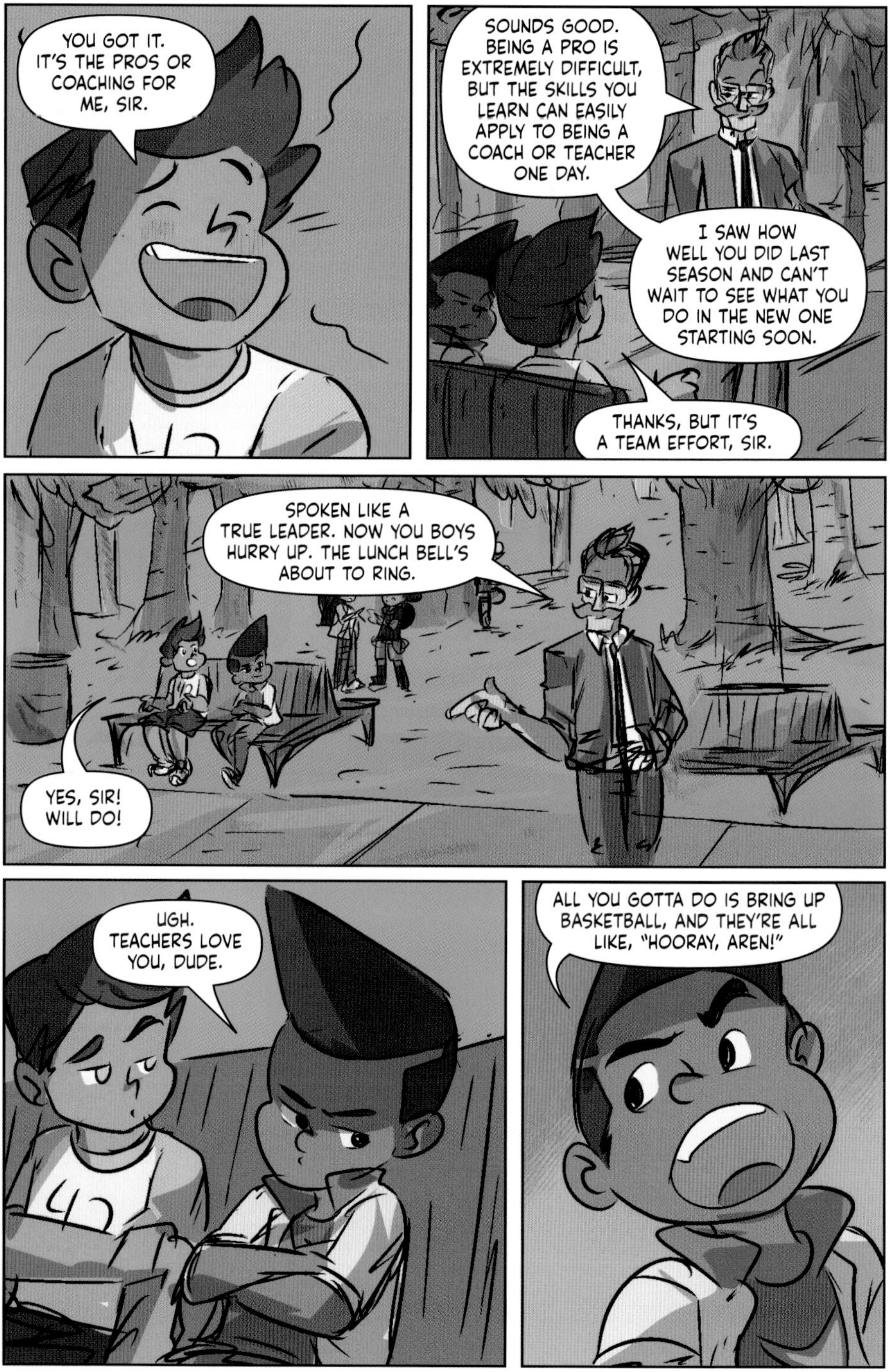
YOU GOT IT. IT'S THE PROS OR COACHING FOR ME, SIR.
SOUNDS GOOD. BEING A PRO IS EXTREMELY DIFFICULT, BUT THE SKILLS YOU LEARN CAN EASILY APPLY TO BEING A COACH OR TEACHER ONE DAY.
I SAW HOW WELL YOU DID LAST SEASON AND CAN'T WAIT TO SEE WHAT YOU DO IN THE NEW ONE STARTING SOON.
THANKS, BUT IT'S A TEAM EFFORT, SIR.
SPOKEN LIKE A TRUE LEADER. NOW YOU BOYS HURRY UP. THE LUNCH BELL'S ABOUT TO RING.
YES, SIR! WILL DO!
UGH. TEACHERS LOVE YOU, DUDE.
ALL YOU GOTTA DO IS BRING UP BASKETBALL, AND THEY'RE ALL LIKE, "HOORAY, AREN!"

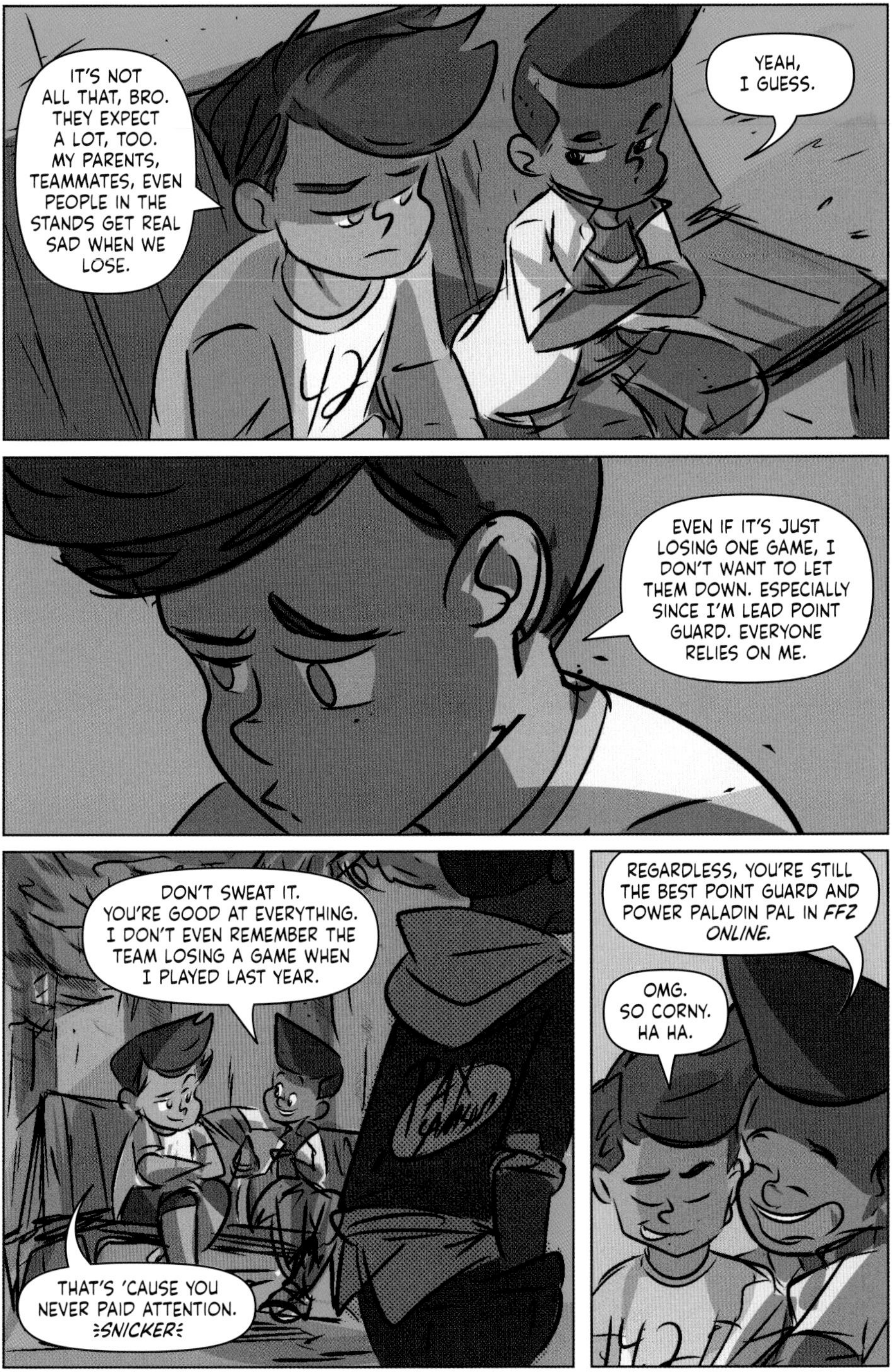
IT'S NOT ALL THAT, BRO. THEY EXPECT A LOT, TOO. MY PARENTS, TEAMMATES, EVEN PEOPLE IN THE STANDS GET REAL SAD WHEN WE LOSE.
YEAH, I GUESS.
EVEN IF IT'S JUST LOSING ONE GAME, I DON'T WANT TO LET THEM DOWN. ESPECIALLY SINCE I'M LEAD POINT GUARD. EVERYONE RELIES ON ME.
DON'T SWEAT IT. YOU'RE GOOD AT EVERYTHING. I DON'T EVEN REMEMBER THE TEAM LOSING A GAME WHEN I PLAYED LAST YEAR.
THAT'S 'CAUSE YOU NEVER PAID ATTENTION. *SNICKER*
REGARDLESS, YOU'RE STILL THE BEST POINT GUARD AND POWER PALADIN PAL IN *FFZ ONLINE.*
OMG. SO CORNY. HA HA.

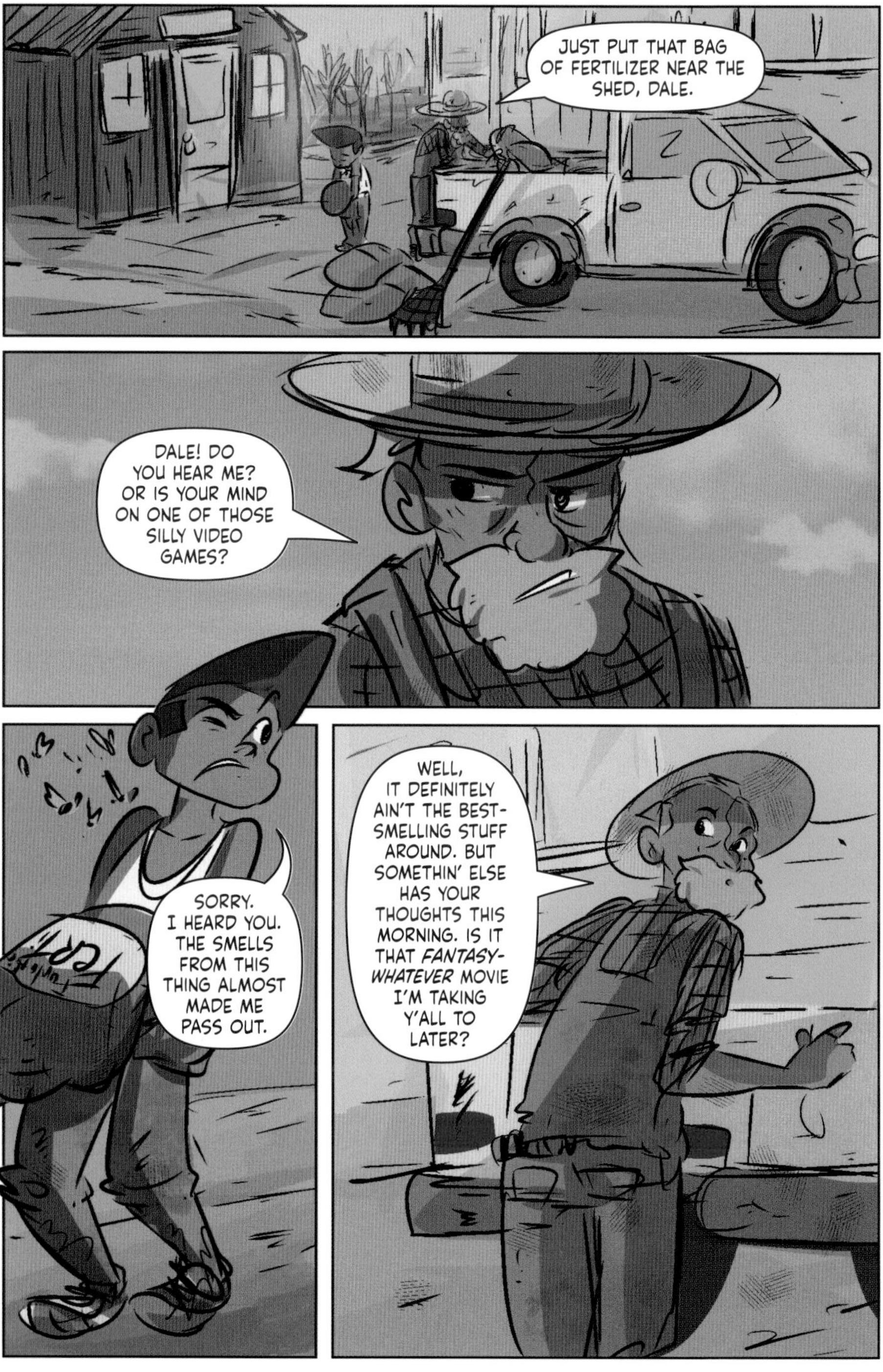
JUST PUT THAT BAG OF FERTILIZER NEAR THE SHED, DALE.
DALE! DO YOU HEAR ME? OR IS YOUR MIND ON ONE OF THOSE SILLY VIDEO GAMES?
SORRY. I HEARD YOU. THE SMELLS FROM THIS THING ALMOST MADE ME PASS OUT.
WELL, IT DEFINITELY AIN'T THE BEST-SMELLING STUFF AROUND. BUT SOMETHIN' ELSE HAS YOUR THOUGHTS THIS MORNING. IS IT THAT *FANTASY-WHATEVER* MOVIE I'M TAKING Y'ALL TO LATER?

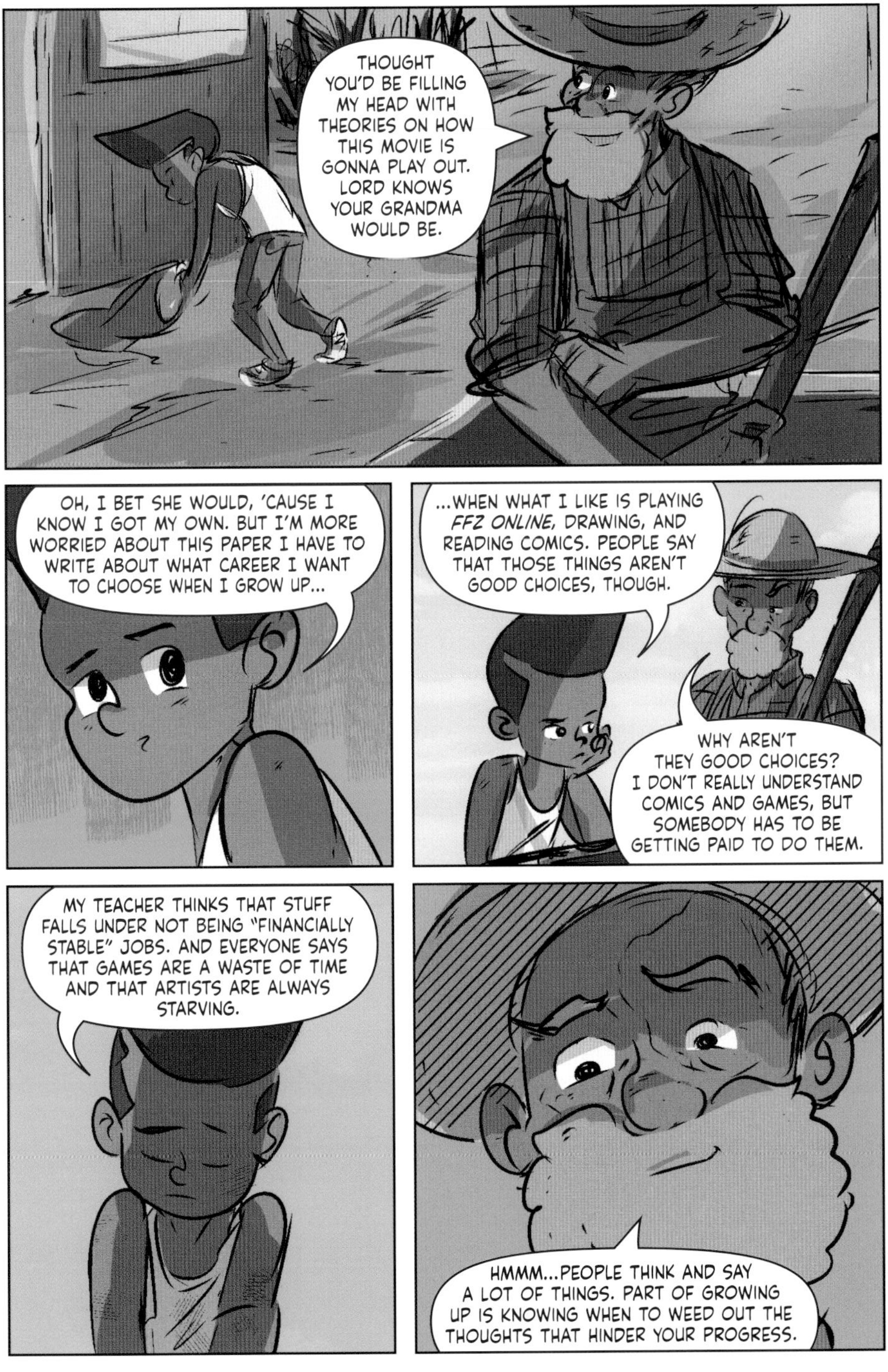
THOUGHT YOU'D BE FILLING MY HEAD WITH THEORIES ON HOW THIS MOVIE IS GONNA PLAY OUT. LORD KNOWS YOUR GRANDMA WOULD BE.
OH, I BET SHE WOULD, 'CAUSE I KNOW I GOT MY OWN. BUT I'M MORE WORRIED ABOUT THIS PAPER I HAVE TO WRITE ABOUT WHAT CAREER I WANT TO CHOOSE WHEN I GROW UP...
...WHEN WHAT I LIKE IS PLAYING *FFZ ONLINE*, DRAWING, AND READING COMICS. PEOPLE SAY THAT THOSE THINGS AREN'T GOOD CHOICES, THOUGH.
WHY AREN'T THEY GOOD CHOICES? I DON'T REALLY UNDERSTAND COMICS AND GAMES, BUT SOMEBODY HAS TO BE GETTING PAID TO DO THEM.
MY TEACHER THINKS THAT STUFF FALLS UNDER NOT BEING "FINANCIALLY STABLE" JOBS. AND EVERYONE SAYS THAT GAMES ARE A WASTE OF TIME AND THAT ARTISTS ARE ALWAYS STARVING.
HMMM...PEOPLE THINK AND SAY A LOT OF THINGS. PART OF GROWING UP IS KNOWING WHEN TO WEED OUT THE THOUGHTS THAT HINDER YOUR PROGRESS.

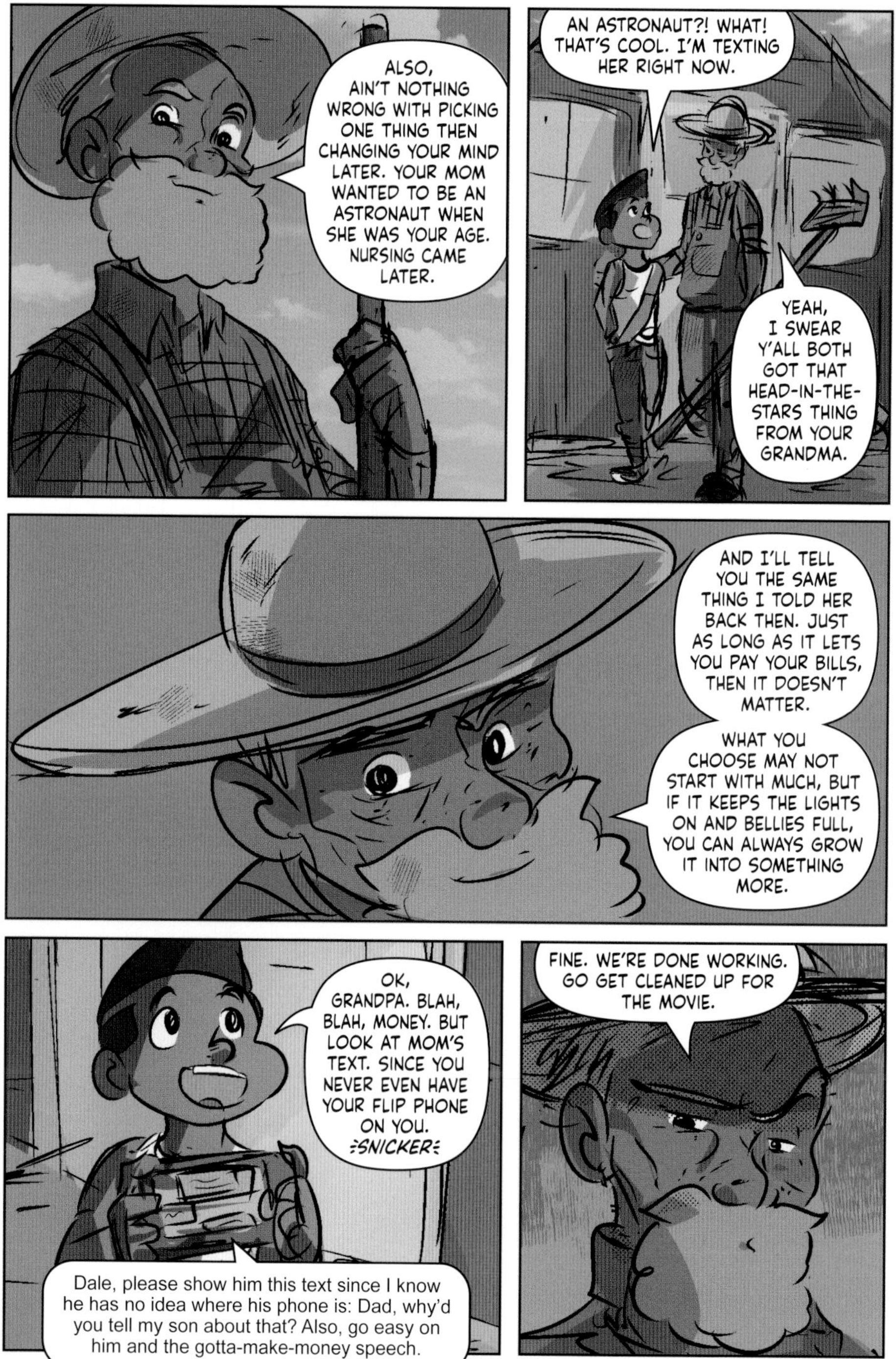
ALSO, AIN'T NOTHING WRONG WITH PICKING ONE THING THEN CHANGING YOUR MIND LATER. YOUR MOM WANTED TO BE AN ASTRONAUT WHEN SHE WAS YOUR AGE. NURSING CAME LATER.
AN ASTRONAUT?! WHAT! THAT'S COOL. I'M TEXTING HER RIGHT NOW.
YEAH, I SWEAR Y'ALL BOTH GOT THAT HEAD-IN-THE-STARS THING FROM YOUR GRANDMA.
AND I'LL TELL YOU THE SAME THING I TOLD HER BACK THEN. JUST AS LONG AS IT LETS YOU PAY YOUR BILLS, THEN IT DOESN'T MATTER.
WHAT YOU CHOOSE MAY NOT START WITH MUCH, BUT IF IT KEEPS THE LIGHTS ON AND BELLIES FULL, YOU CAN ALWAYS GROW IT INTO SOMETHING MORE.
OK, GRANDPA. BLAH, BLAH, MONEY. BUT LOOK AT MOM'S TEXT. SINCE YOU NEVER EVEN HAVE YOUR FLIP PHONE ON YOU. SNICKER
Dale, please show him this text since I know he has no idea where his phone is: Dad, why'd you tell my son about that? Also, go easy on him and the gotta-make-money speech.
FINE. WE'RE DONE WORKING. GO GET CLEANED UP FOR THE MOVIE.

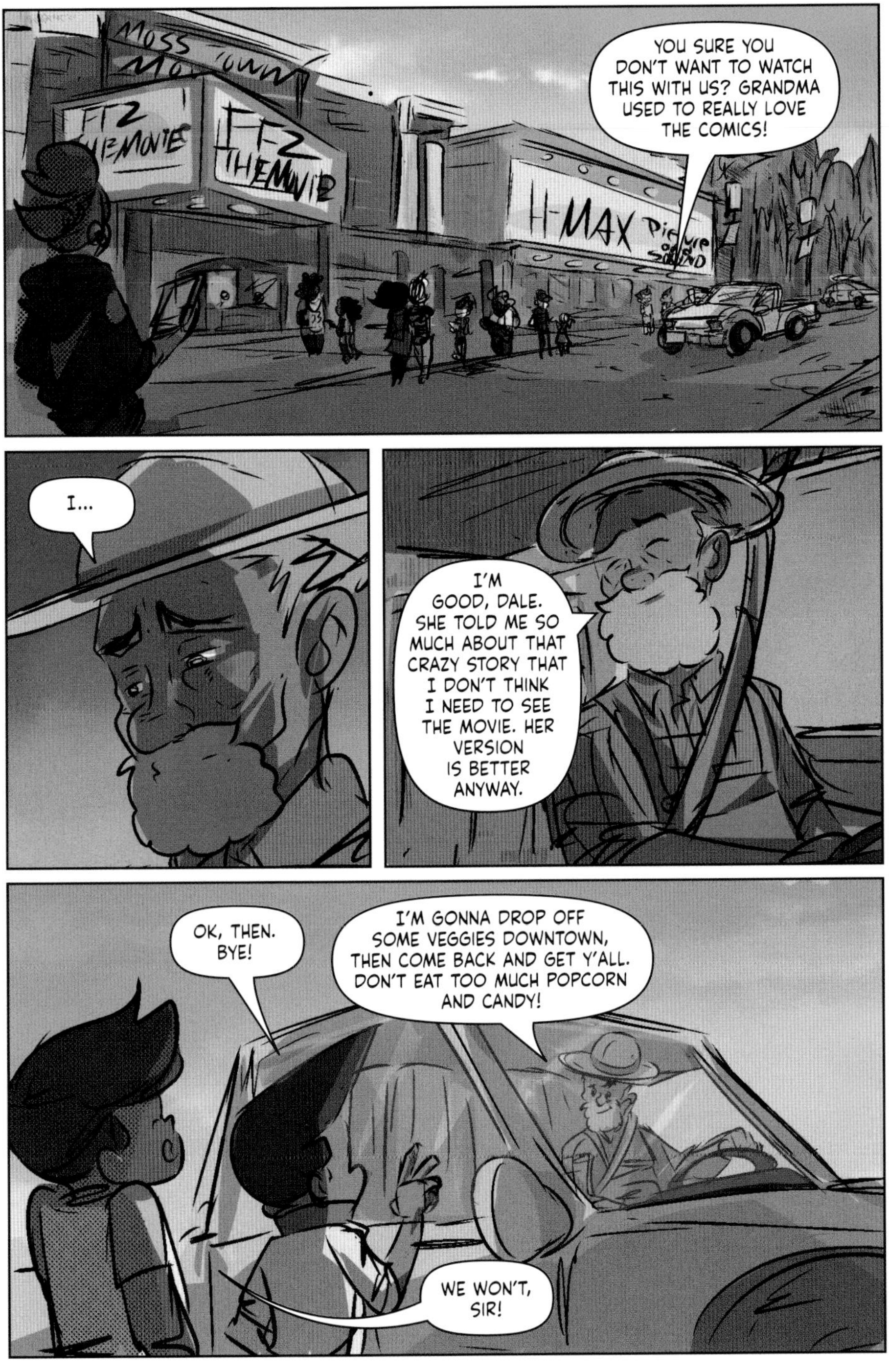
MOSS
FF2 THE MOVIE
FF2 THE MOVIE
H-MAX
YOU SURE YOU DON'T WANT TO WATCH THIS WITH US? GRANDMA USED TO REALLY LOVE THE COMICS!
I...
I'M GOOD, DALE. SHE TOLD ME SO MUCH ABOUT THAT CRAZY STORY THAT I DON'T THINK I NEED TO SEE THE MOVIE. HER VERSION IS BETTER ANYWAY.
OK, THEN. BYE!
I'M GONNA DROP OFF SOME VEGGIES DOWNTOWN, THEN COME BACK AND GET Y'ALL. DON'T EAT TOO MUCH POPCORN AND CANDY!
WE WON'T, SIR!

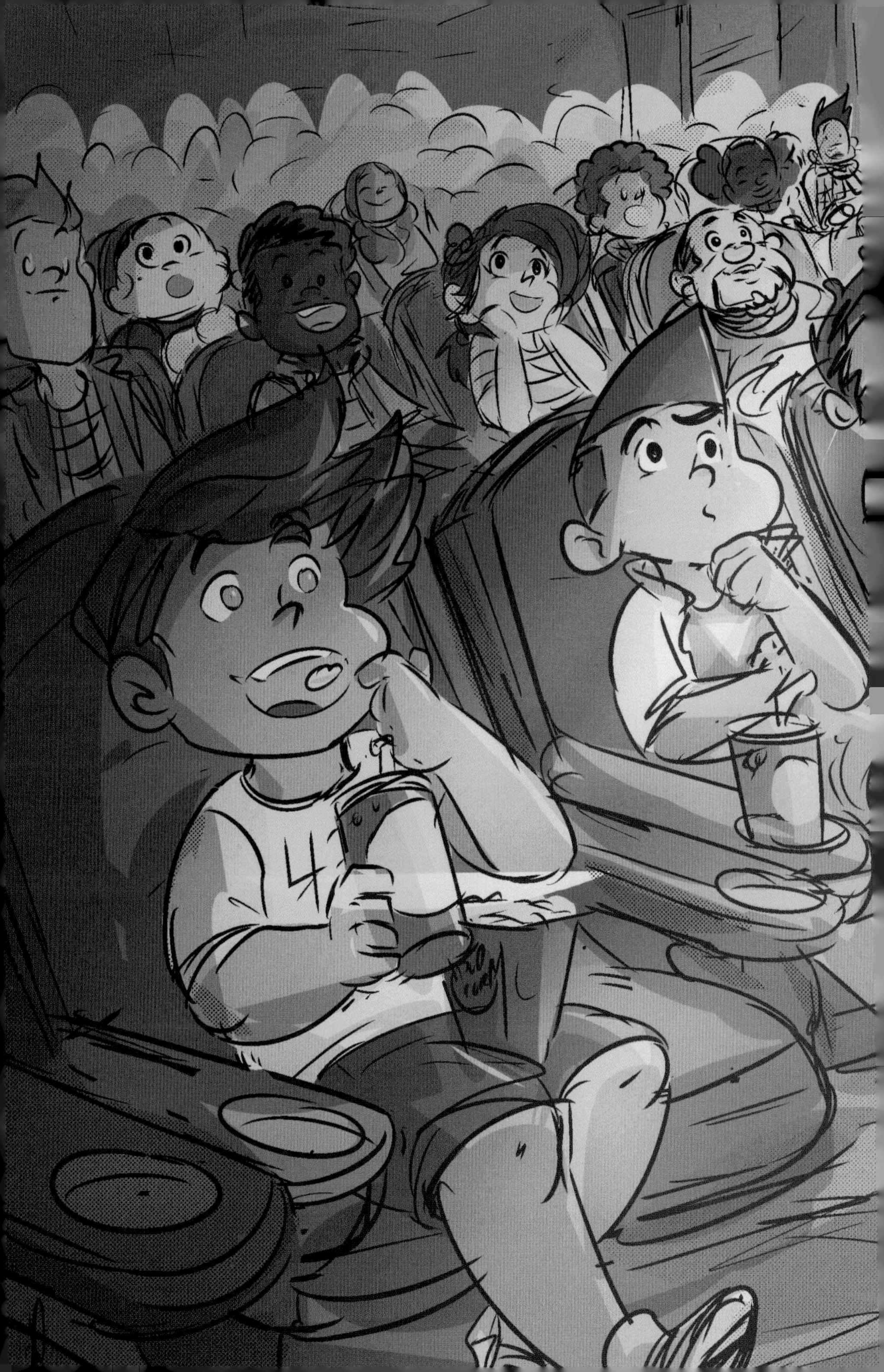

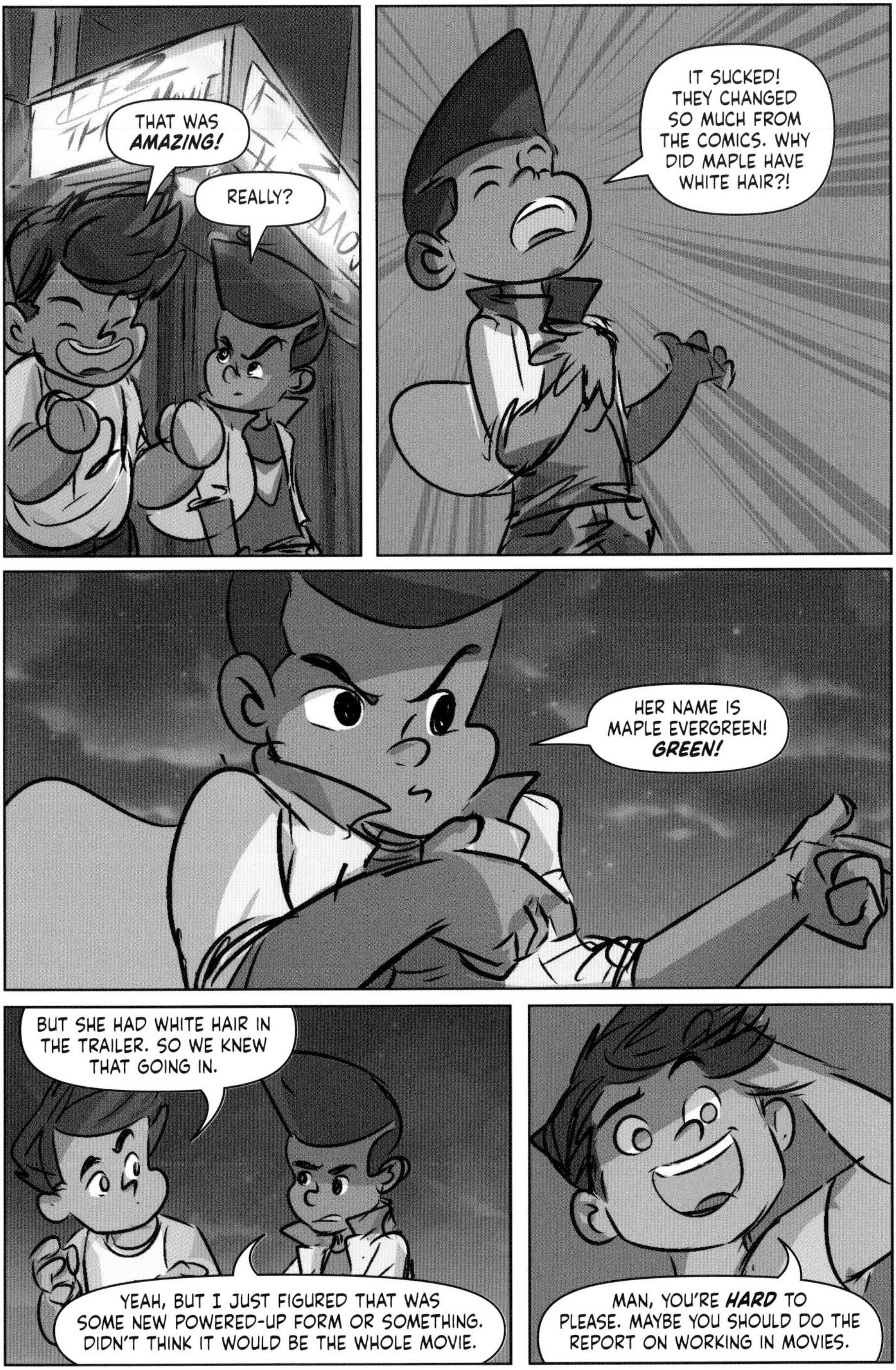
THAT WAS AMAZING!
REALLY?
IT SUCKED! THEY CHANGED SO MUCH FROM THE COMICS. WHY DID MAPLE HAVE WHITE HAIR?!
HER NAME IS MAPLE EVERGREEN! GREEN!
BUT SHE HAD WHITE HAIR IN THE TRAILER. SO WE KNEW THAT GOING IN.
YEAH, BUT I JUST FIGURED THAT WAS SOME NEW POWERED-UP FORM OR SOMETHING. DIDN'T THINK IT WOULD BE THE WHOLE MOVIE.
MAN, YOU'RE HARD TO PLEASE. MAYBE YOU SHOULD DO THE REPORT ON WORKING IN MOVIES.

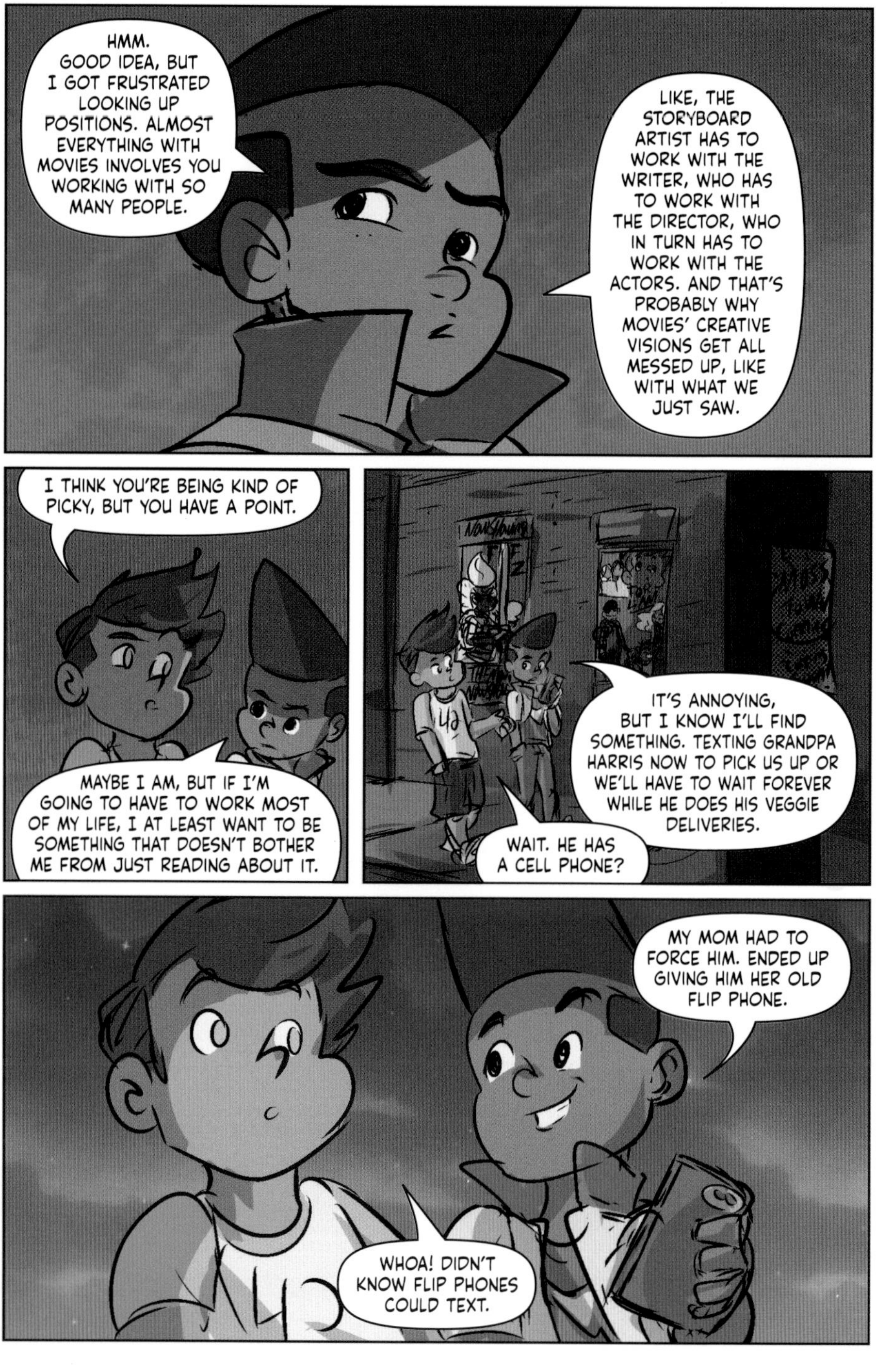
HMM.
GOOD IDEA, BUT I GOT FRUSTRATED LOOKING UP POSITIONS. ALMOST EVERYTHING WITH MOVIES INVOLVES YOU WORKING WITH SO MANY PEOPLE.
LIKE, THE STORYBOARD ARTIST HAS TO WORK WITH THE WRITER, WHO HAS TO WORK WITH THE DIRECTOR, WHO IN TURN HAS TO WORK WITH THE ACTORS. AND THAT'S PROBABLY WHY MOVIES' CREATIVE VISIONS GET ALL MESSED UP, LIKE WITH WHAT WE JUST SAW.
I THINK YOU'RE BEING KIND OF PICKY, BUT YOU HAVE A POINT.
MAYBE I AM, BUT IF I'M GOING TO HAVE TO WORK MOST OF MY LIFE, I AT LEAST WANT TO BE SOMETHING THAT DOESN'T BOTHER ME FROM JUST READING ABOUT IT.
IT'S ANNOYING, BUT I KNOW I'LL FIND SOMETHING. TEXTING GRANDPA HARRIS NOW TO PICK US UP OR WE'LL HAVE TO WAIT FOREVER WHILE HE DOES HIS VEGGIE DELIVERIES.
WAIT. HE HAS A CELL PHONE?
MY MOM HAD TO FORCE HIM. ENDED UP GIVING HIM HER OLD FLIP PHONE.
WHOA! DIDN'T KNOW FLIP PHONES COULD TEXT.

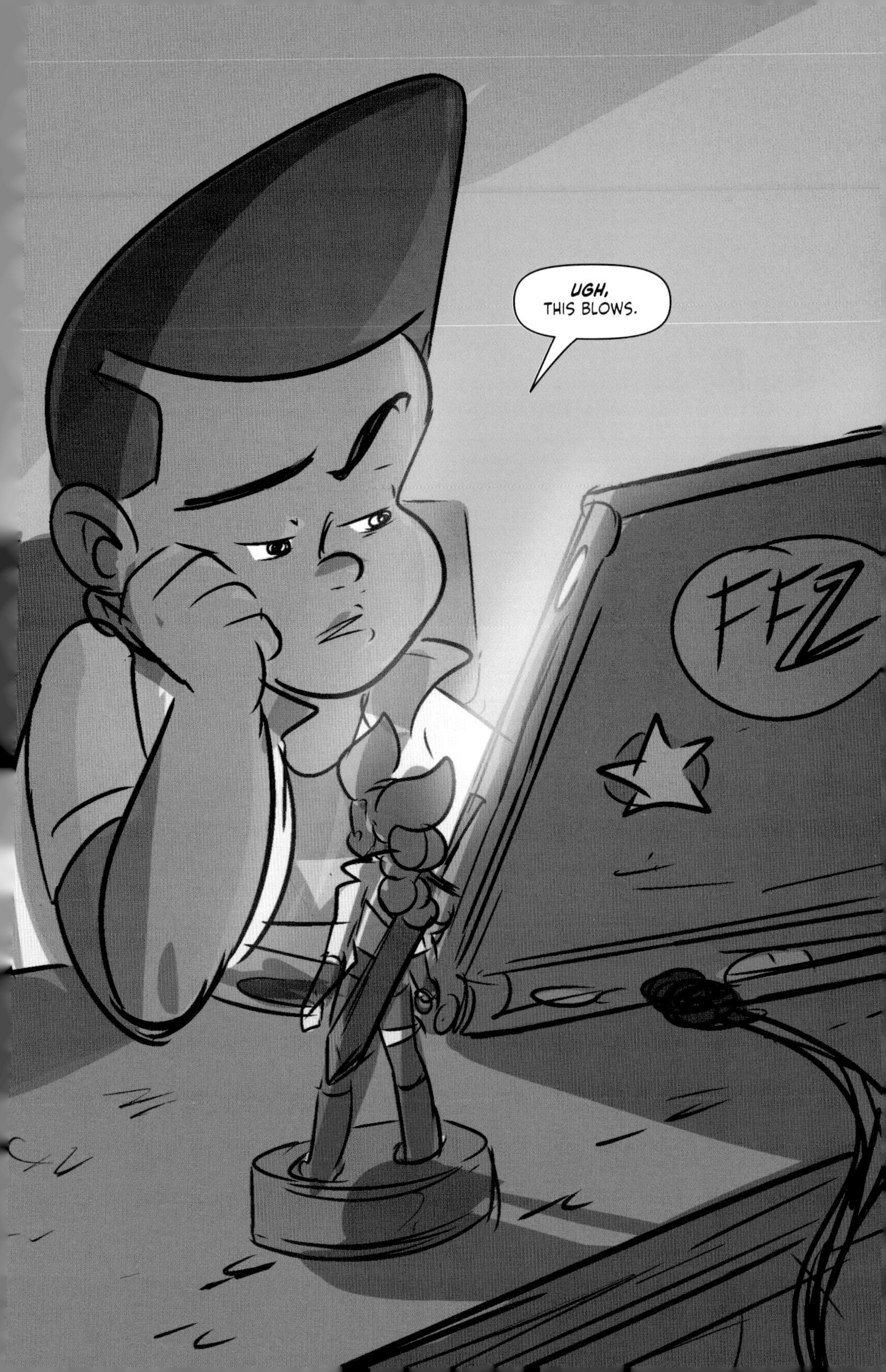
UGH, THIS BLOWS.
FEZ

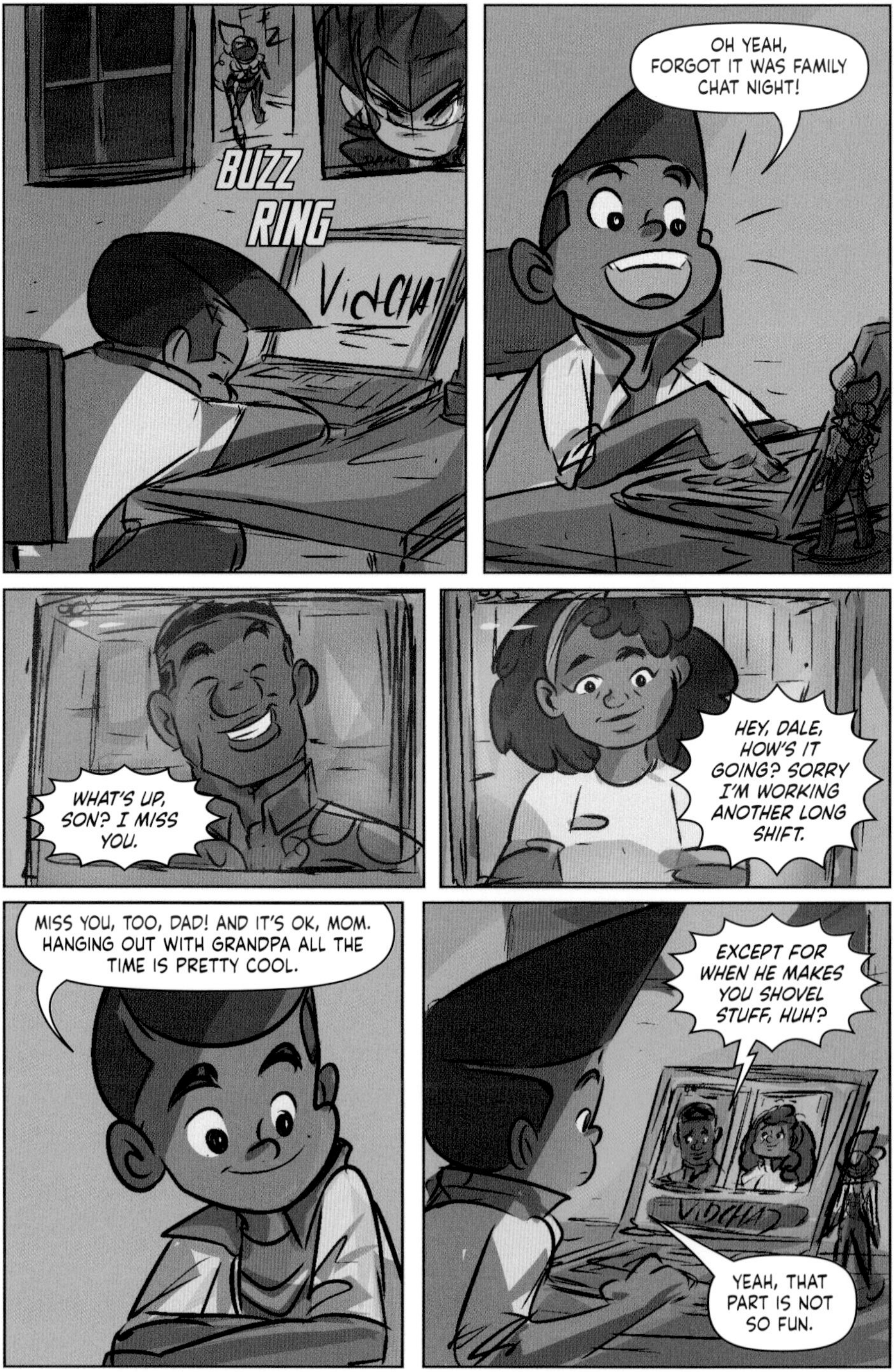
BUZZ
RING
VIDCHAT
OH YEAH, FORGOT IT WAS FAMILY CHAT NIGHT!
WHAT'S UP, SON? I MISS YOU.
HEY, DALE, HOW'S IT GOING? SORRY I'M WORKING ANOTHER LONG SHIFT.
MISS YOU, TOO, DAD! AND IT'S OK, MOM. HANGING OUT WITH GRANDPA ALL THE TIME IS PRETTY COOL.
EXCEPT FOR WHEN HE MAKES YOU SHOVEL STUFF, HUH?
YEAH, THAT PART IS NOT SO FUN.

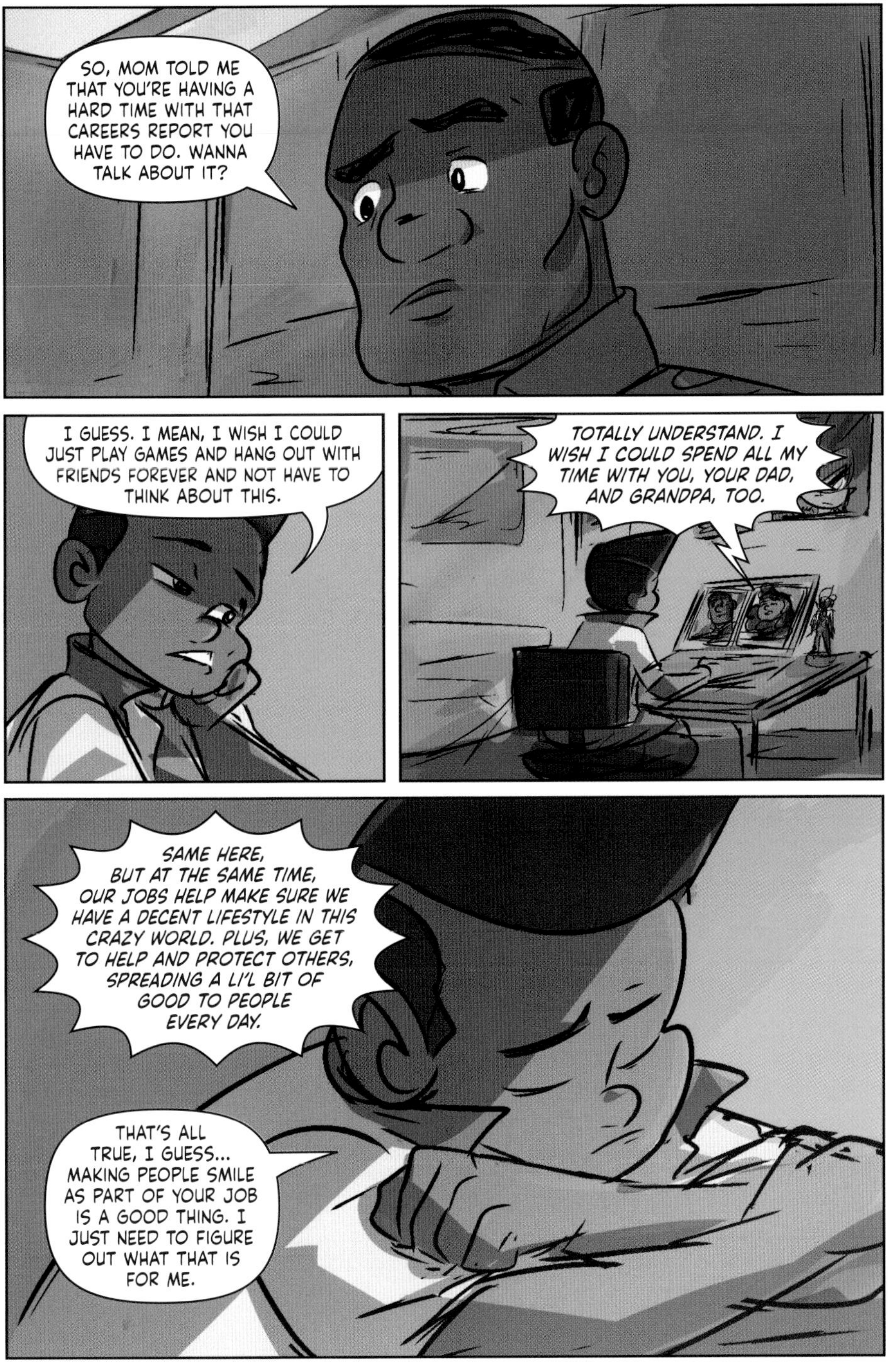
SO, MOM TOLD ME THAT YOU'RE HAVING A HARD TIME WITH THAT CAREERS REPORT YOU HAVE TO DO. WANNA TALK ABOUT IT?
I GUESS. I MEAN, I WISH I COULD JUST PLAY GAMES AND HANG OUT WITH FRIENDS FOREVER AND NOT HAVE TO THINK ABOUT THIS.
TOTALLY UNDERSTAND. I WISH I COULD SPEND ALL MY TIME WITH YOU, YOUR DAD, AND GRANDPA, TOO.
SAME HERE, BUT AT THE SAME TIME, OUR JOBS HELP MAKE SURE WE HAVE A DECENT LIFESTYLE IN THIS CRAZY WORLD. PLUS, WE GET TO HELP AND PROTECT OTHERS, SPREADING A LI'L BIT OF GOOD TO PEOPLE EVERY DAY.
THAT'S ALL TRUE, I GUESS... MAKING PEOPLE SMILE AS PART OF YOUR JOB IS A GOOD THING. I JUST NEED TO FIGURE OUT WHAT THAT IS FOR ME.

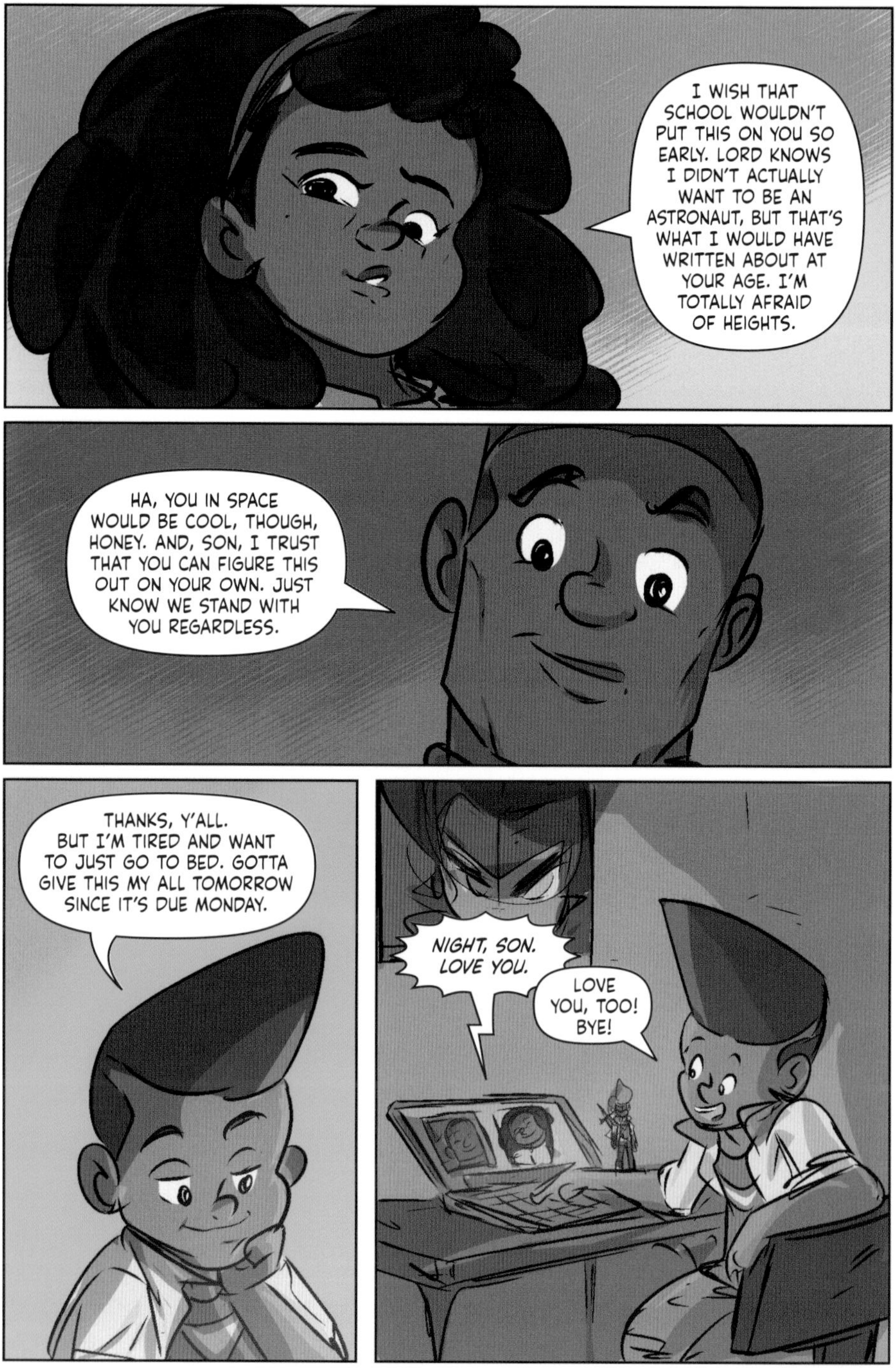
I WISH THAT SCHOOL WOULDN'T PUT THIS ON YOU SO EARLY. LORD KNOWS I DIDN'T ACTUALLY WANT TO BE AN ASTRONAUT, BUT THAT'S WHAT I WOULD HAVE WRITTEN ABOUT AT YOUR AGE. I'M TOTALLY AFRAID OF HEIGHTS.
HA, YOU IN SPACE WOULD BE COOL, THOUGH, HONEY. AND, SON, I TRUST THAT YOU CAN FIGURE THIS OUT ON YOUR OWN. JUST KNOW WE STAND WITH YOU REGARDLESS.
THANKS, Y'ALL. BUT I'M TIRED AND WANT TO JUST GO TO BED. GOTTA GIVE THIS MY ALL TOMORROW SINCE IT'S DUE MONDAY.
NIGHT, SON. LOVE YOU.
LOVE YOU, TOO! BYE!

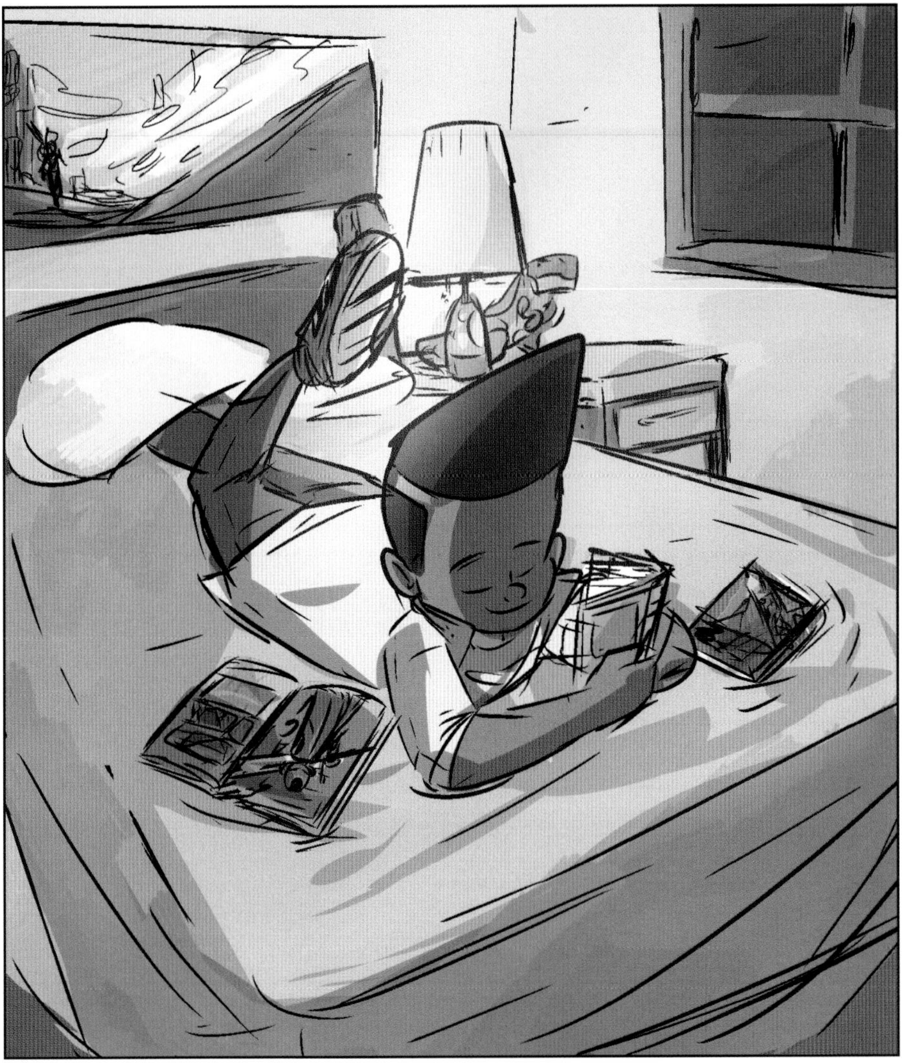

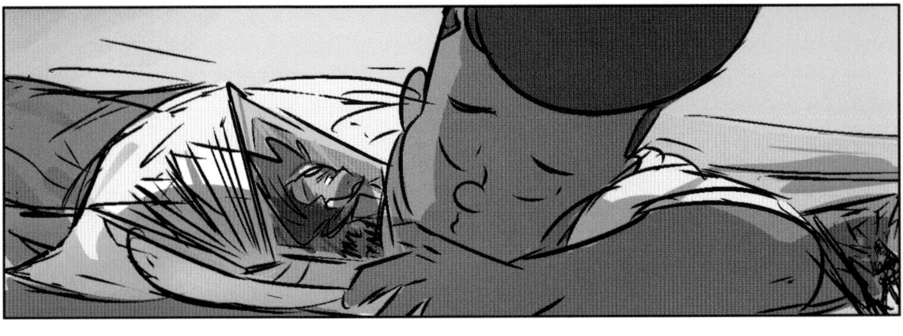

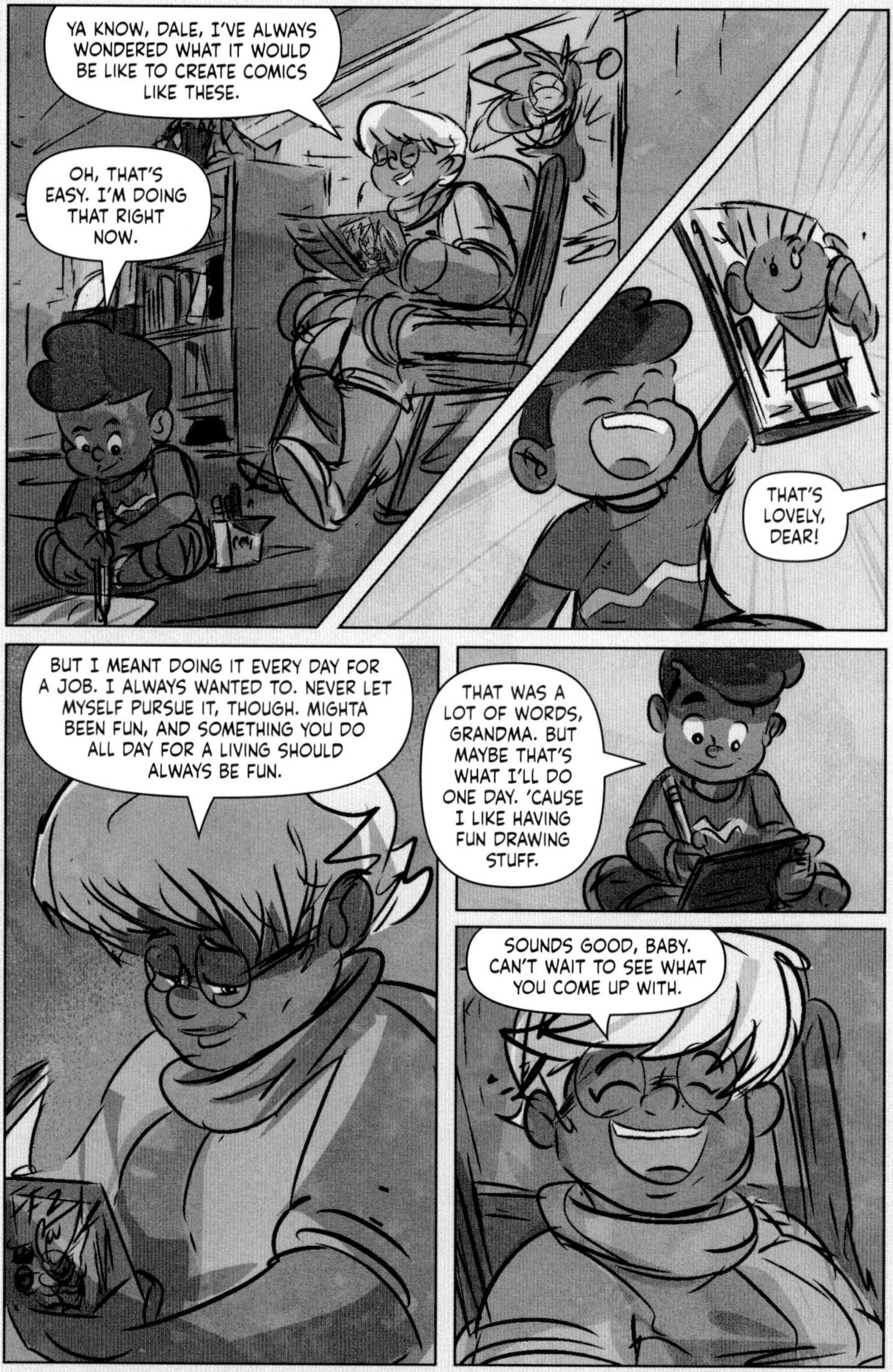
YA KNOW, DALE, I'VE ALWAYS WONDERED WHAT IT WOULD BE LIKE TO CREATE COMICS LIKE THESE.
OH, THAT'S EASY. I'M DOING THAT RIGHT NOW.
THAT'S LOVELY, DEAR!
BUT I MEANT DOING IT EVERY DAY FOR A JOB. I ALWAYS WANTED TO. NEVER LET MYSELF PURSUE IT, THOUGH. MIGHTA BEEN FUN, AND SOMETHING YOU DO ALL DAY FOR A LIVING SHOULD ALWAYS BE FUN.
THAT WAS A LOT OF WORDS, GRANDMA. BUT MAYBE THAT'S WHAT I'LL DO ONE DAY. 'CAUSE I LIKE HAVING FUN DRAWING STUFF.
SOUNDS GOOD, BABY. CAN'T WAIT TO SEE WHAT YOU COME UP WITH.

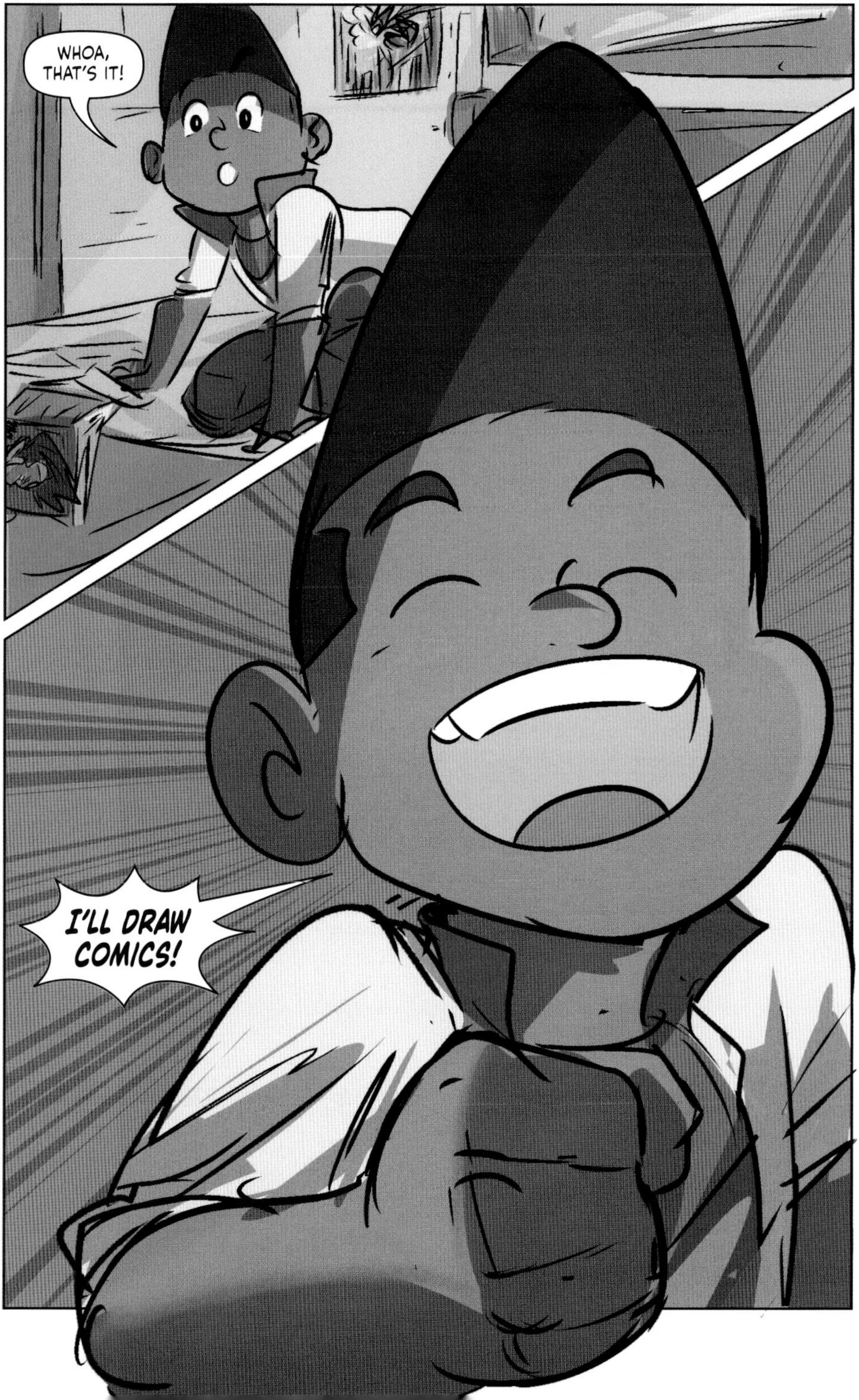
WHOA, THAT'S IT!
I'LL DRAW COMICS!

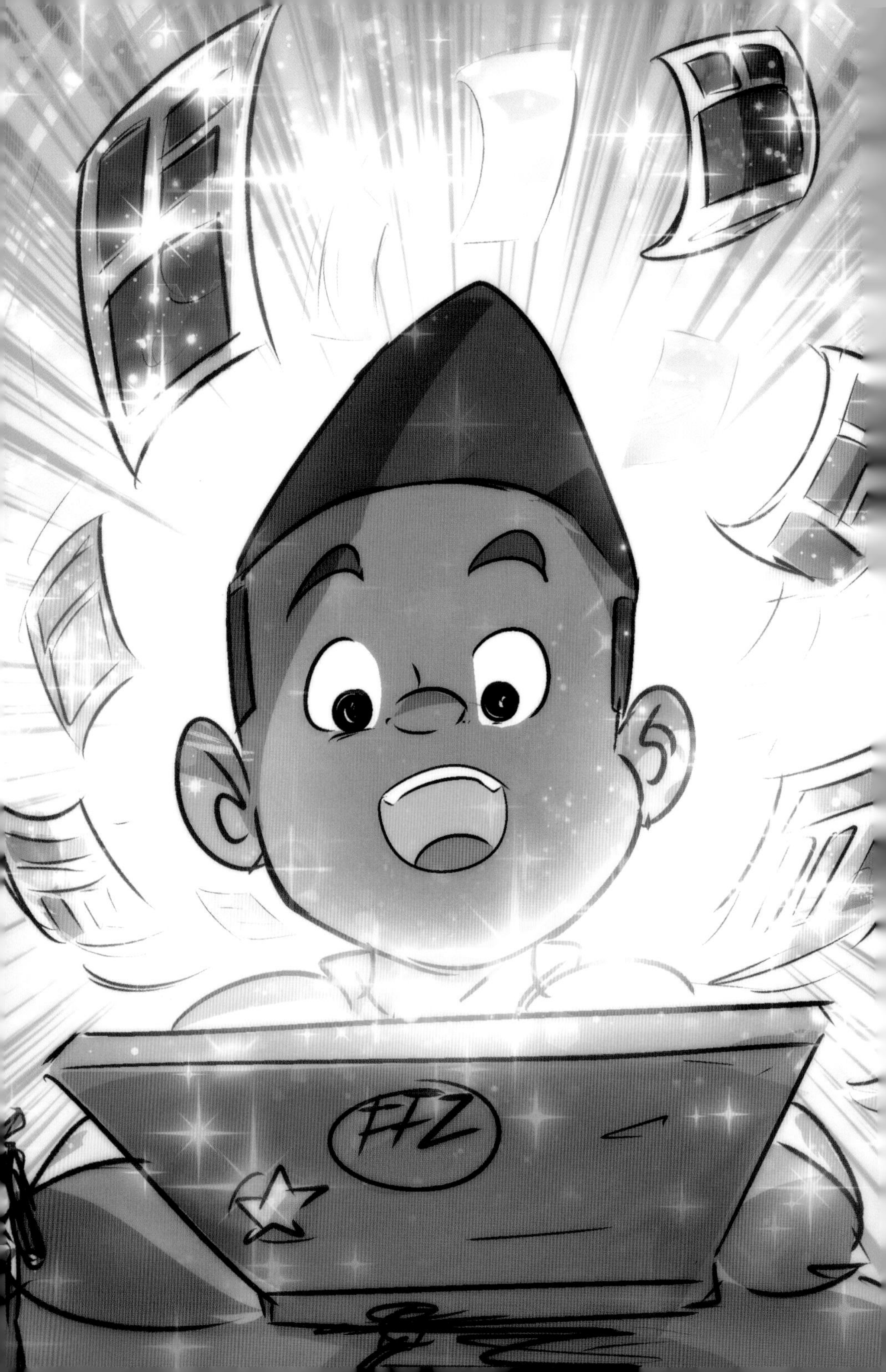

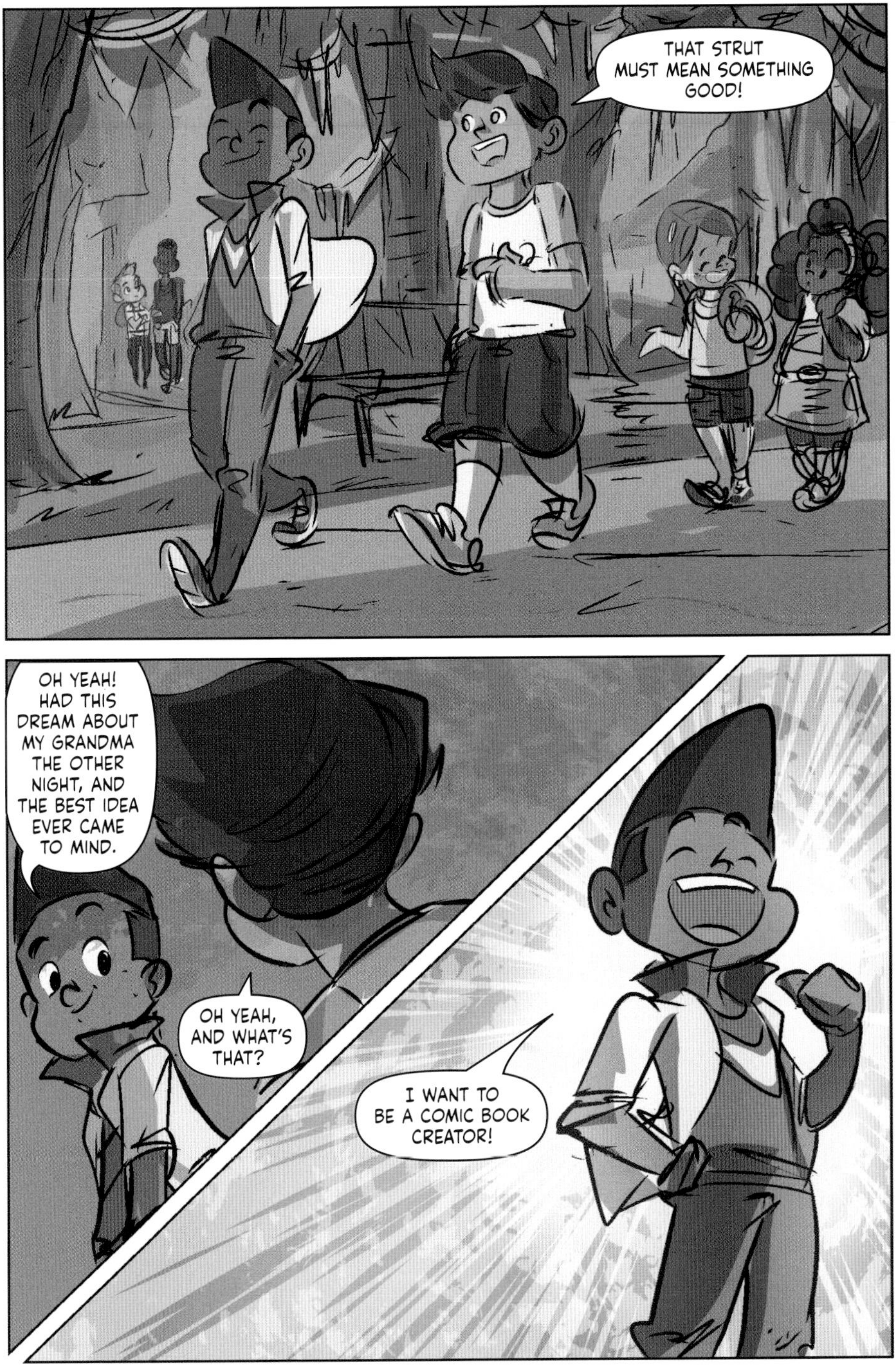
THAT STRUT MUST MEAN SOMETHING GOOD!
OH YEAH! HAD THIS DREAM ABOUT MY GRANDMA THE OTHER NIGHT, AND THE BEST IDEA EVER CAME TO MIND.
OH YEAH, AND WHAT'S THAT?
I WANT TO BE A COMIC BOOK CREATOR!

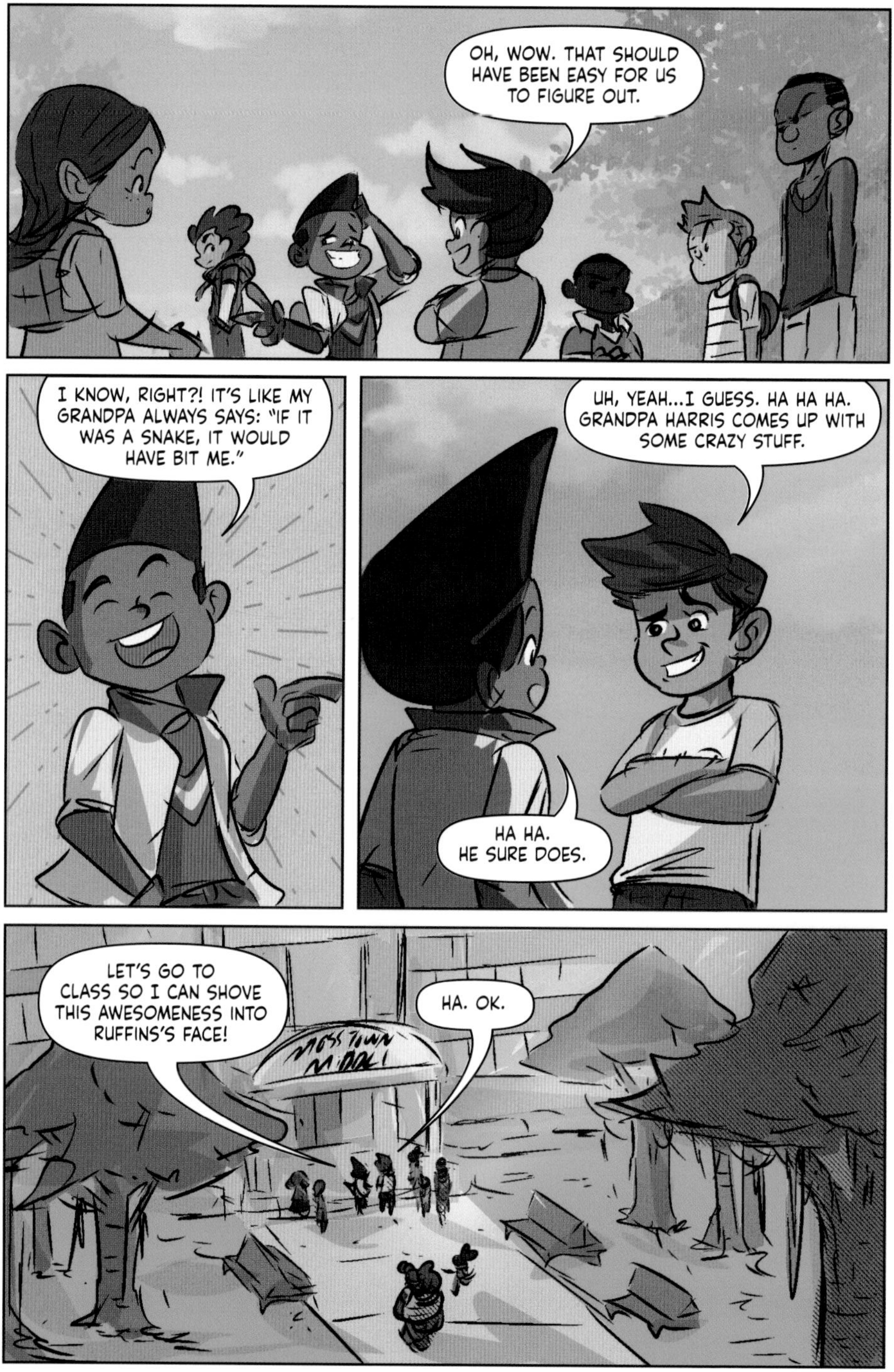
OH, WOW. THAT SHOULD HAVE BEEN EASY FOR US TO FIGURE OUT.
I KNOW, RIGHT?! IT'S LIKE MY GRANDPA ALWAYS SAYS: "IF IT WAS A SNAKE, IT WOULD HAVE BIT ME."
UH, YEAH...I GUESS. HA HA HA. GRANDPA HARRIS COMES UP WITH SOME CRAZY STUFF.
HA HA. HE SURE DOES.
LET'S GO TO CLASS SO I CAN SHOVE THIS AWESOMENESS INTO RUFFINS'S FACE!
HA. OK.

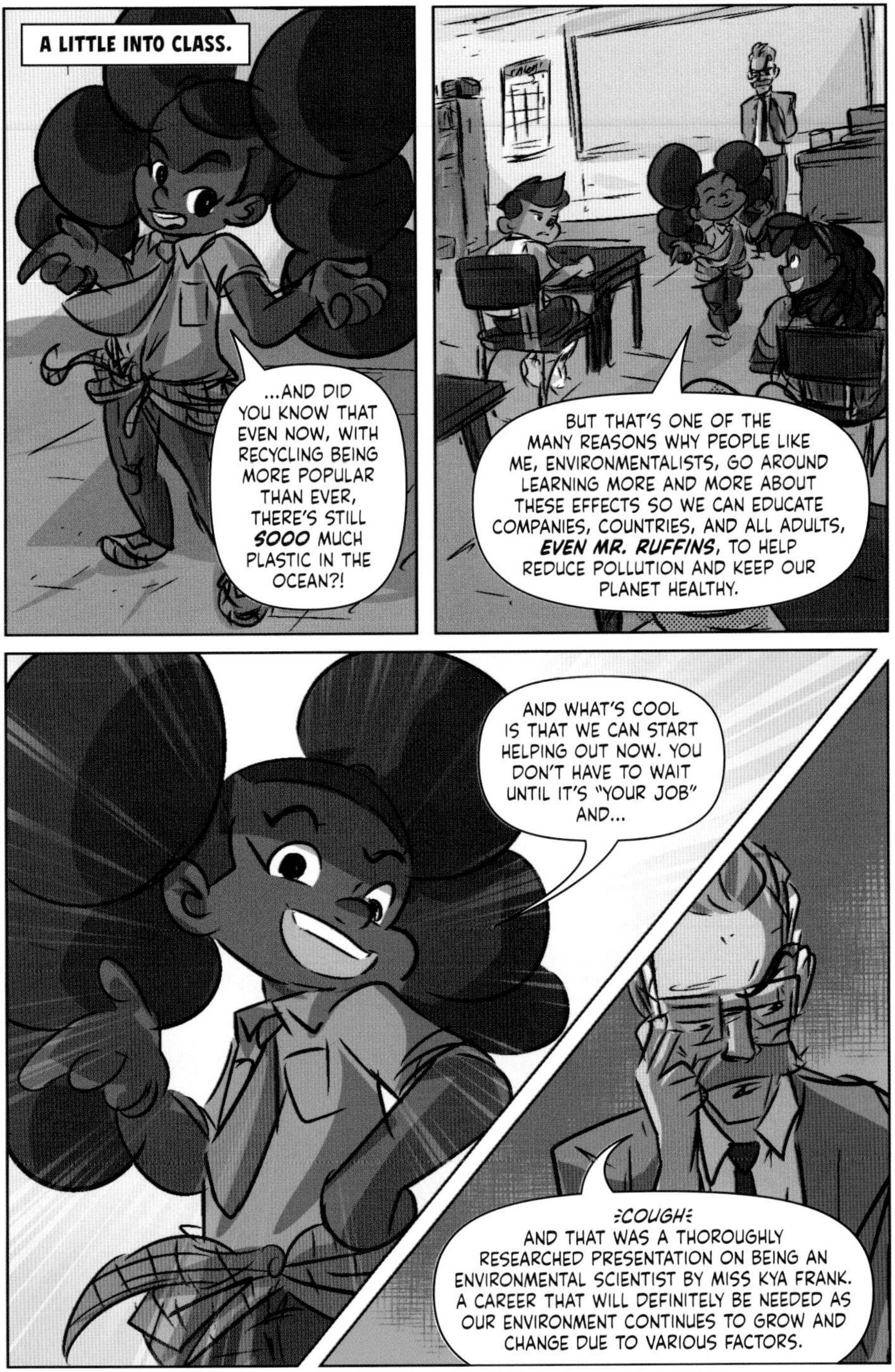
A LITTLE INTO CLASS.
...AND DID YOU KNOW THAT EVEN NOW, WITH RECYCLING BEING MORE POPULAR THAN EVER, THERE'S STILL *SOOO* MUCH PLASTIC IN THE OCEAN?!
BUT THAT'S ONE OF THE MANY REASONS WHY PEOPLE LIKE ME, ENVIRONMENTALISTS, GO AROUND LEARNING MORE AND MORE ABOUT THESE EFFECTS SO WE CAN EDUCATE COMPANIES, COUNTRIES, AND ALL ADULTS, ***EVEN MR. RUFFINS***, TO HELP REDUCE POLLUTION AND KEEP OUR PLANET HEALTHY.
AND WHAT'S COOL IS THAT WE CAN START HELPING OUT NOW. YOU DON'T HAVE TO WAIT UNTIL IT'S "YOUR JOB" AND...
COUGH AND THAT WAS A THOROUGHLY RESEARCHED PRESENTATION ON BEING AN ENVIRONMENTAL SCIENTIST BY MISS KYA FRANK. A CAREER THAT WILL DEFINITELY BE NEEDED AS OUR ENVIRONMENT CONTINUES TO GROW AND CHANGE DUE TO VARIOUS FACTORS.

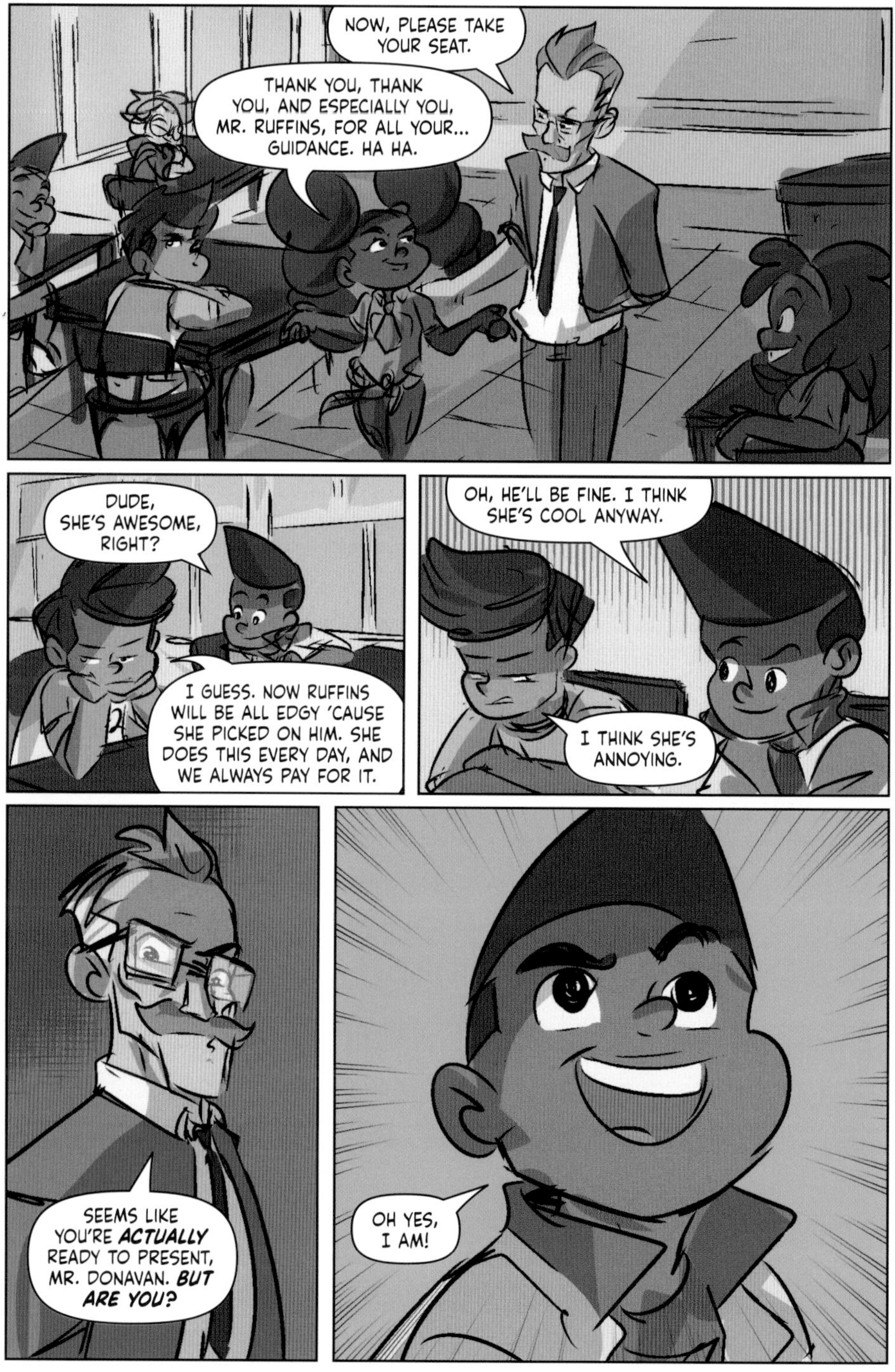
NOW, PLEASE TAKE YOUR SEAT.
THANK YOU, THANK YOU, AND ESPECIALLY YOU, MR. RUFFINS, FOR ALL YOUR... GUIDANCE. HA HA.
DUDE, SHE'S AWESOME, RIGHT?
I GUESS. NOW RUFFINS WILL BE ALL EDGY 'CAUSE SHE PICKED ON HIM. SHE DOES THIS EVERY DAY, AND WE ALWAYS PAY FOR IT.
OH, HE'LL BE FINE. I THINK SHE'S COOL ANYWAY.
I THINK SHE'S ANNOYING.
SEEMS LIKE YOU'RE ***ACTUALLY*** READY TO PRESENT, MR. DONAVAN. ***BUT ARE YOU?***
OH YES, I AM!

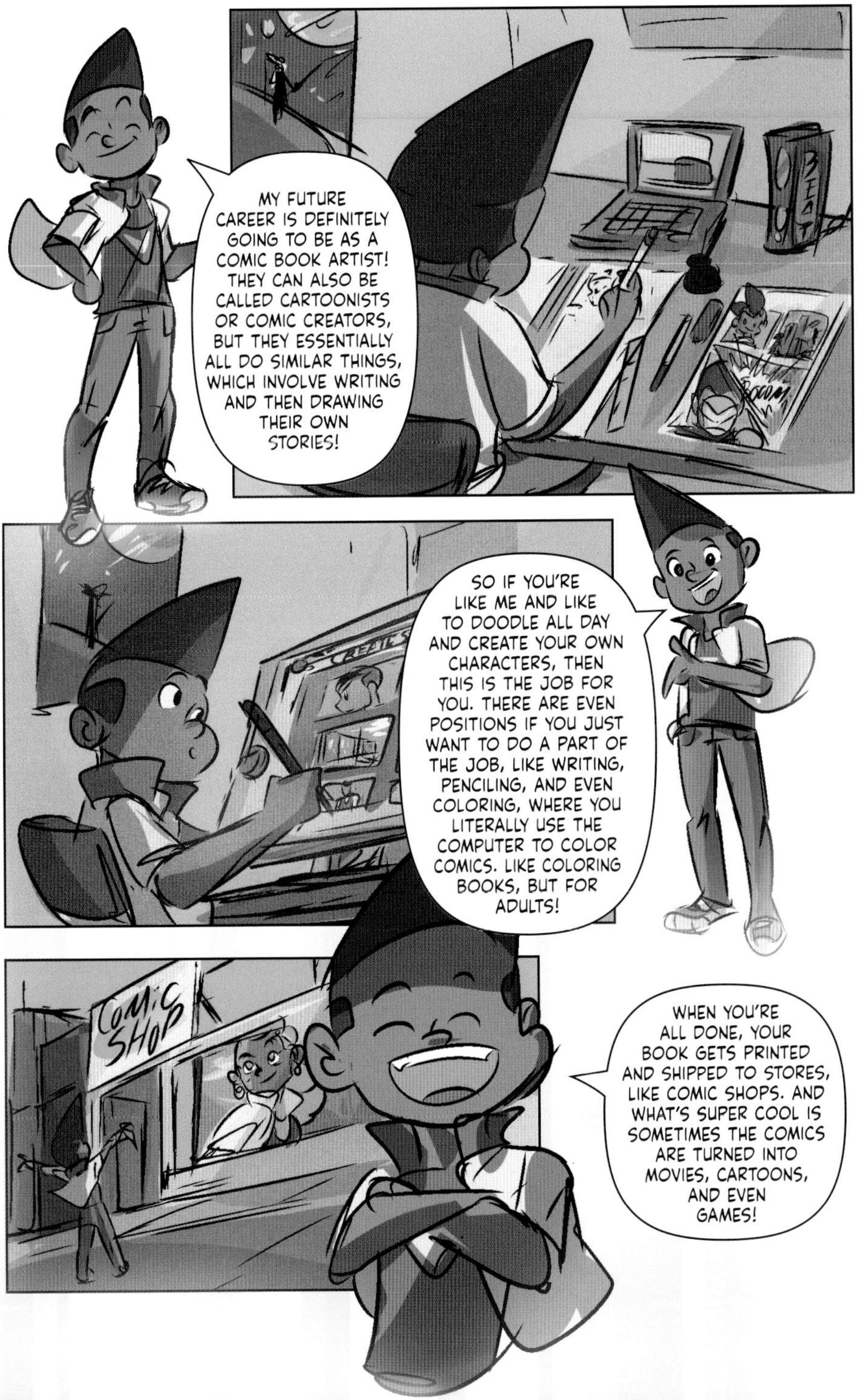
MY FUTURE CAREER IS DEFINITELY GOING TO BE AS A COMIC BOOK ARTIST! THEY CAN ALSO BE CALLED CARTOONISTS OR COMIC CREATORS, BUT THEY ESSENTIALLY ALL DO SIMILAR THINGS, WHICH INVOLVE WRITING AND THEN DRAWING THEIR OWN STORIES!
SO IF YOU'RE LIKE ME AND LIKE TO DOODLE ALL DAY AND CREATE YOUR OWN CHARACTERS, THEN THIS IS THE JOB FOR YOU. THERE ARE EVEN POSITIONS IF YOU JUST WANT TO DO A PART OF THE JOB, LIKE WRITING, PENCILING, AND EVEN COLORING, WHERE YOU LITERALLY USE THE COMPUTER TO COLOR COMICS. LIKE COLORING BOOKS, BUT FOR ADULTS!
COMIC SHOP
WHEN YOU'RE ALL DONE, YOUR BOOK GETS PRINTED AND SHIPPED TO STORES, LIKE COMIC SHOPS. AND WHAT'S SUPER COOL IS SOMETIMES THE COMICS ARE TURNED INTO MOVIES, CARTOONS, AND EVEN GAMES!

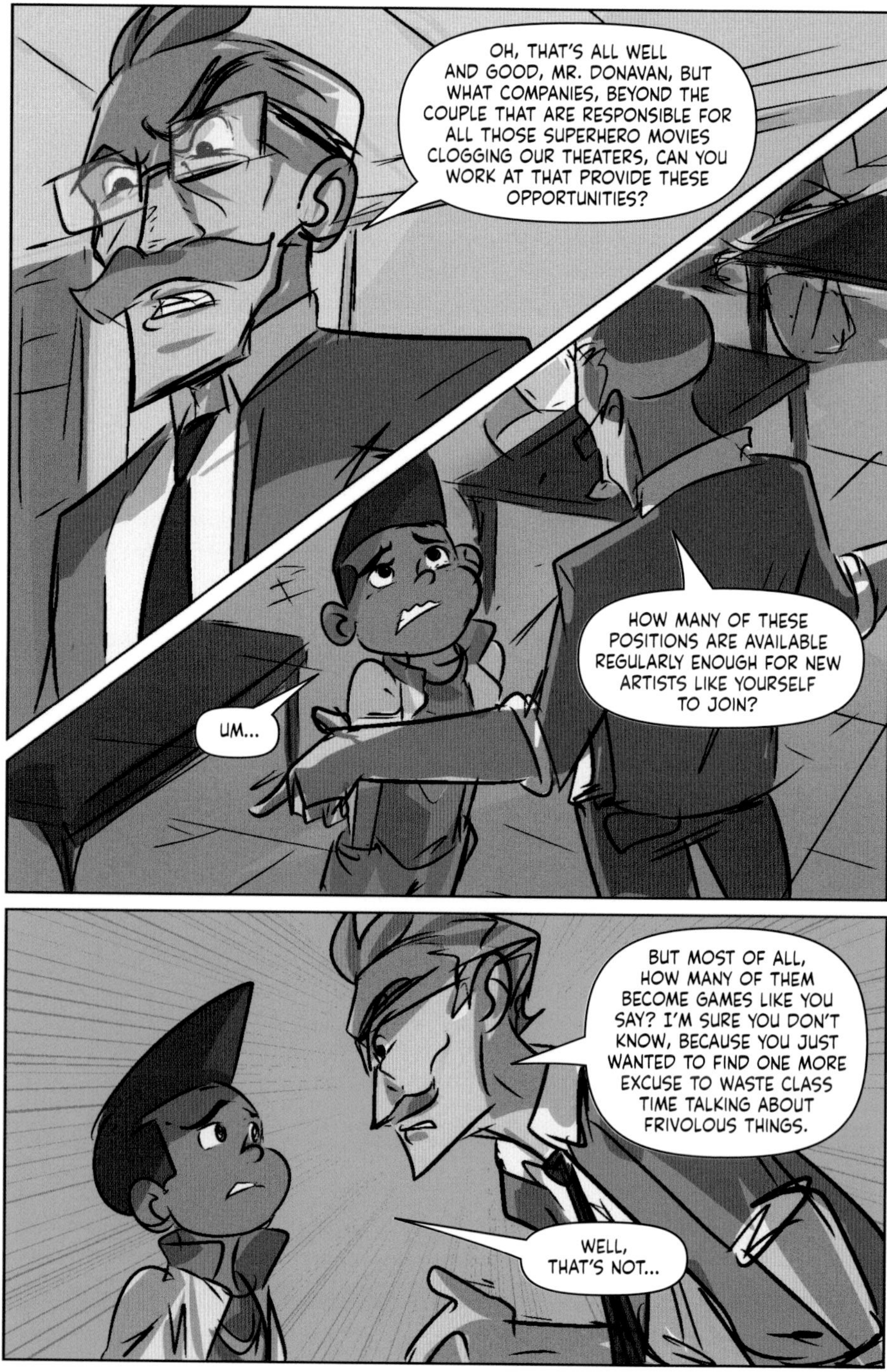

OH, THAT'S ALL WELL AND GOOD, MR. DONAVAN, BUT WHAT COMPANIES, BEYOND THE COUPLE THAT ARE RESPONSIBLE FOR ALL THOSE SUPERHERO MOVIES CLOGGING OUR THEATERS, CAN YOU WORK AT THAT PROVIDE THESE OPPORTUNITIES?
HOW MANY OF THESE POSITIONS ARE AVAILABLE REGULARLY ENOUGH FOR NEW ARTISTS LIKE YOURSELF TO JOIN?
UM...
BUT MOST OF ALL, HOW MANY OF THEM BECOME GAMES LIKE YOU SAY? I'M SURE YOU DON'T KNOW, BECAUSE YOU JUST WANTED TO FIND ONE MORE EXCUSE TO WASTE CLASS TIME TALKING ABOUT FRIVOLOUS THINGS.
WELL, THAT'S NOT...

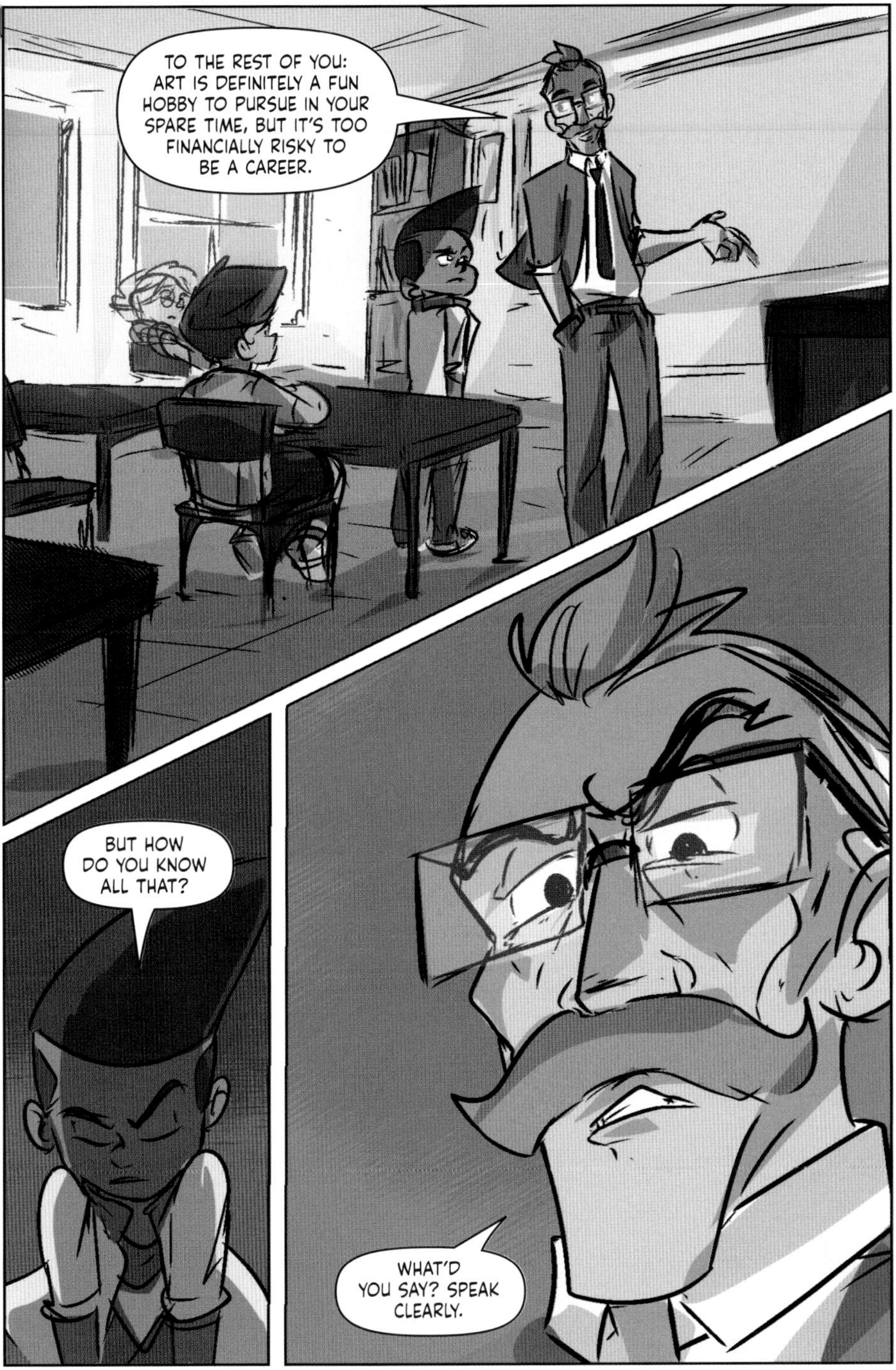
TO THE REST OF YOU: ART IS DEFINITELY A FUN HOBBY TO PURSUE IN YOUR SPARE TIME, BUT IT'S TOO FINANCIALLY RISKY TO BE A CAREER.
BUT HOW DO YOU KNOW ALL THAT?
WHAT'D YOU SAY? SPEAK CLEARLY.

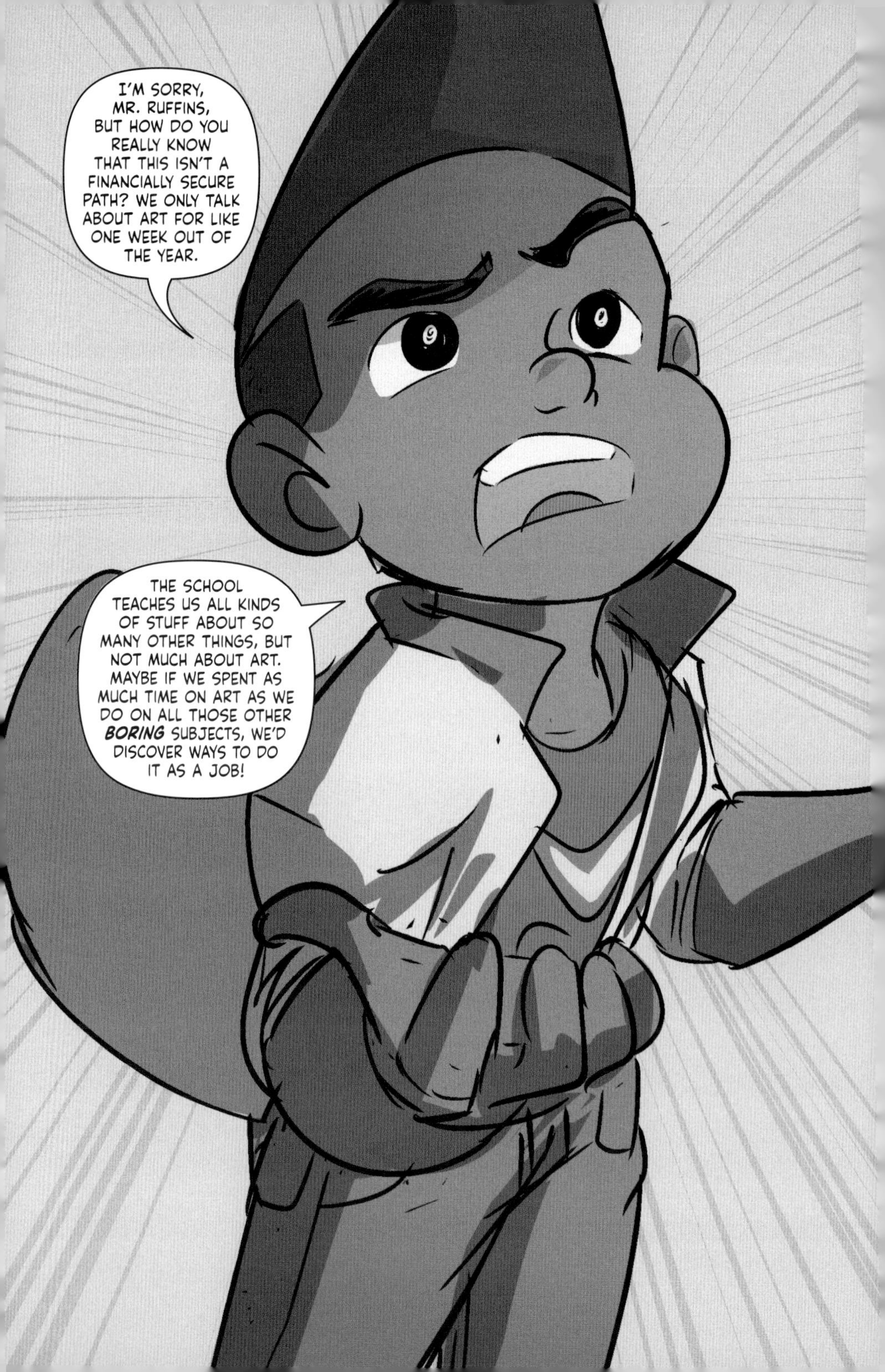
I'M SORRY, MR. RUFFINS, BUT HOW DO YOU REALLY KNOW THAT THIS ISN'T A FINANCIALLY SECURE PATH? WE ONLY TALK ABOUT ART FOR LIKE ONE WEEK OUT OF THE YEAR.
THE SCHOOL TEACHES US ALL KINDS OF STUFF ABOUT SO MANY OTHER THINGS, BUT NOT MUCH ABOUT ART. MAYBE IF WE SPENT AS MUCH TIME ON ART AS WE DO ON ALL THOSE OTHER *BORING* SUBJECTS, WE'D DISCOVER WAYS TO DO IT AS A JOB!

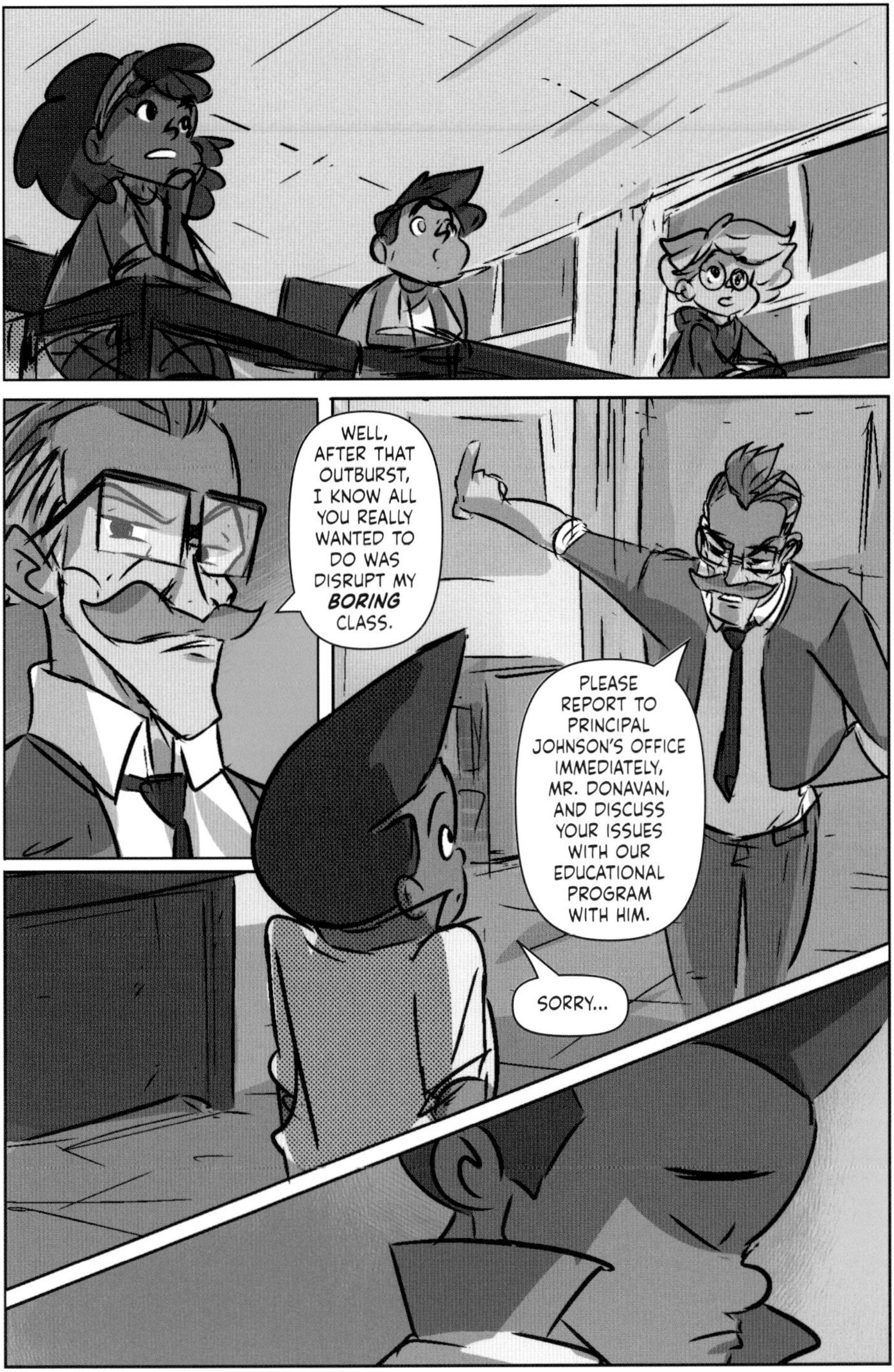
WELL, AFTER THAT OUTBURST, I KNOW ALL YOU REALLY WANTED TO DO WAS DISRUPT MY **BORING** CLASS.
PLEASE REPORT TO PRINCIPAL JOHNSON'S OFFICE IMMEDIATELY, MR. DONAVAN, AND DISCUSS YOUR ISSUES WITH OUR EDUCATIONAL PROGRAM WITH HIM.
SORRY...

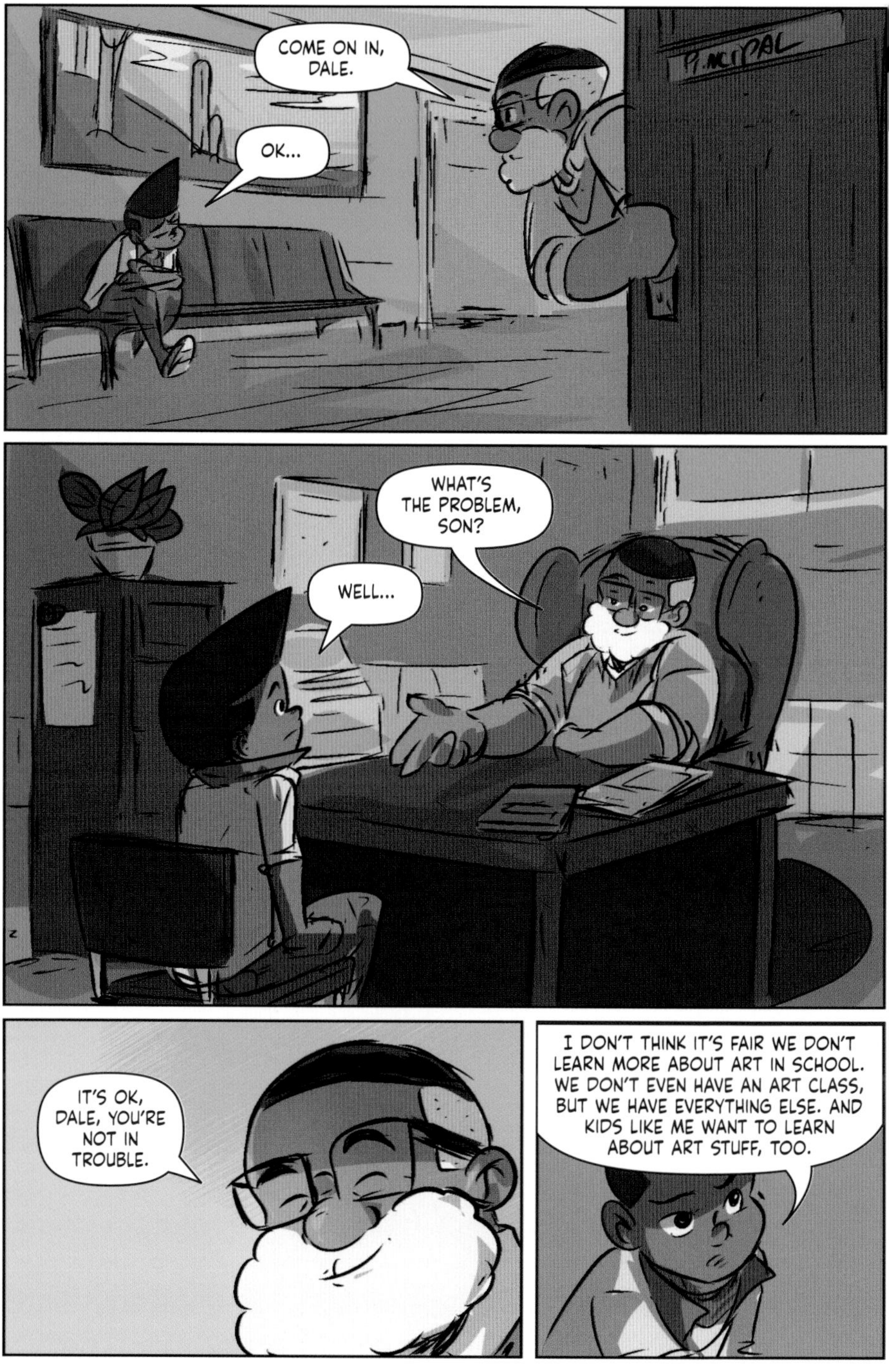
COME ON IN, DALE.
OK...
WHAT'S THE PROBLEM, SON?
WELL...
IT'S OK, DALE, YOU'RE NOT IN TROUBLE.
I DON'T THINK IT'S FAIR WE DON'T LEARN MORE ABOUT ART IN SCHOOL. WE DON'T EVEN HAVE AN ART CLASS, BUT WE HAVE EVERYTHING ELSE. AND KIDS LIKE ME WANT TO LEARN ABOUT ART STUFF, TOO.

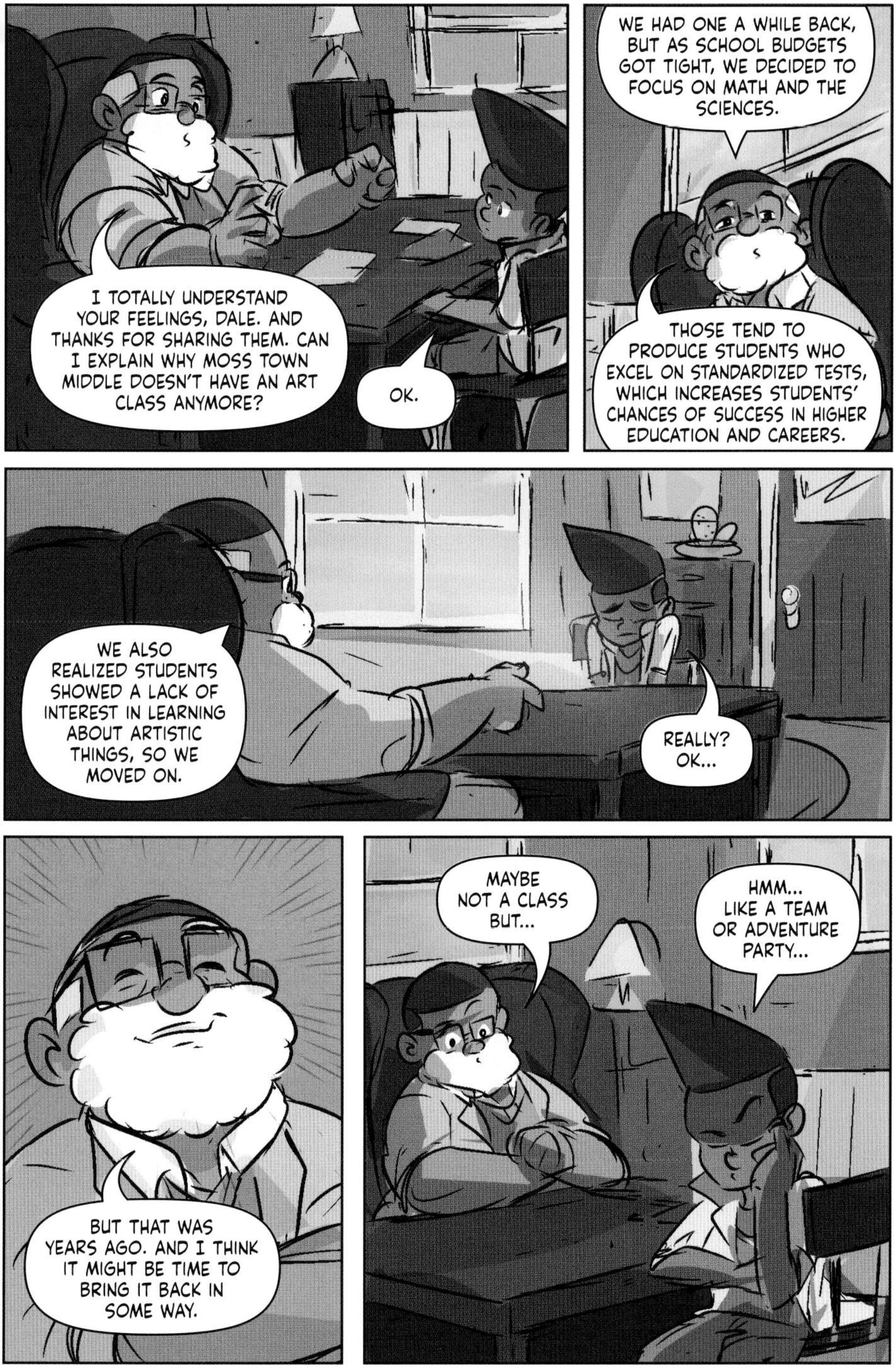
I TOTALLY UNDERSTAND YOUR FEELINGS, DALE. AND THANKS FOR SHARING THEM. CAN I EXPLAIN WHY MOSS TOWN MIDDLE DOESN'T HAVE AN ART CLASS ANYMORE?
OK.
WE HAD ONE A WHILE BACK, BUT AS SCHOOL BUDGETS GOT TIGHT, WE DECIDED TO FOCUS ON MATH AND THE SCIENCES.
THOSE TEND TO PRODUCE STUDENTS WHO EXCEL ON STANDARDIZED TESTS, WHICH INCREASES STUDENTS' CHANCES OF SUCCESS IN HIGHER EDUCATION AND CAREERS.
WE ALSO REALIZED STUDENTS SHOWED A LACK OF INTEREST IN LEARNING ABOUT ARTISTIC THINGS, SO WE MOVED ON.
REALLY? OK...
BUT THAT WAS YEARS AGO. AND I THINK IT MIGHT BE TIME TO BRING IT BACK IN SOME WAY.
MAYBE NOT A CLASS BUT...
HMM... LIKE A TEAM OR ADVENTURE PARTY...

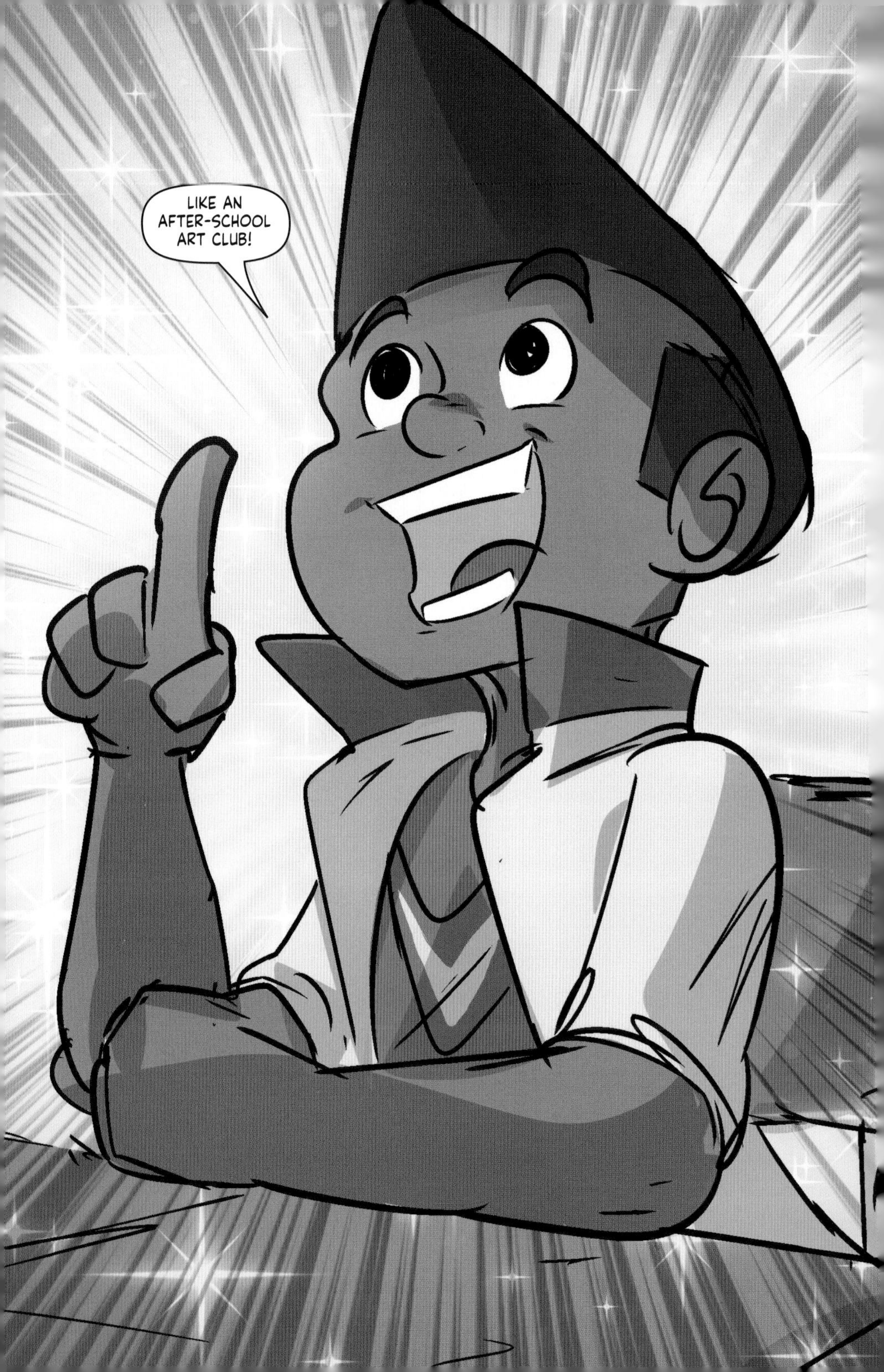
LIKE AN AFTER-SCHOOL ART CLUB!

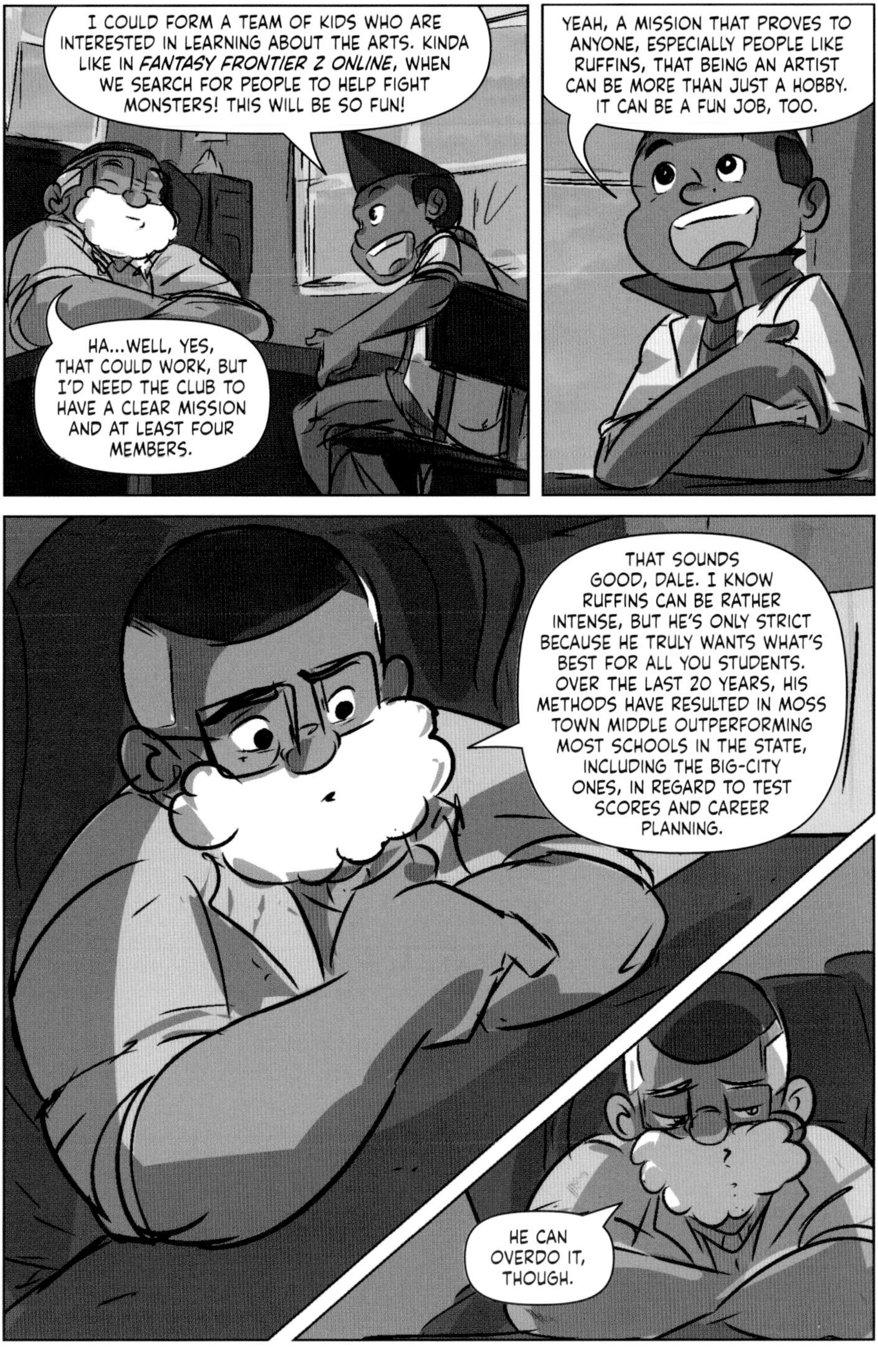
I COULD FORM A TEAM OF KIDS WHO ARE INTERESTED IN LEARNING ABOUT THE ARTS. KINDA LIKE IN *FANTASY FRONTIER Z ONLINE*, WHEN WE SEARCH FOR PEOPLE TO HELP FIGHT MONSTERS! THIS WILL BE SO FUN!
HA...WELL, YES, THAT COULD WORK, BUT I'D NEED THE CLUB TO HAVE A CLEAR MISSION AND AT LEAST FOUR MEMBERS.
YEAH, A MISSION THAT PROVES TO ANYONE, ESPECIALLY PEOPLE LIKE RUFFINS, THAT BEING AN ARTIST CAN BE MORE THAN JUST A HOBBY. IT CAN BE A FUN JOB, TOO.
THAT SOUNDS GOOD, DALE. I KNOW RUFFINS CAN BE RATHER INTENSE, BUT HE'S ONLY STRICT BECAUSE HE TRULY WANTS WHAT'S BEST FOR ALL YOU STUDENTS. OVER THE LAST 20 YEARS, HIS METHODS HAVE RESULTED IN MOSS TOWN MIDDLE OUTPERFORMING MOST SCHOOLS IN THE STATE, INCLUDING THE BIG-CITY ONES, IN REGARD TO TEST SCORES AND CAREER PLANNING.
HE CAN OVERDO IT, THOUGH.

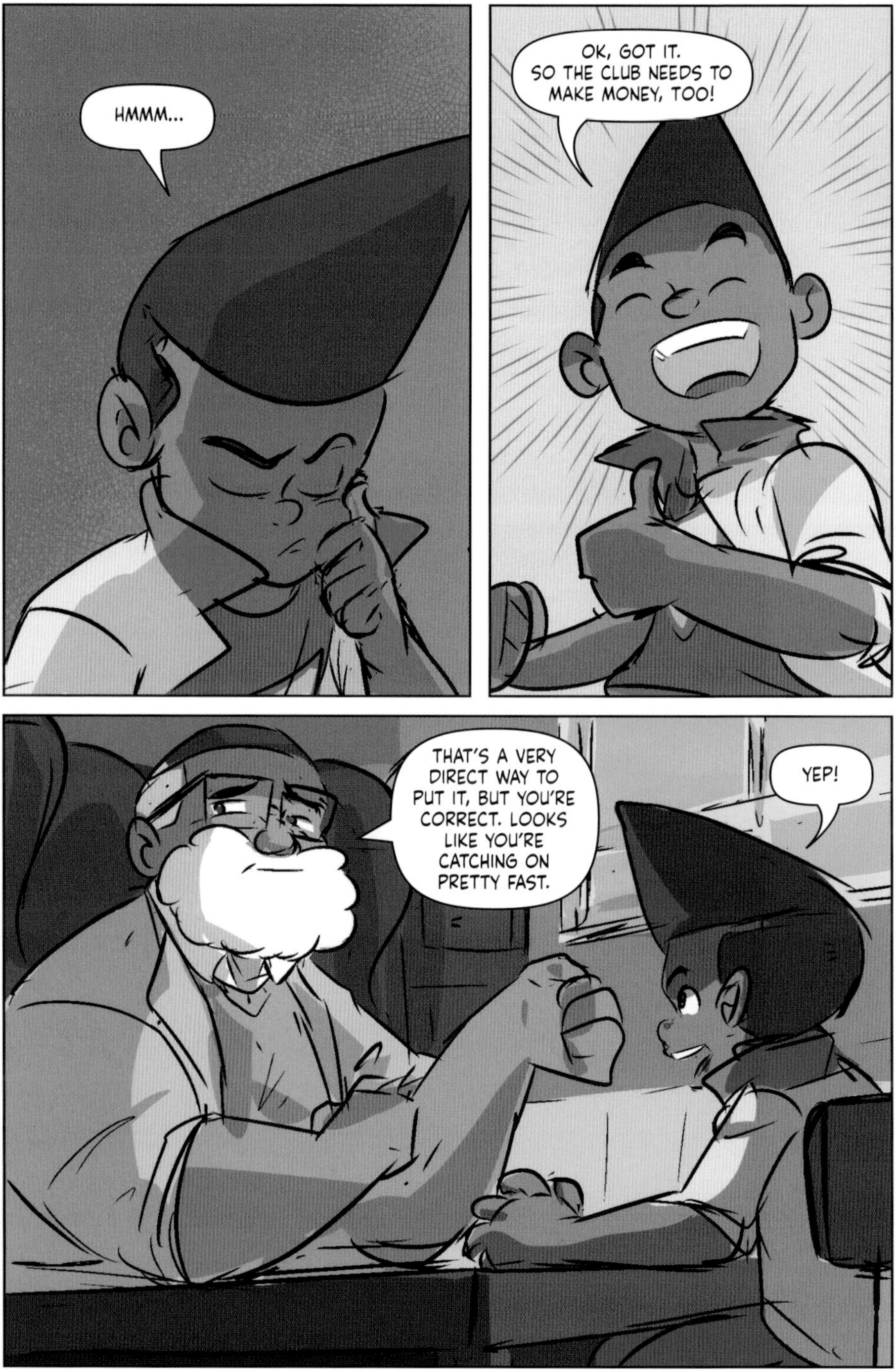
HMMM...
OK, GOT IT. SO THE CLUB NEEDS TO MAKE MONEY, TOO!
THAT'S A VERY DIRECT WAY TO PUT IT, BUT YOU'RE CORRECT. LOOKS LIKE YOU'RE CATCHING ON PRETTY FAST.
YEP!

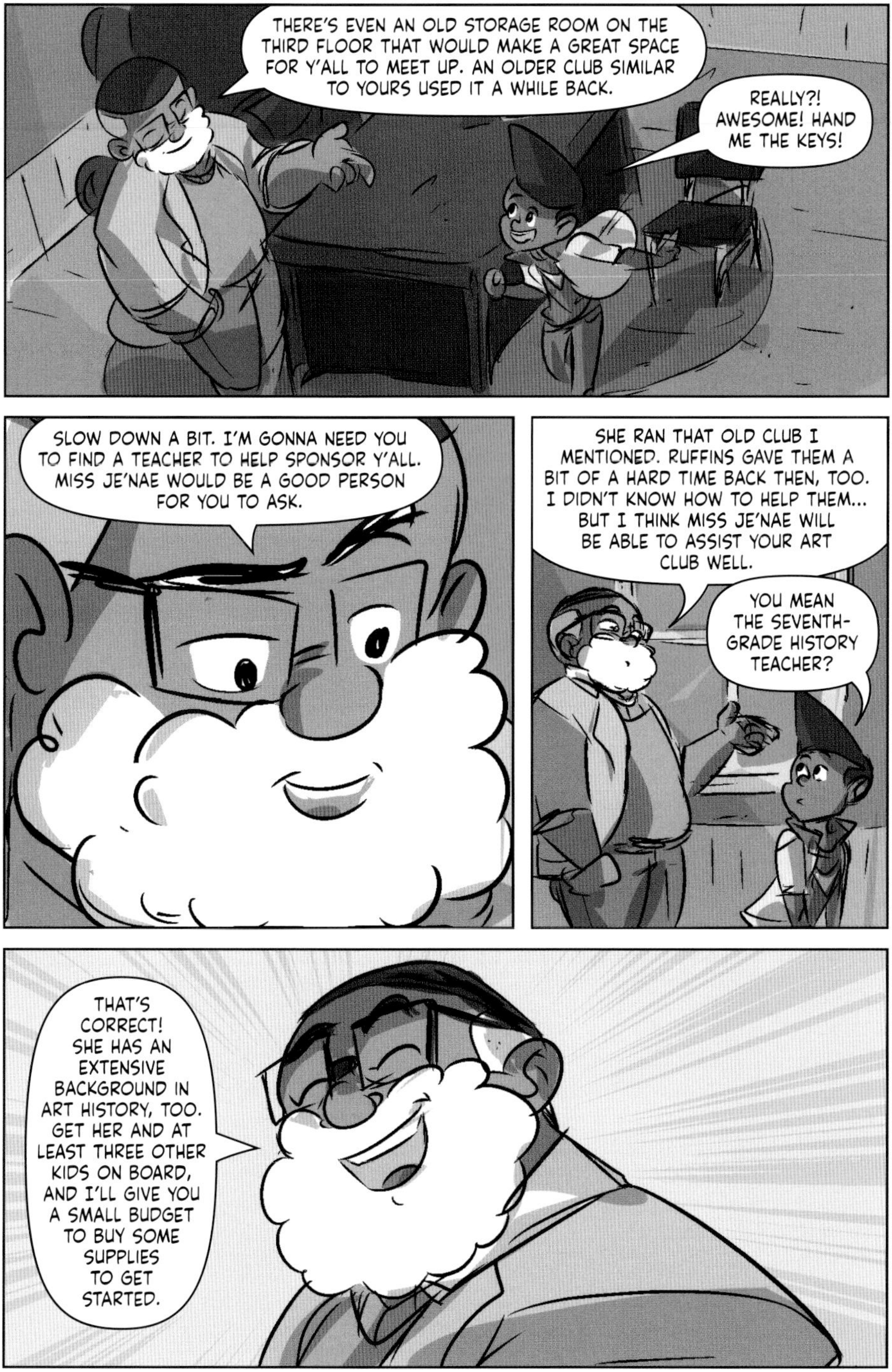
THERE'S EVEN AN OLD STORAGE ROOM ON THE THIRD FLOOR THAT WOULD MAKE A GREAT SPACE FOR Y'ALL TO MEET UP. AN OLDER CLUB SIMILAR TO YOURS USED IT A WHILE BACK.
REALLY?! AWESOME! HAND ME THE KEYS!
SLOW DOWN A BIT. I'M GONNA NEED YOU TO FIND A TEACHER TO HELP SPONSOR Y'ALL. MISS JE'NAE WOULD BE A GOOD PERSON FOR YOU TO ASK.
SHE RAN THAT OLD CLUB I MENTIONED. RUFFINS GAVE THEM A BIT OF A HARD TIME BACK THEN, TOO. I DIDN'T KNOW HOW TO HELP THEM... BUT I THINK MISS JE'NAE WILL BE ABLE TO ASSIST YOUR ART CLUB WELL.
YOU MEAN THE SEVENTH-GRADE HISTORY TEACHER?
THAT'S CORRECT! SHE HAS AN EXTENSIVE BACKGROUND IN ART HISTORY, TOO. GET HER AND AT LEAST THREE OTHER KIDS ON BOARD, AND I'LL GIVE YOU A SMALL BUDGET TO BUY SOME SUPPLIES TO GET STARTED.

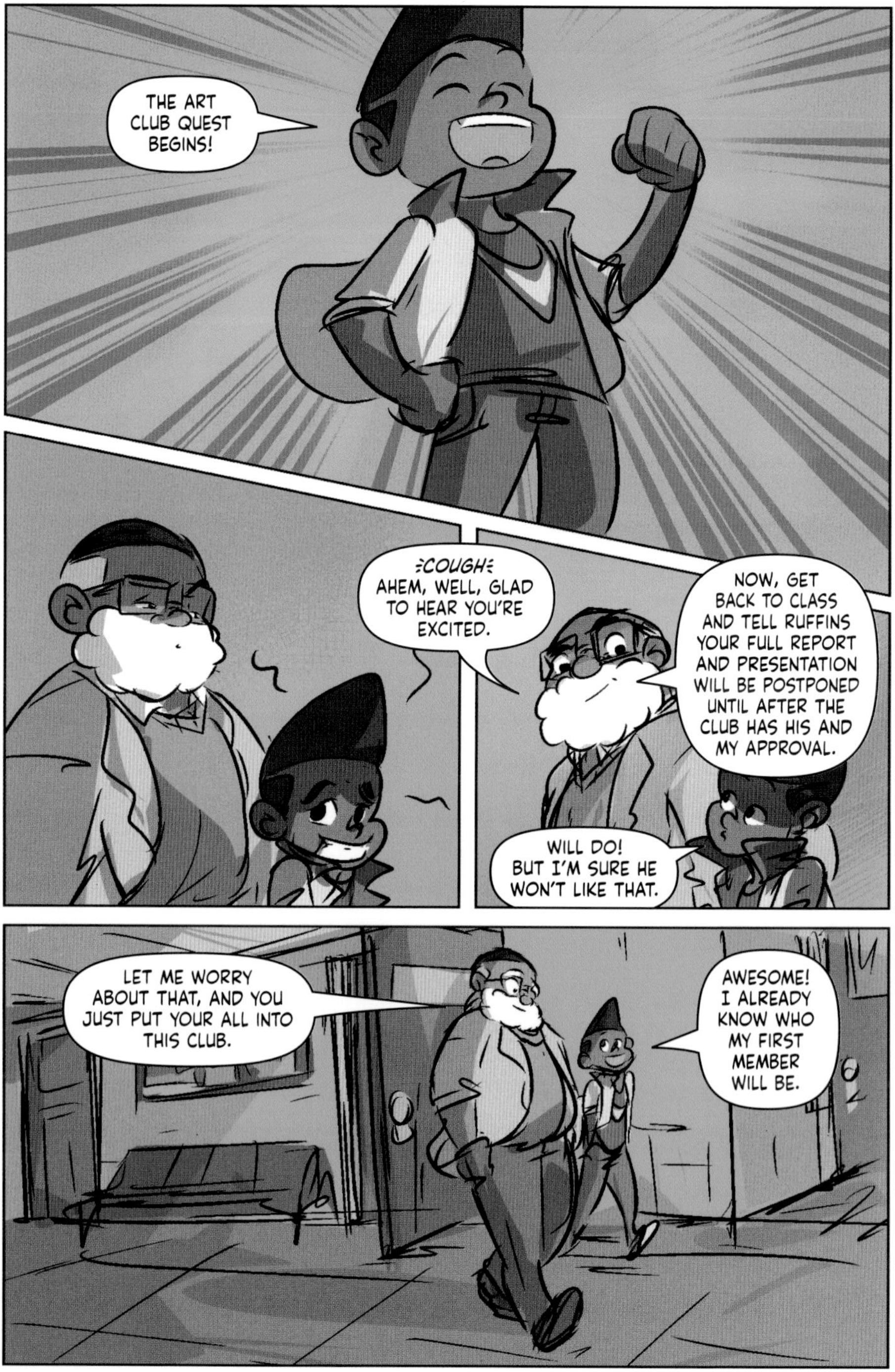
THE ART CLUB QUEST BEGINS!
≈COUGH≈ AHEM, WELL, GLAD TO HEAR YOU'RE EXCITED.
NOW, GET BACK TO CLASS AND TELL RUFFINS YOUR FULL REPORT AND PRESENTATION WILL BE POSTPONED UNTIL AFTER THE CLUB HAS HIS AND MY APPROVAL.
WILL DO! BUT I'M SURE HE WON'T LIKE THAT.
LET ME WORRY ABOUT THAT, AND YOU JUST PUT YOUR ALL INTO THIS CLUB.
AWESOME! I ALREADY KNOW WHO MY FIRST MEMBER WILL BE.

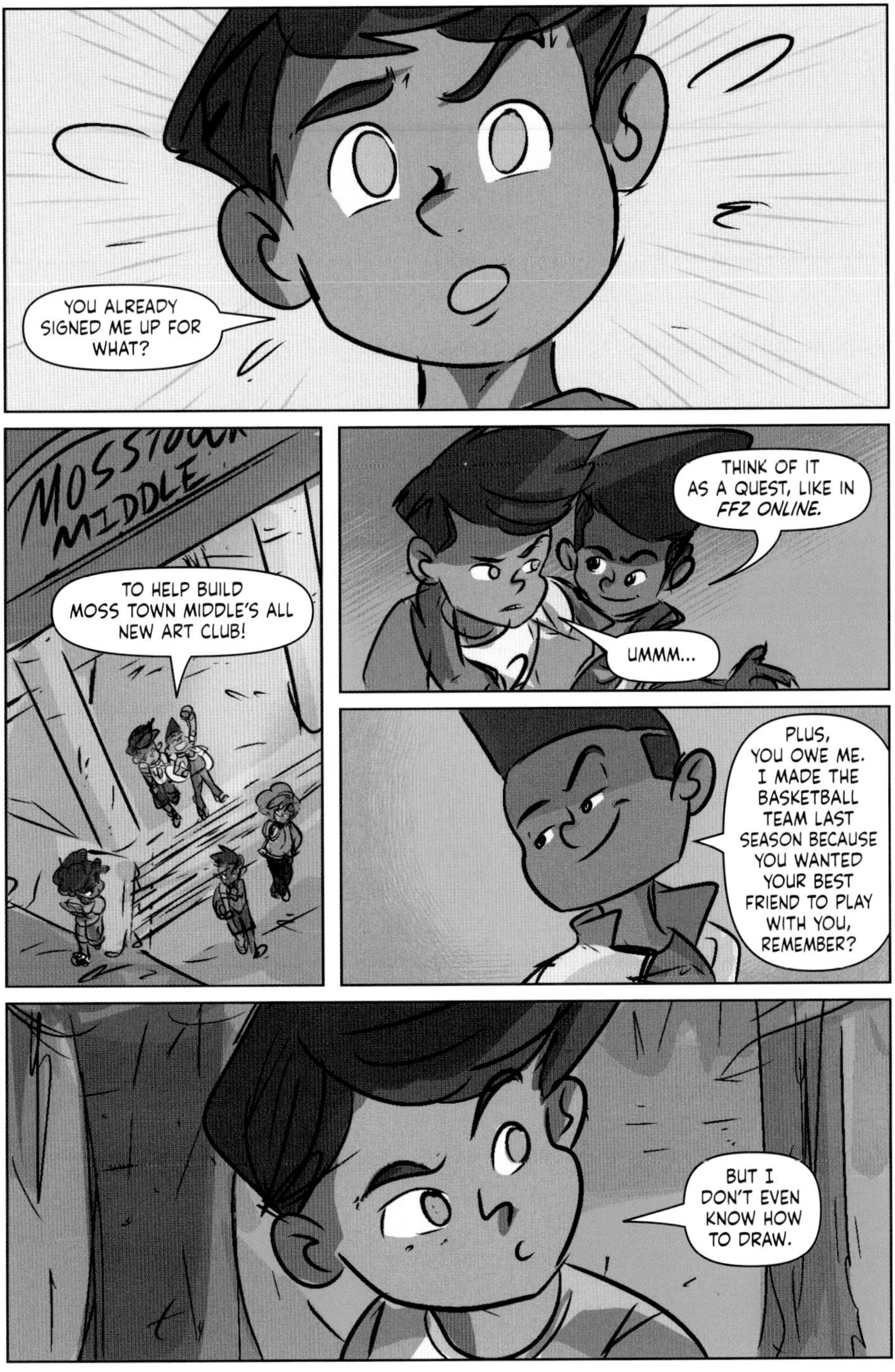
YOU ALREADY SIGNED ME UP FOR WHAT?
MOSSTOWN MIDDLE
TO HELP BUILD MOSS TOWN MIDDLE'S ALL NEW ART CLUB!
THINK OF IT AS A QUEST, LIKE IN *FFZ ONLINE.*
UMMM...
PLUS, YOU OWE ME. I MADE THE BASKETBALL TEAM LAST SEASON BECAUSE YOU WANTED YOUR BEST FRIEND TO PLAY WITH YOU, REMEMBER?
BUT I DON'T EVEN KNOW HOW TO DRAW.

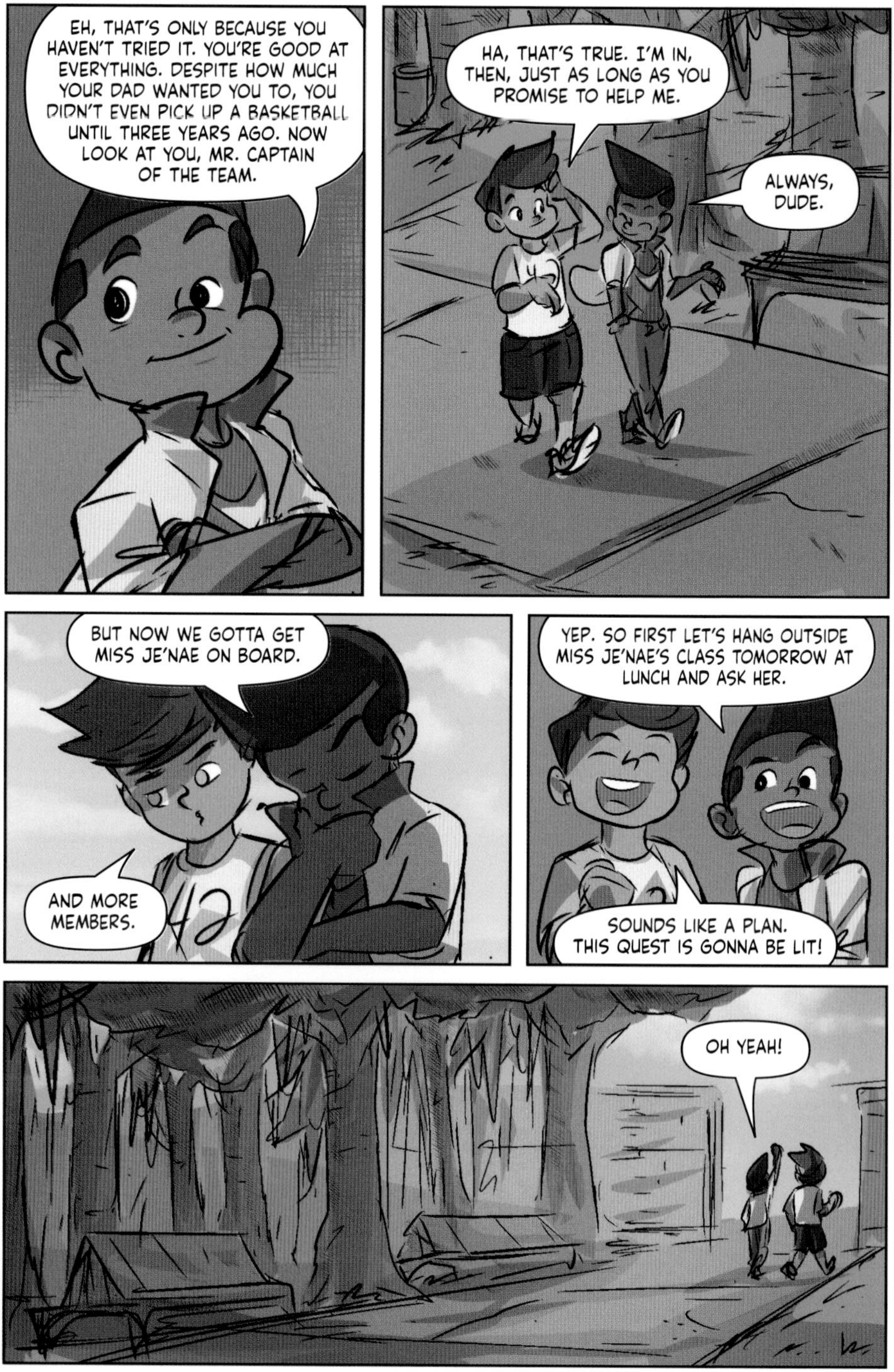
EH, THAT'S ONLY BECAUSE YOU HAVEN'T TRIED IT. YOU'RE GOOD AT EVERYTHING. DESPITE HOW MUCH YOUR DAD WANTED YOU TO, YOU DIDN'T EVEN PICK UP A BASKETBALL UNTIL THREE YEARS AGO. NOW LOOK AT YOU, MR. CAPTAIN OF THE TEAM.
HA, THAT'S TRUE. I'M IN, THEN, JUST AS LONG AS YOU PROMISE TO HELP ME.
ALWAYS, DUDE.
BUT NOW WE GOTTA GET MISS JE'NAE ON BOARD.
AND MORE MEMBERS.
YEP. SO FIRST LET'S HANG OUTSIDE MISS JE'NAE'S CLASS TOMORROW AT LUNCH AND ASK HER.
SOUNDS LIKE A PLAN. THIS QUEST IS GONNA BE LIT!
OH YEAH!

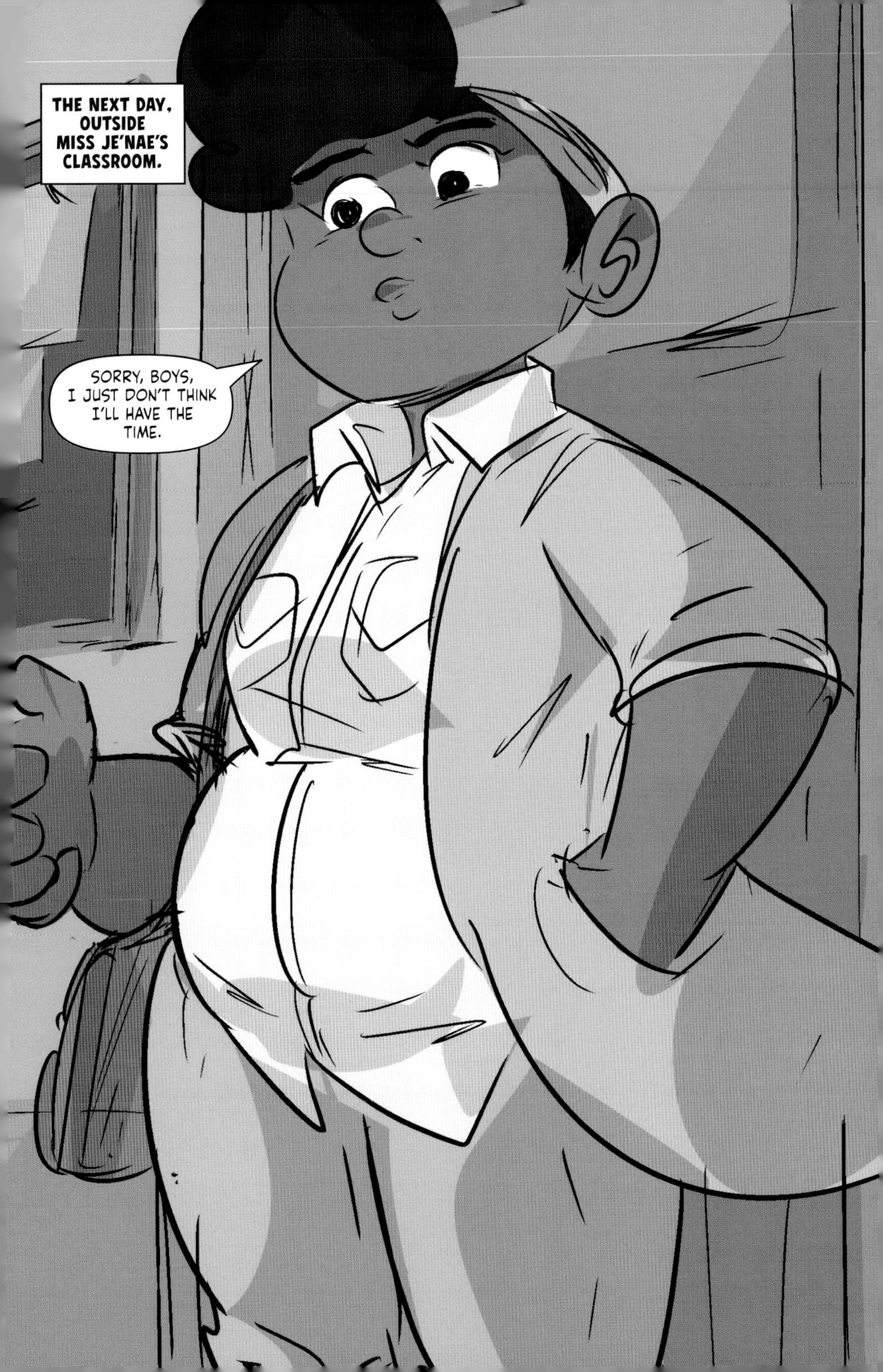
THE NEXT DAY, OUTSIDE MISS JE'NAE'S CLASSROOM.
SORRY, BOYS, I JUST DON'T THINK I'LL HAVE THE TIME.

NOW, IF YOU'LL EXCUSE ME, I NEED TO GRAB A QUICK BITE.

BUT WE REALLY NEED SOMETHING LIKE THIS AT SCHOOL.

THAT MAY BE TRUE. BUT ART WEEK ONCE A YEAR MIGHT BE ALL WE CAN GET RIGHT NOW... *BELIEVE ME*, THIS SCHOOL HAS NO FAITH IN THE ARTS.

BYE, BOYS.

DUDE, LET IT GO. SHE'S NOT UP FOR IT.

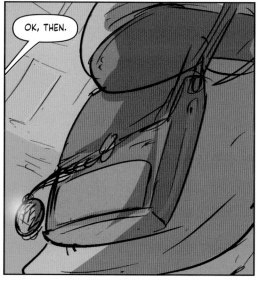

OK, THEN.

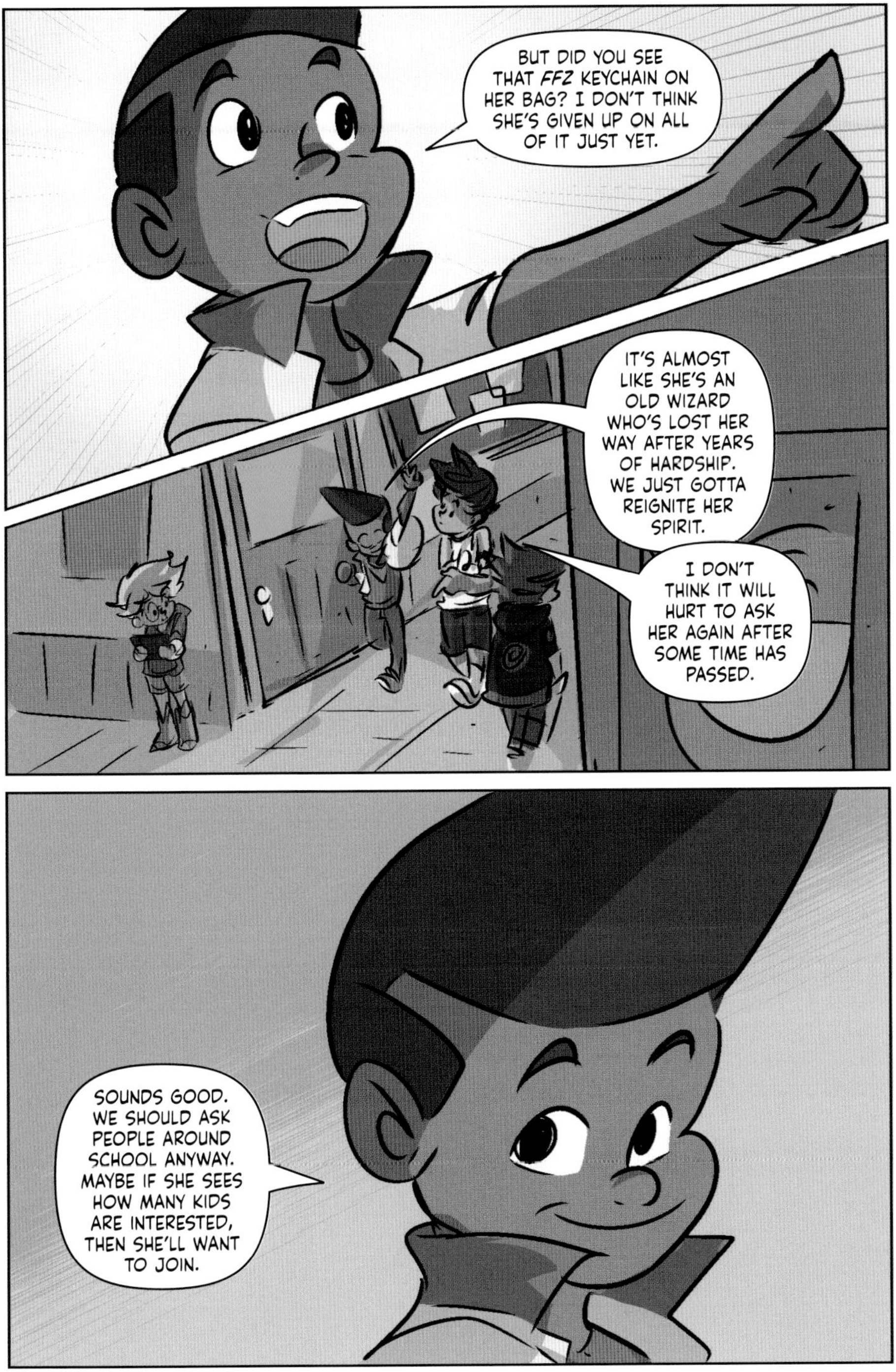
BUT DID YOU SEE THAT FFZ KEYCHAIN ON HER BAG? I DON'T THINK SHE'S GIVEN UP ON ALL OF IT JUST YET.
IT'S ALMOST LIKE SHE'S AN OLD WIZARD WHO'S LOST HER WAY AFTER YEARS OF HARDSHIP. WE JUST GOTTA REIGNITE HER SPIRIT.
I DON'T THINK IT WILL HURT TO ASK HER AGAIN AFTER SOME TIME HAS PASSED.
SOUNDS GOOD. WE SHOULD ASK PEOPLE AROUND SCHOOL ANYWAY. MAYBE IF SHE SEES HOW MANY KIDS ARE INTERESTED, THEN SHE'LL WANT TO JOIN.

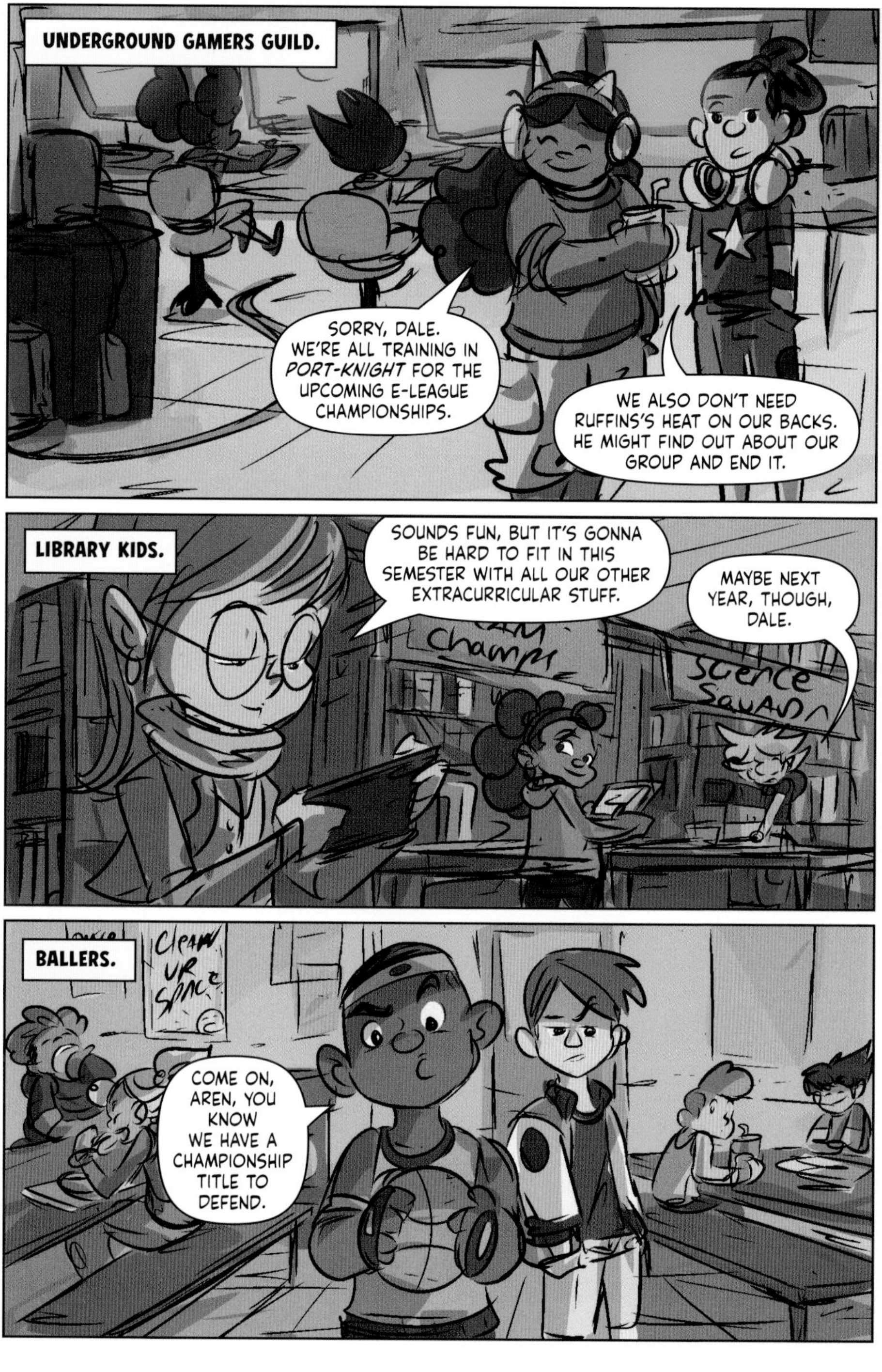
UNDERGROUND GAMERS GUILD.
SORRY, DALE. WE'RE ALL TRAINING IN *PORT-KNIGHT* FOR THE UPCOMING E-LEAGUE CHAMPIONSHIPS.
WE ALSO DON'T NEED RUFFINS'S HEAT ON OUR BACKS. HE MIGHT FIND OUT ABOUT OUR GROUP AND END IT.
LIBRARY KIDS.
SOUNDS FUN, BUT IT'S GONNA BE HARD TO FIT IN THIS SEMESTER WITH ALL OUR OTHER EXTRACURRICULAR STUFF.
MAYBE NEXT YEAR, THOUGH, DALE.
BALLERS.
COME ON, AREN, YOU KNOW WE HAVE A CHAMPIONSHIP TITLE TO DEFEND.

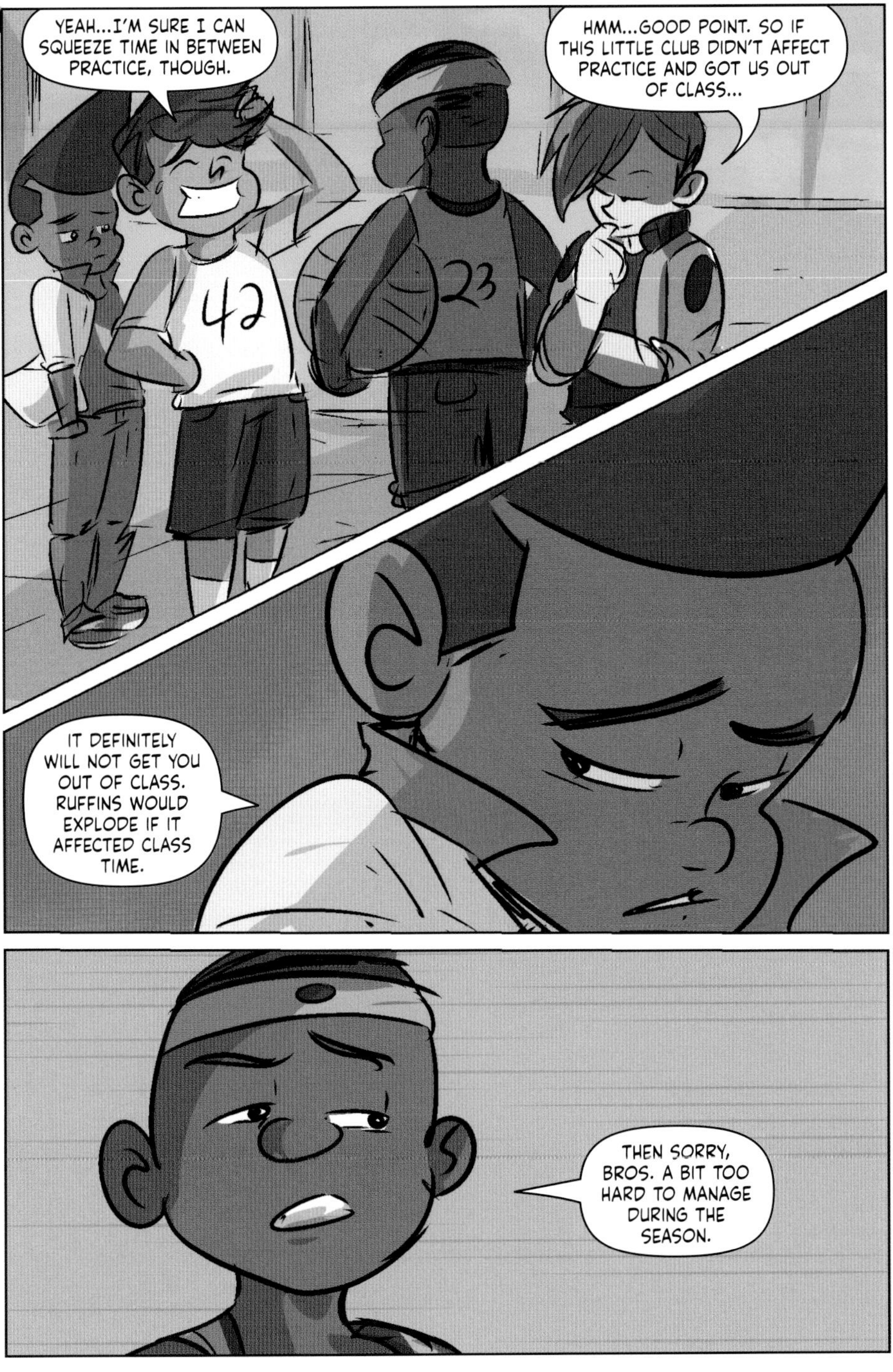
YEAH...I'M SURE I CAN SQUEEZE TIME IN BETWEEN PRACTICE, THOUGH.
HMM...GOOD POINT. SO IF THIS LITTLE CLUB DIDN'T AFFECT PRACTICE AND GOT US OUT OF CLASS...
42
23
IT DEFINITELY WILL NOT GET YOU OUT OF CLASS. RUFFINS WOULD EXPLODE IF IT AFFECTED CLASS TIME.
THEN SORRY, BROS. A BIT TOO HARD TO MANAGE DURING THE SEASON.

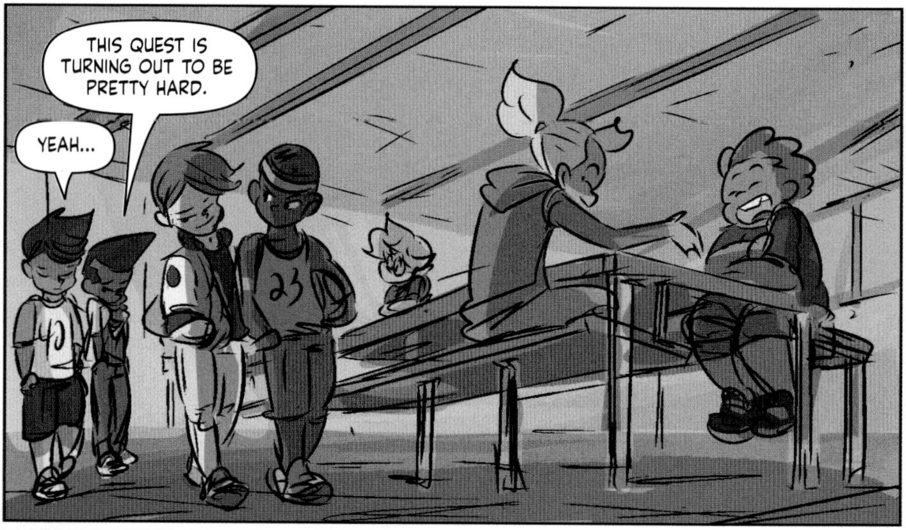
THIS QUEST IS TURNING OUT TO BE PRETTY HARD.
YEAH...

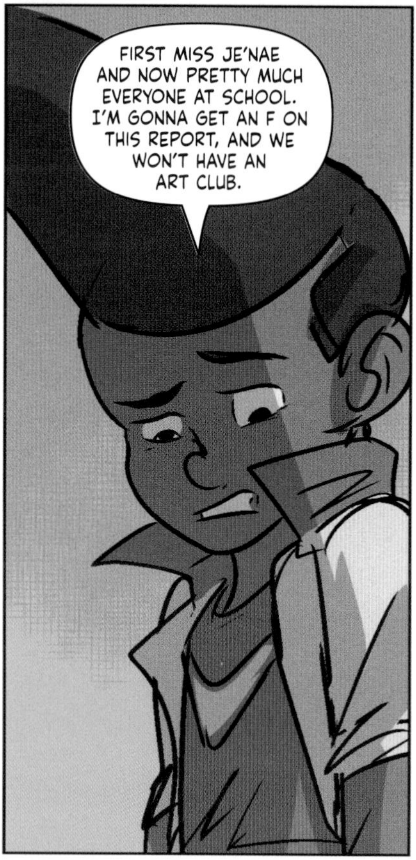
FIRST MISS JE'NAE AND NOW PRETTY MUCH EVERYONE AT SCHOOL. I'M GONNA GET AN F ON THIS REPORT, AND WE WON'T HAVE AN ART CLUB.

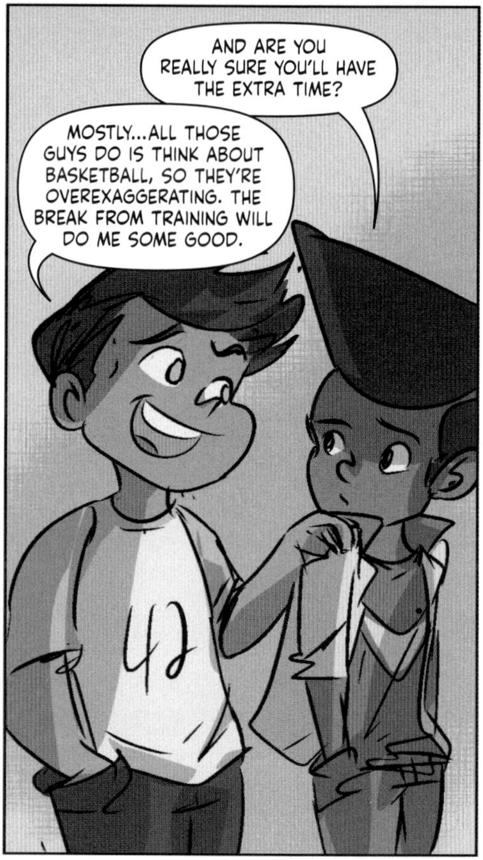
AND ARE YOU REALLY SURE YOU'LL HAVE THE EXTRA TIME?
MOSTLY...ALL THOSE GUYS DO IS THINK ABOUT BASKETBALL, SO THEY'RE OVEREXAGGERATING. THE BREAK FROM TRAINING WILL DO ME SOME GOOD.

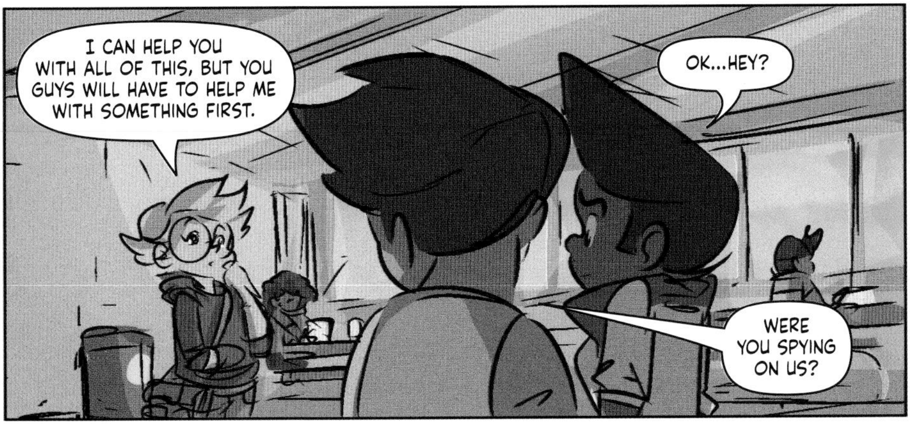
I CAN HELP YOU WITH ALL OF THIS, BUT YOU GUYS WILL HAVE TO HELP ME WITH SOMETHING FIRST.
OK...HEY?
WERE YOU SPYING ON US?

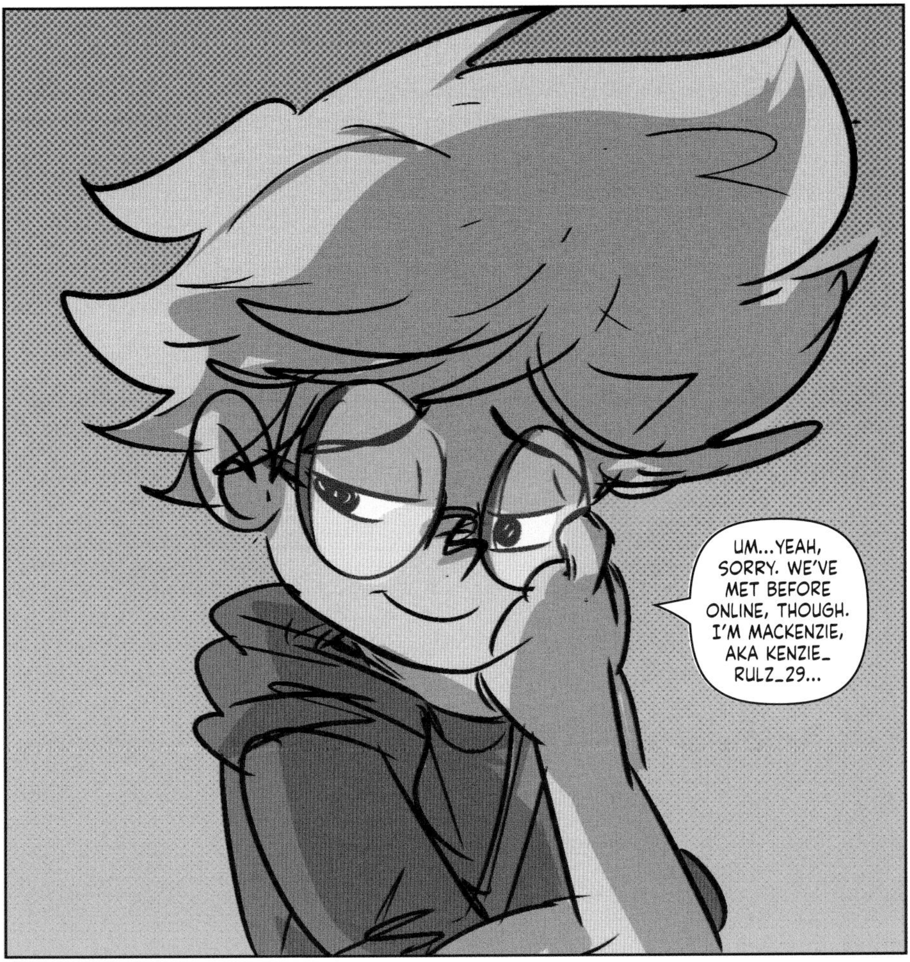
UM...YEAH, SORRY. WE'VE MET BEFORE ONLINE, THOUGH. I'M MACKENZIE, AKA KENZIE_ RULZ_29...

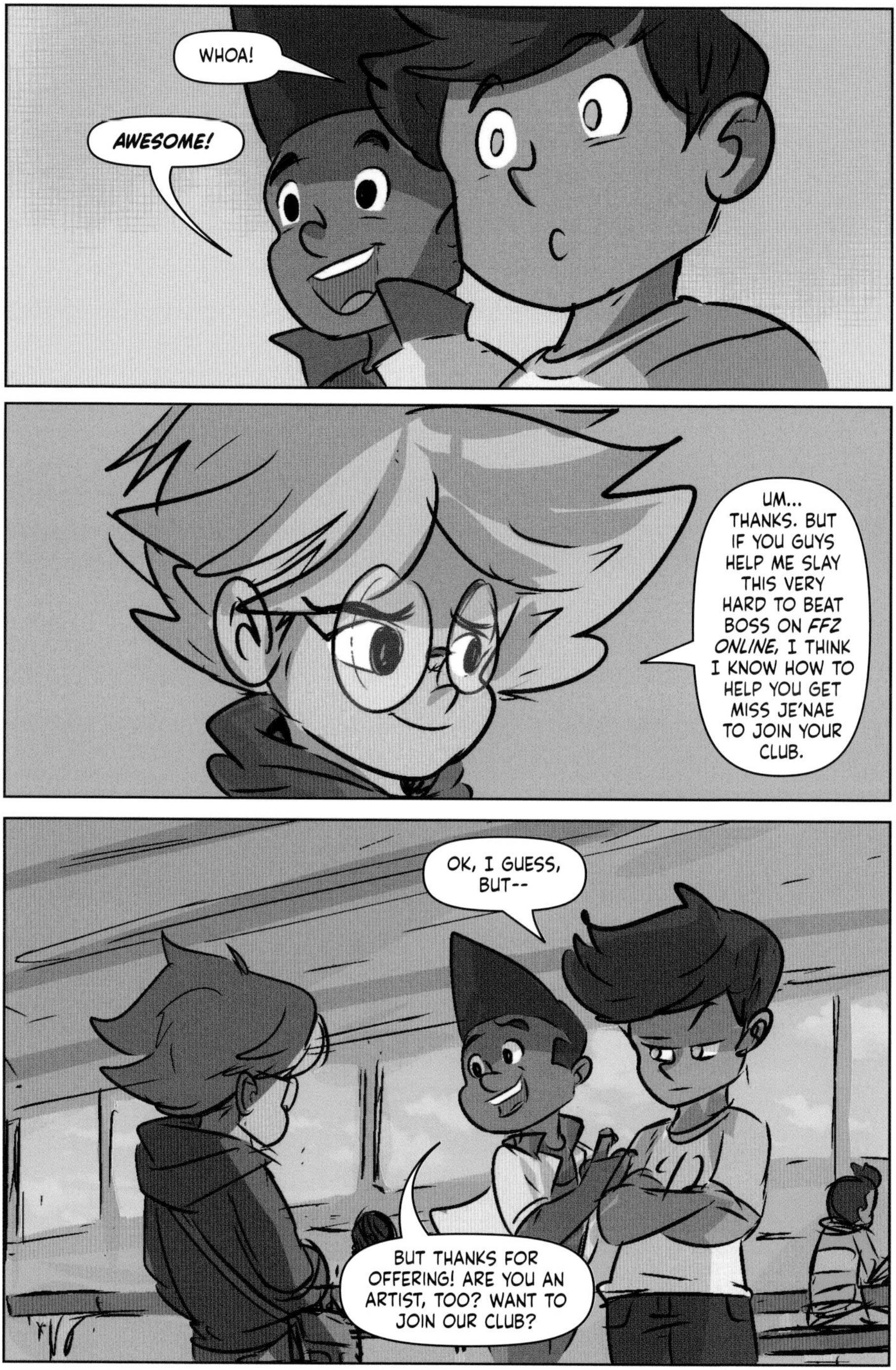
WHOA!
AWESOME!
UM... THANKS. BUT IF YOU GUYS HELP ME SLAY THIS VERY HARD TO BEAT BOSS ON FFZ ONLINE, I THINK I KNOW HOW TO HELP YOU GET MISS JE'NAE TO JOIN YOUR CLUB.
OK, I GUESS, BUT--
BUT THANKS FOR OFFERING! ARE YOU AN ARTIST, TOO? WANT TO JOIN OUR CLUB?

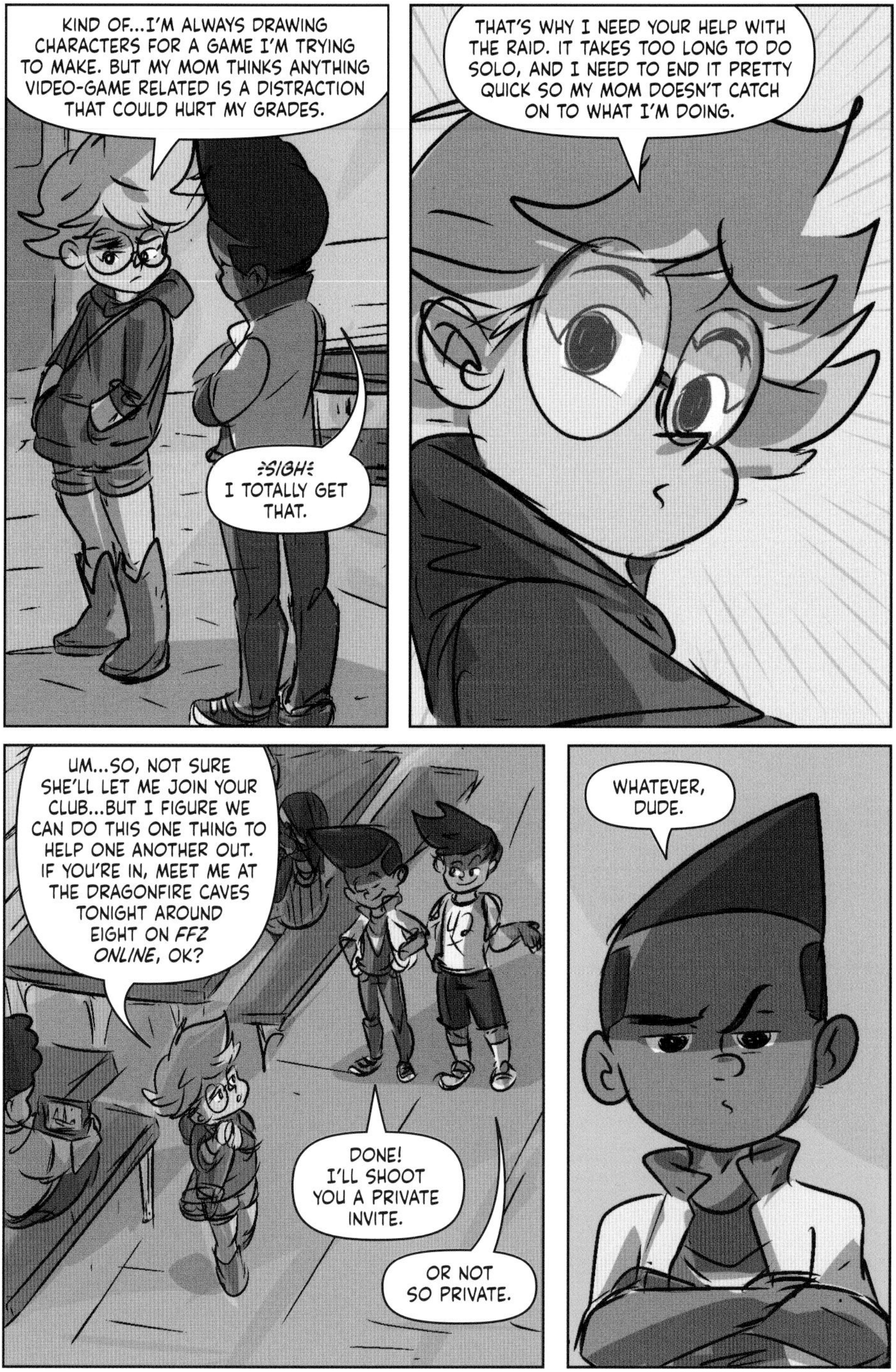
KIND OF...I'M ALWAYS DRAWING CHARACTERS FOR A GAME I'M TRYING TO MAKE. BUT MY MOM THINKS ANYTHING VIDEO-GAME RELATED IS A DISTRACTION THAT COULD HURT MY GRADES.
SIGH
I TOTALLY GET THAT.
THAT'S WHY I NEED YOUR HELP WITH THE RAID. IT TAKES TOO LONG TO DO SOLO, AND I NEED TO END IT PRETTY QUICK SO MY MOM DOESN'T CATCH ON TO WHAT I'M DOING.
UM...SO, NOT SURE SHE'LL LET ME JOIN YOUR CLUB...BUT I FIGURE WE CAN DO THIS ONE THING TO HELP ONE ANOTHER OUT. IF YOU'RE IN, MEET ME AT THE DRAGONFIRE CAVES TONIGHT AROUND EIGHT ON *FFZ ONLINE*, OK?
DONE! I'LL SHOOT YOU A PRIVATE INVITE.
OR NOT SO PRIVATE.
WHATEVER, DUDE.

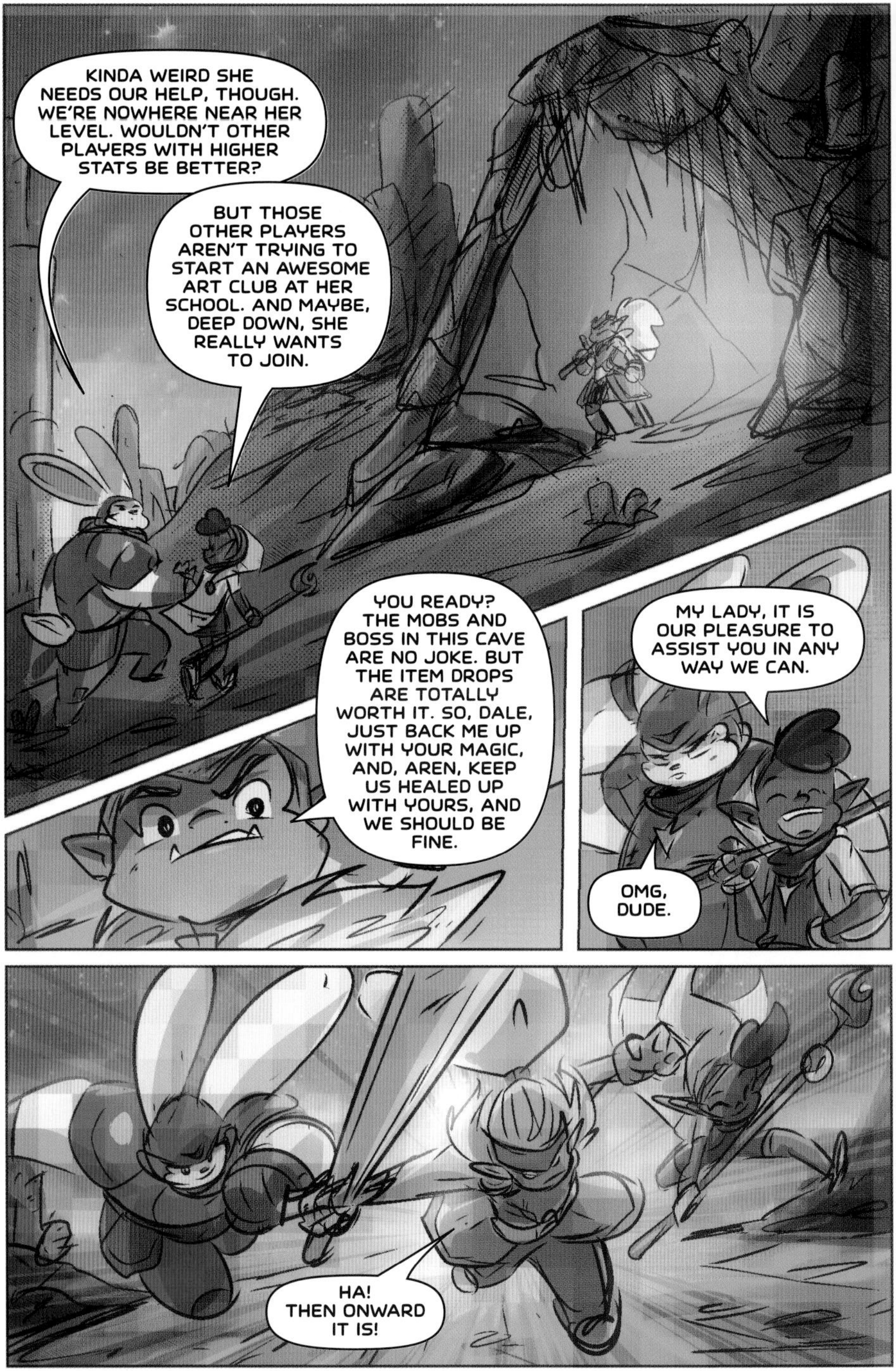
KINDA WEIRD SHE NEEDS OUR HELP, THOUGH. WE'RE NOWHERE NEAR HER LEVEL. WOULDN'T OTHER PLAYERS WITH HIGHER STATS BE BETTER?
BUT THOSE OTHER PLAYERS AREN'T TRYING TO START AN AWESOME ART CLUB AT HER SCHOOL. AND MAYBE, DEEP DOWN, SHE REALLY WANTS TO JOIN.
YOU READY? THE MOBS AND BOSS IN THIS CAVE ARE NO JOKE. BUT THE ITEM DROPS ARE TOTALLY WORTH IT. SO, DALE, JUST BACK ME UP WITH YOUR MAGIC, AND, AREN, KEEP US HEALED UP WITH YOURS, AND WE SHOULD BE FINE.
MY LADY, IT IS OUR PLEASURE TO ASSIST YOU IN ANY WAY WE CAN.
OMG, DUDE.
HA! THEN ONWARD IT IS!

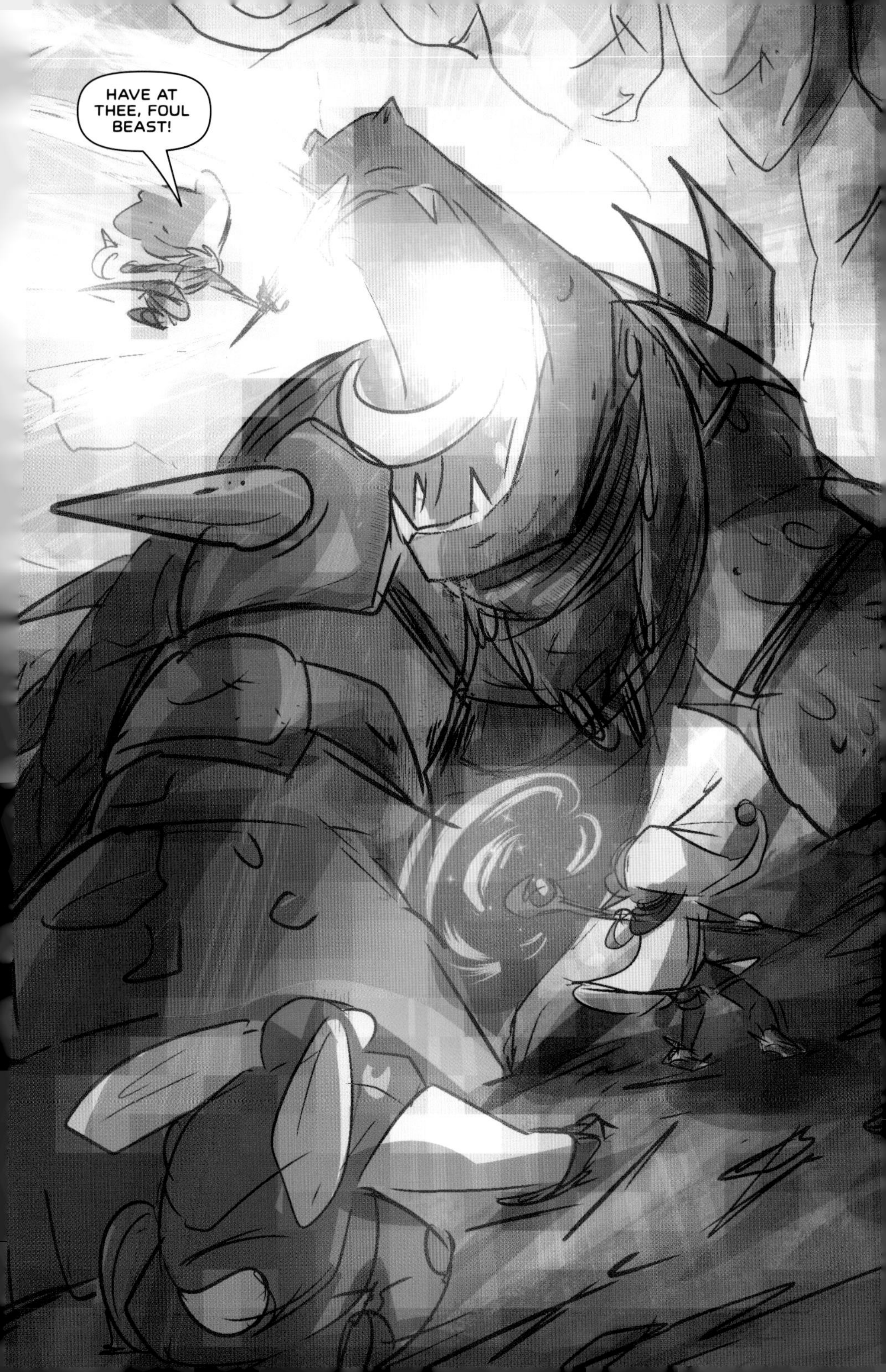
HAVE AT THEE, FOUL BEAST!

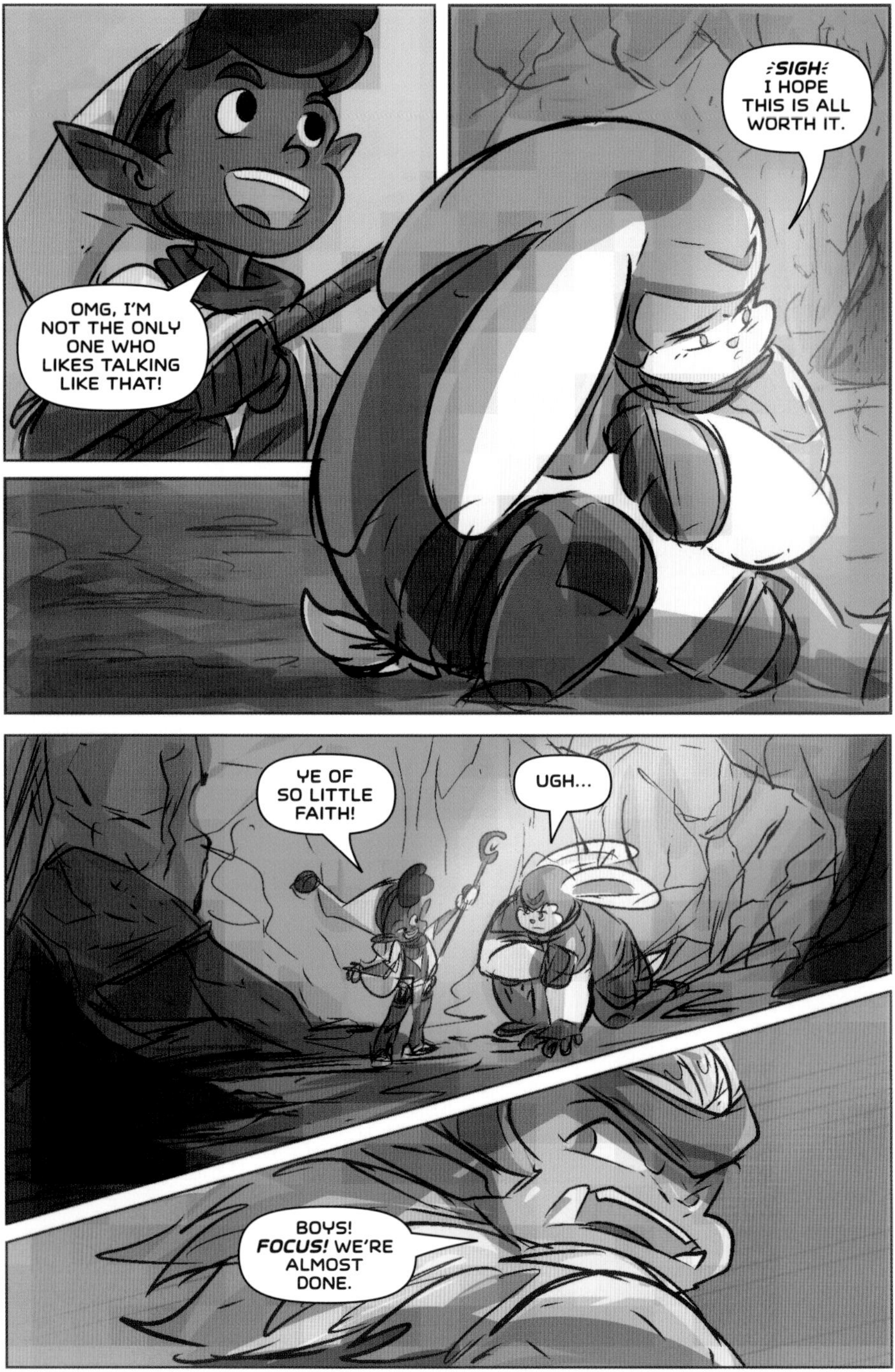
OMG, I'M NOT THE ONLY ONE WHO LIKES TALKING LIKE THAT!
SIGH I HOPE THIS IS ALL WORTH IT.
YE OF SO LITTLE FAITH!
UGH...
BOYS! *FOCUS!* WE'RE ALMOST DONE.

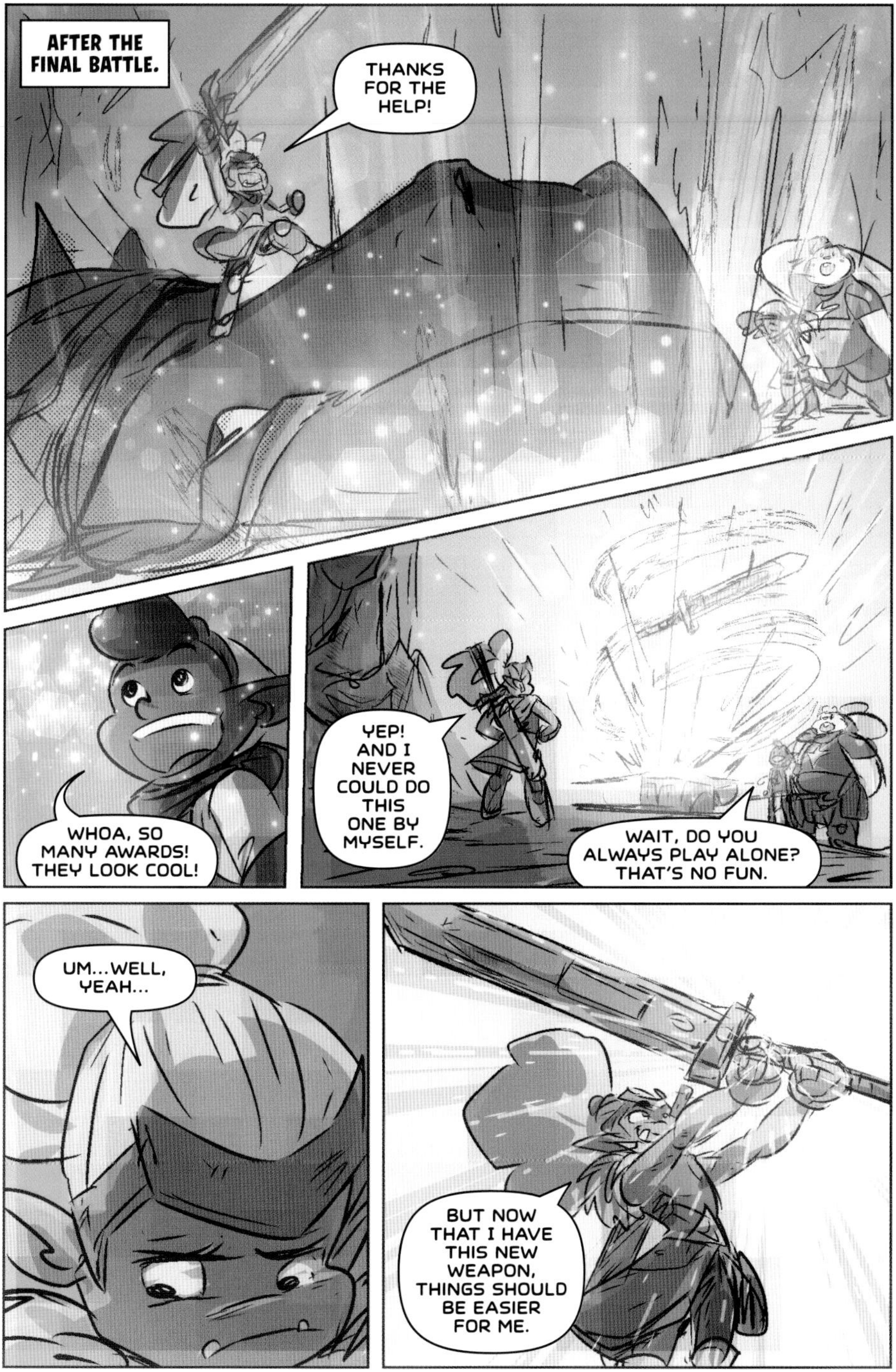
AFTER THE FINAL BATTLE.
THANKS FOR THE HELP!
WHOA, SO MANY AWARDS! THEY LOOK COOL!
YEP! AND I NEVER COULD DO THIS ONE BY MYSELF.
WAIT, DO YOU ALWAYS PLAY ALONE? THAT'S NO FUN.
UM...WELL, YEAH...
BUT NOW THAT I HAVE THIS NEW WEAPON, THINGS SHOULD BE EASIER FOR ME.

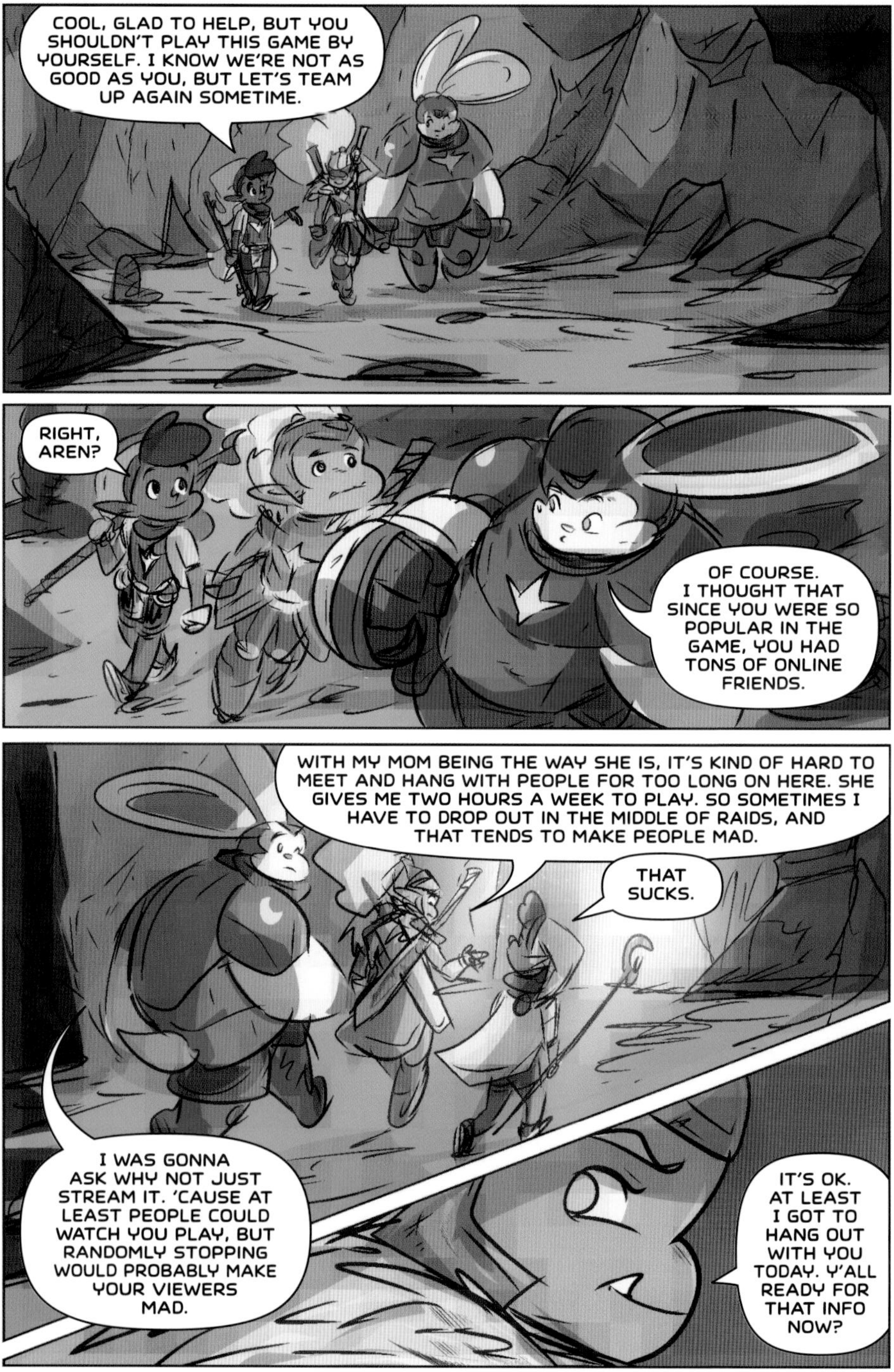
COOL, GLAD TO HELP, BUT YOU SHOULDN'T PLAY THIS GAME BY YOURSELF. I KNOW WE'RE NOT AS GOOD AS YOU, BUT LET'S TEAM UP AGAIN SOMETIME.
RIGHT, AREN?
OF COURSE. I THOUGHT THAT SINCE YOU WERE SO POPULAR IN THE GAME, YOU HAD TONS OF ONLINE FRIENDS.
WITH MY MOM BEING THE WAY SHE IS, IT'S KIND OF HARD TO MEET AND HANG WITH PEOPLE FOR TOO LONG ON HERE. SHE GIVES ME TWO HOURS A WEEK TO PLAY. SO SOMETIMES I HAVE TO DROP OUT IN THE MIDDLE OF RAIDS, AND THAT TENDS TO MAKE PEOPLE MAD.
THAT SUCKS.
I WAS GONNA ASK WHY NOT JUST STREAM IT. 'CAUSE AT LEAST PEOPLE COULD WATCH YOU PLAY, BUT RANDOMLY STOPPING WOULD PROBABLY MAKE YOUR VIEWERS MAD.
IT'S OK. AT LEAST I GOT TO HANG OUT WITH YOU TODAY. Y'ALL READY FOR THAT INFO NOW?

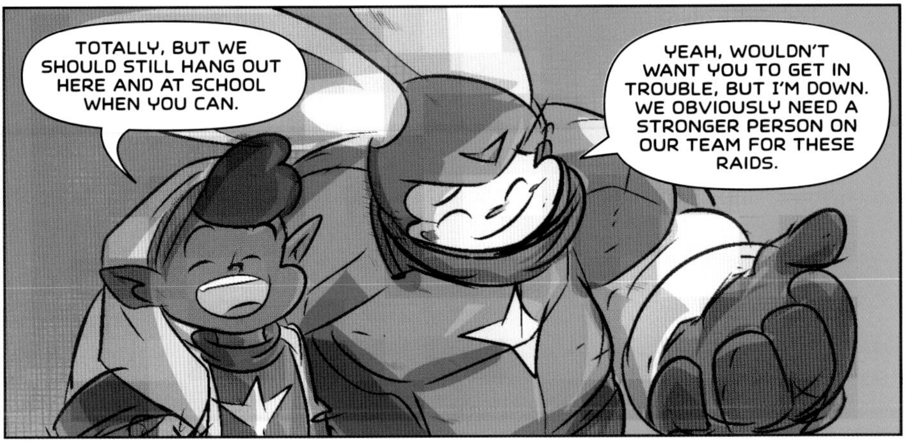
TOTALLY, BUT WE SHOULD STILL HANG OUT HERE AND AT SCHOOL WHEN YOU CAN.
YEAH, WOULDN'T WANT YOU TO GET IN TROUBLE, BUT I'M DOWN. WE OBVIOUSLY NEED A STRONGER PERSON ON OUR TEAM FOR THESE RAIDS.

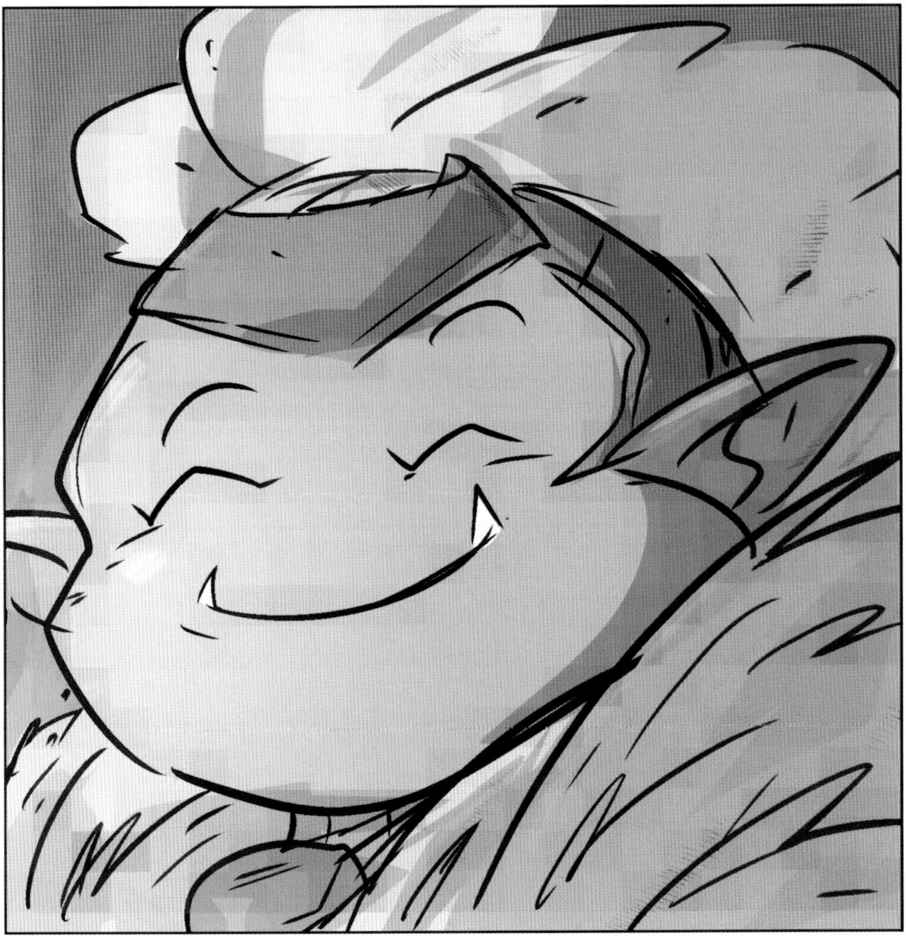

COOL. SO, WHILE DOING MY RESEARCH ON YOU GUYS--

YOU MEAN SPYING.

HA! YEAH, SORRY ABOUT THAT.

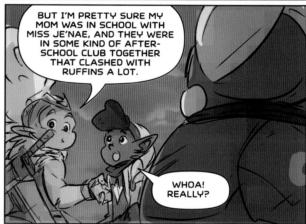

BUT I'M PRETTY SURE MY MOM WAS IN SCHOOL WITH MISS JE'NAE, AND THEY WERE IN SOME KIND OF AFTER-SCHOOL CLUB TOGETHER THAT CLASHED WITH RUFFINS A LOT.

WHOA! REALLY?

FIGURE IF I CAN GET HER TO TELL ME MORE DETAILS, YOU MIGHT BE ABLE TO USE THEM TO CONVINCE JE'NAE TO HELP.

LOVE IT!

DOES THAT MEAN YOU'VE MADE UP YOUR MIND ABOUT JOINING OUR CLUB?

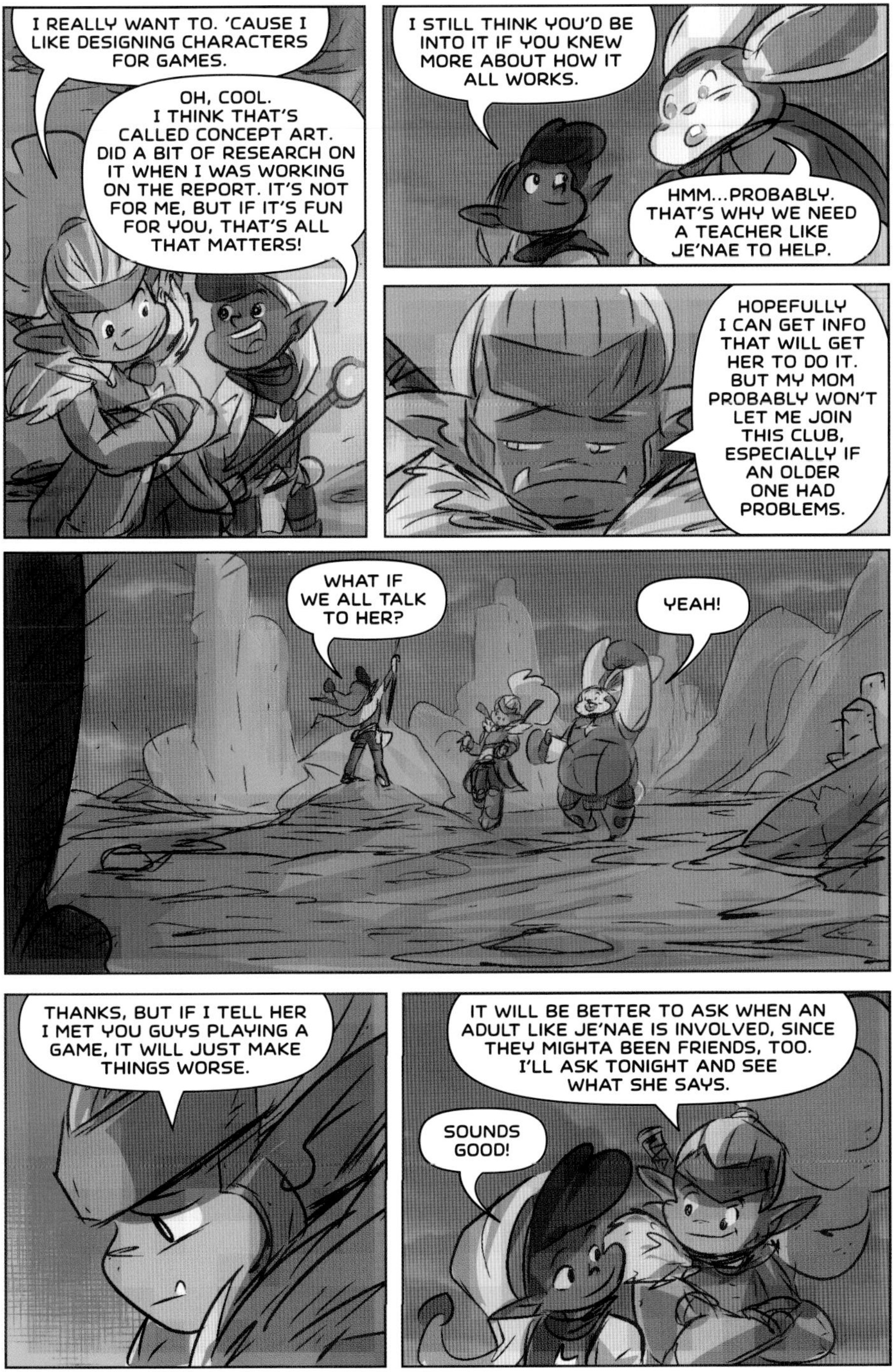
I REALLY WANT TO. 'CAUSE I LIKE DESIGNING CHARACTERS FOR GAMES.
OH, COOL. I THINK THAT'S CALLED CONCEPT ART. DID A BIT OF RESEARCH ON IT WHEN I WAS WORKING ON THE REPORT. IT'S NOT FOR ME, BUT IF IT'S FUN FOR YOU, THAT'S ALL THAT MATTERS!
I STILL THINK YOU'D BE INTO IT IF YOU KNEW MORE ABOUT HOW IT ALL WORKS.
HMM...PROBABLY. THAT'S WHY WE NEED A TEACHER LIKE JE'NAE TO HELP.
HOPEFULLY I CAN GET INFO THAT WILL GET HER TO DO IT. BUT MY MOM PROBABLY WON'T LET ME JOIN THIS CLUB, ESPECIALLY IF AN OLDER ONE HAD PROBLEMS.
WHAT IF WE ALL TALK TO HER?
YEAH!
THANKS, BUT IF I TELL HER I MET YOU GUYS PLAYING A GAME, IT WILL JUST MAKE THINGS WORSE.
IT WILL BE BETTER TO ASK WHEN AN ADULT LIKE JE'NAE IS INVOLVED, SINCE THEY MIGHTA BEEN FRIENDS, TOO. I'LL ASK TONIGHT AND SEE WHAT SHE SAYS.
SOUNDS GOOD!

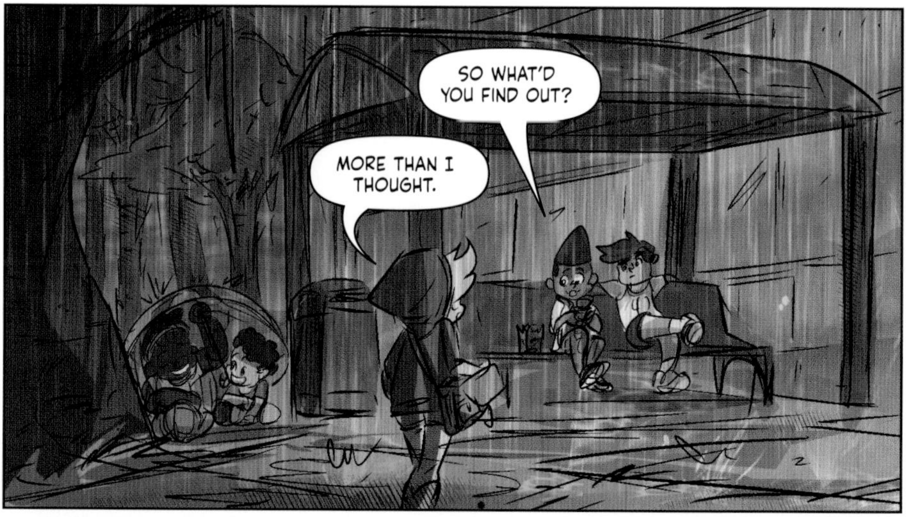
SO WHAT'D YOU FIND OUT?
MORE THAN I THOUGHT.

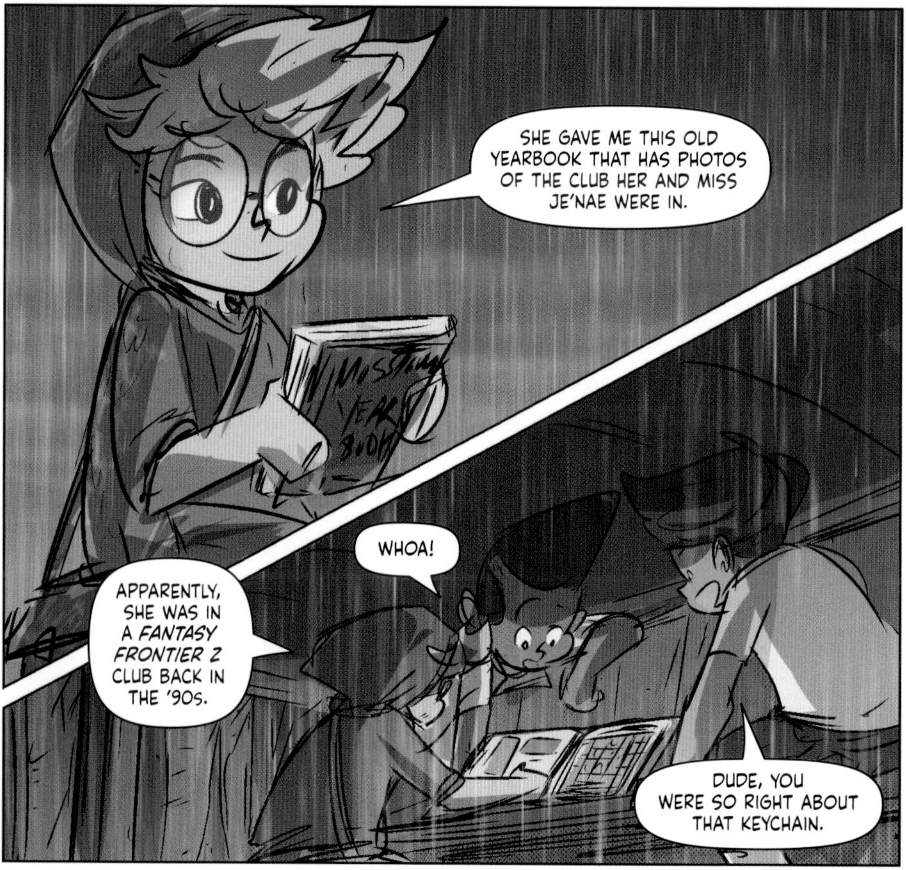
SHE GAVE ME THIS OLD YEARBOOK THAT HAS PHOTOS OF THE CLUB HER AND MISS JE'NAE WERE IN.
APPARENTLY, SHE WAS IN A *FANTASY FRONTIER Z* CLUB BACK IN THE '90s.
WHOA!
DUDE, YOU WERE SO RIGHT ABOUT THAT KEYCHAIN.

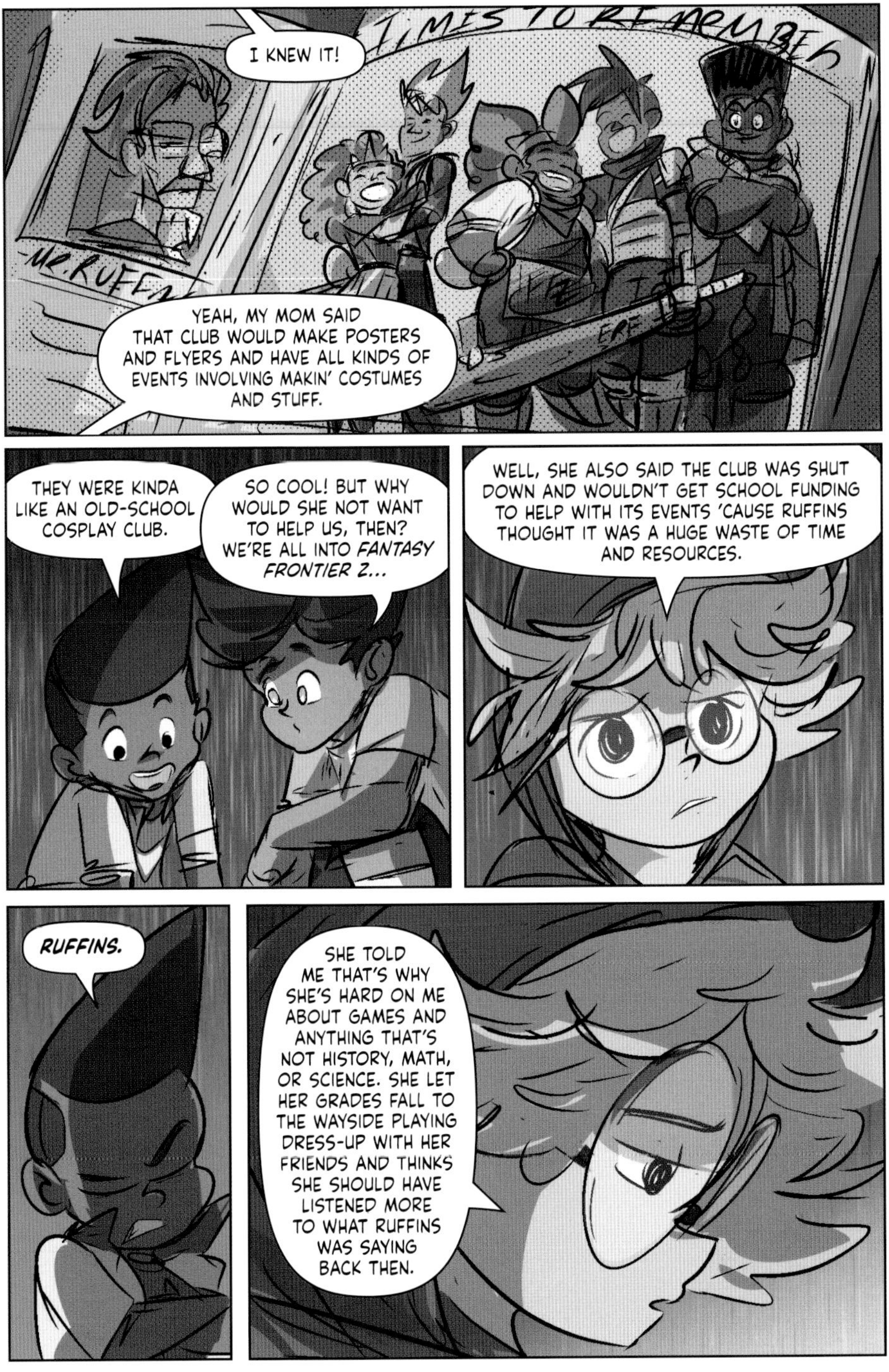
TIMES TO REMEMBER
I KNEW IT!
MR. RUFFINS
YEAH, MY MOM SAID THAT CLUB WOULD MAKE POSTERS AND FLYERS AND HAVE ALL KINDS OF EVENTS INVOLVING MAKIN' COSTUMES AND STUFF.
THEY WERE KINDA LIKE AN OLD-SCHOOL COSPLAY CLUB.
SO COOL! BUT WHY WOULD SHE NOT WANT TO HELP US, THEN? WE'RE ALL INTO *FANTASY FRONTIER 2*...
WELL, SHE ALSO SAID THE CLUB WAS SHUT DOWN AND WOULDN'T GET SCHOOL FUNDING TO HELP WITH ITS EVENTS 'CAUSE RUFFINS THOUGHT IT WAS A HUGE WASTE OF TIME AND RESOURCES.
RUFFINS.
SHE TOLD ME THAT'S WHY SHE'S HARD ON ME ABOUT GAMES AND ANYTHING THAT'S NOT HISTORY, MATH, OR SCIENCE. SHE LET HER GRADES FALL TO THE WAYSIDE PLAYING DRESS-UP WITH HER FRIENDS AND THINKS SHE SHOULD HAVE LISTENED MORE TO WHAT RUFFINS WAS SAYING BACK THEN.

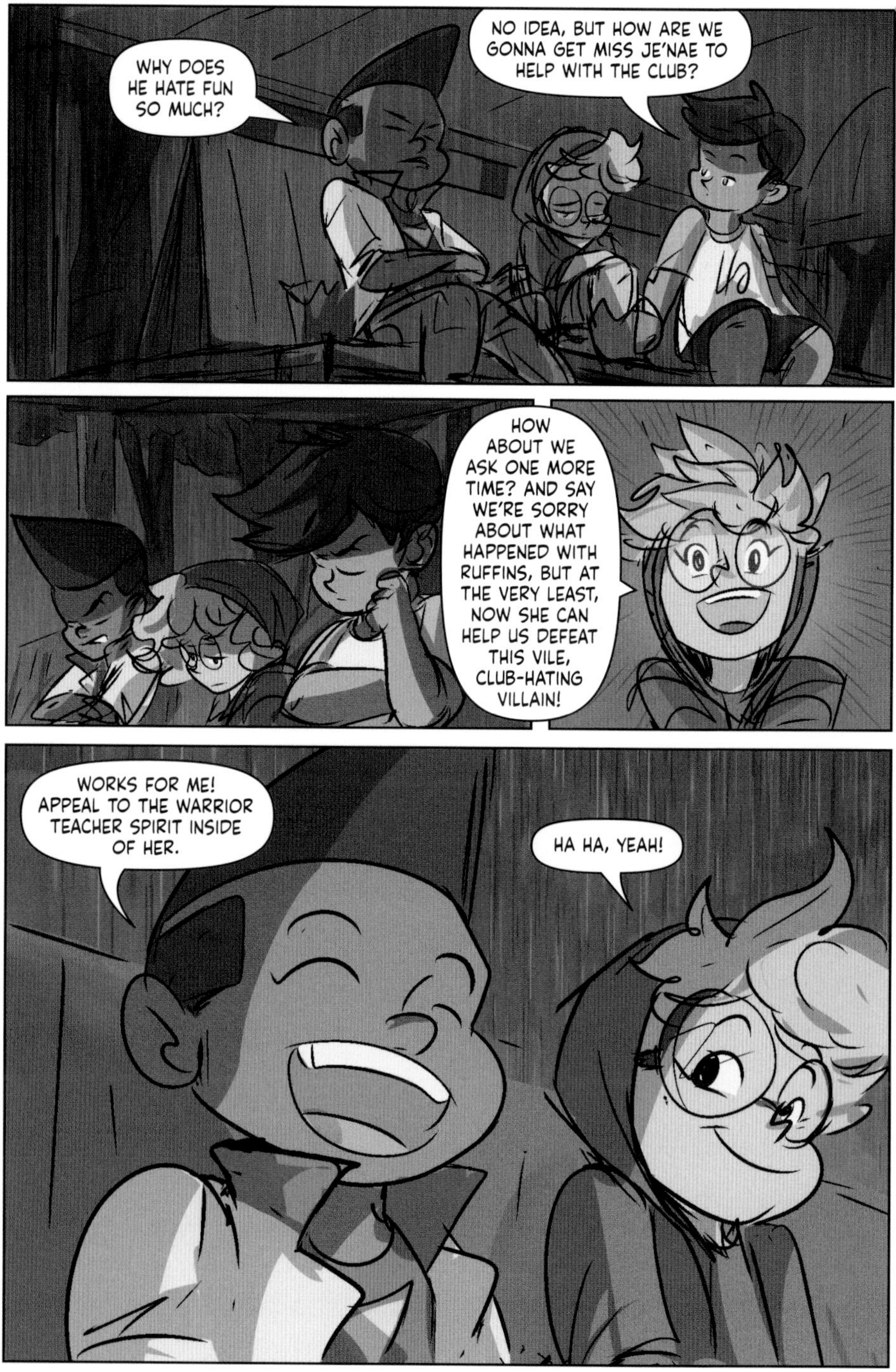

WHY DOES HE HATE FUN SO MUCH?
NO IDEA, BUT HOW ARE WE GONNA GET MISS JE'NAE TO HELP WITH THE CLUB?
HOW ABOUT WE ASK ONE MORE TIME? AND SAY WE'RE SORRY ABOUT WHAT HAPPENED WITH RUFFINS, BUT AT THE VERY LEAST, NOW SHE CAN HELP US DEFEAT THIS VILE, CLUB-HATING VILLAIN!
WORKS FOR ME! APPEAL TO THE WARRIOR TEACHER SPIRIT INSIDE OF HER.
HA HA, YEAH!

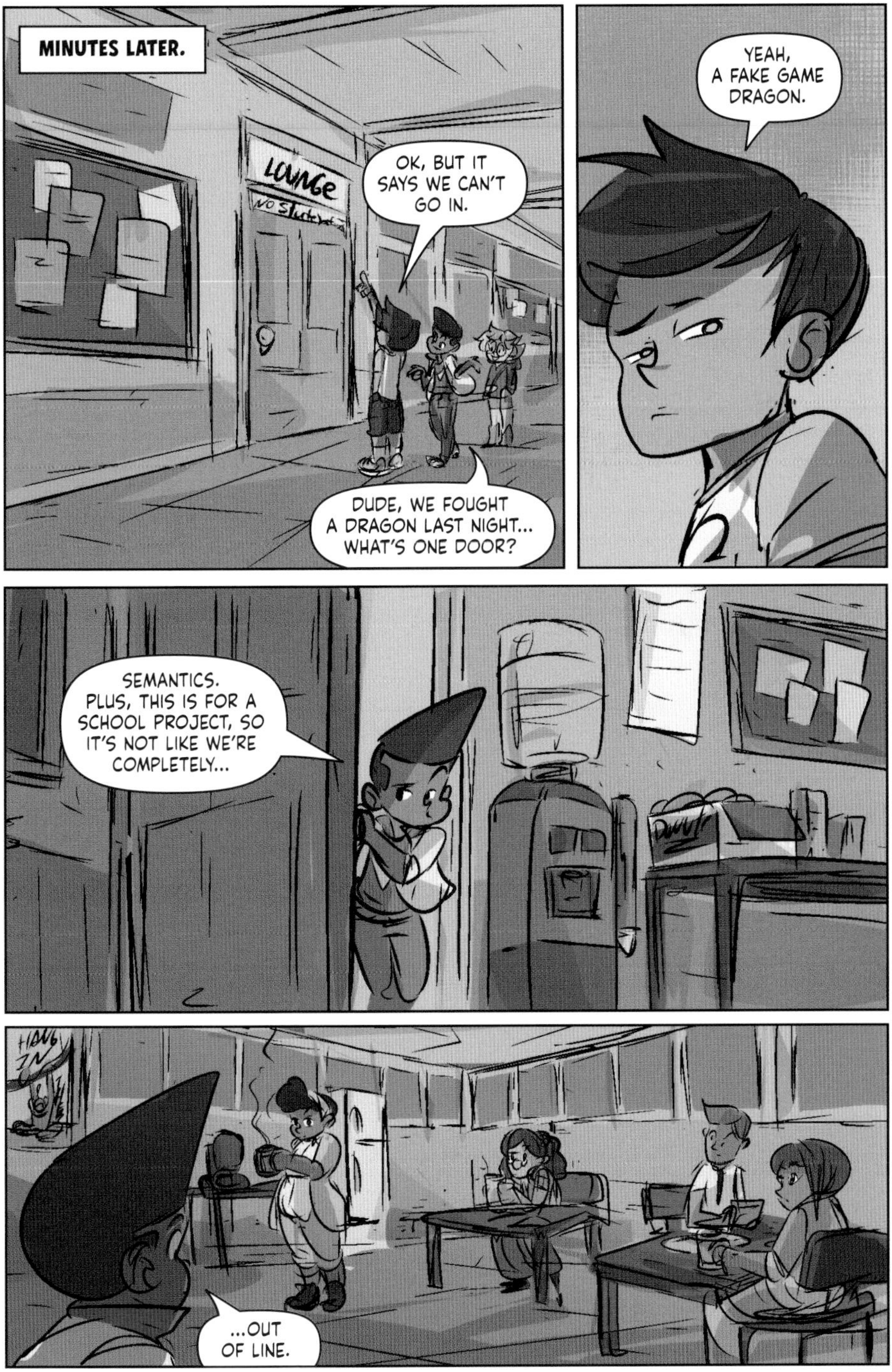
MINUTES LATER.
LOUNGE
OK, BUT IT SAYS WE CAN'T GO IN.
DUDE, WE FOUGHT A DRAGON LAST NIGHT... WHAT'S ONE DOOR?
YEAH, A FAKE GAME DRAGON.
SEMANTICS. PLUS, THIS IS FOR A SCHOOL PROJECT, SO IT'S NOT LIKE WE'RE COMPLETELY...
...OUT OF LINE.

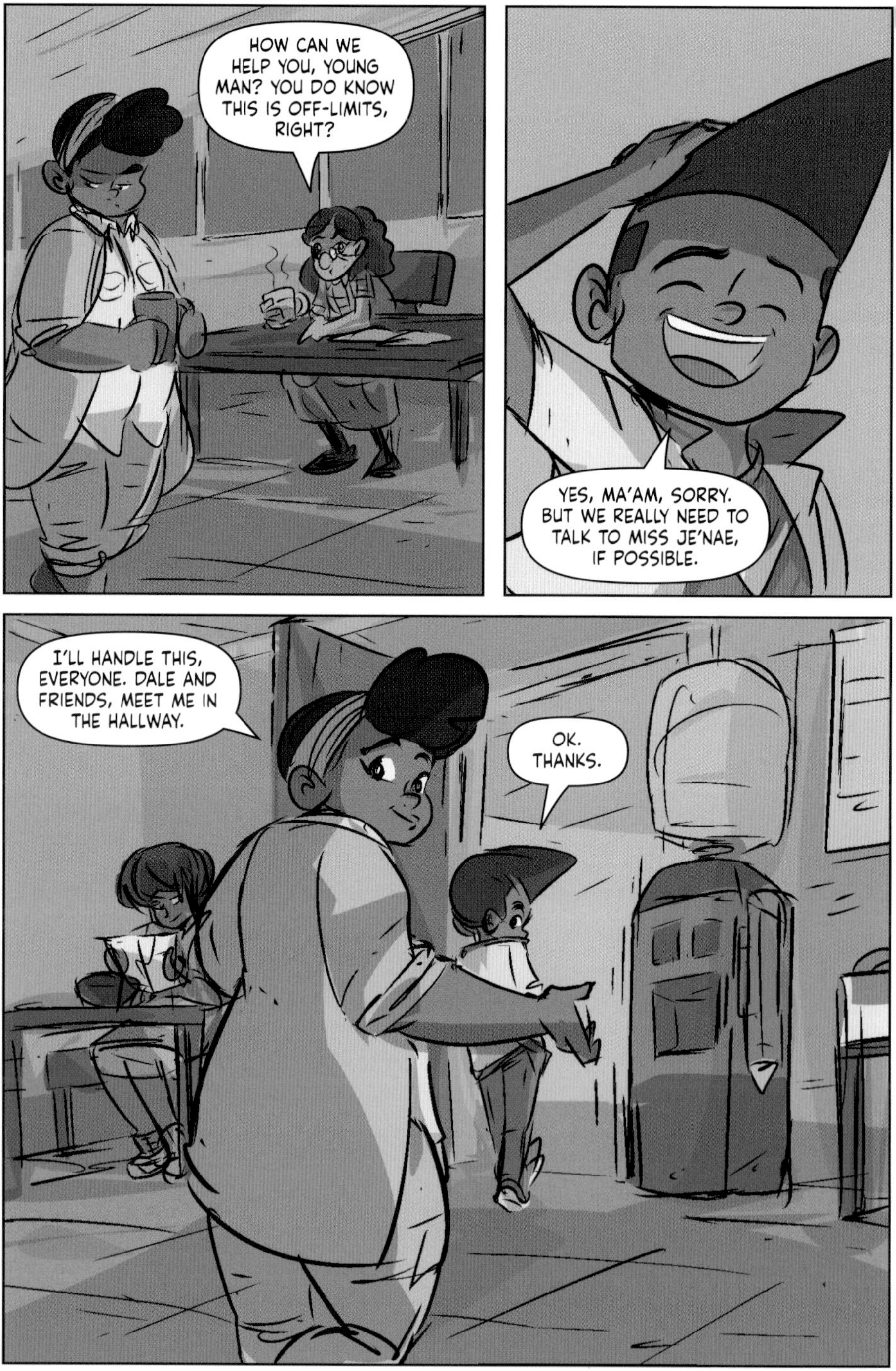
HOW CAN WE HELP YOU, YOUNG MAN? YOU DO KNOW THIS IS OFF-LIMITS, RIGHT?
YES, MA'AM, SORRY. BUT WE REALLY NEED TO TALK TO MISS JE'NAE, IF POSSIBLE.
I'LL HANDLE THIS, EVERYONE. DALE AND FRIENDS, MEET ME IN THE HALLWAY.
OK. THANKS.

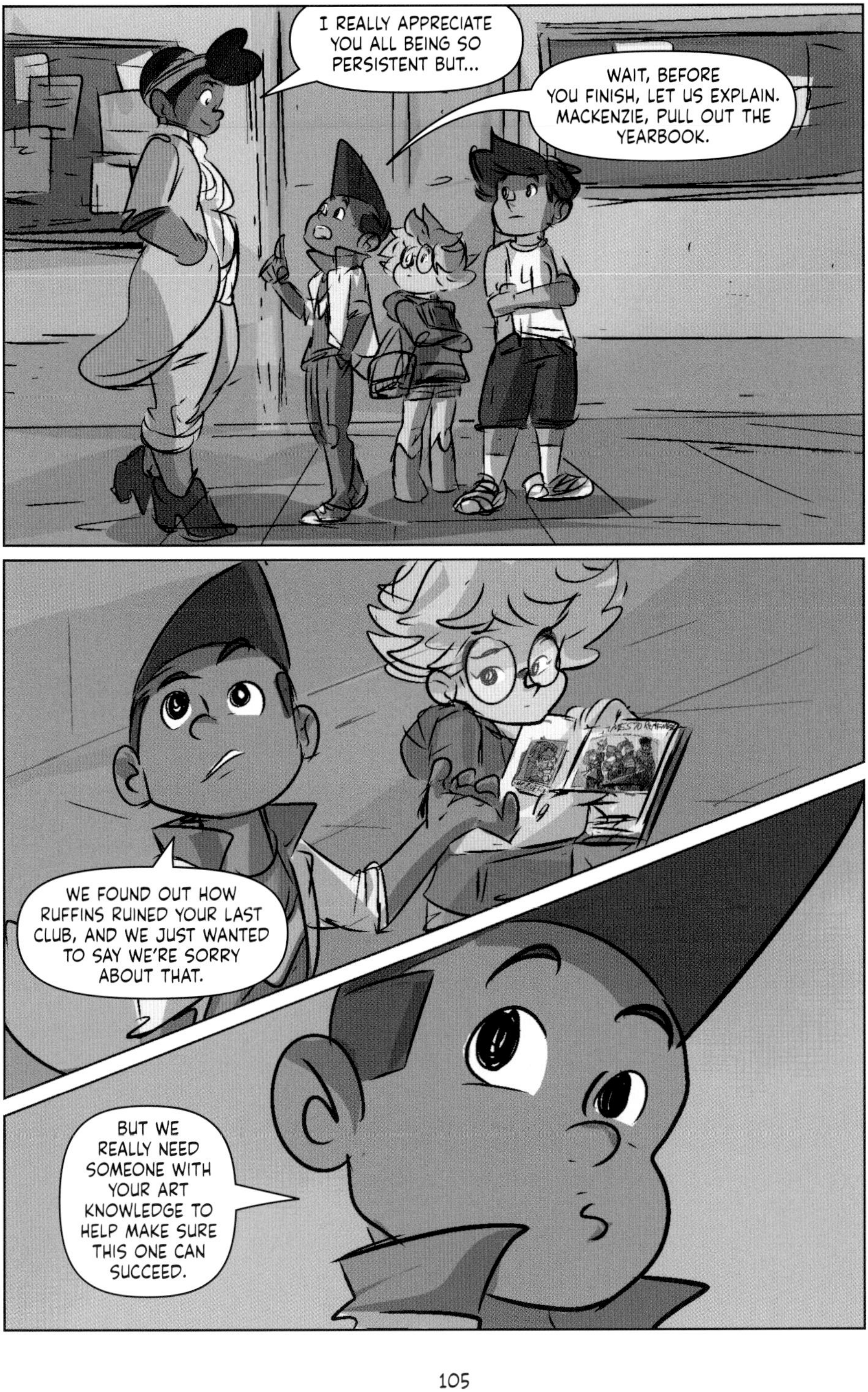
I REALLY APPRECIATE YOU ALL BEING SO PERSISTENT BUT...
WAIT, BEFORE YOU FINISH, LET US EXPLAIN. MACKENZIE, PULL OUT THE YEARBOOK.
WE FOUND OUT HOW RUFFINS RUINED YOUR LAST CLUB, AND WE JUST WANTED TO SAY WE'RE SORRY ABOUT THAT.
BUT WE REALLY NEED SOMEONE WITH YOUR ART KNOWLEDGE TO HELP MAKE SURE THIS ONE CAN SUCCEED.

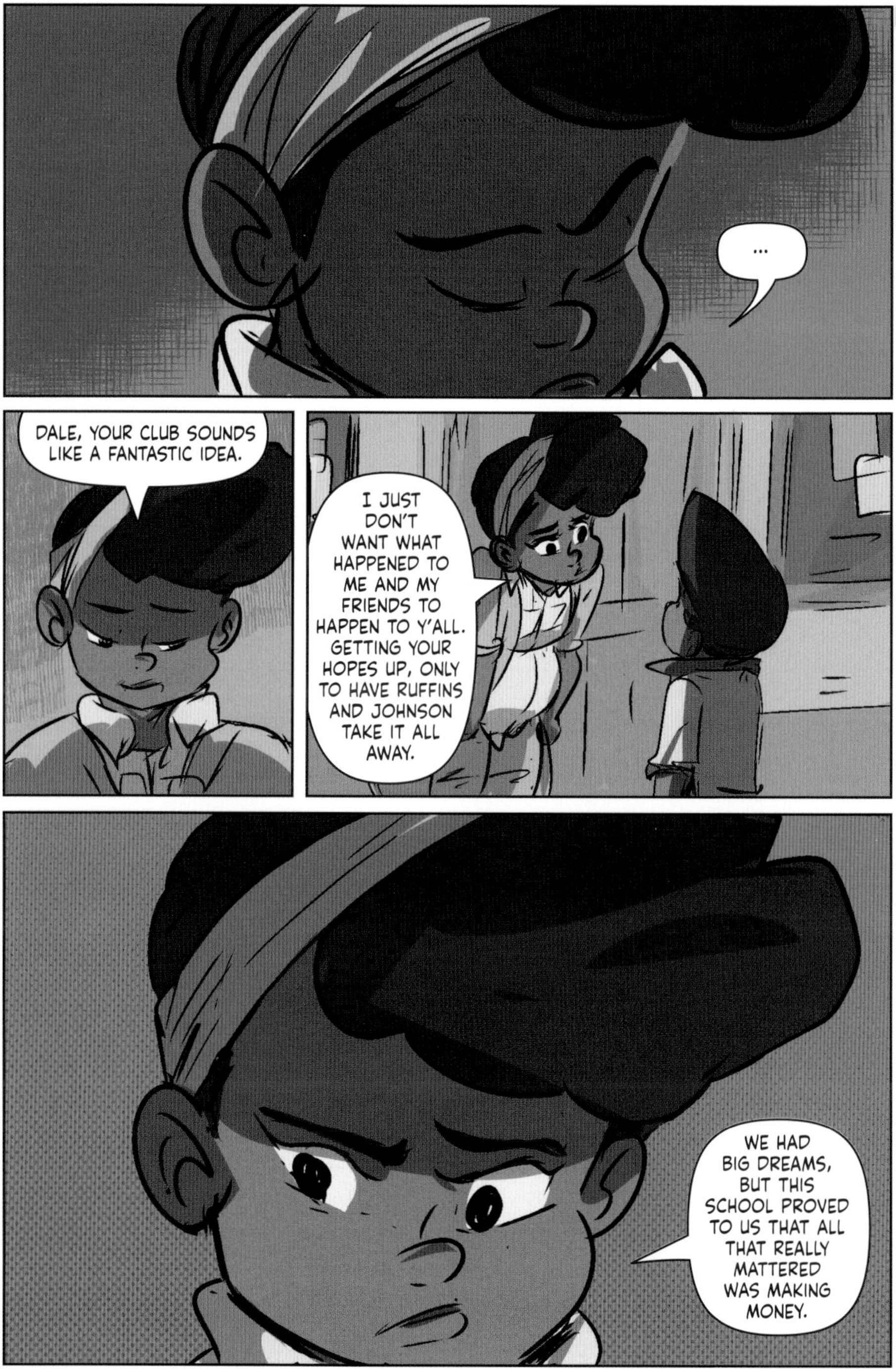
...
DALE, YOUR CLUB SOUNDS LIKE A FANTASTIC IDEA.
I JUST DON'T WANT WHAT HAPPENED TO ME AND MY FRIENDS TO HAPPEN TO Y'ALL. GETTING YOUR HOPES UP, ONLY TO HAVE RUFFINS AND JOHNSON TAKE IT ALL AWAY.
WE HAD BIG DREAMS, BUT THIS SCHOOL PROVED TO US THAT ALL THAT REALLY MATTERED WAS MAKING MONEY.

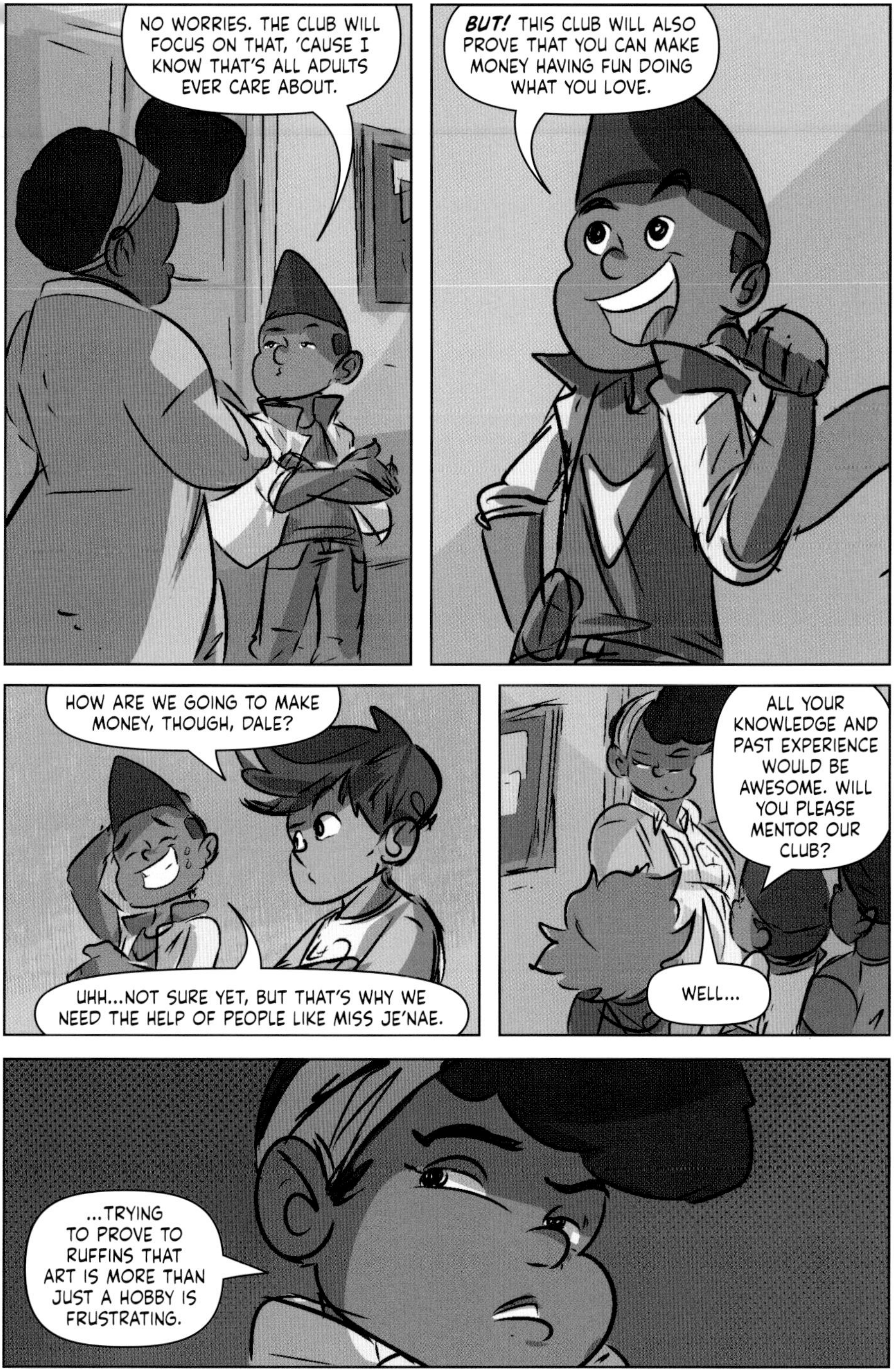
NO WORRIES. THE CLUB WILL FOCUS ON THAT, 'CAUSE I KNOW THAT'S ALL ADULTS EVER CARE ABOUT.
BUT! THIS CLUB WILL ALSO PROVE THAT YOU CAN MAKE MONEY HAVING FUN DOING WHAT YOU LOVE.
HOW ARE WE GOING TO MAKE MONEY, THOUGH, DALE?
UHH...NOT SURE YET, BUT THAT'S WHY WE NEED THE HELP OF PEOPLE LIKE MISS JE'NAE.
ALL YOUR KNOWLEDGE AND PAST EXPERIENCE WOULD BE AWESOME. WILL YOU PLEASE MENTOR OUR CLUB?
WELL...
...TRYING TO PROVE TO RUFFINS THAT ART IS MORE THAN JUST A HOBBY IS FRUSTRATING.

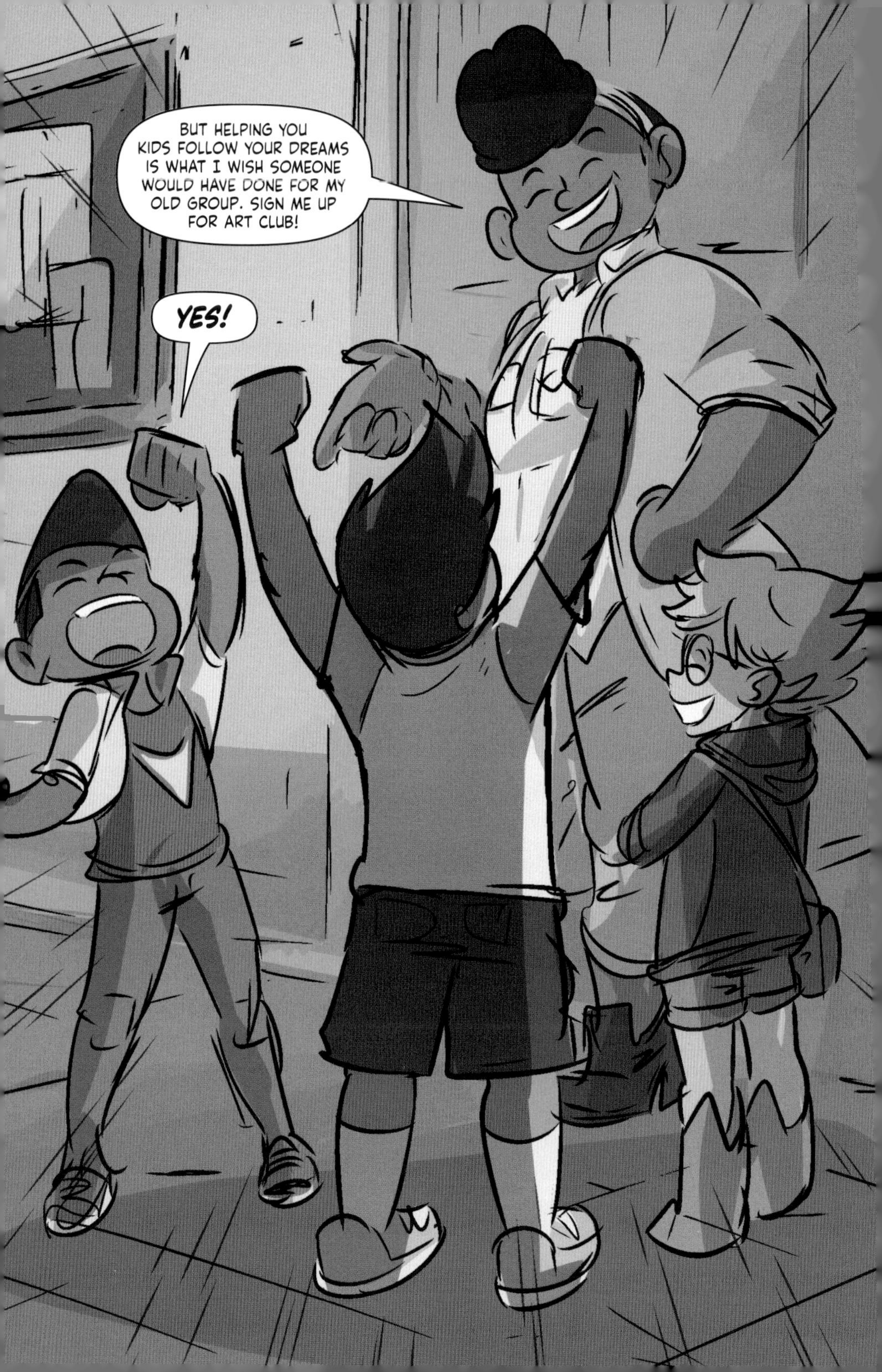
BUT HELPING YOU KIDS FOLLOW YOUR DREAMS IS WHAT I WISH SOMEONE WOULD HAVE DONE FOR MY OLD GROUP. SIGN ME UP FOR ART CLUB!
YES!

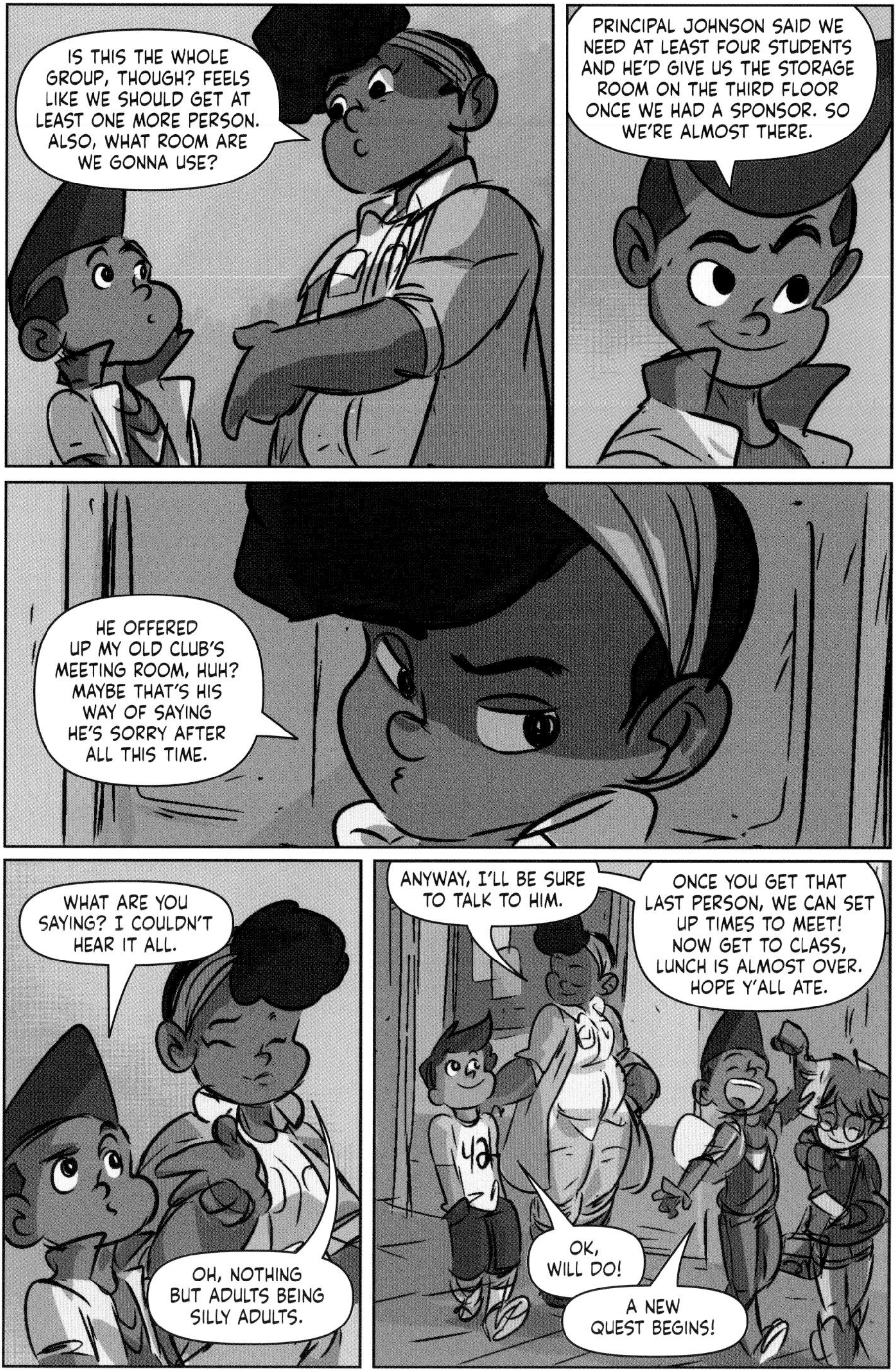
IS THIS THE WHOLE GROUP, THOUGH? FEELS LIKE WE SHOULD GET AT LEAST ONE MORE PERSON. ALSO, WHAT ROOM ARE WE GONNA USE?
PRINCIPAL JOHNSON SAID WE NEED AT LEAST FOUR STUDENTS AND HE'D GIVE US THE STORAGE ROOM ON THE THIRD FLOOR ONCE WE HAD A SPONSOR. SO WE'RE ALMOST THERE.
HE OFFERED UP MY OLD CLUB'S MEETING ROOM, HUH? MAYBE THAT'S HIS WAY OF SAYING HE'S SORRY AFTER ALL THIS TIME.
WHAT ARE YOU SAYING? I COULDN'T HEAR IT ALL.
OH, NOTHING BUT ADULTS BEING SILLY ADULTS.
ANYWAY, I'LL BE SURE TO TALK TO HIM.
ONCE YOU GET THAT LAST PERSON, WE CAN SET UP TIMES TO MEET! NOW GET TO CLASS, LUNCH IS ALMOST OVER. HOPE Y'ALL ATE.
OK, WILL DO!
A NEW QUEST BEGINS!
42

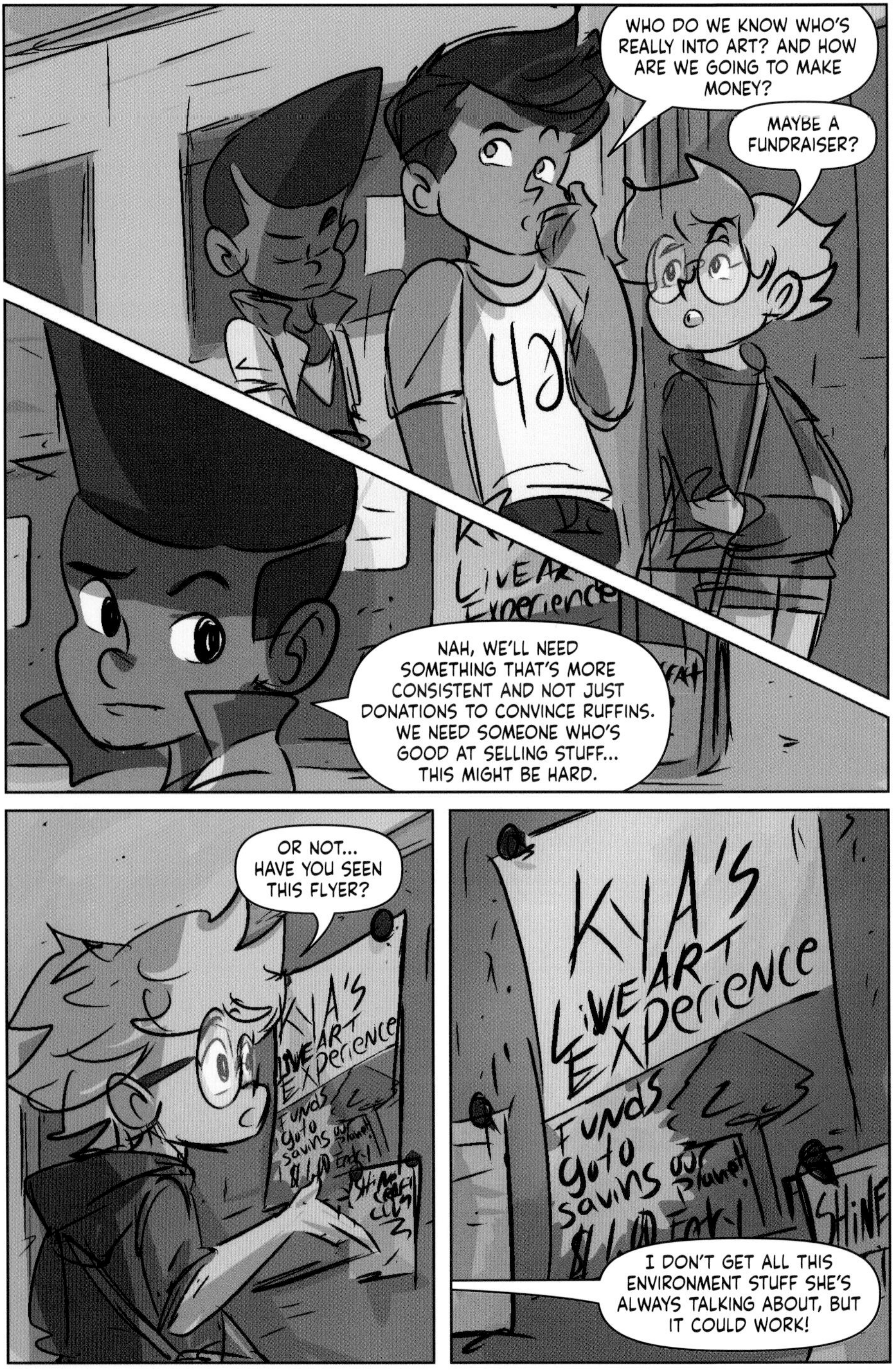
WHO DO WE KNOW WHO'S REALLY INTO ART? AND HOW ARE WE GOING TO MAKE MONEY?
MAYBE A FUNDRAISER?
NAH, WE'LL NEED SOMETHING THAT'S MORE CONSISTENT AND NOT JUST DONATIONS TO CONVINCE RUFFINS. WE NEED SOMEONE WHO'S GOOD AT SELLING STUFF... THIS MIGHT BE HARD.
OR NOT... HAVE YOU SEEN THIS FLYER?
KYA'S LIVE ART EXPERIENCE
I DON'T GET ALL THIS ENVIRONMENT STUFF SHE'S ALWAYS TALKING ABOUT, BUT IT COULD WORK!

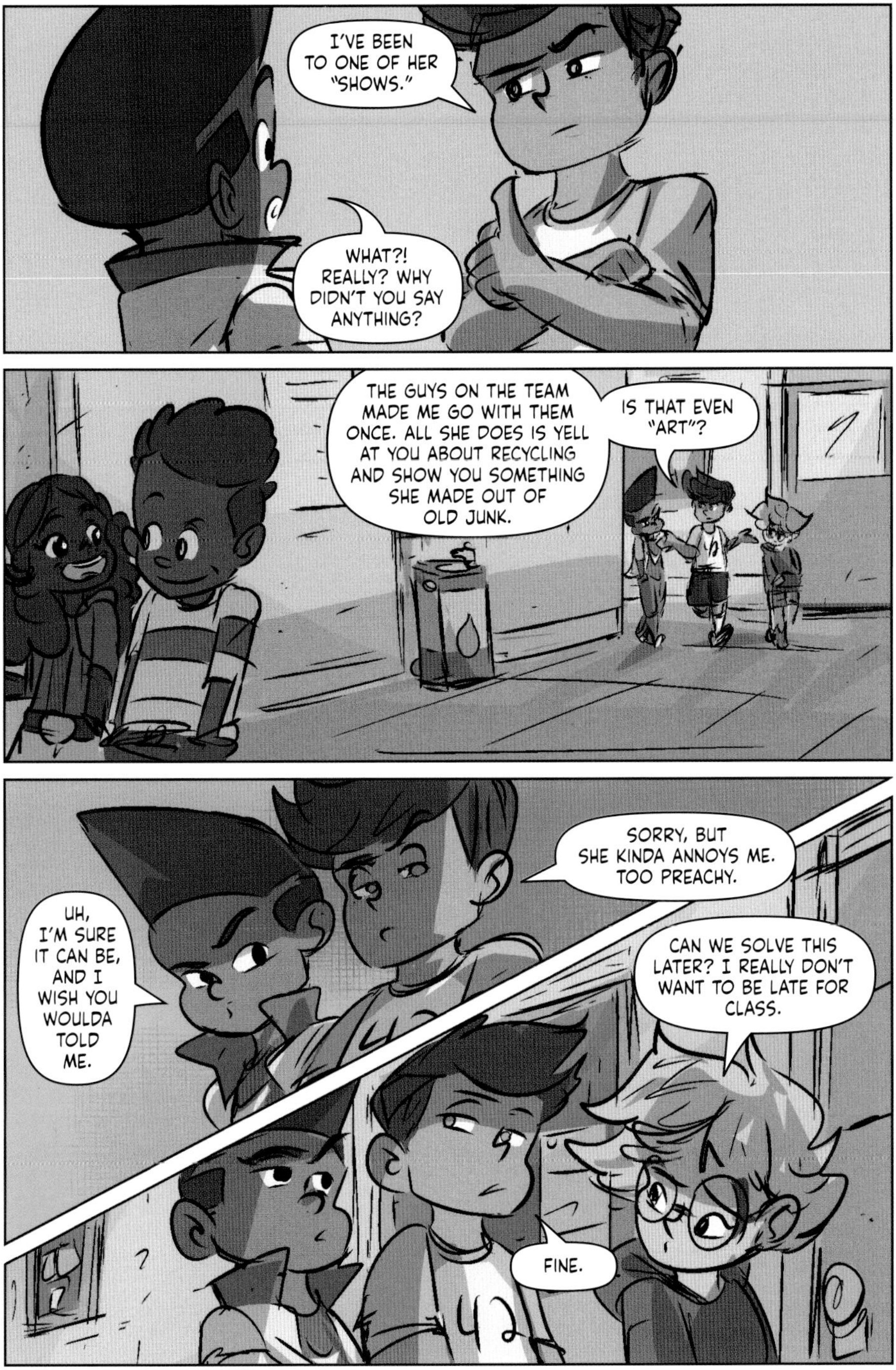
I'VE BEEN TO ONE OF HER "SHOWS."
WHAT?! REALLY? WHY DIDN'T YOU SAY ANYTHING?
THE GUYS ON THE TEAM MADE ME GO WITH THEM ONCE. ALL SHE DOES IS YELL AT YOU ABOUT RECYCLING AND SHOW YOU SOMETHING SHE MADE OUT OF OLD JUNK.
IS THAT EVEN "ART"?
UH, I'M SURE IT CAN BE, AND I WISH YOU WOULDA TOLD ME.
SORRY, BUT SHE KINDA ANNOYS ME. TOO PREACHY.
CAN WE SOLVE THIS LATER? I REALLY DON'T WANT TO BE LATE FOR CLASS.
FINE.

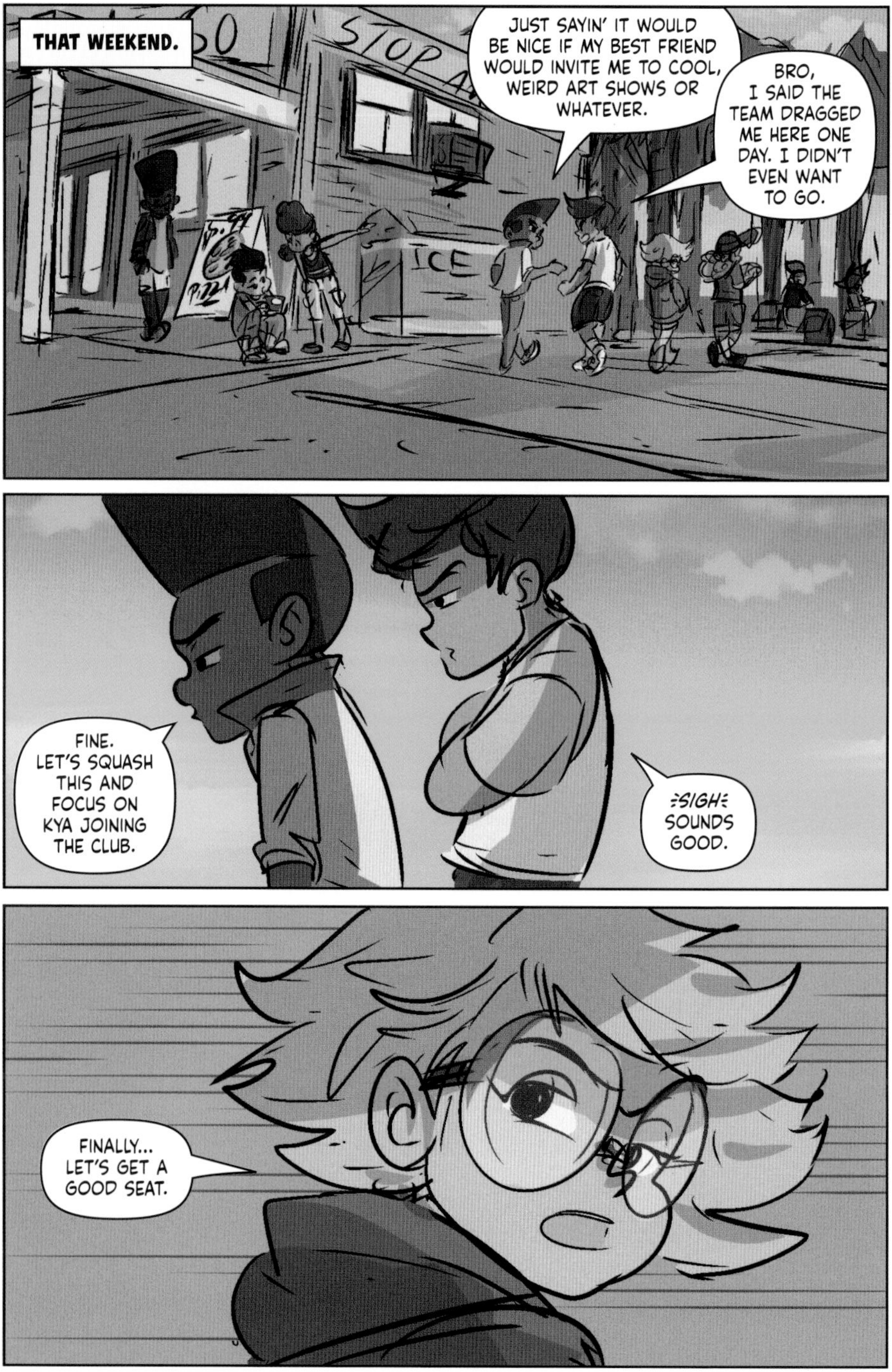
THAT WEEKEND.
JUST SAYIN' IT WOULD BE NICE IF MY BEST FRIEND WOULD INVITE ME TO COOL, WEIRD ART SHOWS OR WHATEVER.
BRO, I SAID THE TEAM DRAGGED ME HERE ONE DAY. I DIDN'T EVEN WANT TO GO.
FINE. LET'S SQUASH THIS AND FOCUS ON KYA JOINING THE CLUB.
SIGH SOUNDS GOOD.
FINALLY... LET'S GET A GOOD SEAT.

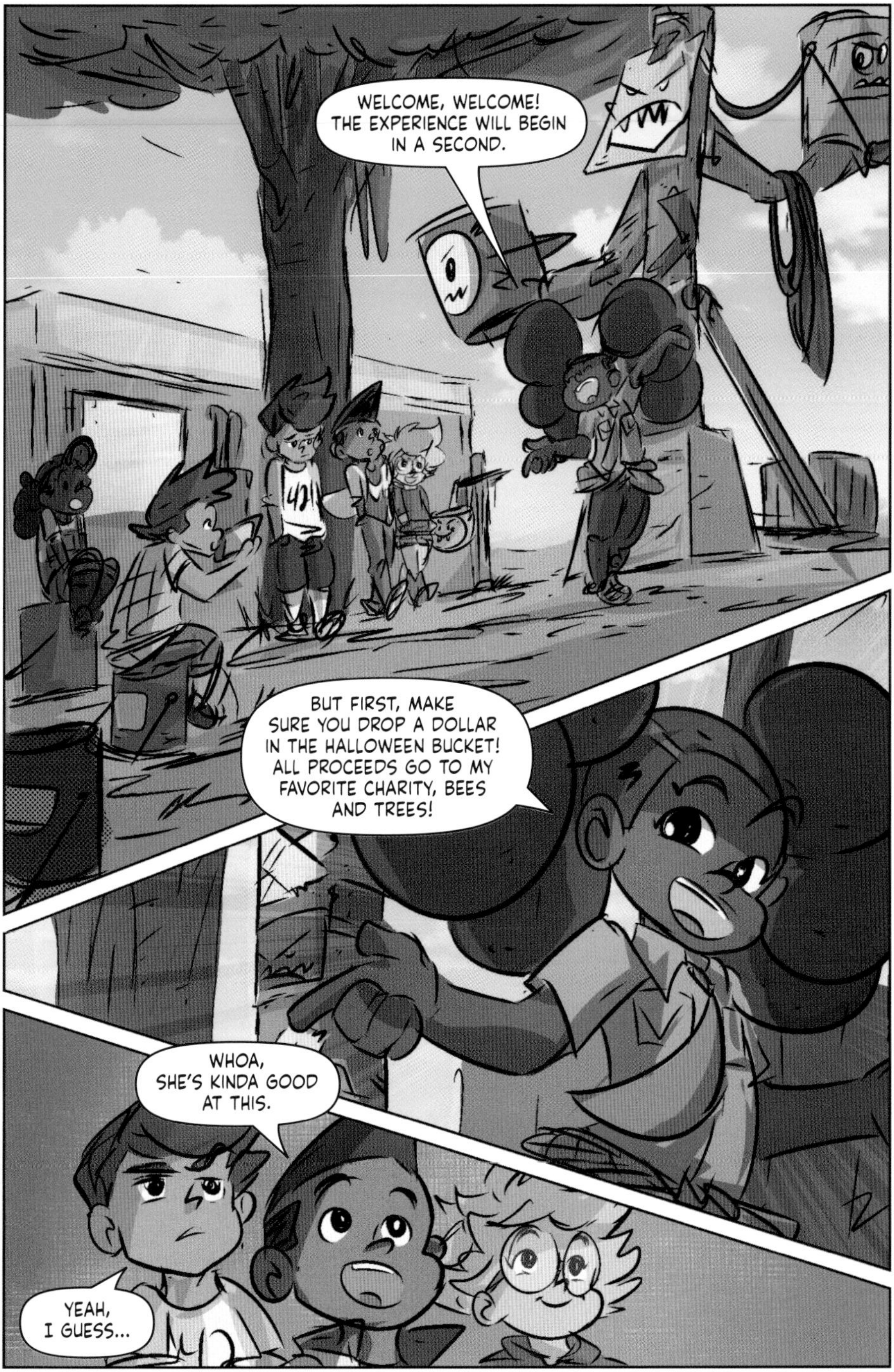
WELCOME, WELCOME! THE EXPERIENCE WILL BEGIN IN A SECOND.
BUT FIRST, MAKE SURE YOU DROP A DOLLAR IN THE HALLOWEEN BUCKET! ALL PROCEEDS GO TO MY FAVORITE CHARITY, BEES AND TREES!
WHOA, SHE'S KINDA GOOD AT THIS.
YEAH, I GUESS...

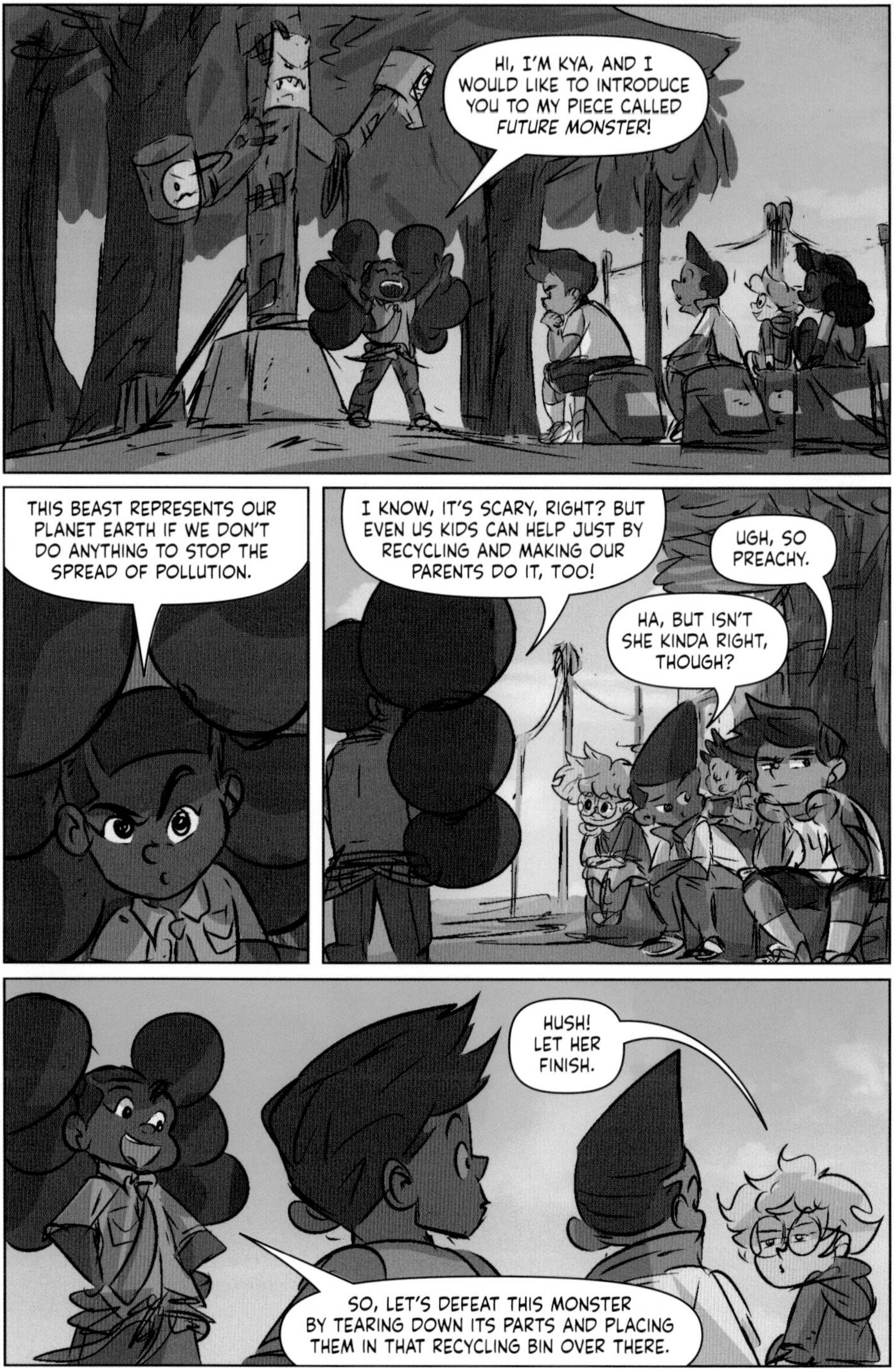
HI, I'M KYA, AND I WOULD LIKE TO INTRODUCE YOU TO MY PIECE CALLED *FUTURE MONSTER!*
THIS BEAST REPRESENTS OUR PLANET EARTH IF WE DON'T DO ANYTHING TO STOP THE SPREAD OF POLLUTION.
I KNOW, IT'S SCARY, RIGHT? BUT EVEN US KIDS CAN HELP JUST BY RECYCLING AND MAKING OUR PARENTS DO IT, TOO!
UGH, SO PREACHY.
HA, BUT ISN'T SHE KINDA RIGHT, THOUGH?
HUSH! LET HER FINISH.
SO, LET'S DEFEAT THIS MONSTER BY TEARING DOWN ITS PARTS AND PLACING THEM IN THAT RECYCLING BIN OVER THERE.

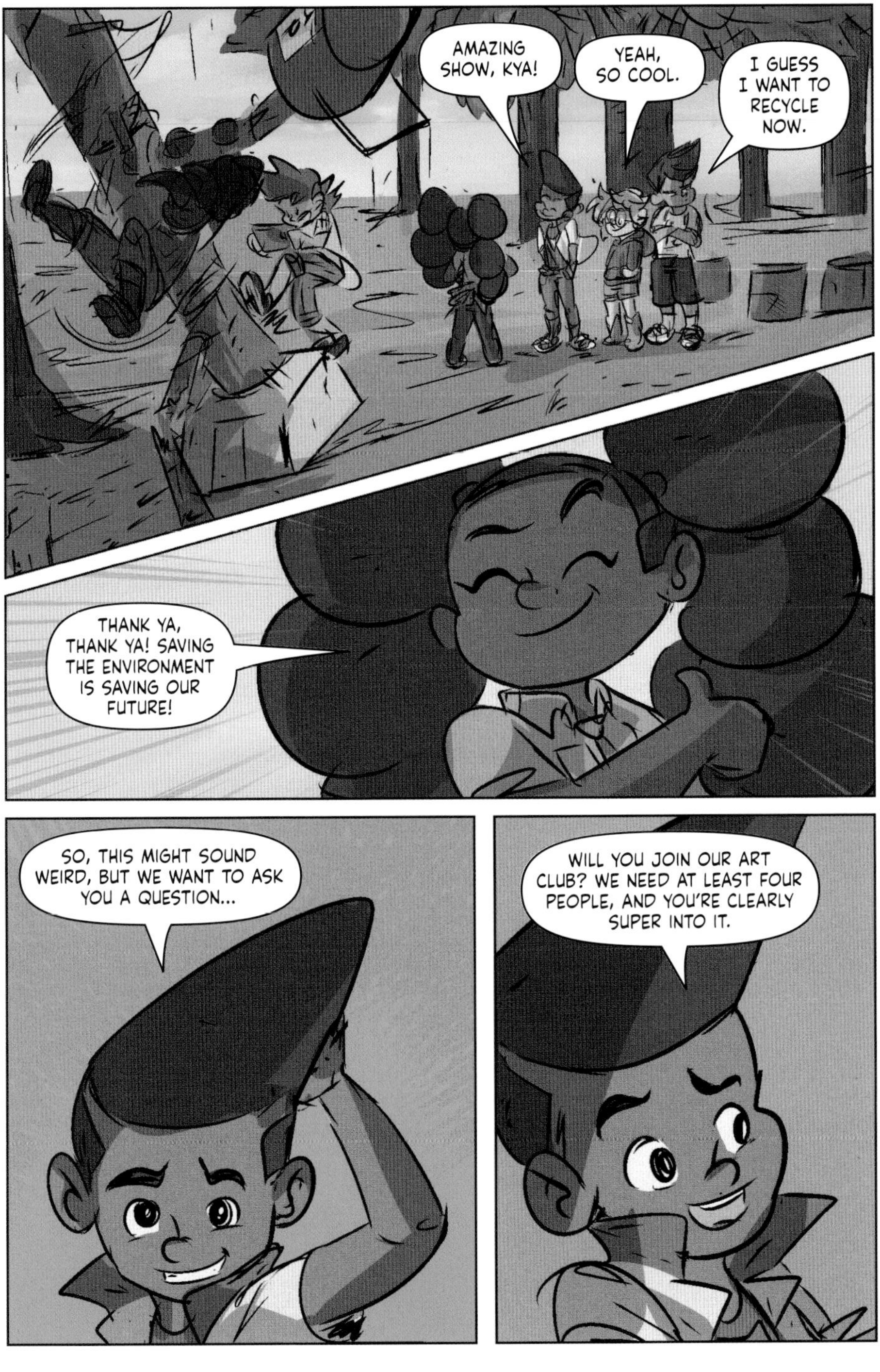
AMAZING SHOW, KYA!
YEAH, SO COOL.
I GUESS I WANT TO RECYCLE NOW.
THANK YA, THANK YA! SAVING THE ENVIRONMENT IS SAVING OUR FUTURE!
SO, THIS MIGHT SOUND WEIRD, BUT WE WANT TO ASK YOU A QUESTION...
WILL YOU JOIN OUR ART CLUB? WE NEED AT LEAST FOUR PEOPLE, AND YOU'RE CLEARLY SUPER INTO IT.

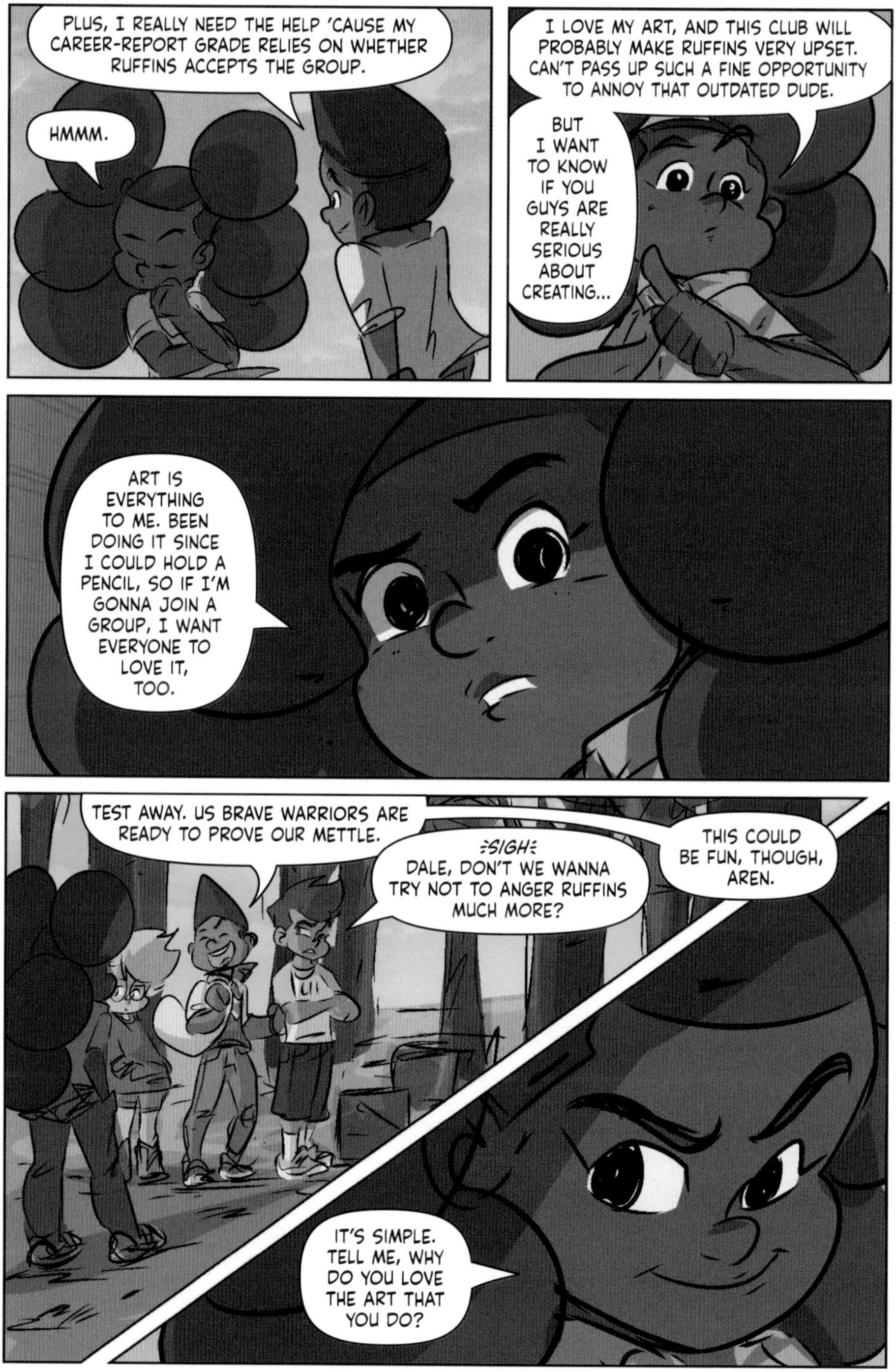
PLUS, I REALLY NEED THE HELP 'CAUSE MY CAREER-REPORT GRADE RELIES ON WHETHER RUFFINS ACCEPTS THE GROUP.
HMMM.
I LOVE MY ART, AND THIS CLUB WILL PROBABLY MAKE RUFFINS VERY UPSET. CAN'T PASS UP SUCH A FINE OPPORTUNITY TO ANNOY THAT OUTDATED DUDE.
BUT I WANT TO KNOW IF YOU GUYS ARE REALLY SERIOUS ABOUT CREATING...
ART IS EVERYTHING TO ME. BEEN DOING IT SINCE I COULD HOLD A PENCIL, SO IF I'M GONNA JOIN A GROUP, I WANT EVERYONE TO LOVE IT, TOO.
TEST AWAY. US BRAVE WARRIORS ARE READY TO PROVE OUR METTLE.
SIGH
DALE, DON'T WE WANNA TRY NOT TO ANGER RUFFINS MUCH MORE?
THIS COULD BE FUN, THOUGH, AREN.
IT'S SIMPLE. TELL ME, WHY DO YOU LOVE THE ART THAT YOU DO?

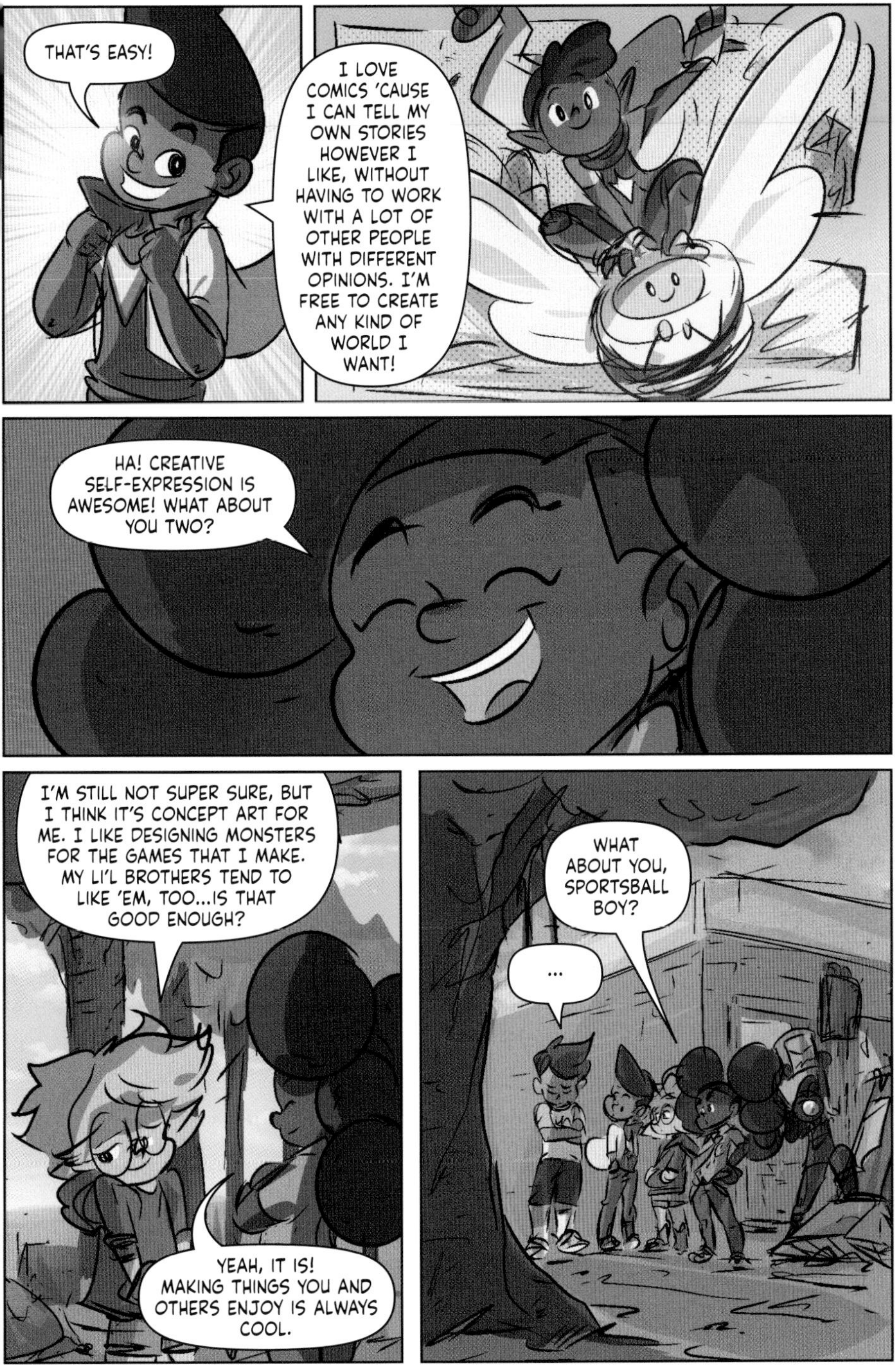
THAT'S EASY!
I LOVE COMICS 'CAUSE I CAN TELL MY OWN STORIES HOWEVER I LIKE, WITHOUT HAVING TO WORK WITH A LOT OF OTHER PEOPLE WITH DIFFERENT OPINIONS. I'M FREE TO CREATE ANY KIND OF WORLD I WANT!
HA! CREATIVE SELF-EXPRESSION IS AWESOME! WHAT ABOUT YOU TWO?
I'M STILL NOT SUPER SURE, BUT I THINK IT'S CONCEPT ART FOR ME. I LIKE DESIGNING MONSTERS FOR THE GAMES THAT I MAKE. MY LI'L BROTHERS TEND TO LIKE 'EM, TOO...IS THAT GOOD ENOUGH?
YEAH, IT IS! MAKING THINGS YOU AND OTHERS ENJOY IS ALWAYS COOL.
WHAT ABOUT YOU, SPORTSBALL BOY?
...

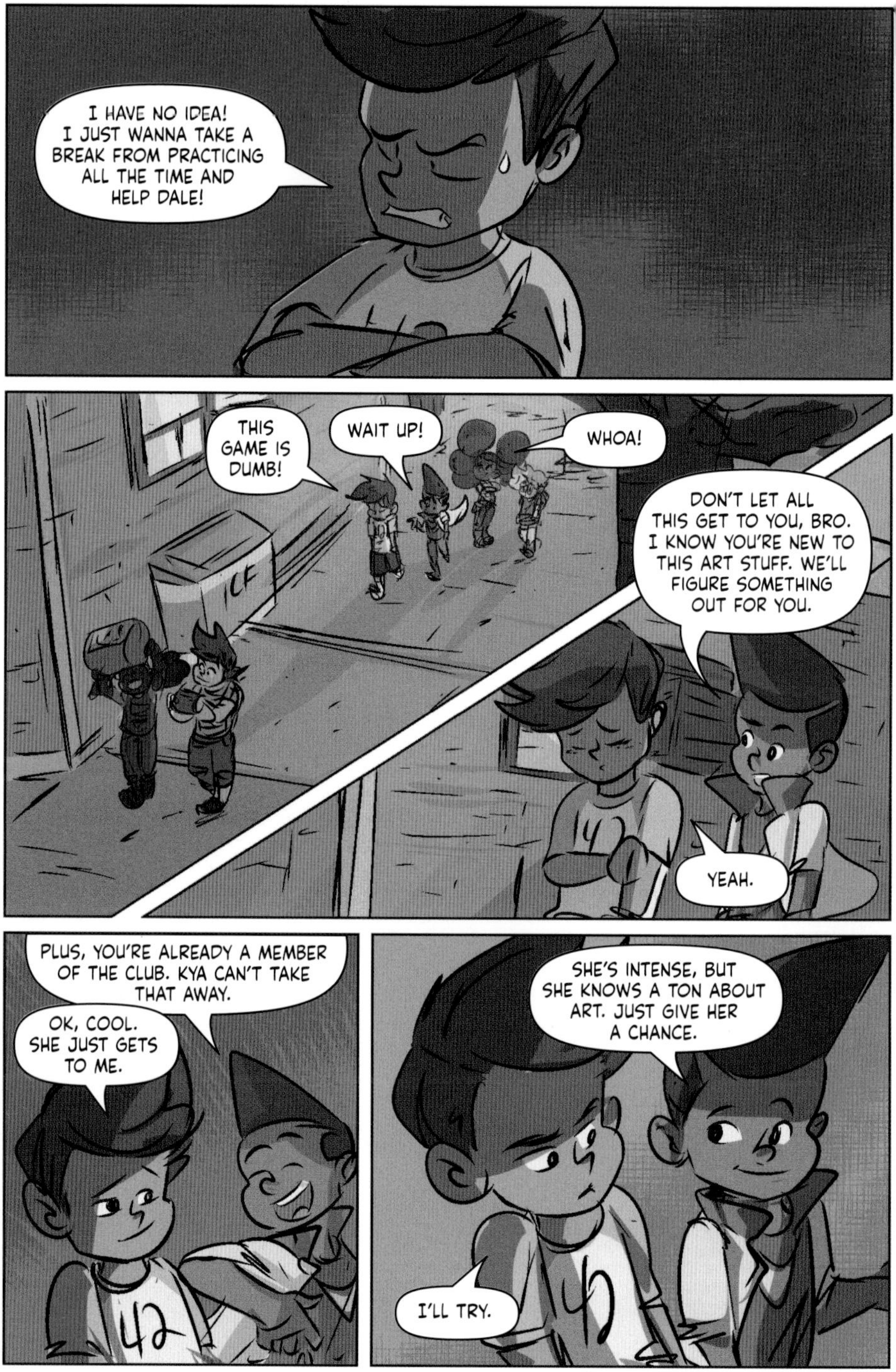
I HAVE NO IDEA! I JUST WANNA TAKE A BREAK FROM PRACTICING ALL THE TIME AND HELP DALE!
THIS GAME IS DUMB!
WAIT UP!
WHOA!
ICE
DON'T LET ALL THIS GET TO YOU, BRO. I KNOW YOU'RE NEW TO THIS ART STUFF. WE'LL FIGURE SOMETHING OUT FOR YOU.
YEAH.
PLUS, YOU'RE ALREADY A MEMBER OF THE CLUB. KYA CAN'T TAKE THAT AWAY.
OK, COOL. SHE JUST GETS TO ME.
SHE'S INTENSE, BUT SHE KNOWS A TON ABOUT ART. JUST GIVE HER A CHANCE.
I'LL TRY.

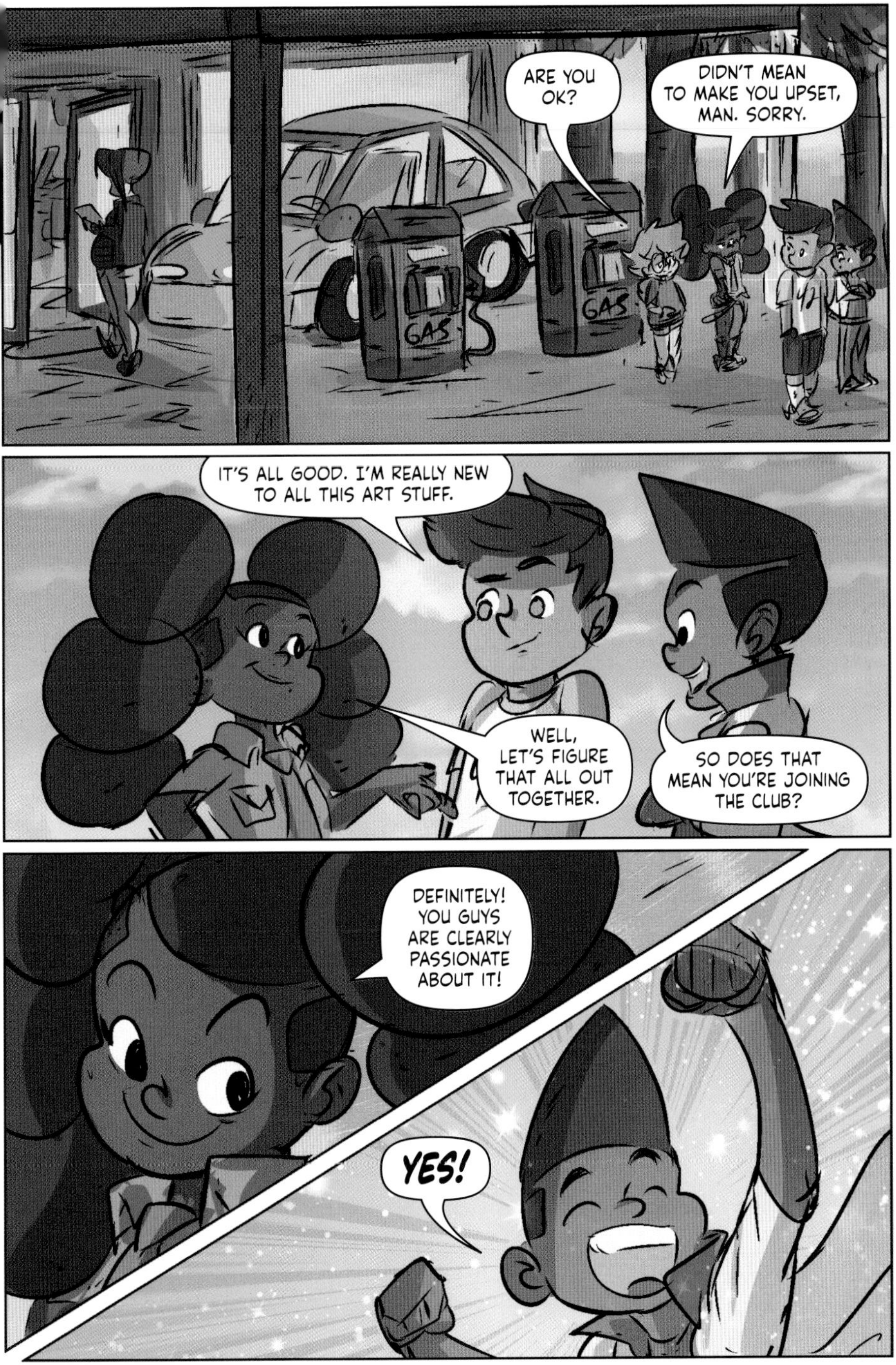
ARE YOU OK?
DIDN'T MEAN TO MAKE YOU UPSET, MAN. SORRY.
IT'S ALL GOOD. I'M REALLY NEW TO ALL THIS ART STUFF.
WELL, LET'S FIGURE THAT ALL OUT TOGETHER.
SO DOES THAT MEAN YOU'RE JOINING THE CLUB?
DEFINITELY! YOU GUYS ARE CLEARLY PASSIONATE ABOUT IT!
YES!

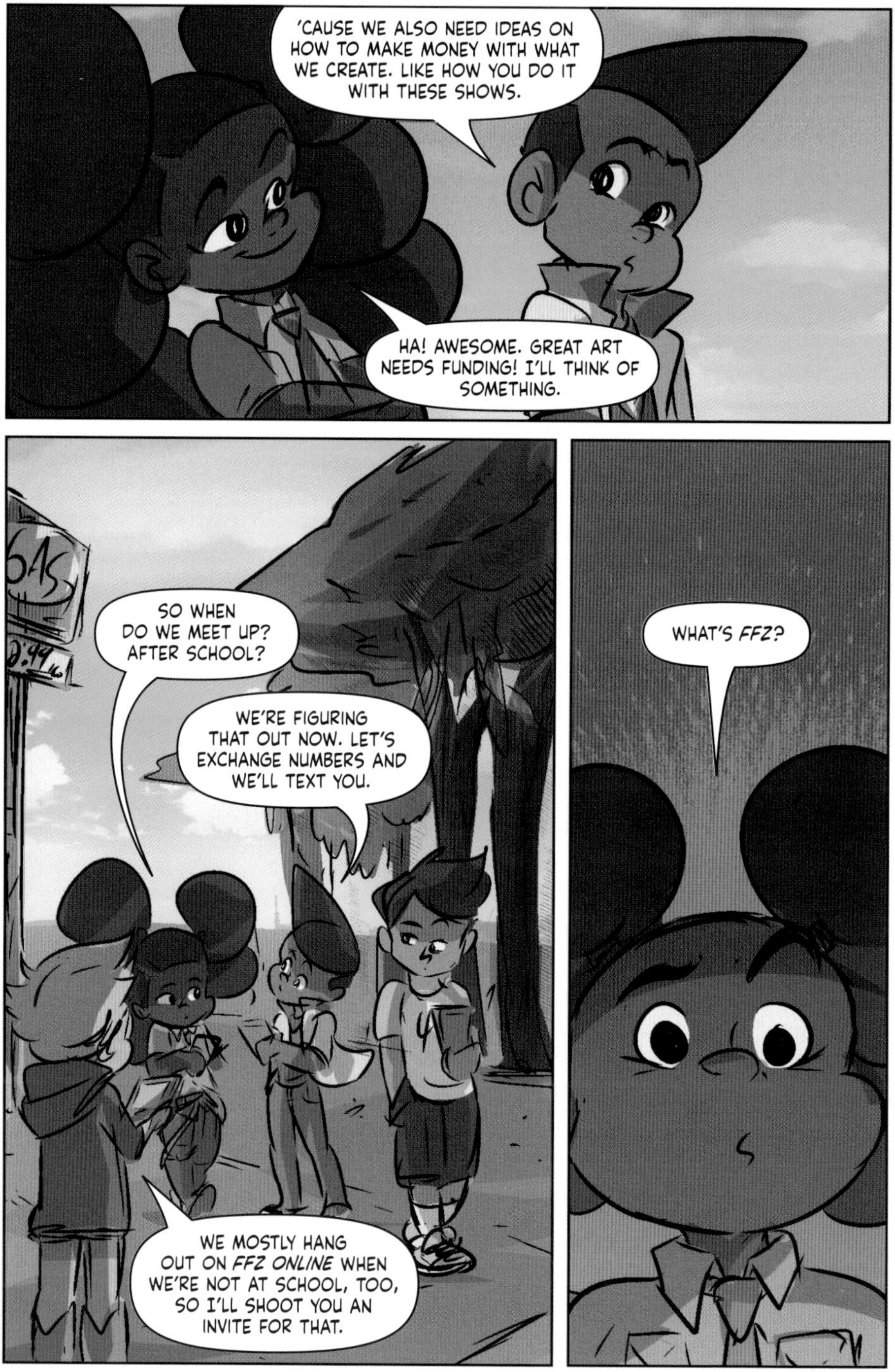
'CAUSE WE ALSO NEED IDEAS ON HOW TO MAKE MONEY WITH WHAT WE CREATE. LIKE HOW YOU DO IT WITH THESE SHOWS.
HA! AWESOME. GREAT ART NEEDS FUNDING! I'LL THINK OF SOMETHING.
SO WHEN DO WE MEET UP? AFTER SCHOOL?
WE'RE FIGURING THAT OUT NOW. LET'S EXCHANGE NUMBERS AND WE'LL TEXT YOU.
WE MOSTLY HANG OUT ON *FFZ ONLINE* WHEN WE'RE NOT AT SCHOOL, TOO, SO I'LL SHOOT YOU AN INVITE FOR THAT.
WHAT'S *FFZ*?

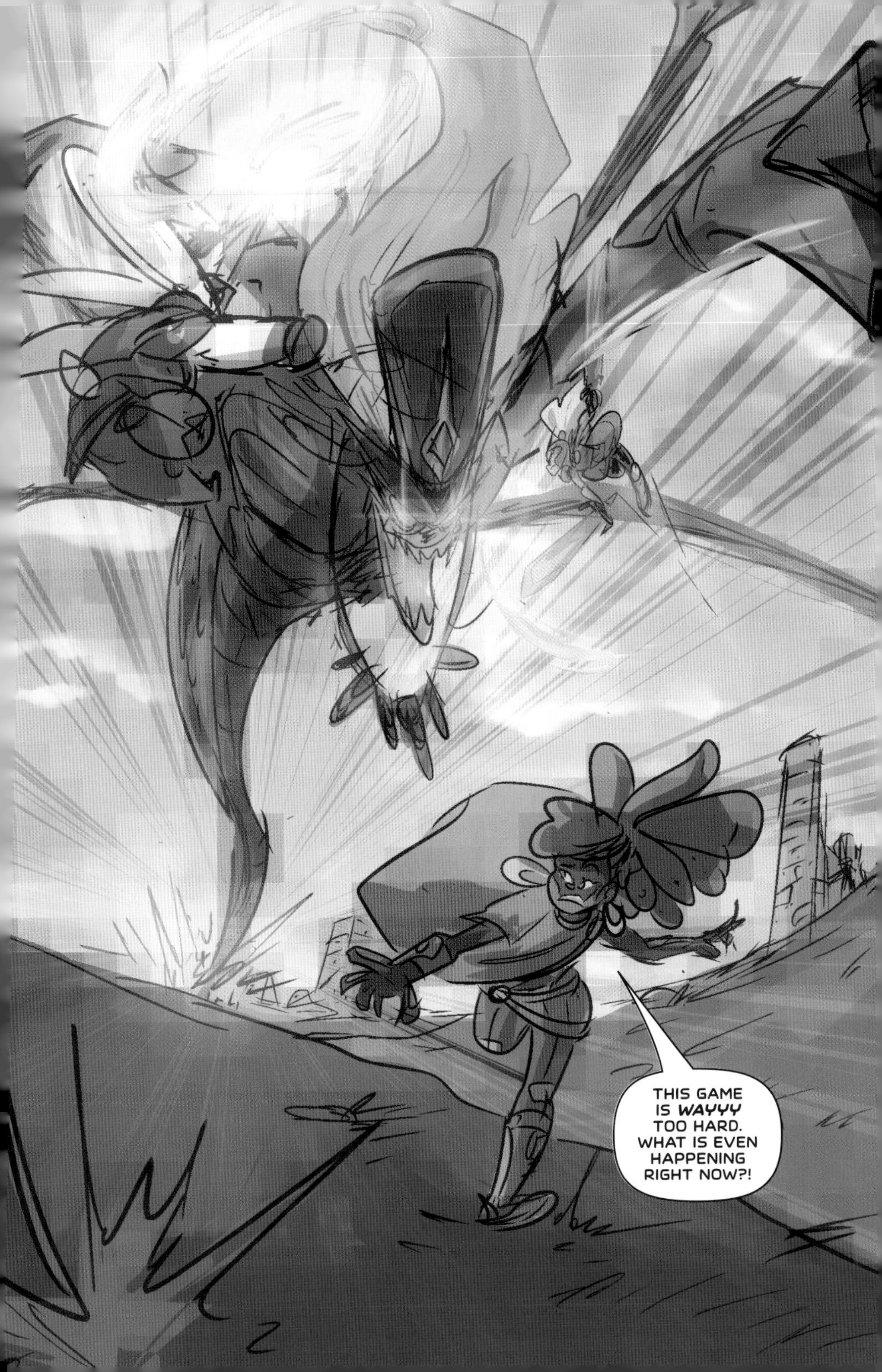
THIS GAME IS WAYYY TOO HARD. WHAT IS EVEN HAPPENING RIGHT NOW?!

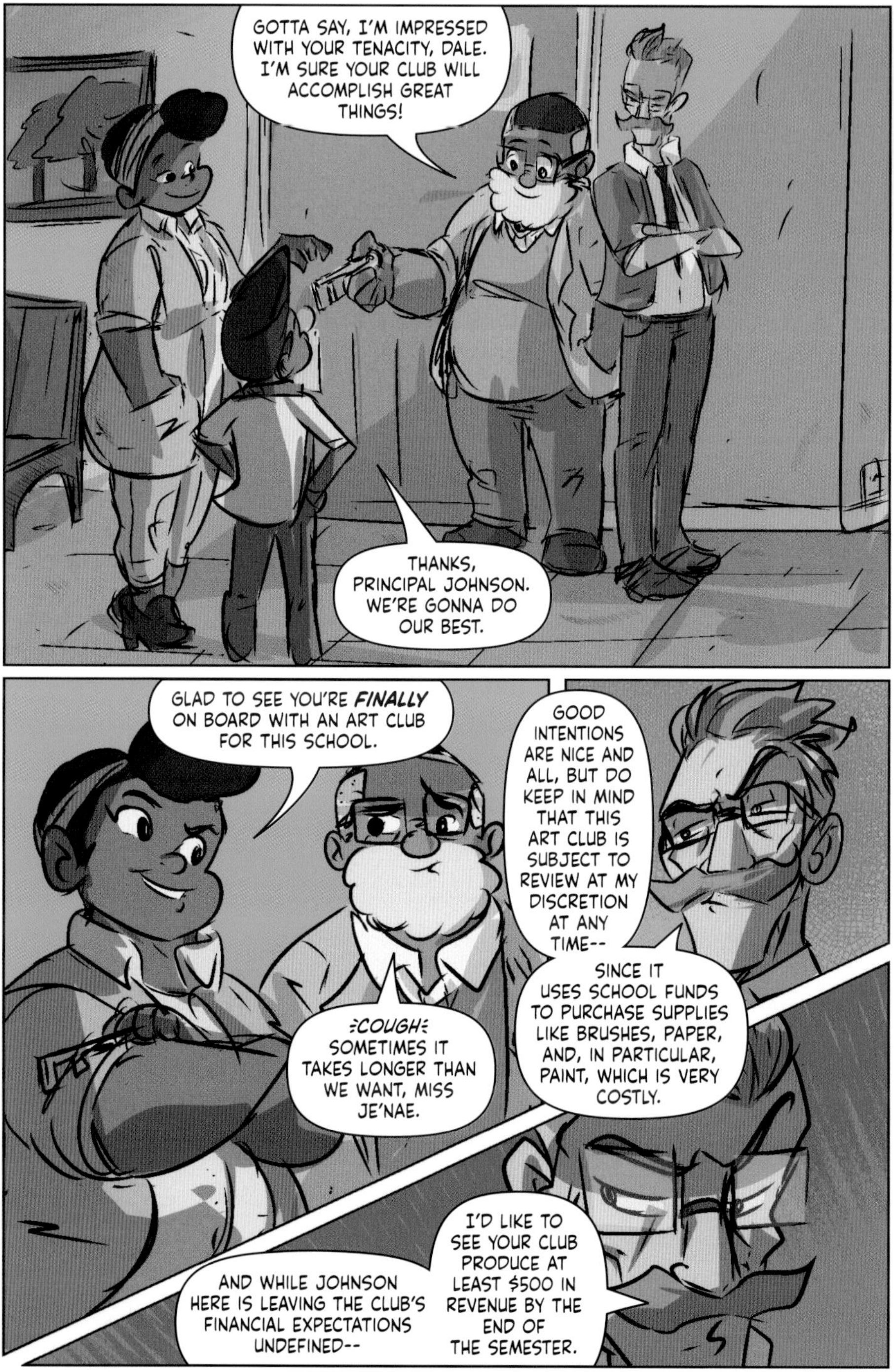
GOTTA SAY, I'M IMPRESSED WITH YOUR TENACITY, DALE. I'M SURE YOUR CLUB WILL ACCOMPLISH GREAT THINGS!
THANKS, PRINCIPAL JOHNSON. WE'RE GONNA DO OUR BEST.
GLAD TO SEE YOU'RE *FINALLY* ON BOARD WITH AN ART CLUB FOR THIS SCHOOL.
COUGH SOMETIMES IT TAKES LONGER THAN WE WANT, MISS JE'NAE.
GOOD INTENTIONS ARE NICE AND ALL, BUT DO KEEP IN MIND THAT THIS ART CLUB IS SUBJECT TO REVIEW AT MY DISCRETION AT ANY TIME--
SINCE IT USES SCHOOL FUNDS TO PURCHASE SUPPLIES LIKE BRUSHES, PAPER, AND, IN PARTICULAR, PAINT, WHICH IS VERY COSTLY.
AND WHILE JOHNSON HERE IS LEAVING THE CLUB'S FINANCIAL EXPECTATIONS UNDEFINED--
I'D LIKE TO SEE YOUR CLUB PRODUCE AT LEAST $500 IN REVENUE BY THE END OF THE SEMESTER.

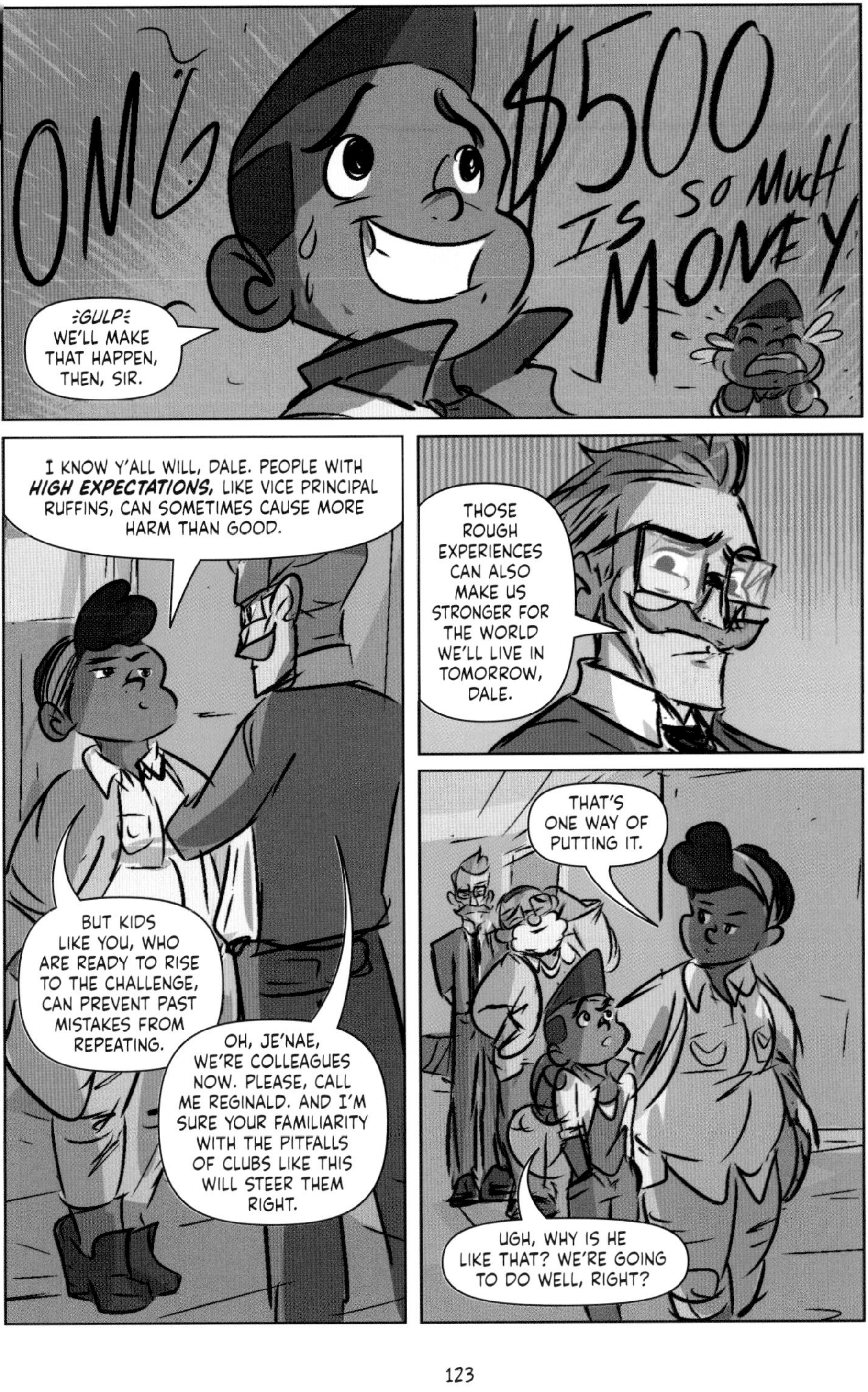
OMG $500 IS SO MUCH MONEY
GULP WE'LL MAKE THAT HAPPEN, THEN, SIR.
I KNOW Y'ALL WILL, DALE. PEOPLE WITH ***HIGH EXPECTATIONS,*** LIKE VICE PRINCIPAL RUFFINS, CAN SOMETIMES CAUSE MORE HARM THAN GOOD.
BUT KIDS LIKE YOU, WHO ARE READY TO RISE TO THE CHALLENGE, CAN PREVENT PAST MISTAKES FROM REPEATING.
OH, JE'NAE, WE'RE COLLEAGUES NOW. PLEASE, CALL ME REGINALD. AND I'M SURE YOUR FAMILIARITY WITH THE PITFALLS OF CLUBS LIKE THIS WILL STEER THEM RIGHT.
THOSE ROUGH EXPERIENCES CAN ALSO MAKE US STRONGER FOR THE WORLD WE'LL LIVE IN TOMORROW, DALE.
THAT'S ONE WAY OF PUTTING IT.
UGH, WHY IS HE LIKE THAT? WE'RE GOING TO DO WELL, RIGHT?

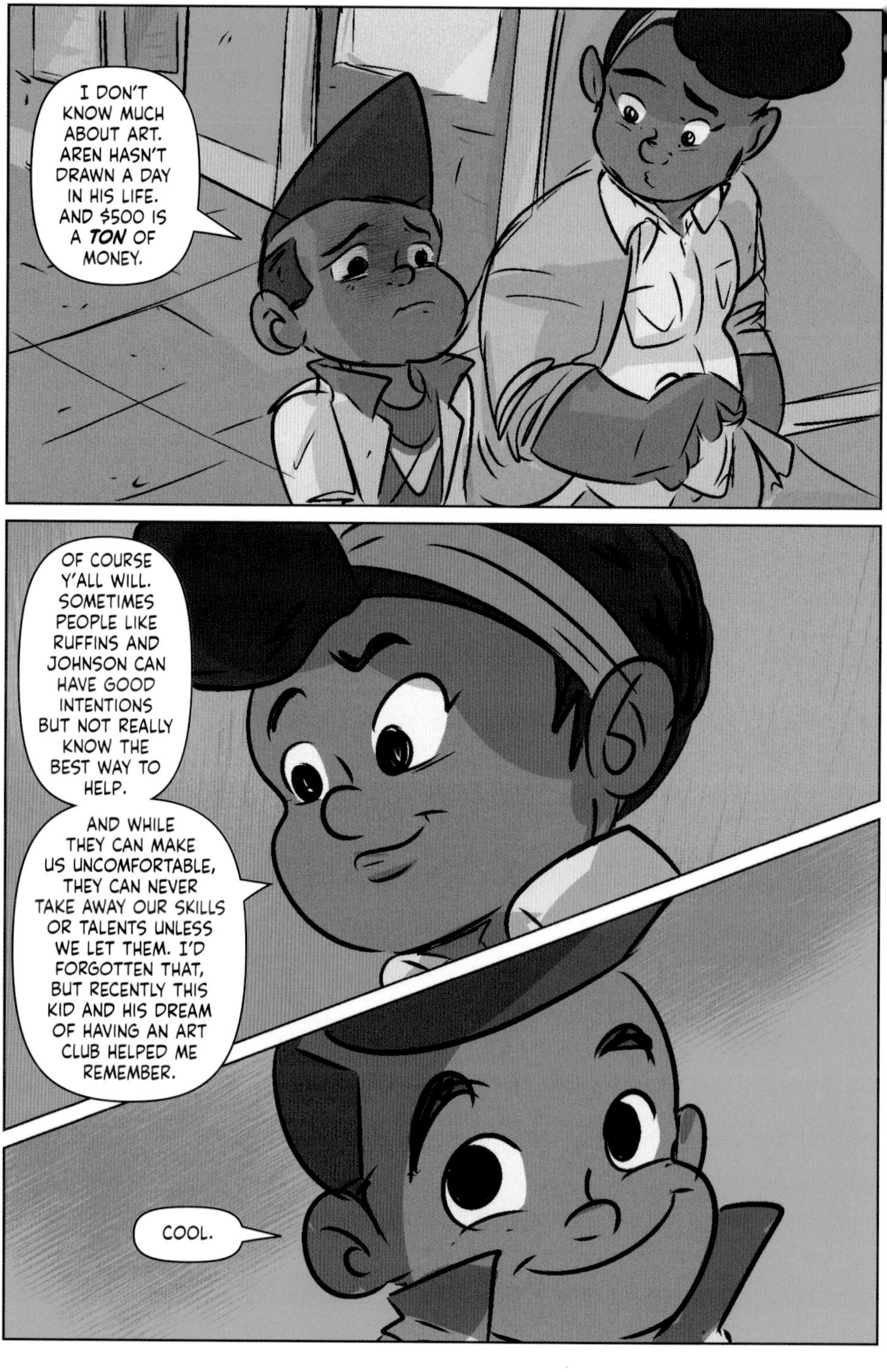
I DON'T KNOW MUCH ABOUT ART. AREN HASN'T DRAWN A DAY IN HIS LIFE. AND $500 IS A TON OF MONEY.
OF COURSE Y'ALL WILL. SOMETIMES PEOPLE LIKE RUFFINS AND JOHNSON CAN HAVE GOOD INTENTIONS BUT NOT REALLY KNOW THE BEST WAY TO HELP.
AND WHILE THEY CAN MAKE US UNCOMFORTABLE, THEY CAN NEVER TAKE AWAY OUR SKILLS OR TALENTS UNLESS WE LET THEM. I'D FORGOTTEN THAT, BUT RECENTLY THIS KID AND HIS DREAM OF HAVING AN ART CLUB HELPED ME REMEMBER.
COOL.

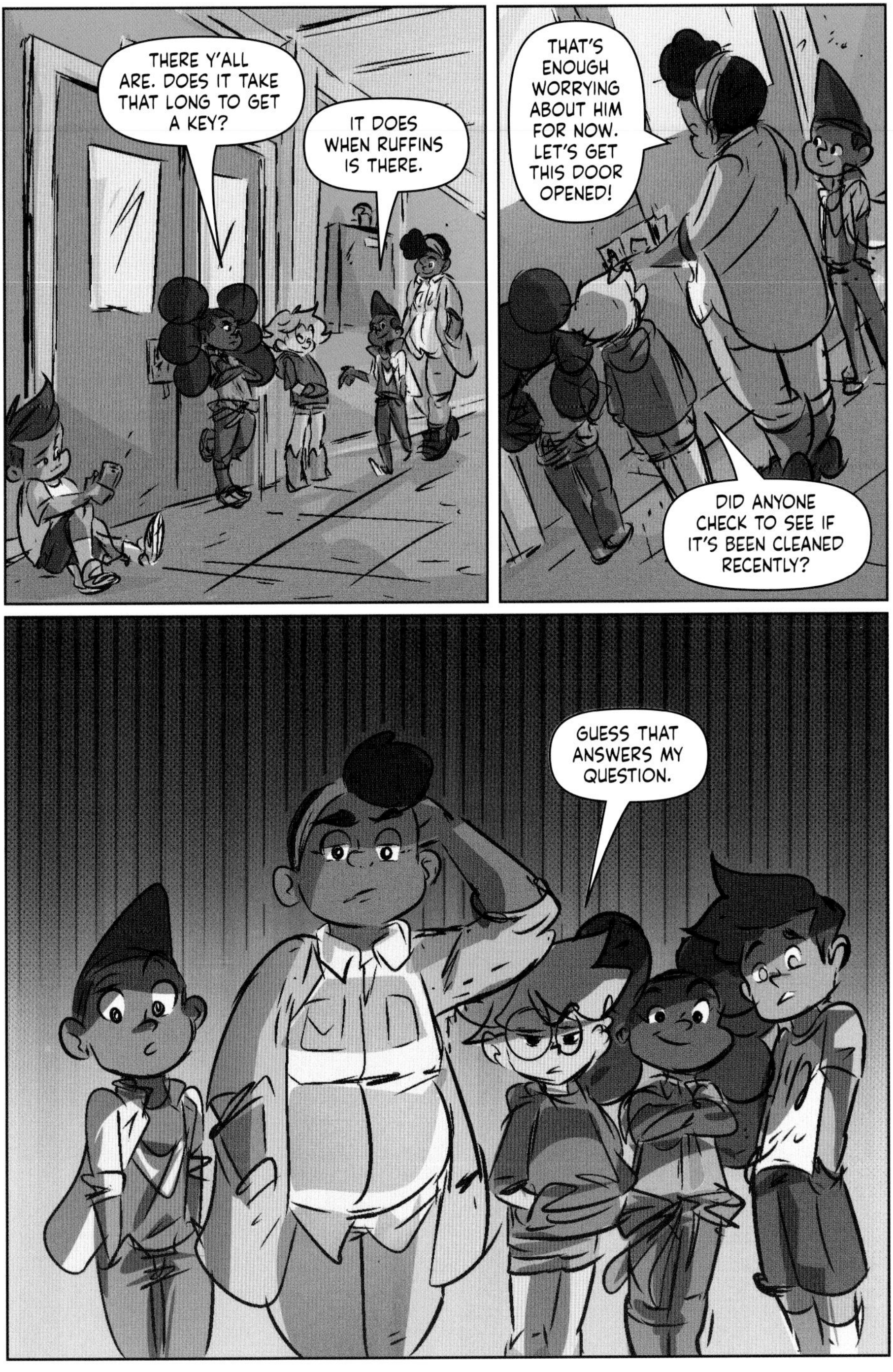
THERE Y'ALL ARE. DOES IT TAKE THAT LONG TO GET A KEY?
IT DOES WHEN RUFFINS IS THERE.
THAT'S ENOUGH WORRYING ABOUT HIM FOR NOW. LET'S GET THIS DOOR OPENED!
DID ANYONE CHECK TO SEE IF IT'S BEEN CLEANED RECENTLY?
GUESS THAT ANSWERS MY QUESTION.

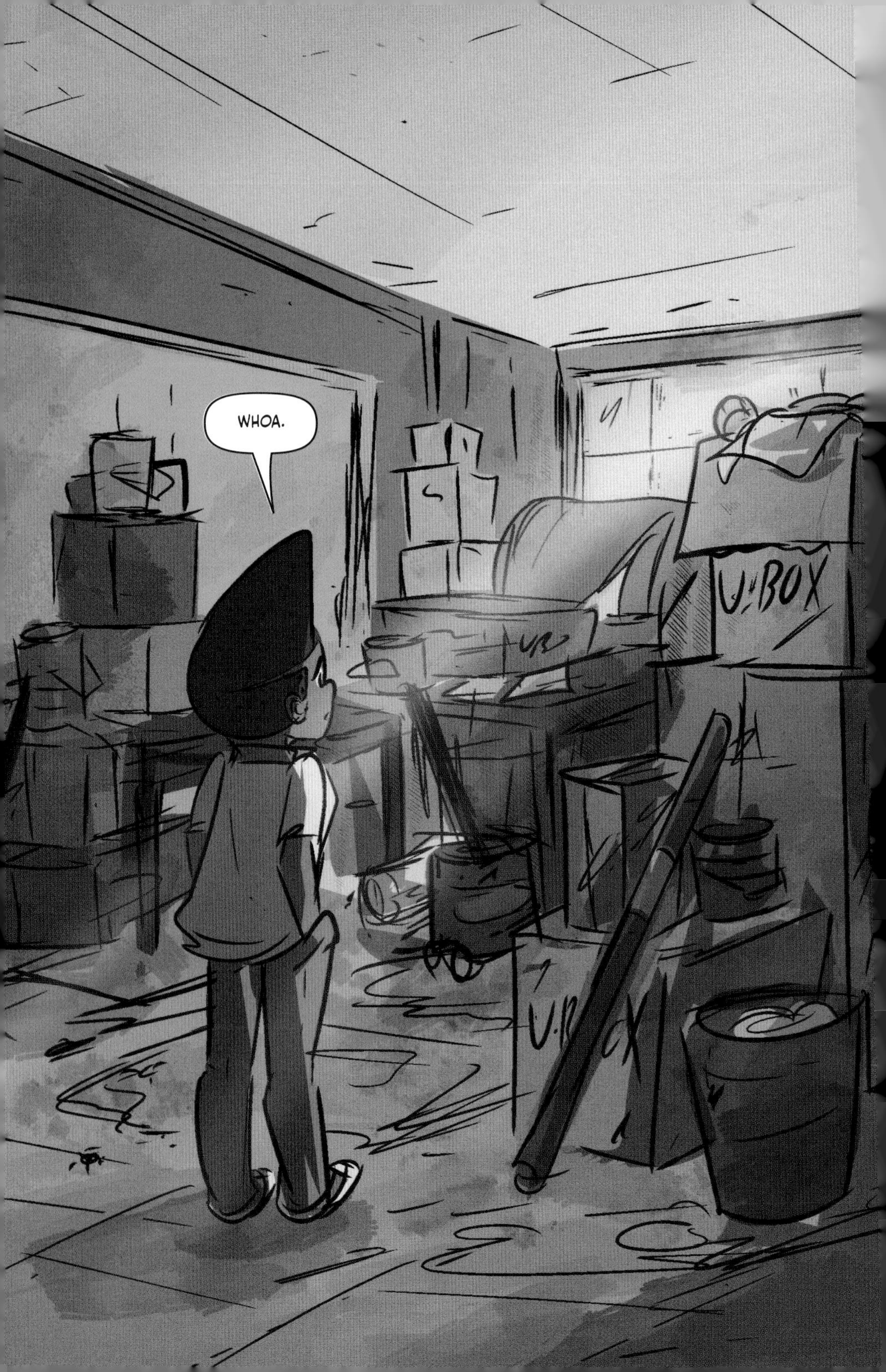
WHOA.
U-BOX

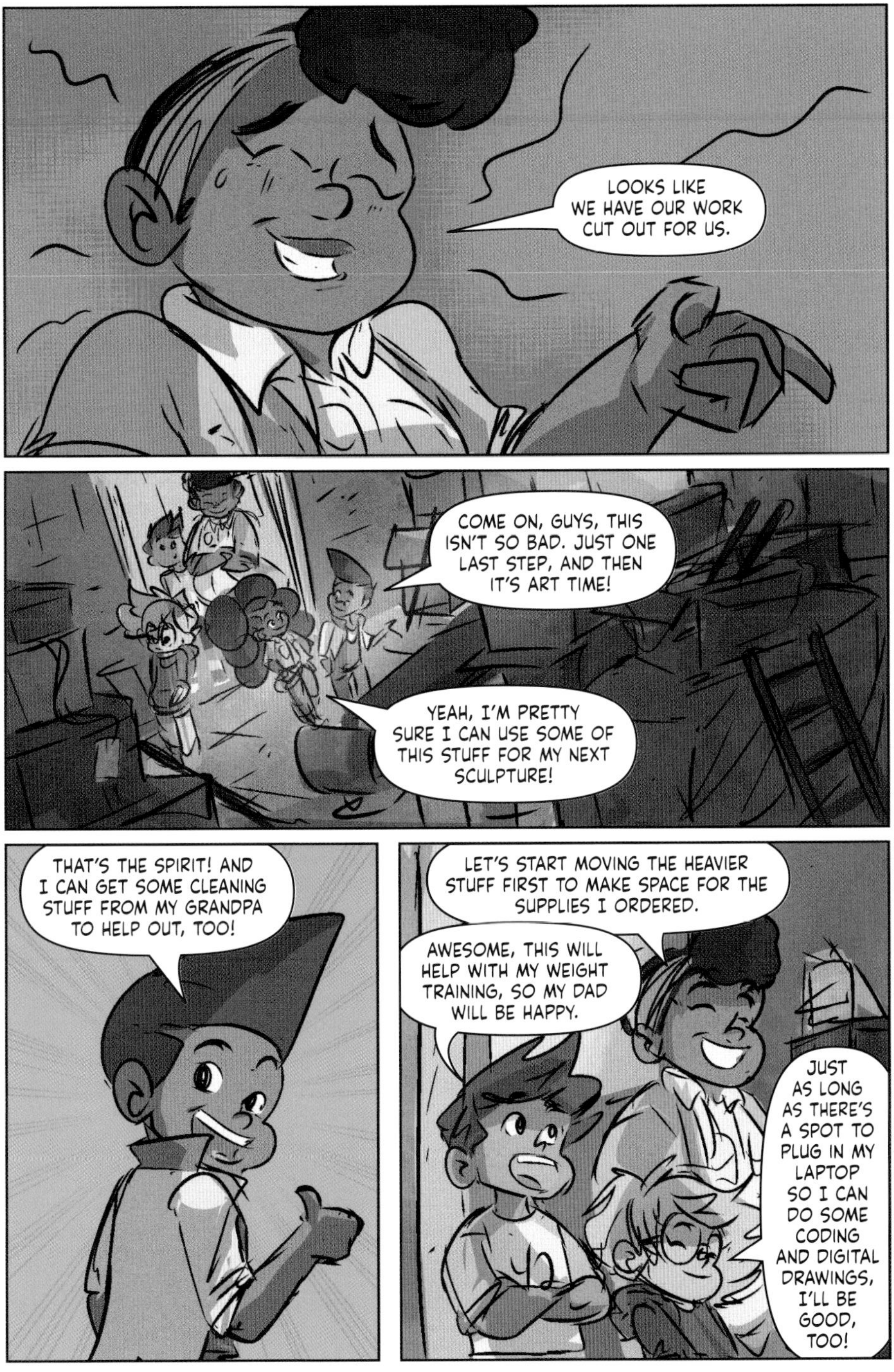
LOOKS LIKE WE HAVE OUR WORK CUT OUT FOR US.
COME ON, GUYS, THIS ISN'T SO BAD. JUST ONE LAST STEP, AND THEN IT'S ART TIME!
YEAH, I'M PRETTY SURE I CAN USE SOME OF THIS STUFF FOR MY NEXT SCULPTURE!
THAT'S THE SPIRIT! AND I CAN GET SOME CLEANING STUFF FROM MY GRANDPA TO HELP OUT, TOO!
LET'S START MOVING THE HEAVIER STUFF FIRST TO MAKE SPACE FOR THE SUPPLIES I ORDERED.
AWESOME, THIS WILL HELP WITH MY WEIGHT TRAINING, SO MY DAD WILL BE HAPPY.
JUST AS LONG AS THERE'S A SPOT TO PLUG IN MY LAPTOP SO I CAN DO SOME CODING AND DIGITAL DRAWINGS, I'LL BE GOOD, TOO!

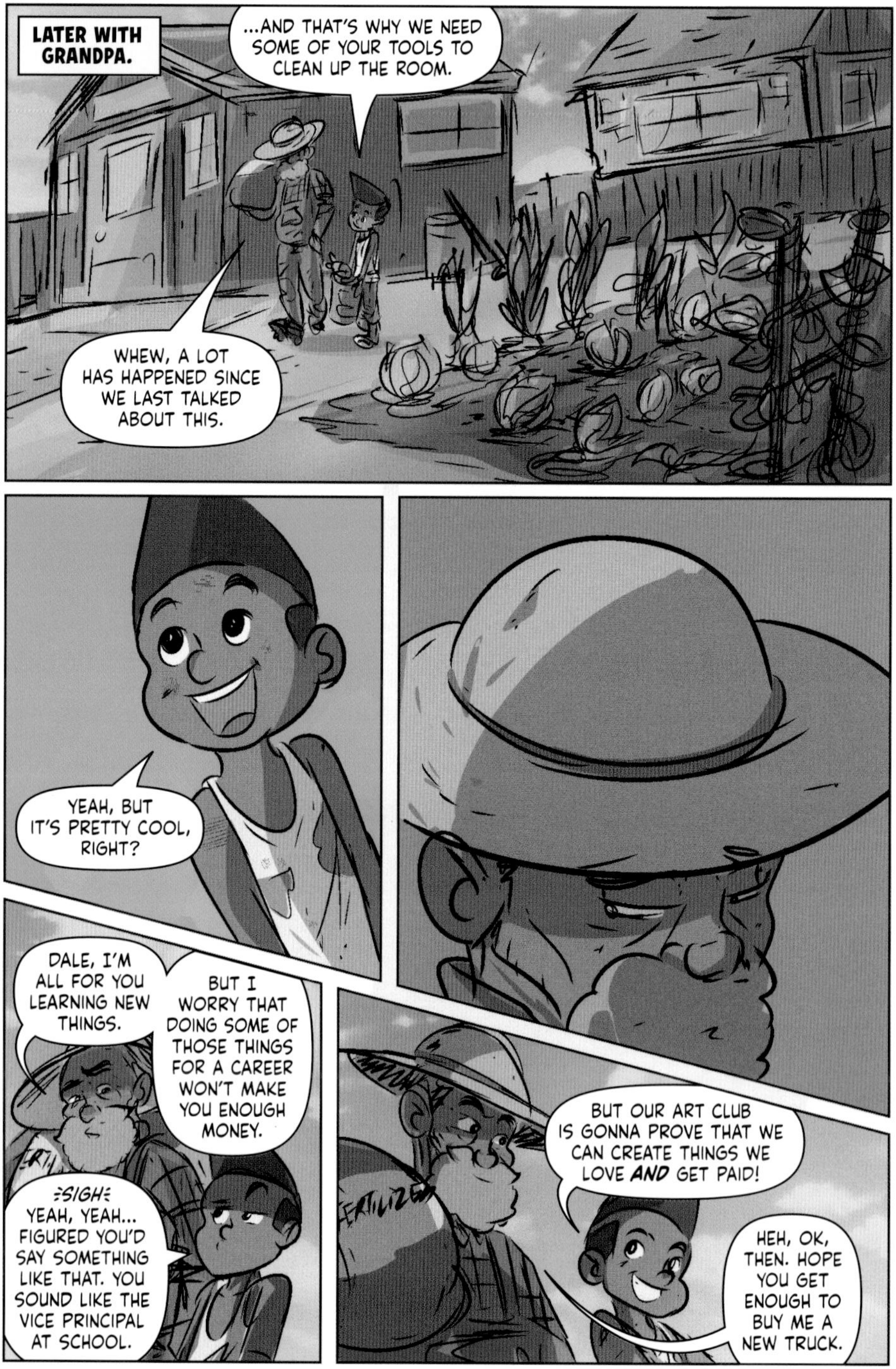
LATER WITH GRANDPA.
...AND THAT'S WHY WE NEED SOME OF YOUR TOOLS TO CLEAN UP THE ROOM.
WHEW, A LOT HAS HAPPENED SINCE WE LAST TALKED ABOUT THIS.
YEAH, BUT IT'S PRETTY COOL, RIGHT?
DALE, I'M ALL FOR YOU LEARNING NEW THINGS.
BUT I WORRY THAT DOING SOME OF THOSE THINGS FOR A CAREER WON'T MAKE YOU ENOUGH MONEY.
SIGH
YEAH, YEAH... FIGURED YOU'D SAY SOMETHING LIKE THAT. YOU SOUND LIKE THE VICE PRINCIPAL AT SCHOOL.
BUT OUR ART CLUB IS GONNA PROVE THAT WE CAN CREATE THINGS WE LOVE ***AND*** GET PAID!
HEH, OK, THEN. HOPE YOU GET ENOUGH TO BUY ME A NEW TRUCK.

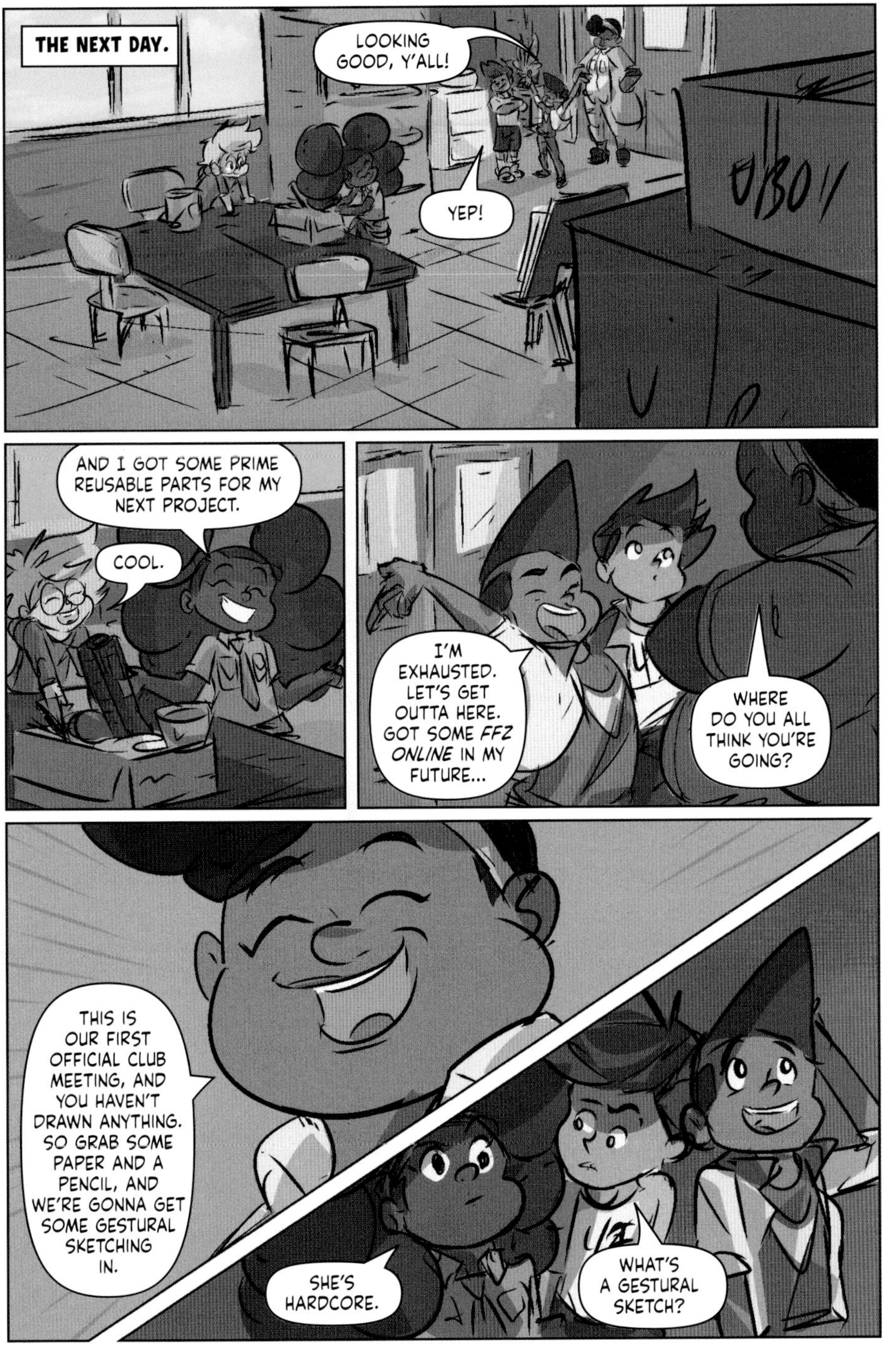
THE NEXT DAY.
LOOKING GOOD, Y'ALL!
YEP!
AND I GOT SOME PRIME REUSABLE PARTS FOR MY NEXT PROJECT.
COOL.
I'M EXHAUSTED. LET'S GET OUTTA HERE. GOT SOME *FFZ ONLINE* IN MY FUTURE...
WHERE DO YOU ALL THINK YOU'RE GOING?
THIS IS OUR FIRST OFFICIAL CLUB MEETING, AND YOU HAVEN'T DRAWN ANYTHING. SO GRAB SOME PAPER AND A PENCIL, AND WE'RE GONNA GET SOME GESTURAL SKETCHING IN.
SHE'S HARDCORE.
WHAT'S A GESTURAL SKETCH?

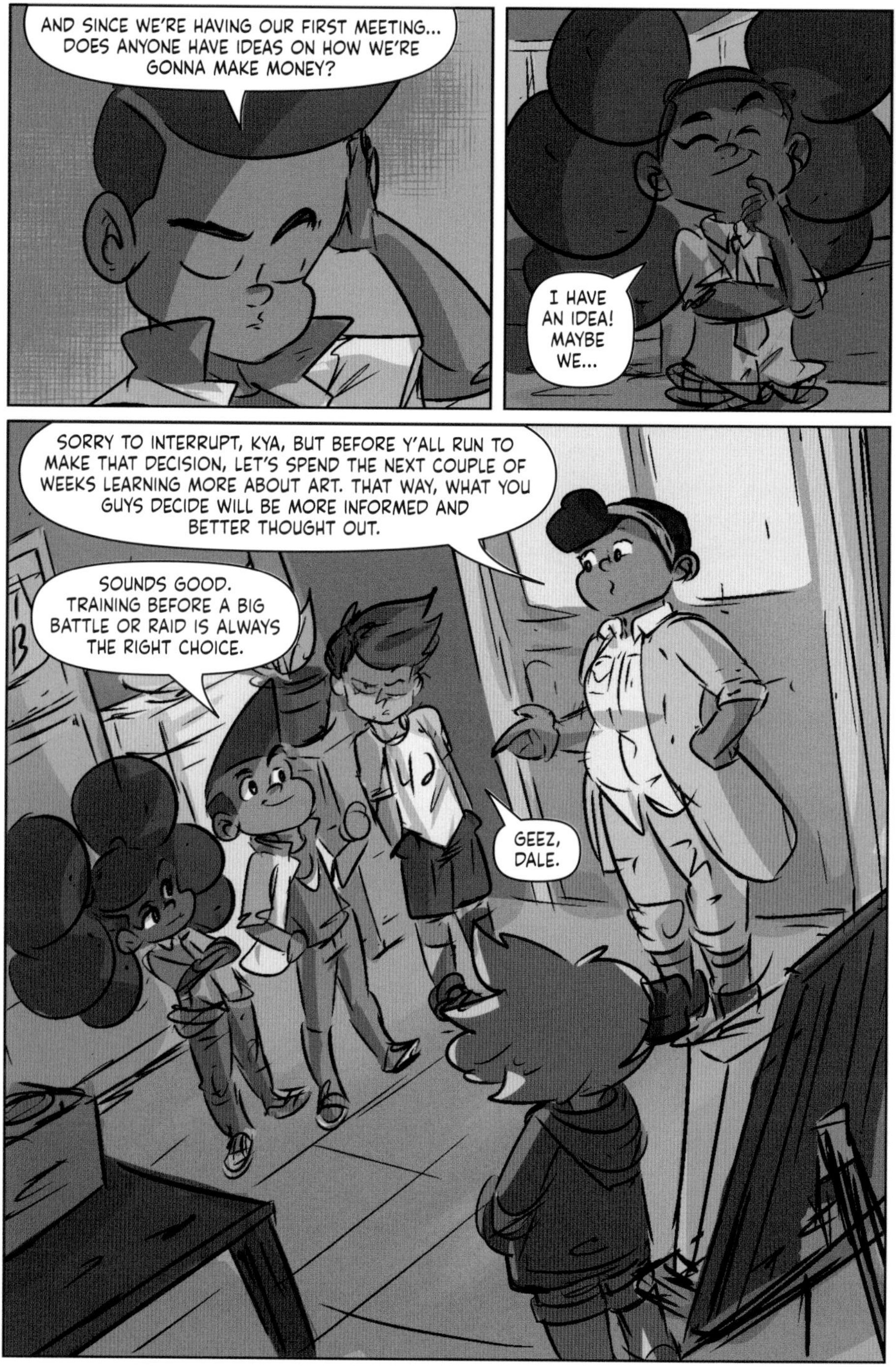
AND SINCE WE'RE HAVING OUR FIRST MEETING... DOES ANYONE HAVE IDEAS ON HOW WE'RE GONNA MAKE MONEY?
I HAVE AN IDEA! MAYBE WE...
SORRY TO INTERRUPT, KYA, BUT BEFORE Y'ALL RUN TO MAKE THAT DECISION, LET'S SPEND THE NEXT COUPLE OF WEEKS LEARNING MORE ABOUT ART. THAT WAY, WHAT YOU GUYS DECIDE WILL BE MORE INFORMED AND BETTER THOUGHT OUT.
SOUNDS GOOD. TRAINING BEFORE A BIG BATTLE OR RAID IS ALWAYS THE RIGHT CHOICE.
GEEZ, DALE.

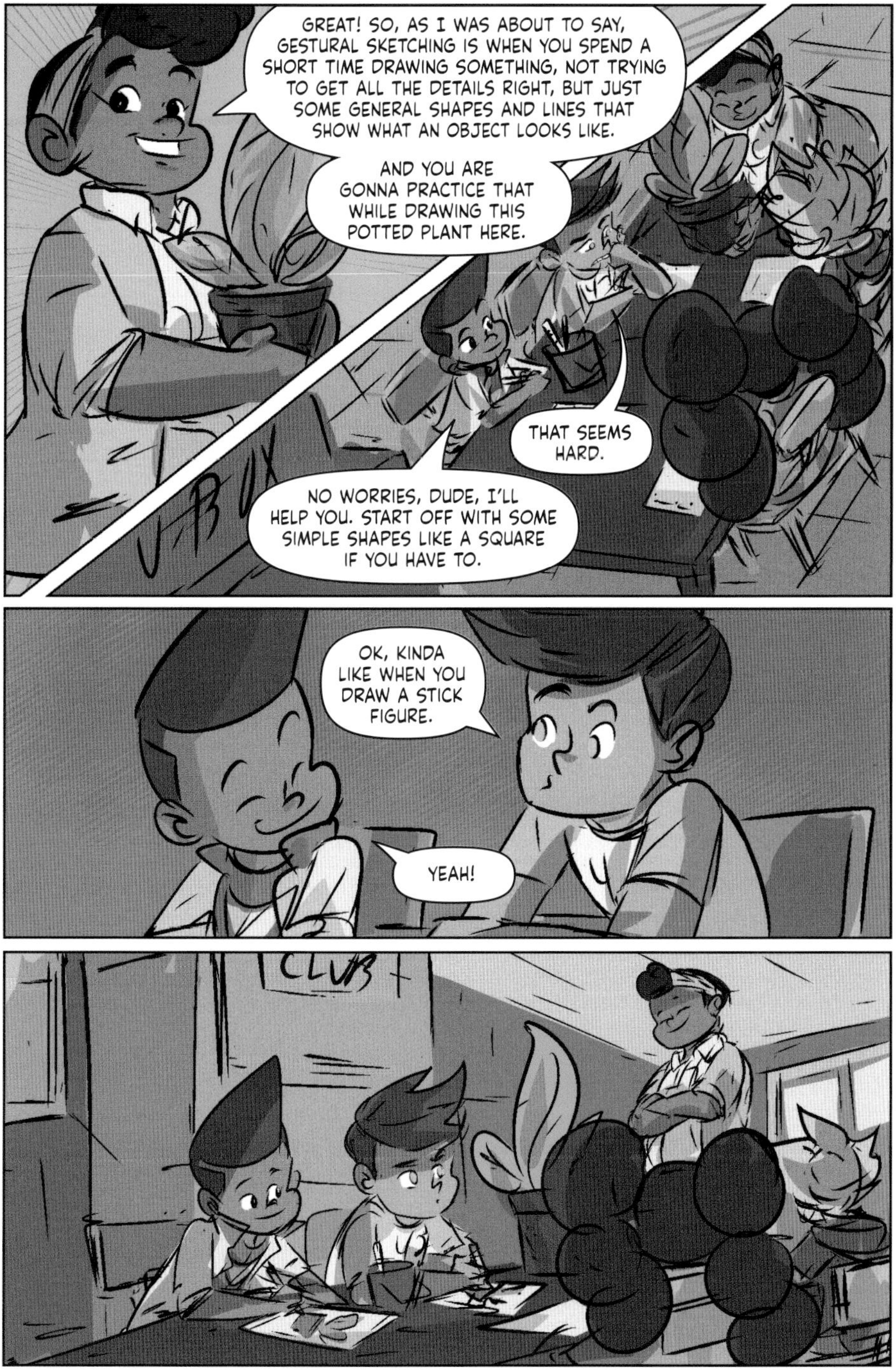
GREAT! SO, AS I WAS ABOUT TO SAY, GESTURAL SKETCHING IS WHEN YOU SPEND A SHORT TIME DRAWING SOMETHING, NOT TRYING TO GET ALL THE DETAILS RIGHT, BUT JUST SOME GENERAL SHAPES AND LINES THAT SHOW WHAT AN OBJECT LOOKS LIKE.
AND YOU ARE GONNA PRACTICE THAT WHILE DRAWING THIS POTTED PLANT HERE.
THAT SEEMS HARD.
NO WORRIES, DUDE, I'LL HELP YOU. START OFF WITH SOME SIMPLE SHAPES LIKE A SQUARE IF YOU HAVE TO.
OK, KINDA LIKE WHEN YOU DRAW A STICK FIGURE.
YEAH!
CLUB

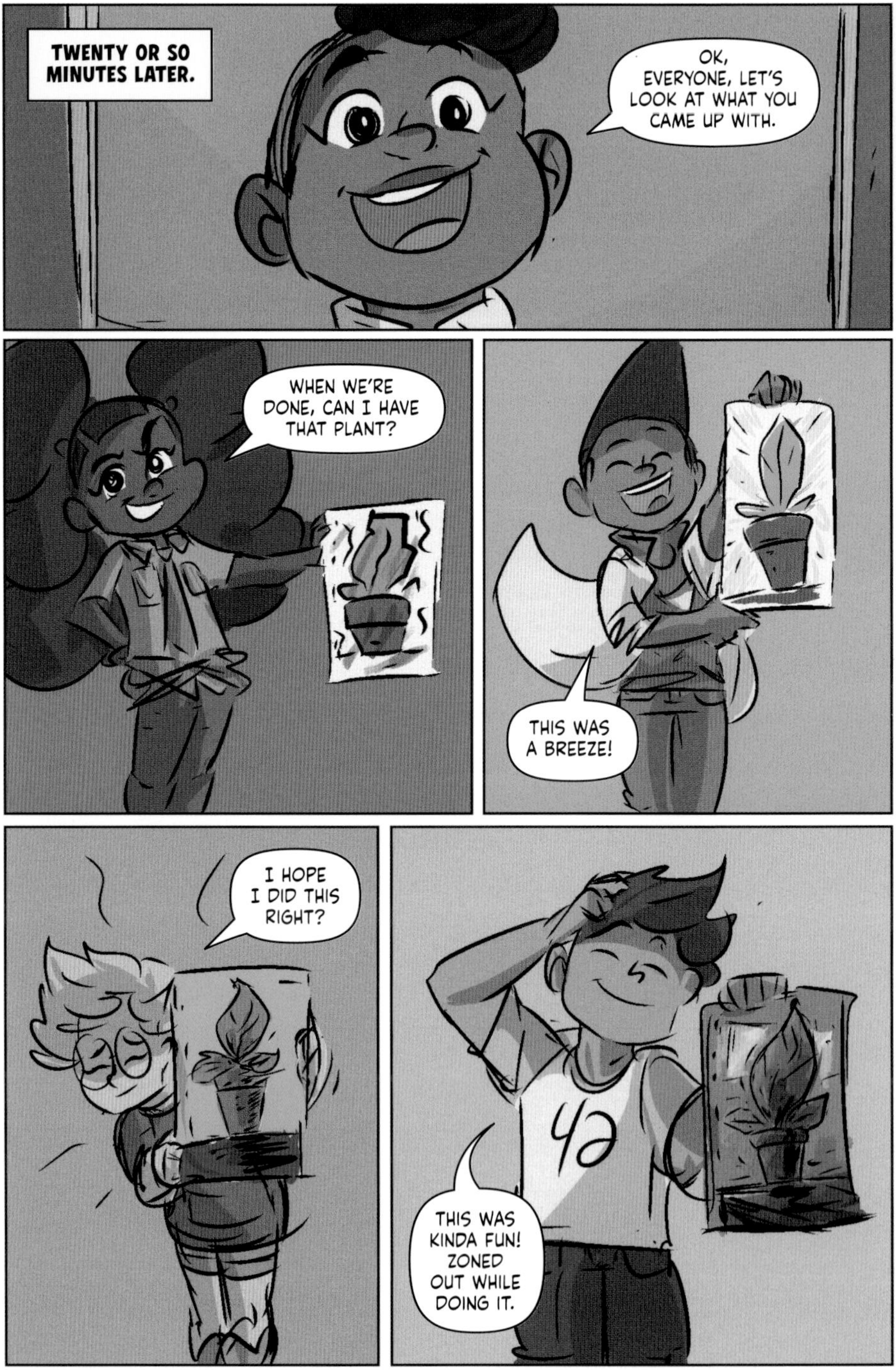
TWENTY OR SO MINUTES LATER.
OK, EVERYONE, LET'S LOOK AT WHAT YOU CAME UP WITH.
WHEN WE'RE DONE, CAN I HAVE THAT PLANT?
THIS WAS A BREEZE!
I HOPE I DID THIS RIGHT?
THIS WAS KINDA FUN! ZONED OUT WHILE DOING IT.

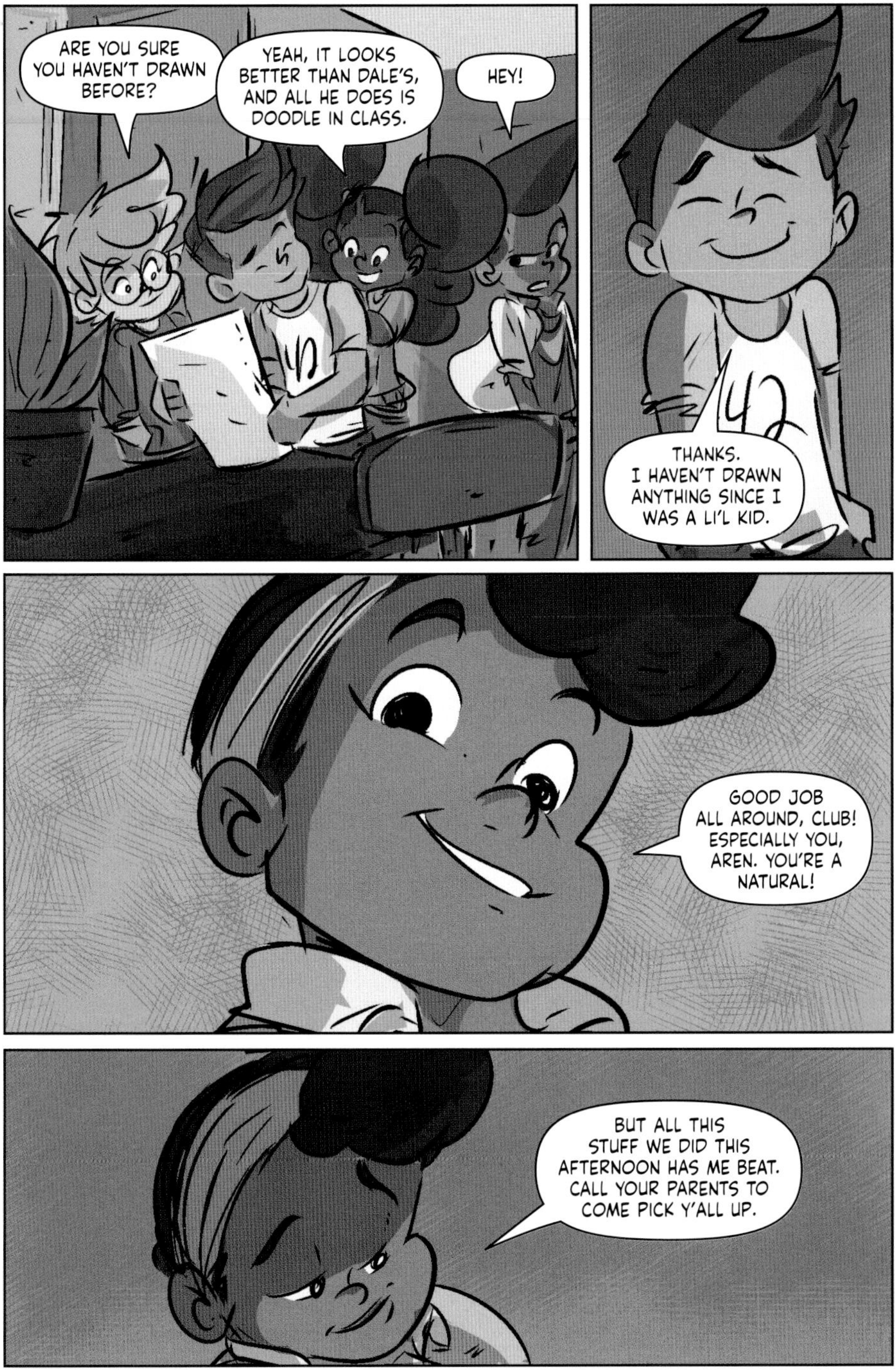
ARE YOU SURE YOU HAVEN'T DRAWN BEFORE?
YEAH, IT LOOKS BETTER THAN DALE'S, AND ALL HE DOES IS DOODLE IN CLASS.
HEY!
THANKS. I HAVEN'T DRAWN ANYTHING SINCE I WAS A LI'L KID.
GOOD JOB ALL AROUND, CLUB! ESPECIALLY YOU, AREN. YOU'RE A NATURAL!
BUT ALL THIS STUFF WE DID THIS AFTERNOON HAS ME BEAT. CALL YOUR PARENTS TO COME PICK Y'ALL UP.

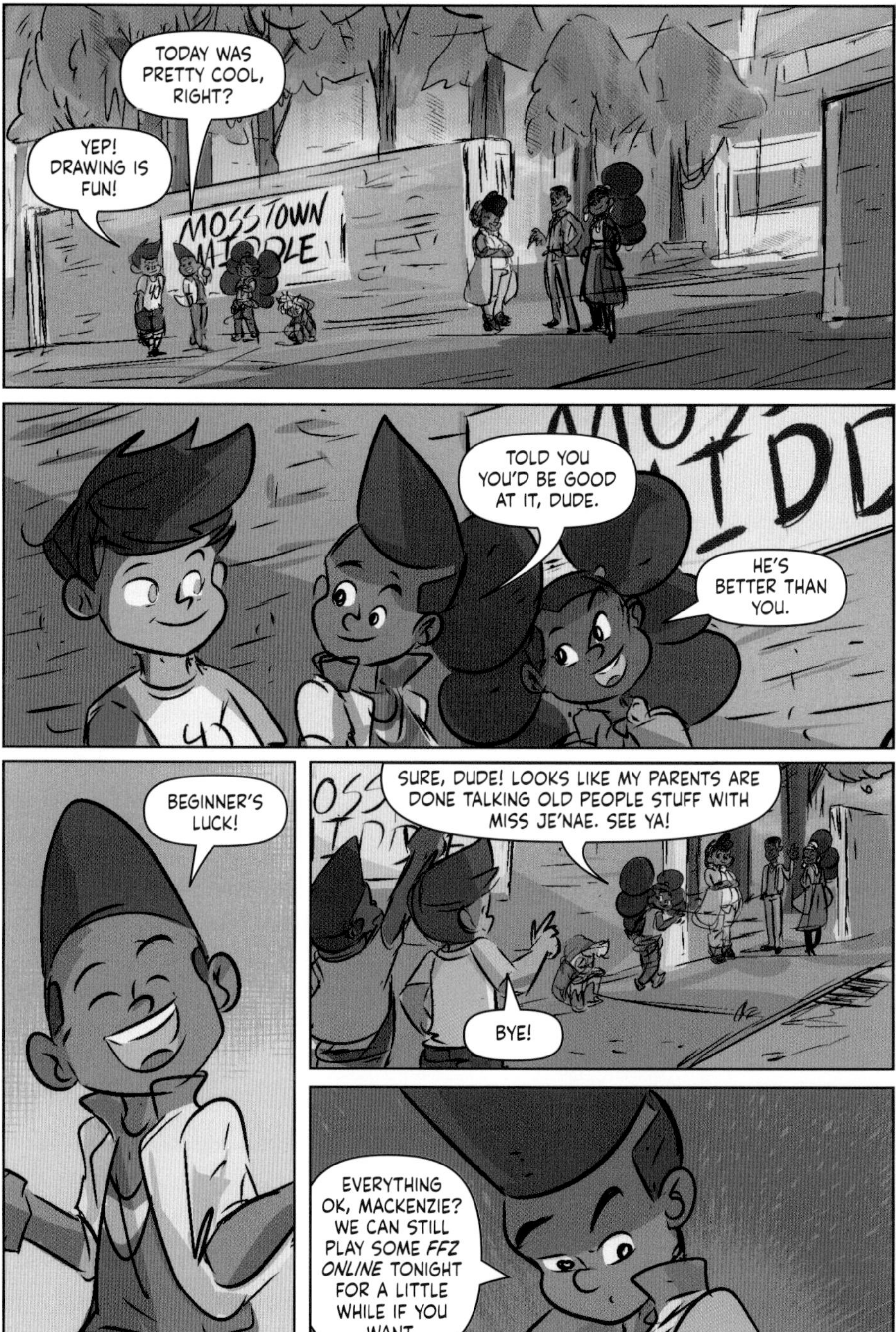
TODAY WAS PRETTY COOL, RIGHT?
YEP! DRAWING IS FUN!
MOSSTOWN MIDDLE
TOLD YOU YOU'D BE GOOD AT IT, DUDE.
HE'S BETTER THAN YOU.
BEGINNER'S LUCK!
SURE, DUDE! LOOKS LIKE MY PARENTS ARE DONE TALKING OLD PEOPLE STUFF WITH MISS JE'NAE. SEE YA!
BYE!
EVERYTHING OK, MACKENZIE? WE CAN STILL PLAY SOME *FFZ ONLINE* TONIGHT FOR A LITTLE WHILE IF YOU WANT.

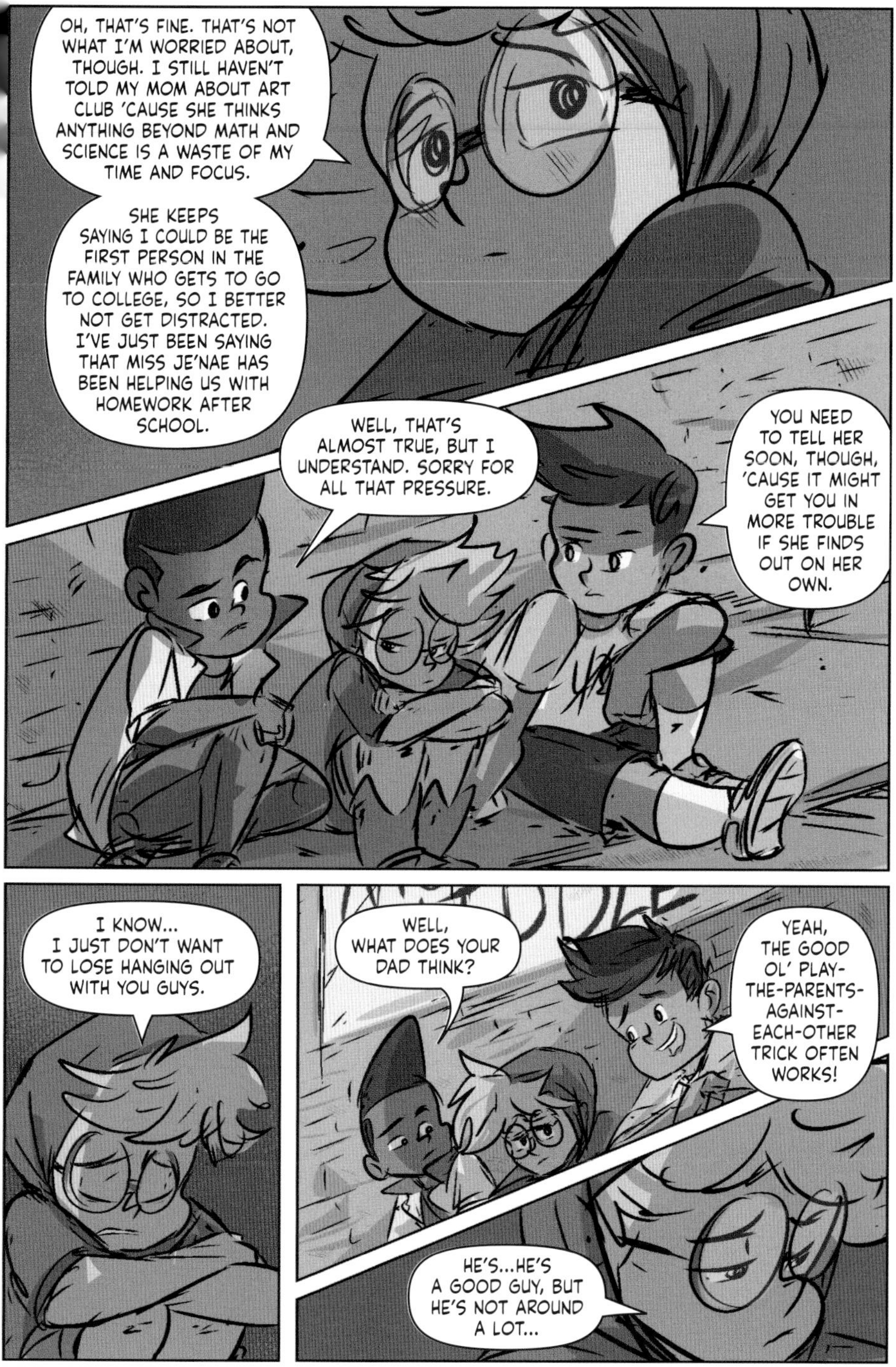
OH, THAT'S FINE. THAT'S NOT WHAT I'M WORRIED ABOUT, THOUGH. I STILL HAVEN'T TOLD MY MOM ABOUT ART CLUB 'CAUSE SHE THINKS ANYTHING BEYOND MATH AND SCIENCE IS A WASTE OF MY TIME AND FOCUS.
SHE KEEPS SAYING I COULD BE THE FIRST PERSON IN THE FAMILY WHO GETS TO GO TO COLLEGE, SO I BETTER NOT GET DISTRACTED. I'VE JUST BEEN SAYING THAT MISS JE'NAE HAS BEEN HELPING US WITH HOMEWORK AFTER SCHOOL.
WELL, THAT'S ALMOST TRUE, BUT I UNDERSTAND. SORRY FOR ALL THAT PRESSURE.
YOU NEED TO TELL HER SOON, THOUGH, 'CAUSE IT MIGHT GET YOU IN MORE TROUBLE IF SHE FINDS OUT ON HER OWN.
I KNOW... I JUST DON'T WANT TO LOSE HANGING OUT WITH YOU GUYS.
WELL, WHAT DOES YOUR DAD THINK?
YEAH, THE GOOD OL' PLAY-THE-PARENTS-AGAINST-EACH-OTHER TRICK OFTEN WORKS!
HE'S...HE'S A GOOD GUY, BUT HE'S NOT AROUND A LOT...

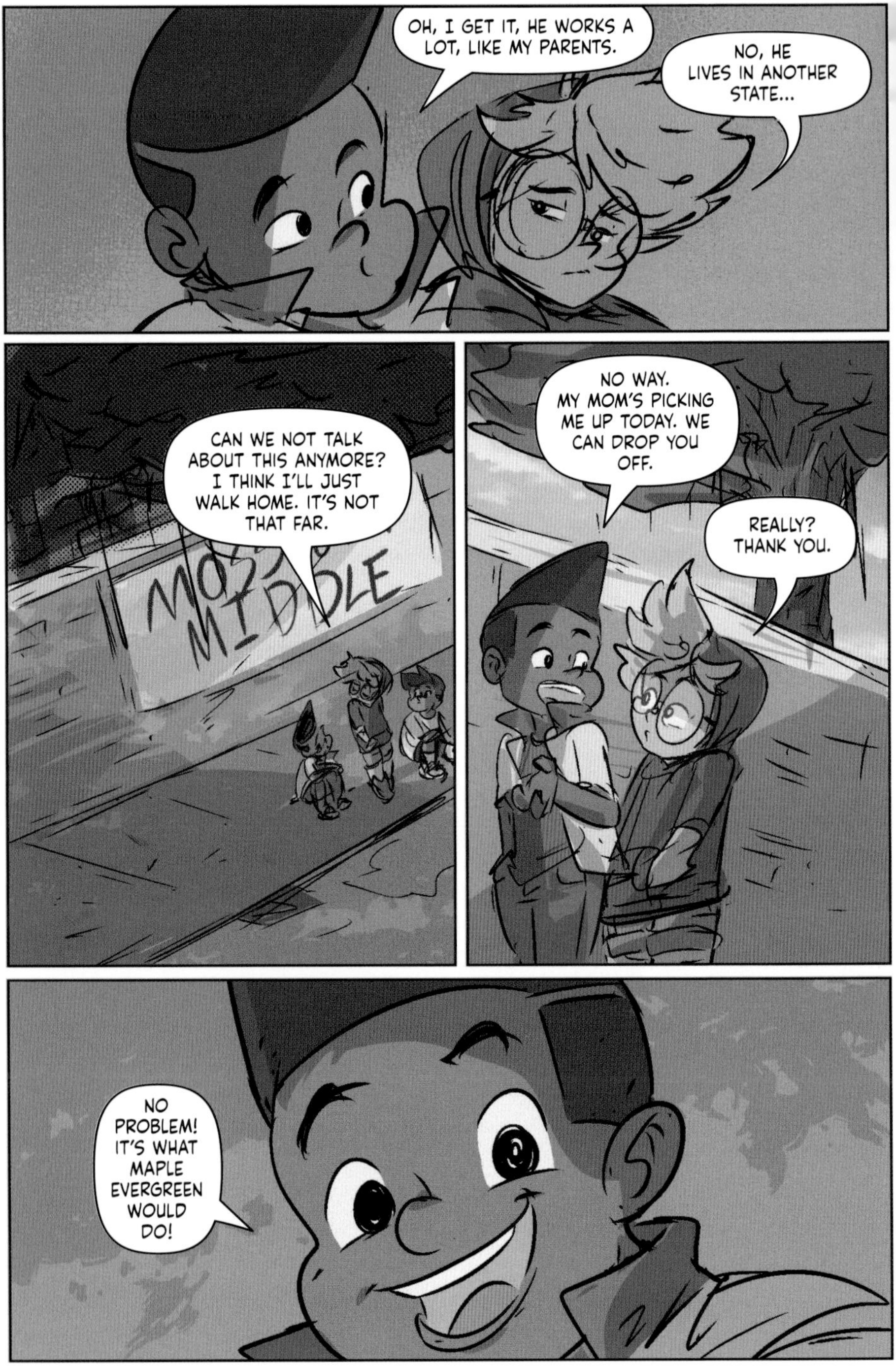
OH, I GET IT, HE WORKS A LOT, LIKE MY PARENTS.
NO, HE LIVES IN ANOTHER STATE...
CAN WE NOT TALK ABOUT THIS ANYMORE? I THINK I'LL JUST WALK HOME. IT'S NOT THAT FAR.
MIDDLE
NO WAY. MY MOM'S PICKING ME UP TODAY. WE CAN DROP YOU OFF.
REALLY? THANK YOU.
NO PROBLEM! IT'S WHAT MAPLE EVERGREEN WOULD DO!

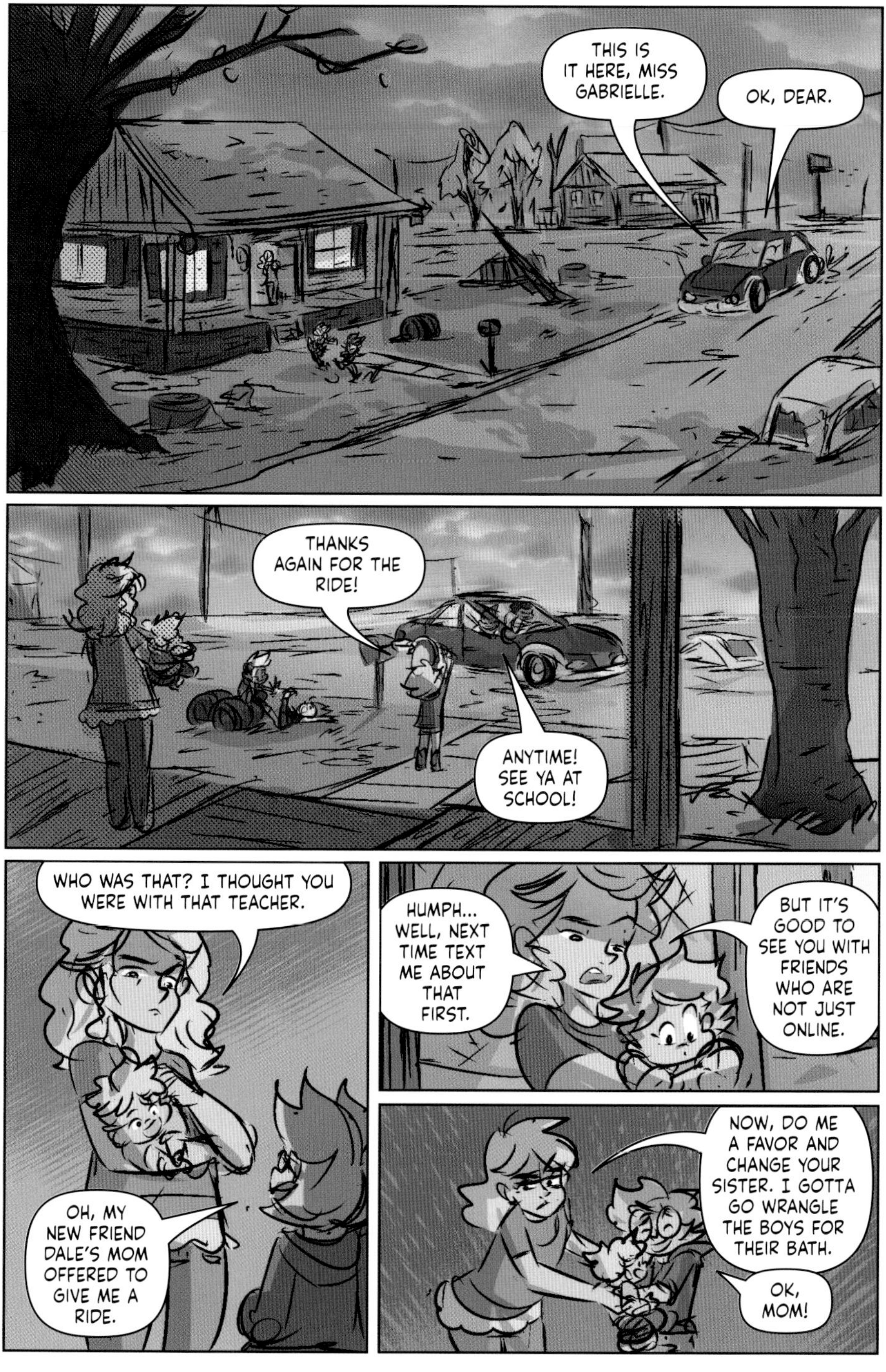
THIS IS IT HERE, MISS GABRIELLE.
OK, DEAR.
THANKS AGAIN FOR THE RIDE!
ANYTIME! SEE YA AT SCHOOL!
WHO WAS THAT? I THOUGHT YOU WERE WITH THAT TEACHER.
OH, MY NEW FRIEND DALE'S MOM OFFERED TO GIVE ME A RIDE.
HUMPH... WELL, NEXT TIME TEXT ME ABOUT THAT FIRST.
BUT IT'S GOOD TO SEE YOU WITH FRIENDS WHO ARE NOT JUST ONLINE.
NOW, DO ME A FAVOR AND CHANGE YOUR SISTER. I GOTTA GO WRANGLE THE BOYS FOR THEIR BATH.
OK, MOM!

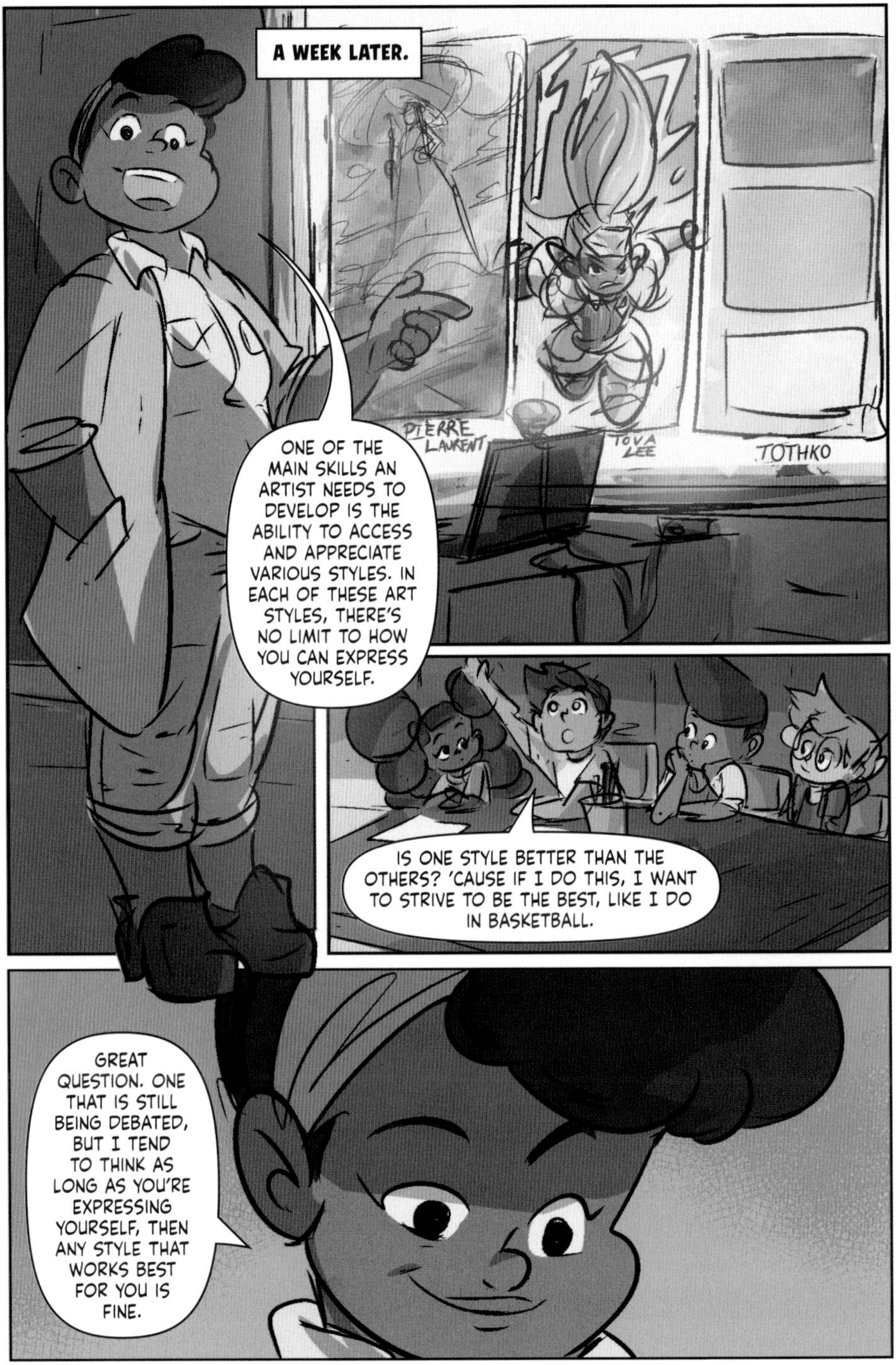
A WEEK LATER.
PIERRE LAURENT
TOVA LEE
TOTHKO
ONE OF THE MAIN SKILLS AN ARTIST NEEDS TO DEVELOP IS THE ABILITY TO ACCESS AND APPRECIATE VARIOUS STYLES. IN EACH OF THESE ART STYLES, THERE'S NO LIMIT TO HOW YOU CAN EXPRESS YOURSELF.
IS ONE STYLE BETTER THAN THE OTHERS? 'CAUSE IF I DO THIS, I WANT TO STRIVE TO BE THE BEST, LIKE I DO IN BASKETBALL.
GREAT QUESTION. ONE THAT IS STILL BEING DEBATED, BUT I TEND TO THINK AS LONG AS YOU'RE EXPRESSING YOURSELF, THEN ANY STYLE THAT WORKS BEST FOR YOU IS FINE.

WOW! THESE KINDA LOOK LIKE CONCEPT ART FROM GAMES, BUT WITHOUT ALL THE FANTASY STUFF.

THIS PIECE IS CONSIDERED CLASSICAL REALISM. BEFORE THE INTERNET, TV, AND EVEN PHOTOGRAPHS, THIS WAS A WAY FOR ARTISTS TO REPLICATE THE WORLD AS REALISTICALLY AS POSSIBLE, AS WELL AS IMMORTALIZE MOMENTS FOR OTHERS TO APPRECIATE.

GREAT CONNECTION, MACKENZIE! VIDEO-GAME CONCEPT ART OFTEN COMBINES REALITY WITH FICTIONAL ASPECTS.

AND BELIEVE IT OR NOT, A LOT OF ARTISTS FROM THIS TIME WERE KNOWN TO EXAGGERATE THE REALITY THEY WERE PAINTING.

NEXT IS ABSTRACT EXPRESSIONISM, IN WHICH ARTISTS TRIED LESS TO REPLICATE THE WORLD WE SEE AND TRIED MORE INNOVATIVE WAYS TO EXPRESS WHAT THEY FELT OR BELIEVED.

WHOA, THIS IS GETTING DEEP.

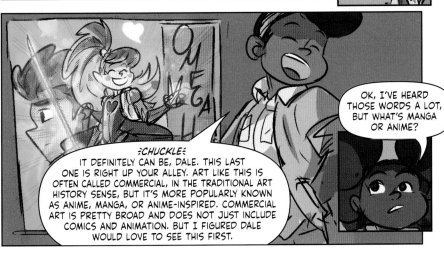

OK, I'VE HEARD THOSE WORDS A LOT, BUT WHAT'S MANGA OR ANIME?

≥CHUCKLE≤
IT DEFINITELY CAN BE, DALE. THIS LAST ONE IS RIGHT UP YOUR ALLEY. ART LIKE THIS IS OFTEN CALLED COMMERCIAL, IN THE TRADITIONAL ART HISTORY SENSE, BUT IT'S MORE POPULARLY KNOWN AS ANIME, MANGA, OR ANIME-INSPIRED. COMMERCIAL ART IS PRETTY BROAD AND DOES NOT JUST INCLUDE COMICS AND ANIMATION. BUT I FIGURED DALE WOULD LOVE TO SEE THIS FIRST.

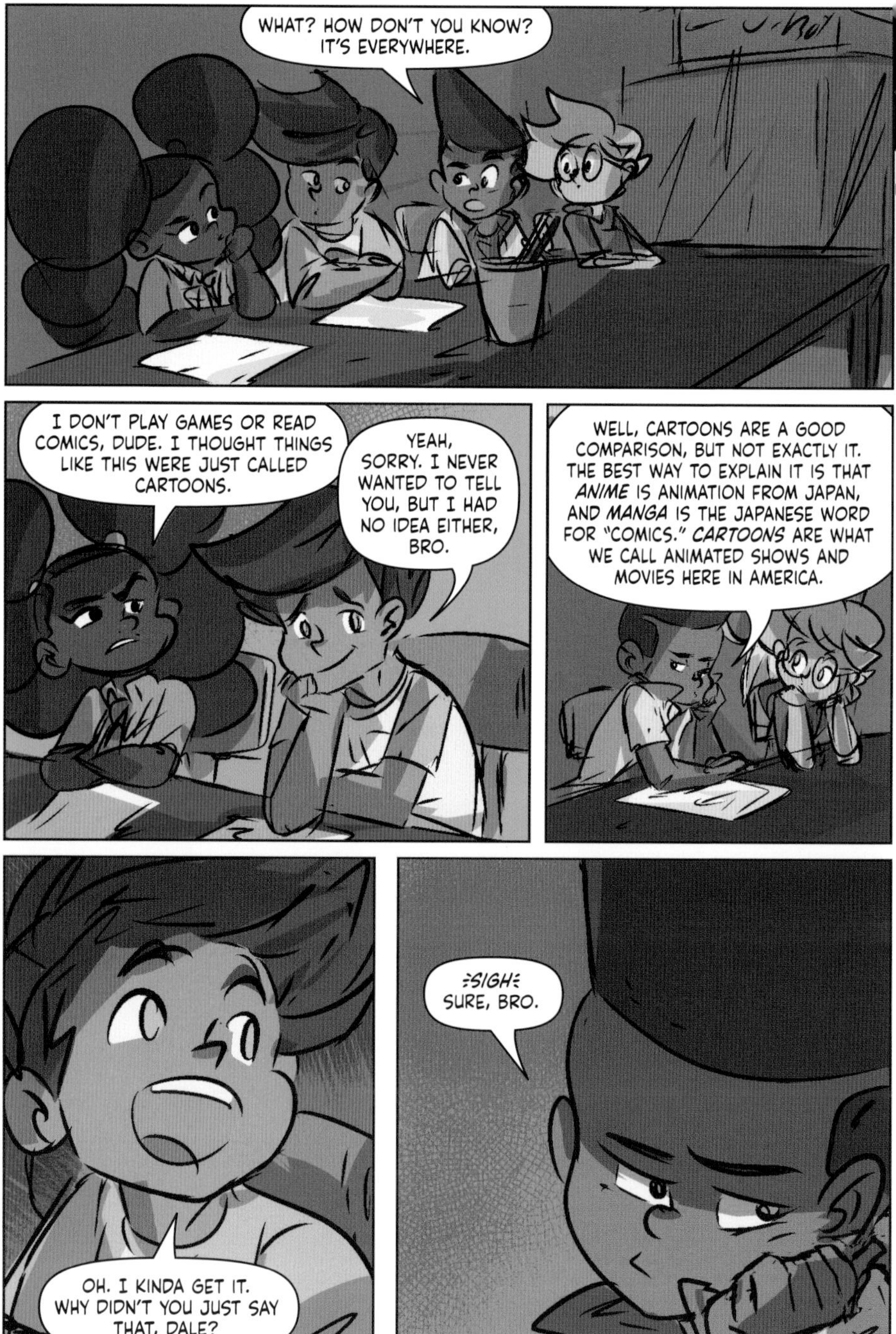
WHAT? HOW DON'T YOU KNOW? IT'S EVERYWHERE.
I DON'T PLAY GAMES OR READ COMICS, DUDE. I THOUGHT THINGS LIKE THIS WERE JUST CALLED CARTOONS.
YEAH, SORRY. I NEVER WANTED TO TELL YOU, BUT I HAD NO IDEA EITHER, BRO.
WELL, CARTOONS ARE A GOOD COMPARISON, BUT NOT EXACTLY IT. THE BEST WAY TO EXPLAIN IT IS THAT *ANIME* IS ANIMATION FROM JAPAN, AND *MANGA* IS THE JAPANESE WORD FOR "COMICS." *CARTOONS* ARE WHAT WE CALL ANIMATED SHOWS AND MOVIES HERE IN AMERICA.
OH. I KINDA GET IT. WHY DIDN'T YOU JUST SAY THAT, DALE?
SIGH SURE, BRO.

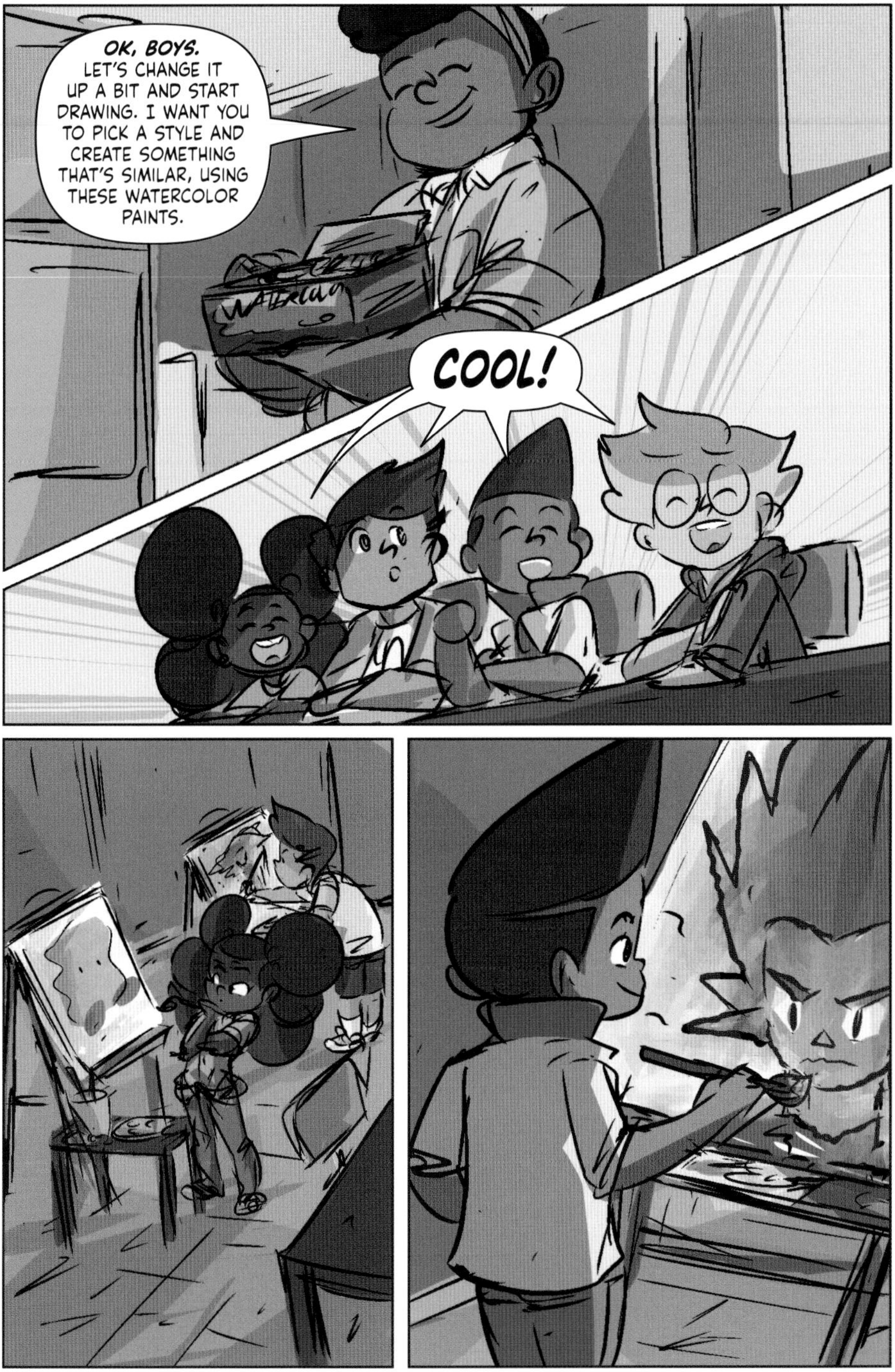
OK, BOYS. LET'S CHANGE IT UP A BIT AND START DRAWING. I WANT YOU TO PICK A STYLE AND CREATE SOMETHING THAT'S SIMILAR, USING THESE WATERCOLOR PAINTS.
COOL!

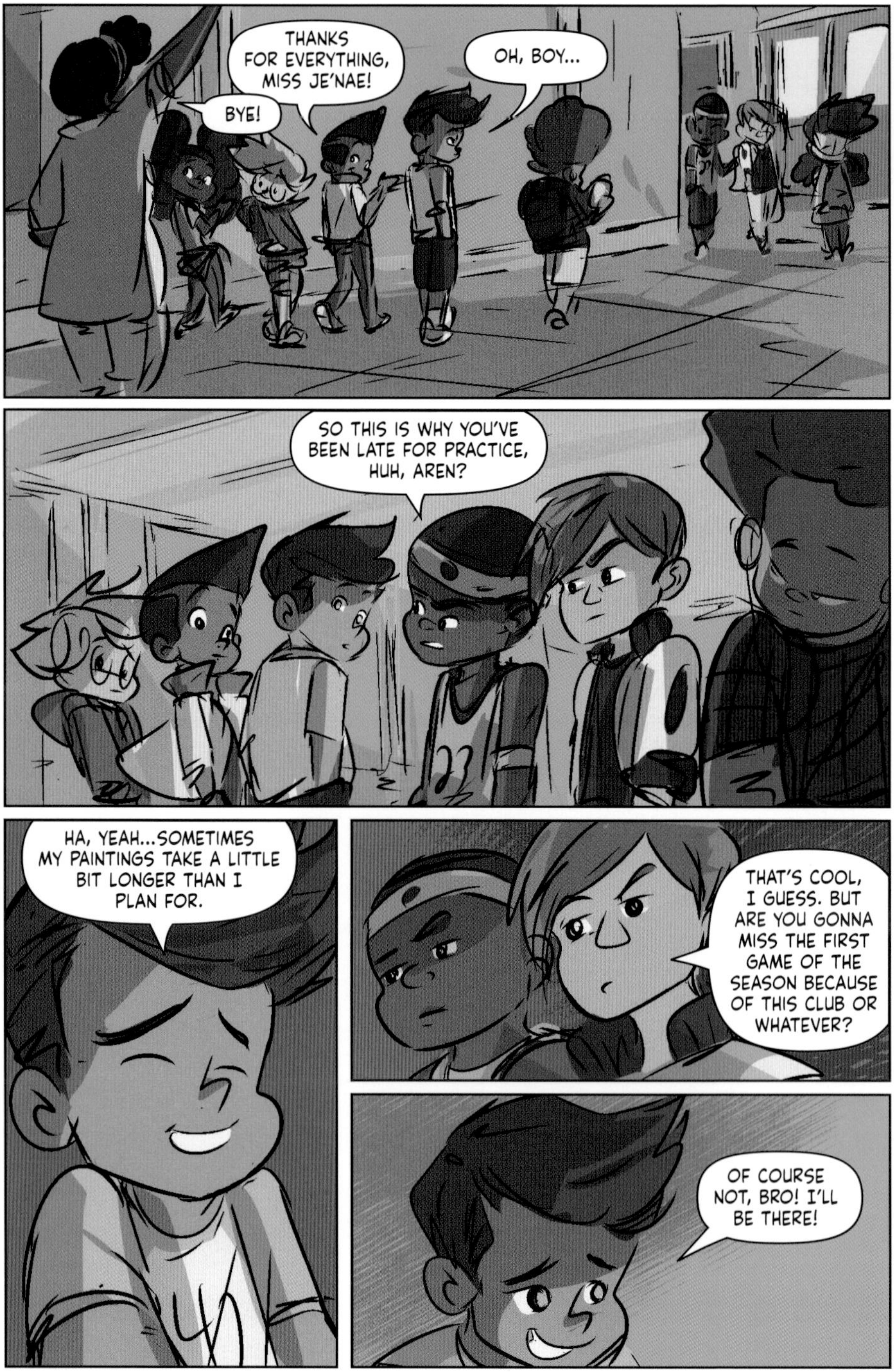
BYE!
THANKS FOR EVERYTHING, MISS JE'NAE!
OH, BOY...
SO THIS IS WHY YOU'VE BEEN LATE FOR PRACTICE, HUH, AREN?
HA, YEAH...SOMETIMES MY PAINTINGS TAKE A LITTLE BIT LONGER THAN I PLAN FOR.
THAT'S COOL, I GUESS. BUT ARE YOU GONNA MISS THE FIRST GAME OF THE SEASON BECAUSE OF THIS CLUB OR WHATEVER?
OF COURSE NOT, BRO! I'LL BE THERE!

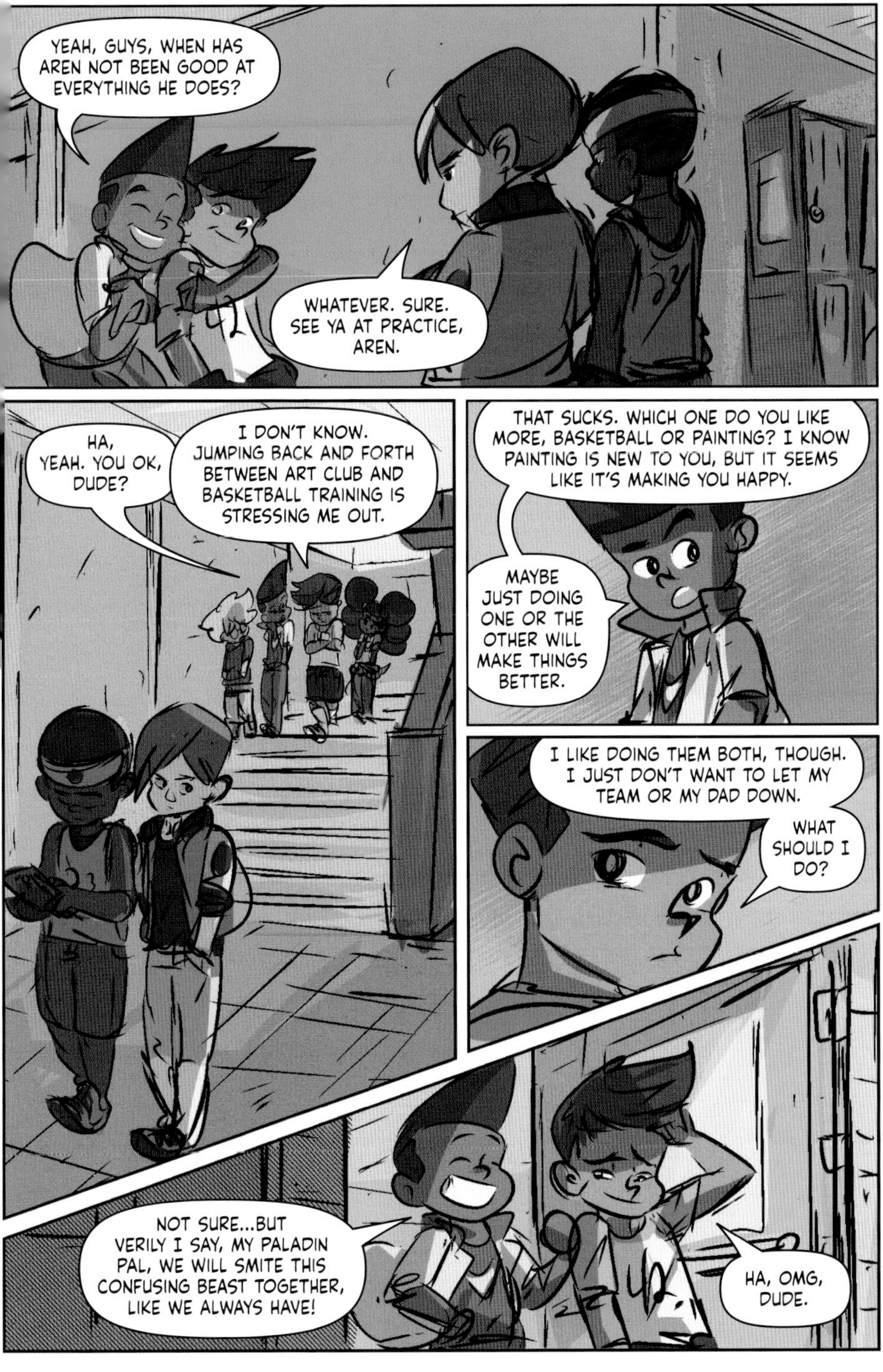
YEAH, GUYS, WHEN HAS AREN NOT BEEN GOOD AT EVERYTHING HE DOES?
WHATEVER. SURE. SEE YA AT PRACTICE, AREN.
HA, YEAH. YOU OK, DUDE?
I DON'T KNOW. JUMPING BACK AND FORTH BETWEEN ART CLUB AND BASKETBALL TRAINING IS STRESSING ME OUT.
THAT SUCKS. WHICH ONE DO YOU LIKE MORE, BASKETBALL OR PAINTING? I KNOW PAINTING IS NEW TO YOU, BUT IT SEEMS LIKE IT'S MAKING YOU HAPPY.
MAYBE JUST DOING ONE OR THE OTHER WILL MAKE THINGS BETTER.
I LIKE DOING THEM BOTH, THOUGH. I JUST DON'T WANT TO LET MY TEAM OR MY DAD DOWN.
WHAT SHOULD I DO?
NOT SURE...BUT VERILY I SAY, MY PALADIN PAL, WE WILL SMITE THIS CONFUSING BEAST TOGETHER, LIKE WE ALWAYS HAVE!
HA, OMG, DUDE.

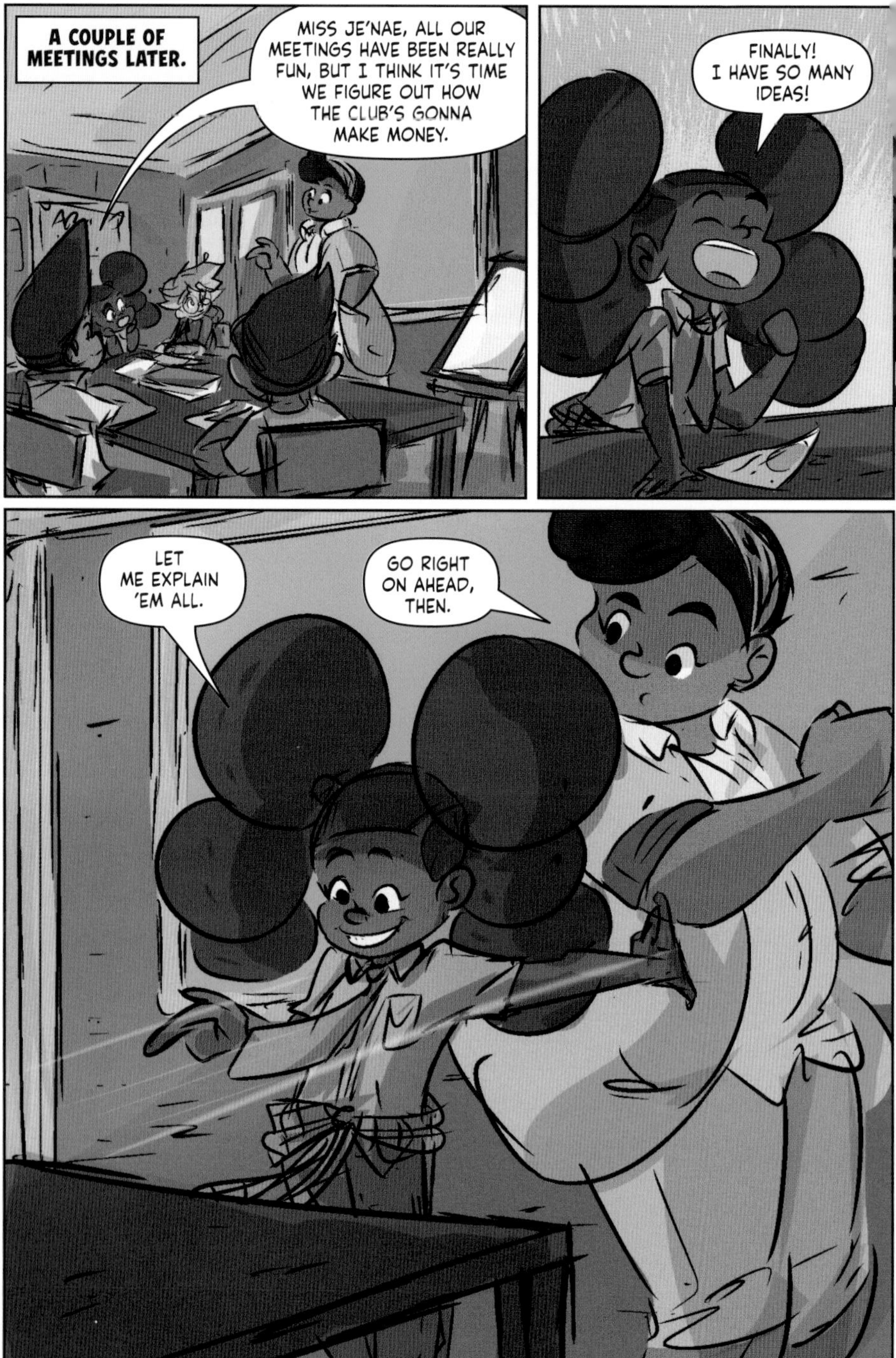
A COUPLE OF MEETINGS LATER.
MISS JE'NAE, ALL OUR MEETINGS HAVE BEEN REALLY FUN, BUT I THINK IT'S TIME WE FIGURE OUT HOW THE CLUB'S GONNA MAKE MONEY.
FINALLY! I HAVE SO MANY IDEAS!
LET ME EXPLAIN 'EM ALL.
GO RIGHT ON AHEAD, THEN.

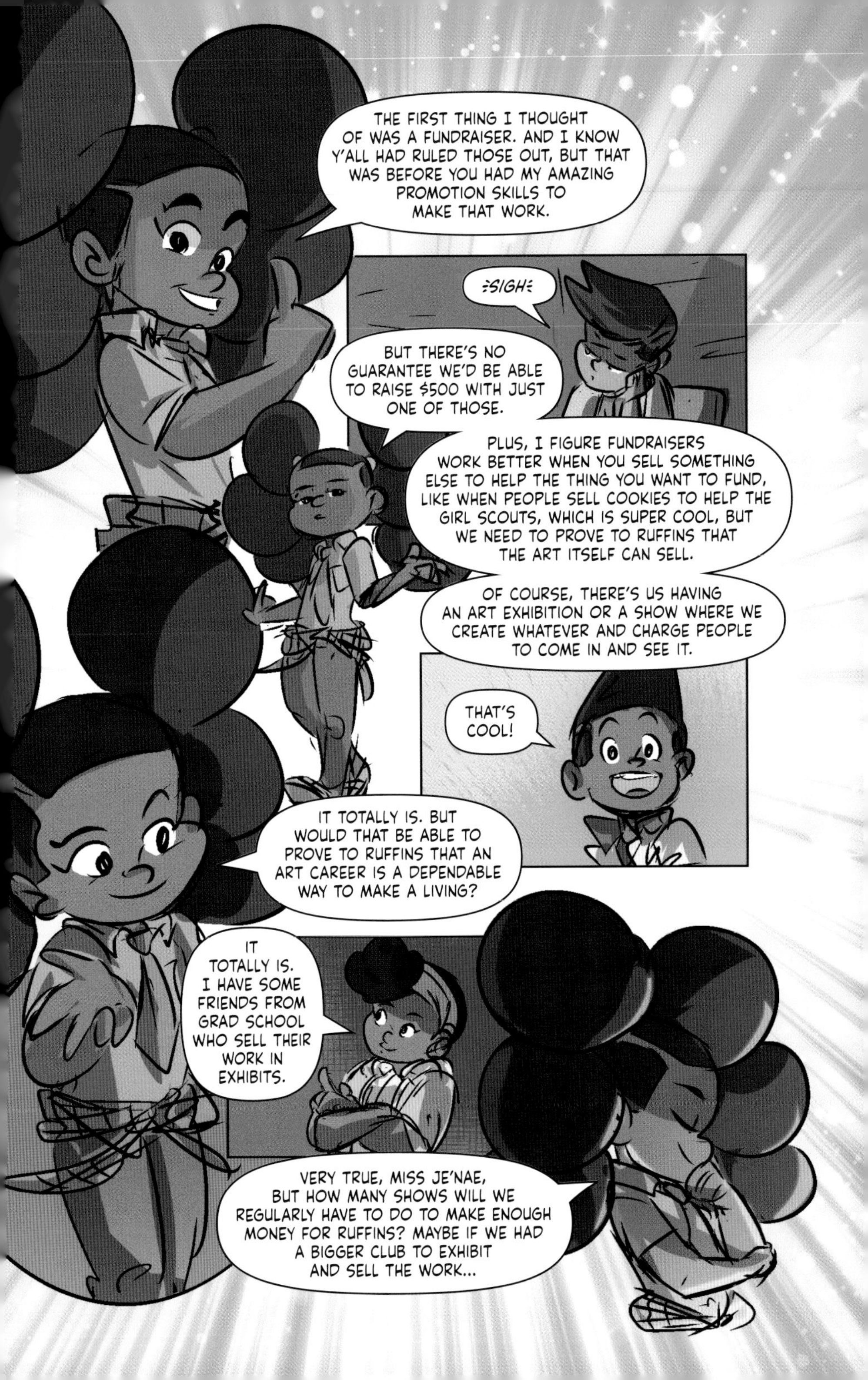
THE FIRST THING I THOUGHT OF WAS A FUNDRAISER. AND I KNOW Y'ALL HAD RULED THOSE OUT, BUT THAT WAS BEFORE YOU HAD MY AMAZING PROMOTION SKILLS TO MAKE THAT WORK.
SIGH
BUT THERE'S NO GUARANTEE WE'D BE ABLE TO RAISE $500 WITH JUST ONE OF THOSE.
PLUS, I FIGURE FUNDRAISERS WORK BETTER WHEN YOU SELL SOMETHING ELSE TO HELP THE THING YOU WANT TO FUND, LIKE WHEN PEOPLE SELL COOKIES TO HELP THE GIRL SCOUTS, WHICH IS SUPER COOL, BUT WE NEED TO PROVE TO RUFFINS THAT THE ART ITSELF CAN SELL.
OF COURSE, THERE'S US HAVING AN ART EXHIBITION OR A SHOW WHERE WE CREATE WHATEVER AND CHARGE PEOPLE TO COME IN AND SEE IT.
THAT'S COOL!
IT TOTALLY IS. BUT WOULD THAT BE ABLE TO PROVE TO RUFFINS THAT AN ART CAREER IS A DEPENDABLE WAY TO MAKE A LIVING?
IT TOTALLY IS. I HAVE SOME FRIENDS FROM GRAD SCHOOL WHO SELL THEIR WORK IN EXHIBITS.
VERY TRUE, MISS JE'NAE, BUT HOW MANY SHOWS WILL WE REGULARLY HAVE TO DO TO MAKE ENOUGH MONEY FOR RUFFINS? MAYBE IF WE HAD A BIGGER CLUB TO EXHIBIT AND SELL THE WORK...

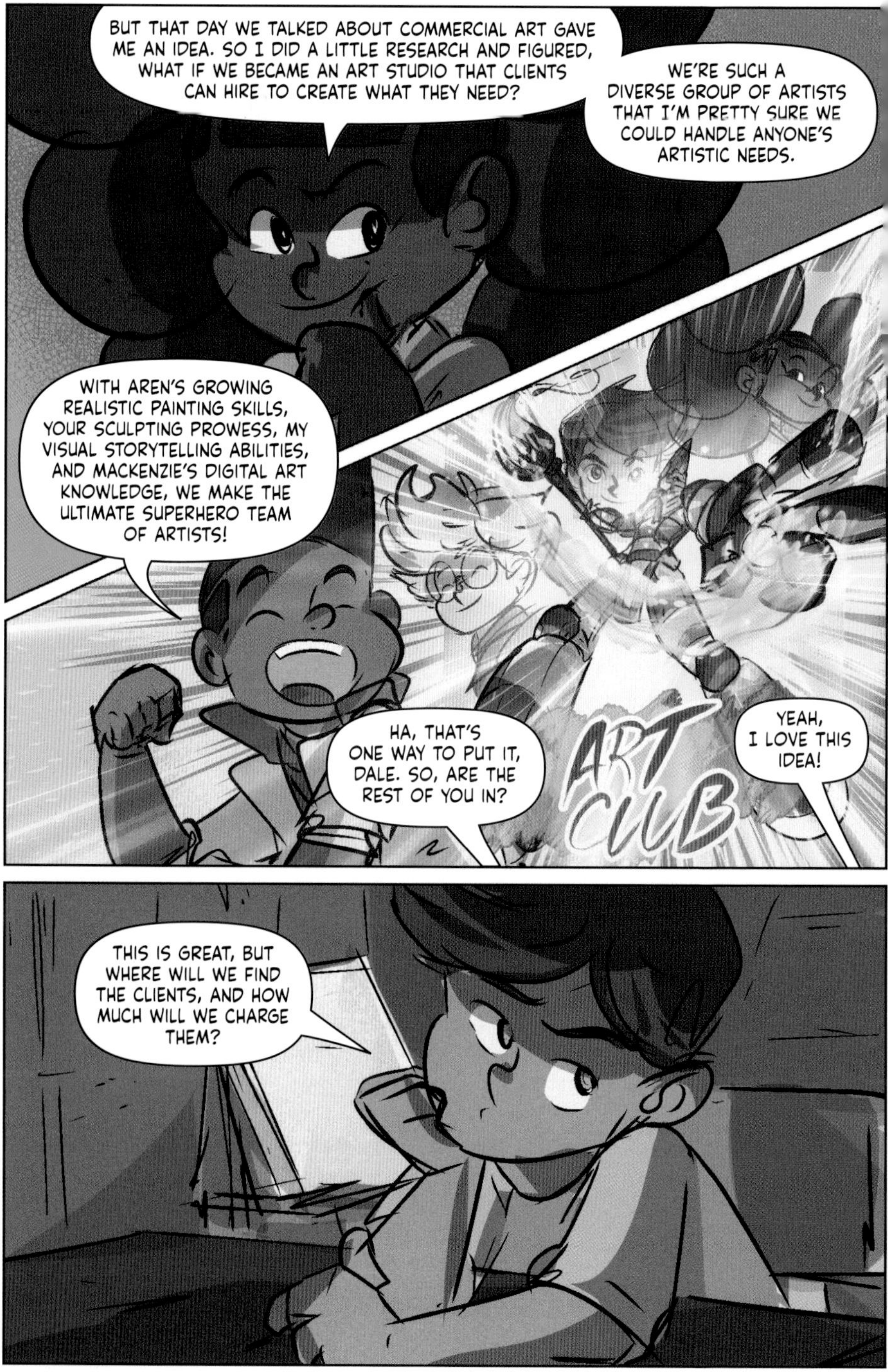

BUT THAT DAY WE TALKED ABOUT COMMERCIAL ART GAVE ME AN IDEA. SO I DID A LITTLE RESEARCH AND FIGURED, WHAT IF WE BECAME AN ART STUDIO THAT CLIENTS CAN HIRE TO CREATE WHAT THEY NEED?
WE'RE SUCH A DIVERSE GROUP OF ARTISTS THAT I'M PRETTY SURE WE COULD HANDLE ANYONE'S ARTISTIC NEEDS.
WITH AREN'S GROWING REALISTIC PAINTING SKILLS, YOUR SCULPTING PROWESS, MY VISUAL STORYTELLING ABILITIES, AND MACKENZIE'S DIGITAL ART KNOWLEDGE, WE MAKE THE ULTIMATE SUPERHERO TEAM OF ARTISTS!
HA, THAT'S ONE WAY TO PUT IT, DALE. SO, ARE THE REST OF YOU IN?
ART CLUB
YEAH, I LOVE THIS IDEA!
THIS IS GREAT, BUT WHERE WILL WE FIND THE CLIENTS, AND HOW MUCH WILL WE CHARGE THEM?

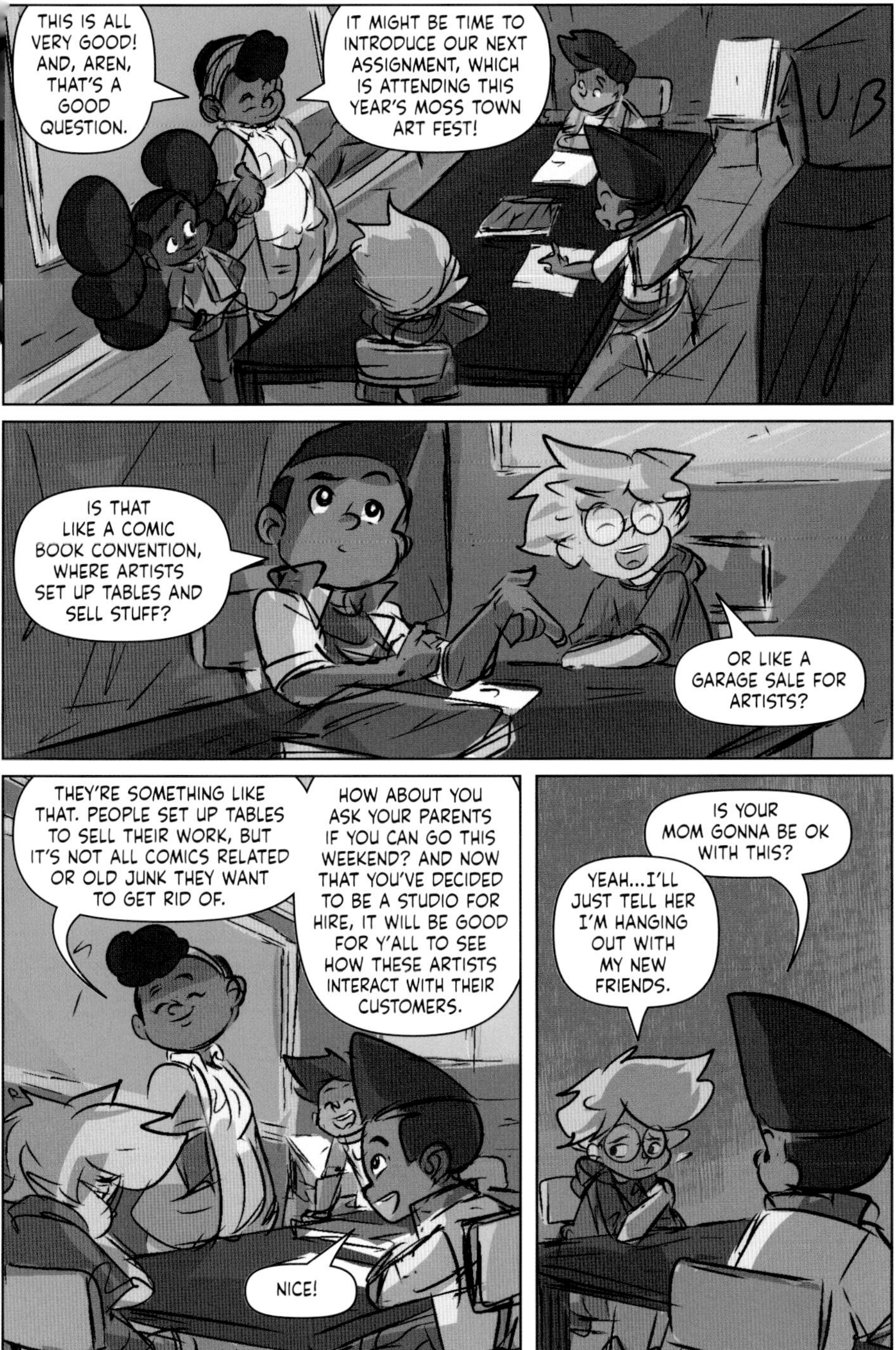
THIS IS ALL VERY GOOD! AND, AREN, THAT'S A GOOD QUESTION.
IT MIGHT BE TIME TO INTRODUCE OUR NEXT ASSIGNMENT, WHICH IS ATTENDING THIS YEAR'S MOSS TOWN ART FEST!
IS THAT LIKE A COMIC BOOK CONVENTION, WHERE ARTISTS SET UP TABLES AND SELL STUFF?
OR LIKE A GARAGE SALE FOR ARTISTS?
THEY'RE SOMETHING LIKE THAT. PEOPLE SET UP TABLES TO SELL THEIR WORK, BUT IT'S NOT ALL COMICS RELATED OR OLD JUNK THEY WANT TO GET RID OF.
HOW ABOUT YOU ASK YOUR PARENTS IF YOU CAN GO THIS WEEKEND? AND NOW THAT YOU'VE DECIDED TO BE A STUDIO FOR HIRE, IT WILL BE GOOD FOR Y'ALL TO SEE HOW THESE ARTISTS INTERACT WITH THEIR CUSTOMERS.
NICE!
IS YOUR MOM GONNA BE OK WITH THIS?
YEAH...I'LL JUST TELL HER I'M HANGING OUT WITH MY NEW FRIENDS.

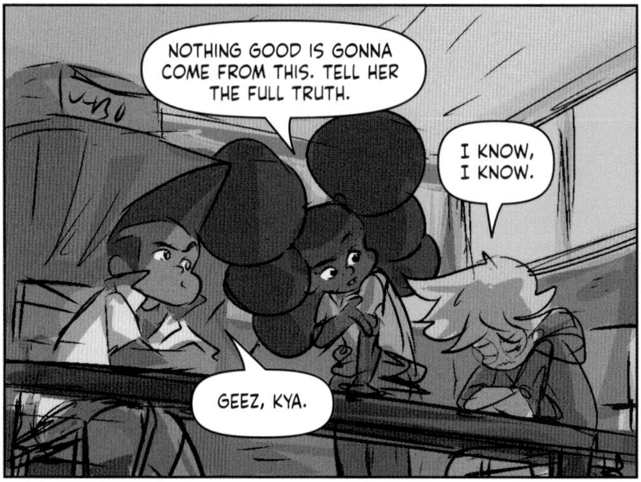
NOTHING GOOD IS GONNA COME FROM THIS. TELL HER THE FULL TRUTH.
I KNOW, I KNOW.
GEEZ, KYA.
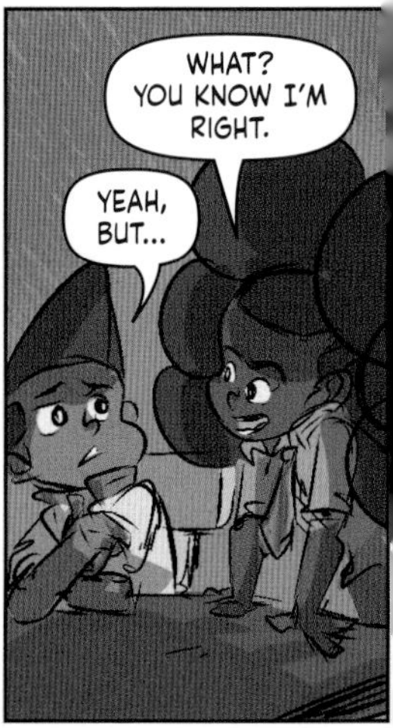
WHAT? YOU KNOW I'M RIGHT.
YEAH, BUT...
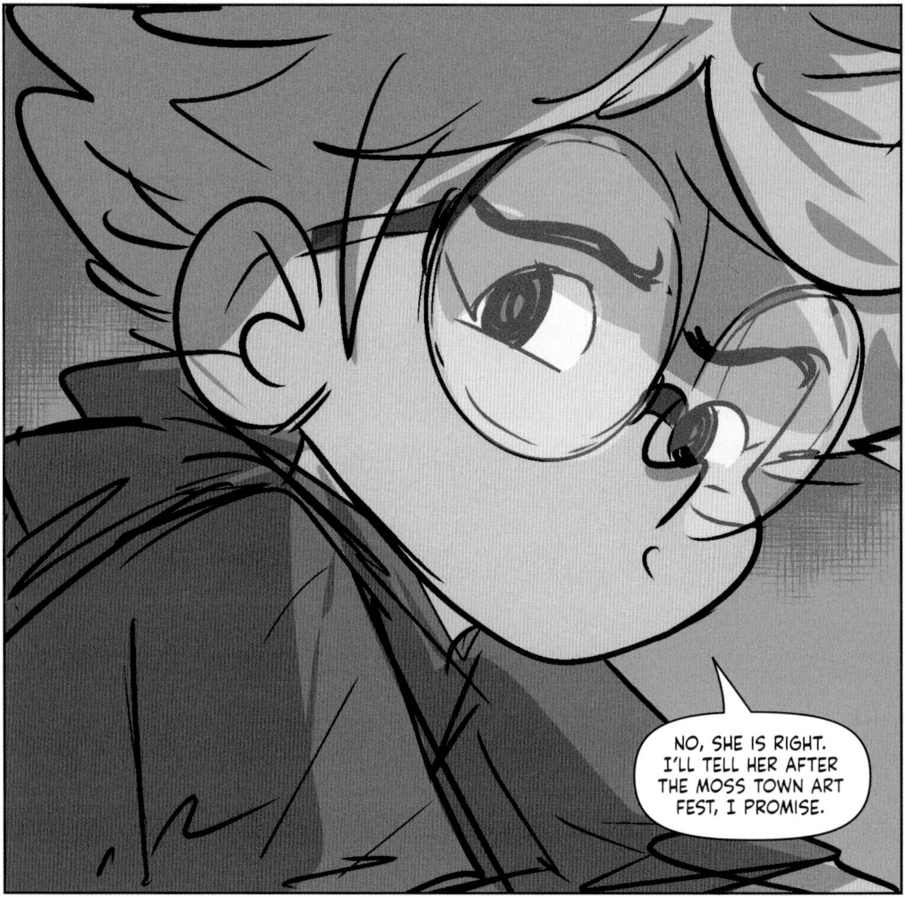
NO, SHE IS RIGHT. I'LL TELL HER AFTER THE MOSS TOWN ART FEST, I PROMISE.

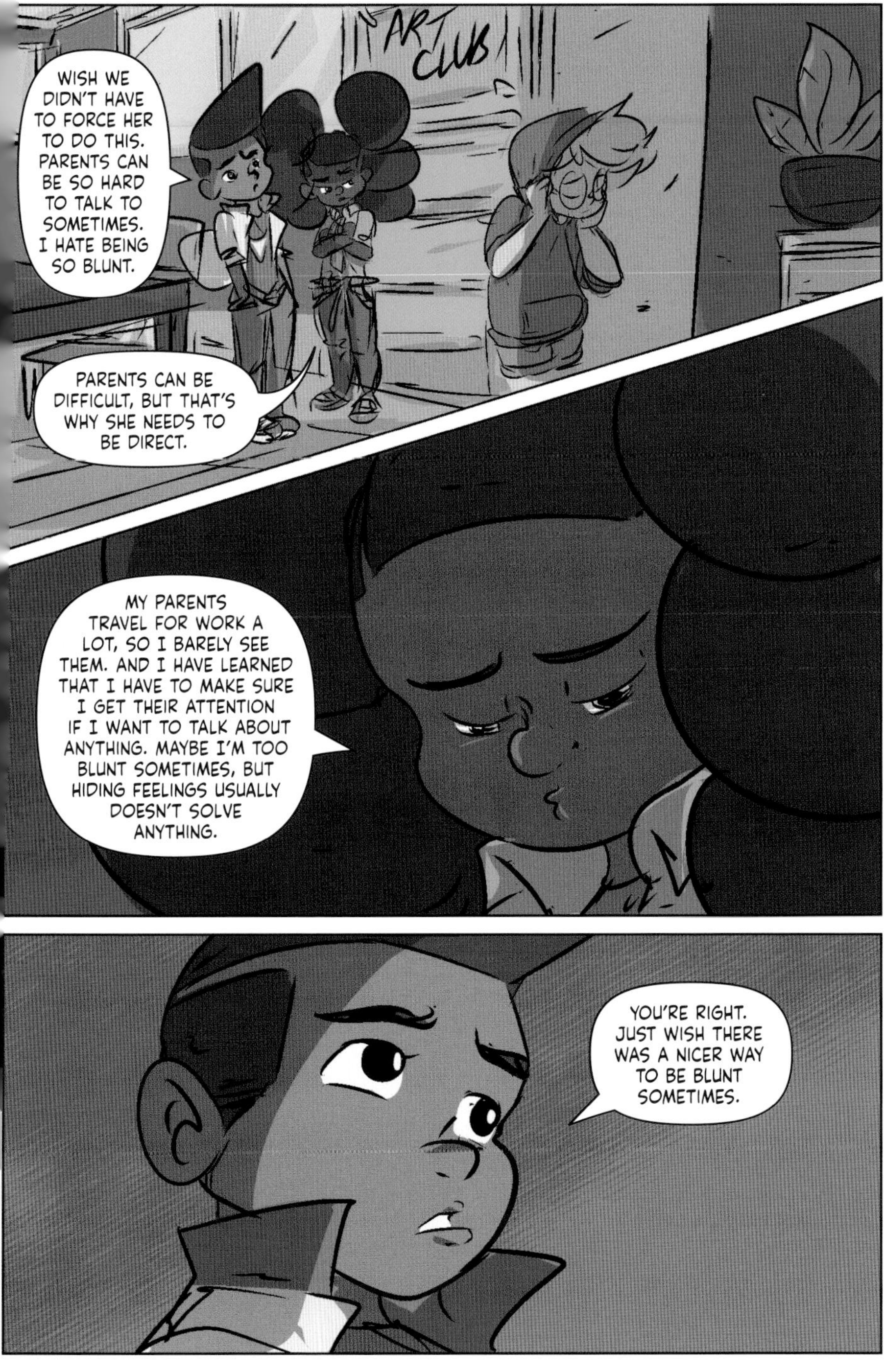
ART CLUB
WISH WE DIDN'T HAVE TO FORCE HER TO DO THIS. PARENTS CAN BE SO HARD TO TALK TO SOMETIMES. I HATE BEING SO BLUNT.
PARENTS CAN BE DIFFICULT, BUT THAT'S WHY SHE NEEDS TO BE DIRECT.
MY PARENTS TRAVEL FOR WORK A LOT, SO I BARELY SEE THEM. AND I HAVE LEARNED THAT I HAVE TO MAKE SURE I GET THEIR ATTENTION IF I WANT TO TALK ABOUT ANYTHING. MAYBE I'M TOO BLUNT SOMETIMES, BUT HIDING FEELINGS USUALLY DOESN'T SOLVE ANYTHING.
YOU'RE RIGHT. JUST WISH THERE WAS A NICER WAY TO BE BLUNT SOMETIMES.

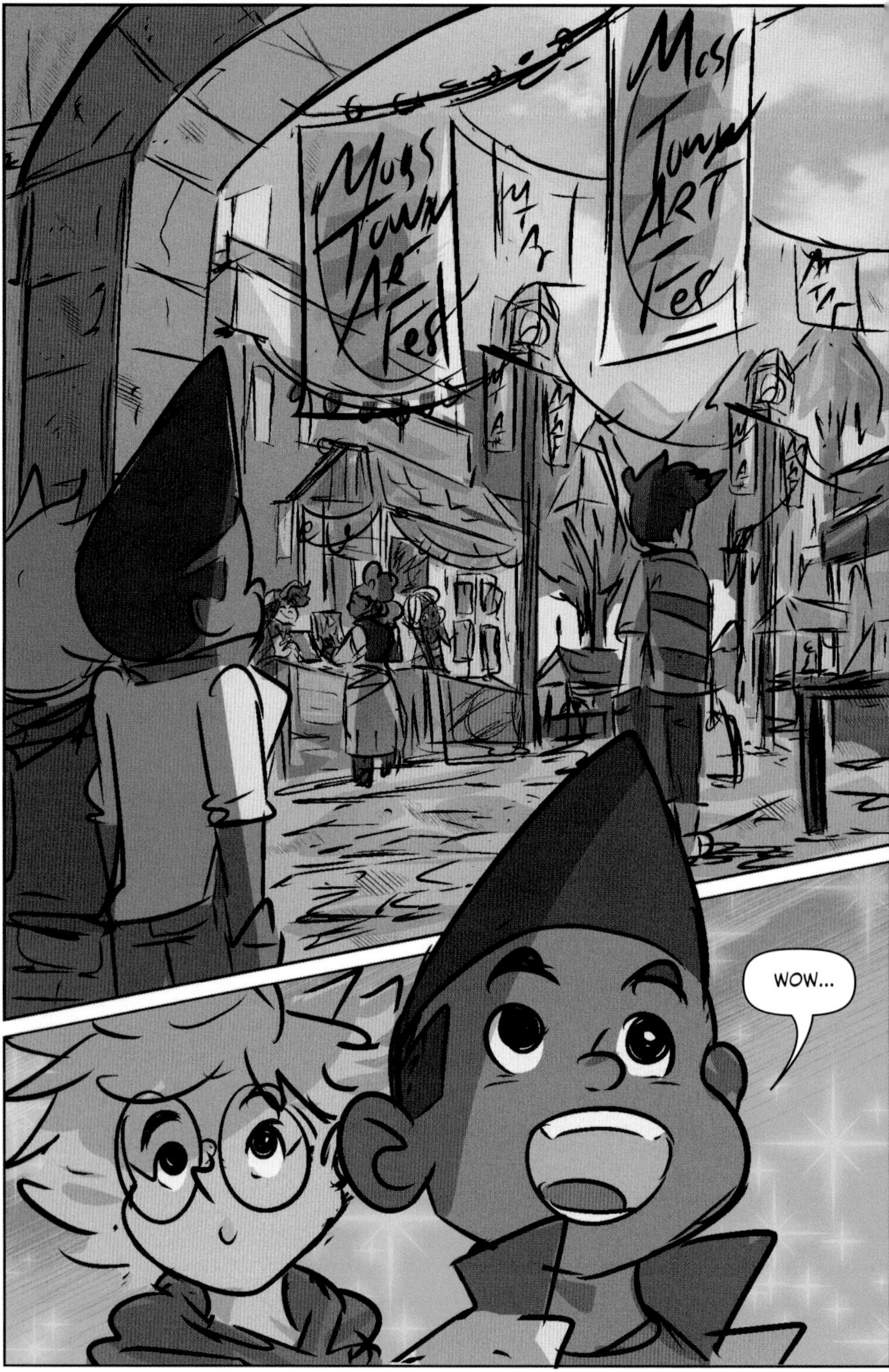
Moss Town ART Fest
WOW...

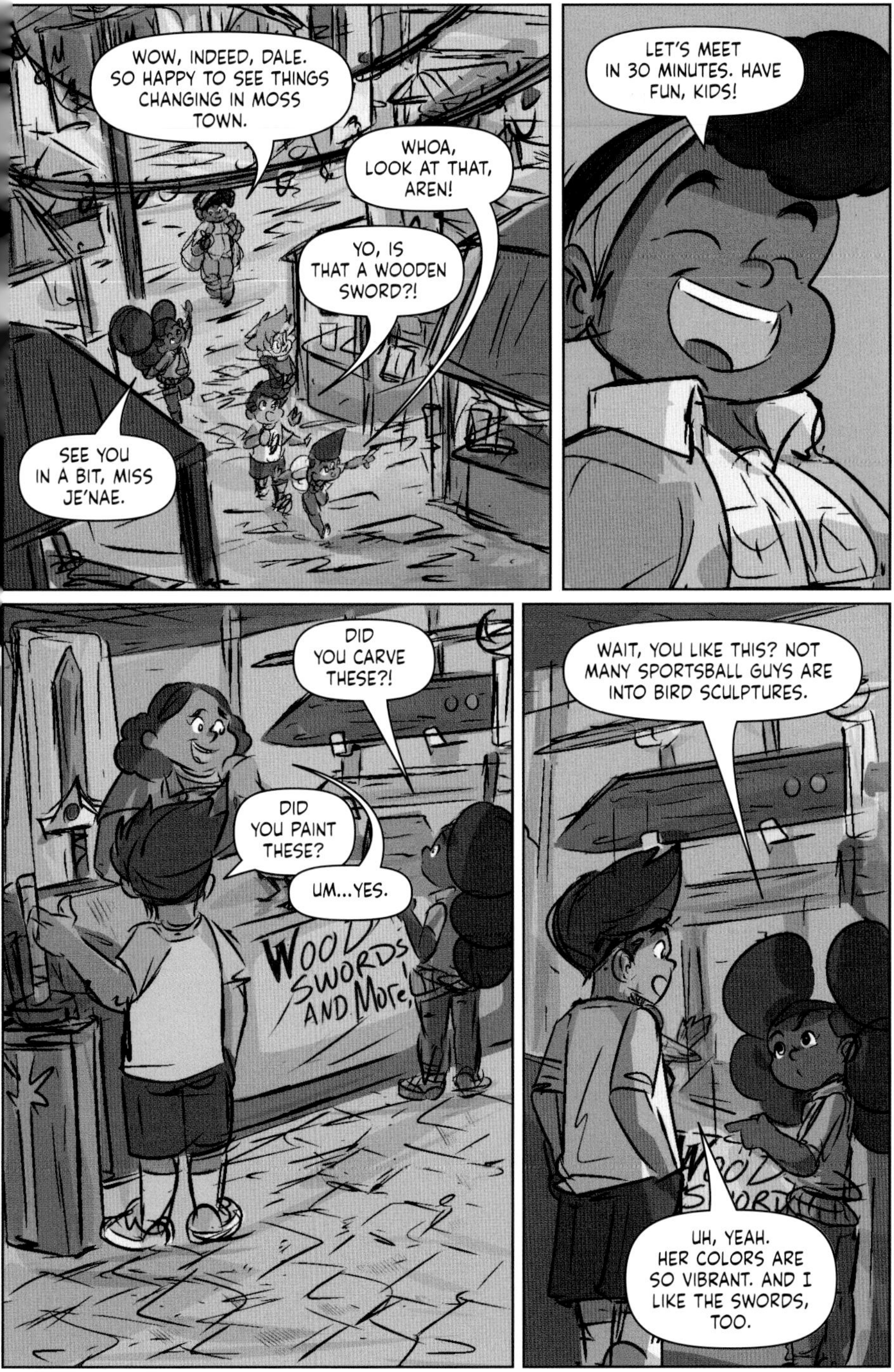
WOW, INDEED, DALE. SO HAPPY TO SEE THINGS CHANGING IN MOSS TOWN.
WHOA, LOOK AT THAT, AREN!
YO, IS THAT A WOODEN SWORD?!
SEE YOU IN A BIT, MISS JE'NAE.
LET'S MEET IN 30 MINUTES. HAVE FUN, KIDS!
DID YOU CARVE THESE?!
DID YOU PAINT THESE?
UM...YES.
WOOD SWORDS AND More!
WAIT, YOU LIKE THIS? NOT MANY SPORTSBALL GUYS ARE INTO BIRD SCULPTURES.
UH, YEAH. HER COLORS ARE SO VIBRANT. AND I LIKE THE SWORDS, TOO.

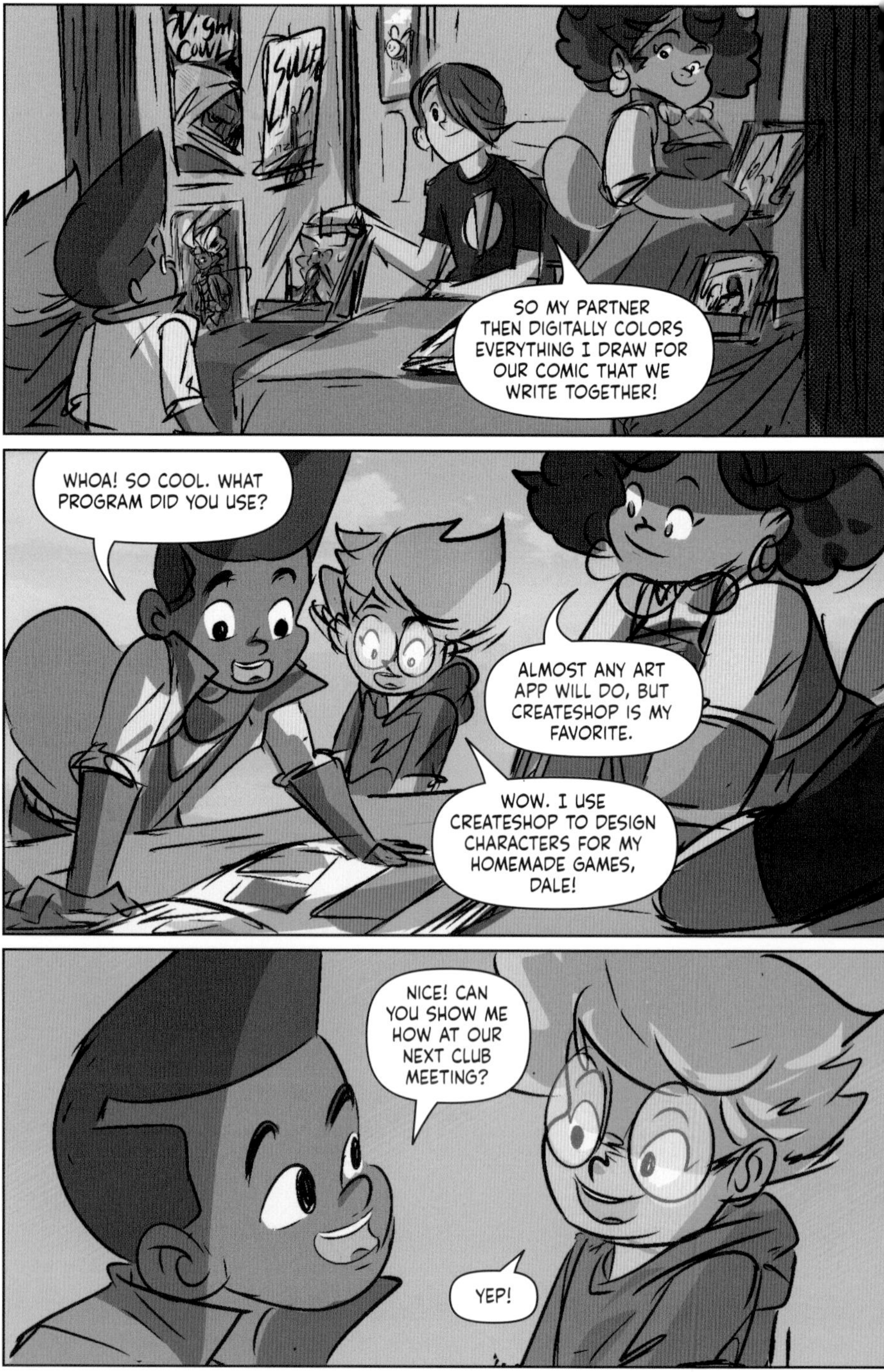
SO MY PARTNER THEN DIGITALLY COLORS EVERYTHING I DRAW FOR OUR COMIC THAT WE WRITE TOGETHER!
WHOA! SO COOL. WHAT PROGRAM DID YOU USE?
ALMOST ANY ART APP WILL DO, BUT CREATESHOP IS MY FAVORITE.
WOW. I USE CREATESHOP TO DESIGN CHARACTERS FOR MY HOMEMADE GAMES, DALE!
NICE! CAN YOU SHOW ME HOW AT OUR NEXT CLUB MEETING?
YEP!

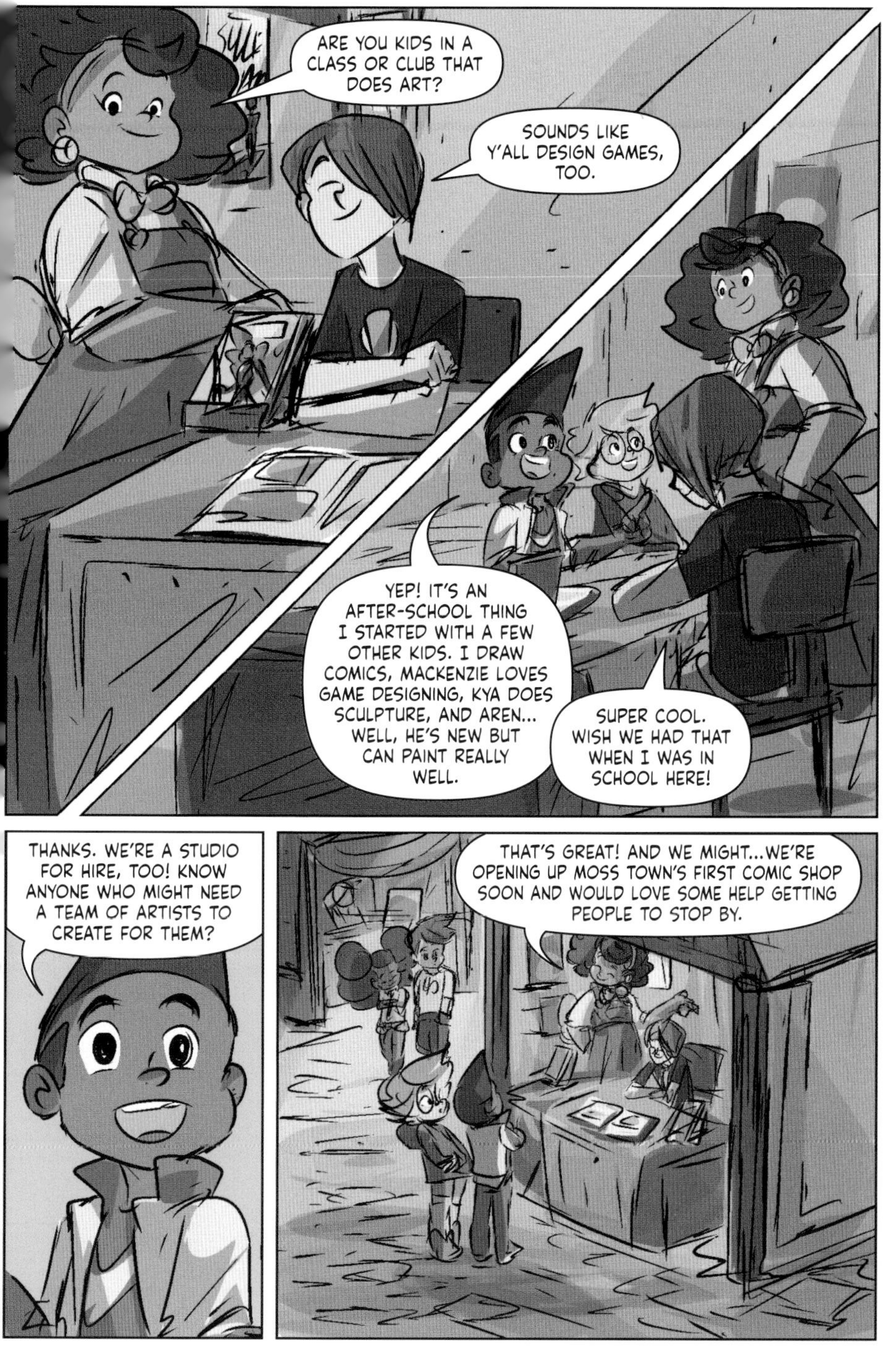
ARE YOU KIDS IN A CLASS OR CLUB THAT DOES ART?
SOUNDS LIKE Y'ALL DESIGN GAMES, TOO.
YEP! IT'S AN AFTER-SCHOOL THING I STARTED WITH A FEW OTHER KIDS. I DRAW COMICS, MACKENZIE LOVES GAME DESIGNING, KYA DOES SCULPTURE, AND AREN... WELL, HE'S NEW BUT CAN PAINT REALLY WELL.
SUPER COOL. WISH WE HAD THAT WHEN I WAS IN SCHOOL HERE!
THANKS. WE'RE A STUDIO FOR HIRE, TOO! KNOW ANYONE WHO MIGHT NEED A TEAM OF ARTISTS TO CREATE FOR THEM?
THAT'S GREAT! AND WE MIGHT...WE'RE OPENING UP MOSS TOWN'S FIRST COMIC SHOP SOON AND WOULD LOVE SOME HELP GETTING PEOPLE TO STOP BY.

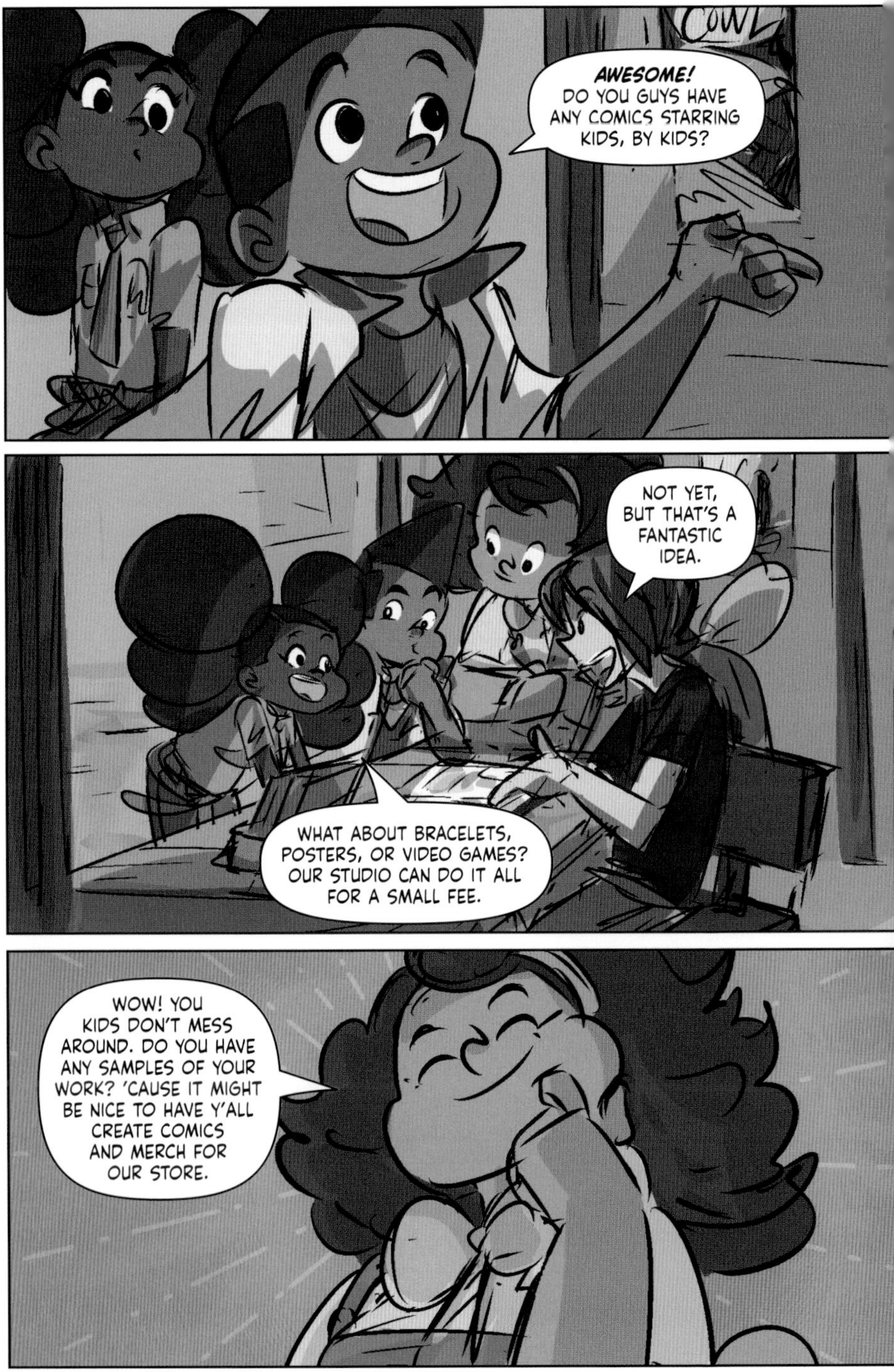
COWL
AWESOME! DO YOU GUYS HAVE ANY COMICS STARRING KIDS, BY KIDS?
NOT YET, BUT THAT'S A FANTASTIC IDEA.
WHAT ABOUT BRACELETS, POSTERS, OR VIDEO GAMES? OUR STUDIO CAN DO IT ALL FOR A SMALL FEE.
WOW! YOU KIDS DON'T MESS AROUND. DO YOU HAVE ANY SAMPLES OF YOUR WORK? 'CAUSE IT MIGHT BE NICE TO HAVE Y'ALL CREATE COMICS AND MERCH FOR OUR STORE.

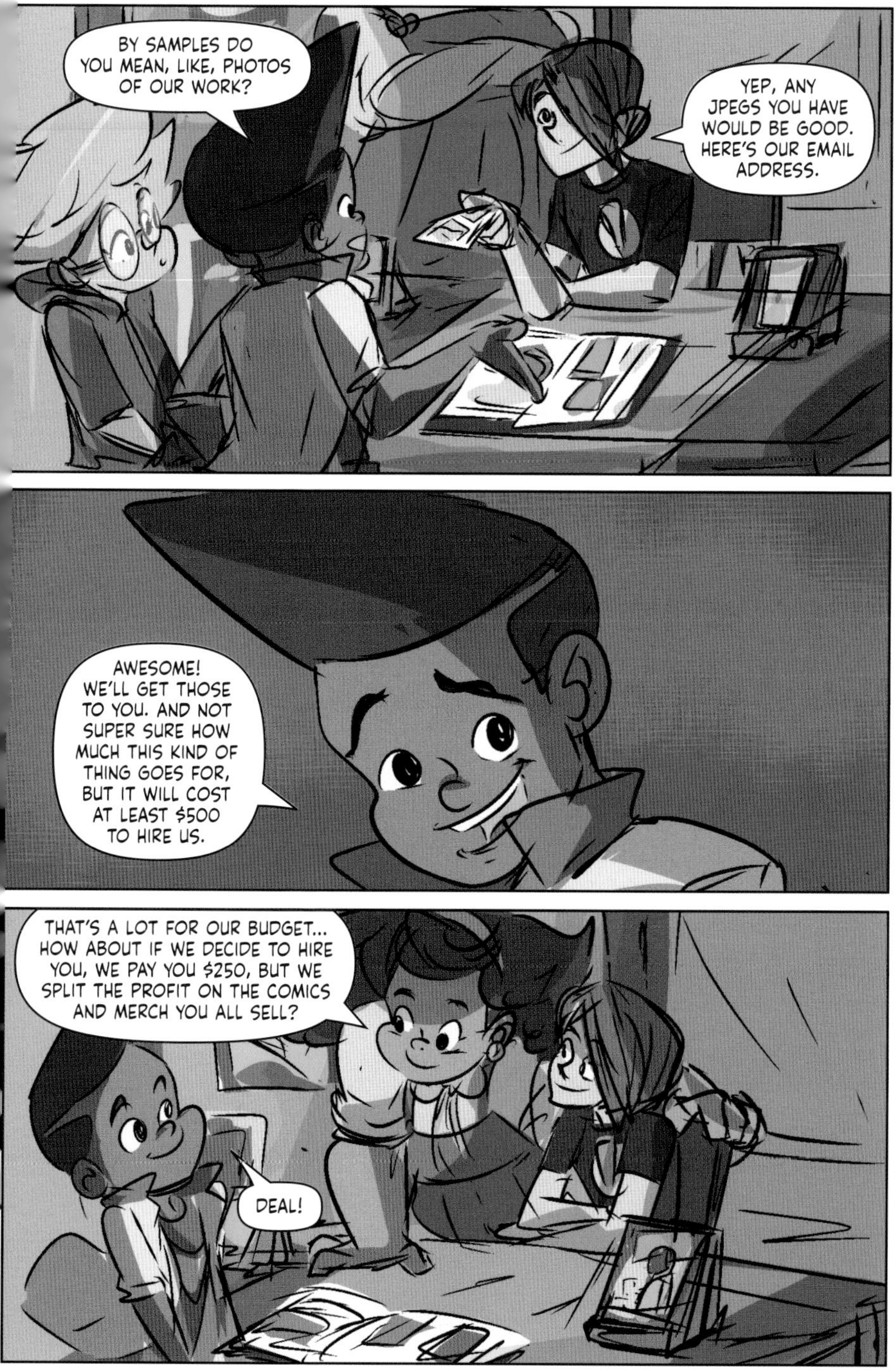
BY SAMPLES DO YOU MEAN, LIKE, PHOTOS OF OUR WORK?
YEP, ANY JPEGS YOU HAVE WOULD BE GOOD. HERE'S OUR EMAIL ADDRESS.
AWESOME! WE'LL GET THOSE TO YOU. AND NOT SUPER SURE HOW MUCH THIS KIND OF THING GOES FOR, BUT IT WILL COST AT LEAST $500 TO HIRE US.
THAT'S A LOT FOR OUR BUDGET... HOW ABOUT IF WE DECIDE TO HIRE YOU, WE PAY YOU $250, BUT WE SPLIT THE PROFIT ON THE COMICS AND MERCH YOU ALL SELL?
DEAL!

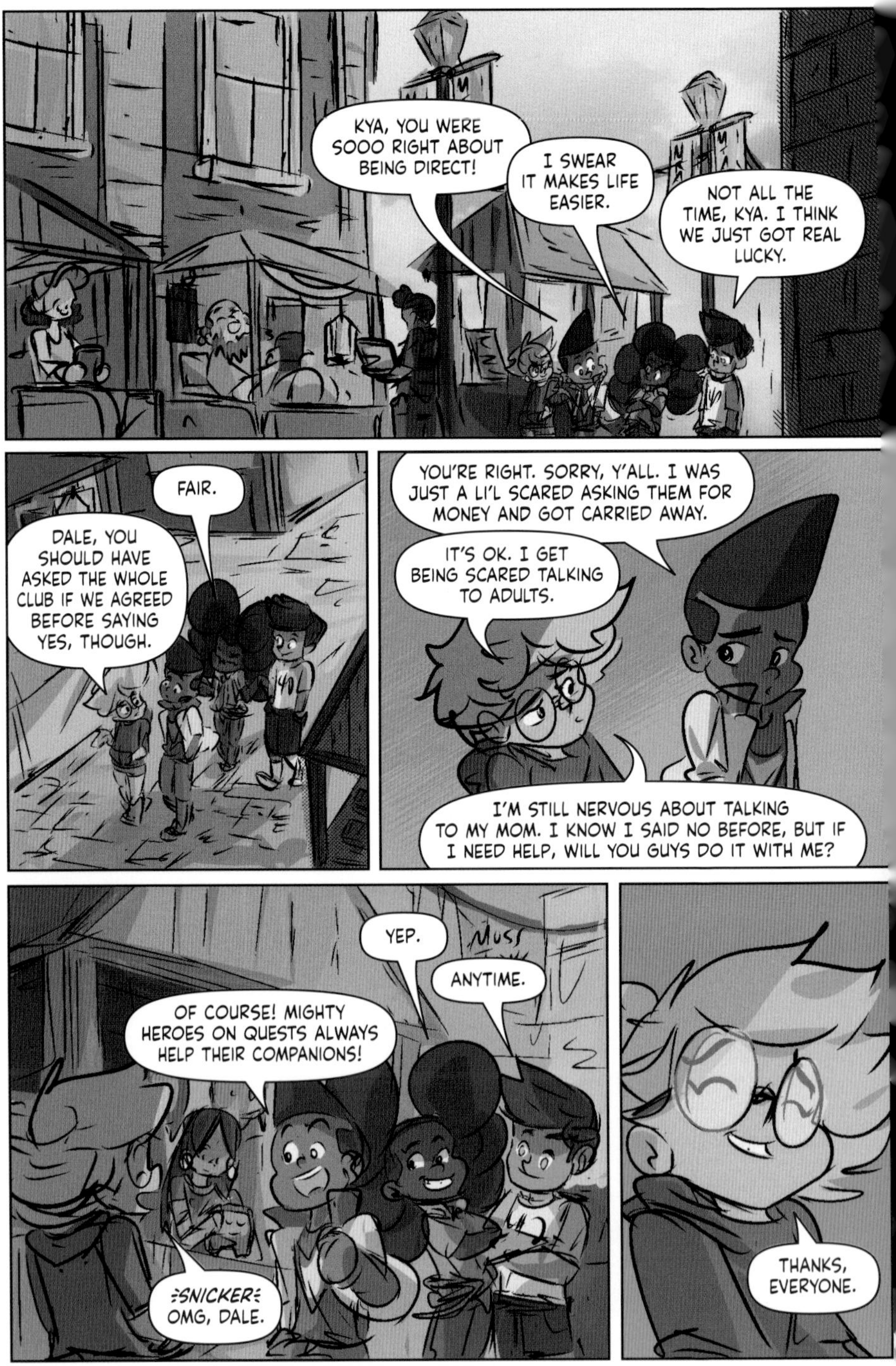
KYA, YOU WERE SOOO RIGHT ABOUT BEING DIRECT!
I SWEAR IT MAKES LIFE EASIER.
NOT ALL THE TIME, KYA. I THINK WE JUST GOT REAL LUCKY.
FAIR.
DALE, YOU SHOULD HAVE ASKED THE WHOLE CLUB IF WE AGREED BEFORE SAYING YES, THOUGH.
YOU'RE RIGHT. SORRY, Y'ALL. I WAS JUST A LI'L SCARED ASKING THEM FOR MONEY AND GOT CARRIED AWAY.
IT'S OK. I GET BEING SCARED TALKING TO ADULTS.
I'M STILL NERVOUS ABOUT TALKING TO MY MOM. I KNOW I SAID NO BEFORE, BUT IF I NEED HELP, WILL YOU GUYS DO IT WITH ME?
YEP.
ANYTIME.
OF COURSE! MIGHTY HEROES ON QUESTS ALWAYS HELP THEIR COMPANIONS!
SNICKER OMG, DALE.
THANKS, EVERYONE.

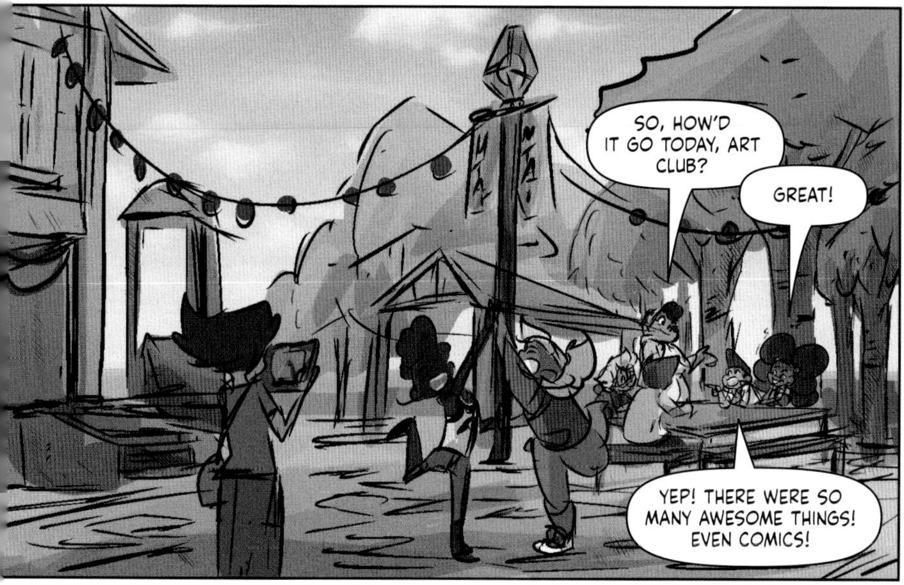
SO, HOW'D IT GO TODAY, ART CLUB?
GREAT!
YEP! THERE WERE SO MANY AWESOME THINGS! EVEN COMICS!

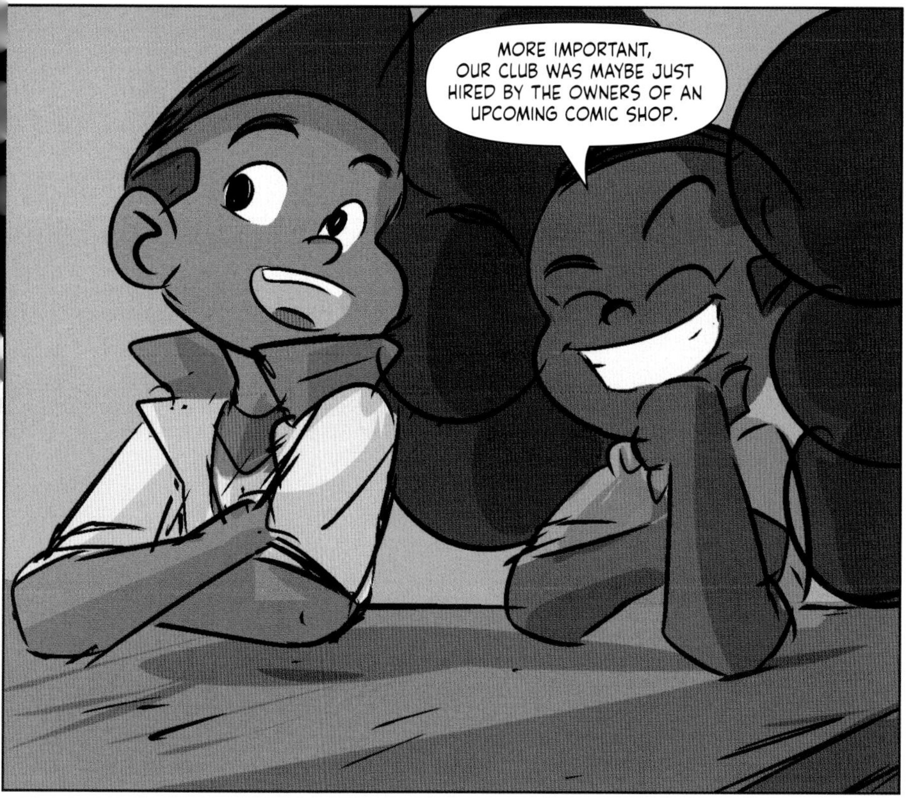
MORE IMPORTANT, OUR CLUB WAS MAYBE JUST HIRED BY THE OWNERS OF AN UPCOMING COMIC SHOP.

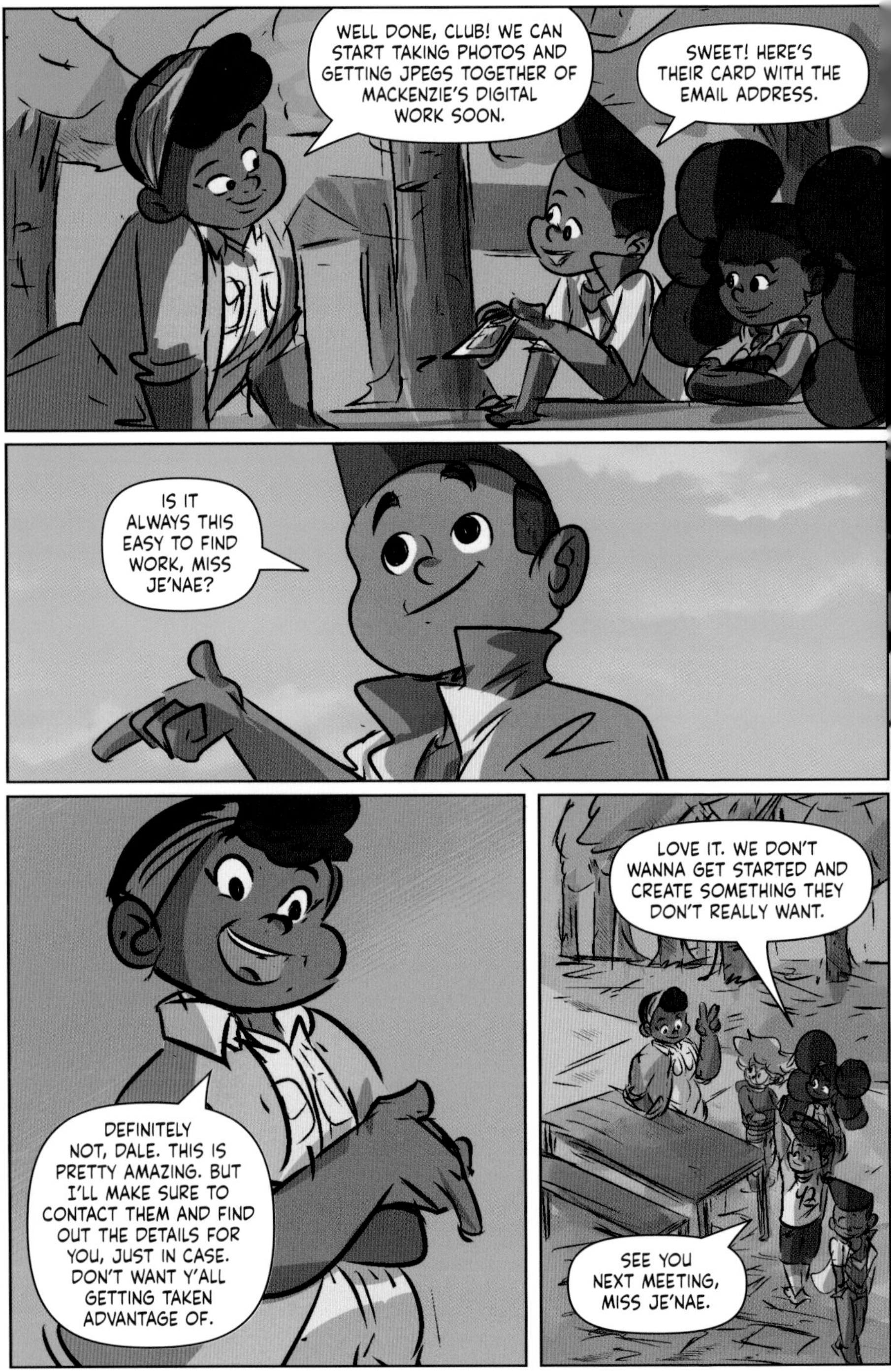
WELL DONE, CLUB! WE CAN START TAKING PHOTOS AND GETTING JPEGS TOGETHER OF MACKENZIE'S DIGITAL WORK SOON.
SWEET! HERE'S THEIR CARD WITH THE EMAIL ADDRESS.
IS IT ALWAYS THIS EASY TO FIND WORK, MISS JE'NAE?
DEFINITELY NOT, DALE. THIS IS PRETTY AMAZING. BUT I'LL MAKE SURE TO CONTACT THEM AND FIND OUT THE DETAILS FOR YOU, JUST IN CASE. DON'T WANT Y'ALL GETTING TAKEN ADVANTAGE OF.
LOVE IT. WE DON'T WANNA GET STARTED AND CREATE SOMETHING THEY DON'T REALLY WANT.
SEE YOU NEXT MEETING, MISS JE'NAE.

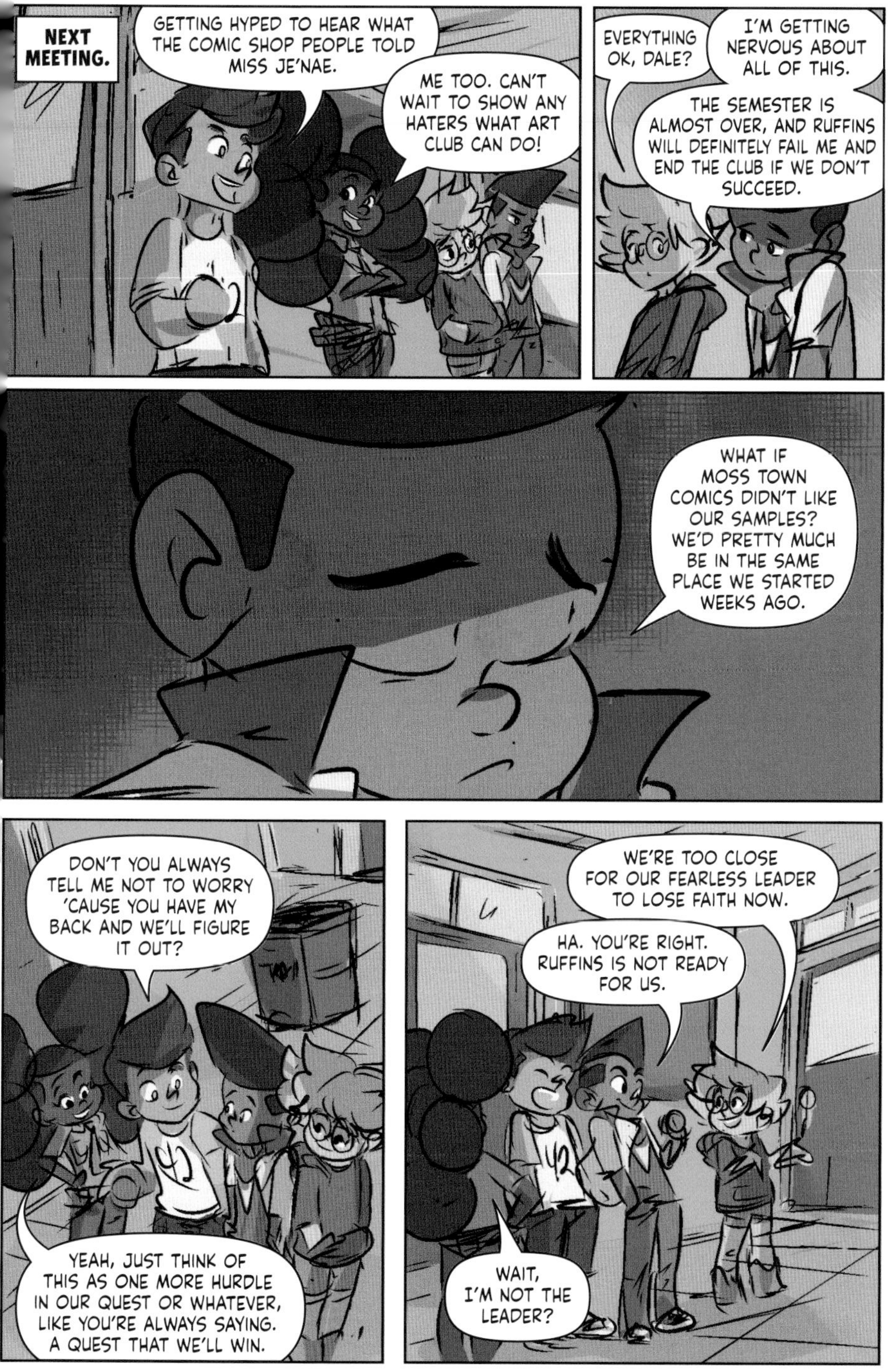
NEXT MEETING.
GETTING HYPED TO HEAR WHAT THE COMIC SHOP PEOPLE TOLD MISS JE'NAE.
ME TOO. CAN'T WAIT TO SHOW ANY HATERS WHAT ART CLUB CAN DO!
EVERYTHING OK, DALE?
I'M GETTING NERVOUS ABOUT ALL OF THIS.
THE SEMESTER IS ALMOST OVER, AND RUFFINS WILL DEFINITELY FAIL ME AND END THE CLUB IF WE DON'T SUCCEED.
WHAT IF MOSS TOWN COMICS DIDN'T LIKE OUR SAMPLES? WE'D PRETTY MUCH BE IN THE SAME PLACE WE STARTED WEEKS AGO.
DON'T YOU ALWAYS TELL ME NOT TO WORRY 'CAUSE YOU HAVE MY BACK AND WE'LL FIGURE IT OUT?
YEAH, JUST THINK OF THIS AS ONE MORE HURDLE IN OUR QUEST OR WHATEVER, LIKE YOU'RE ALWAYS SAYING. A QUEST THAT WE'LL WIN.
WE'RE TOO CLOSE FOR OUR FEARLESS LEADER TO LOSE FAITH NOW.
HA. YOU'RE RIGHT. RUFFINS IS NOT READY FOR US.
WAIT, I'M NOT THE LEADER?

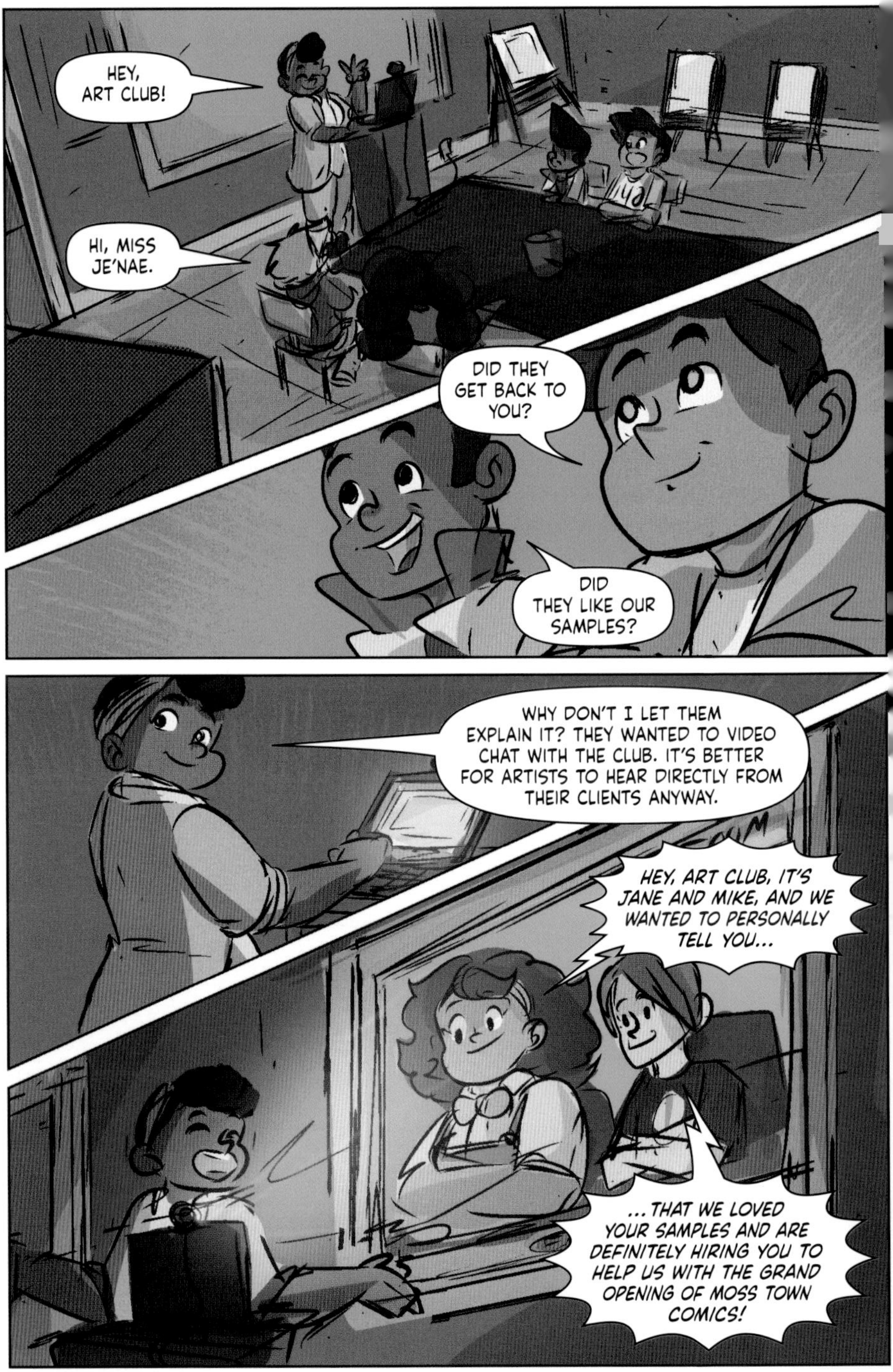
HEY, ART CLUB!
HI, MISS JE'NAE.
DID THEY GET BACK TO YOU?
DID THEY LIKE OUR SAMPLES?
WHY DON'T I LET THEM EXPLAIN IT? THEY WANTED TO VIDEO CHAT WITH THE CLUB. IT'S BETTER FOR ARTISTS TO HEAR DIRECTLY FROM THEIR CLIENTS ANYWAY.
HEY, ART CLUB, IT'S JANE AND MIKE, AND WE WANTED TO PERSONALLY TELL YOU...
...THAT WE LOVED YOUR SAMPLES AND ARE DEFINITELY HIRING YOU TO HELP US WITH THE GRAND OPENING OF MOSS TOWN COMICS!

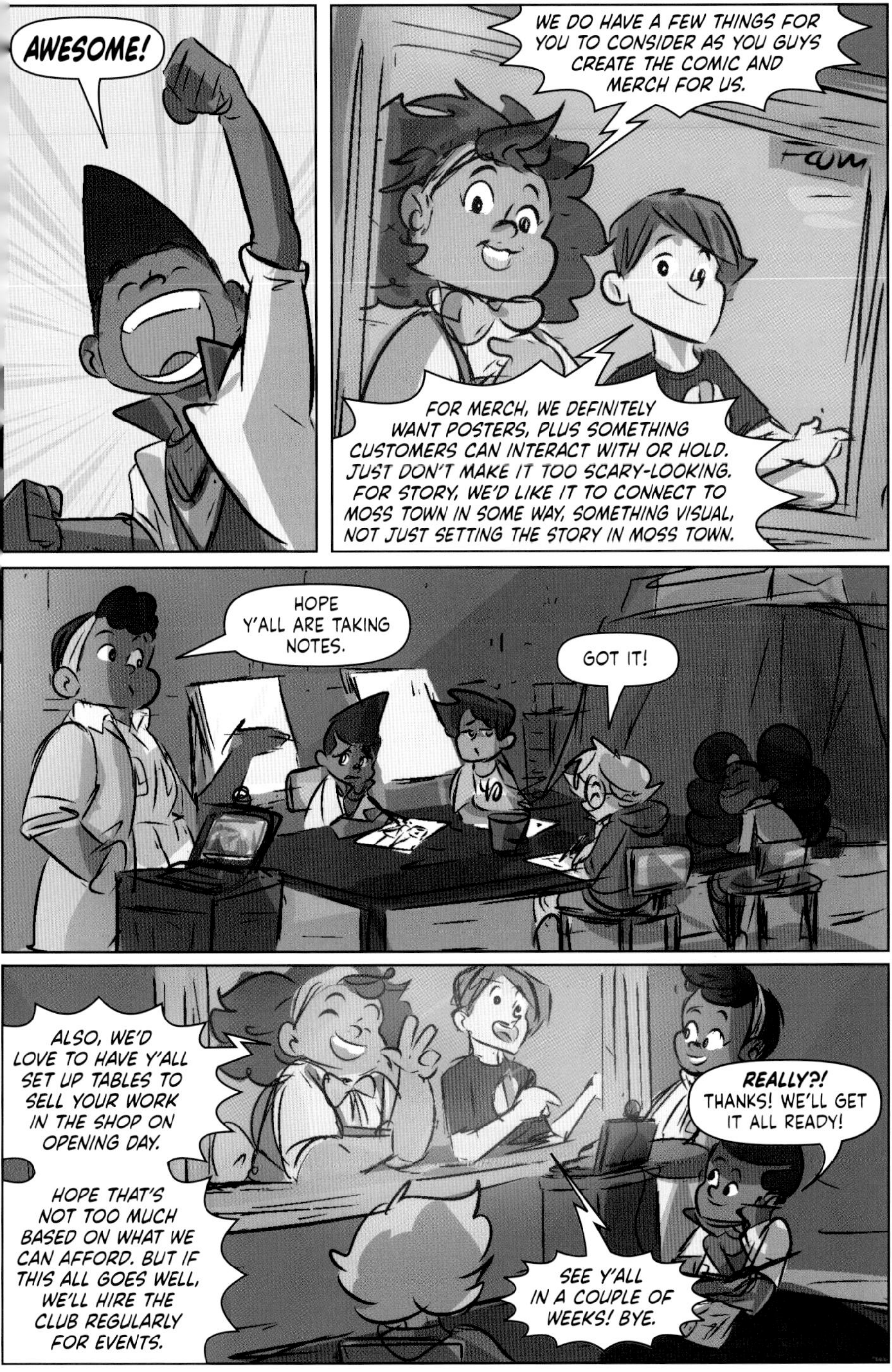
AWESOME!
WE DO HAVE A FEW THINGS FOR YOU TO CONSIDER AS YOU GUYS CREATE THE COMIC AND MERCH FOR US.
FOR MERCH, WE DEFINITELY WANT POSTERS, PLUS SOMETHING CUSTOMERS CAN INTERACT WITH OR HOLD. JUST DON'T MAKE IT TOO SCARY-LOOKING. FOR STORY, WE'D LIKE IT TO CONNECT TO MOSS TOWN IN SOME WAY, SOMETHING VISUAL, NOT JUST SETTING THE STORY IN MOSS TOWN.
HOPE Y'ALL ARE TAKING NOTES.
GOT IT!
ALSO, WE'D LOVE TO HAVE Y'ALL SET UP TABLES TO SELL YOUR WORK IN THE SHOP ON OPENING DAY.
HOPE THAT'S NOT TOO MUCH BASED ON WHAT WE CAN AFFORD. BUT IF THIS ALL GOES WELL, WE'LL HIRE THE CLUB REGULARLY FOR EVENTS.
REALLY?! THANKS! WE'LL GET IT ALL READY!
SEE Y'ALL IN A COUPLE OF WEEKS! BYE.

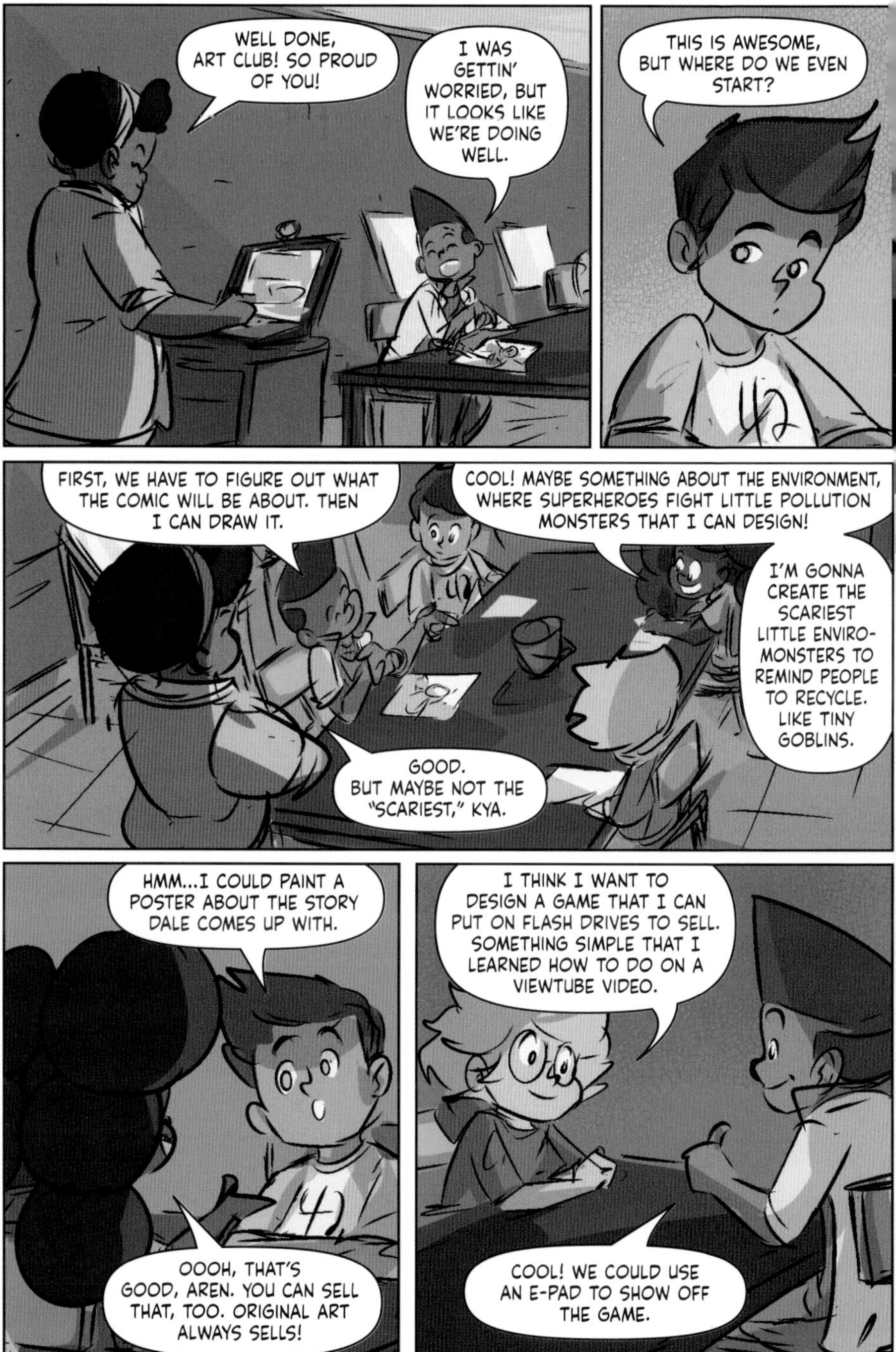
WELL DONE, ART CLUB! SO PROUD OF YOU!
I WAS GETTIN' WORRIED, BUT IT LOOKS LIKE WE'RE DOING WELL.
THIS IS AWESOME, BUT WHERE DO WE EVEN START?
FIRST, WE HAVE TO FIGURE OUT WHAT THE COMIC WILL BE ABOUT. THEN I CAN DRAW IT.
COOL! MAYBE SOMETHING ABOUT THE ENVIRONMENT, WHERE SUPERHEROES FIGHT LITTLE POLLUTION MONSTERS THAT I CAN DESIGN!
I'M GONNA CREATE THE SCARIEST LITTLE ENVIRO-MONSTERS TO REMIND PEOPLE TO RECYCLE. LIKE TINY GOBLINS.
GOOD. BUT MAYBE NOT THE "SCARIEST," KYA.
HMM...I COULD PAINT A POSTER ABOUT THE STORY DALE COMES UP WITH.
OOOH, THAT'S GOOD, AREN. YOU CAN SELL THAT, TOO. ORIGINAL ART ALWAYS SELLS!
I THINK I WANT TO DESIGN A GAME THAT I CAN PUT ON FLASH DRIVES TO SELL. SOMETHING SIMPLE THAT I LEARNED HOW TO DO ON A VIEWTUBE VIDEO.
COOL! WE COULD USE AN E-PAD TO SHOW OFF THE GAME.

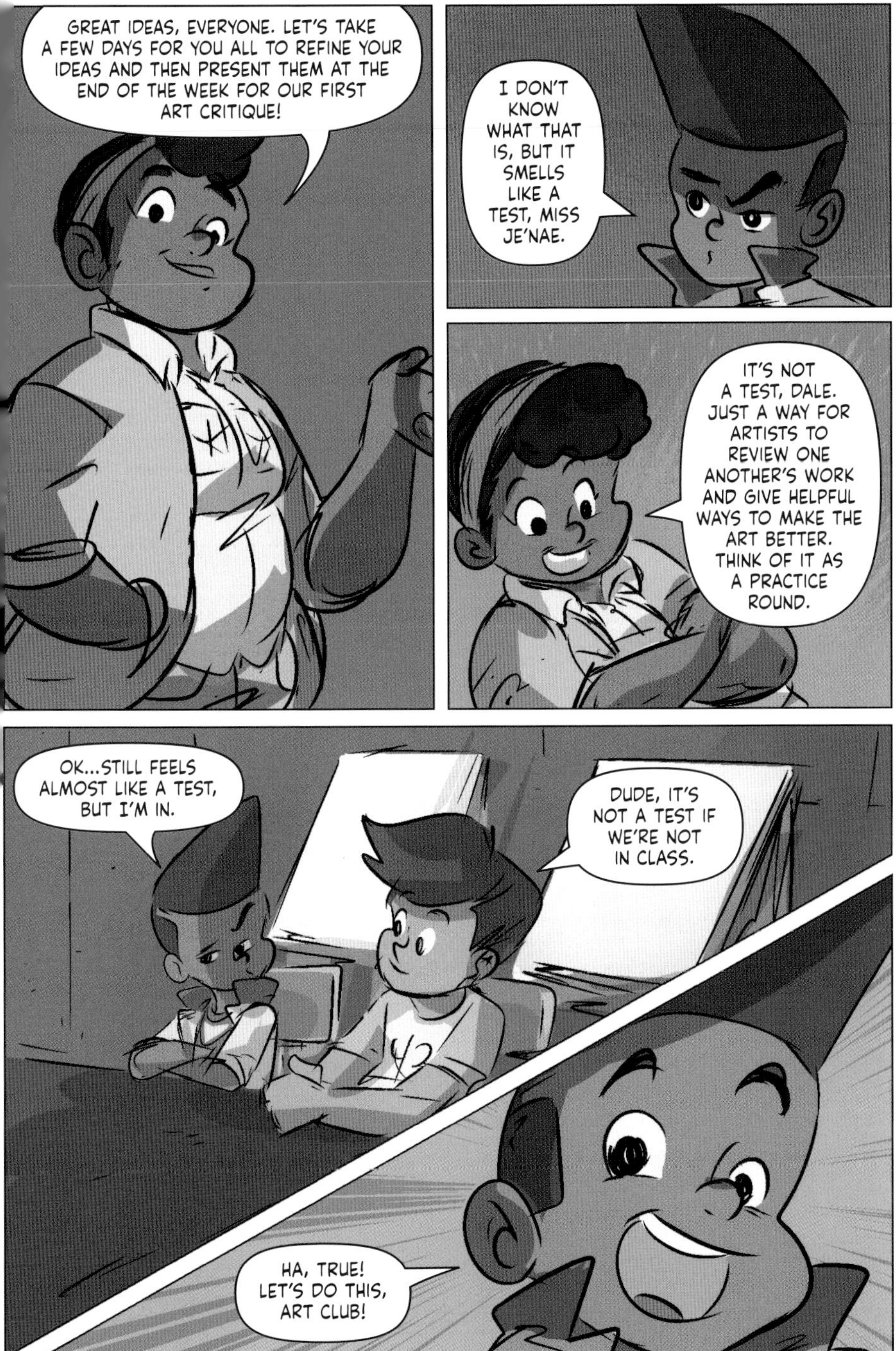
GREAT IDEAS, EVERYONE. LET'S TAKE A FEW DAYS FOR YOU ALL TO REFINE YOUR IDEAS AND THEN PRESENT THEM AT THE END OF THE WEEK FOR OUR FIRST ART CRITIQUE!
I DON'T KNOW WHAT THAT IS, BUT IT SMELLS LIKE A TEST, MISS JE'NAE.
IT'S NOT A TEST, DALE. JUST A WAY FOR ARTISTS TO REVIEW ONE ANOTHER'S WORK AND GIVE HELPFUL WAYS TO MAKE THE ART BETTER. THINK OF IT AS A PRACTICE ROUND.
OK...STILL FEELS ALMOST LIKE A TEST, BUT I'M IN.
DUDE, IT'S NOT A TEST IF WE'RE NOT IN CLASS.
HA, TRUE! LET'S DO THIS, ART CLUB!

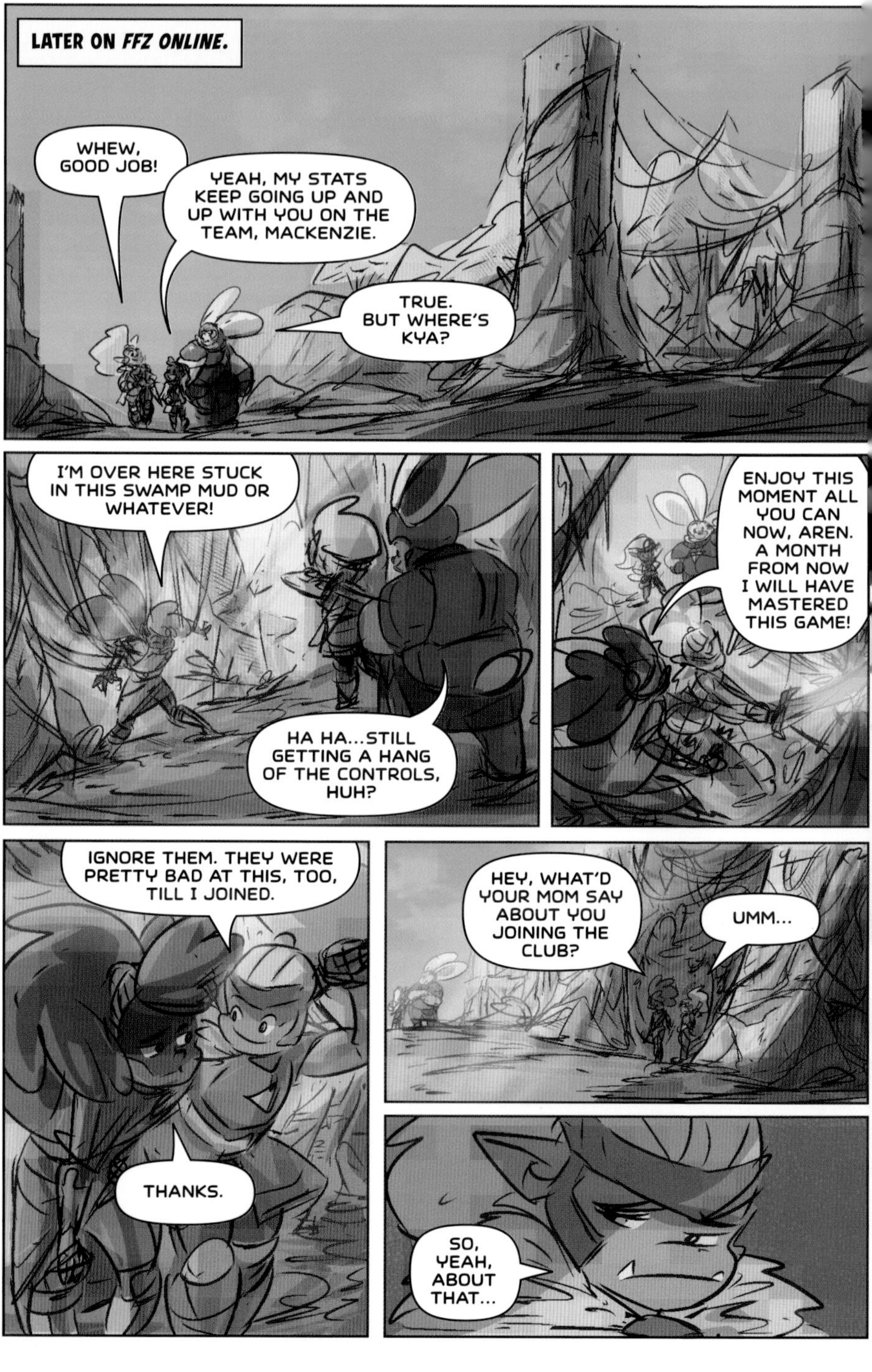
LATER ON FFZ ONLINE.
WHEW, GOOD JOB!
YEAH, MY STATS KEEP GOING UP AND UP WITH YOU ON THE TEAM, MACKENZIE.
TRUE. BUT WHERE'S KYA?
I'M OVER HERE STUCK IN THIS SWAMP MUD OR WHATEVER!
HA HA...STILL GETTING A HANG OF THE CONTROLS, HUH?
ENJOY THIS MOMENT ALL YOU CAN NOW, AREN. A MONTH FROM NOW I WILL HAVE MASTERED THIS GAME!
IGNORE THEM. THEY WERE PRETTY BAD AT THIS, TOO, TILL I JOINED.
THANKS.
HEY, WHAT'D YOUR MOM SAY ABOUT YOU JOINING THE CLUB?
UMM...
SO, YEAH, ABOUT THAT...

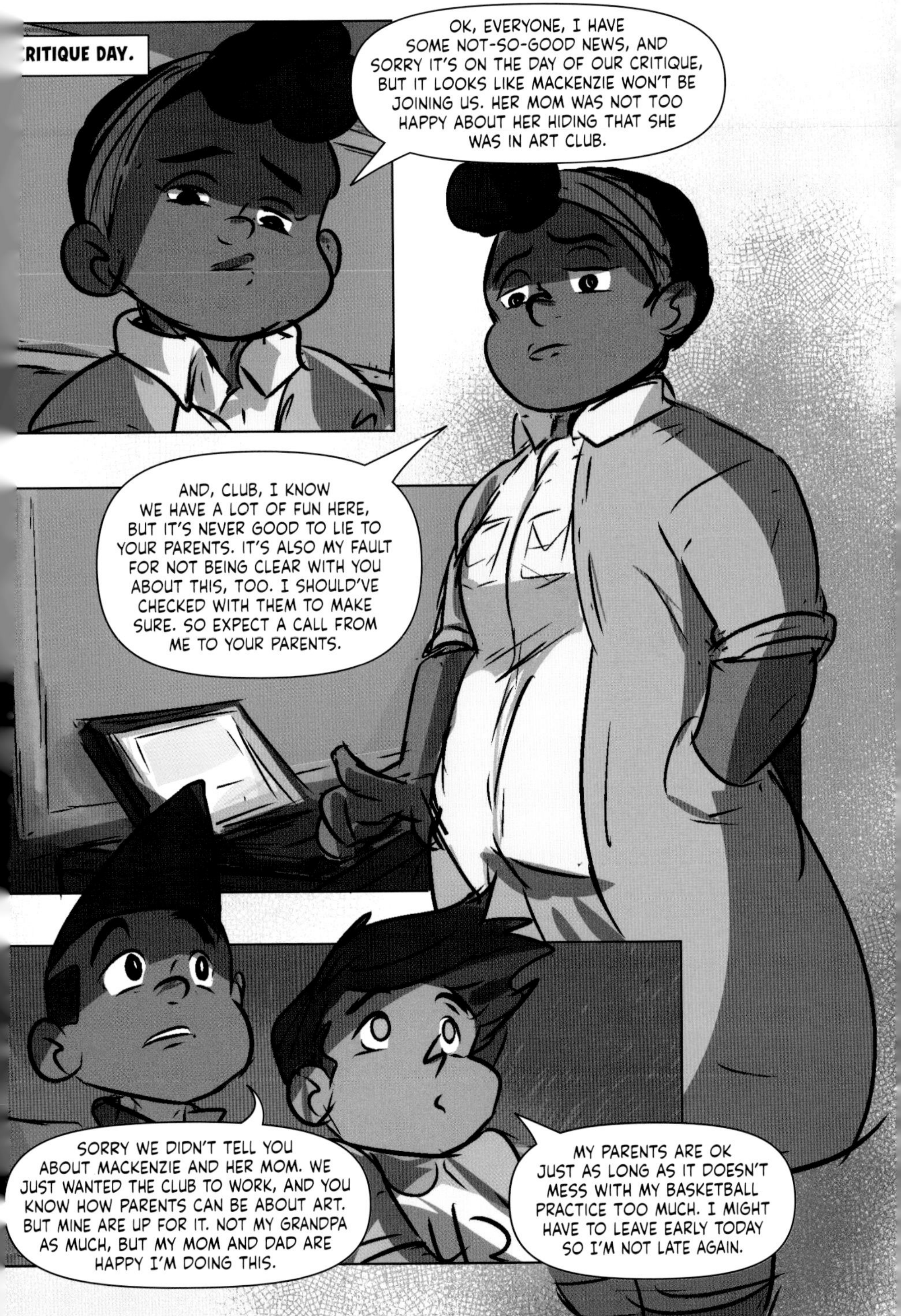
CRITIQUE DAY.
OK, EVERYONE, I HAVE SOME NOT-SO-GOOD NEWS, AND SORRY IT'S ON THE DAY OF OUR CRITIQUE, BUT IT LOOKS LIKE MACKENZIE WON'T BE JOINING US. HER MOM WAS NOT TOO HAPPY ABOUT HER HIDING THAT SHE WAS IN ART CLUB.
AND, CLUB, I KNOW WE HAVE A LOT OF FUN HERE, BUT IT'S NEVER GOOD TO LIE TO YOUR PARENTS. IT'S ALSO MY FAULT FOR NOT BEING CLEAR WITH YOU ABOUT THIS, TOO. I SHOULD'VE CHECKED WITH THEM TO MAKE SURE. SO EXPECT A CALL FROM ME TO YOUR PARENTS.
SORRY WE DIDN'T TELL YOU ABOUT MACKENZIE AND HER MOM. WE JUST WANTED THE CLUB TO WORK, AND YOU KNOW HOW PARENTS CAN BE ABOUT ART. BUT MINE ARE UP FOR IT. NOT MY GRANDPA AS MUCH, BUT MY MOM AND DAD ARE HAPPY I'M DOING THIS.
MY PARENTS ARE OK JUST AS LONG AS IT DOESN'T MESS WITH MY BASKETBALL PRACTICE TOO MUCH. I MIGHT HAVE TO LEAVE EARLY TODAY SO I'M NOT LATE AGAIN.

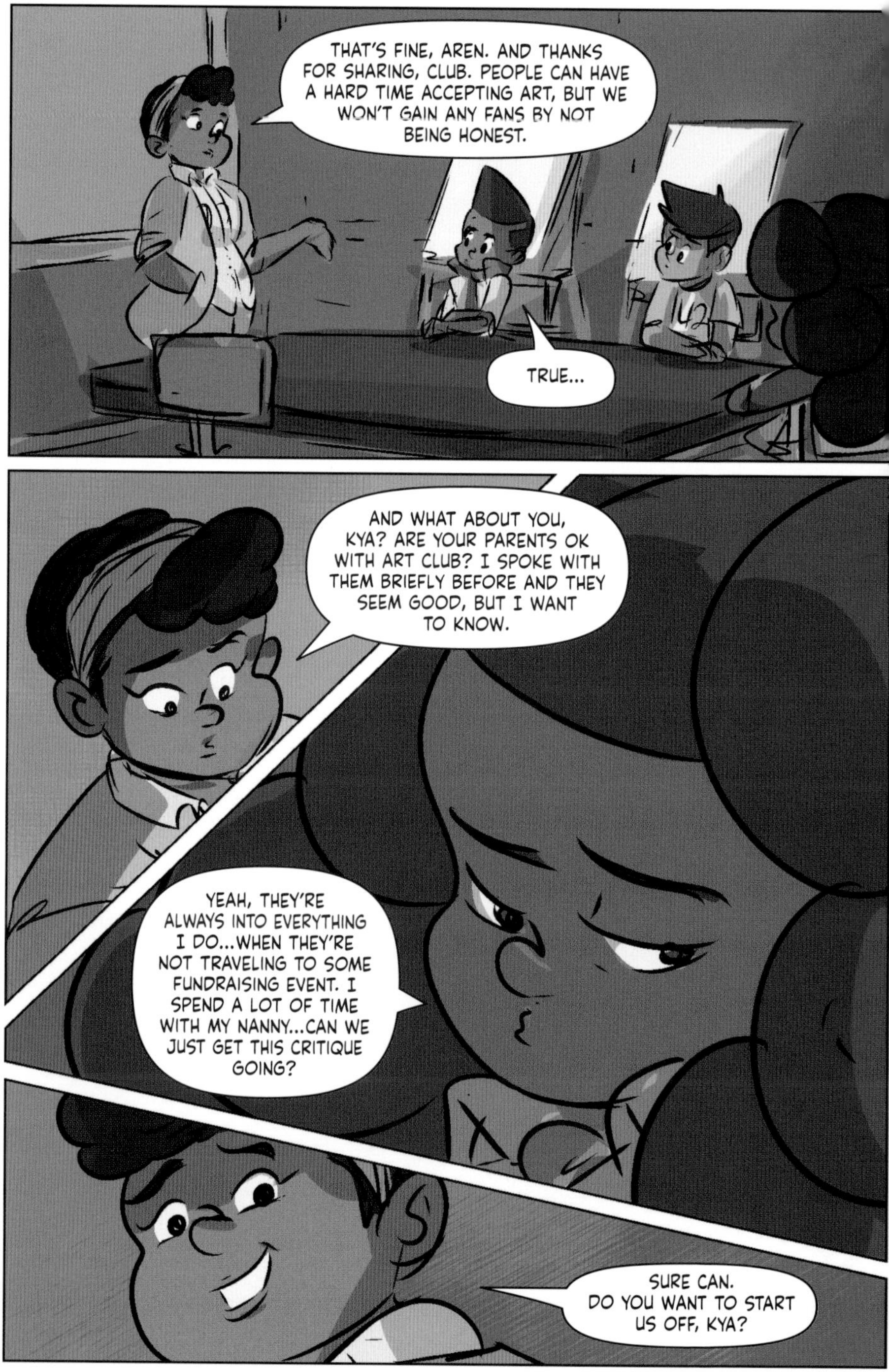
THAT'S FINE, AREN. AND THANKS FOR SHARING, CLUB. PEOPLE CAN HAVE A HARD TIME ACCEPTING ART, BUT WE WON'T GAIN ANY FANS BY NOT BEING HONEST.
TRUE...
AND WHAT ABOUT YOU, KYA? ARE YOUR PARENTS OK WITH ART CLUB? I SPOKE WITH THEM BRIEFLY BEFORE AND THEY SEEM GOOD, BUT I WANT TO KNOW.
YEAH, THEY'RE ALWAYS INTO EVERYTHING I DO...WHEN THEY'RE NOT TRAVELING TO SOME FUNDRAISING EVENT. I SPEND A LOT OF TIME WITH MY NANNY...CAN WE JUST GET THIS CRITIQUE GOING?
SURE CAN. DO YOU WANT TO START US OFF, KYA?

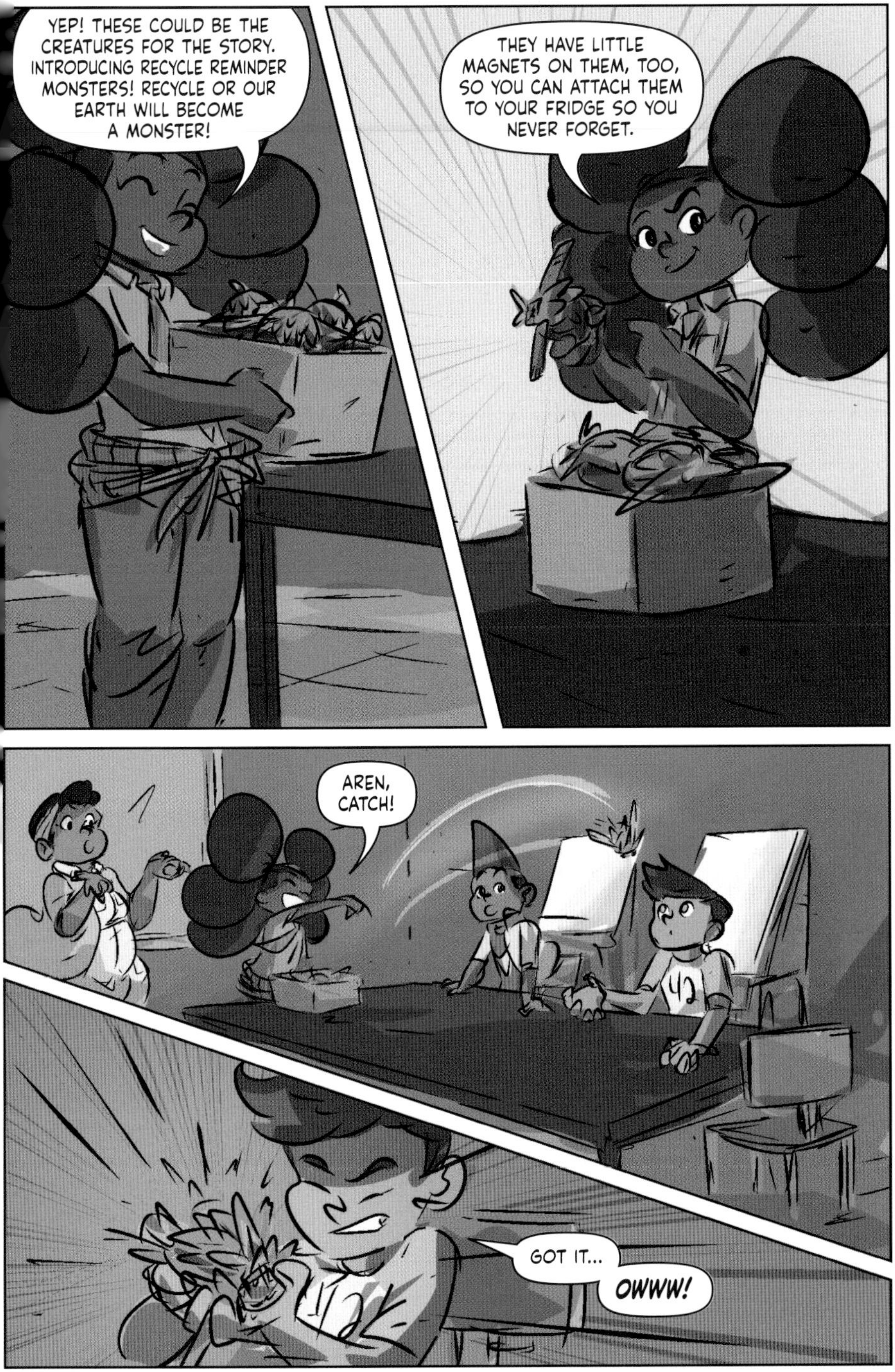
YEP! THESE COULD BE THE CREATURES FOR THE STORY. INTRODUCING RECYCLE REMINDER MONSTERS! RECYCLE OR OUR EARTH WILL BECOME A MONSTER!
THEY HAVE LITTLE MAGNETS ON THEM, TOO, SO YOU CAN ATTACH THEM TO YOUR FRIDGE SO YOU NEVER FORGET.
AREN, CATCH!
42
GOT IT...
OWWW!

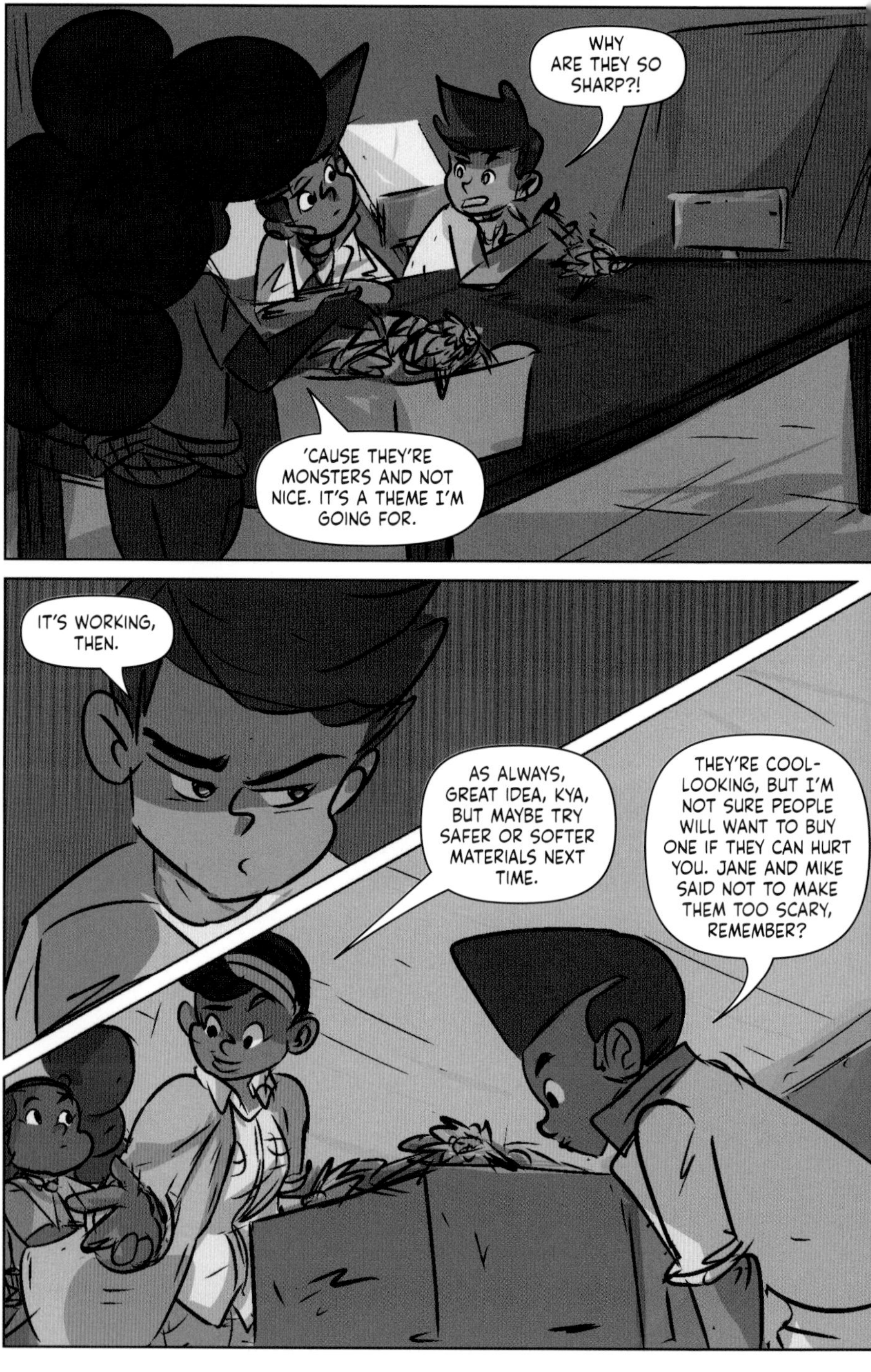
WHY ARE THEY SO SHARP?!
'CAUSE THEY'RE MONSTERS AND NOT NICE. IT'S A THEME I'M GOING FOR.
IT'S WORKING, THEN.
AS ALWAYS, GREAT IDEA, KYA, BUT MAYBE TRY SAFER OR SOFTER MATERIALS NEXT TIME.
THEY'RE COOL-LOOKING, BUT I'M NOT SURE PEOPLE WILL WANT TO BUY ONE IF THEY CAN HURT YOU. JANE AND MIKE SAID NOT TO MAKE THEM TOO SCARY, REMEMBER?

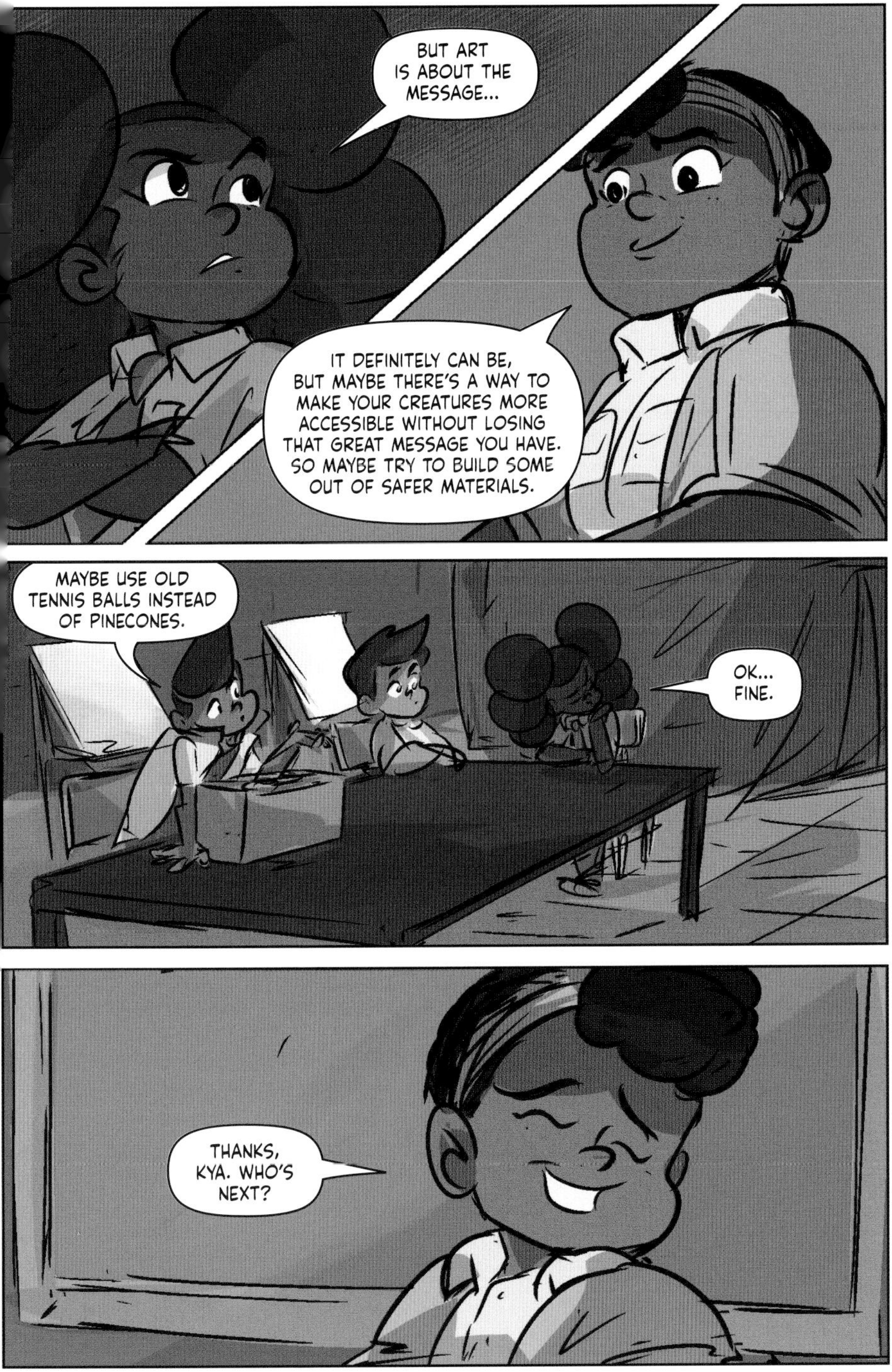
BUT ART IS ABOUT THE MESSAGE...
IT DEFINITELY CAN BE, BUT MAYBE THERE'S A WAY TO MAKE YOUR CREATURES MORE ACCESSIBLE WITHOUT LOSING THAT GREAT MESSAGE YOU HAVE. SO MAYBE TRY TO BUILD SOME OUT OF SAFER MATERIALS.
MAYBE USE OLD TENNIS BALLS INSTEAD OF PINECONES.
OK... FINE.
THANKS, KYA. WHO'S NEXT?

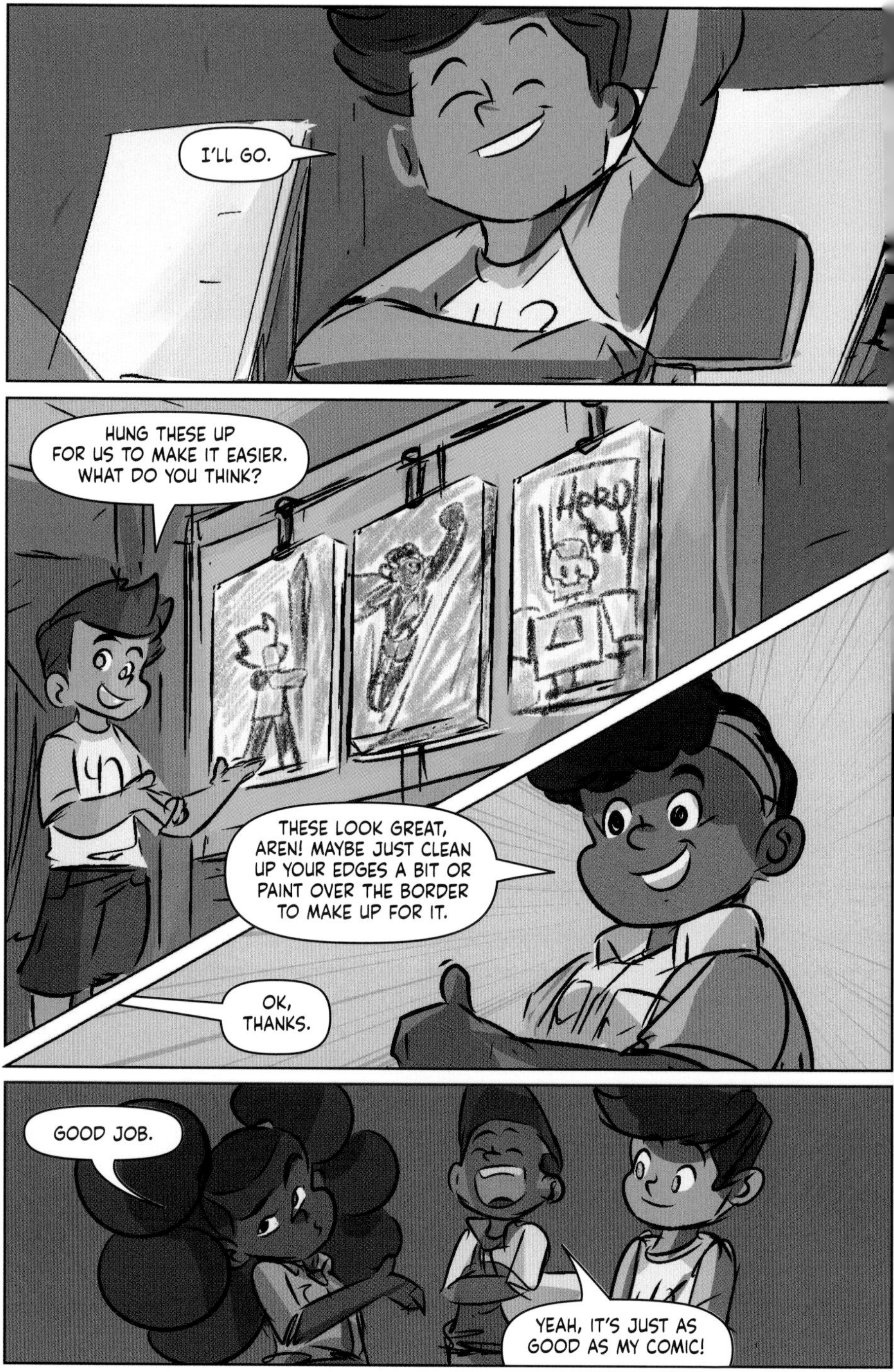
I'LL GO.
HUNG THESE UP FOR US TO MAKE IT EASIER. WHAT DO YOU THINK?
THESE LOOK GREAT, AREN! MAYBE JUST CLEAN UP YOUR EDGES A BIT OR PAINT OVER THE BORDER TO MAKE UP FOR IT.
OK, THANKS.
GOOD JOB.
YEAH, IT'S JUST AS GOOD AS MY COMIC!

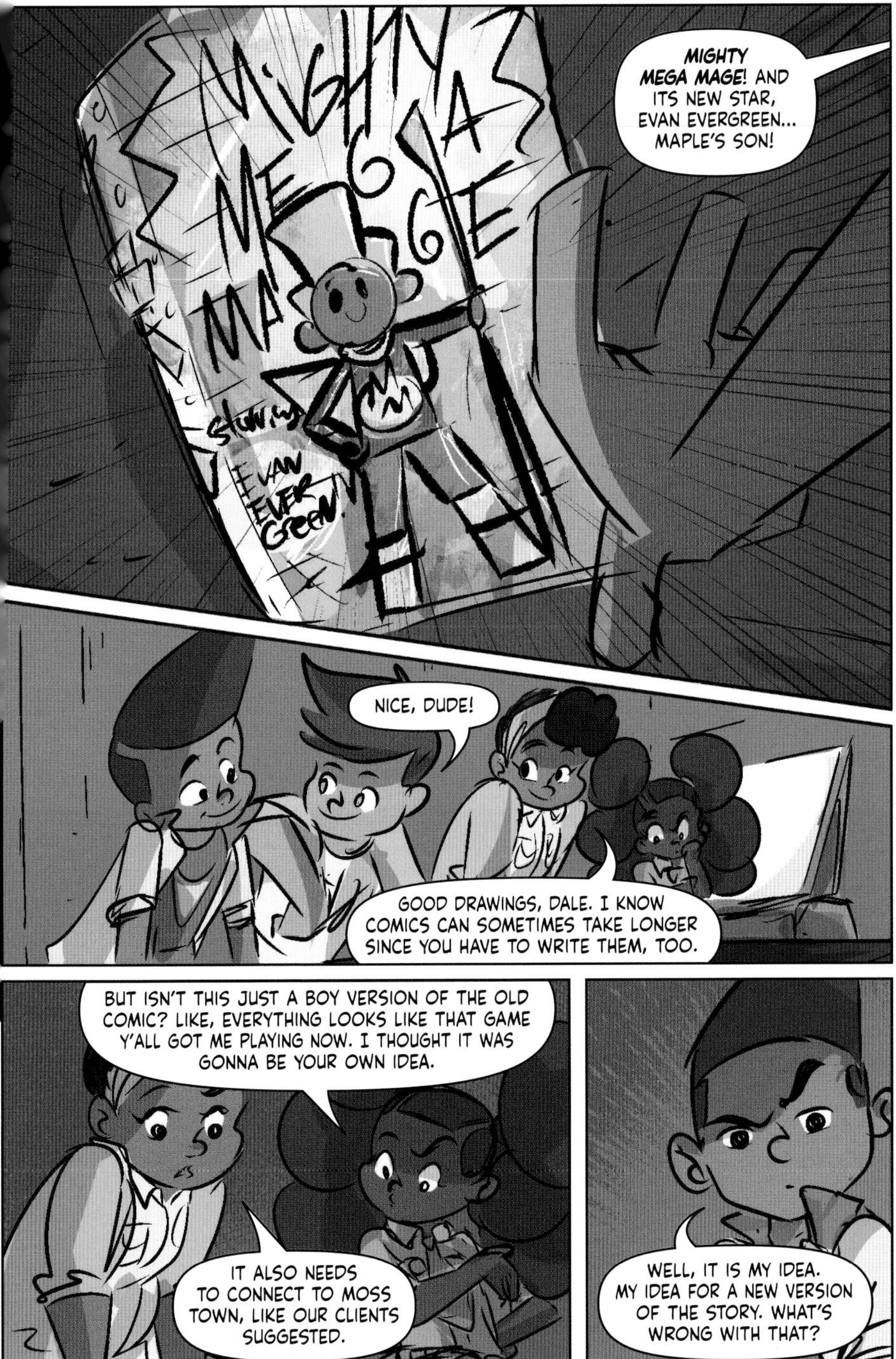
MIGHTY
MEGA
MAGE
starring
EVAN
EVERGREEN
MIGHTY MEGA MAGE! AND ITS NEW STAR, EVAN EVERGREEN... MAPLE'S SON!
NICE, DUDE!
GOOD DRAWINGS, DALE. I KNOW COMICS CAN SOMETIMES TAKE LONGER SINCE YOU HAVE TO WRITE THEM, TOO.
BUT ISN'T THIS JUST A BOY VERSION OF THE OLD COMIC? LIKE, EVERYTHING LOOKS LIKE THAT GAME Y'ALL GOT ME PLAYING NOW. I THOUGHT IT WAS GONNA BE YOUR OWN IDEA.
IT ALSO NEEDS TO CONNECT TO MOSS TOWN, LIKE OUR CLIENTS SUGGESTED.
WELL, IT IS MY IDEA. MY IDEA FOR A NEW VERSION OF THE STORY. WHAT'S WRONG WITH THAT?

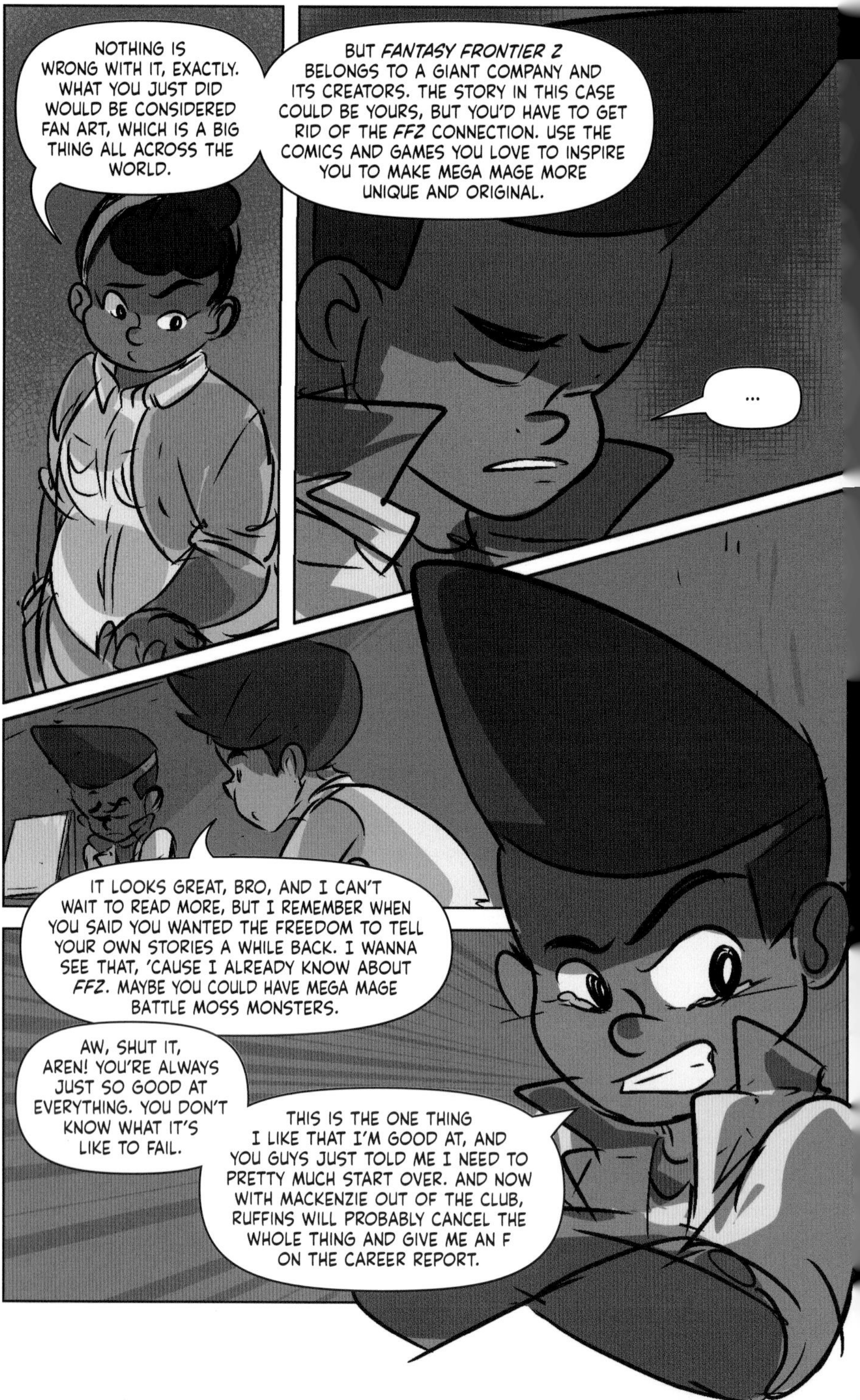
NOTHING IS WRONG WITH IT, EXACTLY. WHAT YOU JUST DID WOULD BE CONSIDERED FAN ART, WHICH IS A BIG THING ALL ACROSS THE WORLD.
BUT *FANTASY FRONTIER 2* BELONGS TO A GIANT COMPANY AND ITS CREATORS. THE STORY IN THIS CASE COULD BE YOURS, BUT YOU'D HAVE TO GET RID OF THE *FF2* CONNECTION. USE THE COMICS AND GAMES YOU LOVE TO INSPIRE YOU TO MAKE MEGA MAGE MORE UNIQUE AND ORIGINAL.
...
IT LOOKS GREAT, BRO, AND I CAN'T WAIT TO READ MORE, BUT I REMEMBER WHEN YOU SAID YOU WANTED THE FREEDOM TO TELL YOUR OWN STORIES A WHILE BACK. I WANNA SEE THAT, 'CAUSE I ALREADY KNOW ABOUT *FF2*. MAYBE YOU COULD HAVE MEGA MAGE BATTLE MOSS MONSTERS.
AW, SHUT IT, AREN! YOU'RE ALWAYS JUST SO GOOD AT EVERYTHING. YOU DON'T KNOW WHAT IT'S LIKE TO FAIL.
THIS IS THE ONE THING I LIKE THAT I'M GOOD AT, AND YOU GUYS JUST TOLD ME I NEED TO PRETTY MUCH START OVER. AND NOW WITH MACKENZIE OUT OF THE CLUB, RUFFINS WILL PROBABLY CANCEL THE WHOLE THING AND GIVE ME AN F ON THE CAREER REPORT.

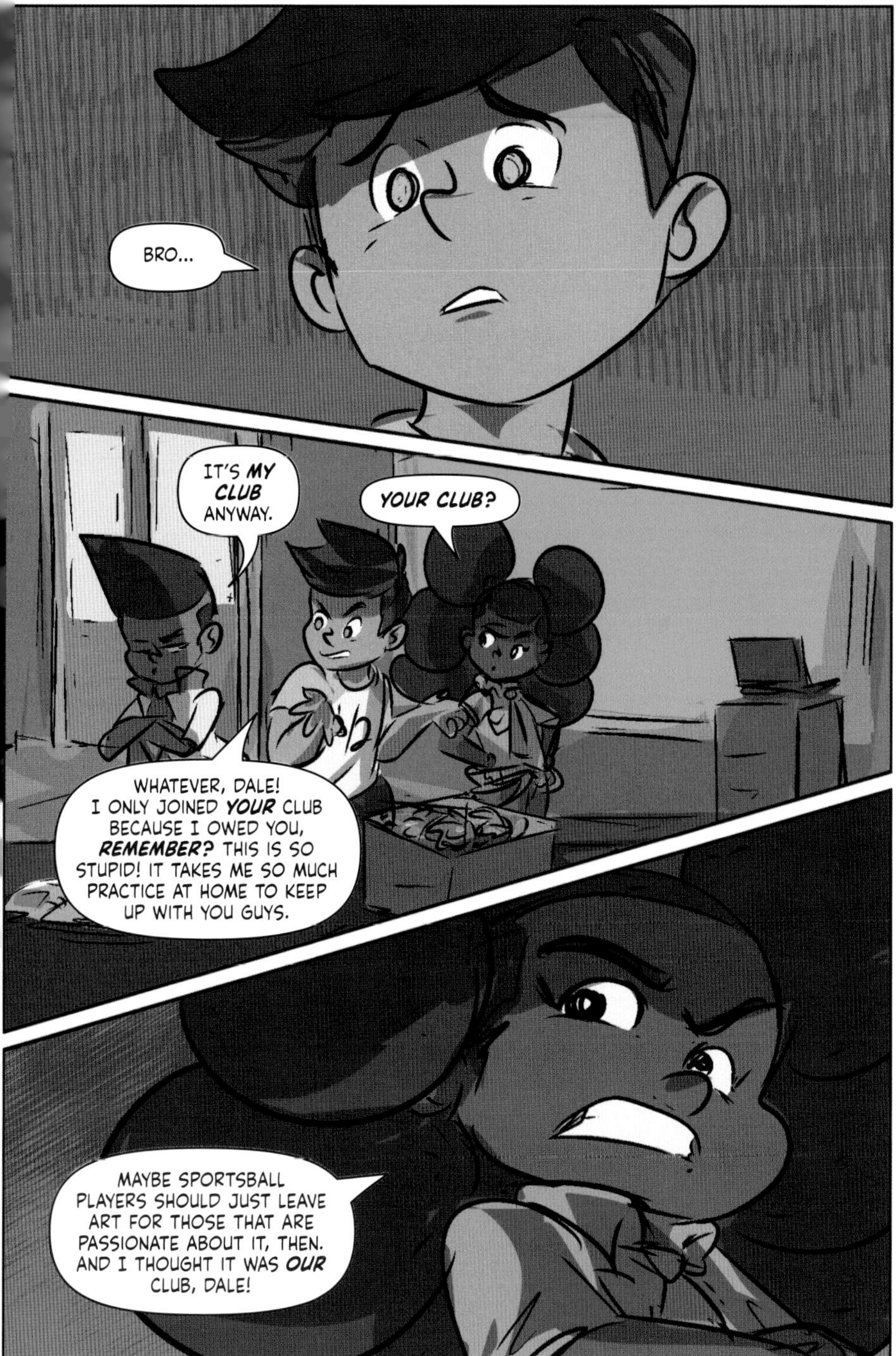
BRO...
IT'S MY CLUB ANYWAY.
YOUR CLUB?
WHATEVER, DALE! I ONLY JOINED YOUR CLUB BECAUSE I OWED YOU, REMEMBER? THIS IS SO STUPID! IT TAKES ME SO MUCH PRACTICE AT HOME TO KEEP UP WITH YOU GUYS.
MAYBE SPORTSBALL PLAYERS SHOULD JUST LEAVE ART FOR THOSE THAT ARE PASSIONATE ABOUT IT, THEN. AND I THOUGHT IT WAS OUR CLUB, DALE!

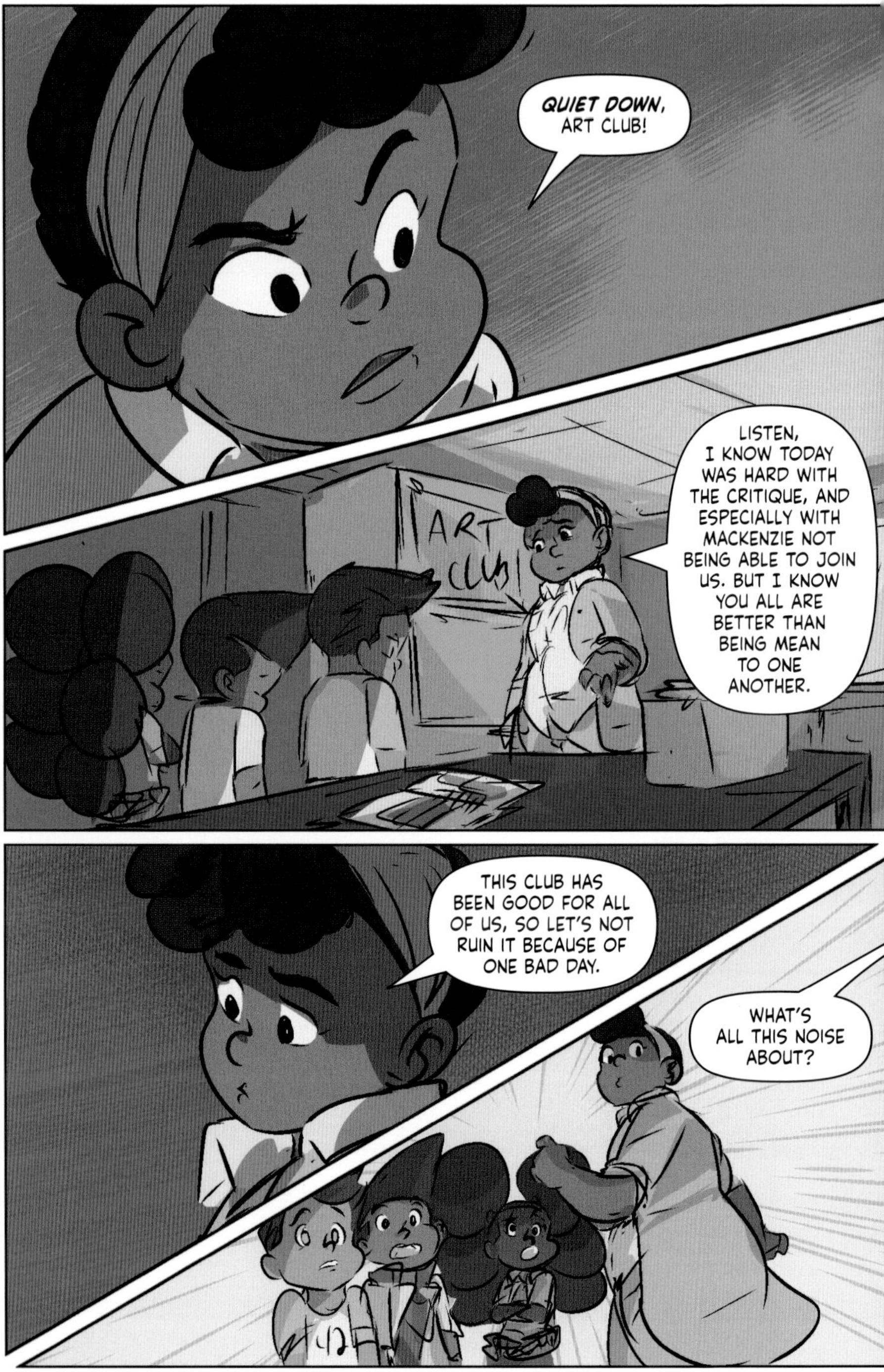
QUIET DOWN, ART CLUB!
ART CLUB
LISTEN, I KNOW TODAY WAS HARD WITH THE CRITIQUE, AND ESPECIALLY WITH MACKENZIE NOT BEING ABLE TO JOIN US. BUT I KNOW YOU ALL ARE BETTER THAN BEING MEAN TO ONE ANOTHER.
THIS CLUB HAS BEEN GOOD FOR ALL OF US, SO LET'S NOT RUIN IT BECAUSE OF ONE BAD DAY.
WHAT'S ALL THIS NOISE ABOUT?

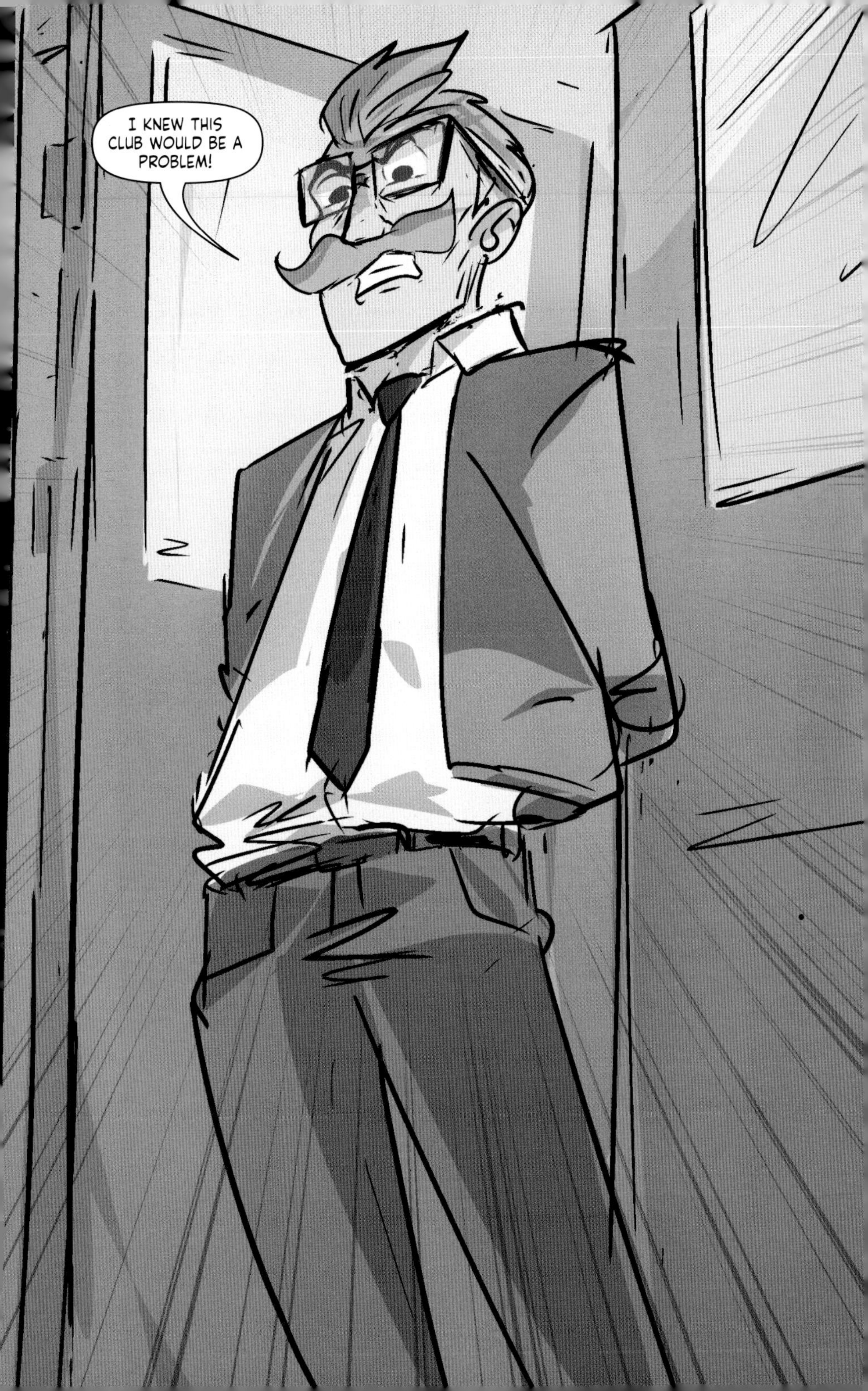
I KNEW THIS CLUB WOULD BE A PROBLEM!

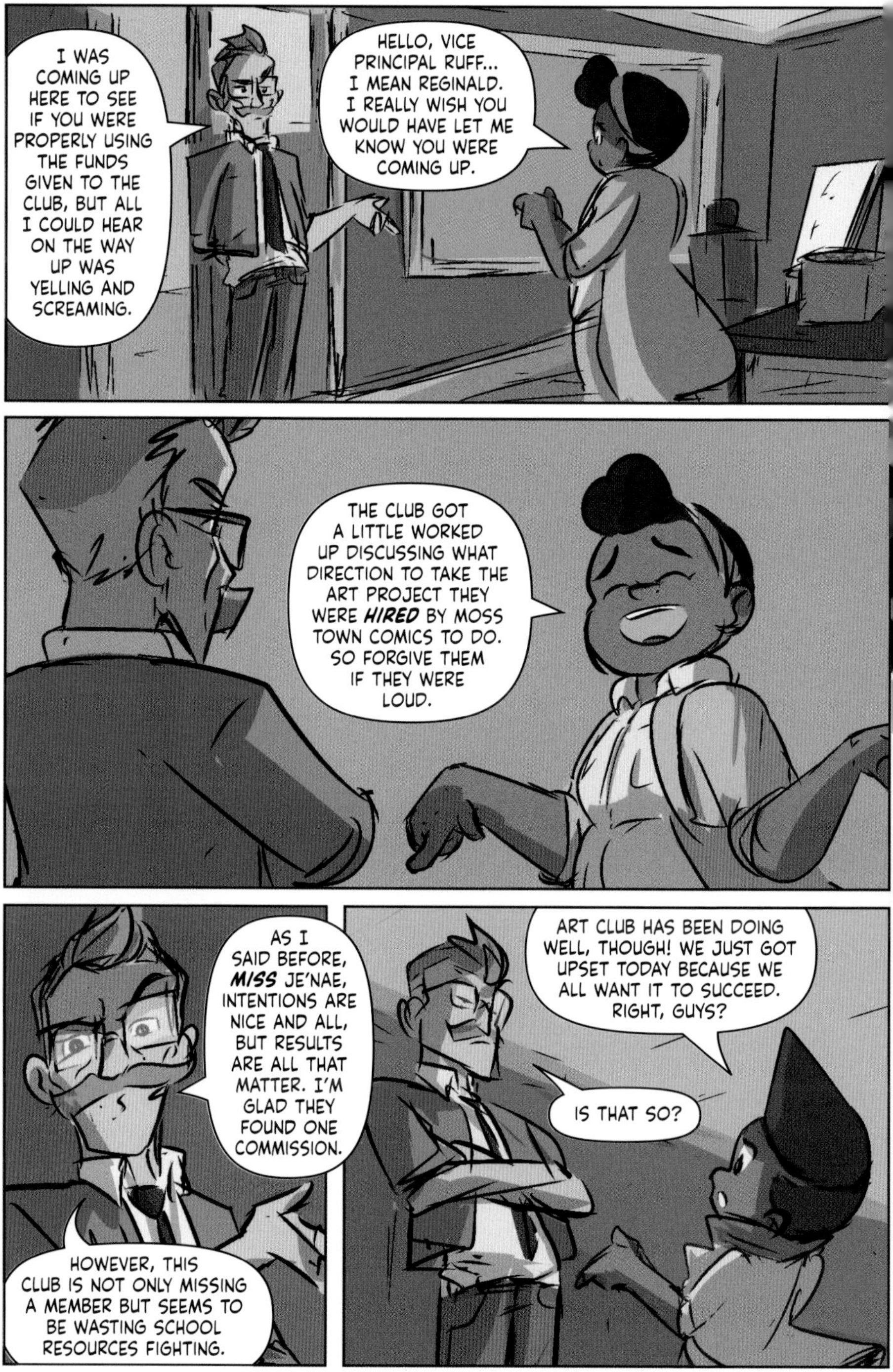
I WAS COMING UP HERE TO SEE IF YOU WERE PROPERLY USING THE FUNDS GIVEN TO THE CLUB, BUT ALL I COULD HEAR ON THE WAY UP WAS YELLING AND SCREAMING.
HELLO, VICE PRINCIPAL RUFF... I MEAN REGINALD. I REALLY WISH YOU WOULD HAVE LET ME KNOW YOU WERE COMING UP.
THE CLUB GOT A LITTLE WORKED UP DISCUSSING WHAT DIRECTION TO TAKE THE ART PROJECT THEY WERE *HIRED* BY MOSS TOWN COMICS TO DO. SO FORGIVE THEM IF THEY WERE LOUD.
AS I SAID BEFORE, *MISS* JE'NAE, INTENTIONS ARE NICE AND ALL, BUT RESULTS ARE ALL THAT MATTER. I'M GLAD THEY FOUND ONE COMMISSION.
HOWEVER, THIS CLUB IS NOT ONLY MISSING A MEMBER BUT SEEMS TO BE WASTING SCHOOL RESOURCES FIGHTING.
ART CLUB HAS BEEN DOING WELL, THOUGH! WE JUST GOT UPSET TODAY BECAUSE WE ALL WANT IT TO SUCCEED. RIGHT, GUYS?
IS THAT SO?

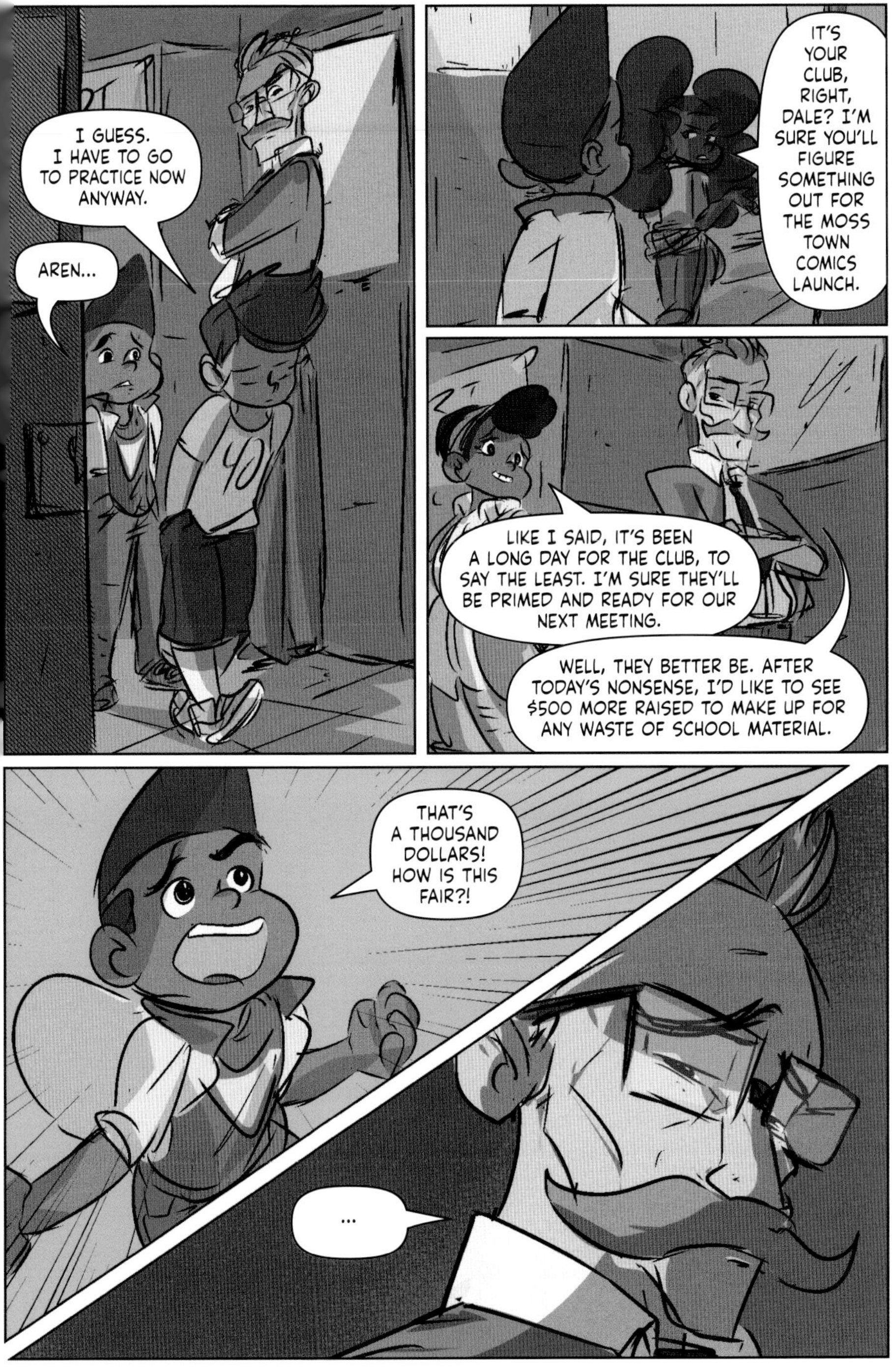
I GUESS. I HAVE TO GO TO PRACTICE NOW ANYWAY.
AREN...
IT'S YOUR CLUB, RIGHT, DALE? I'M SURE YOU'LL FIGURE SOMETHING OUT FOR THE MOSS TOWN COMICS LAUNCH.
LIKE I SAID, IT'S BEEN A LONG DAY FOR THE CLUB, TO SAY THE LEAST. I'M SURE THEY'LL BE PRIMED AND READY FOR OUR NEXT MEETING.
WELL, THEY BETTER BE. AFTER TODAY'S NONSENSE, I'D LIKE TO SEE $500 MORE RAISED TO MAKE UP FOR ANY WASTE OF SCHOOL MATERIAL.
THAT'S A THOUSAND DOLLARS! HOW IS THIS FAIR?!
...

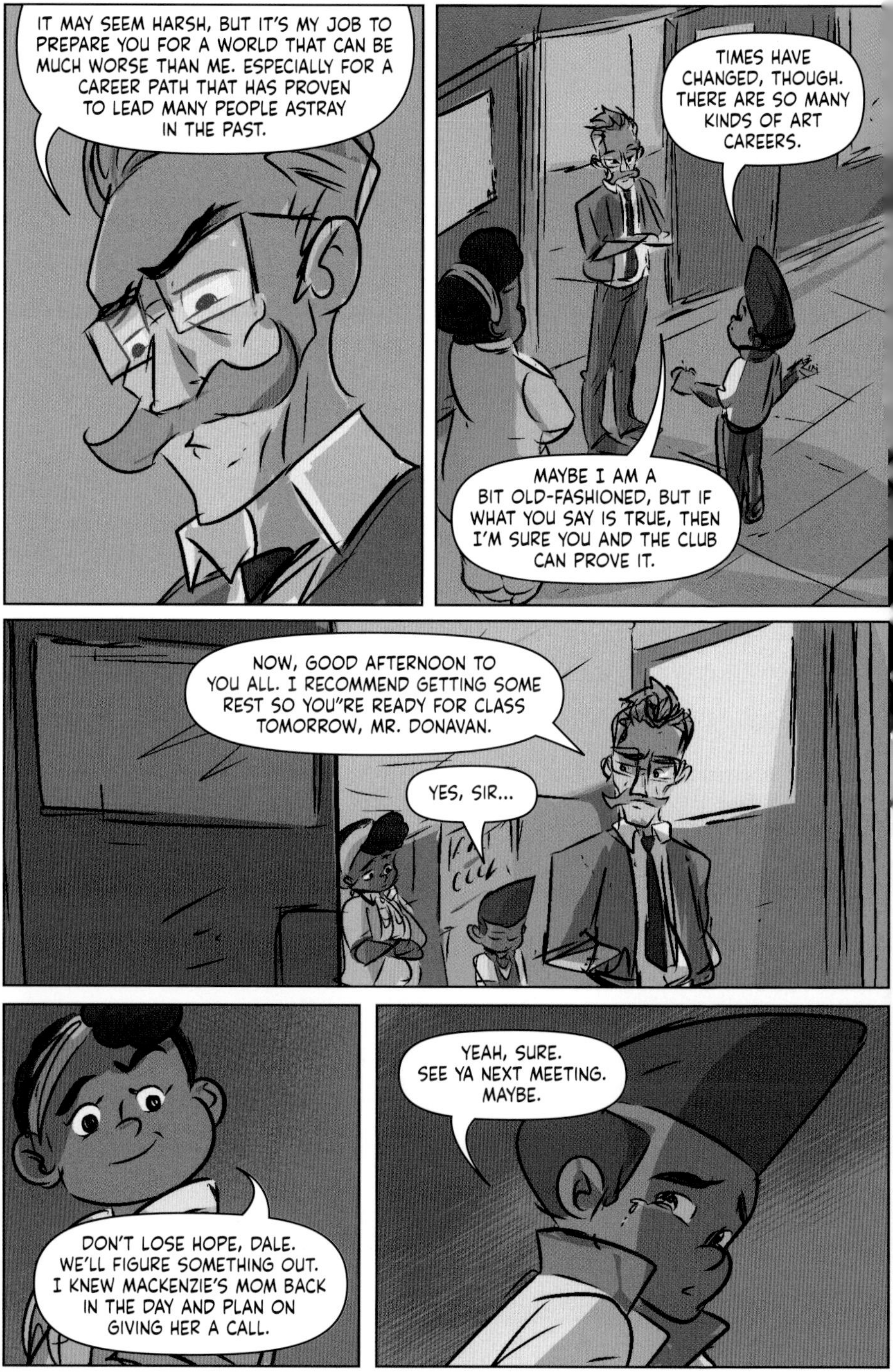

IT MAY SEEM HARSH, BUT IT'S MY JOB TO PREPARE YOU FOR A WORLD THAT CAN BE MUCH WORSE THAN ME. ESPECIALLY FOR A CAREER PATH THAT HAS PROVEN TO LEAD MANY PEOPLE ASTRAY IN THE PAST.
TIMES HAVE CHANGED, THOUGH. THERE ARE SO MANY KINDS OF ART CAREERS.
MAYBE I AM A BIT OLD-FASHIONED, BUT IF WHAT YOU SAY IS TRUE, THEN I'M SURE YOU AND THE CLUB CAN PROVE IT.
NOW, GOOD AFTERNOON TO YOU ALL. I RECOMMEND GETTING SOME REST SO YOU"RE READY FOR CLASS TOMORROW, MR. DONAVAN.
YES, SIR...
DON'T LOSE HOPE, DALE. WE'LL FIGURE SOMETHING OUT. I KNEW MACKENZIE'S MOM BACK IN THE DAY AND PLAN ON GIVING HER A CALL.
YEAH, SURE. SEE YA NEXT MEETING. MAYBE.

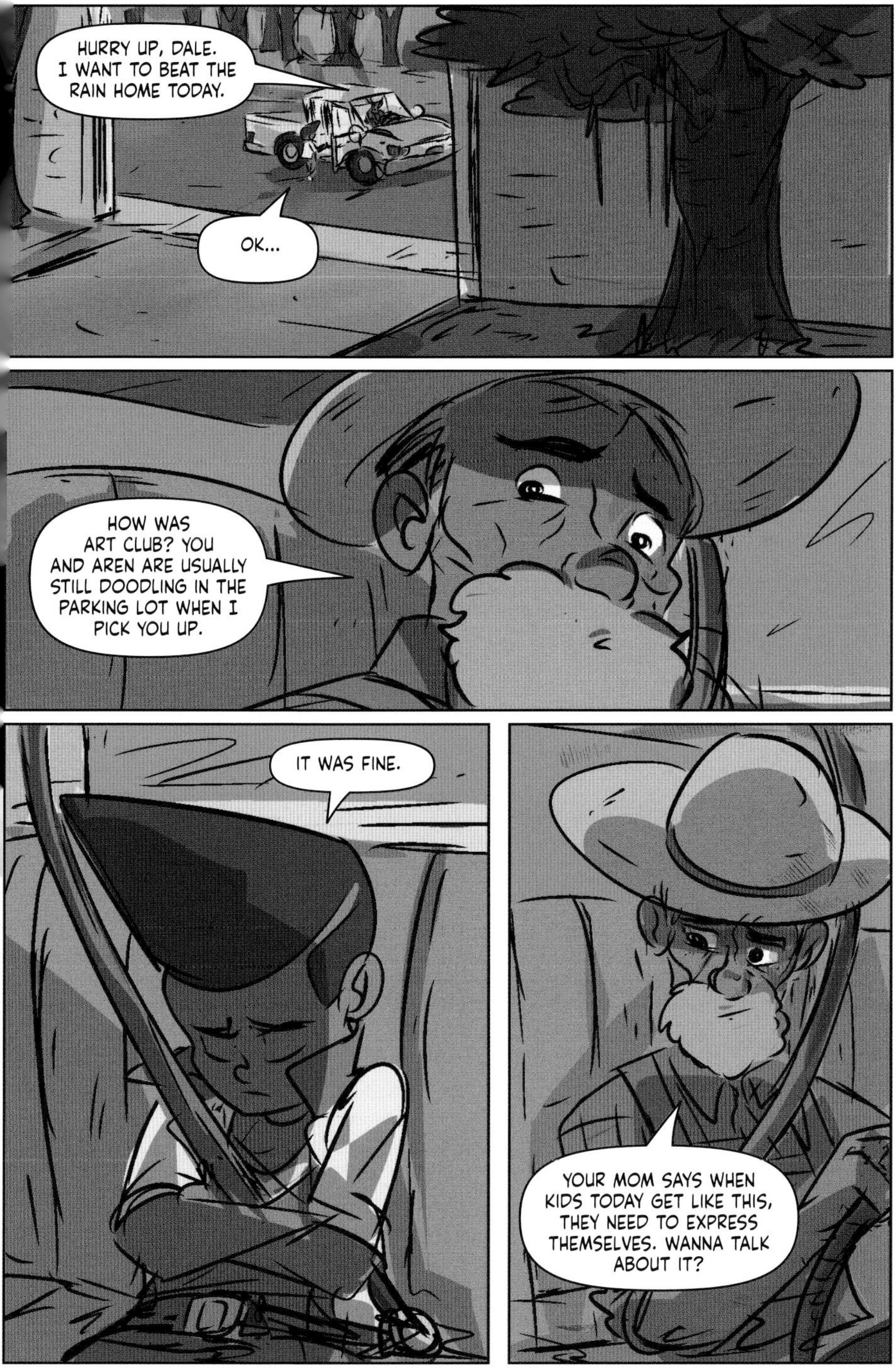
HURRY UP, DALE. I WANT TO BEAT THE RAIN HOME TODAY.
OK...
HOW WAS ART CLUB? YOU AND AREN ARE USUALLY STILL DOODLING IN THE PARKING LOT WHEN I PICK YOU UP.
IT WAS FINE.
YOUR MOM SAYS WHEN KIDS TODAY GET LIKE THIS, THEY NEED TO EXPRESS THEMSELVES. WANNA TALK ABOUT IT?

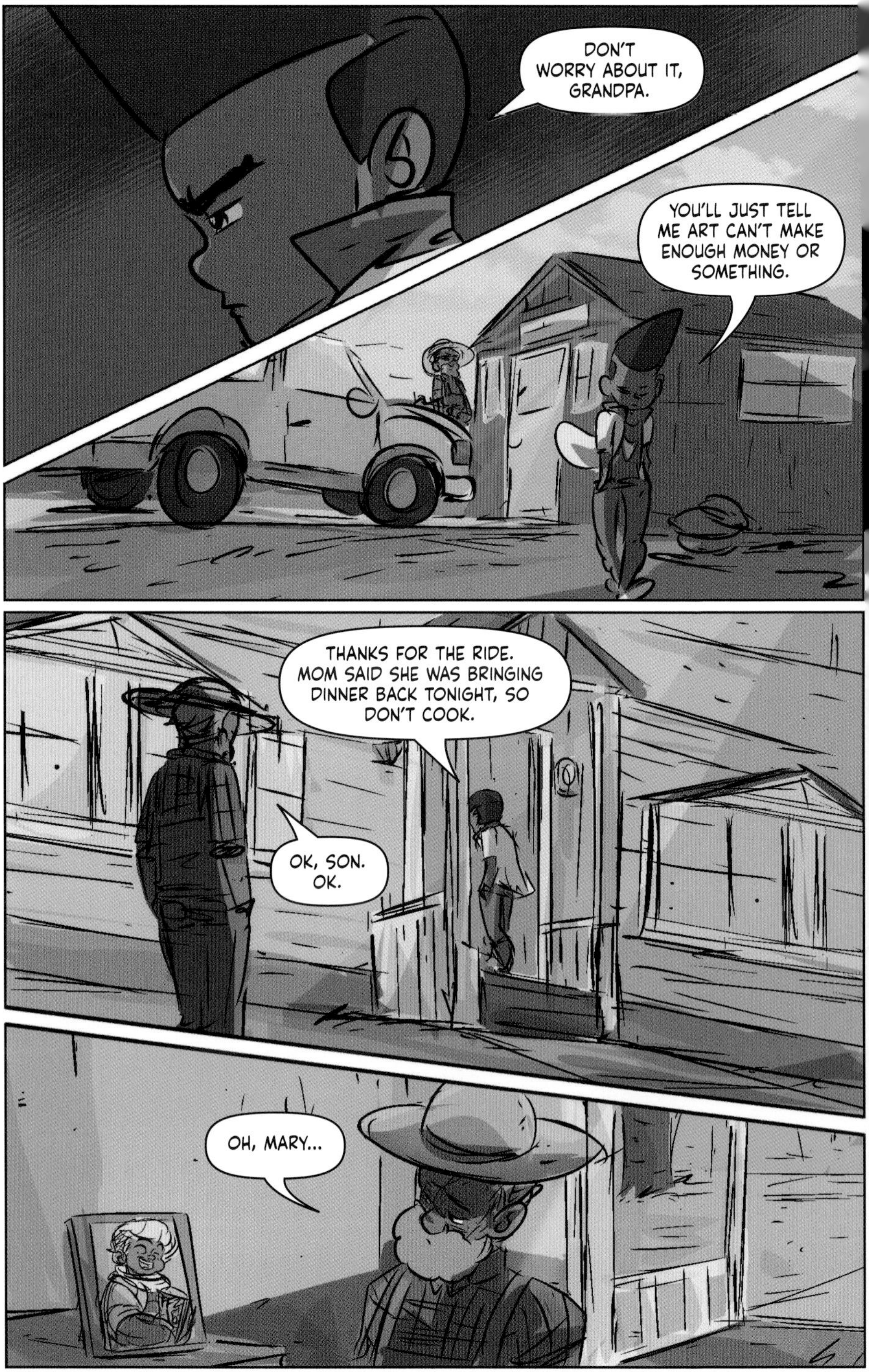
DON'T WORRY ABOUT IT, GRANDPA.
YOU'LL JUST TELL ME ART CAN'T MAKE ENOUGH MONEY OR SOMETHING.
THANKS FOR THE RIDE. MOM SAID SHE WAS BRINGING DINNER BACK TONIGHT, SO DON'T COOK.
OK, SON. OK.
OH, MARY...

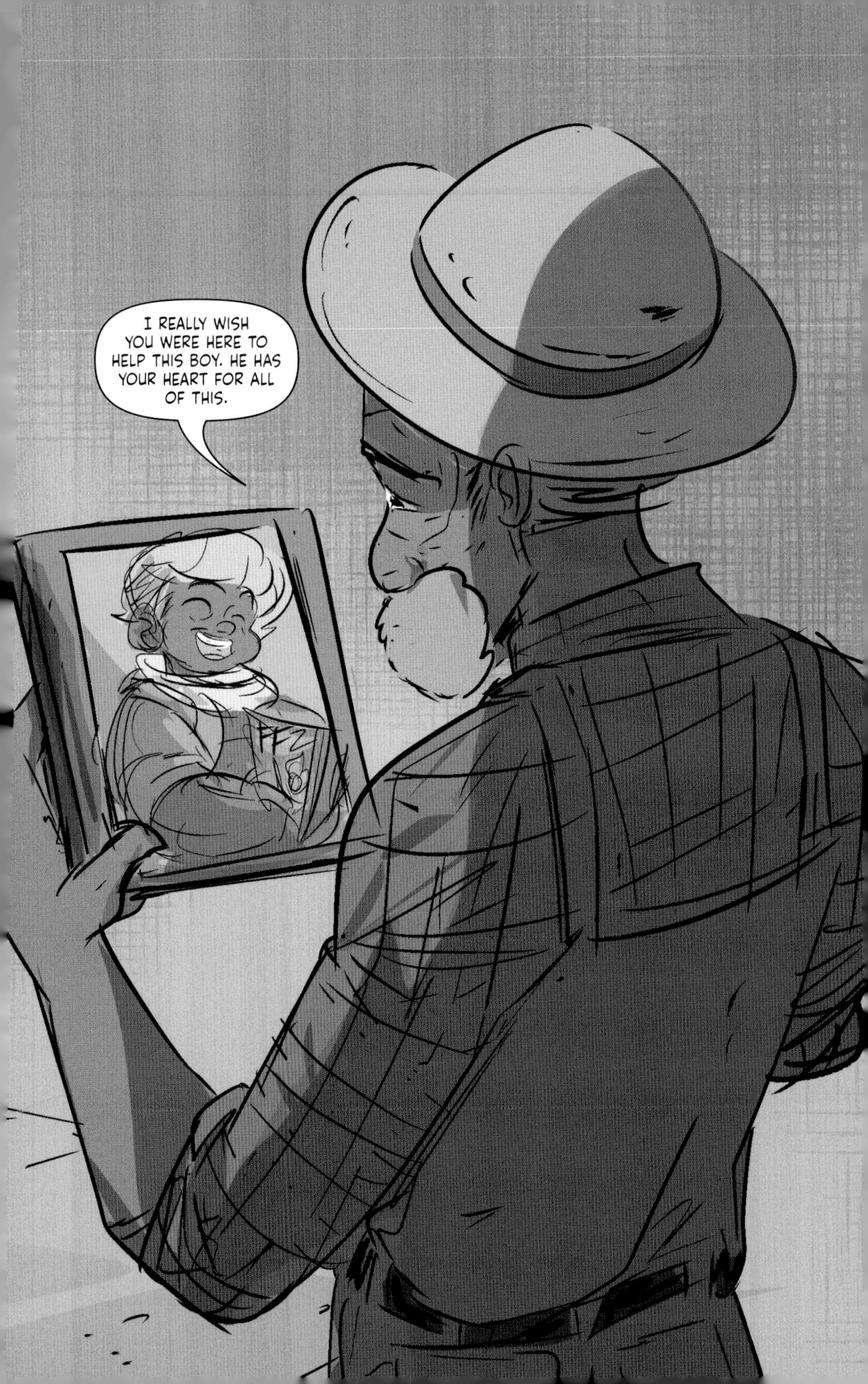
I REALLY WISH YOU WERE HERE TO HELP THIS BOY. HE HAS YOUR HEART FOR ALL OF THIS.

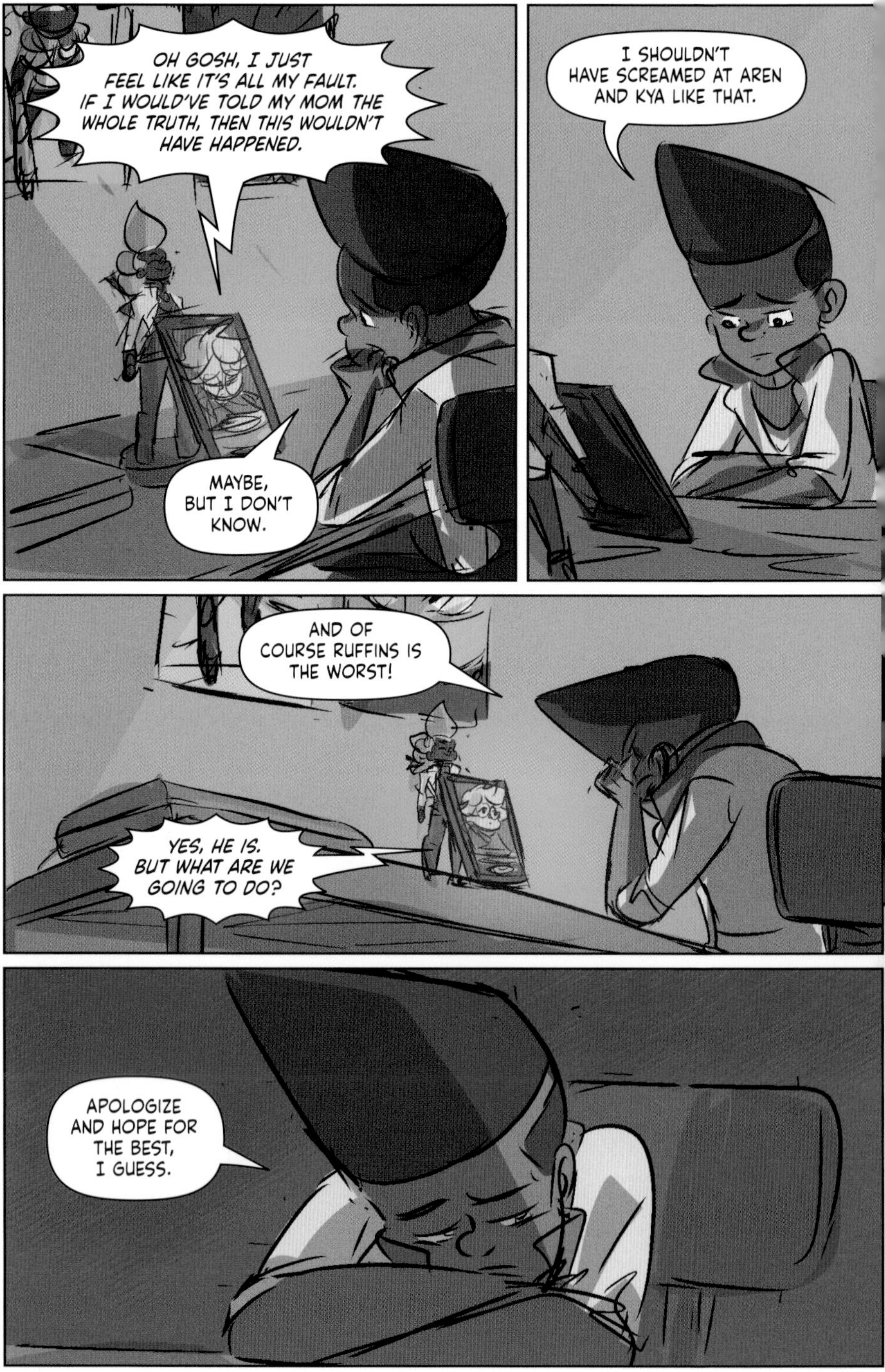
OH GOSH, I JUST FEEL LIKE IT'S ALL MY FAULT. IF I WOULD'VE TOLD MY MOM THE WHOLE TRUTH, THEN THIS WOULDN'T HAVE HAPPENED.
MAYBE, BUT I DON'T KNOW.
I SHOULDN'T HAVE SCREAMED AT AREN AND KYA LIKE THAT.
AND OF COURSE RUFFINS IS THE WORST!
YES, HE IS. BUT WHAT ARE WE GOING TO DO?
APOLOGIZE AND HOPE FOR THE BEST, I GUESS.

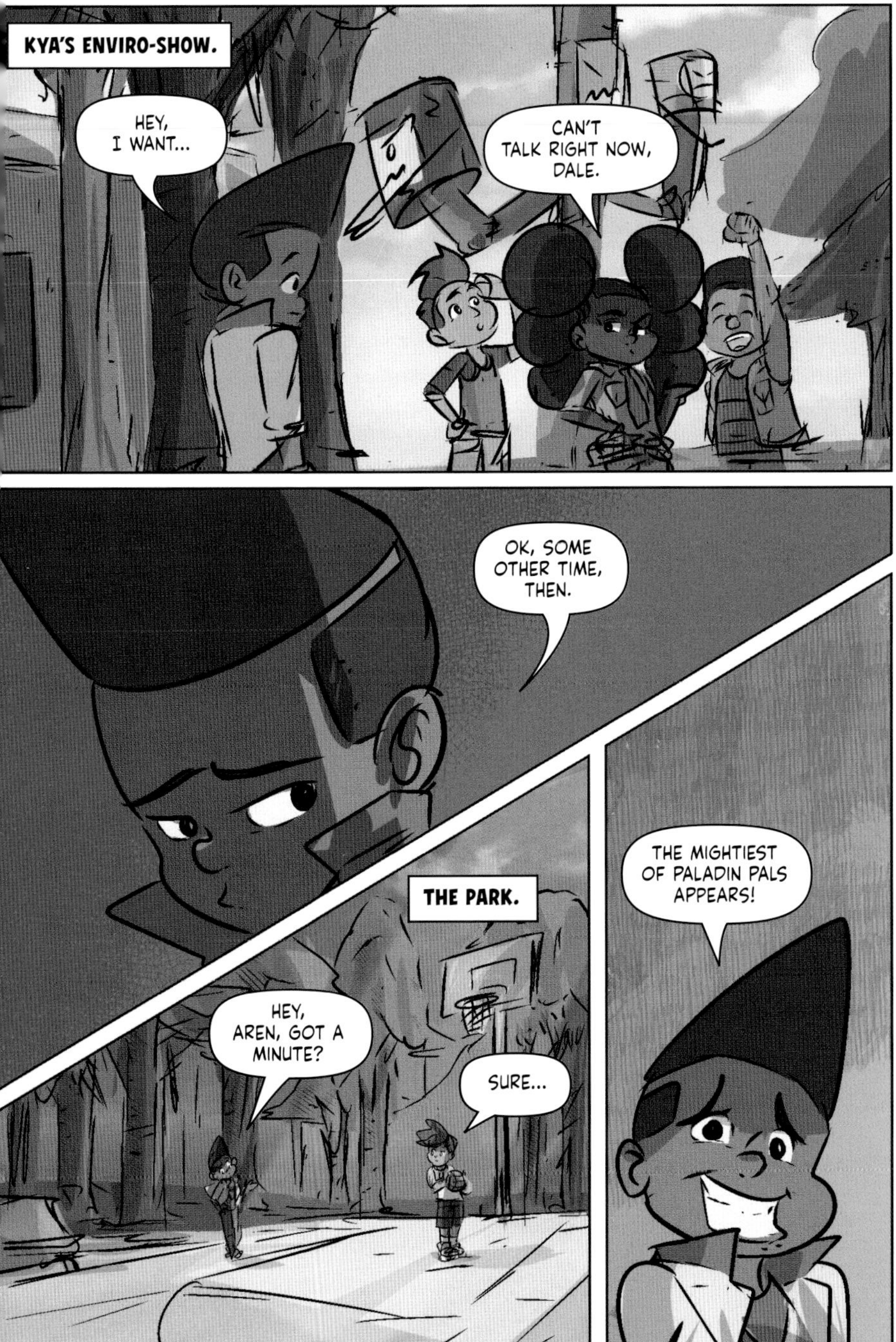
KYA'S ENVIRO-SHOW.
HEY, I WANT...
CAN'T TALK RIGHT NOW, DALE.
OK, SOME OTHER TIME, THEN.
THE PARK.
HEY, AREN, GOT A MINUTE?
SURE...
THE MIGHTIEST OF PALADIN PALS APPEARS!

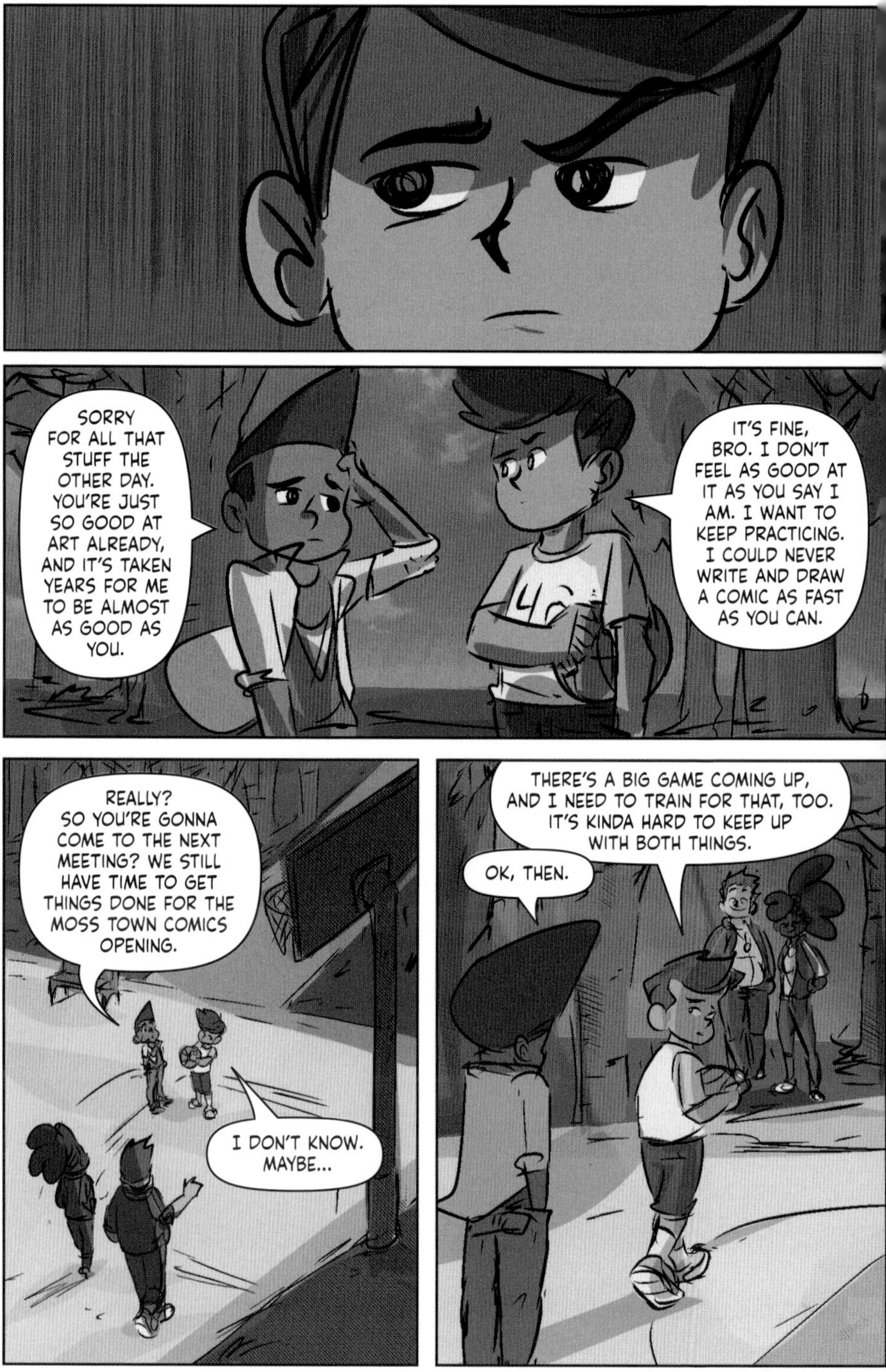
SORRY FOR ALL THAT STUFF THE OTHER DAY. YOU'RE JUST SO GOOD AT ART ALREADY, AND IT'S TAKEN YEARS FOR ME TO BE ALMOST AS GOOD AS YOU.
IT'S FINE, BRO. I DON'T FEEL AS GOOD AT IT AS YOU SAY I AM. I WANT TO KEEP PRACTICING. I COULD NEVER WRITE AND DRAW A COMIC AS FAST AS YOU CAN.
REALLY? SO YOU'RE GONNA COME TO THE NEXT MEETING? WE STILL HAVE TIME TO GET THINGS DONE FOR THE MOSS TOWN COMICS OPENING.
I DON'T KNOW. MAYBE...
THERE'S A BIG GAME COMING UP, AND I NEED TO TRAIN FOR THAT, TOO. IT'S KINDA HARD TO KEEP UP WITH BOTH THINGS.
OK, THEN.

OK, SON, YOU'VE NOT BEEN TOO ENTHUSED LATELY WITH YOUR OTHER HALF. WHAT'S GOING ON BETWEEN YOU TWO?

YEAH, CHIEF, I THOUGHT ART WAS A GOOD LITTLE HOBBY FOR YOU.

I LOVE BASKETBALL...

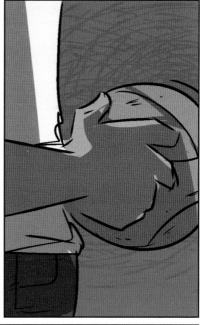

ART'S MORE THAN A HOBBY, THOUGH. I THINK I COULD BE REALLY GOOD AT IT IF I KEEP PRACTICING. BUT IT'S CUTTING INTO BASKETBALL TIME, AND I DON'T WANT TO LET YOU GUYS OR THE TEAM DOWN.

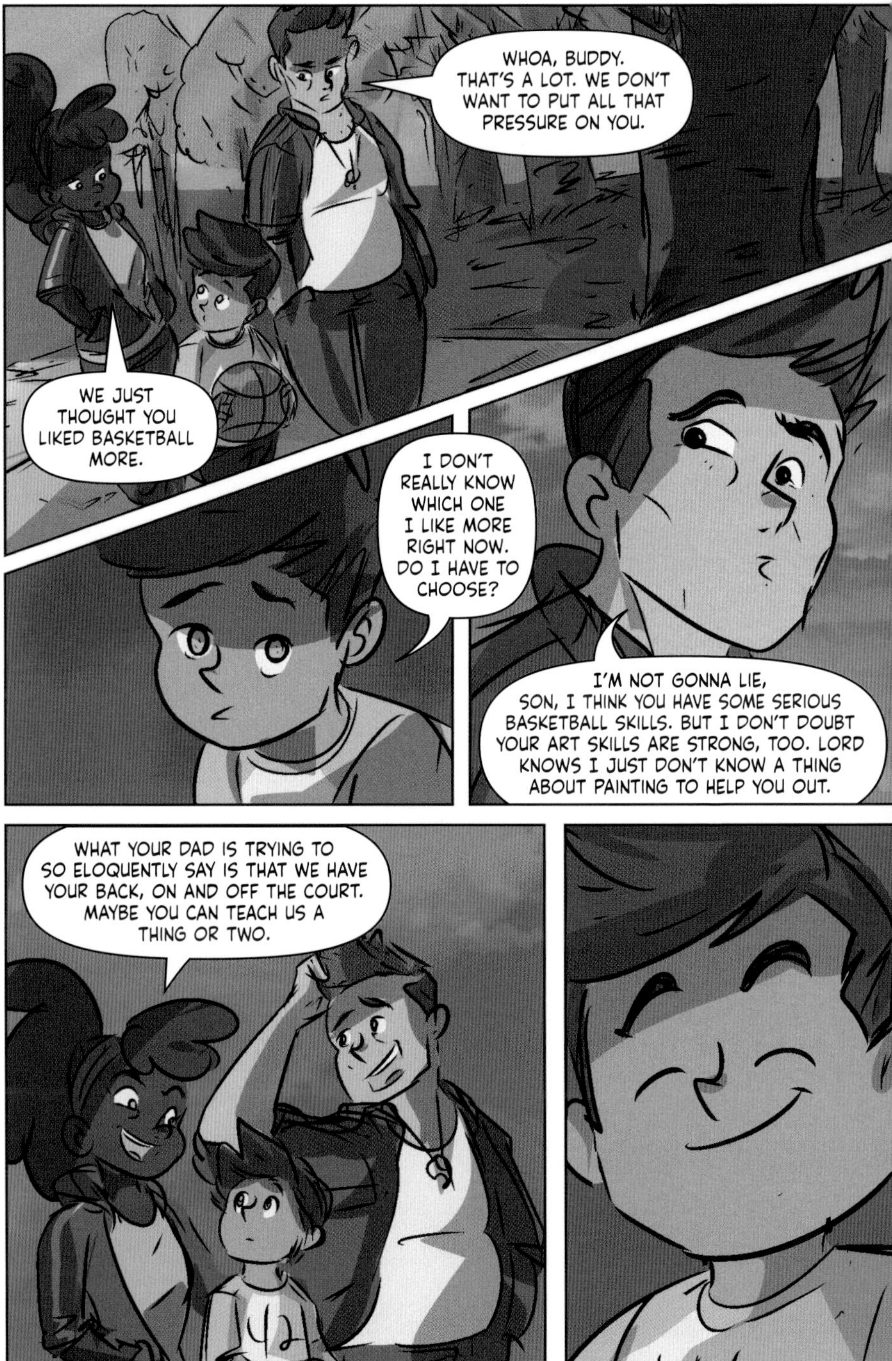
WHOA, BUDDY. THAT'S A LOT. WE DON'T WANT TO PUT ALL THAT PRESSURE ON YOU.
WE JUST THOUGHT YOU LIKED BASKETBALL MORE.
I DON'T REALLY KNOW WHICH ONE I LIKE MORE RIGHT NOW. DO I HAVE TO CHOOSE?
I'M NOT GONNA LIE, SON, I THINK YOU HAVE SOME SERIOUS BASKETBALL SKILLS. BUT I DON'T DOUBT YOUR ART SKILLS ARE STRONG, TOO. LORD KNOWS I JUST DON'T KNOW A THING ABOUT PAINTING TO HELP YOU OUT.
WHAT YOUR DAD IS TRYING TO SO ELOQUENTLY SAY IS THAT WE HAVE YOUR BACK, ON AND OFF THE COURT. MAYBE YOU CAN TEACH US A THING OR TWO.
42

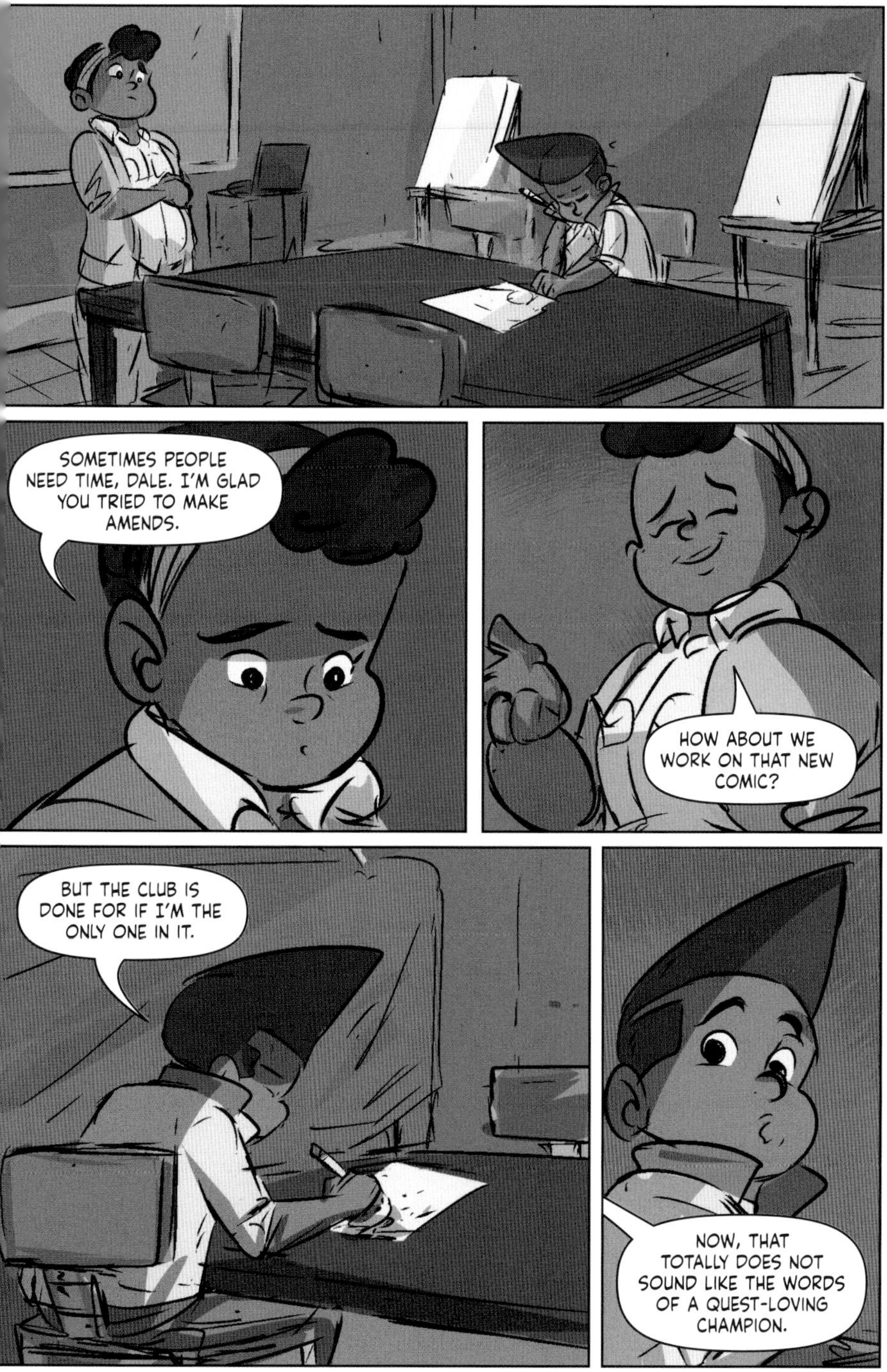
SOMETIMES PEOPLE NEED TIME, DALE. I'M GLAD YOU TRIED TO MAKE AMENDS.
HOW ABOUT WE WORK ON THAT NEW COMIC?
BUT THE CLUB IS DONE FOR IF I'M THE ONLY ONE IN IT.
NOW, THAT TOTALLY DOES NOT SOUND LIKE THE WORDS OF A QUEST-LOVING CHAMPION.

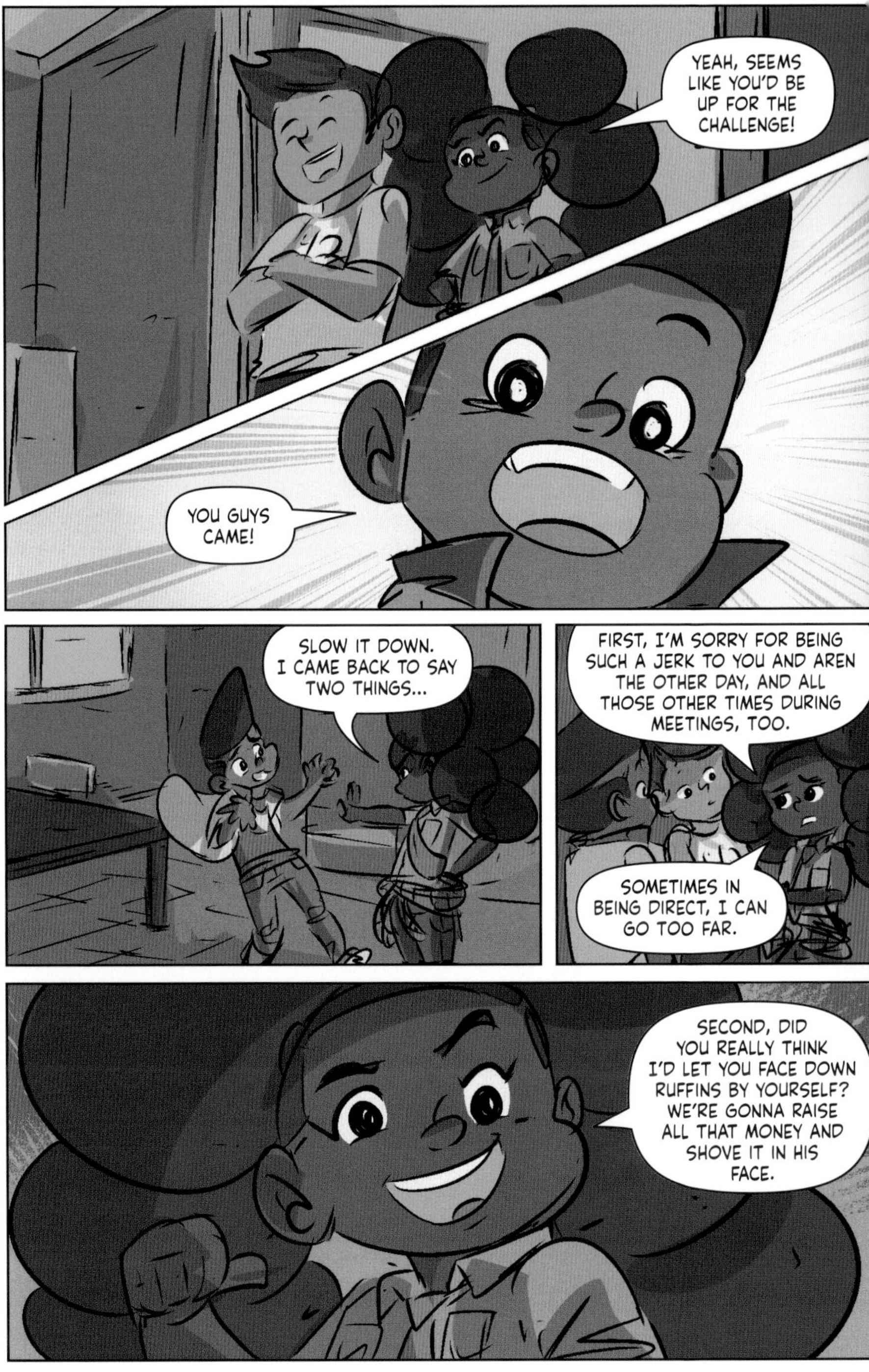
YEAH, SEEMS LIKE YOU'D BE UP FOR THE CHALLENGE!
YOU GUYS CAME!
SLOW IT DOWN. I CAME BACK TO SAY TWO THINGS...
FIRST, I'M SORRY FOR BEING SUCH A JERK TO YOU AND AREN THE OTHER DAY, AND ALL THOSE OTHER TIMES DURING MEETINGS, TOO.
SOMETIMES IN BEING DIRECT, I CAN GO TOO FAR.
SECOND, DID YOU REALLY THINK I'D LET YOU FACE DOWN RUFFINS BY YOURSELF? WE'RE GONNA RAISE ALL THAT MONEY AND SHOVE IT IN HIS FACE.

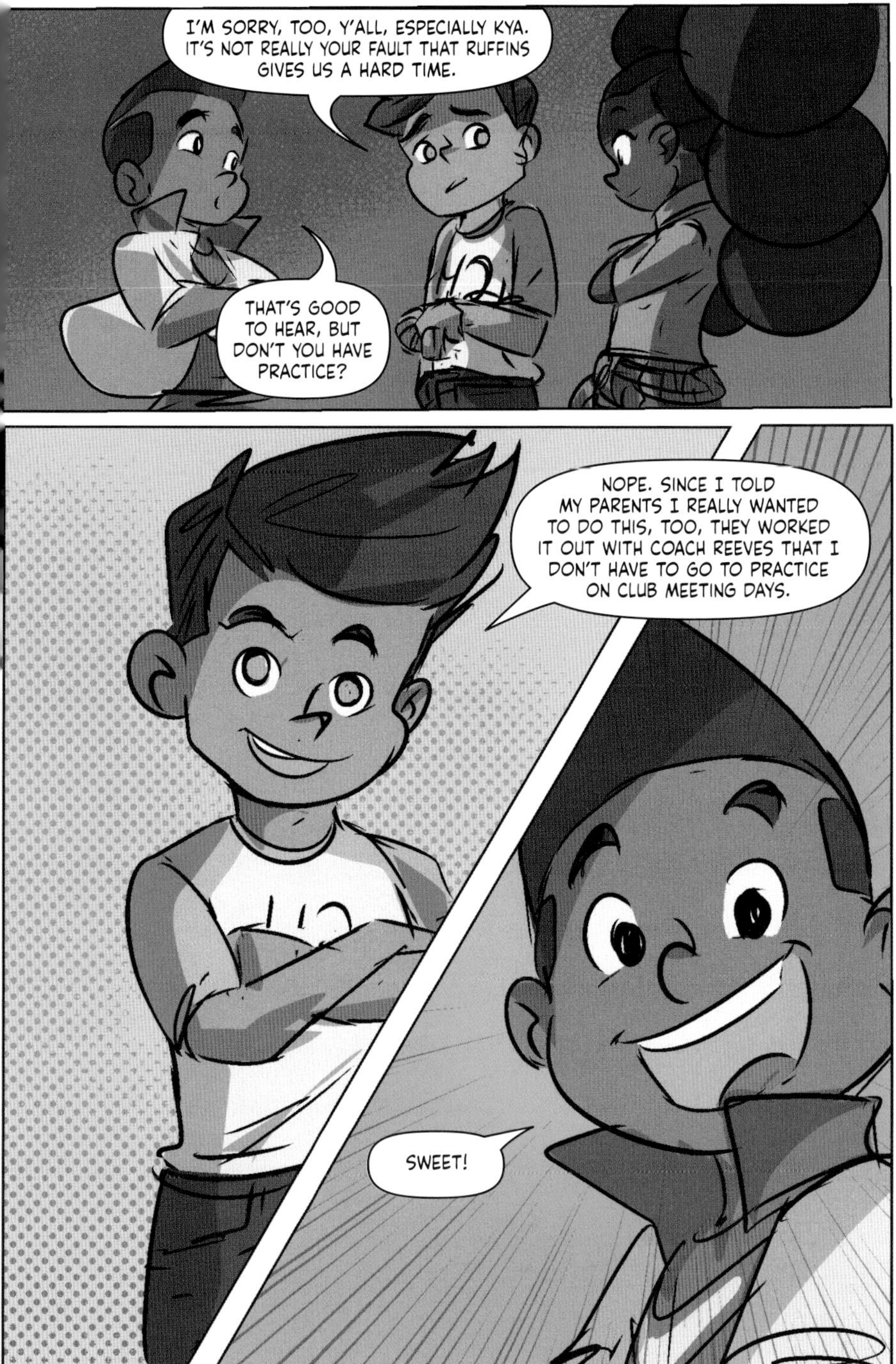
I'M SORRY, TOO, Y'ALL, ESPECIALLY KYA. IT'S NOT REALLY YOUR FAULT THAT RUFFINS GIVES US A HARD TIME.
THAT'S GOOD TO HEAR, BUT DON'T YOU HAVE PRACTICE?
NOPE. SINCE I TOLD MY PARENTS I REALLY WANTED TO DO THIS, TOO, THEY WORKED IT OUT WITH COACH REEVES THAT I DON'T HAVE TO GO TO PRACTICE ON CLUB MEETING DAYS.
SWEET!

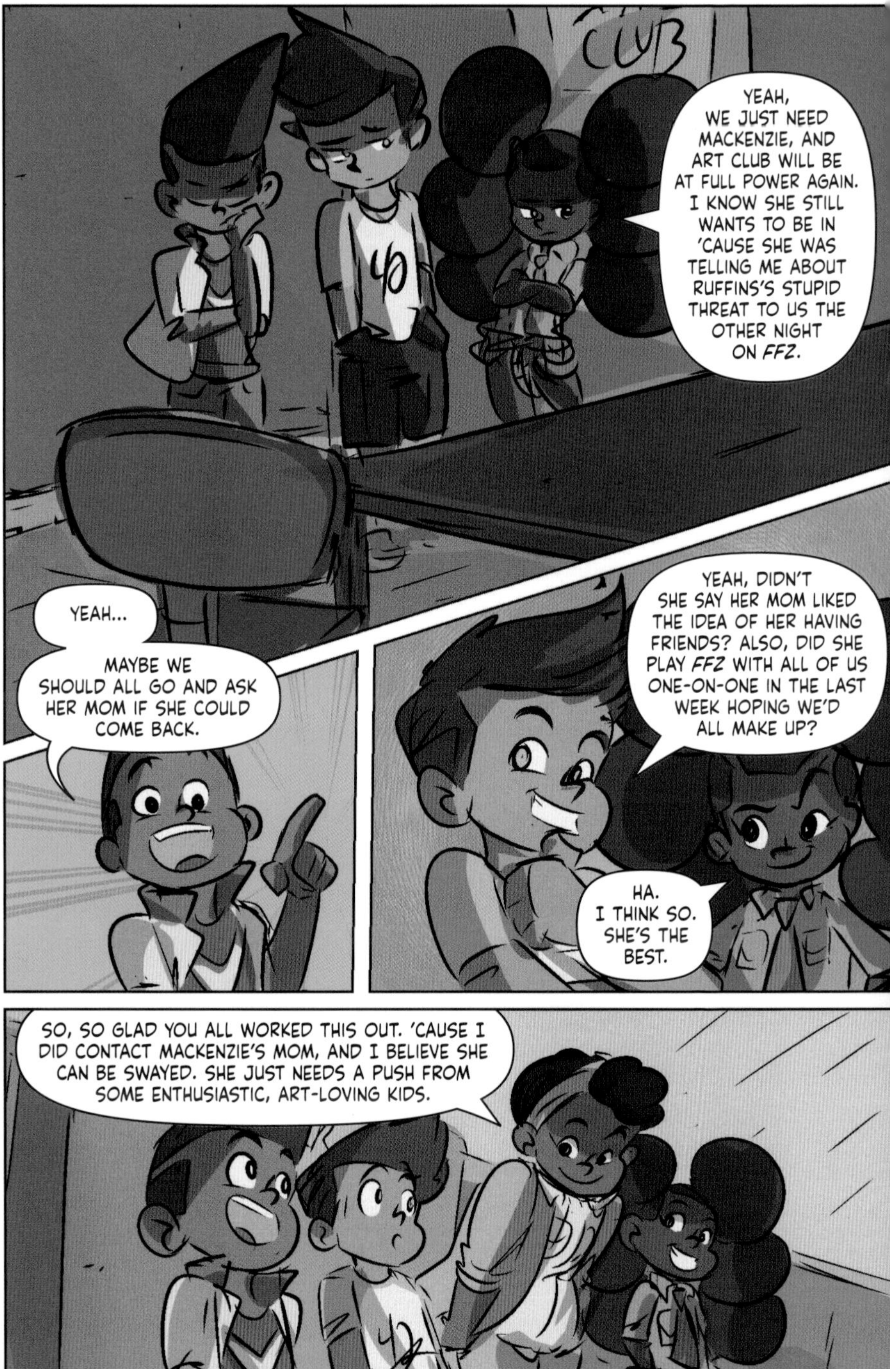
CLUB
YEAH, WE JUST NEED MACKENZIE, AND ART CLUB WILL BE AT FULL POWER AGAIN. I KNOW SHE STILL WANTS TO BE IN 'CAUSE SHE WAS TELLING ME ABOUT RUFFINS'S STUPID THREAT TO US THE OTHER NIGHT ON *FFZ*.
YEAH...
MAYBE WE SHOULD ALL GO AND ASK HER MOM IF SHE COULD COME BACK.
YEAH, DIDN'T SHE SAY HER MOM LIKED THE IDEA OF HER HAVING FRIENDS? ALSO, DID SHE PLAY *FFZ* WITH ALL OF US ONE-ON-ONE IN THE LAST WEEK HOPING WE'D ALL MAKE UP?
HA. I THINK SO. SHE'S THE BEST.
SO, SO GLAD YOU ALL WORKED THIS OUT. 'CAUSE I DID CONTACT MACKENZIE'S MOM, AND I BELIEVE SHE CAN BE SWAYED. SHE JUST NEEDS A PUSH FROM SOME ENTHUSIASTIC, ART-LOVING KIDS.

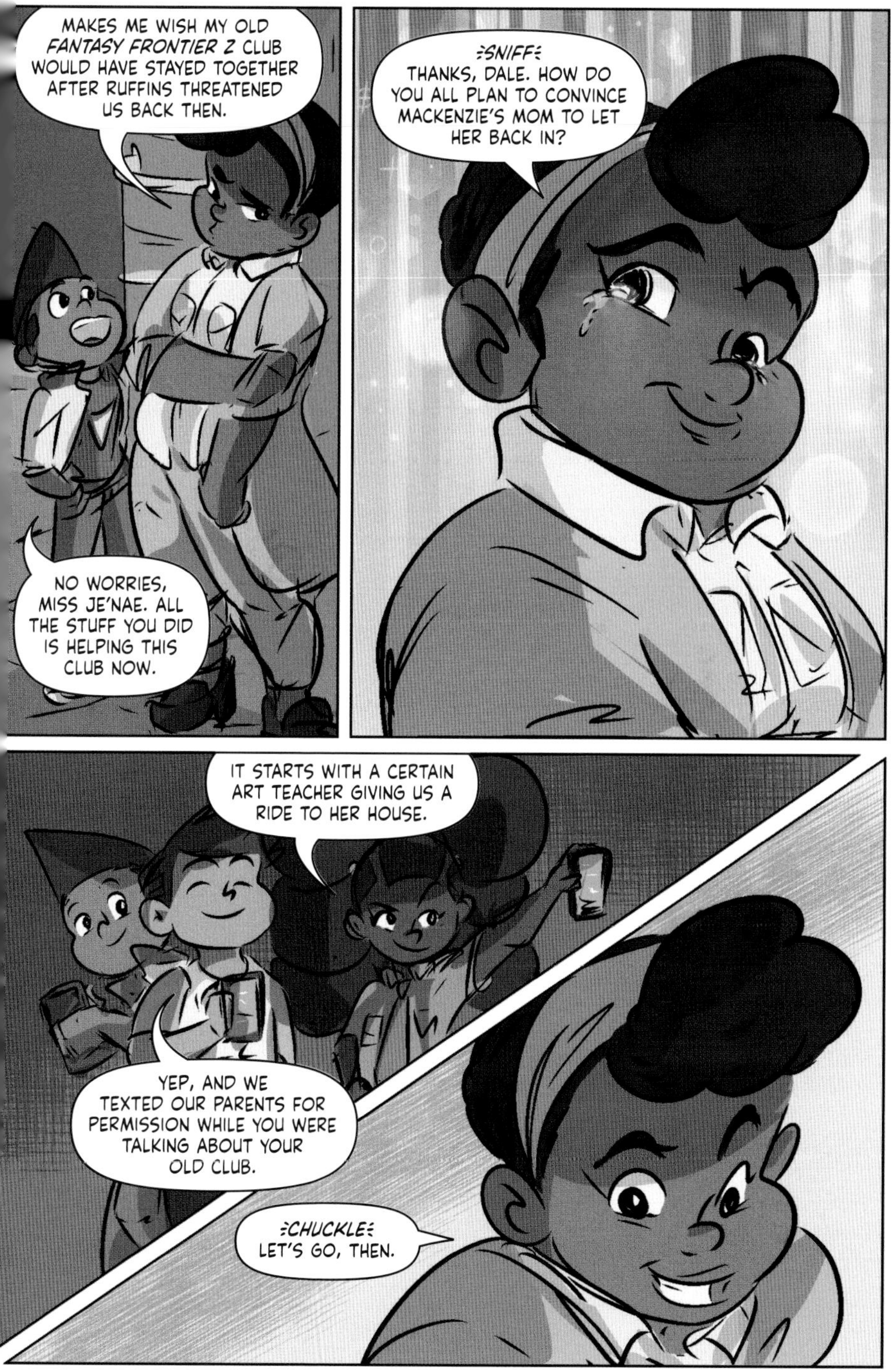
MAKES ME WISH MY OLD *FANTASY FRONTIER Z* CLUB WOULD HAVE STAYED TOGETHER AFTER RUFFINS THREATENED US BACK THEN.
NO WORRIES, MISS JE'NAE. ALL THE STUFF YOU DID IS HELPING THIS CLUB NOW.
SNIFF THANKS, DALE. HOW DO YOU ALL PLAN TO CONVINCE MACKENZIE'S MOM TO LET HER BACK IN?
IT STARTS WITH A CERTAIN ART TEACHER GIVING US A RIDE TO HER HOUSE.
YEP, AND WE TEXTED OUR PARENTS FOR PERMISSION WHILE YOU WERE TALKING ABOUT YOUR OLD CLUB.
CHUCKLE LET'S GO, THEN.

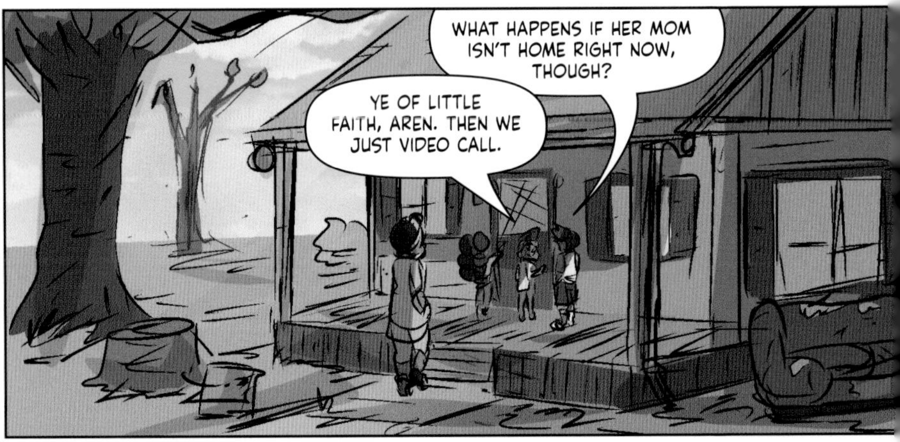
WHAT HAPPENS IF HER MOM ISN'T HOME RIGHT NOW, THOUGH?
YE OF LITTLE FAITH, AREN. THEN WE JUST VIDEO CALL.

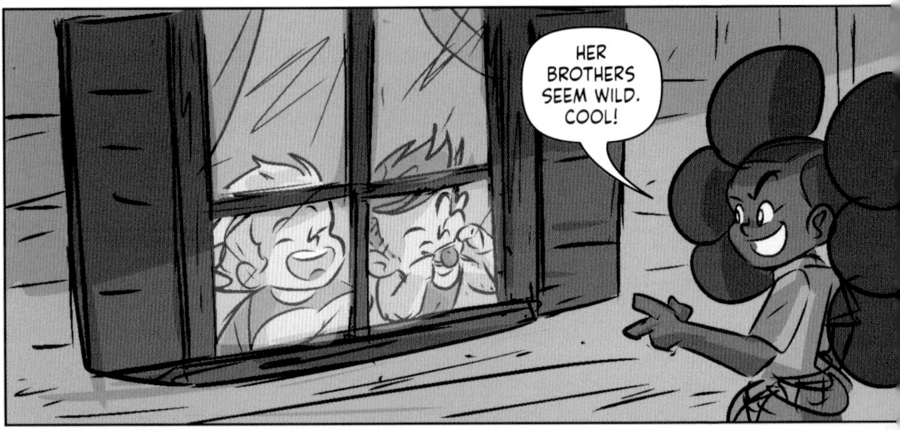
HER BROTHERS SEEM WILD. COOL!

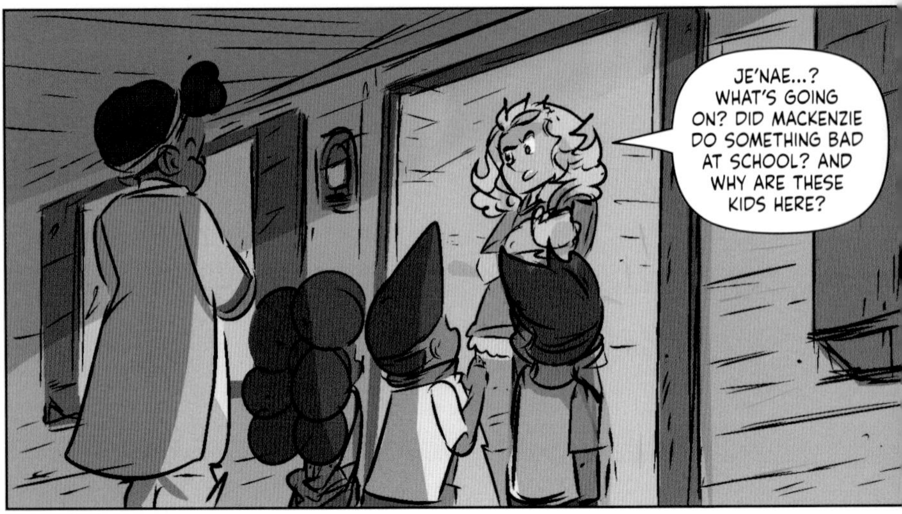
JE'NAE...? WHAT'S GOING ON? DID MACKENZIE DO SOMETHING BAD AT SCHOOL? AND WHY ARE THESE KIDS HERE?

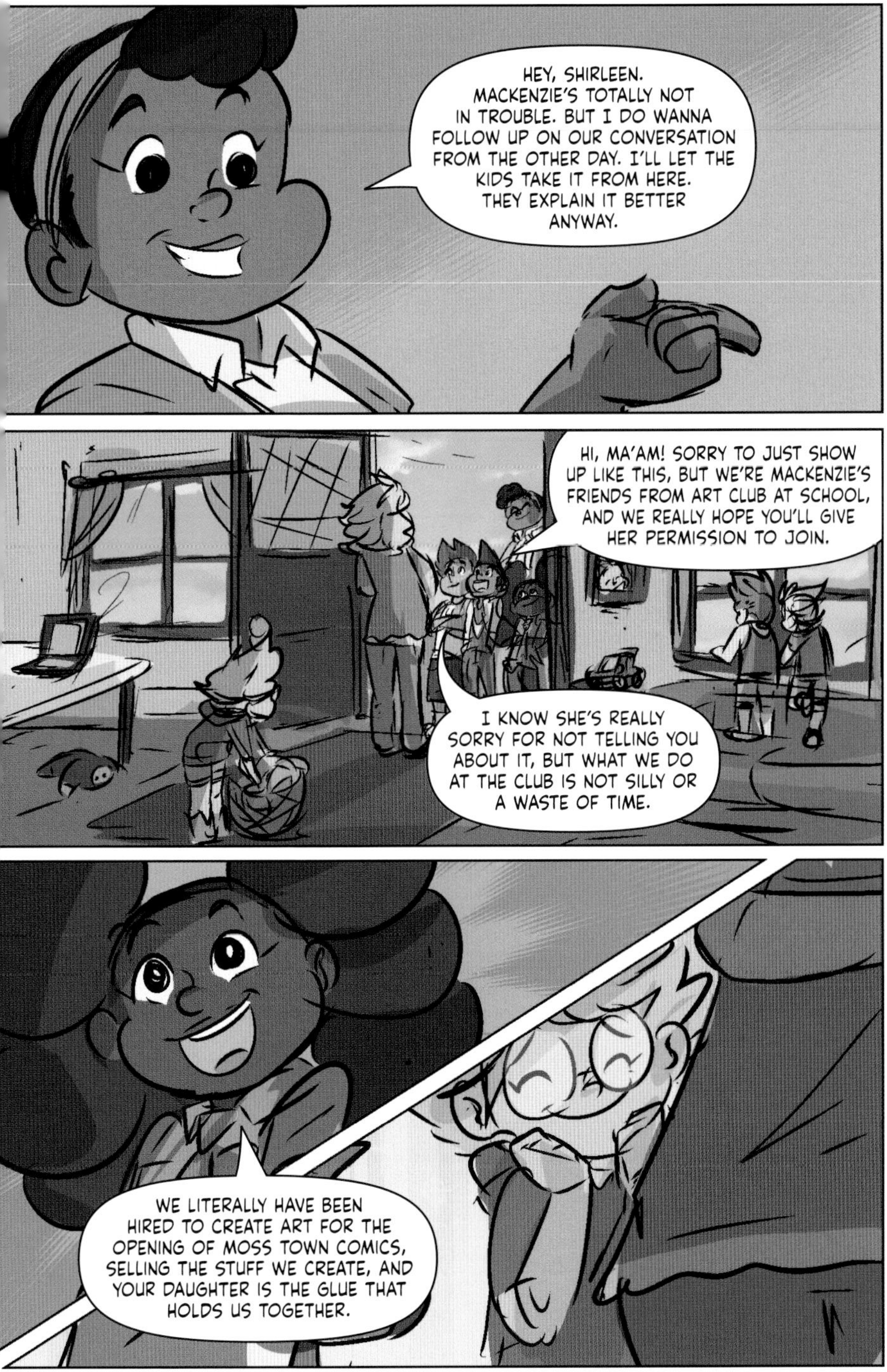
HEY, SHIRLEEN. MACKENZIE'S TOTALLY NOT IN TROUBLE. BUT I DO WANNA FOLLOW UP ON OUR CONVERSATION FROM THE OTHER DAY. I'LL LET THE KIDS TAKE IT FROM HERE. THEY EXPLAIN IT BETTER ANYWAY.
HI, MA'AM! SORRY TO JUST SHOW UP LIKE THIS, BUT WE'RE MACKENZIE'S FRIENDS FROM ART CLUB AT SCHOOL, AND WE REALLY HOPE YOU'LL GIVE HER PERMISSION TO JOIN.
I KNOW SHE'S REALLY SORRY FOR NOT TELLING YOU ABOUT IT, BUT WHAT WE DO AT THE CLUB IS NOT SILLY OR A WASTE OF TIME.
WE LITERALLY HAVE BEEN HIRED TO CREATE ART FOR THE OPENING OF MOSS TOWN COMICS, SELLING THE STUFF WE CREATE, AND YOUR DAUGHTER IS THE GLUE THAT HOLDS US TOGETHER.

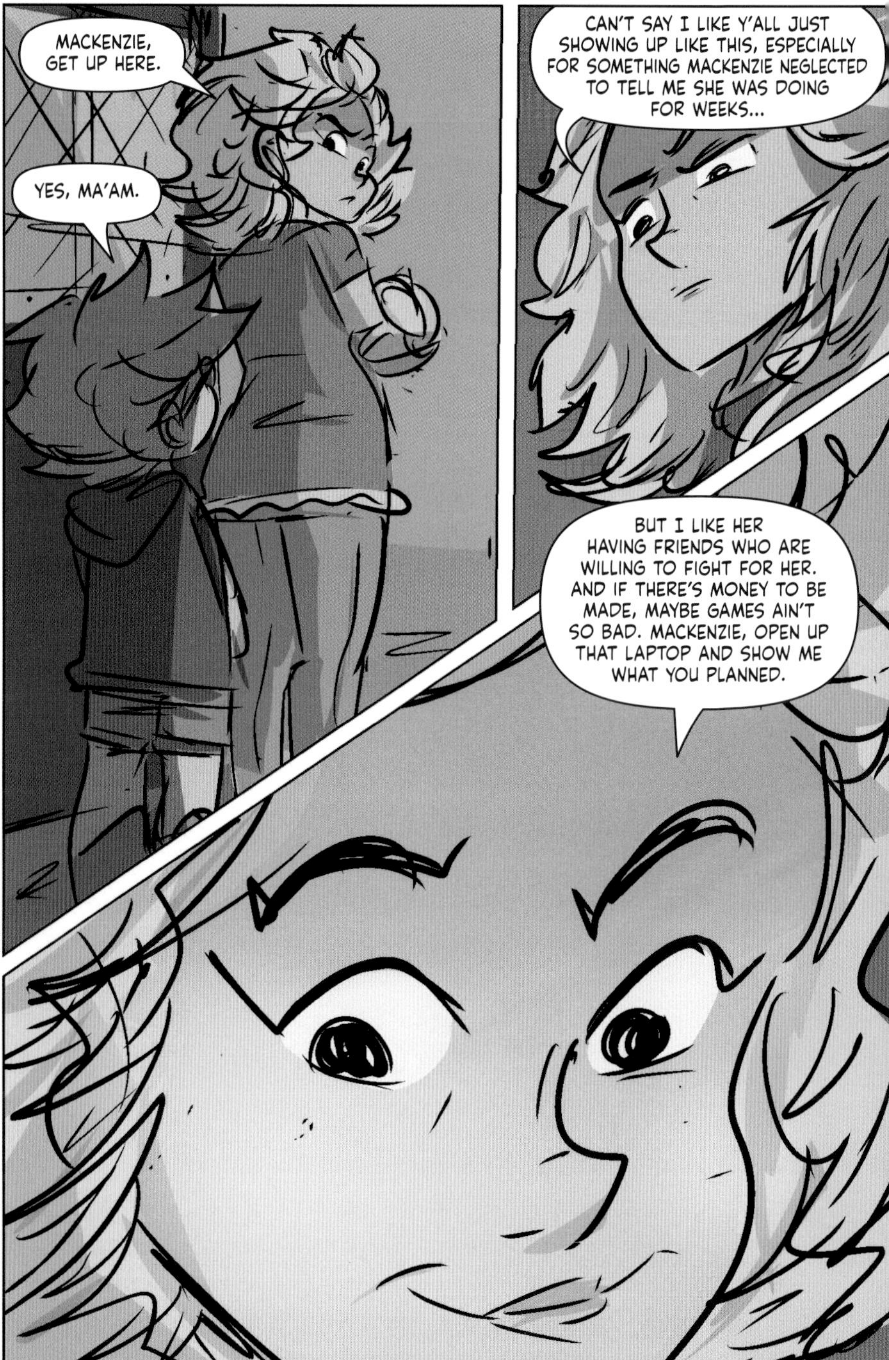
MACKENZIE, GET UP HERE.
YES, MA'AM.
CAN'T SAY I LIKE Y'ALL JUST SHOWING UP LIKE THIS, ESPECIALLY FOR SOMETHING MACKENZIE NEGLECTED TO TELL ME SHE WAS DOING FOR WEEKS...
BUT I LIKE HER HAVING FRIENDS WHO ARE WILLING TO FIGHT FOR HER. AND IF THERE'S MONEY TO BE MADE, MAYBE GAMES AIN'T SO BAD. MACKENZIE, OPEN UP THAT LAPTOP AND SHOW ME WHAT YOU PLANNED.

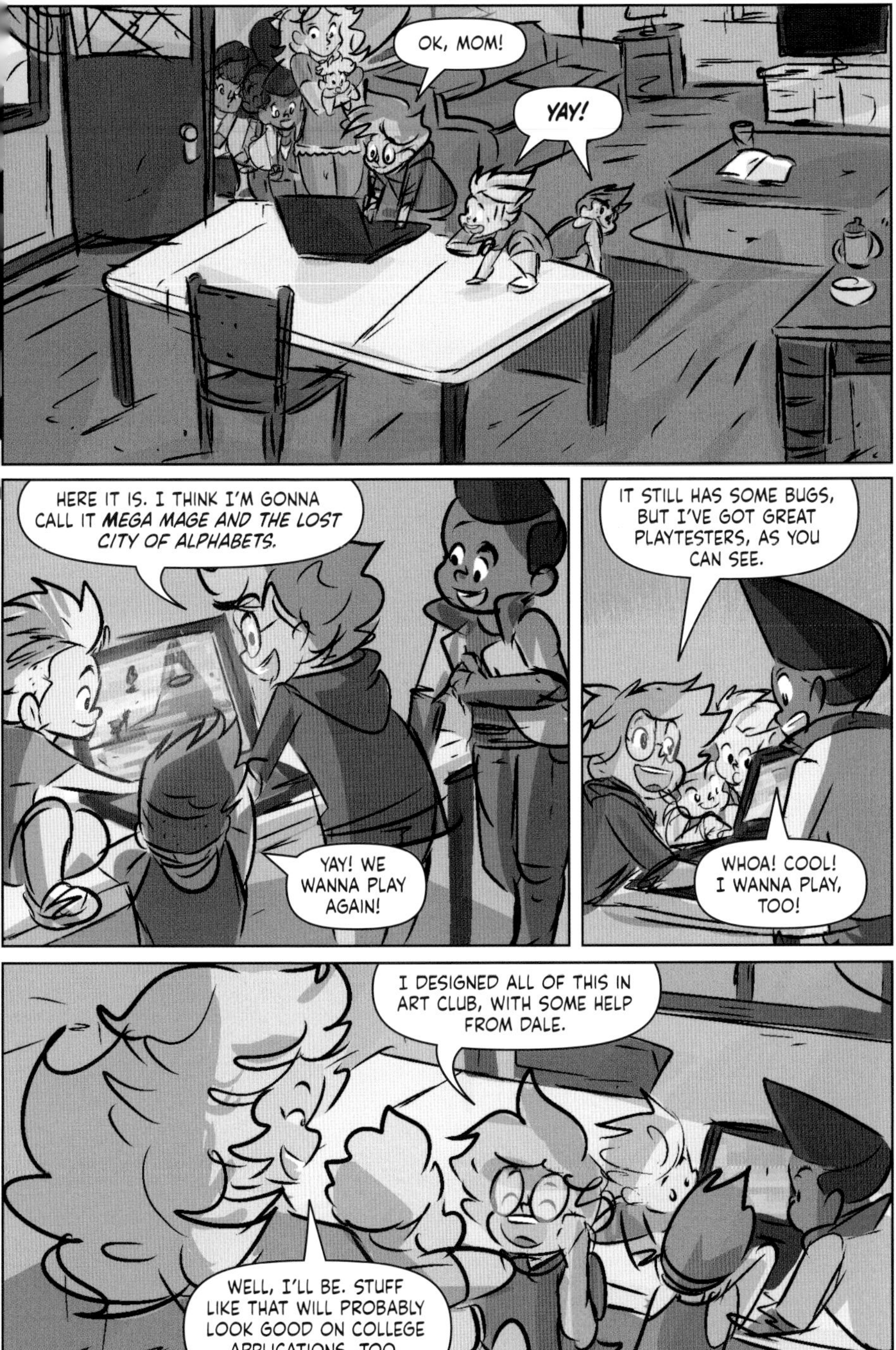
OK, MOM!
YAY!
HERE IT IS. I THINK I'M GONNA CALL IT MEGA MAGE AND THE LOST CITY OF ALPHABETS.
YAY! WE WANNA PLAY AGAIN!
IT STILL HAS SOME BUGS, BUT I'VE GOT GREAT PLAYTESTERS, AS YOU CAN SEE.
WHOA! COOL! I WANNA PLAY, TOO!
I DESIGNED ALL OF THIS IN ART CLUB, WITH SOME HELP FROM DALE.
WELL, I'LL BE. STUFF LIKE THAT WILL PROBABLY LOOK GOOD ON COLLEGE APPLICATIONS, TOO.

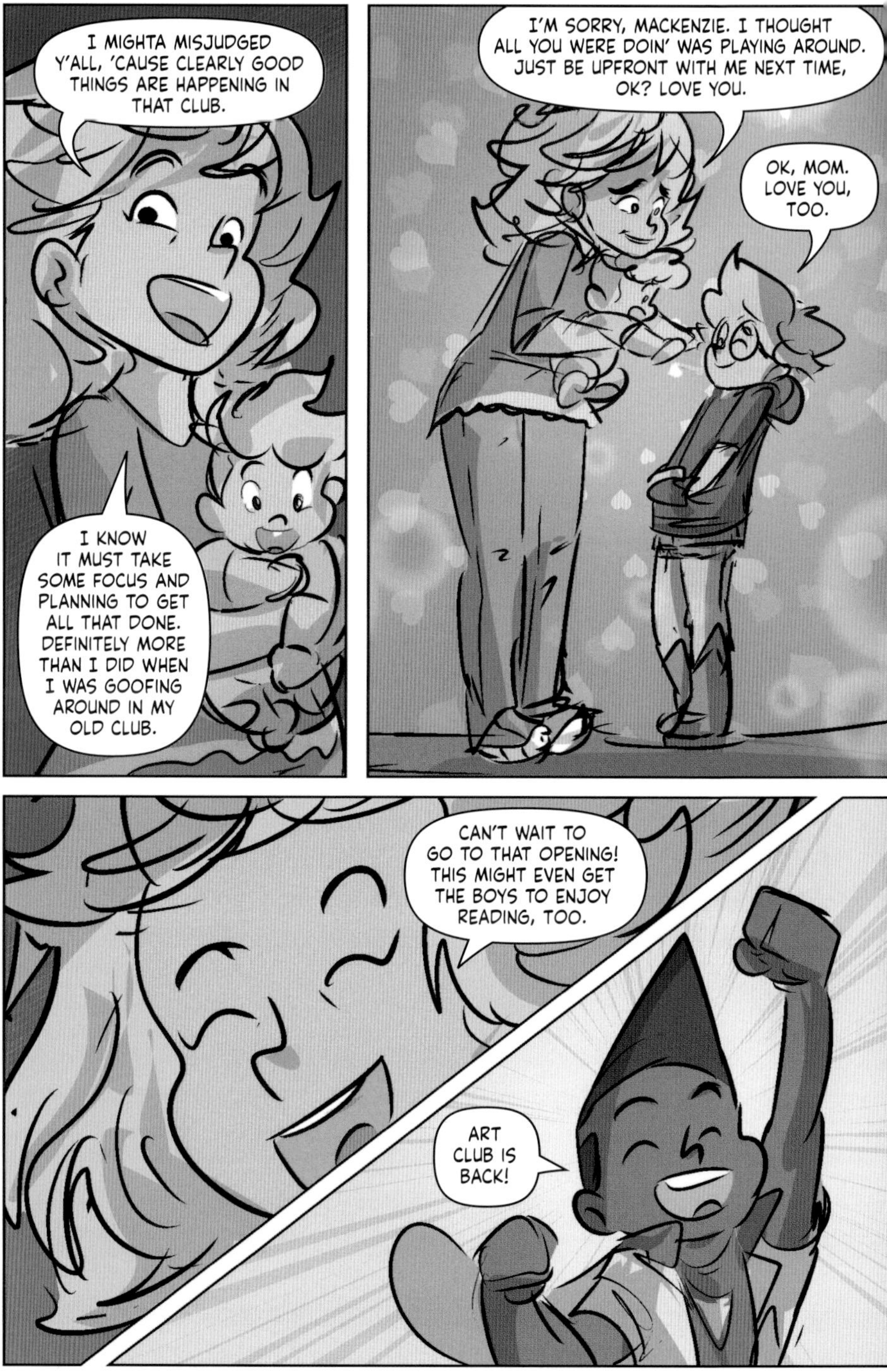
I MIGHTA MISJUDGED Y'ALL, 'CAUSE CLEARLY GOOD THINGS ARE HAPPENING IN THAT CLUB.
I KNOW IT MUST TAKE SOME FOCUS AND PLANNING TO GET ALL THAT DONE. DEFINITELY MORE THAN I DID WHEN I WAS GOOFING AROUND IN MY OLD CLUB.
I'M SORRY, MACKENZIE. I THOUGHT ALL YOU WERE DOIN' WAS PLAYING AROUND. JUST BE UPFRONT WITH ME NEXT TIME, OK? LOVE YOU.
OK, MOM. LOVE YOU, TOO.
CAN'T WAIT TO GO TO THAT OPENING! THIS MIGHT EVEN GET THE BOYS TO ENJOY READING, TOO.
ART CLUB IS BACK!

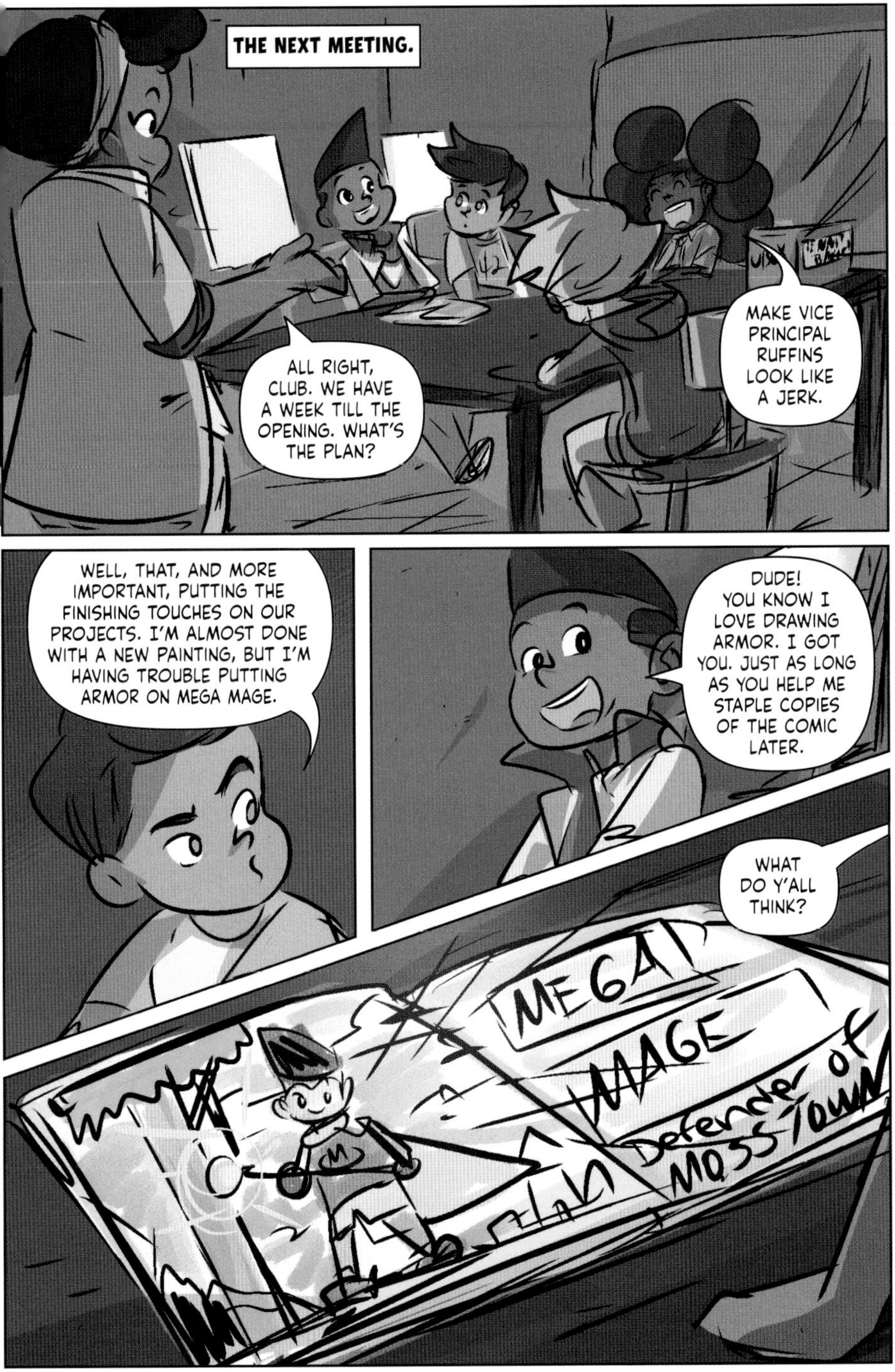
THE NEXT MEETING.
ALL RIGHT, CLUB. WE HAVE A WEEK TILL THE OPENING. WHAT'S THE PLAN?
MAKE VICE PRINCIPAL RUFFINS LOOK LIKE A JERK.
WELL, THAT, AND MORE IMPORTANT, PUTTING THE FINISHING TOUCHES ON OUR PROJECTS. I'M ALMOST DONE WITH A NEW PAINTING, BUT I'M HAVING TROUBLE PUTTING ARMOR ON MEGA MAGE.
DUDE! YOU KNOW I LOVE DRAWING ARMOR. I GOT YOU. JUST AS LONG AS YOU HELP ME STAPLE COPIES OF THE COMIC LATER.
WHAT DO Y'ALL THINK?
MEGA MAGE
Defender of MOSSTOWN

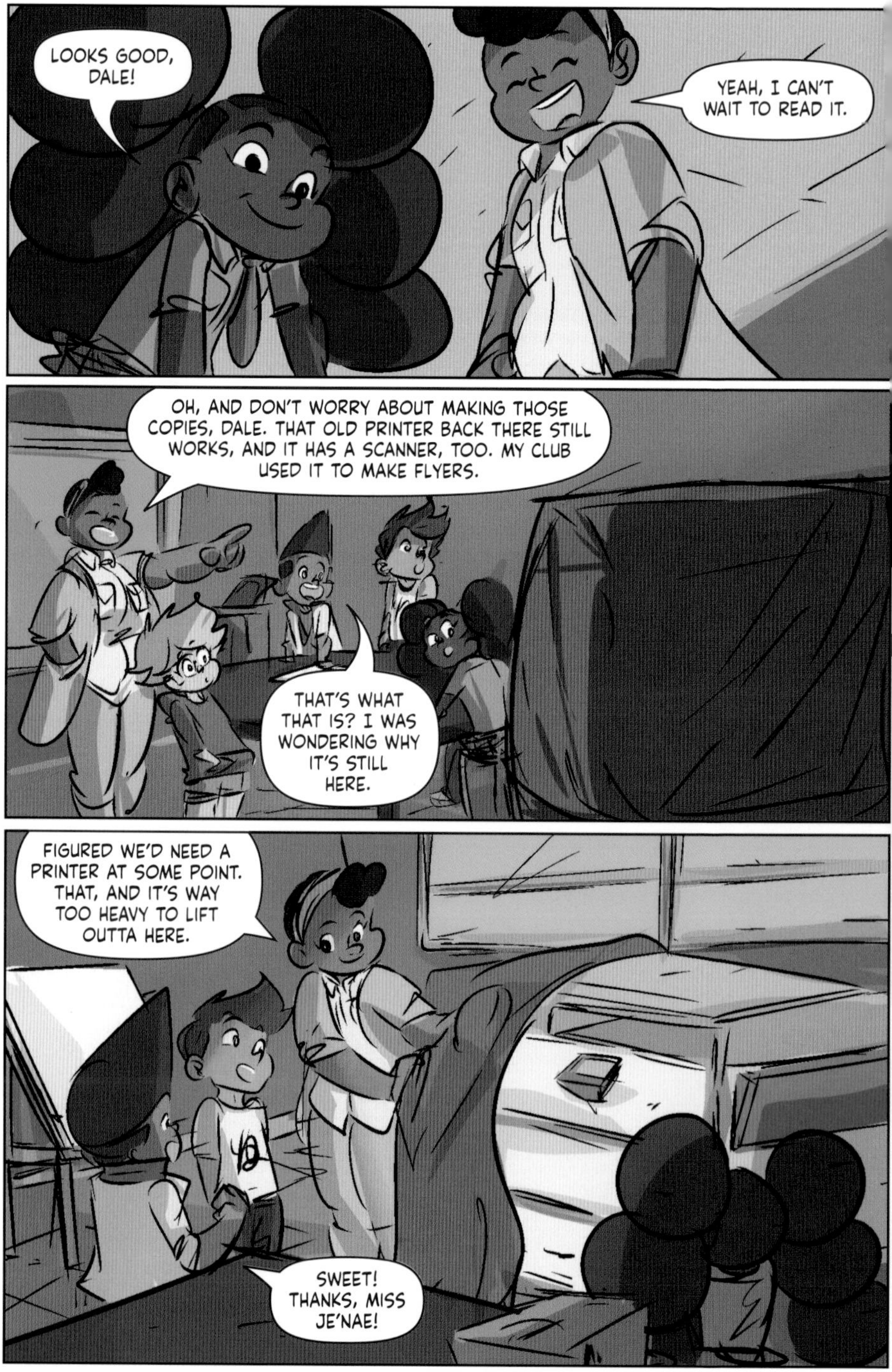
LOOKS GOOD, DALE!
YEAH, I CAN'T WAIT TO READ IT.
OH, AND DON'T WORRY ABOUT MAKING THOSE COPIES, DALE. THAT OLD PRINTER BACK THERE STILL WORKS, AND IT HAS A SCANNER, TOO. MY CLUB USED IT TO MAKE FLYERS.
THAT'S WHAT THAT IS? I WAS WONDERING WHY IT'S STILL HERE.
FIGURED WE'D NEED A PRINTER AT SOME POINT. THAT, AND IT'S WAY TOO HEAVY TO LIFT OUTTA HERE.
SWEET! THANKS, MISS JE'NAE!

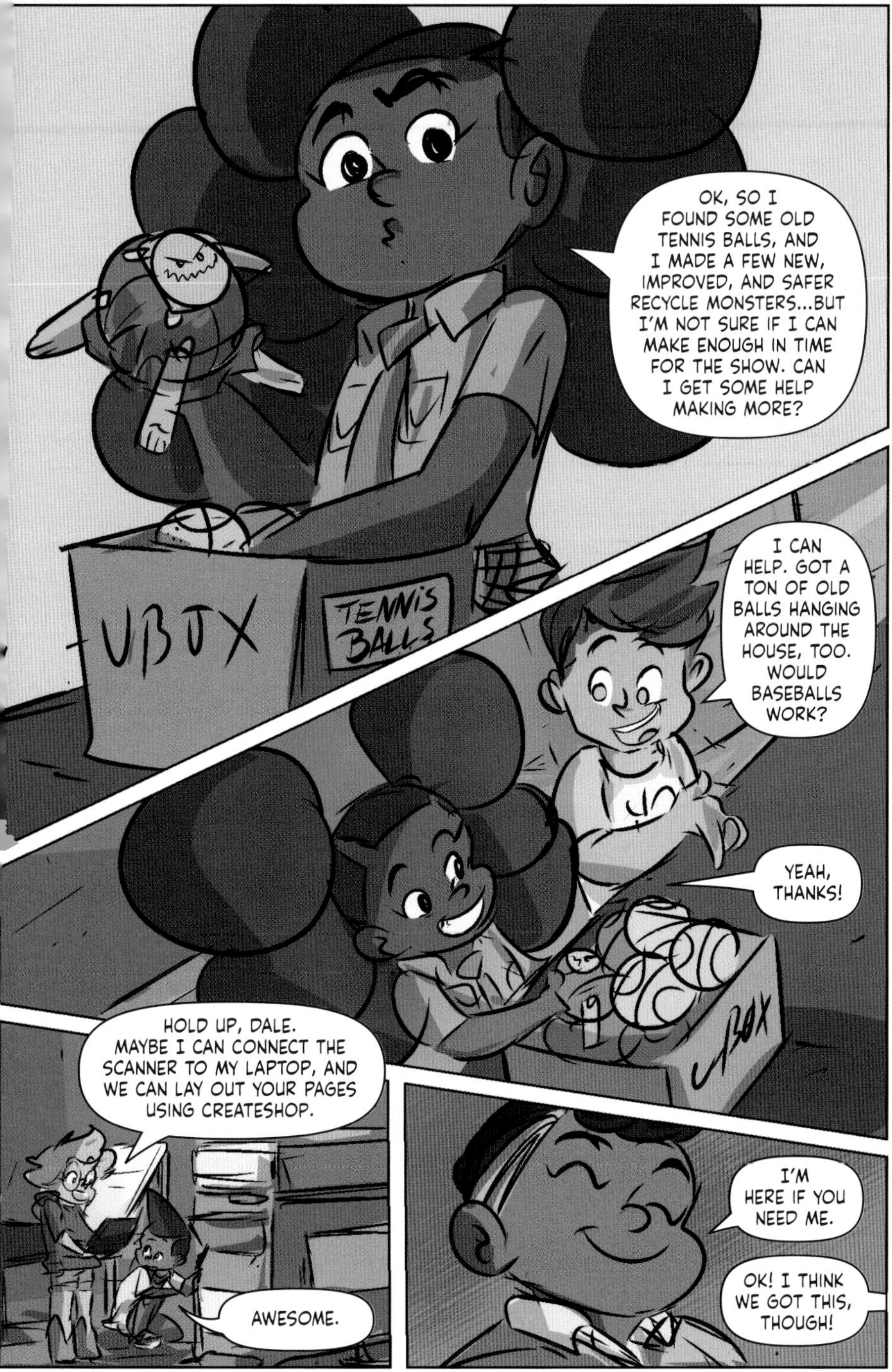
OK, SO I FOUND SOME OLD TENNIS BALLS, AND I MADE A FEW NEW, IMPROVED, AND SAFER RECYCLE MONSTERS...BUT I'M NOT SURE IF I CAN MAKE ENOUGH IN TIME FOR THE SHOW. CAN I GET SOME HELP MAKING MORE?
UBOX
TENNIS BALLS
I CAN HELP. GOT A TON OF OLD BALLS HANGING AROUND THE HOUSE, TOO. WOULD BASEBALLS WORK?
YEAH, THANKS!
UBOX
HOLD UP, DALE. MAYBE I CAN CONNECT THE SCANNER TO MY LAPTOP, AND WE CAN LAY OUT YOUR PAGES USING CREATESHOP.
AWESOME.
I'M HERE IF YOU NEED ME.
OK! I THINK WE GOT THIS, THOUGH!

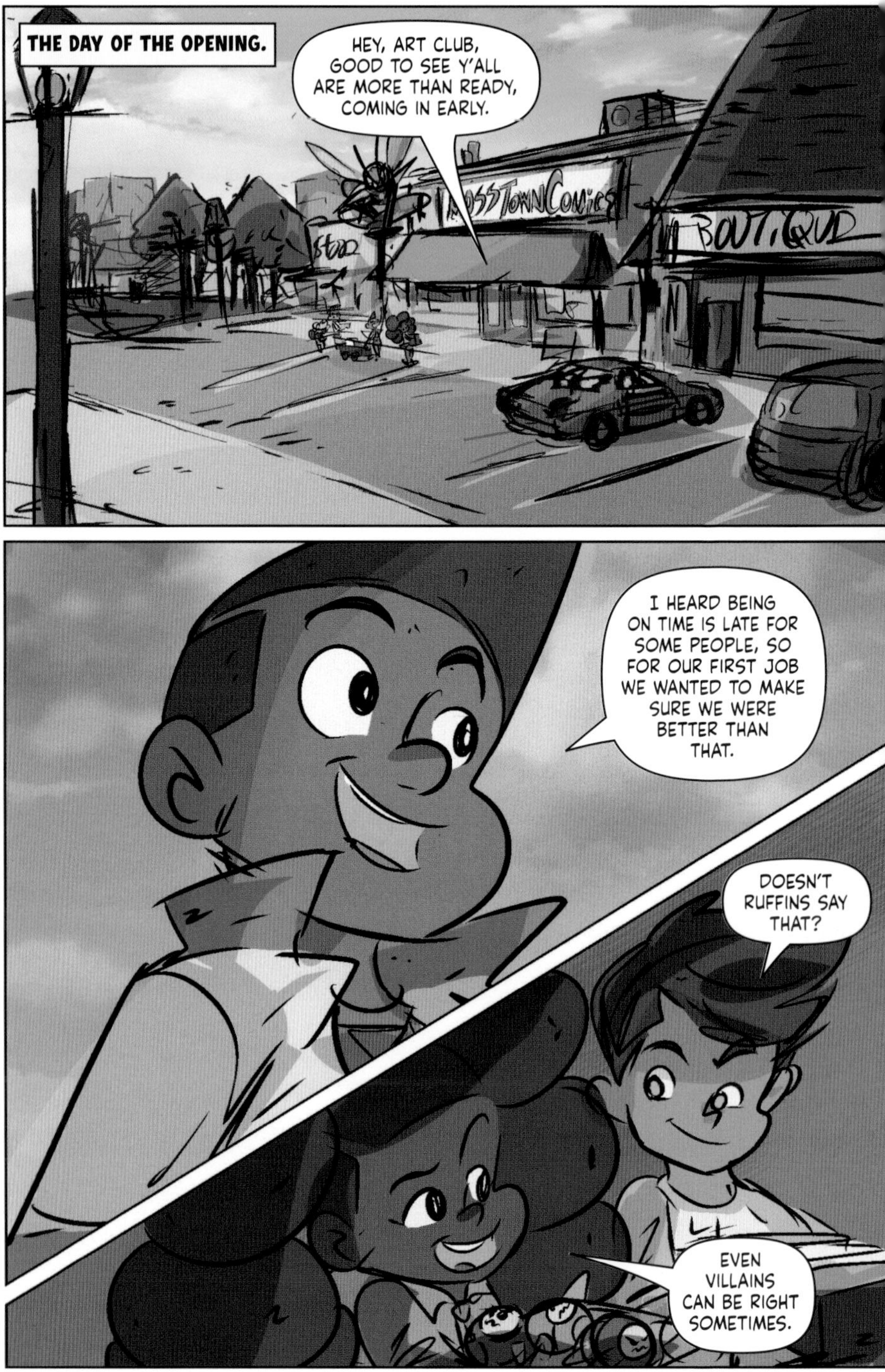
THE DAY OF THE OPENING.
HEY, ART CLUB, GOOD TO SEE Y'ALL ARE MORE THAN READY, COMING IN EARLY.
I HEARD BEING ON TIME IS LATE FOR SOME PEOPLE, SO FOR OUR FIRST JOB WE WANTED TO MAKE SURE WE WERE BETTER THAN THAT.
DOESN'T RUFFINS SAY THAT?
EVEN VILLAINS CAN BE RIGHT SOMETIMES.

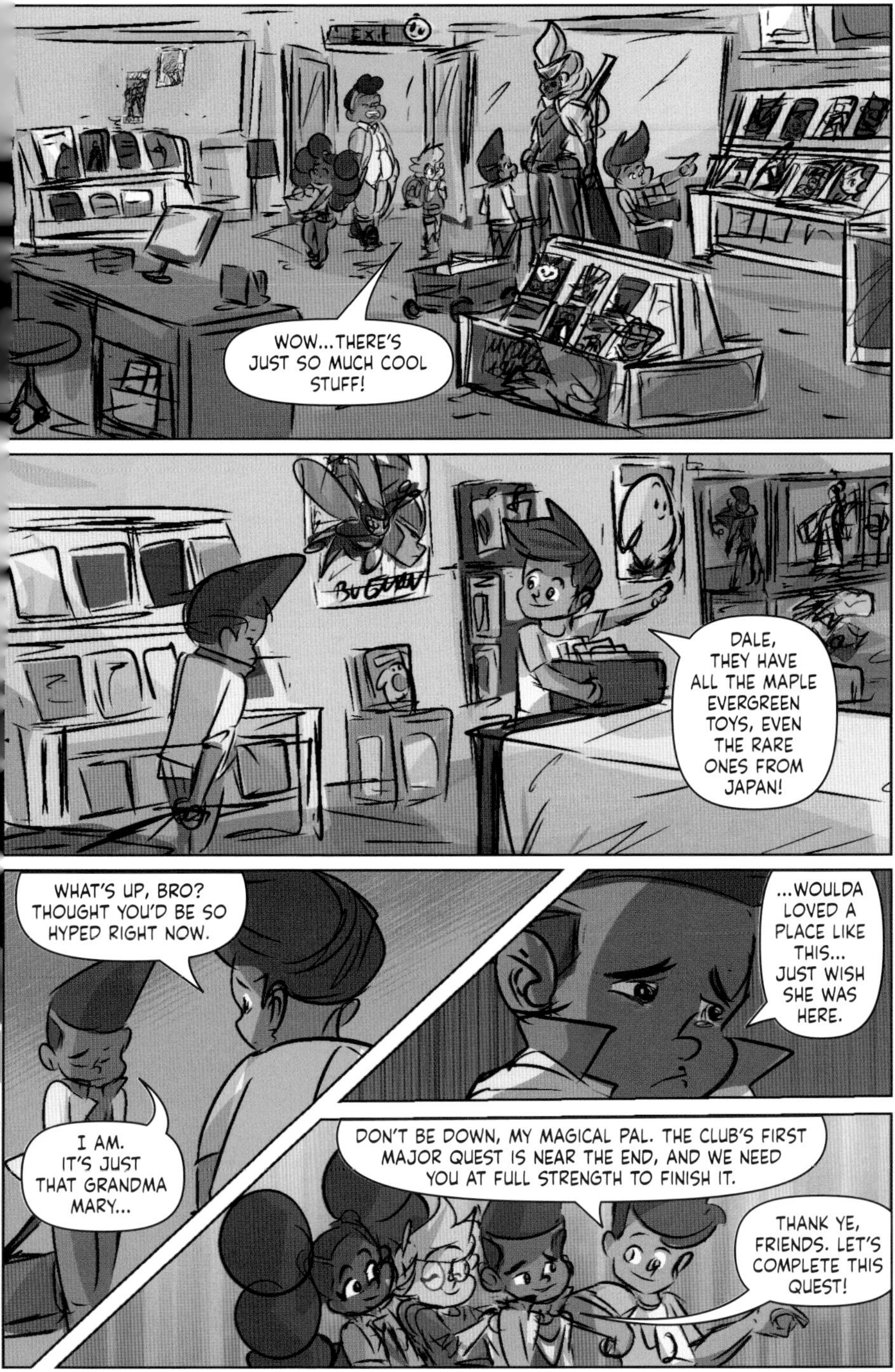
WOW...THERE'S JUST SO MUCH COOL STUFF!
DALE, THEY HAVE ALL THE MAPLE EVERGREEN TOYS, EVEN THE RARE ONES FROM JAPAN!
WHAT'S UP, BRO? THOUGHT YOU'D BE SO HYPED RIGHT NOW.
I AM. IT'S JUST THAT GRANDMA MARY...
...WOULDA LOVED A PLACE LIKE THIS... JUST WISH SHE WAS HERE.
DON'T BE DOWN, MY MAGICAL PAL. THE CLUB'S FIRST MAJOR QUEST IS NEAR THE END, AND WE NEED YOU AT FULL STRENGTH TO FINISH IT.
THANK YE, FRIENDS. LET'S COMPLETE THIS QUEST!

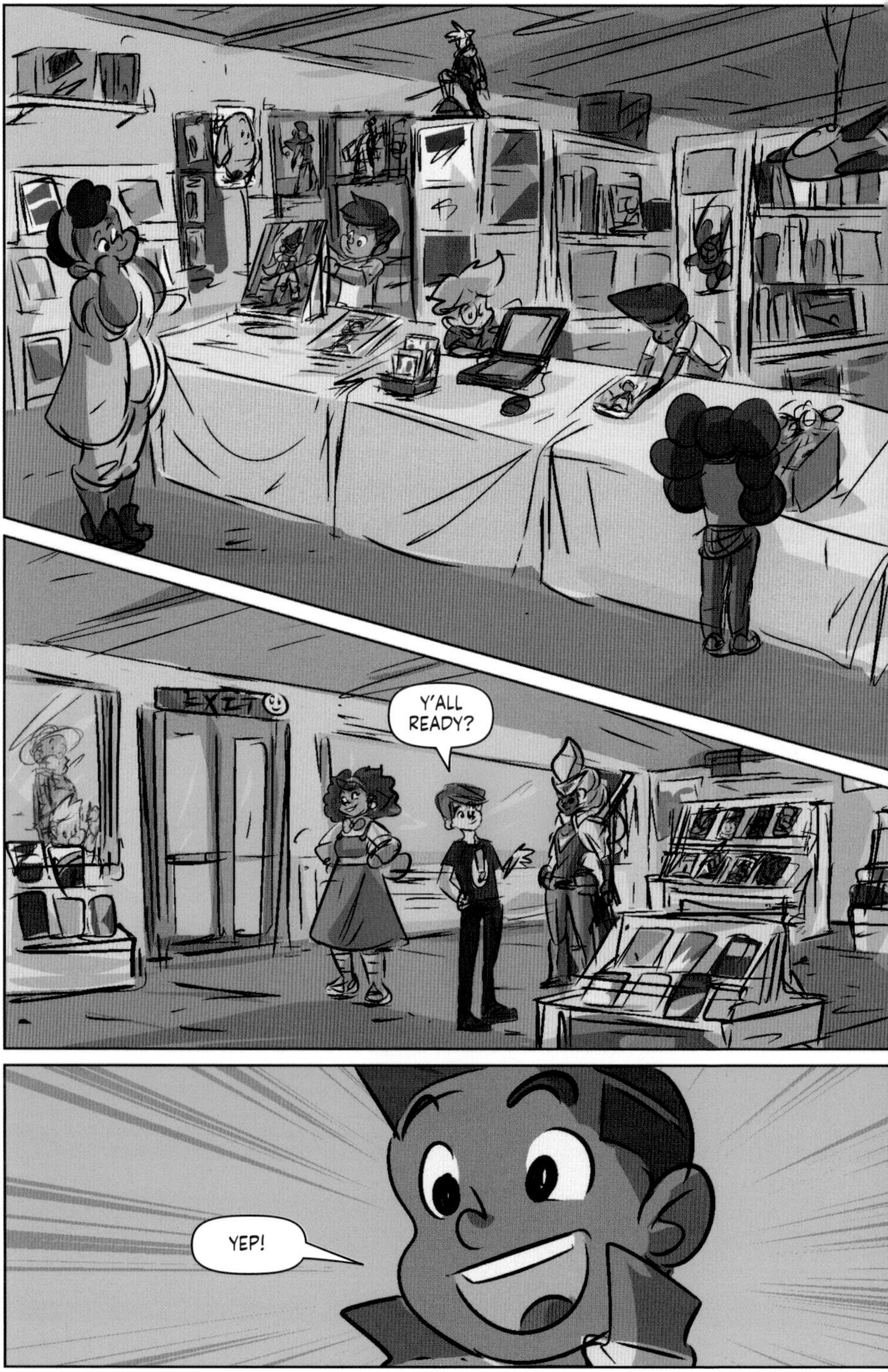
EXIT
Y'ALL READY?
YEP!

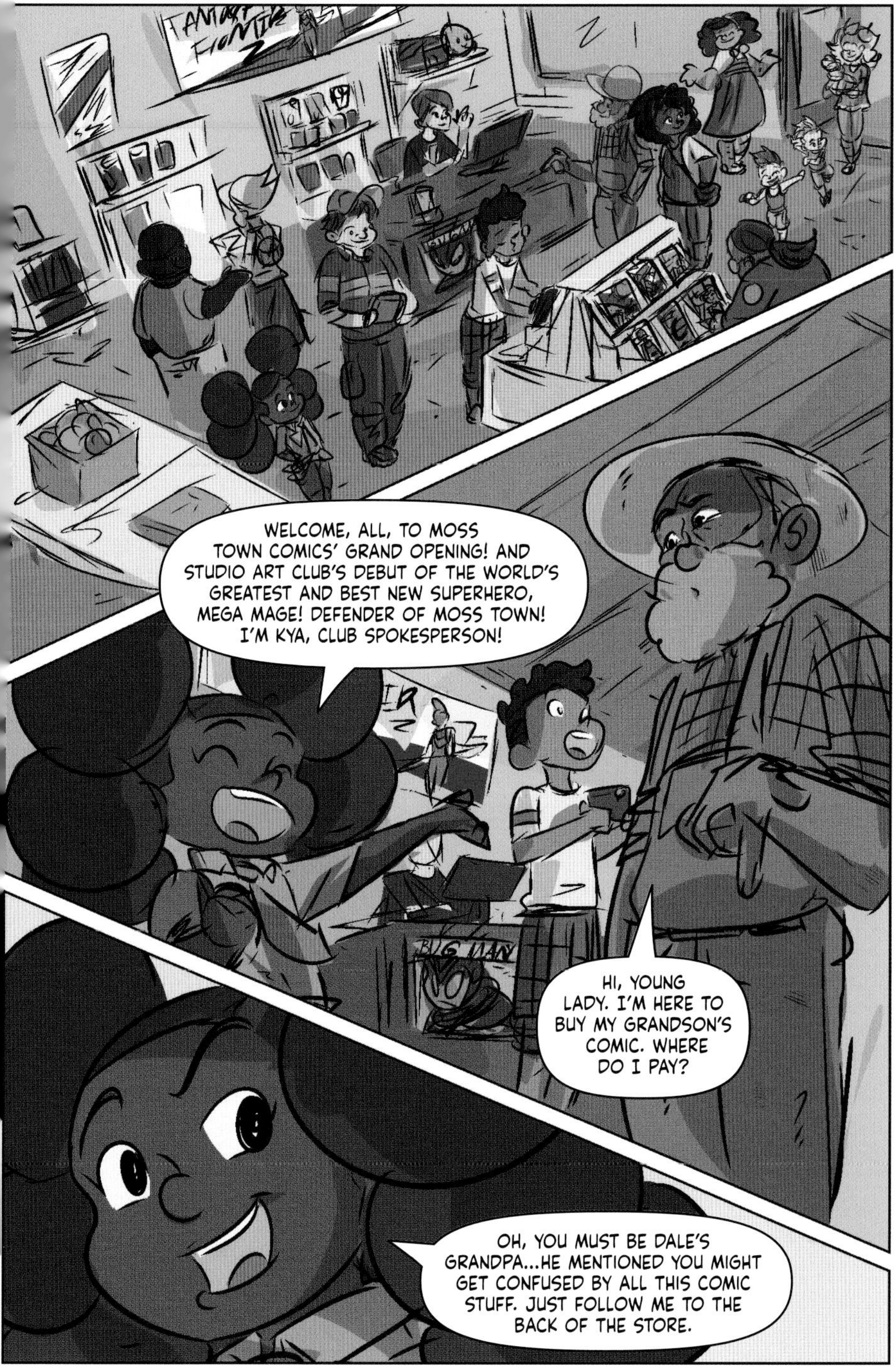
FANTASY FRONTIER
WELCOME, ALL, TO MOSS TOWN COMICS' GRAND OPENING! AND STUDIO ART CLUB'S DEBUT OF THE WORLD'S GREATEST AND BEST NEW SUPERHERO, MEGA MAGE! DEFENDER OF MOSS TOWN! I'M KYA, CLUB SPOKESPERSON!
HI, YOUNG LADY. I'M HERE TO BUY MY GRANDSON'S COMIC. WHERE DO I PAY?
OH, YOU MUST BE DALE'S GRANDPA...HE MENTIONED YOU MIGHT GET CONFUSED BY ALL THIS COMIC STUFF. JUST FOLLOW ME TO THE BACK OF THE STORE.

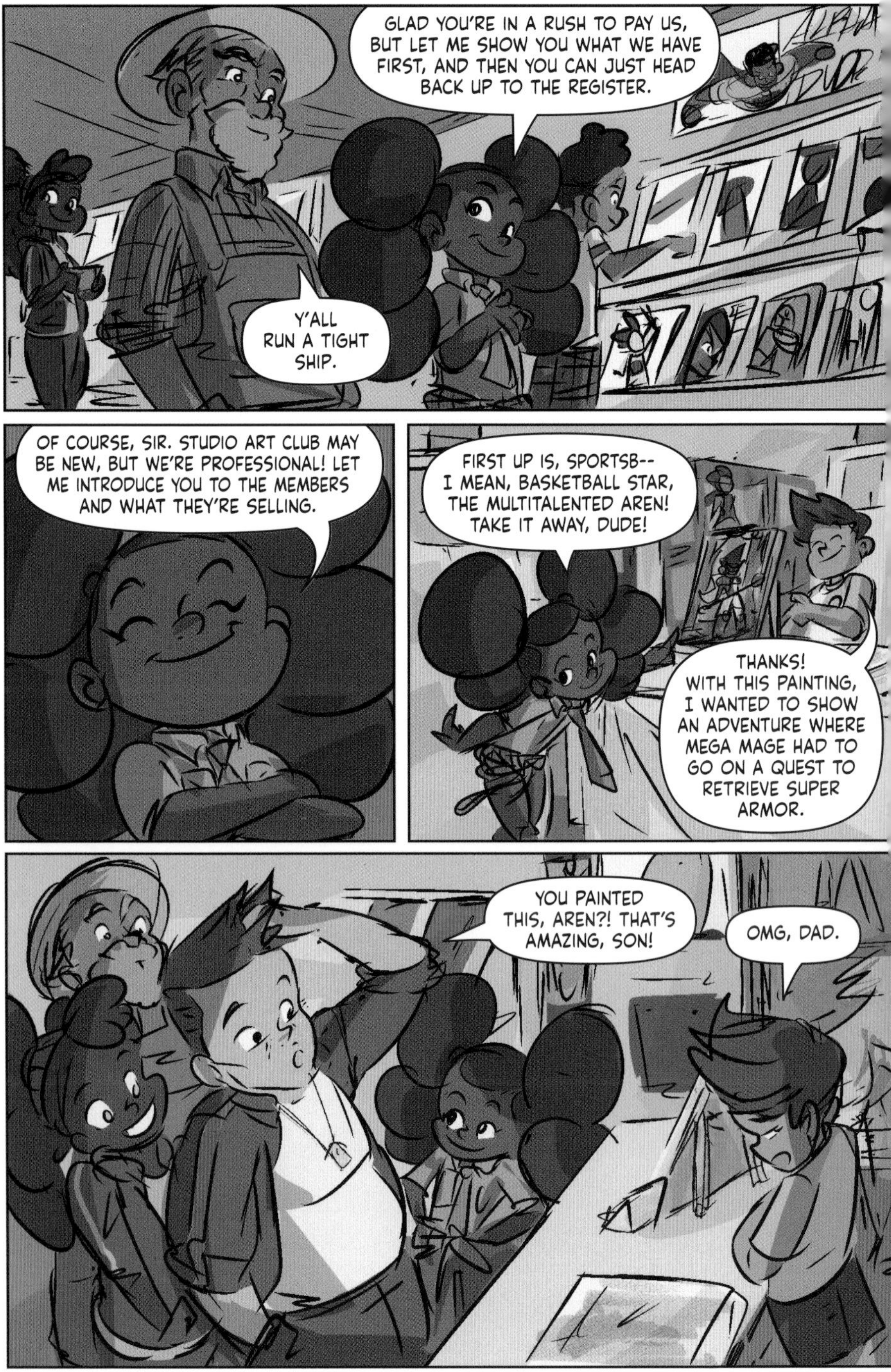
GLAD YOU'RE IN A RUSH TO PAY US, BUT LET ME SHOW YOU WHAT WE HAVE FIRST, AND THEN YOU CAN JUST HEAD BACK UP TO THE REGISTER.
Y'ALL RUN A TIGHT SHIP.
OF COURSE, SIR. STUDIO ART CLUB MAY BE NEW, BUT WE'RE PROFESSIONAL! LET ME INTRODUCE YOU TO THE MEMBERS AND WHAT THEY'RE SELLING.
FIRST UP IS, SPORTSB-- I MEAN, BASKETBALL STAR, THE MULTITALENTED AREN! TAKE IT AWAY, DUDE!
THANKS! WITH THIS PAINTING, I WANTED TO SHOW AN ADVENTURE WHERE MEGA MAGE HAD TO GO ON A QUEST TO RETRIEVE SUPER ARMOR.
YOU PAINTED THIS, AREN?! THAT'S AMAZING, SON!
OMG, DAD.

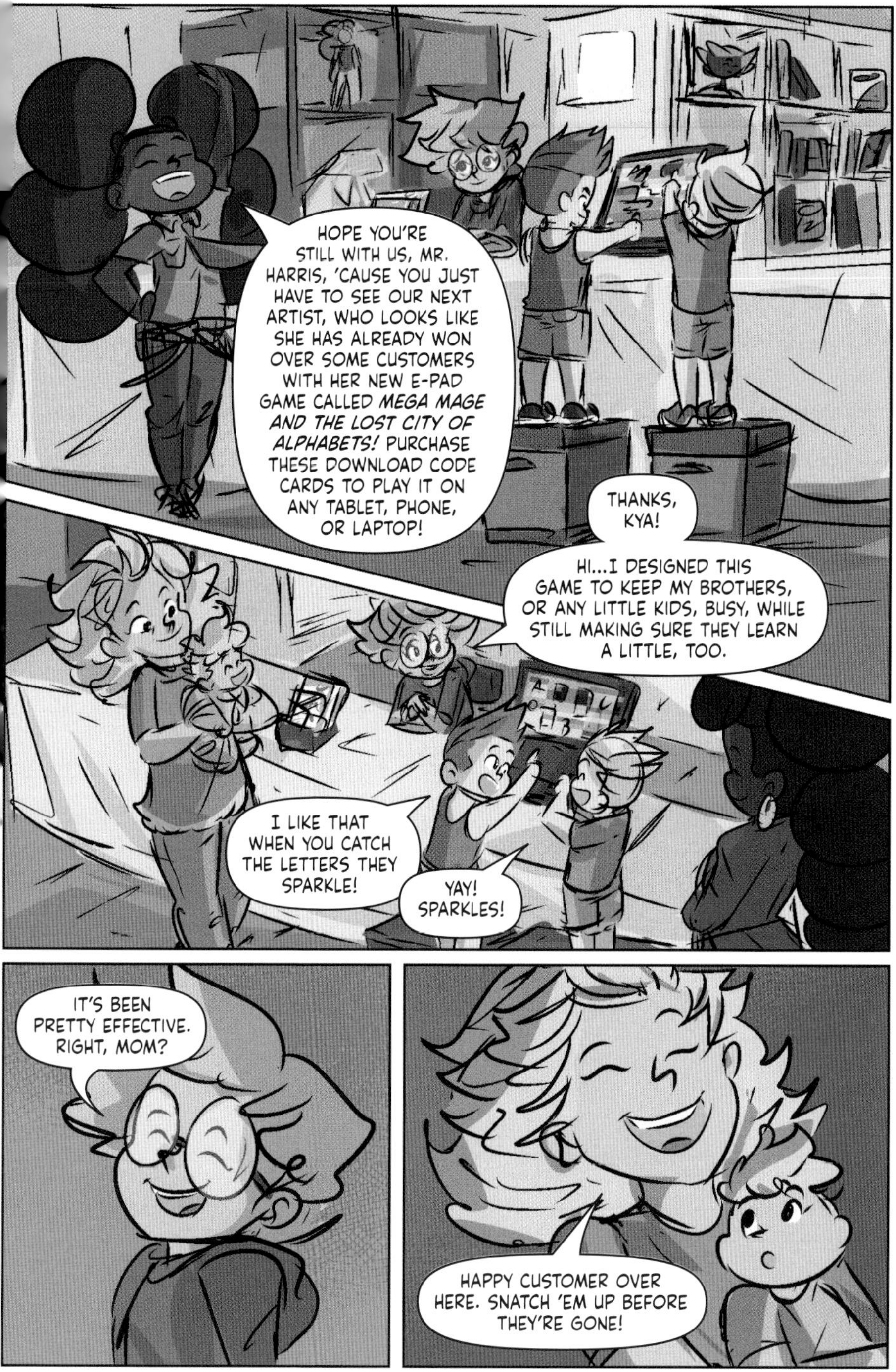
HOPE YOU'RE STILL WITH US, MR. HARRIS, 'CAUSE YOU JUST HAVE TO SEE OUR NEXT ARTIST, WHO LOOKS LIKE SHE HAS ALREADY WON OVER SOME CUSTOMERS WITH HER NEW E-PAD GAME CALLED *MEGA MAGE AND THE LOST CITY OF ALPHABETS!* PURCHASE THESE DOWNLOAD CODE CARDS TO PLAY IT ON ANY TABLET, PHONE, OR LAPTOP!
THANKS, KYA!
HI...I DESIGNED THIS GAME TO KEEP MY BROTHERS, OR ANY LITTLE KIDS, BUSY, WHILE STILL MAKING SURE THEY LEARN A LITTLE, TOO.
I LIKE THAT WHEN YOU CATCH THE LETTERS THEY SPARKLE!
YAY! SPARKLES!
IT'S BEEN PRETTY EFFECTIVE. RIGHT, MOM?
HAPPY CUSTOMER OVER HERE. SNATCH 'EM UP BEFORE THEY'RE GONE!

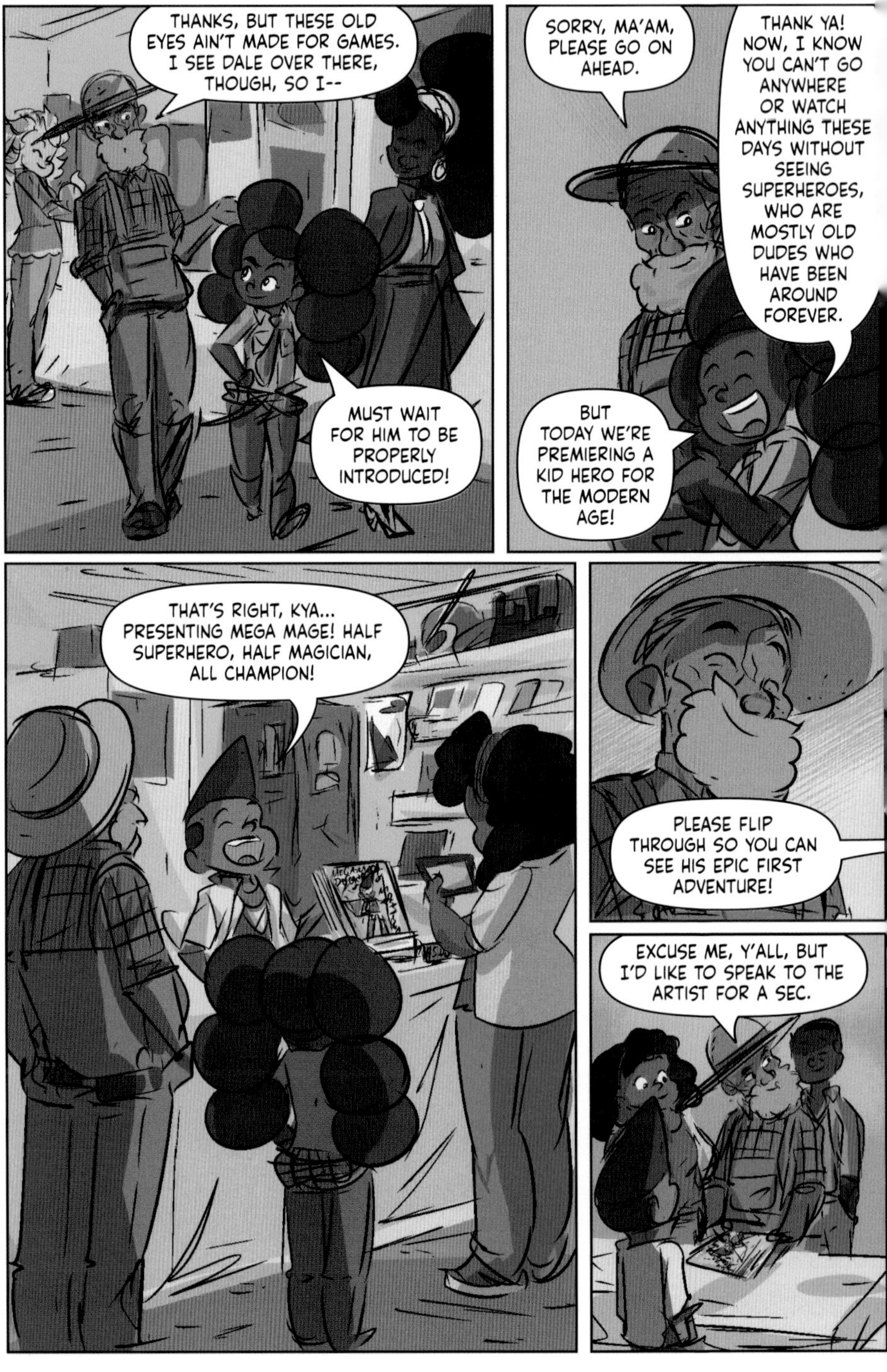
THANKS, BUT THESE OLD EYES AIN'T MADE FOR GAMES. I SEE DALE OVER THERE, THOUGH, SO I--
MUST WAIT FOR HIM TO BE PROPERLY INTRODUCED!
SORRY, MA'AM, PLEASE GO ON AHEAD.
THANK YA! NOW, I KNOW YOU CAN'T GO ANYWHERE OR WATCH ANYTHING THESE DAYS WITHOUT SEEING SUPERHEROES, WHO ARE MOSTLY OLD DUDES WHO HAVE BEEN AROUND FOREVER.
BUT TODAY WE'RE PREMIERING A KID HERO FOR THE MODERN AGE!
THAT'S RIGHT, KYA... PRESENTING MEGA MAGE! HALF SUPERHERO, HALF MAGICIAN, ALL CHAMPION!
PLEASE FLIP THROUGH SO YOU CAN SEE HIS EPIC FIRST ADVENTURE!
EXCUSE ME, Y'ALL, BUT I'D LIKE TO SPEAK TO THE ARTIST FOR A SEC.

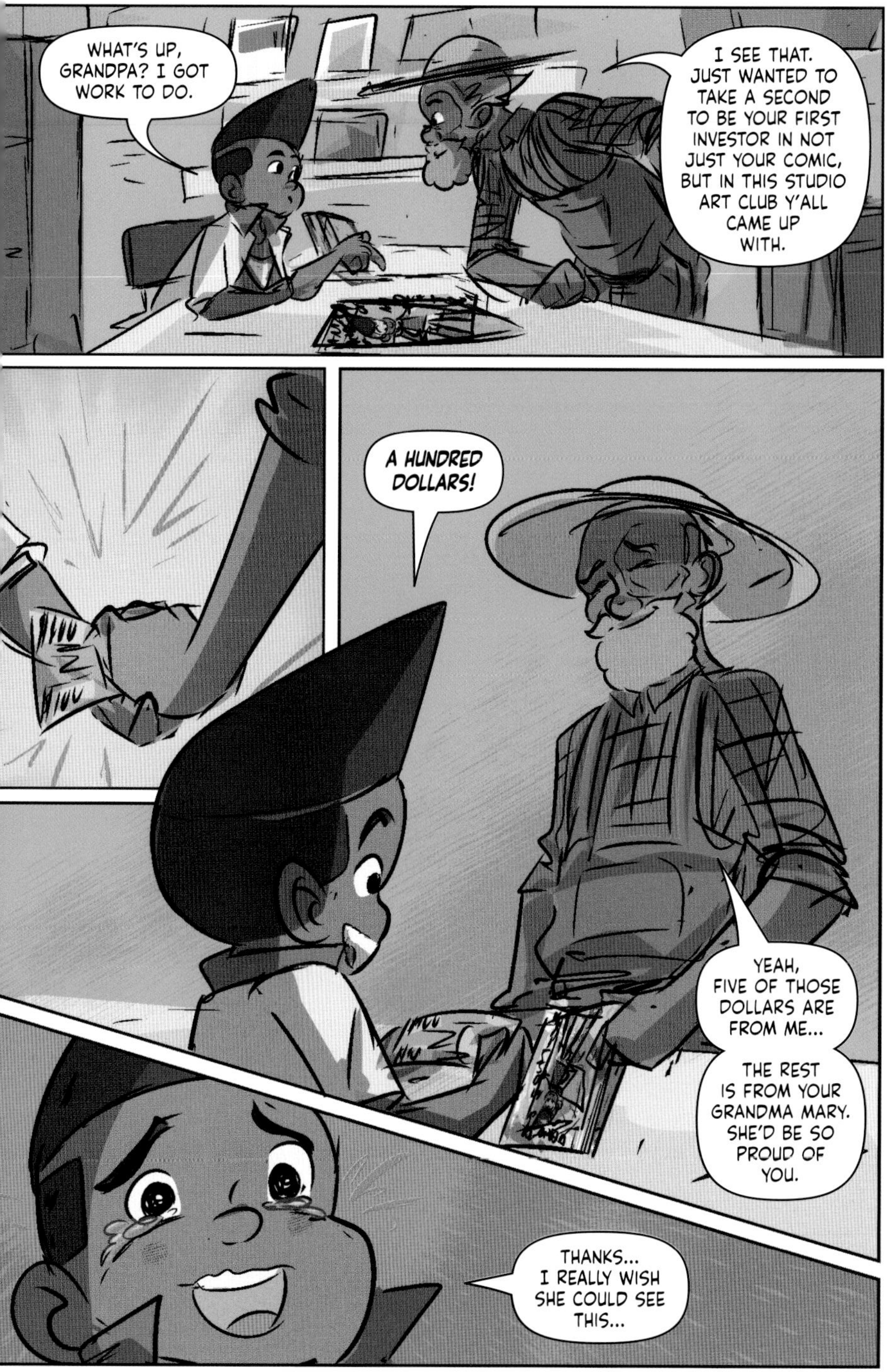
WHAT'S UP, GRANDPA? I GOT WORK TO DO.
I SEE THAT. JUST WANTED TO TAKE A SECOND TO BE YOUR FIRST INVESTOR IN NOT JUST YOUR COMIC, BUT IN THIS STUDIO ART CLUB Y'ALL CAME UP WITH.
A HUNDRED DOLLARS!
YEAH, FIVE OF THOSE DOLLARS ARE FROM ME...
THE REST IS FROM YOUR GRANDMA MARY. SHE'D BE SO PROUD OF YOU.
THANKS... I REALLY WISH SHE COULD SEE THIS...

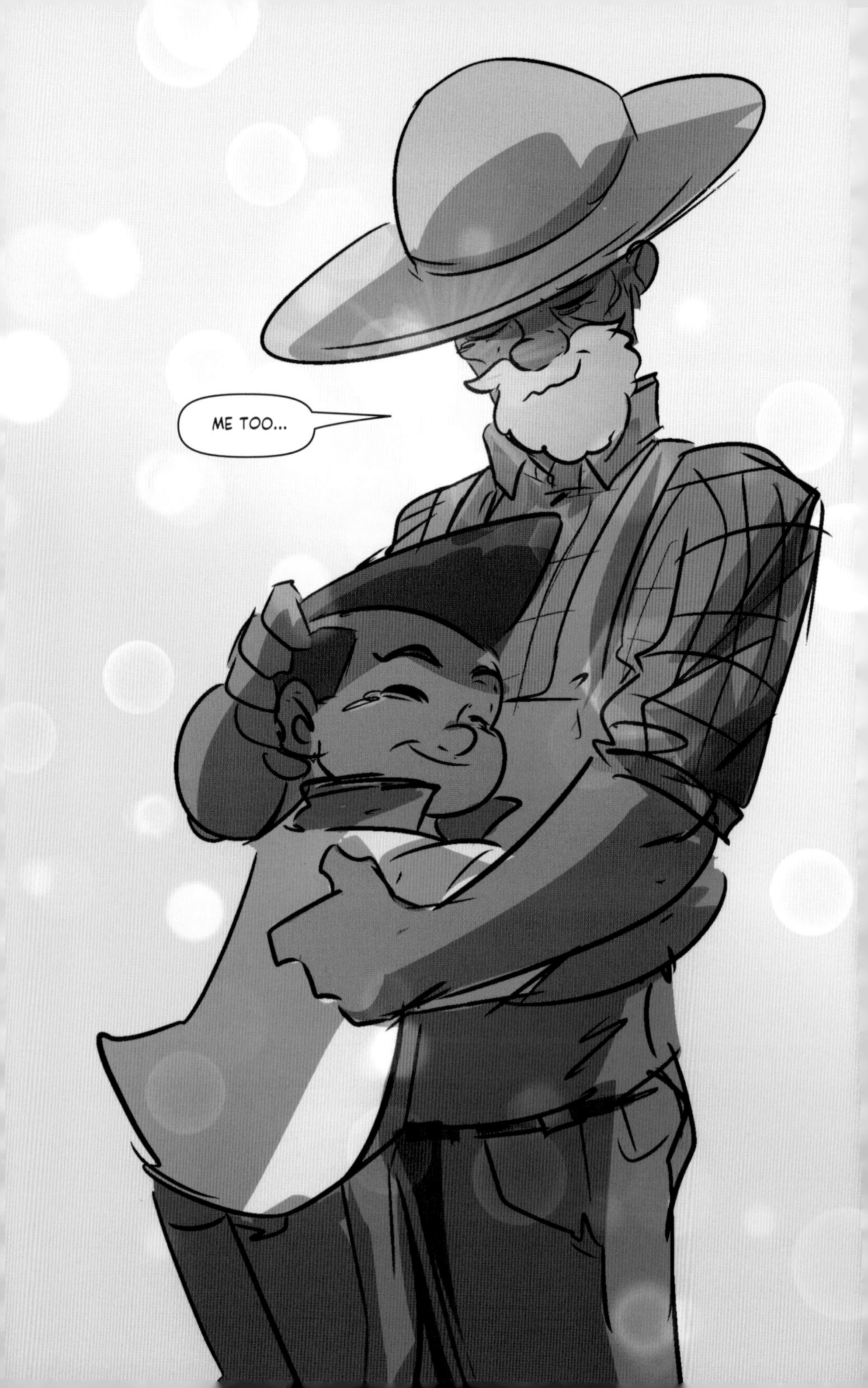
ME TOO...

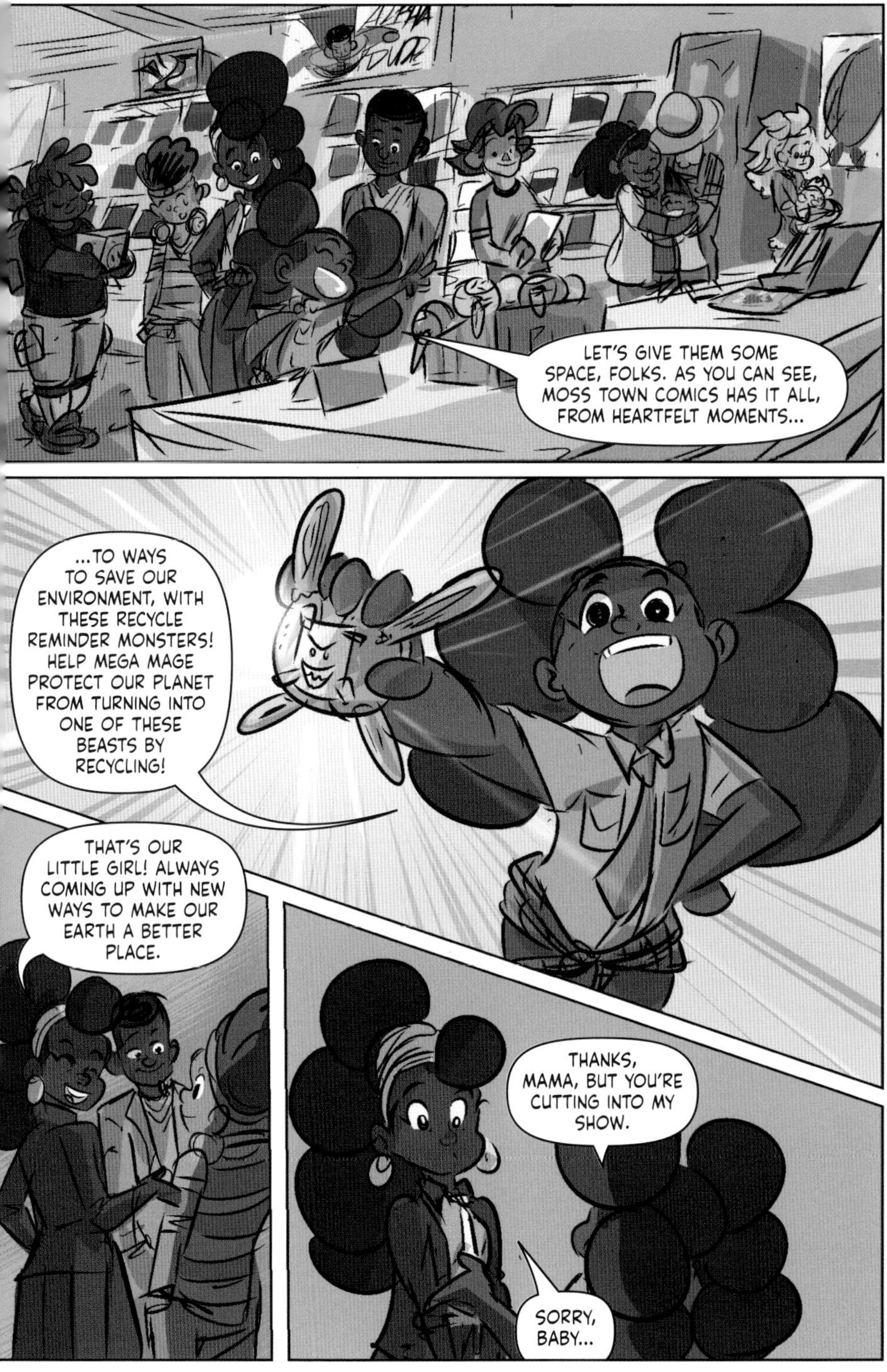
LET'S GIVE THEM SOME SPACE, FOLKS. AS YOU CAN SEE, MOSS TOWN COMICS HAS IT ALL, FROM HEARTFELT MOMENTS...
...TO WAYS TO SAVE OUR ENVIRONMENT, WITH THESE RECYCLE REMINDER MONSTERS! HELP MEGA MAGE PROTECT OUR PLANET FROM TURNING INTO ONE OF THESE BEASTS BY RECYCLING!
THAT'S OUR LITTLE GIRL! ALWAYS COMING UP WITH NEW WAYS TO MAKE OUR EARTH A BETTER PLACE.
THANKS, MAMA, BUT YOU'RE CUTTING INTO MY SHOW.
SORRY, BABY...

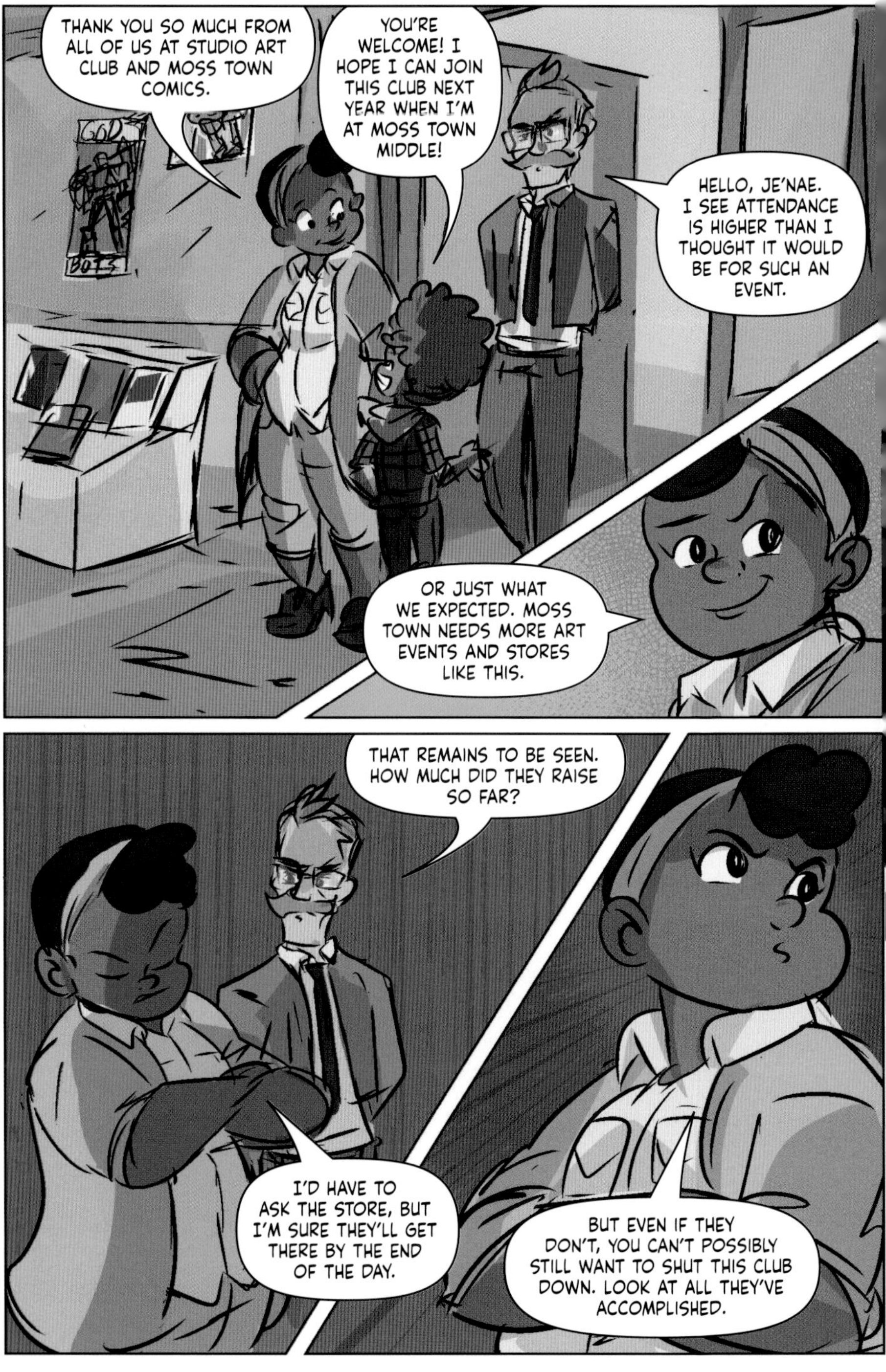
THANK YOU SO MUCH FROM ALL OF US AT STUDIO ART CLUB AND MOSS TOWN COMICS.
YOU'RE WELCOME! I HOPE I CAN JOIN THIS CLUB NEXT YEAR WHEN I'M AT MOSS TOWN MIDDLE!
HELLO, JE'NAE. I SEE ATTENDANCE IS HIGHER THAN I THOUGHT IT WOULD BE FOR SUCH AN EVENT.
OR JUST WHAT WE EXPECTED. MOSS TOWN NEEDS MORE ART EVENTS AND STORES LIKE THIS.
THAT REMAINS TO BE SEEN. HOW MUCH DID THEY RAISE SO FAR?
I'D HAVE TO ASK THE STORE, BUT I'M SURE THEY'LL GET THERE BY THE END OF THE DAY.
BUT EVEN IF THEY DON'T, YOU CAN'T POSSIBLY STILL WANT TO SHUT THIS CLUB DOWN. LOOK AT ALL THEY'VE ACCOMPLISHED.

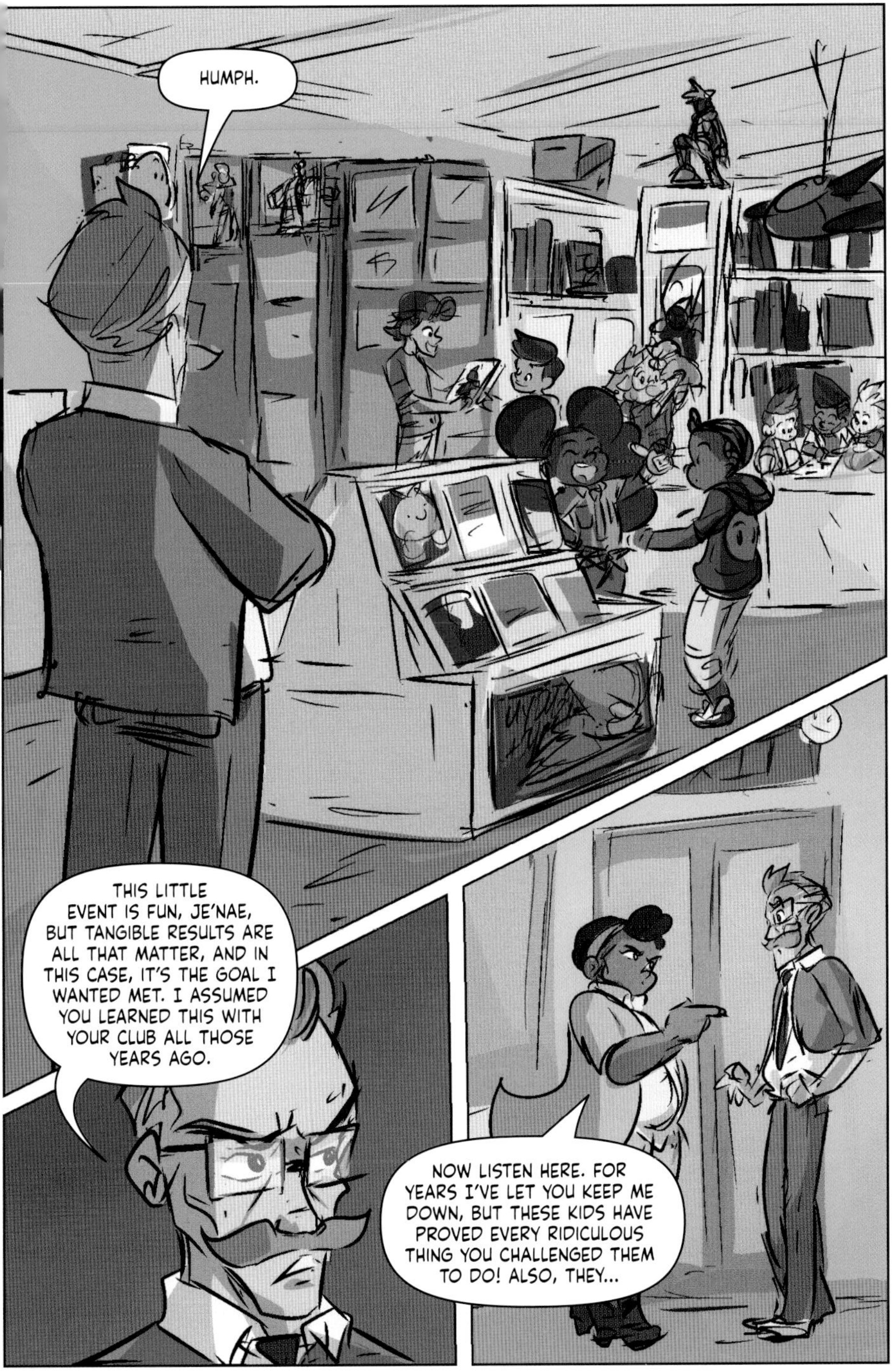
HUMPH.
THIS LITTLE EVENT IS FUN, JE'NAE, BUT TANGIBLE RESULTS ARE ALL THAT MATTER, AND IN THIS CASE, IT'S THE GOAL I WANTED MET. I ASSUMED YOU LEARNED THIS WITH YOUR CLUB ALL THOSE YEARS AGO.
NOW LISTEN HERE. FOR YEARS I'VE LET YOU KEEP ME DOWN, BUT THESE KIDS HAVE PROVED EVERY RIDICULOUS THING YOU CHALLENGED THEM TO DO! ALSO, THEY...

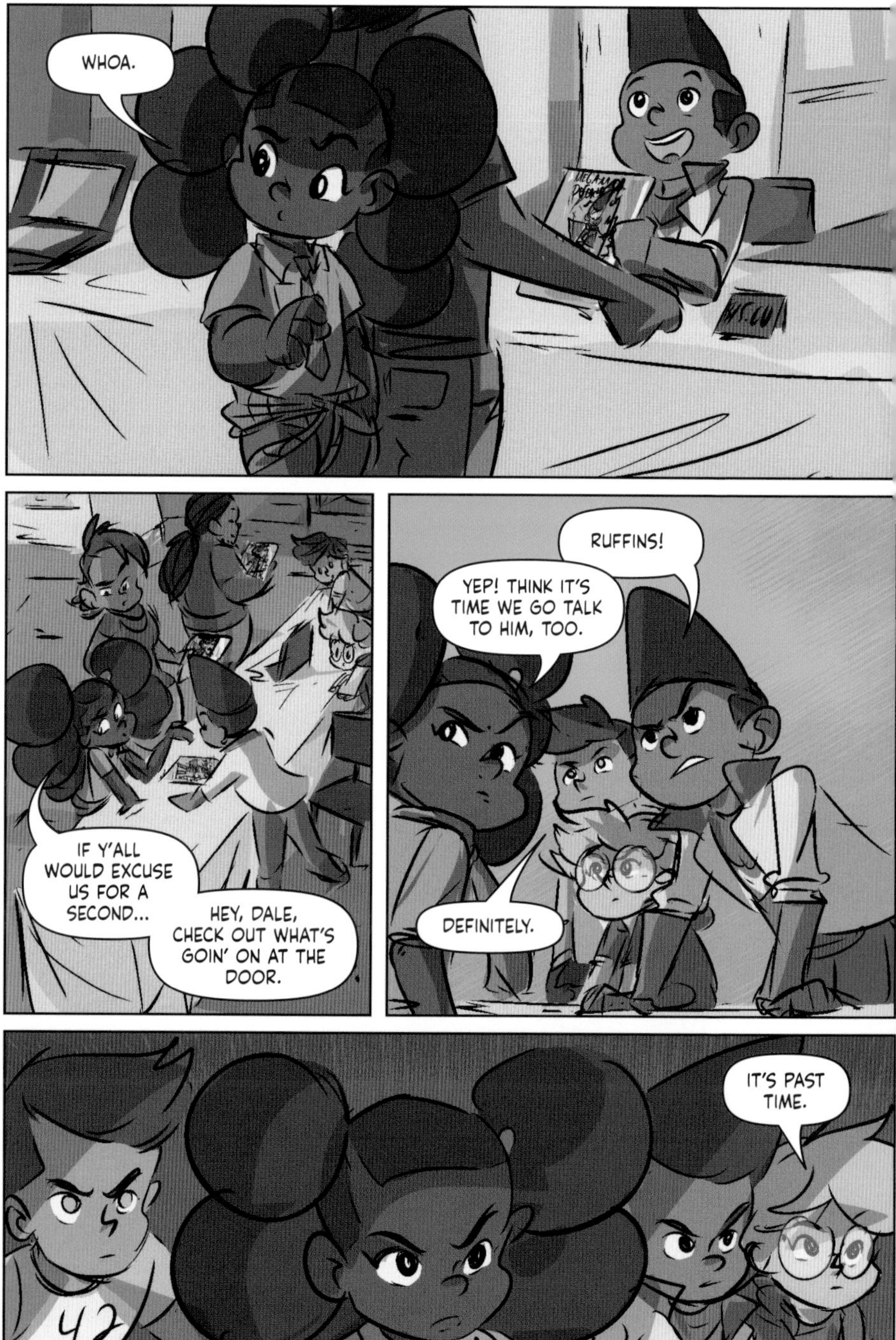
WHOA.
IF Y'ALL WOULD EXCUSE US FOR A SECOND...
HEY, DALE, CHECK OUT WHAT'S GOIN' ON AT THE DOOR.
RUFFINS!
YEP! THINK IT'S TIME WE GO TALK TO HIM, TOO.
DEFINITELY.
IT'S PAST TIME.

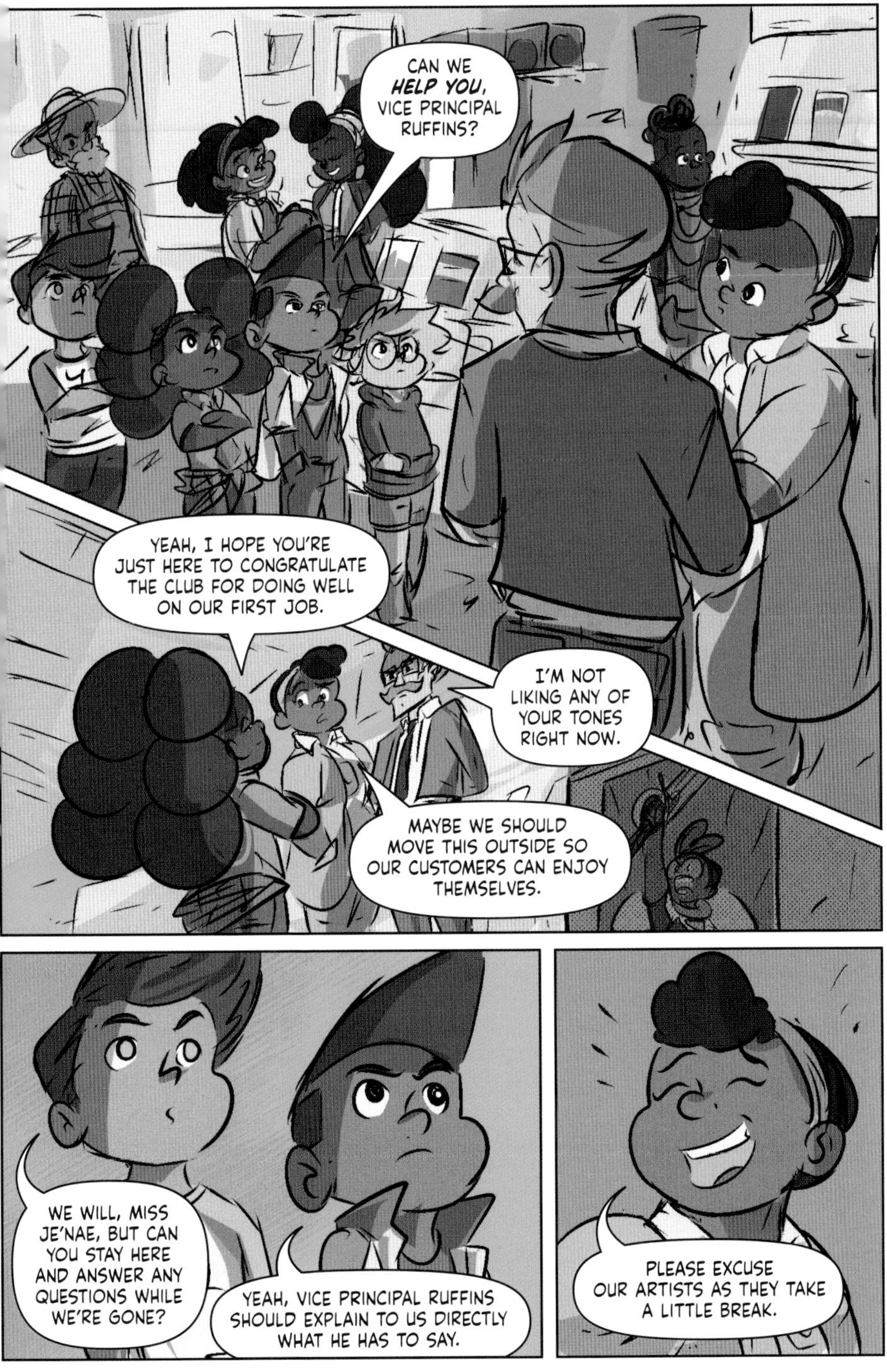
CAN WE ***HELP YOU***, VICE PRINCIPAL RUFFINS?
YEAH, I HOPE YOU'RE JUST HERE TO CONGRATULATE THE CLUB FOR DOING WELL ON OUR FIRST JOB.
I'M NOT LIKING ANY OF YOUR TONES RIGHT NOW.
MAYBE WE SHOULD MOVE THIS OUTSIDE SO OUR CUSTOMERS CAN ENJOY THEMSELVES.
WE WILL, MISS JE'NAE, BUT CAN YOU STAY HERE AND ANSWER ANY QUESTIONS WHILE WE'RE GONE?
YEAH, VICE PRINCIPAL RUFFINS SHOULD EXPLAIN TO US DIRECTLY WHAT HE HAS TO SAY.
PLEASE EXCUSE OUR ARTISTS AS THEY TAKE A LITTLE BREAK.

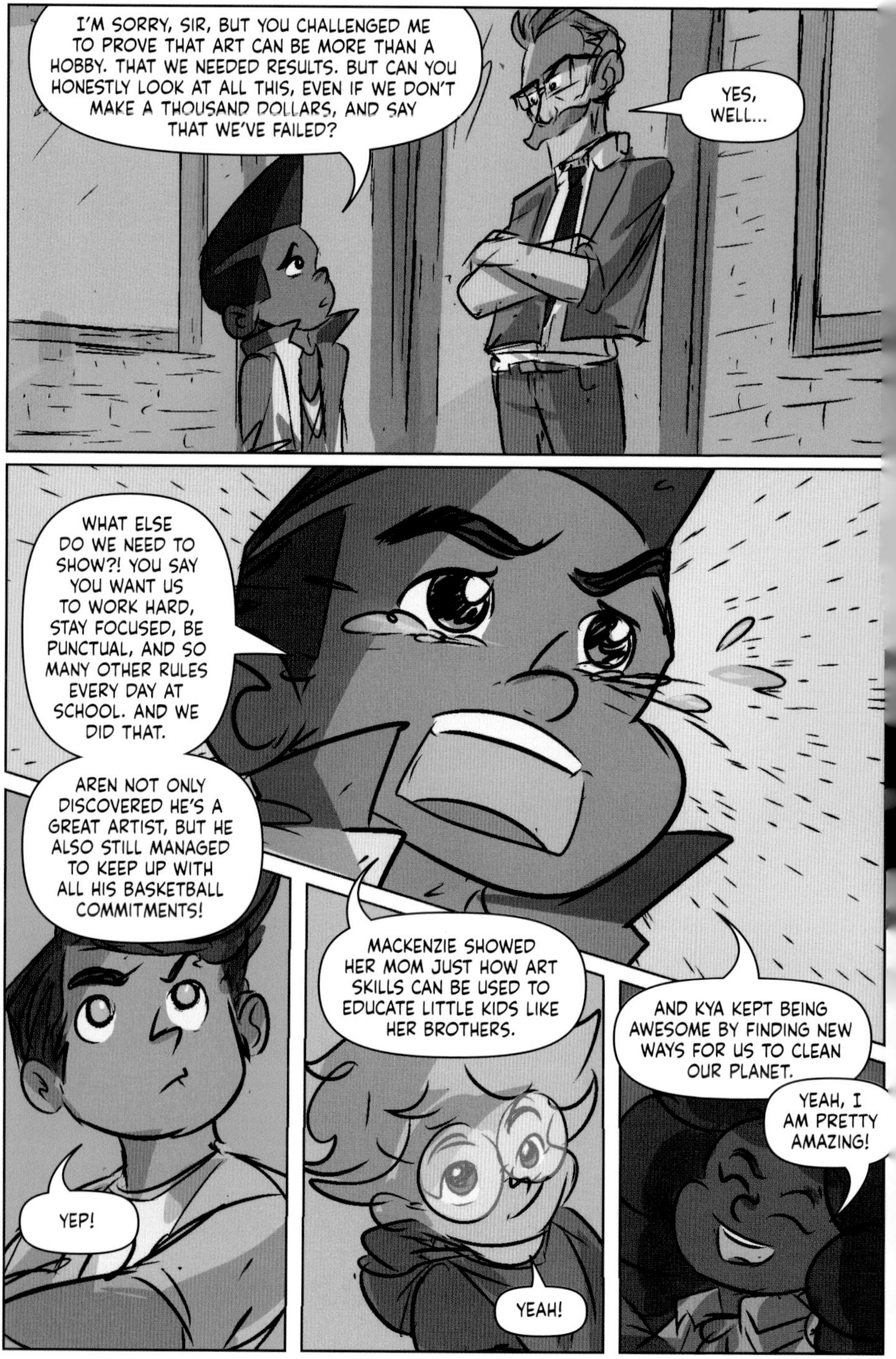
I'M SORRY, SIR, BUT YOU CHALLENGED ME TO PROVE THAT ART CAN BE MORE THAN A HOBBY. THAT WE NEEDED RESULTS. BUT CAN YOU HONESTLY LOOK AT ALL THIS, EVEN IF WE DON'T MAKE A THOUSAND DOLLARS, AND SAY THAT WE'VE FAILED?
YES, WELL...
WHAT ELSE DO WE NEED TO SHOW?! YOU SAY YOU WANT US TO WORK HARD, STAY FOCUSED, BE PUNCTUAL, AND SO MANY OTHER RULES EVERY DAY AT SCHOOL. AND WE DID THAT.
AREN NOT ONLY DISCOVERED HE'S A GREAT ARTIST, BUT HE ALSO STILL MANAGED TO KEEP UP WITH ALL HIS BASKETBALL COMMITMENTS!
YEP!
MACKENZIE SHOWED HER MOM JUST HOW ART SKILLS CAN BE USED TO EDUCATE LITTLE KIDS LIKE HER BROTHERS.
YEAH!
AND KYA KEPT BEING AWESOME BY FINDING NEW WAYS FOR US TO CLEAN OUR PLANET.
YEAH, I AM PRETTY AMAZING!

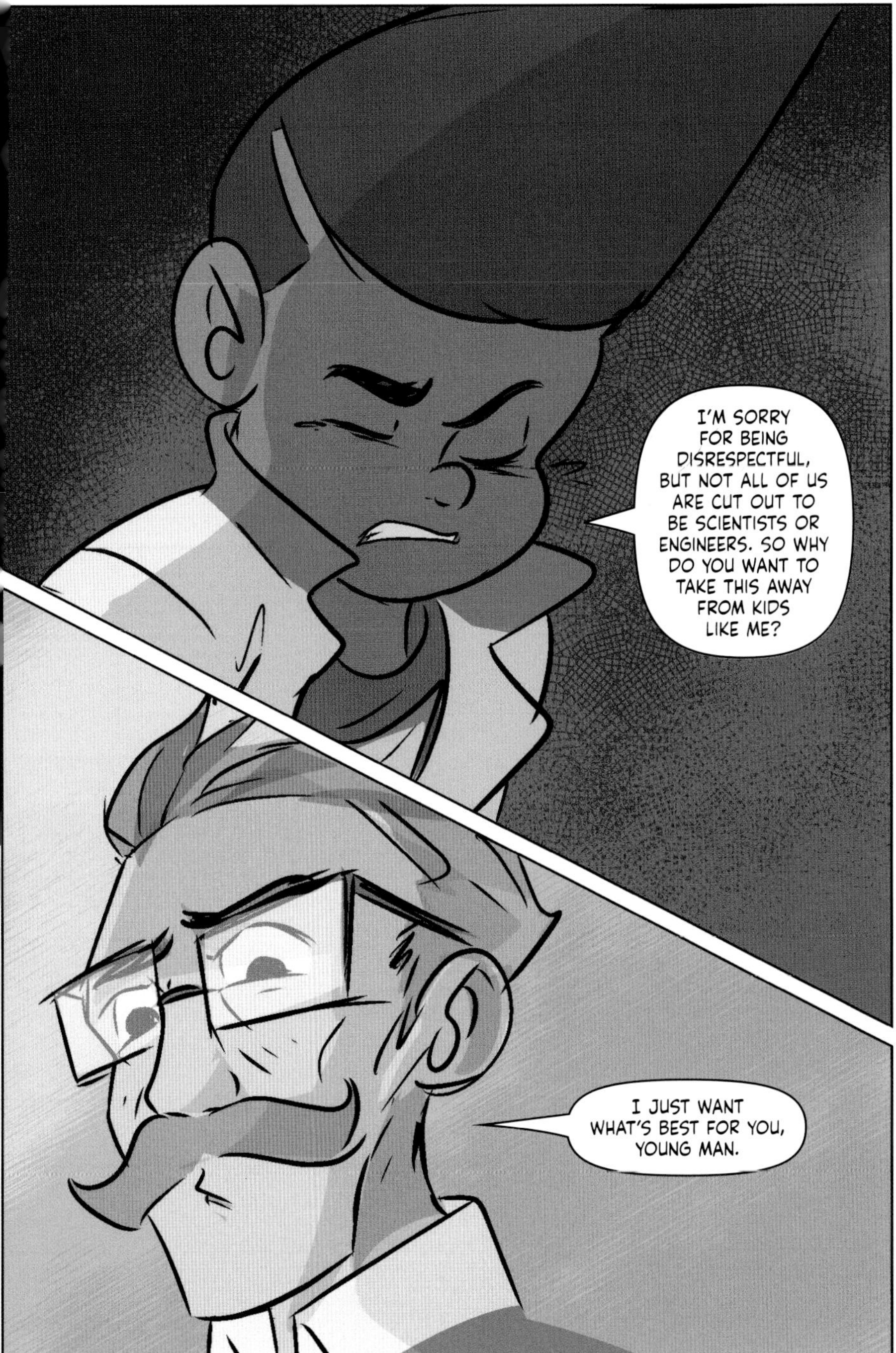
I'M SORRY FOR BEING DISRESPECTFUL, BUT NOT ALL OF US ARE CUT OUT TO BE SCIENTISTS OR ENGINEERS. SO WHY DO YOU WANT TO TAKE THIS AWAY FROM KIDS LIKE ME?
I JUST WANT WHAT'S BEST FOR YOU, YOUNG MAN.

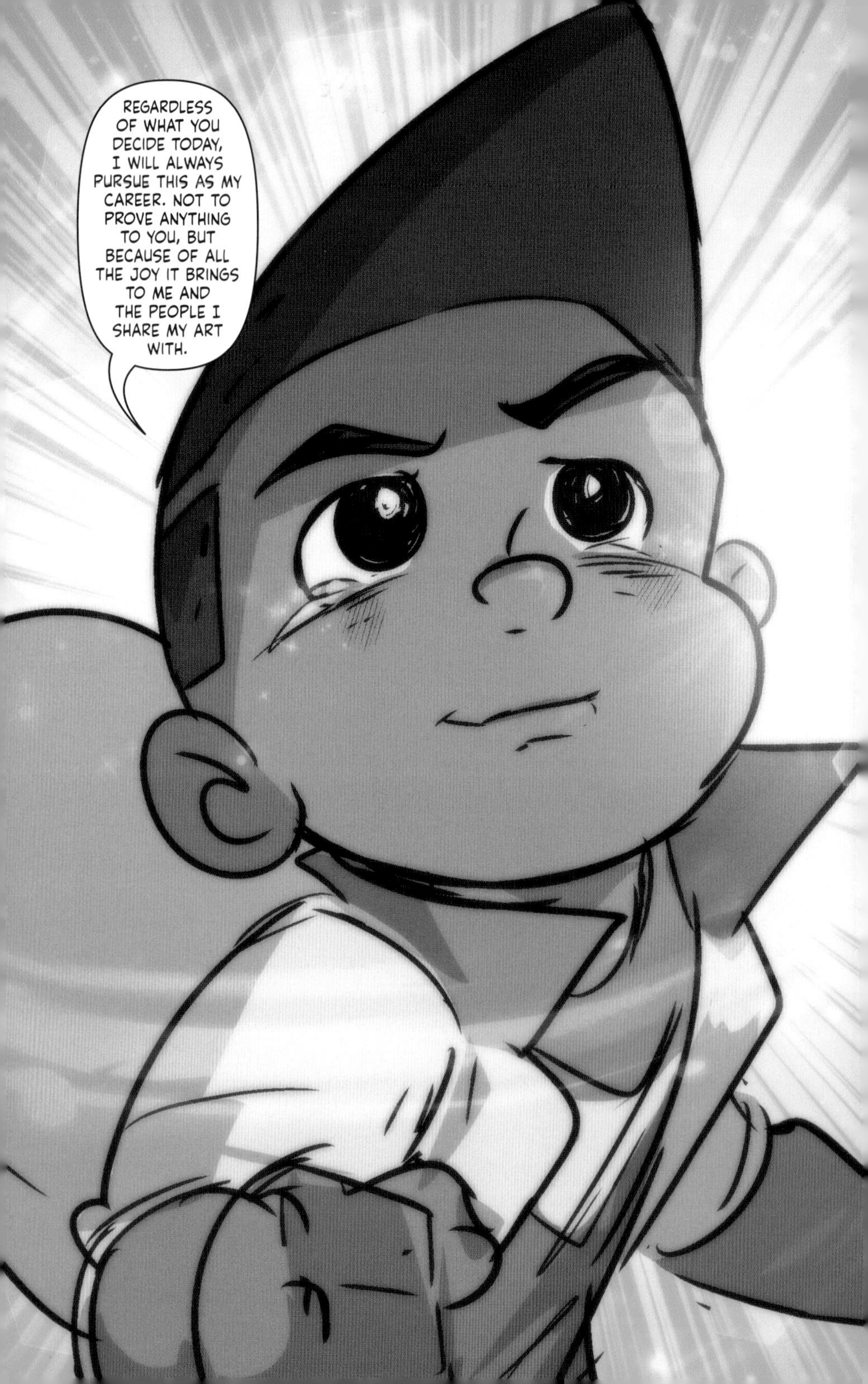
REGARDLESS OF WHAT YOU DECIDE TODAY, I WILL ALWAYS PURSUE THIS AS MY CAREER. NOT TO PROVE ANYTHING TO YOU, BUT BECAUSE OF ALL THE JOY IT BRINGS TO ME AND THE PEOPLE I SHARE MY ART WITH.

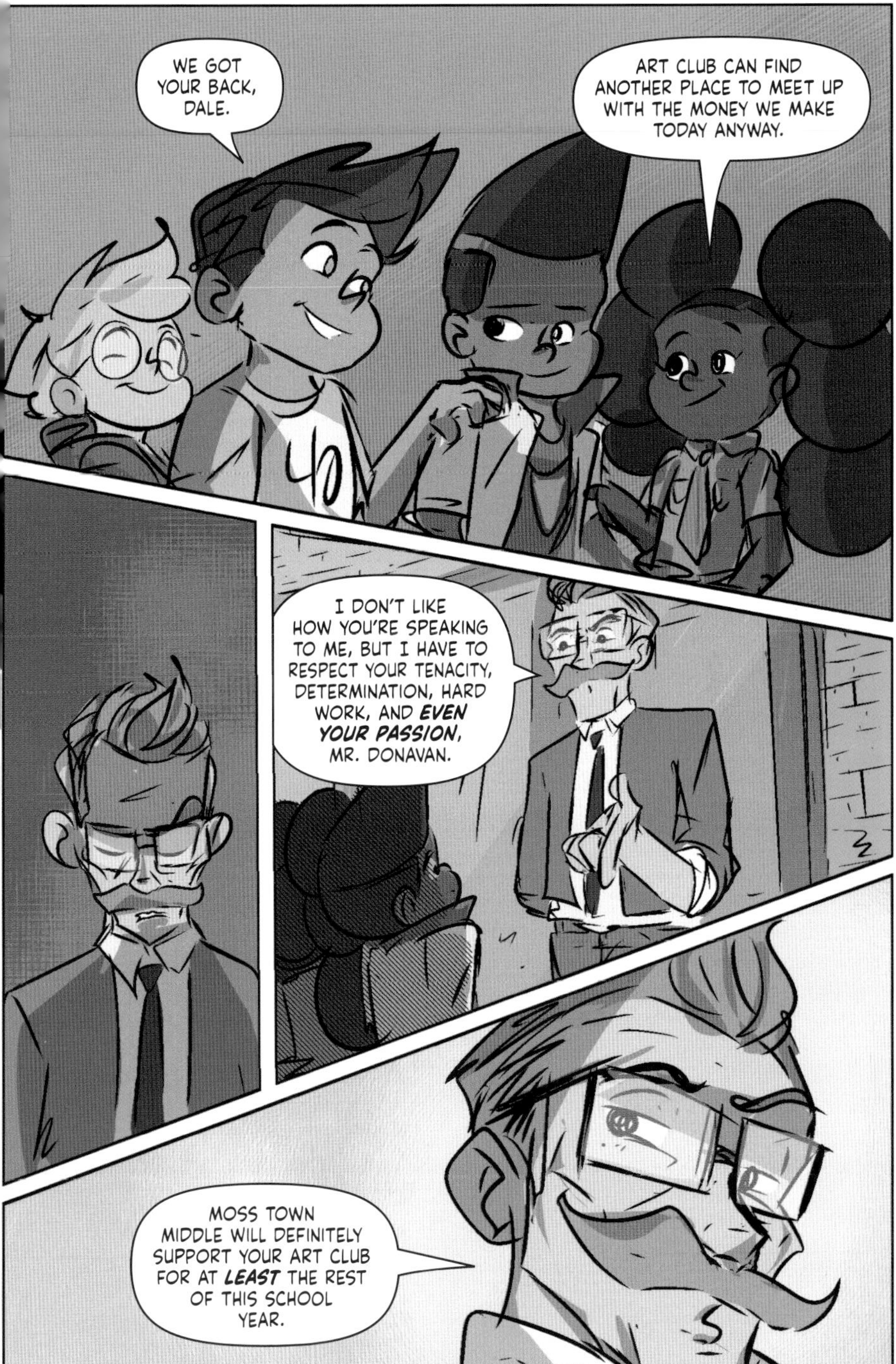
WE GOT YOUR BACK, DALE.
ART CLUB CAN FIND ANOTHER PLACE TO MEET UP WITH THE MONEY WE MAKE TODAY ANYWAY.
I DON'T LIKE HOW YOU'RE SPEAKING TO ME, BUT I HAVE TO RESPECT YOUR TENACITY, DETERMINATION, HARD WORK, AND ***EVEN YOUR PASSION***, MR. DONAVAN.
MOSS TOWN MIDDLE WILL DEFINITELY SUPPORT YOUR ART CLUB FOR AT ***LEAST*** THE REST OF THIS SCHOOL YEAR.

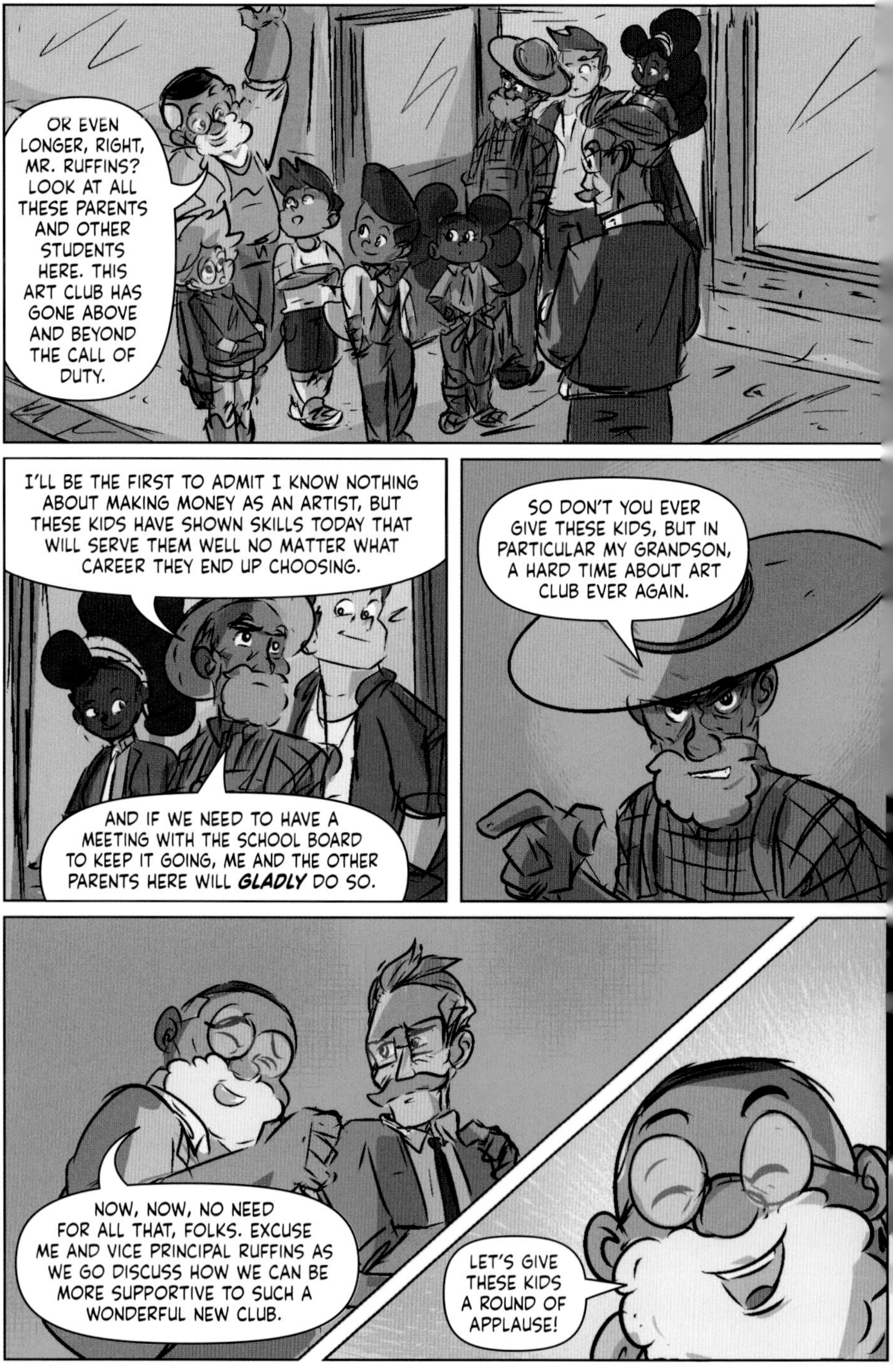
OR EVEN LONGER, RIGHT, MR. RUFFINS? LOOK AT ALL THESE PARENTS AND OTHER STUDENTS HERE. THIS ART CLUB HAS GONE ABOVE AND BEYOND THE CALL OF DUTY.
I'LL BE THE FIRST TO ADMIT I KNOW NOTHING ABOUT MAKING MONEY AS AN ARTIST, BUT THESE KIDS HAVE SHOWN SKILLS TODAY THAT WILL SERVE THEM WELL NO MATTER WHAT CAREER THEY END UP CHOOSING.
AND IF WE NEED TO HAVE A MEETING WITH THE SCHOOL BOARD TO KEEP IT GOING, ME AND THE OTHER PARENTS HERE WILL *GLADLY* DO SO.
SO DON'T YOU EVER GIVE THESE KIDS, BUT IN PARTICULAR MY GRANDSON, A HARD TIME ABOUT ART CLUB EVER AGAIN.
NOW, NOW, NO NEED FOR ALL THAT, FOLKS. EXCUSE ME AND VICE PRINCIPAL RUFFINS AS WE GO DISCUSS HOW WE CAN BE MORE SUPPORTIVE TO SUCH A WONDERFUL NEW CLUB.
LET'S GIVE THESE KIDS A ROUND OF APPLAUSE!

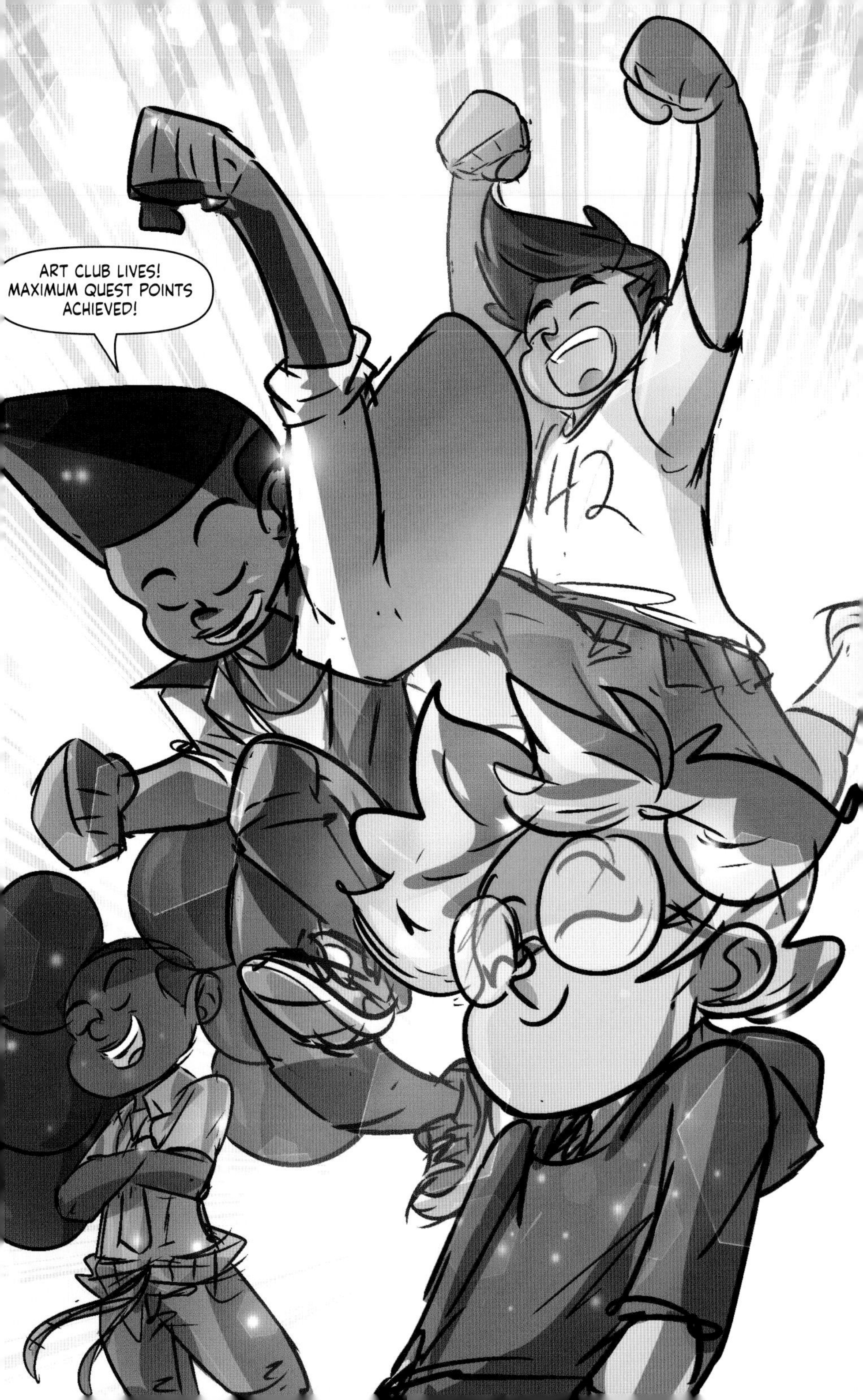
ART CLUB LIVES! MAXIMUM QUEST POINTS ACHIEVED!

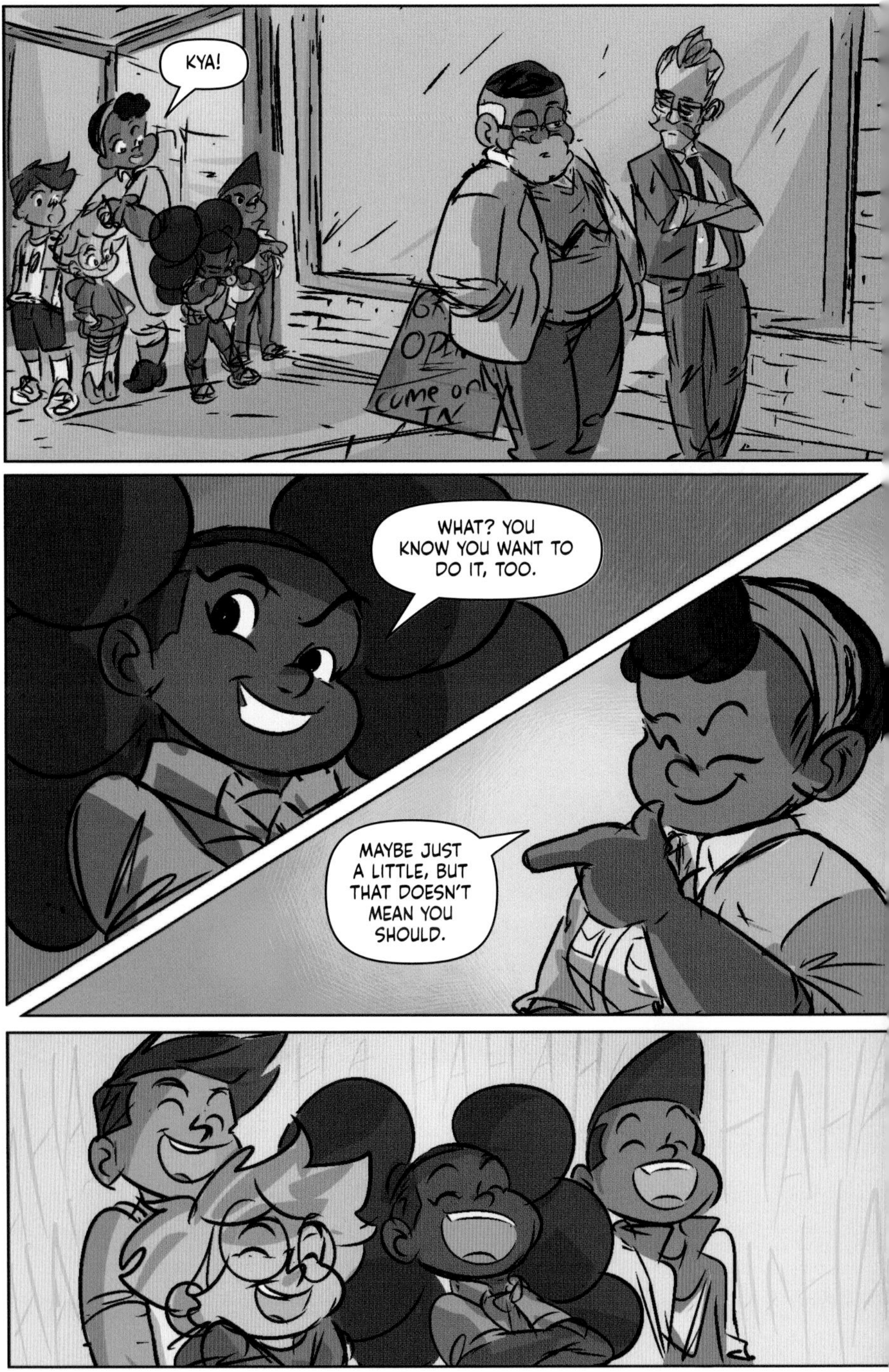
KYA!
WHAT? YOU KNOW YOU WANT TO DO IT, TOO.
MAYBE JUST A LITTLE, BUT THAT DOESN'T MEAN YOU SHOULD.

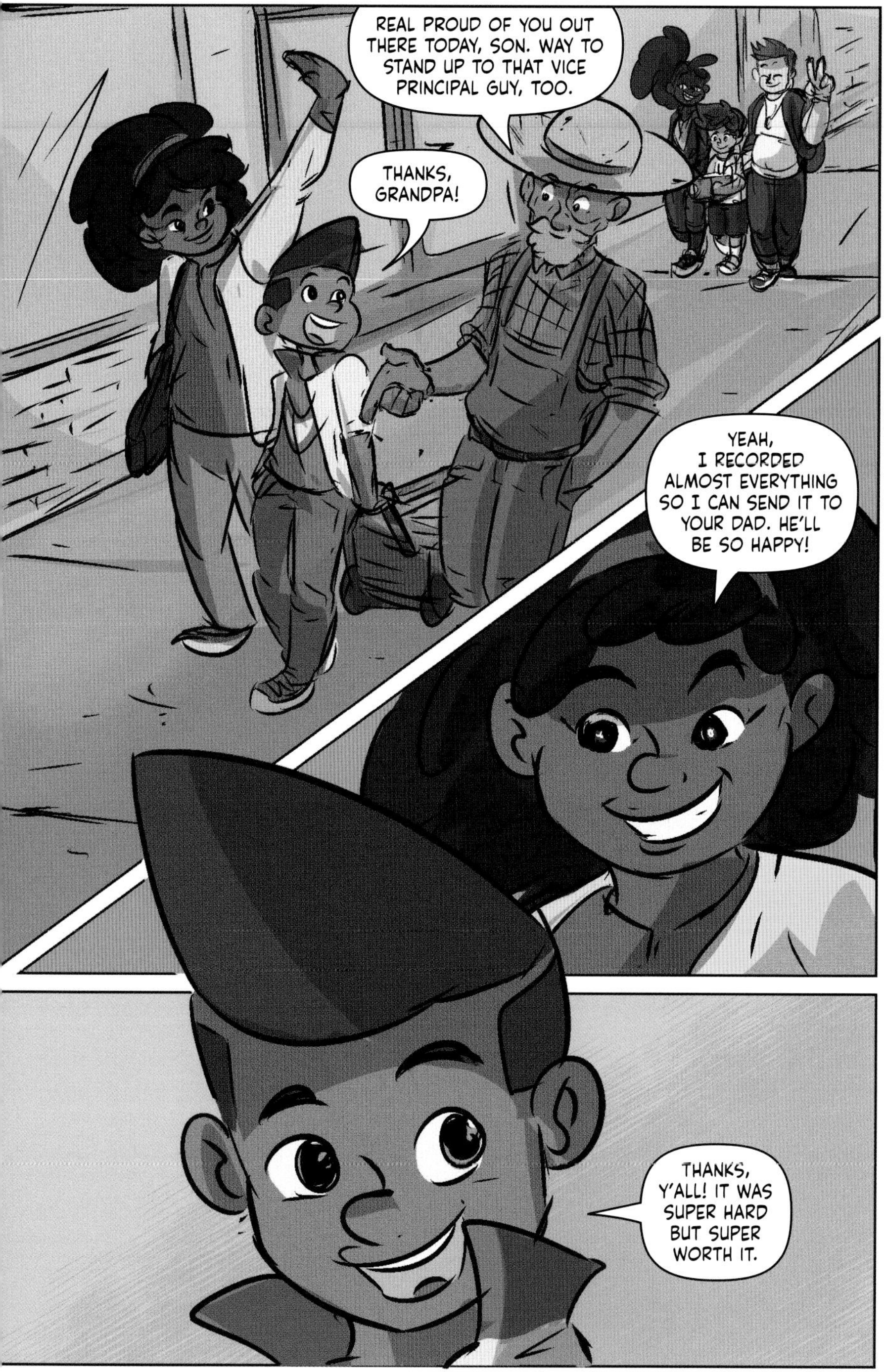
REAL PROUD OF YOU OUT THERE TODAY, SON. WAY TO STAND UP TO THAT VICE PRINCIPAL GUY, TOO.
THANKS, GRANDPA!
YEAH, I RECORDED ALMOST EVERYTHING SO I CAN SEND IT TO YOUR DAD. HE'LL BE SO HAPPY!
THANKS, Y'ALL! IT WAS SUPER HARD BUT SUPER WORTH IT.

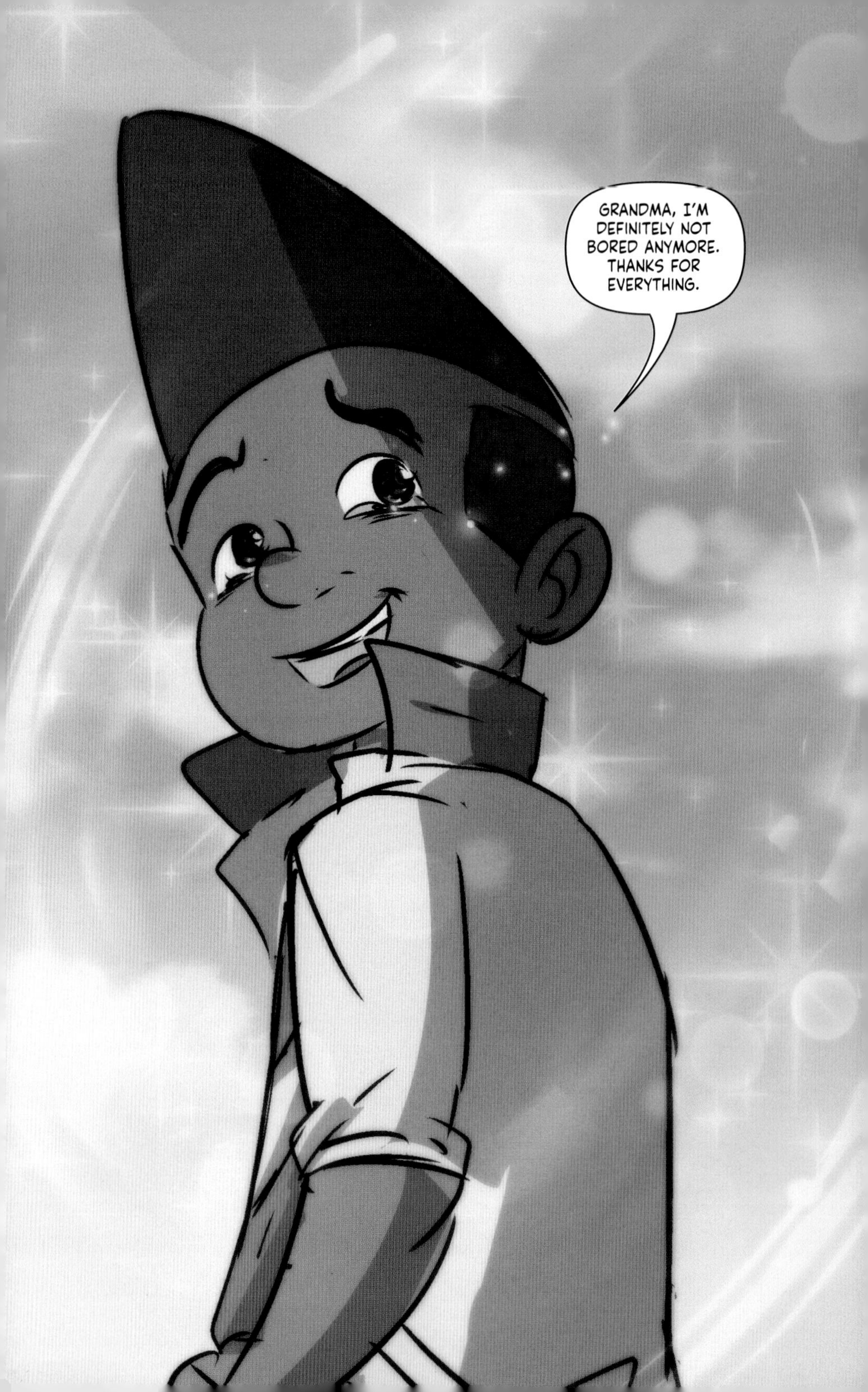
GRANDMA, I'M DEFINITELY NOT BORED ANYMORE. THANKS FOR EVERYTHING.

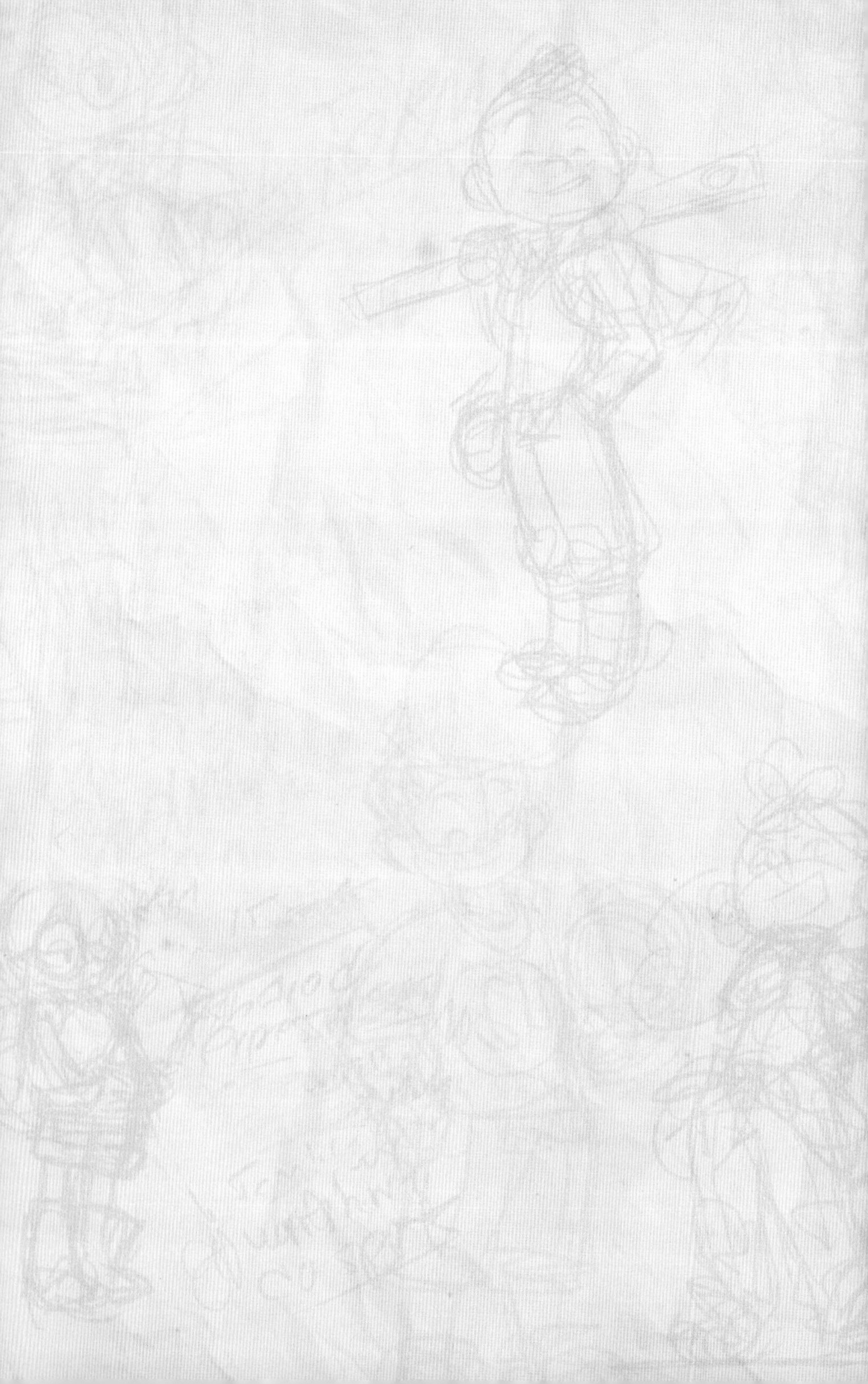

THE MAKING OF
Art Club

Hey, everyone!

Creating comics is super fun, but it can be a daunting task! Here's a peek into how this book was created to hopefully help you create your own comics.

It all starts with a simple idea or concept. In this case, the idea came from my editor, Andrea Colvin, who suggested that I create a story focused on some part of my life without it being centered around fantasy or superheroes—which is something I don't normally do but was very excited to try!

And much like Dale, I thought long and hard about what to create, ultimately settling on turning my decision to create comics for a living into a story that would be fun to read. *Art Club* is in no way a direct retelling of my life, though. In real life, I didn't start drawing comics until I was almost twenty years old.

Dale and his friends are mixes of myself with ideas I had for characters. With the exception of his parents and grandparents, who are loosely based on my own, they are not based on real people.

I also thought it would be fun if Dale put together a team of artists—each with a specific talent, similar to superhero teams like the Avengers—that way the story would still be based in reality but have elements I'm familiar with creating.

After coming up with a short summary of the story, I started designing the characters.

These are the first drawings of Dale.

I like to sketch in light blue because it makes cleaning up the work with black lines look less messy. This cleanup process is called inking.

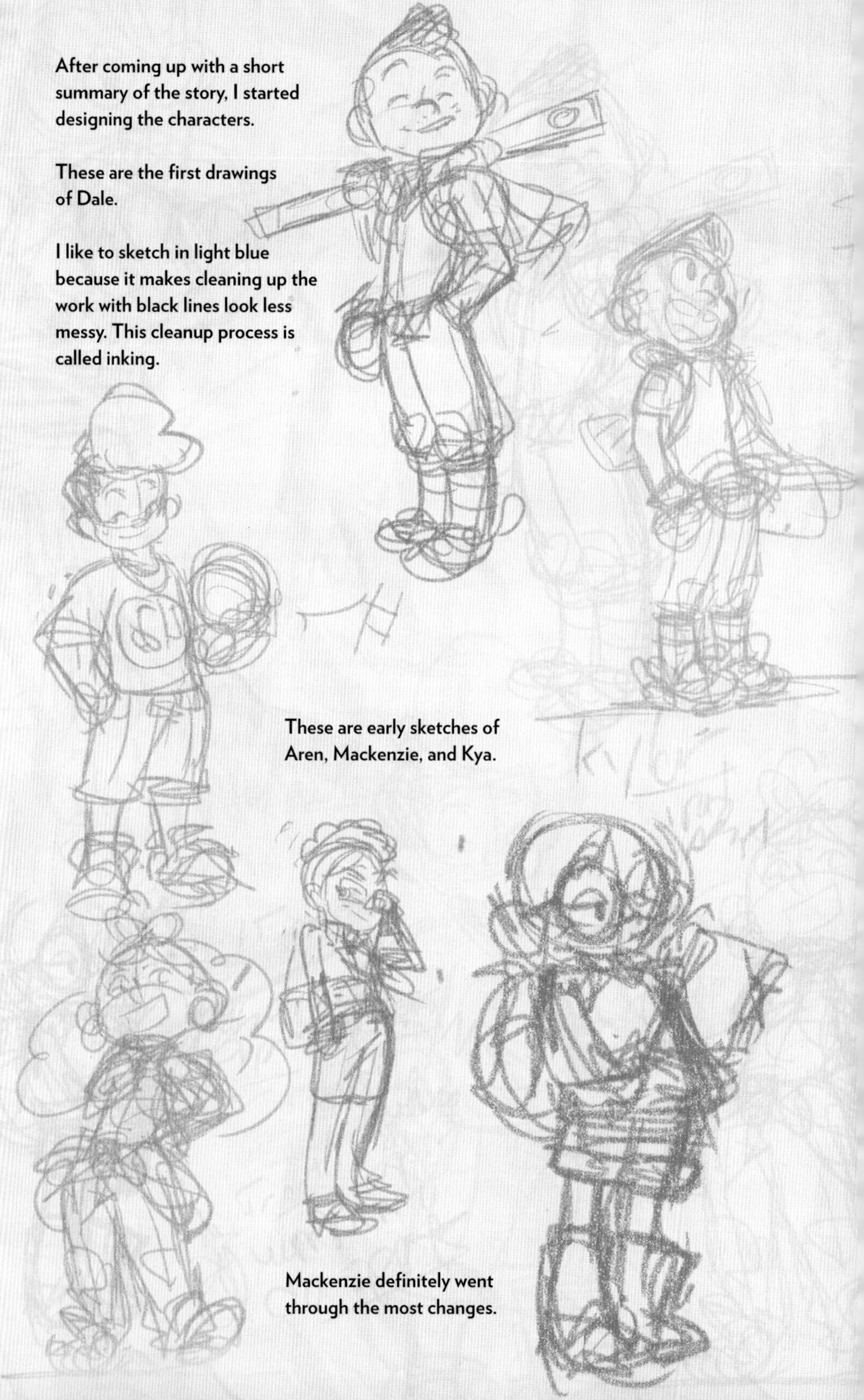

These are early sketches of Aren, Mackenzie, and Kya.

Mackenzie definitely went through the most changes.

Here's a finished look at the main cast, which was used in the pitch to the publisher. A pitch is a document consisting of character designs and a story summary. It's sent to book publishers to see if they want to mass-produce your story.

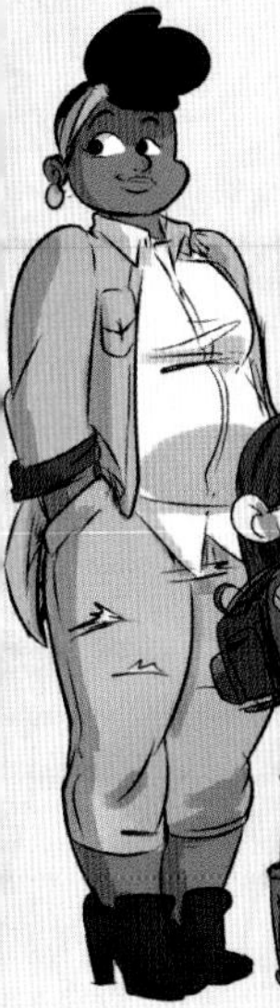

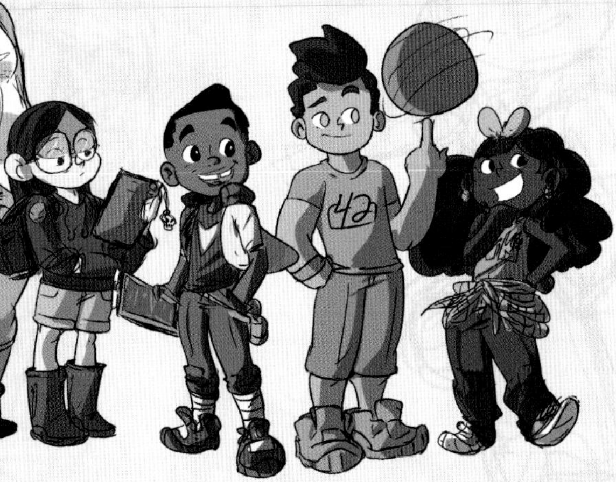
42

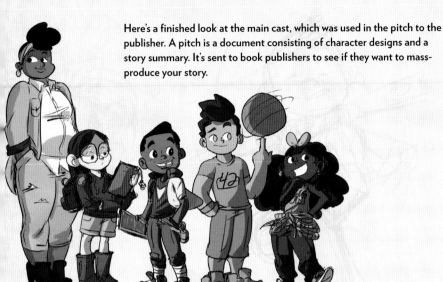

One of the main aspects of creating comics is updating character designs as you further polish an idea and receive feedback from the editor and/or publisher.

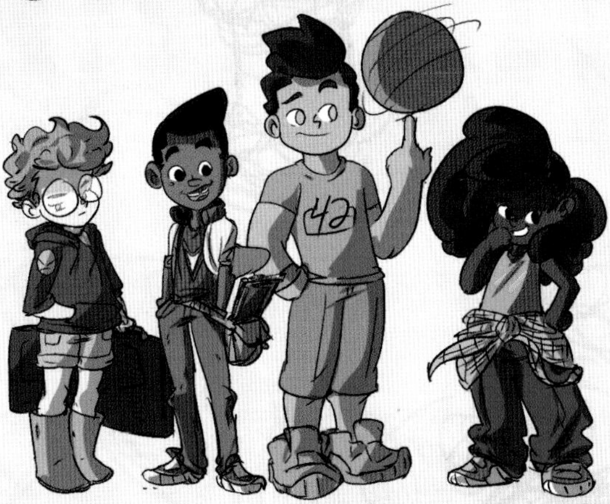
42

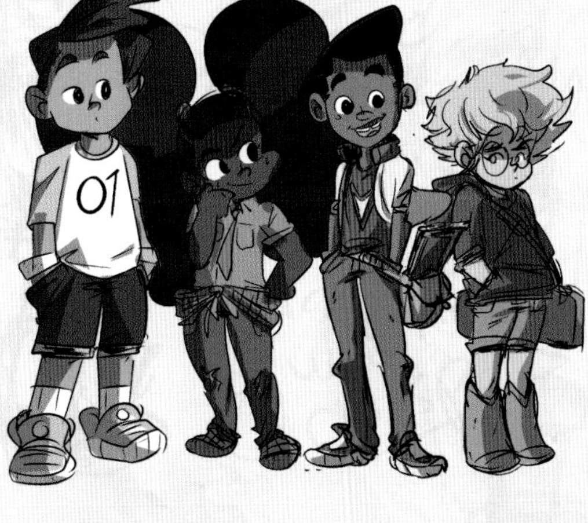
01

Dale's final design didn't change much from the original, but the rest had some major tweaks. Most of these were finding clothing colors that made each character stand out.

It was also really fun to design the characters' *Fantasy Frontier Z* avatars. This was the reference sheet used to make sure my color assistant, Andy Gordon, and I didn't forget what everyone looked like.

Reference sheets are super important when working on comics. They help keep the characters' costumes consistent throughout a book.

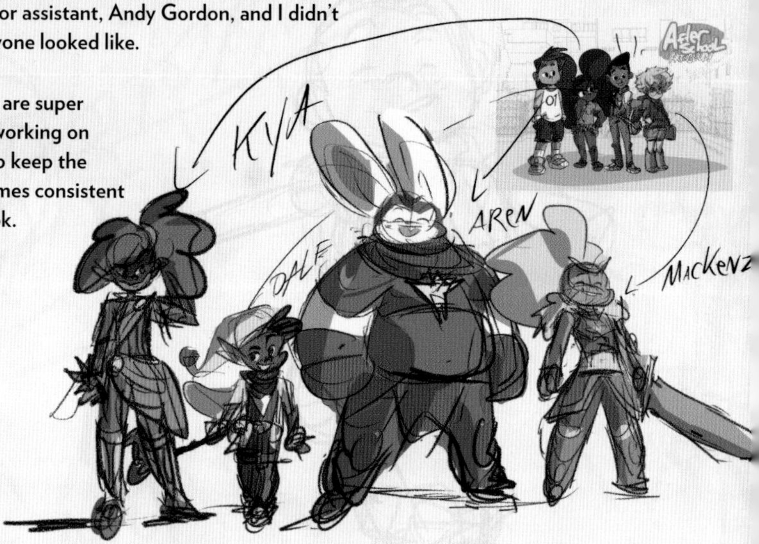
KYA
DALE
AREN
MACKENZ

Writing the script was the next step in creating this comic. It's always best to have this done before drawing. Knowing what your characters are saying and where they are can focus your imagination when creating the pages. You'll end up erasing and changing things way less often because you've specifically decided how things will look while scripting.

PAGE 1 (4 panels)

Panel 1: Big panel close on Dale, he's bored. He's screaming it.

DALE: I'm sooo bored grandma!

Panel 2: We can see grandma with the laundry, walking past Dale in the living room. Surrounded by toys. Kid ipad/tablet

GRANDMA: What about your new e-pad? or all those toys you need to pick up.

DALE: They're all boring, there's nothin new to watch and all my toys say they're tired of going on adventures today.

Panel 3: A bit close on Grandma, laughing to herself a bit.

GRANDMA: 'chuckle' I understand. Hmmm... I guess it's time I show you my secret lair. Just head up into the attic.

Panel 4: Dale is ecstatic! She has a secret lair?! What? How? He runs almost off panel in the foreground. Grandma, still smirking.

GRANDMA: But you have to promise to be a big boy and be careful with my secret lair stuff ok.

DALE: A secret lair!!! I promise! don't worry!

Once the script was done, it was finally time to work on the actual comic. The following page details some of those steps: pencils, inks, flat colors (done by Andy Gordon), and finished colors.

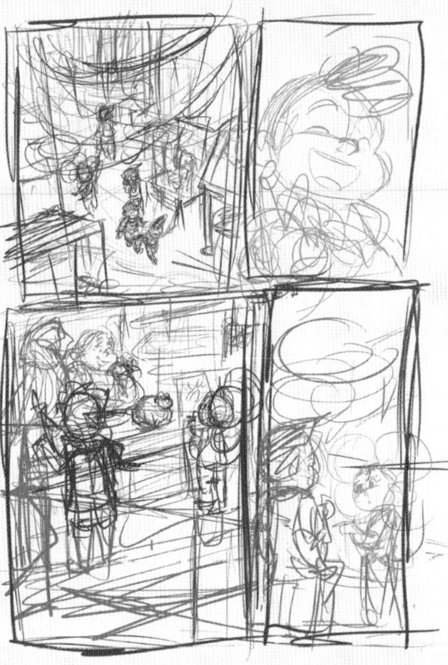

pencils

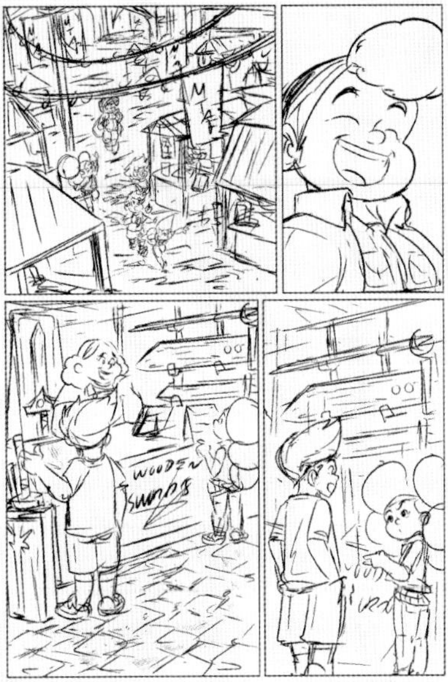
WOODEN

inks

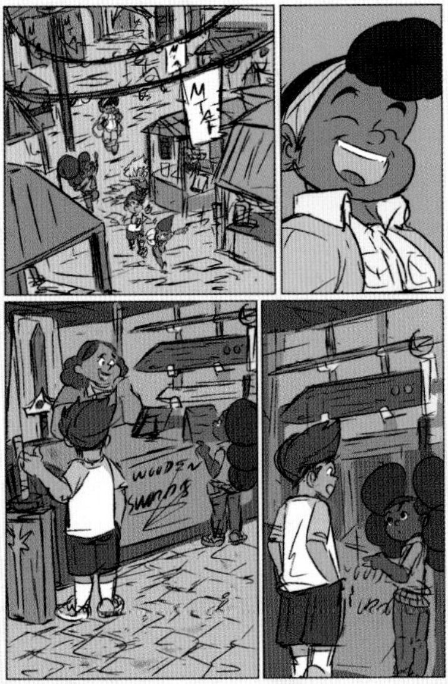
WOODEN

flat colors

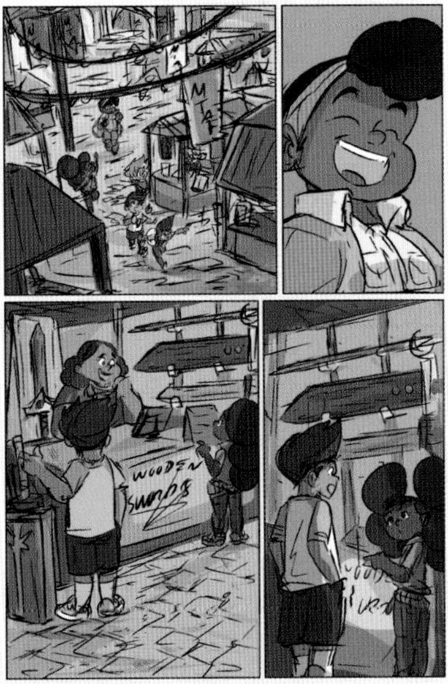
WOODEN

finished colors

There are a lot of reasons why creating comics is awesome, but one of the best is that it can be done all alone or with a team of people, each bringing their own creativity to the finished book! The next few pages include some extra images from Dale's favorite comics and games.

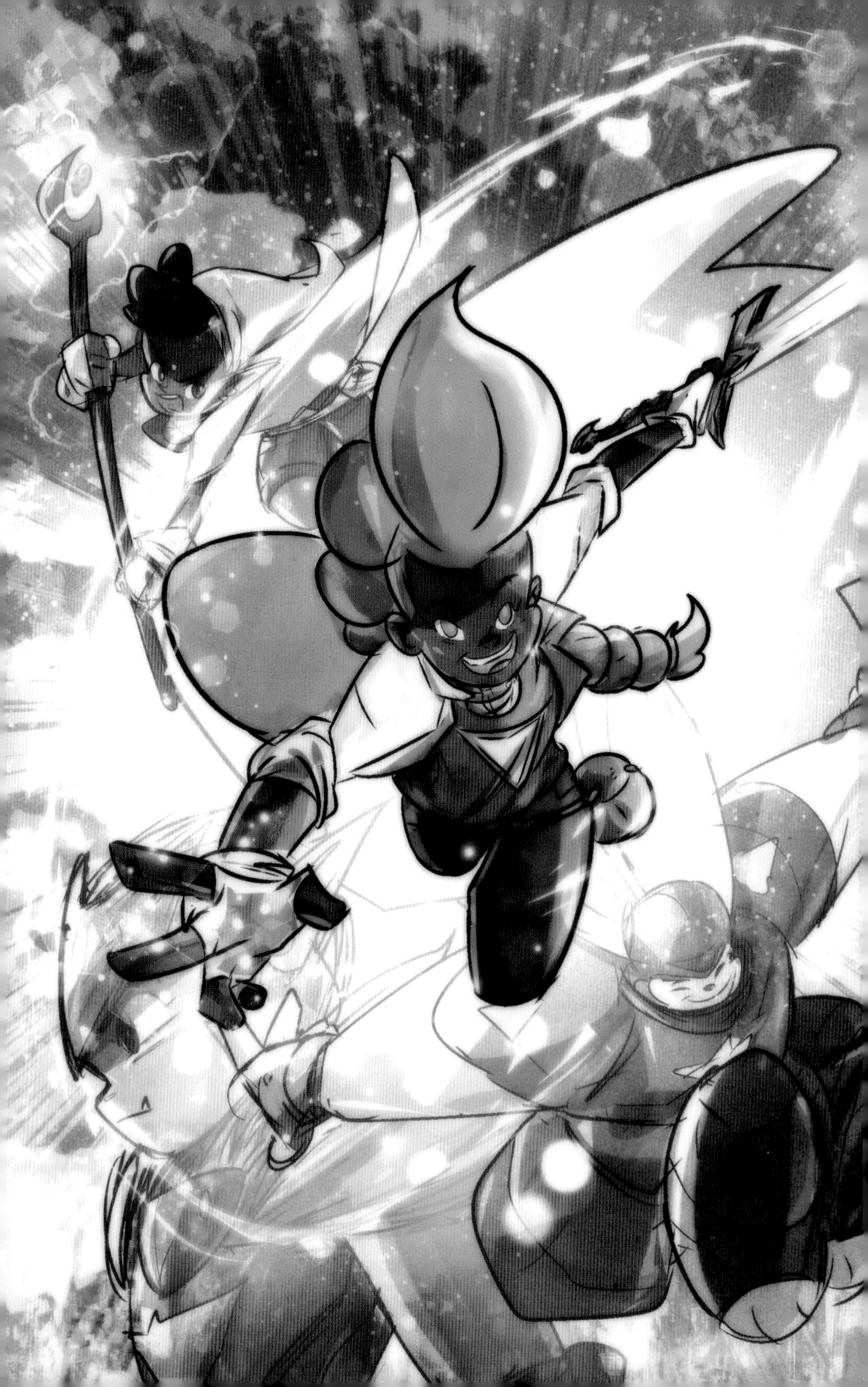

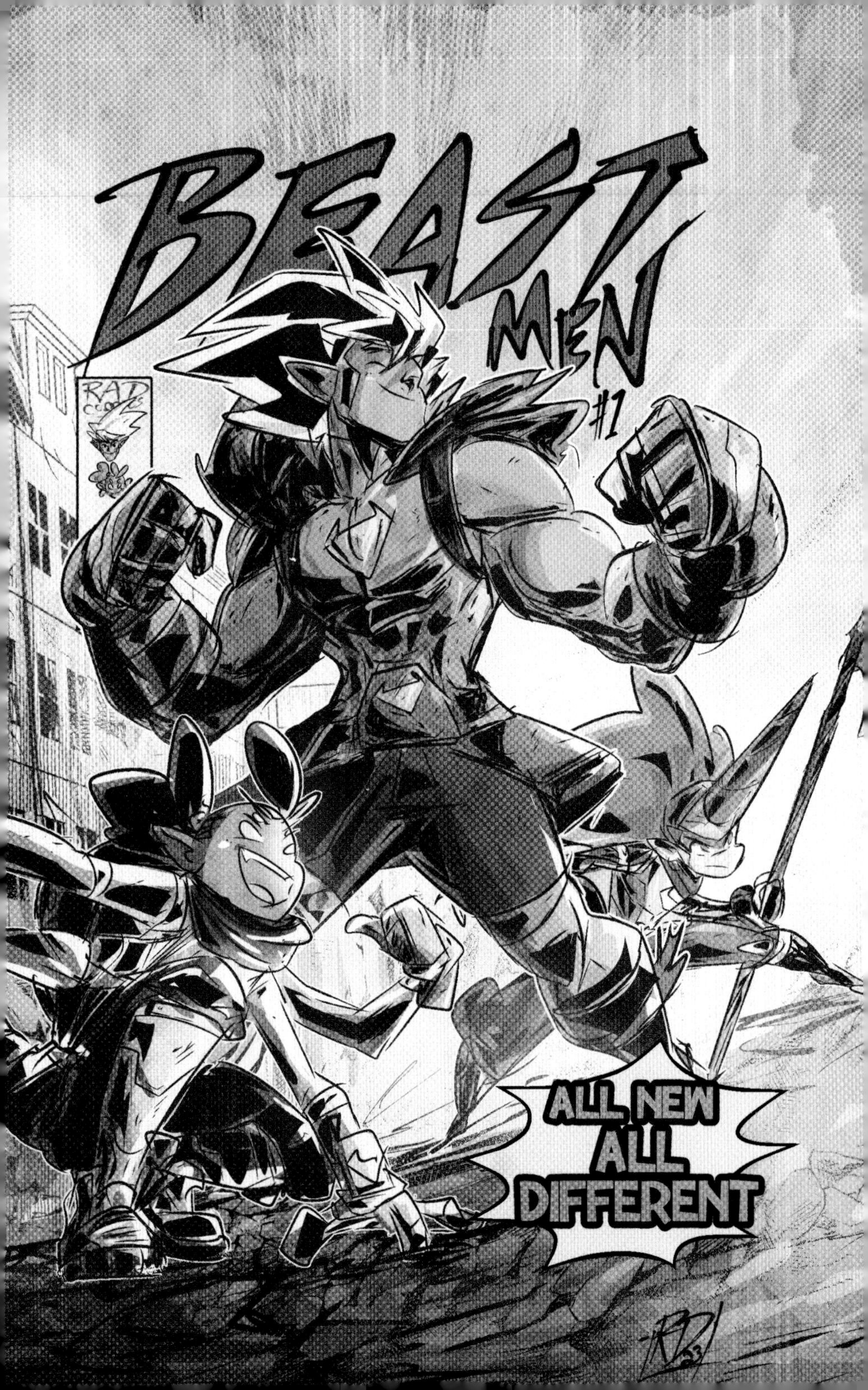
BEAST MEN
#1
RAD COMICS
ALL NEW
ALL
DIFFERENT

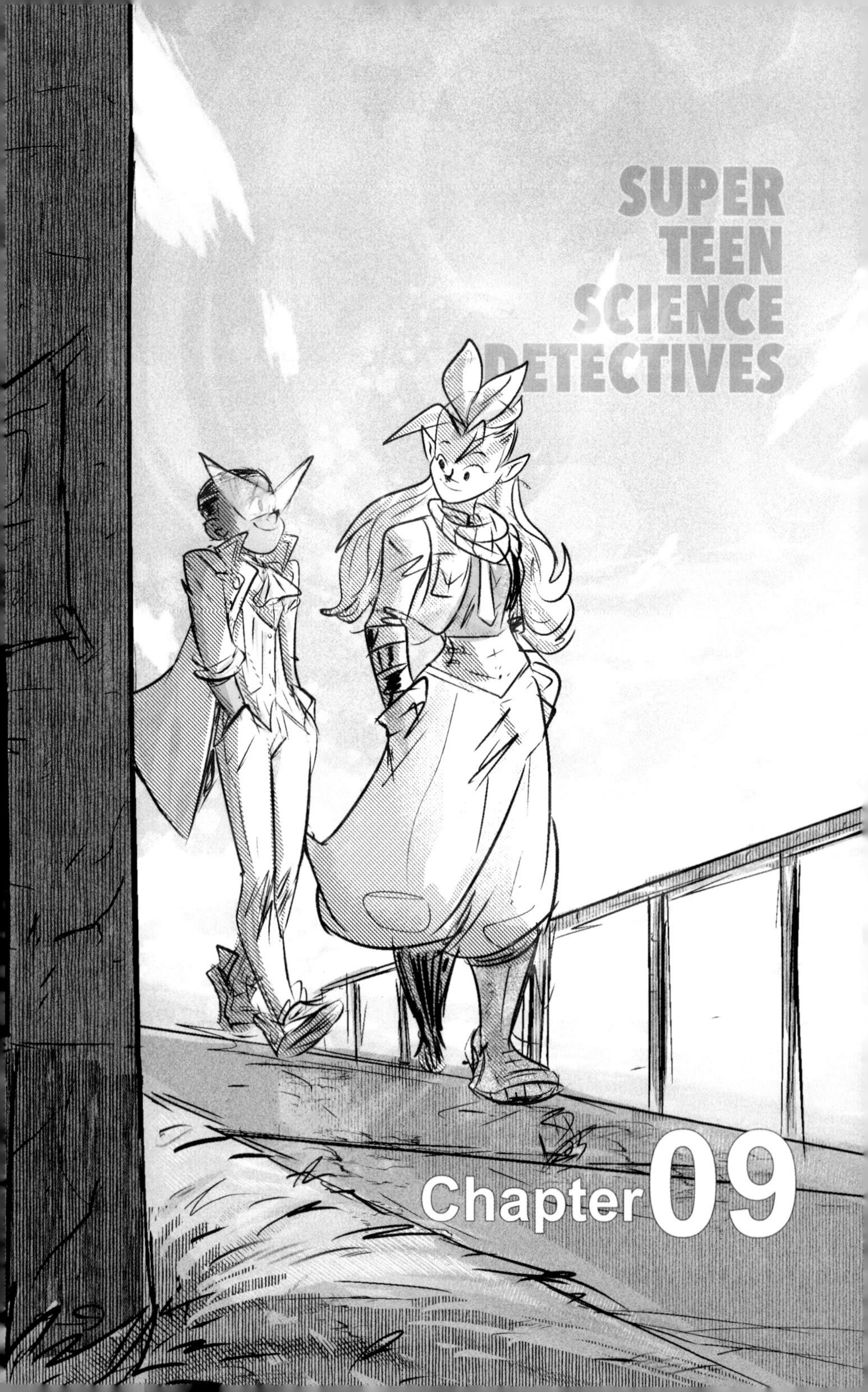
SUPER
TEEN
SCIENCE
DETECTIVES
Chapter 09

Acknowledgments

Ultra thank you to Andrea Colvin for always believing in my work, helping me focus my zany ideas, and helping me realize I can actually write stories without explosions (well, mostly without explosions).

Thanks to my friends and family, who listen to me rant and rave about my ideas, frustrations, and love of the comic industry.

Shout-out to my students, who keep me up to date with what the next generation of creators wants. Now I truly appreciate the power of romance comics starring half demons, lol.

Thanks to all the awesome art professors I had during college. We're all colleagues now, but every day I appreciate the positive art culture and vibes you have cultivated in our halls.

And lastly, I want to say shout-out to all the kids, both young and old, striving to get their work out there. Who cares if it's cliché— keep dreaming! Just adapt, grow, learn more about your industry, and keep going. There's only one you, and your voice needs to be heard.

About the Author

Rashad Doucet

Rashad Doucet is from New Orleans by way of Eunice
and Ville Platte, Louisiana. He's been drawing comics since his
grandma gave him a pencil and some paper to keep quiet during
church. Rashad is currently a professor of sequential art at SCAD in
Savannah, Georgia, where he can often be found listening to
K-pop and watching way too much anime.